SOLITARY JOURNEY

Emperor Gallienus' Sole Reign
During the Chaos of
Third Century Rome

Skip Carter

Copyright © 2025 by Lynn Carter

All rights reserved. No part of this publication may be reproduced, distributed or transmitted in any form or by any means, without prior written permission.

Skip Carter/Carter House Press
https://skipcarter.biz

Author's Note: This is a work of historical fiction. Names, characters, places, and incidents conform to historical records where available, although fictitious characters have been added to enrich the story and are noted in the cast of characters. Where sources are lacking or contradictory, creative assumptions were made.

Website Design Traci Bisson, 2025

Book Layout © 2016 BookDesignTemplates.com

Solitary Journey, Emperor Gallienus Sole Reign During the Chaos of Third Century Rome/ Skip Carter

Printed in the United States

Available in these formats
ISBN 979-89870654-0-2   Paperback
ISBN 979-89870654-8-8   Kindle
ISBN 979-89870654-9-5   Ebook - EPUB

Dedication

In times long past, a few people made decisions and took actions that have had measurable impacts on the course of civilization, both past and present. What dangers did these people face? How did they react? What were their fears, doubts, insecurities, their flaws, shortcomings? Answers to these questions would have made history more dramatic and memorable. Yet many of these questions were not directly addressed in history books I read, perhaps because many cannot be answered historically. I was inspired to address those questions during a visit to Istanbul. I decided to write a story about the last assault on what was then known as Byzantium, later Constantinople, and planned to title it "The 22nd Siege." Research for a credible back story eventually led me to Gallienus' and Valerian's succession as co-emperors of Rome in 253 AD. The turbulent time they lived in inspired me to write a historical novel about these men and how they dealt with threats to the empire, both external and internal. Why did each man deal with the challenges as they did, since each man approached leadership very differently? And what were the results of their different styles? I am extremely grateful for all who read my drafts and suggested ways to make this story better. Below are people who were instrumental in shaping this writing into its current form.

Eric Ratinoff made me believe this story could be told, that I might be able to tell it, and patiently shepherded me through the entire first draft.

My wife, Pam, supported and encouraged me throughout this long creative writing effort. She also assisted in selecting the design for this book cover.

My brother, Dave, a medical doctor and bow and arrow hunter, ensured that hunting scenes were authentic and advised me in medical matters pertaining to plague, infections, and wounds which I used throughout the story. An English major, he also proved to be a most thorough editor.

Many stimulating discussions with Martha Paull over the course of the story's evolution covered a wide range of topics including editing, characters' motivations and behavior, food, dress, lodging, diseases, and gardens - what flowers might be blooming in Thessalonica in September, for example. She also translated several documents from Italian and Greek for me. The story is far richer as a result of her thoughts and suggestions.

Jean Lambert, an English and drama teacher, made significant contributions during ten years of editing assistance, improving organization and giving me ideas on use of body language and non-verbal reactions.

Joanna Saidel provided a thorough review of grammar, punctuation, plot consistency, and offered paragraph restructuring ideas which greatly improved readability. She also assisted in design of this book cover. Her thorough research skills also kept the story historically accurate.

Cindi Barbeau's high-speed reading style focused my attention on the story flow.

Robin Baskerville shared insights in the professional aspects of editing and helped bring my story closer to publication. Her positive critique of the manuscript was very reassuring.

The Picture of Gallienus' Bust is reproduced with permission of Carole Raddato under Creative Commons license CC BY-SA

About the Maps

Map segments used in this book are reproduced with permission of Mr. Peter Kay, UNRV website administrator.

UNRV.com History of Ancient Rome, is the source of the complete full-color map of the Roman Empire, along with an outstanding and extensive collection of information about ancient Rome. Visit UNRV.com to purchase a complete map of the Roman Empire at the time of its greatest expansion. This is by far the most comprehensive map of the Empire that I have been able to find. I referred to it extensively when writing this story.

The complete map shows Rome's greatest extent, c. 117 AD. By 253AD, several legions had been relocated.

Dacia   V Macedonia replaces XIII Gemina
Germania Inferior XXX Ulpia Victrix replaces I Minervia
Moesia Superior IV Flavia Felix replaces VII Claudia Pia
  Fidelis

Noricum   II Italica added.
Rhaetia   III Italica added.

Pityus, the northernmost city on the eastern Euxine Sea, settled around the 6th century BC, does not appear on this map. All cities and towns named in the story existed then and I believe still exist under different names. See Grant, *A Guide to the Ancient World.*

About the Runes

All information regarding rune casting techniques and interpretations in this story comes from *Runic Journey*, specifically discussed in chapters Salonina, the Dream and Andrasta. Interpretations of each rune are mentioned throughout the book.

Jennifer Smith, *Raido, The Runic Journey*, Tara Hill Designs, Milton, Ontario, Canada. 1993.

About Historical References

Where historical information was sparse or non-existent, I created careers and spouses for some of the actual characters. Refer to the "Characters" section for details. Historical facts have not been altered, with the following qualifications. Large gaps, confusions, and contradictions sometimes exist in available historical sources. Scholars often do not know or disagree on chronology and validity of some data. Most emperors are historically introduced with, "little or nothing is known of his career before..." I have constructed event timelines and backstories, filling historical gaps with conjectures and educated guesses to create a richer and more complete story.

About Roman names, briefly

During this period women had two names, men had three. For this story, the last name for each person is the one to remember.

Preface

The story of Emperor Gallienus' reign in imperial Rome begins in *Perilous Privilege* and continues in *Solitary Journey*.

This is a dangerous time to be emperor. Fourteen Roman emperors died violently in the previous forty-two years, all but one killed by Romans. Yet, in the fall of 253, Gallienus, a 35-year old patrician, is proclaimed co-emperor by the Senate, along with his father, Valerian, a former leader of the Senate.

Gallienus is an unlikely choice for emperor (a position he never aspired to), with his Greek education and sardonic personality. He also has a reputation for frequenting brothels and taverns, behavior considered scandalous by his contemporaries. In the spring of 254, Valerian takes much of the army and most experienced generals east to face Shapur, an aggressive Persian king, leaving Gallienus in command of the entire western half of the empire with insufficient soldiers and inexperienced leaders.

Gallienus is forced to defend against invading tribes and suppress multiple civil wars. When not on the battlefield, he must deal with intrigues of ambitious men in a restive Senate. He enjoys women's company and values their counsel. Yet among these tempting women are those willing to use any means available to advance their personal interests.

During the two years prior to the beginning of Solitary Journey, Emperor Gallienus has defeated three invading armies in the western half of the empire and survived two revolts by provincial governors. He plans a punitive attack across the Danube River late in 260, followed by a well-deserved rest for himself and his army.

As *Solitary Journey* begins, Emperor Valerian confronts a Persian army attacking his eastern frontier, despite losses in legions due to a plague.

Figure 1 Rhine Frontier and Gaul

Figure 2 Rome and Western Danube

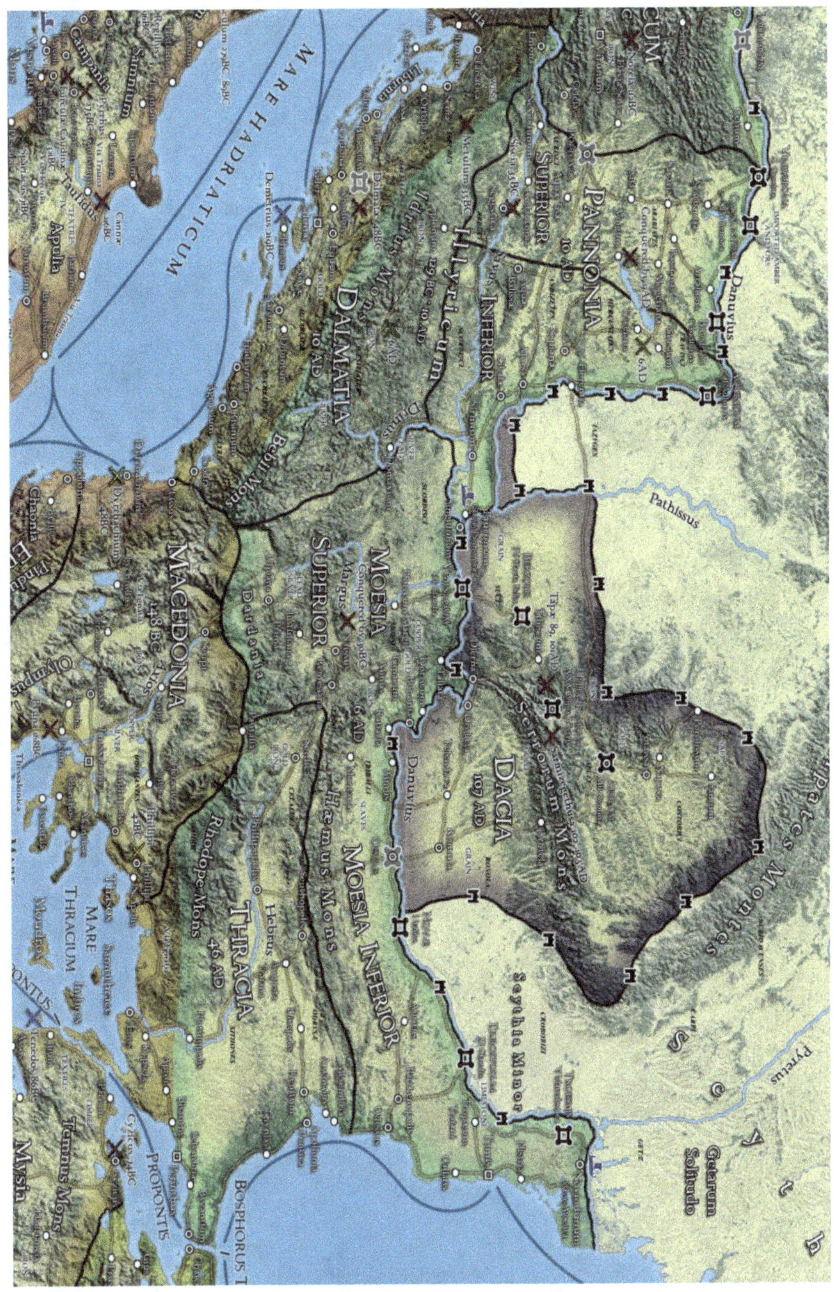

Figure 3 Eastern Danube

Figure 4 Black Sea

Figure 5 Greece and Western Turkey

Figure 6 Syria and Persia

CONTENTS

Chapter One______________________________________ 14

Chapter Two______________________________________49

Chapter Three____________________________________99

Chapter Four____________________________________133

Chapter Five____________________________________191

Chapter Six_____________________________________233

Chapter Seven___________________________________291

Chapter Eight___________________________________339

Chapter Nine____________________________________383

Chapter Ten_____________________________________449

Postscript_____________________________________515

Timeline____521

Characters______________________________________529

Bibliography____________________________________536

About the Author________________________________540

1-1
No Alternatives
Approaching Carrhae, Mesopotamia
21 June, 260

"We still don't know where the Persian army is." Successianus, emperor Valerian's chief of staff, spat on the ground in front of Victor, Valerian's brother-in-law, to emphasize his reply. "That's why I sent scouts to the east." He'd long ago tired of Victor's second guessing his every move during these morning staff meetings.

"Of course we know where the Persians are," Victor contradicted, "they're besieging Edessa."

"For all we know, Edessa may have already fallen," Successianus said, "and since their scouts know where we are, then Shapur (the Persian king) knows where we are. Has it occurred to you that he might decide to move his army?"

Instead of answering, Victor broached another topic, speaking exclusively to Valerian. Successianus ignored their chatter and looked east from their campsite. He welcomed the morning sun on his face while it gradually banished the chill of the desert night, but he knew that well before midday, he and the army would be cursing the heat. Last night the army had descended from a region of higher ground with rivers and arable land to camp on the desert's edge west of the city of Carrhae.

Successianus could clearly see distant hills, but nearer, undulating ground meant he would temporarily lose sight of parts of his army during their march. The road ran almost due east from their campsite until it came to Carrhae, nearly twelve miles away. Even at Valerian's slow marching pace, they should reach Carrhae by late this afternoon, if Valerian would finish this interminable meeting.

Once in Carrhae, they could strip the city of its garrison and march north across another twenty miles of this barren land, before reaching Edessa from the south. For the last two days Successianus had seen no one on the road coming from the east. He suspected the Persians had blocked it.

"Do you have any objections to that?" Valerian's question jarred him from his thoughts.

"To what?" he asked. Both Valerian and Victor were staring at him.

"I asked if you had a problem with putting Julianus' forces at the head of the march today," Valerian said.

Successianus preferred to have Julianus, Victor's son and also Valerian's cousin, close by to keep an eye on him, but realized that Julianus' father and uncle were trying to give him a chance to redeem his reputation. Any objection he raised would probably be overruled. Successianus nodded glumly. "I'll have a word with him first."

Just before the army embarked on the morning march Successianus gave Julianus a bit of advice. "Persians sometimes feign a retreat to lure their enemy into a chase. It's usually a trap. Don't let that ploy deceive you." He stood only inches from Julianus and hoped his harsh tone would be effective in getting his message across. During the march Successianus would be halfway back in the column where Valerian preferred to ride. Due to the size of their army, their column stretched over three miles along the road and Successianus had no hope of controlling an impulsive leader marching at the front. "Your job is to lead the column, just that, not to win any battles yourself. Is that clear?"

Around midday Julianus crested another of the road's many rises. In the depression just ahead of him, he saw a group of dismounted Persians warriors. They looked up at Julianus and the lead element of his column. Their leader made an obscene gesture, then they all leapt onto their horses and started to gallop up the far side of the hill.

I know Successianus warned me about traps, Julianus thought. *But clearly I've taken them by surprise. This is my chance to show everyone what I can do!* "After them," he shouted, and raced toward the fleeing Persians.

It took nearly five minutes for the messenger to reach Successianus with news of Julianus' precipitous charge into the desert. Without waiting for consent from Valerian, he grabbed the arm of the nearest tribune. "Ride to the front. Halt the march. Tell the centurions to spread out and expect an attack from the front. Then find the nearest legate and put him in charge. Go quickly!" Successianus silently thanked the gods for his foresight to place messengers at both ends of the column.

"What are you doing?" Victor shouted. "We should be moving ahead, not stopping."

Successianus looked at him coldly. "You wouldn't be calling for an advance, if Julianus wasn't leading the charge."

"If he's surprised the Persians, we have a chance for a quick victory." Victor spoke urgently to Valerian. "If it's a trap then we can't leave him exposed and unsupported."

Successianus was unmoved. "He exposed himself against my orders. I'm not willing to jeopardize the rest of the army because of Julianus' disobedience and bad judgment."

"Successianus may not be willing to support his men," Victor pleaded with Valerian, "but I am. Give me a legion, even a few cohorts, and I'll share in Julianus' victory or help him return to you."

"Not while I'm in command," Successianus snapped, seeing indecision on Valerian's face. "In fact, I'd rather fall back a mile or more, where ground's more favorable for a battle."

"Retreat is out of the question," Victor challenged Successianus' proposal as if he were in command of the army himself.

Valerian looked at both men. As he started to speak, Successianus raised his hand and pointed wordlessly to the north, on the left side of their column. A dust cloud was rising from behind the distant hillocks. Valerian stared at it, open-mouthed.

"We can't win this battle with three people commanding the army," Successianus said to Valerian. "Pick one of us, before we all die." Valerian hesitated. A scout galloped over the closest hill to their left shouting that a Persian attack was imminent.

"You." Valerian nodded at his Praetorian Prefect. Successianus drew in a quick breath then wheeled about shouting orders to deploy the army before Persian horsemen spilled over the dunes and were among them. Trumpets blared. Centurions barked orders. Legionnaires ran from the road, hurrying to change from a marching column into a defensive formation. By now everyone knew the situation, yet the only sounds were shouts of the centurions, crunching of men's sandals running across gravel, and clanking armor.

A deep rumble of Persian kettle drums reached them from tops of the distant dunes. At first only dust from their galloping horses was visual. Then came a faraway thunder of charging horses and still-faint shouts of Persian horsemen. When angry whizzing sounds of arrows began, centurions halted their legionnaires, ordering them to prepare for an arrow attack. The first of the three rows held their shields directly in front of them while second and third rows held theirs over their heads. The sound of arrows reminded Successianus of a deadly rainstorm. Some clanged off armor; others thudded into the legionnaires' wooden shields. Occasionally, the "thunk" of an arrow was followed immediately by the screams of wounded, both men and horses.

Successianus surveyed their situation. The army had formed in the shape of a large rectangle, three ranks deep. The longer sides of the rectangle, each about two miles long, ran parallel to the road and faced north and south. The shorter sides, each about a mile long, ran perpendicular to the road and faced east and west. As long as Successianus stayed somewhere near the center of this rectangle, he would be able to see most of what was happening across the whole formation. He had deployed his cavalry to disrupt the Persian attacks. A second Persian attack came almost simultaneously from the south.

Light Persian cavalry galloped continuously around his army showering them with arrows. Sometimes they rushed in toward the Romans, then quickly withdrew before coming within range of the Roman javelins.

"They'll run out of arrows soon," Victor predicted confidently.

Valerian looked at Successianus. "What are you going to do?"

"A small-scale attack, there." Successianus pointed to the center of the long, north-facing rank, where the first attack had come from. He trotted toward the line. Valerian and Victor followed with Valerian's Praetorian Guards. Successianus' tribunes gathered three legates commanding the legions on the northern side and explained his plan. They had dismounted and stood between their horses as protection against the arrow attacks, which had unexpectedly stopped.

Instead, the Persian commander had seen the emperor riding toward the Roman front ranks, and into the range of his archers. He'd ordered them to cease firing and wait, hoping for an opportunity to catch the exposed emperor in a volley of arrows.

While Successianus issued orders to his legates, Valerian and his contingent, emboldened by the cessation of the arrow assault, rode closer, to provide encouragement. Successianus looked up at the motion of horses, cursed, then shouted and desperately waved Valerian away.

A sudden shower of arrows whizzed over his head and rained down on Valerian, striking five men and three horses closest to him. Valerian ducked instinctively behind his shield, which was struck repeatedly. His horse was not so fortunate. Hit with at least five arrows, it fell to the ground, writhing, until one of the Praetorians ended its suffering. Valerian rolled clear of the horse during the fall and lay motionless a few feet away from the unfortunate animal. Praetorians flocked around him with their horses, shields, and armor. Successianus ran across the open space between his group and the emperor and pushed his way into the throng. Someone had rolled Valerian onto his back and held him in his arms. Successianus elbowed Victor roughly aside and knelt beside the unmoving emperor. He reached for Valerian's wrist, at the same time looking for blood or signs of wounds. He found neither. Then he looked and felt for broken bones. Nothing seemed abnormal. Successianus was about to shout for the medicus when Valerian opened his eyes. He looked around with a vacant stare and began gasping for a breath. Successianus stood, taking a deep breath himself, which he let out slowly. He looked through the crowd of soldiers to where Victor stared at him anxiously. "No wounds, nothing broken," he said. "Probably had the wind knocked out of him."

Successianus promptly dismissed the emperor from his mind and looked for his aides. "Sound the trumpets," he shouted. "I want the middle group of cavalry to attack the Persians, now."

Successianus realized almost immediately that his attack would fail. Persian archers fled from the initial charge. Roman cavalry was lured over dunes where Persian heavy cavalry was waiting and were quickly overwhelmed. Retreating Romans, while generally organized, still suffered considerable casualties.

While the Romans reformed ranks, Successianus rode back to Valerian. "Are you well enough to ride?" The emperor rose unsteadily, leaned against one of his tribunes. "Help me to mount." The man looked a bit uncertain, then knelt to allow Valerian to put one foot on his shoulder. His horse was immediately surrounded by Praetorians, shielding him from another volley of arrows.

Successianus grabbed Victor's shoulder. "Get Valerian away from the front line."

Again, he surveyed the battlefield. Persian heavy cavalry had moved in close and held the remaining Roman cavalry and legionnaires in check, while Persian light cavalry continued shooting arrows into Roman formation. He felt hot, dry wind on his face and grit in his mouth from desert dust, and struggled to suppress a sudden wave of fatigue. Sweat from his hands mixed with windblown dirt. There was blood on his uniform. He looked quickly to see if he'd been wounded, but found nothing. An overwhelming sense of thirst came over him which he realized was a combination of heat, exertion, and anxiety of battle. He felt pity for his soldiers, who had been forced to begin battle before eating their midday meal. An arrow struck his shield. Successianus shook his head; more than food, drink, or rest, he needed a plan.

He considered his options, then urged his horse toward the center of the formation.

"We need to break through their line and retreat," he said to Valerian. "We can't continue to take these losses." He glanced at Victor.

"I thought not," Valerian agreed.

"You have a plan?" Victor asked Successianus.

"Breakthrough on the east side and retreat to Carrhae. I've just ordered the west side to withdraw inward." He looked west. "It's already begun. I hope that distraction draws off some of their cavalry. In the meantime, we ride east, and use Praetorians to break through their lines."

Valerian glanced at Victor. "Maybe we'll find Julianus and his legionnaires." He actually sounded hopeful.

"Not likely, now," Victor said, thinking of his son's probable fate, "but we have to try something."

Successianus looked over when the commander of the eastern legion answered his summons. It was Cledonius, the lead centurion of XVI Flavia Firma Legion, the most senior man in the legion not dead or wounded. Cledonius saluted after the plan had been explained then galloped back to prepare his legionnaires. Successianus gave him a short time to prepare his men, and also let the retreat of the formation on the west end develop. He closed his eyes, turned his face toward the sun, and offered a brief prayer to Sol Invictus, the invincible sun god, asking that his plan would succeed. When he opened his eyes, he looked at Valerian. The emperor gave him a barely perceptible nod. Successianus raised his arm and signaled for the Praetorians to follow him. Sixteen hundred horsemen rode behind him at a trot, toward Persian cavalry beyond them, and ultimately toward their objective, the distant city of Carrhae.

The ranks of Cledonius' men opened, allowing two wings of Praetorians to pass through their ranks. The third wing stopped behind Roman lines protecting the emperor. Once through, the Praetorians advanced toward Persian heavy cavalry at a trot. The Persians had seen this maneuver developing, but had not been able to contain it. They fell back, denying the Romans a chance for battle. Persian archers flanked heavy cavalry, and showered Roman horsemen with arrows.

Successianus desperately wanted to close with the heavy cavalry. He needed to defeat them before he could extricate the rest of the army. But instead of facing him, the Persians retreated, then turned at the top of the next rise. They appeared ready to do battle there. When the Romans closed in on them, the Persians wheeled about and repeated their retreat. After yet another Persian retreat, an image of Julianus came to his mind. For a few moments he could not understand why. Then he knew—and his own warning to Julianus ran through his head: They're luring me away from the legions and waiting for reinforcements to arrive. He cursed himself for not recognizing it sooner despite his fatigue and the heat of battle. The next time the Persians wheeled and started galloping away, Successianus halted his Praetorians and turned them around. He had to get back to the Roman lines before he was attacked from both sides or, worse, met head-on by Persian reinforcements. He knew the retreating Persians would quickly realize they were no longer being pursued and would turn to attack from behind. How many hills have we crossed? Successianus couldn't remember.

He turned to a tribune. "Give the order to retreat at a gallop," A trumpet blared out the order and men urged their horses back toward the Roman army at a gallop. Successianus knew he was sacrificing all order and discipline, but he needed to reach the legions' protection before the Persians closed their trap on him. They galloped to the top of one hill, then a second. Still no legions in sight. So it must be at least three, Successianus thought grimly, as they plunged over the crest and into the next depression. Thei horses were starting to tire from heat and exertion. Foam formed on their necks, shoulders and chests and ran from the sides of their mouths. None had the strength to race up the next hill. As he approached the top of the third hill, Successianus decided to halt their retreat. When he reached the top, he saw the line of Roman legions in the distance—and between him and the Romans, was a line of Persian heavy cavalry.

Successianus looked behind him and saw dust from Persian cavalry now in pursuit. He had only a short time to attack the

Persians ahead of him before he was attacked from the rear.

"Ahead at a trot," he ordered to his tribune. No time for a plan. *And it doesn't matter how many of them there are. We fight our way through, or die trying.* The attack seemed almost dream-like to Successianus. He couldn't remember any time in his life when he felt so close to death—except maybe during his very first battle. He was beyond fearing for his life. It was liberating.

They rode straight into the Persians—no charge, no feints. Shouts and insults were exchanged just before the clash of metal against metal. Horses shoved against horses, pikes and javelins thrust against shields, armor, flesh, and horses. Swords hacked at each other. Shouts and screams of men and horses filled the air. The Romans fought with a grim determination born of desperation. After what seemed an eternity, Successianus heard a trumpet blaring. He couldn't tell from where, although it sounded familiar. He heard horses galloping and more men shouting, but dared not look away from his opponent, even for a second. He heard shouts in a foreign tongue. Fear in their voices gave him hope. The man he was struggling with suddenly sagged in his saddle, a Roman javelin stuck in his back. Successianus glanced beyond him. *More Praetorians, fresh soldiers! Valerian must have released the men left to protect him, to aid the retreating Praetorians.* Persian horsemen started to slip away from the fight. Those that were slow to leave or chose to stay and fight died quickly. A warning flashed through Successianus' mind. *What about the horsemen behind us?* He looked over his shoulder in time to see them rounding the crest of a hill he had so recently passed over. *They have to be tired, but they might rally the others to return.*

"Back to our lines, quickly," he bellowed to the tribune near him. A trumpet blew. They began retiring to the safety of the legionnaires. Successianus lingered in the field, urging his men to hurry. When the last man had ridden past, Successianus followed toward Roman line. Arrows began whizzing past his head. *Less than fifty yards to go.* An arrow struck his horse's right flank. It staggered and cried out in pain, but continued running. *Maybe twenty-five yards now.* Successianus felt a searing pain in his left thigh. He looked down. The arrow that grazed his leg was lodged in his horse's chest. The animal took two more steps before pitching forward and collapsing on the ground. Successianus was thrown clear and landed hard and lay where he had fallen, unmoving.

What am I doing on the ground? He couldn't remember where he was or why he was there. *Had there really been a battle with the Persians—or had it just been a dream?* The pain in his left thigh brought Successianus back to his senses with a start. He looked up at the sound of horses racing toward him, so he did not see who grabbed him by the shoulders and pulled him roughly to his feet. He was not sure if he had been lifted by a Roman dragging him to safety, or by a Persian about to end his life, but there was no fight left in him. The last thing he remembered was that several other men clustered around him and started dragging him, he did not know where.

1-2
Conference With a King
Near Carrhae, Mesopotamia
21 June, 260

A familiar voice spoke near Successianus' head. "I think he's regaining consciousness." He opened his eyes and saw one of his aides staring anxiously down at him. Without thinking, he tried to sit up, but the tribune held him back gently.

"Just take it easy for a few minutes, sir," the aide pleaded.

Successianus lay back dizzy and nauseated. He grabbed his aide by the sleeve. "Where am I? How did I get here?"

"You're on a battlefield." Successianus stared at him blankly. "We've just fought against the Persian army." The aide added hopefully.

Pain shot through Successianus' left leg. Surprised, he looked at his bandaged thigh, then remembered being struck by a Persian arrow. Although his wound had been treated, blood still seeped from around the dressing and ran down his leg mixing with sweat and dirt. He resisted the urge to wipe it clean and tried to stand.

"No need to do anything right now," the aide assured him. Successianus rubbed a hand across his face, tried to clear his head.

"What happened?"

"When Cledonius saw you fall, he ordered his legionaries to advance in a line toward you. Then he ran ahead of them and dragged you back to our line," the aide said casually.

While Successianus considered the acts of quick thinking and bravery that had undoubtedly saved his life, he suddenly became aware of an unnatural stillness on the battlefield. "Why is it so quiet?"

"A delegation went to talk with Shapur, under a flag of truce," the tribune explained. "We're waiting for his response."

Successianus' eyes widened. He grasped his aide's arm. "The emperor didn't go himself, did he?"

"He sent Victor, who's trying to negotiate our way out of…the current situation," the tribune spoke delicately of their predicament. "A payment of gold perhaps, a promise of further tribute, there's certainly a precedent for it."

"You're referring to a promise that Philip made then later reneged on." Successianus considered the Persian reaction. "Shapur doesn't strike me as a man who'd forget that sort of thing."

"They've been gone quite a while. Do you think that's an encouraging sign?" the tribune asked.

It must be late in the afternoon, Successianus thought. "Have the men been fed?" he asked, suddenly hungry himself.

The tribune nodded. "Would you like something to eat?"

Successianus shook his head. "Water." After drinking deeply, he fired a volley of questions at the tribune. How many casualties? How many of the cavalry were left? How many archers? Did they have arrows? What were the Praetorians' losses during their retreat?

Casualty estimates ran between one-half to one-third of the men, the tribune informed him. Just over a hundred cavalry and only twenty-five archers remained. Arrows were in short supply.

The Praetorians had lost about three hundred men during their foray, most during the final battle just beyond the Roman lines. Successianus nodded, wondering what he could do next if the negotiations failed.

The tribune pointed to the north, where a group of men rode slowly through Persian lines. "We should have an answer shortly." The lead rider carried a javelin pointed high in the air. A white piece of cloth tied on its tip signified that they rode under a flag of truce.

Victor met Valerian at the center of the army's defenses. "He kept me waiting, then refused to deal with me," Victor complained in response to Valerian's questioning look.

"I can't understand why." Valerian scratched his head, then nodded at Successianus to acknowledge his presence but neglected to ask of his condition. "Didn't he say anything?"

"One of his deputies told me you must come yourself."

Valerian pondered the remark. "I suppose that makes sense—ruler dealing with ruler."

"What else did he say?" Successianus asked.

"He said to come with your senior officers and no more than twenty-five soldiers, since you'd be dealing directly with him."

"I wouldn't advise that," Successianus said quickly.

"What choice do we have?" Valerian asked. He interpreted Successianus' silence as a validation of his plan.

"Shouldn't a senior officer remain to command the army?" Successianus asked, feeling uneasy about these arrangements.

"I'll appoint Cledonius," Valerian said. "He's one of the senior centurions, and he's certainly distinguished himself in battle today. Besides," Valerian smiled, "I don't expect this to take all that much time, and I may want your opinion on some point of order."

He ignored my military advice but might want my opinion on negotiations, Successianus thought. "I still don't feel comfortable with this," he said. "I'd recommend you take at least a hundred Praetorians, maybe more."

"Very well," Valerian agreed. "A hundred it will be."

The answer should have satisfied Successianus, but his soldier's instinct still flashed alarm. He started to speak, but

Valerian held up a hand.

A short time later, Valerian, Victor, Successianus, a number of senators, and a hundred Praetorian guards rode through Persian lines under a flag of truce. Their Persian escorts led them to a place where the rolling dunes gave way to a flat expanse of ground. Scores of multi-colored tents stood in contrast to the stark surroundings. Their escorts led the Romans through this encampment, past curious onlookers, and approached a central tent separated from others by a respectful distance, and surrounded by Shapur's elite bodyguard. Successianus assumed the tents on either side housed his harem and he briefly wondered how many women Shapur had brought with him.

Directly in front of Shapur's tent, a portable throne had been set on a wooden staging about two feet high. As the Romans drew nearer, Successianus saw the gold-colored throne and assumed it was made to appear like gold to impress anyone who came into Shapur's presence.

The Romans dismounted and were told to stand in front of the throne. They fanned out in the open area behind Valerian. None of the Persians had made any comment about the number of escorts they had brought and Successianus now wished he had pressed Valerian to bring more. The Persian guides led the Romans' horses away and didn't return.

"Is this where you were before?" Valerian asked Victor while they waited for Shapur to appear. Victor nodded. The only sounds breaking the stillness were routine camp noises: bustling slaves doing their masters' biddings, an occasional bleating of a goat somewhere in the distance, a horse whinnying nearby. The heat was becoming more bearable, but Successianus still felt grimy and sweat-stained beneath his armor. His wound was throbbing.

The flaps of Shapur's tent swayed briefly and the guards on either side snapped to attention. Two burly soldiers walked deliberately to either side of the throne. Behind them a lone figure came to the tent's opening and stood surveying the scene expressionlessly for several moments. Shapur was tall, lean, dressed in black ceremonial robes lined with red silk, his feet covered with soft, jewel-encrusted slippers. A long sword at his left hip swayed as he walked toward the throne. Black hair spilled from beneath his ceremonial headdress. He had a straight nose, penetrating black eyes, a curly short-trimmed black beard, and a mustache that highlighted his thin, determined mouth. Trumpeters trilled a salutation while the King of Kings walked to the throne and seated himself deliberately. When he deemed himself comfortable, he casually waved a hand to his bowing subjects. Then, Shapur held up a finger to one side summoning his interpreter. While he spoke to the interpreter, he looked down at the Romans as if seeing them for the first time. A slight smile played briefly across his face.

"The King of Kings bids you greetings," the interpreter began in accented but acceptable Latin, "and wishes to know the reason you have sought an audience with him."

Successianus studied the men beside Shapur and assumed one was Shapur's son. Probably a general, or maybe he actually commands the army, Successianus thought, since the man was still wearing battle dress. The other man seemed to be Shapur's advisor, or maybe the head of his body guard. Valerian was speaking now.

"The Emperor of Rome bids greetings to the King of the Persians," Valerian began.

Valerian seems comfortable in this sort of situation, Successianus thought, although the hairs on the back of his neck stood on end. *Negotiations and speeches are Valerian's talents and passions. He certainly shows neither as a battlefield commander.*

"We come to suggest an alternative conclusion to this unfortunate conflict," Valerian swept both hands out in a grand gesture, a pleasant expression on his face, as if he, himself, were offering Shapur an exit from a painfully difficult situation.

"The King feels that events have evolved satisfactorily," the interpreter replied. "Nevertheless, he's willing to listen to your suggestions." The interpreter gestured for Valerian to continue.

Valerian nodded, as if encouraged by Shapur's remark. "Rather than both our nations spilling so much blood of our youth, I propose we resolve this matter to our mutual satisfaction, shall we say, in a financial way?" He stopped and nodded approvingly at his own suggestion.

Shapur's eyes darted quickly left and right without making the slightest movement of his head. While the translator was droning on, he leaned casually to his deputy, Maricq. "How many men do you think he has with him? Seventy-five?"

"Nearer a hundred, lord. I've been counting," Maricq whispered back.

"In fact, I'm prepared to offer you a considerable sum of gold," Valerian concluded.

"How large a sum, and when would it be available to me?" the interpreter asked.

Shapur whispered to Maricq. "Bring twice as many men here, quickly and quietly."

"It shall be done, lord," Maricq whispered back.

Shapur looked at Maricq. "Kill anyone that resists, but I want Valerian alive. When I clap my hands, that will be your signal to act." Maricq bowed his head to retire. "Have refreshments sent to us," Shapur smiled at Maricq. "It will give you a reason to absent yourself." Maricq smiled at Shapur, who raised a hand before he left. "And musicians, Maricq, to mask the sound of your men's movements."

"The sum of five hundred thousand denarii was agreed on when Emperor Philip negotiated a peace with you," Valerian was saying. He pursed his lips and nodded to himself. "I'm prepared to make a similar offer to you today."

Shapur leaned forward on his throne, as if the offer interested him.

"Philip offered me an annual tribute as well," the interpreter relayed.

"It's a possibility we could explore," Valerian agreed.

"Philip never made good on his promise of tribute," the interpreter continued. "Why should I believe you would behave differently?"

"Philip wasn't the emperor when he made that promise; I am."

"You're not the only emperor," Shapur mused.

"But I am the senior emperor. Therefore, my word is obeyed.

We're both men of our word, you and I," he spoke with conviction.

Negotiations were interrupted by the arrival of slaves carrying silver trays of dates and drinks of honeyed wine. While the men ate and drank, musicians played their mandolin-shaped ouds and hollow-caned neys, accompanied by the rhythmic drumbeats of large hourglass-shaped darboukas.

When the Romans had been served, Shapur leaned back on his throne, a golden goblet in his hand, and resumed the conversation.

"Philip also conceded lands to me," Shapur said through his interpreter. "Lands that Rome has since tried to reclaim."

"I'm willing to put my seal on whatever agreement we finally reach," Valerian said. "The word of the Emperor of Rome," he added for emphasis.

Shapur sat impassively, as if considering Valerian's pledge, while he scanned the area for a sign of Maricq. He found him standing behind some of the Praetorian guards on his far left. Their eyes met. Maricq nodded. Shapur appeared to make a decision. He held his goblet out to his side. A slave appeared with a pitcher. He shook his head and the slave retired carrying both pitcher and goblet. Then Shapur stood, took a step toward Valerian, and looked coldly down on him. When he spoke to the interpreter, the man looked startled. Shapur nodded for him to proceed.

"The King of Kings says, 'Why should I negotiate with you when I can take whatever I want.'"

Shapur clapped his hands; Maricq shouted orders from behind the Praetorians. The Persians had all been alerted to the King's signal. They poured from behind surrounding tents and rushed to confront the Praetorians. Valerian's jaw dropped in surprise.

"Protect the emperor," Successianus shouted, drawing his sword. Just as he pulled it free from the scabbard, three arrows pierced his torso. His sword clattered on the gravel. Successianus was dead before his body hit the ground. Twenty other Praetorians who had followed Successianus' lead also died quickly. The rest stood sullenly, realizing the futility of their efforts.

"Fetch my horse," Shapur said to one of the Imperial guards.

During the short wait, no one spoke nor moved. A tall black stallion was led into the opening from beside Shapur's tent with a snort and a toss of its head. Shapur smiled at the animal and signaled for it to be brought to where he now stood in front of Valerian. Shapur impatiently waved the interpreter to come to him as well.

"The King commands you to help him to mount," the interpreter said to Valerian.

Valerian looked at the interpreter incredulously. Then he looked into Shapur's expressionless eyes. His face burned with the shame of this humiliation, but he realized he had no choice and slowly he knelt before Shapur. The King put a foot on Valerian's shoulder, then spoke to his interpreter.

"You are now my prisoner," the man translated to Valerian as Shapur swung his other leg over his mount. The Persians burst into cheers and waved their arms wildly while Shapur raised his right arm high over his head, waved back at his men, and allowed himself a rare smile.

That evening the Persian soldiers withdrew from the battlefield, as was their custom. Before leaving, they shouted insults at the Romans and vowed to return the next day to complete their victory.

When Valerian and his retinue failed to return that night, rumors ran rampant through the army. Some speculated that he'd been murdered, or had even sought refuge with the Persians. Cledonius heard these rumors. As the senior officer in charge of the remnants of the army, many men came to him during the night asking if he knew any more than they did. And, although deeply troubled by the rumors, he could not offer anyone words of consolation. He rejected their suggestions that he abandon the battlefield that night and lead them to somewhere, anywhere but here. Instead, he said he had been placed in command of the army and would honor that trust and remain where he was until the emperor returned.

Despite his counsel, nearly half of the men felt that no good would come from waiting for Persians to return in the morning.

Those fit enough fled in the darkness.

The next morning, all who remained with Cledonius were killed or enslaved by the Persians.

1-3

A Strange Request
Samosata, Commagene
24 June, 260

Afternoon shadows, cast by hills north of the city, stretched over distant fields of barley and darkened three arches of a recently completed aqueduct. Macrianus, manager of Valerian's supplies and temporarily in command of the remaining Roman soldiers, frowned and drummed his fingers on the fortress wall as he gazed along the road from the bridge below the fortress walls until it disappeared in the rising terrain on the far shore. This was part of the ancient Persian "Royal Road." Xerxes had crossed that bridge on his way to invade Greece over seven centuries earlier. Valerian's messenger, now two days overdue, would come along that road and over that bridge, Macrianus was sure of it.

The last message from Valerian arrived on the 22nd and told Macrianus to expect the next correspondence from Edessa, first city east along the Royal Road. A message from Edessa would mean Valerian had relieved the siege and defeated Shapur. Macrianus imagined the "Triumph" they would hold in Rome to celebrate a victory over the Persians: he and Valerian at the head of the army, marching down streets to a cheering crowd, spoils of victory towed in carts behind them for everyone to see, Shapur walking in chains behind Valerian. But the messenger from Edessa had not arrived as expected. Macrianus dismissed his concern as absurd. Romans expected victory, even against superior forces, and history had proven them right countless times. Many unexpected events could have arisen to delay the messenger.

Instead of word from Valerian, a message came yesterday from the half of Julianus' legion, IV Scythica, just returned to

Zeugma from training in the desert. Macrianus smiled as he thought of Successianus' reaction to Julianus not having his entire legion ready to march.

"A messenger to see you, sir."

"From whom?"

"He says he's from the emperor, sir."

Macrianus felt a sense of relief wash over him. "Bring him to me."

"Here, sir?"

"No, at Valerian's headquarters. Keep the man waiting for a few minutes," Macrianus added, then signaled for his horse.

On reaching Valerian's headquarters, Macrianus sprawled comfortably in a chair next to a large cedar table that Valerian favored for discussions with his staff. A full goblet of wine sat untouched in front of him, beside a plate piled with grapes, dates, and figs. When the man entered the room it took Macrianus a few moments to realize who he was, although Macrianus knew him. His face was drawn, his hair matted. Dirt covering his clothes was mixed with sweat, or maybe dried blood. Macrianus wrinkled his nose. Apparently this man hadn't bathed in days. He stood erect and silent in front of Macrianus, awaiting' permission to speak. Why has Cledonius come, Macrianus wondered, instead of one of the usual messengers? He rested his elbow on the table and rubbed his chin.

"Wine, Cledonius?" he asked.

"I'd prefer water."

"Of course." Macrianus gestured to a tribune at the far end of the room.

Soon a servant appeared carrying a silver tray with a glass goblet and a crystal pitcher of water. She set the tray on a table near Cledonius and filled his goblet before slipping out of the room. Macrianus nodded toward the tray. Cledonius lifted the pitcher to his lips with both hands, and drank deeply, spilling water over his face as he drank. Finally, he took several deep breaths before setting the empty pitcher onto the table.

"A fig perhaps?" Macrianus reached for a date himself. He took a small bite before looking up at Cledonius.

Cledonius' eyes dropped momentarily to the offered fruit, then looked straight ahead. "No." There was no expression in his voice.

Macrianus sat up in his chair. "What news do you bring me? I assume Valerian has sent me something in writing." He held out a hand expectantly.

Cledonius scowled. "There was no time to put his wishes on parchment. The emperor instructs you to come to him. He should be outside Edessa by now."

"He wants me to come?" Macrianus gasped. "When?"

"As quickly as possible."

"There must have been more."

"You're to bring the reserve forces, and the balance of the imperial treasury."

"A strange request, indeed, Cledonius," Macrianus temporized. "It was quite clear when Valerian left that I was to remain here, to manage the reserves and keep the army supplied."

Cledonius shrugged. "The situation has changed."

"He wants all the reserves?" Macrianus sounded incredulous.

"And the balance of the treasury."

"Why would he want the balance of the treasury at Edessa?" Macrianus stared at Cledonius suspiciously. *How quickly can I ready the legionaries and make the treasury suitable for traveling?* Macrianus wondered. A knock at the door interrupted him. "Later," he barked impatiently.

The tribune stood stubbornly at the threshold. "It's urgent, sir."

"I'm busy.

"A man here insists that the emperor has been defeated!" the tribune persisted.

Before he said anything further to the tribune, Macrianus stared at Cledonius. "Was there a battle?" he asked.

"For the better part of two days."

Now he understood Cledonius' appearance. Macrianus considered Cledonius' answer for a few moments before nodding to his tribune. "Send the man in."

Macrianus recognized the man as the leader of the most recent supply train to leave Samosata. His appearance resembled

Cledonius'—except for the blood stains. "Your report, centurion," he said.

"Our supply train met stragglers from the army. They said there'd been a battle with the Persians." After the centurion related his story, Macrianus looked questioningly at Cledonius.

"That's essentially what happened."

"Why didn't you tell me?" Macrianus glared at Cledonius, his anger rising.

"I was coming to that part."

Fear suddenly gripped Macrianus. Shapur's victorious army was out there somewhere, and the reserve forces here at Samosata were undoubtedly his next objective. What should I do now? he wondered, acutely aware that all decisions were now his to make, and that he would bear the responsibility for their outcome. A saying he'd once heard from a Chinese merchant came to mind. "Crisis," the man had said, "was opportunity riding on a dangerous wind." An opportunity. Macrianus thought.

"Was he killed?" he asked Cledonius, referring to Valerian.

"No."

"Then he's Shapur's prisoner?"

"He is."

Macrianus was incredulous. "This has never happened before, Cledonius. Never!" He thought a moment more. "Successianus?"

"I was told he died defending the emperor."

"Victor?"

"With Valerian."

"What about Julianus?" Macrianus asked, curious, rather than concerned.

"Lured into a Persian trap before the battle began." Cledonius made no effort to hide his disgust. "We never saw him, or his legionaries, again."

Macrianus leaned back, his composure returning. A thin smile played across his face. "So Valerian wants me to bring him the Imperial treasury, and the rest of the army."

"He said a ransom was the only way to gain his freedom and that the reserves would keep Shapur from simply taking it."

Macrianus clasped his hands behind his head and regarded Cledonius. "Shapur may not have any intention of settling for a ransom."

"Then you'll abandon Valerian to the Persians?"

"I could go myself, along with the gold and soldiers, of course. But perhaps that's Shapur's plan—to lure our reserves out of Samosata and defeat them, too." He shrugged. "Then we'd lose both the treasury and what's left of the army."

"And your own freedom," Cledonius sneered, reading Macrianus' mind. "I didn't think you'd have the courage to come."

Macrianus flushed briefly. "Don't tell me you trust Shapur's word, despite what Valerian said. I find that preposterous."

"I am sent by the emperor with his orders," Cledonius said.

"Indeed!" Macrianus leaned forward, placing one elbow on the table and resting his chin on his hand. "Then you understand the predicament better than I first thought." Macrianus stared straight ahead, lost in thought. *I owe my current position and authority to Valerian. Yet Valerian's indecisiveness led to his current predicament. As emperor, Valerian wasn't strong enough to hold what the Senate had granted to him.* "There is another option."

"I expected that refusing to send relief would have been your first thought."

Macrianus frowned. "We seem compelled to respond to Shapur's demands without knowing his intentions."

"Then the rumors were true," Cledonius interrupted.

"They seldom are," Macrianus replied. "Which rumors are you speaking about, exactly?"

"Some say you urged Valerian to confront Shapur, yet arranged to stay safely behind the walls of Samosata with a large part of the emperor's army." Cledonius watched Macrianus' face closely.

Macrianus flinched, this accusation taking him completely by surprise, then smiled at Cledonius. "And what if I did?"

Silence settled oppressively over the room. They stared at each other, neither blinking nor speaking. "Will you come?" Cledonius asked finally.

"Who would be so mad as to prefer to be a slave rather than

a free man?" Macrianus demanded. "You come to me from two men, neither of whom is my master. One is an enemy and the other is not even master of himself."

"Then the emperor will die in captivity." Cledonius' shoulders sagged slightly, although his voice betrayed no emotion. He suddenly looked very tired. "You have it in your power to free him."

"I doubt it." Macrianus held Cledonius' gaze, confident in his decision. "If I were you, Cledonius, I wouldn't go back to Shapur. He doesn't strike me as the type to take a refusal gracefully. There's also the question of your own freedom."

"Honor compels me to return."

Macrianus rose slowly and held out his hand. "Then good bye, Cledonius." He wasn't surprised when Cledonius refused his hand, turned without being dismissed, and stalked out of the room.

Stillness filled the chamber after Cledonius' departure. Macrianus forced himself to face the situation as he now understood it. The army had been defeated. Valerian was Shapur's prisoner—his slave, in essence. Successianus was dead. Victor was a prisoner. He didn't know if Callistus still held Edessa, if the city had fallen to Shapur's siege, or if the garrison had starved to death. *Why didn't I think to ask him about that?* Macrianus chided himself. This meant he was the senior Roman official in the East, and his reserve soldiers, plus Julianus' half-legion, were the only forces he could count on to resist the Persians. *If I were Shapur, I'd attack Samosata and destroy what's left of the Roman army. I'll withdraw to Zeugma and combine Julianus' forces with mine. Then I can withdraw to Antioch. I should be able to withstand a siege there. How much time do I have? It should take Cledonius a day to reach Edessa, and at least two for Shapur's army to march here.* Macrianus signaled for his tribune. "We'll go south to Zeugma with all the reserves in two days," he said.

"Then who will defend Samosata?" the tribune asked.

The question surprised Macrianus. he shrugged. "They'll have to fend for themselves."

1-4
Anticipating a Siege
Edessa
26 June, 260

Callistus, a senior general under Valerian's command, stood on the ramparts of Edessa trying to count the Persian campfires flickering beyond the city. He gave up when he couldn't determine where fires ended and stars began. The night was cold, clear, and still. He pulled his cloak closer around his shoulders.

"Would you like another, sir?" his aide asked, starting to remove his own.

Callistus held up a hand and shook his head, grateful for the offer. "You need it more than I do."

"What does it mean?" the aide asked, pointing at the host of campfires.

Callistus looked at his young aide for a moment. He was barely twenty, with no battle experience beyond this siege. "It means Shapur will launch a major assault on the city tomorrow."

"What do you think will happen?" the aide asked, expecting some reassurance from his general.

Callistus' reply was noncommittal. "We've held them off so far."

"Maybe the emperor will arrive with his reinforcements," the aide suggested.

Callistus nodded. "Maybe. Get some rest," he said, dismissing the aide. "We'll be up before dawn."

Callistus stared at the campfires long after the aide had gone. His men were weakened from days of half-rations. They would not have the strength to resist an all-out attack. *Without Valerian's relief column*, Callistus thought dispassionately, *it will probably be over in a day, two at the most.* He had faced the prospect of death many times in his career. Most were in the desperate moments of battle—an arrow splitting the top of his shield, a Persian lance penetrating part of his body armor, a last-second glimpse of a sword swung at his head. Better not to know that certain death lies just a day or two away. Callistus thought of his wife and family. *Had they known their fates in advance? Or had death come quickly, after Shapur overran their city, could it have been eighteen years ago*? His thoughts drifted to the emperor. Callistus held out little hope of relief, since Valerian had not come by now. He didn't know if the emperor had lost his nerve, changed his mind about relieving the city, or was just moving too slowly. In a few more days, the answer would not matter. When Valerian arrived, if he came at all, he would find a sacked city, defenders dead to the last man. Callistus stretched and sighed. He desperately needed a few hours' sleep.

By daybreak Callistus had resumed his watch on the ramparts, his legionaries bravely deployed, ready to receive a Persian assault. Despite their weakened condition, Callistus knew his men would fight courageously and resolutely to the end. But instead of being attacked he stared in disbelief at what he saw.

The Persian army was marching past Edessa, outwardly unconcerned that the city still stood, as if the last forty-two days of siege had been an unfortunate mistake, or had never happened at all.

"Do you think it's a trick, sir?" his aide asked.

"I don't think so." A sense of relief washed over Callistus. He exhaled knowing that the siege had been lifted and he wouldn't die today.

"What else could it be?"

Callistus wondered the same thing, but his soldier's instinct told him that something else was happening. *What's changed? Where are the Persians going*? The answers were obvious when he put himself in Shapur's position.

"Shapur must have won a victory," he said gravely, "so decisive that he's willing to bypass an enemy-held city and leave remnants of a Roman garrison behind him."

"Then they're heading for Samosata," the aide speculated. His grasp of the situation impressed Callistus.

"Yes. To defeat our reserves," Callistus agreed.

"Then where?"

"Either he'll attack Antioch again, or invade the provinces—Commagene and Cilicia."

"Why go back to Antioch when he could attack so many wealthy and under-protected cities?" the aide asked rhetorically. "What will we do next, sir?" he looked at his general.

Callistus considered the question. *Foolhardy to pursue the Persians with six cohorts of half-starved legionaries.* He wondered how Macrianus would fare against the full force of Shapur's assault. "We'll go to Carrhae, refit the soldiers' equipment, have a good meal." He half-smiled at the aide's reaction to the mention of food. "Then we'll go west to Zeugma. Maybe we'll find stragglers from the army and learn what happened to Valerian, and maybe Macrianus as well, he thought. "Pass the word," he said to his aide. "We leave tomorrow at dawn."

1-5
Unexpected Reunion
Zeugma, Commagene
3 July, 260

Callistus shook his head when he reached the eastern edge of the Euphrates River and stared at the plumes of smoke rising above Zeugma on the opposite shore. It was clear that many of the city's buildings lay in ruins.

"The Persians have burned the city!" one of his tribunes exclaimed.

Shapur must have made short work of Samosata, Callistus thought, with a mixture of admiration at Shapur's efficiency and scorn at Macrianus' rapid capitulation. A Persian victory at Samosata would mean the loss of reserve forces left there under Macrianus' command. *If Shapur's already destroyed Samosata and now Zeugma, then we're too late to defend Antioch. Strange that Shapur didn't burn the bridge*, Callistus thought. A hot dry wind blew dust across the road in front of him and onto the barren landscape behind him. He wiped his brow, then turned to and spoke to his deputy.

"Have the men make camp here. I'll cross the river with a

small detachment and evaluate the situation."

Half an hour later, the group reached Zeugma's eastern gate. "Take me to your commanding officer," Callistus shouted after identifying himself to the sentry atop the wall. While the sentry instructed legionnaires to open the gate, he suppressed his irritation at not being recognized then wondered why someone would be standing guard after the Persians had sacked the city. "What are you doing here?" Callistus demanded of the first legionnaire he met when the gate swung open.

The man looked surprised by the question. "No one's relieved us, sir."

Callistus brushed past him then stopped directly beneath the east gate's great stone arch and stared at the spectacle in front of him. Most nearby buildings lay in ruins. Upper floors having fallen successively onto the ones below. Fires still burned through wooden debris from apartments on the top floors. Since he heard no cries for help, Callistus realized people trapped in the rubble must have been overcome by smoke, or died horribly. He assumed from bodies lying in the street that some had jumped to their death rather than die in the fire. Survivors leaned against the few intact buildings or wandered aimlessly about.

"Earthquake," a legionnaire said at Callistus' shoulder. The voice startled him.

So... Shapur hasn't been here after all. Maybe Antioch has been spared. Instead of us getting support from Zeugma, we're going to be the ones providing help to the city. Callistus thought a moment, then summoned a messenger. "Return to camp. Tell the lead centurion I want all medical personnel he can get and legionnaires to help fight the fires."

"How many, sir?"

"A hundred to start with. He can decide what he needs after he sees what we're dealing with." Callistus motioned to the gate sentry. "Lead me to your commanding officer." The man hesitated, reluctant to leave his post. "There's nothing to guard against here," Callistus waved his hand around the rubble.

Once his men passed underneath the arch, they were forced to dismount and lead their horses on foot, picking their way through buckled streets. Some stones that had comprised the pavement were thrust upward while others hung precariously over gaping chasms where the earth had opened. Dust filled the air, its musty odor contrasting with an acrid smell of smoke.

"When did this happen?" Callistus asked the sentry, while they pushed grimly through streets packed with stunned people.

"Just after daybreak, sir. Dogs began barking, the horses became restless. Some broke out of their stalls and raced through the streets. Then we heard it too, like a distant thunder at first, then like a strong wind blowing through trees in the orchards. Walls began to shake. Buildings began to fall. We were thrown to the ground. The roar was deafening." He shuddered. "After that…the fires began."

They came upon an old man sitting at the edge of the street, stroking the head of a young woman clutched in his arms. Three small children lay motionless around him. Callistus stopped and bent down on one knee. He put a finger to the woman's neck, then did the same to each of the children. "I know… they're all dead," the man said hoarsely. Callistus rose wordlessly.

"Why haven't the soldiers been sent out to help these people?" Callistus glared at the sentry. The man shrugged. Of course he would have no way of answering that question. And then Callistus realized he had no idea who was in charge at Zeugma. "Who is your commanding officer now?" he asked.

"The legate of IV Scythica Legion, sir."

"Julianus! I thought he was dead." When Callistus approached ruins of the city prefect's villa he saw signs of organized activity. As they drew closer, Callistus' surprise turned to anger, then to fury. The man who seemed to be in charge wore the scarlet cape of a general. Why would Julianus settle for the mere rank of a general? Callistus fumed. Why not the purple cape of the emperor? His hand tightened on the hilt of his sword.

An aide spoke hurriedly to the man with the red cape when Callistus' group approached, and he wheeled about to face them.

"Callistus! I see you survived the siege at Edessa," Macrianus nodded with a thin smile.

"I see you survived the siege of Samosata."

Callistus' comment surprised Macrianus. "There was no

siege of Samosata, at least not while I was there."

"I saw the battlefield near Carrhae," Callistus said, "but no signs of Valerian or Successianus."

"Captured and killed—in that order. Cledonius told me." Callistus said nothing. "He came to Samosata," Macrianus continued, "saying Valerian wanted the treasury and reserves brought to him."

"Obviously you declined."

"I'd have been a fool to go."

"As well as Shapur's prisoner yourself," Callistus agreed.

"I intended to take my forces to Antioch, but, as you can see," Macrianus looked around at destruction everywhere around him, "this interrupted my plans."

"The prefect?" Callistus nodded at the city prefect's collapsed home behind Macrianus.

Macrianus shrugged. "Dead. It was rumored that a statue of Jupiter crushed him. Actually, he and his whole family died when their villa collapsed."

"Where's Julianus?" Callistus asked. "I thought he was with Valerian, but I was told he was here."

"He was with Valerian," Macrianus confirmed. "But he's here, somewhere in the city. No one seems to know his whereabouts this morning."

Callistus turned his attention to more pressing matters. "I've sent for medical people and legionnaires to help fight the fires."

"Mine are doing the same," Macrianus said. "They started in the north, closest to my campsite. It seems that damage runs south and west from the city. My campsite only suffered tremors." He looked across the city. Ruins of the prefect's villa sat high on the hill, affording them an excellent view.

"We need to talk," Callistus said. He pointed to a fallen column a few paces away, part of what once had been the prefect's villa, and started walking toward it. Callistus smiled inwardly as he thought how his wife would sometimes say that to him. Nothing pleasant ever seemed to follow those words. "Alone," he said sharply, when Macrianus' aide moved to join them.

"I've never cared for you personally," Callistus began,

poking a finger into Macrianus' chest. "Nor do I think you're a competent general." Macrianus retreated under Callistus' assault until he became pinned against the column then found himself sitting on it. He flushed at Callistus' insults and tried to rise. Callistus grabbed his shoulder forcing him to remain seated. "This is a time for truths," Callistus said. "And the truth is this: we're all that's left in the East."

"Not necessarily," Macrianus interrupted. "We're not sure if Odenathus (king of Palmyra and a Roman citizen) is still our ally."

"He won't side with Shapur," Callistus scoffed. "He's already tried that."

Macrianus stared at him, amazed at this revelation. "When did this happen?"

"Years ago," Callistus smiled at his surprise. "It failed spectacularly."

A dog barked furiously somewhere nearby, joined quickly by others. The two men stared in awe at an olive grove on the edge of a nearby hill. Trees rose and fell as if the land were an angry sea. Then, a noise like a thousand galloping horses approached them from the olive grove, rushed past where they sat, and moved on toward the northern part of the city. As suddenly as it came, the sound was gone. An unnatural stillness settled over the area.

Macrianus let out a deep breath. "Who knows how many more tremors there'll be."

Callistus returned to their discussion. "We can work together, or we can challenge each other for supremacy. Here's my suggestion: you manage the logistics and the administration. Let me fight the Persians.":

"Do you have a plan?"

"Not yet," Callistus admitted. "We should work on that together, after we learn what Shapur does, and what kind of forces we can bring to bear."

"Agreed," Macrianus conceded.

"Good." Callistus nodded. "Then there's just one other issue that needs to be resolved."

Macrianus was suddenly suspicious. "And that would be?"

"Julianus. I'll deal with him personally."

"You don't plan to kill him, do you?" Macrianus looked only mildly concerned. "He is related to…I guess it would be Emperor Gallienus now."

Callistus shook his head. "Death would be too kind a punishment."

Julianus finally sauntered into what remained of the legion's headquarters around midday. He suppressed a look of surprise when he saw Callistus, then smiled. "Hello, general. I hadn't expected to see you here."

Callistus stood in front of him and glared. "Tell me what happened."

Julianus summarized events of the battle from his perspective as he lounged comfortably on a dining couch that he had managed to find somewhere in the city.

"What did you do after you chased the Persian light cavalry?" Callistus growled.

"When the Persians abandoned us, I thought it prudent to make for Carrhae to seek reinforcements."

"You had half a legion with you at the time."

Julianus dismissed the question with the wave of a hand.

"You left the army in the middle of a battle. On whose authority?"

"My own, of course." Julianus frowned. "We were isolated from the rest of the army."

"And when did you rejoin the battle?"

"There was a problem mobilizing the reserves in Carrhae," Julianus protested. He avoided Callistus' unwavering gaze.

"So you waited in Carrhae?" Callistus sounded almost sympathetic.

"What else could we do at that point?" Julianus held up the palms of his hands.

Callistus waited until it was clear Julianus had nothing further to add. "I passed through Carrhae after leaving Edessa," he said quietly. "It's curious that no one there thought to mention your visit."

Julianus shrugged then poured himself a glass of wine from a bottle he had recently obtained. "Outpost cities, local garrison troops. What do you expect?"

"What did you expect?" Callistus countered. "You said you went there for reinforcements." Julianus made no comment. Instead, he raised the glass of wine to his lips. Callistus sprang forward and grabbed his wrist. The goblet fell to the ground shattering on the tiles. He struck Julianus across the face with the back of his other hand. "After Carrhae I went to that battlefield," Callistus growled. "It was hot. Bodies lay everywhere, stripped and bloated. The stench was overpowering. I had to leave them lying on that god-forsaken plain." He stopped, breathing deeply while the memory flooded over him. "Friends of mine lay there, Julianus. Men I'd known for most of my life, had fought with in countless battles. You deserted them! You abandoned your emperor on the field of battle." Julianus met Callistus' disgust with an insolent glare. "You deserted your father. What will your mother think when she learns of that?"

"I've brought back half a legion of soldiers," Julianus protested, rubbing his cheek and trying to wrench himself free of Callistus' grip. "Nearly a whole legion, when you count the men who stayed at Zeugma."

"You're a coward and a slacker, Julianus." Callistus threw him back onto his couch. "You're relieved as legate of the IV Scythica."

"I serve at the pleasure of the emperor," Julianus answered haughtily.

"There is no emperor in the East now," Callistus shouted. "When I write to Emperor Gallienus and tell him how you deserted his father on the battlefield, I think he'll support my decision. If not, I'll reinstate you as legate—if you're still alive. In the meantime," Callistus paused to take several deep breaths, veins on his neck bulged, his eyes wide, "if I see you anywhere near any military unit, I'll kill you myself, not with my sword, but with my bare hands."

News From the East
Rome
22 July, 260

Humid afternoon heat hung over the capitol, oppressive even here on the Palatine Hill. Saecularis, sat at a small ivory-inlaid ebony desk he had given to his daughter years before. He was living in the Imperial Palace at the invitation of his son-in-law, Gallienus, while performing his duties as senior Consul and Prefect of Rome. It was to be expected, therefore, that a message from Syria would have been delivered to him.

After reading details of Valerian's defeat, Saecularis rolled up the scroll and stared straight ahead, unconsciously drumming his fingers on the table. He wondered if the messenger was aware of its contents, even though the wax seal had been intact when he received it. Then he shook his head: everyone in the east, he realized, knew about the contents of the message. And by now, everyone in the port of Ostia must know it. Soon news will be all over Rome.

He thought of Valerian for a moment. The message said he had been seized by the Persians after a disastrous battle. There were few details and no indication if he were still alive. As a general, Saecularis would like to have known details of the battle. As a Consul, his first concern was the implication of this Roman defeat. Shapur, the message also indicated, was reported to be moving into the provinces of Commagene and Cilicia with his victorious army and no serious opposition. *How far will Shapur go?* Saecularis wondered. *Will he try to capture all of Asia Minor, restore the ancient Persian boundaries? Who could stop him, if he tried?*

Defeat of a Roman army and capture of an emperor would be seen as a sign of weakness, encouraging invasions externally and revolts internally. The empire needed competent leaders to maintain order and discipline in the provinces and to defend borders against hostile armies. Yet, these competent men, accustomed to acting on their own and with one or more legions under their command, also posed the greatest threat of rebellion. *Who might try to seize power?* Saecularis worked his way through the empire: *Fortunatianus in Numidia? Doubtful. Postumus in Germania? Possible. But General Silvanus and Gallienus' son, Saloninus, should keep him in check. No one along the Danuvius is likely to revolt with Gallienus and most of the army nearby. Aemilianus in Egypt? That would be serious, considering grain supplies we import, but he only has part of a legion at Alexandria for support. Macrianus in Syria? With Shapur running unchecked through the region, he's likely to have other things on his mind. One of Gallienus' generals? I've heard nothing from my sources to suggest their dissatisfaction. Saecularis took a deep breath and exhaled slowly. Maybe,* he hoped against his better judgment, *it won't be as bad as I first feared.*

He dipped one of his daughter Salonina's pens into a nearby inkwell and started writing a message to Gallienus.

2-1
A Plan and a Summons
Antioch, Syria
23 July, 260

"You want to do what?" Macrianus stared skeptically at Callistus and Gnaeus Pompieus Rubius, commander of the naval fleet based at nearby Seleucia.

"Emperor Trajan once moved a legion by sea during his eastern campaign. We could do something similar ourselves," Callistus said.

"How many ships did he use?"

"Over sixty, but for a much longer distance. We're looking at less than one hundred miles, around twenty-four hours' sailing time as long as the winds remain favorable."

"Do you happen to have sixty ships at your disposal?" Macrianus asked Rubius.

"I've commandeered twenty merchant ships and four large grain ships from Egypt—all in the harbor now. Between those and my ten warships, I estimate we could transport over twenty-five hundred legionnaires."

Macrianus shook his head. "Valerian attacked Shapur with a whole army. Now you're proposing to attack him with half a legion!"

"We could send the ships back to Seleucia and bring another

twenty-five hundred men in three days," Rubius suggested.

They sat around a square cedar table in a small room at Antioch's Imperial palace, a room Valerian had favored for personal discussions. Callistus looked at the mosaic map on the floor wishing it were of the province of Cilicia, where he intended to land his legionnaires, instead of Syria. He thought about how uncertain and indefinite their path was at this point. *What would be the outcome of the war? Who would eventually gain control of the east? Even though there was uncertainty and hesitation with Valerian*, Callistus thought, *Valerian was the unquestioned leader*. He cleared his throat.

"You heard Rubius, yourself," Callistus reiterated his argument. "One of his ships fled a Persian attack at Aigeai three days ago. And Severus, the ship's captain, said the Persian army has dispersed into looting parties."

"Neither of you," Macrianus waved at Callistus and Rubius, "has any experience moving such a large force by sea. Putting that difficulty aside for a moment, you'd have to disembark this force somewhere along an unfamiliar shore against an enemy force much larger than your own."

"We'll have the advantage of surprise," Callistus said. "Maybe we can rescue the emperor at the same time we defeat Shapur."

"We don't even know if Valerian is still alive," Macrianus said, suddenly fearful of Valerian's wrath if Callistus rescued him when he, Macrianus, had refused Cledonius' entreaties to come to Valerian's aid.

"We don't know that he's dead either. I presume you want Valerian freed, even though you refused his ransom?"

The reproach hung in the air, but Macrianus forced himself to ignore Callistus' barb. "We should keep the army near Antioch. That was our initial plan: to protect the city and confront Shapur when he returned loaded down with spoils and prisoners."

"Protect Antioch from what?" Callistus asked. "We know where Shapur is now."

"What about Odenathus?" Macrianus asked.

"Valerian gave him the title of consul—and made him

governor of lower Syria," Callistus said. "We were both there when he did it!"

"Which put a legion under his command," Macrianus reminded him. "He might be tempted to attack Antioch himself, if we deplete our defenses."

"At my last count, we'd assembled over twenty-three thousand men, nearly five legions," Callistus said. "I'll be leaving you eighteen thousand men. That should be sufficient for you to defend against Odenathus' one legion."

"He has an army of his own, too," Macrianus sniffed.

Callistus stared at him, thinking about how quickly Macrianus had assumed the role of "proconsul" of the east. *You govern your subjects with a heavy hand*, he thought, *yet you're tentative, maybe even fearful, about battles with the enemy—just like Valerian.*

"Dealing with Odenathus is your responsibility," Callistus said finally. "Dealing with Persians is mine."

Macrianus studied Callistus and the fleet commander for some time before reluctantly reaching his decision. "You'll take my sons with you, of course." Macrianus' suggestion took Callistus by surprise.

"They have no combat experience whatsoever!" Callistus thought of Macrianus' two sons: Quietus, the younger and Macrianus the elder, both unremarkable men in their early thirties. "You were content to have them remain at Samosata with you."

"I've been training them to follow in my footsteps as quartermasters and supply officers," Macrianus said defensively. "Under the circumstances, I think they could benefit from some battle experience."

"Maybe their real purpose would be to act as spies for their father," Callistus suggested.

"The thought never entered my mind," Macrianus protested unconvincingly. "Is there something you'd rather I not know about?"

"I've got nothing to hide from you," Callistus growled. "But having one of your sons along should protect me from any of your intrigues. I'll take young Macrianus with me," Callistus said, "provided he understands he's under my authority. Quietus stays with you."

Macrianus nodded, smiled, and leaned back in his chair, satisfied with this arrangement. *My son will also understand the difficulties our family would face if Valerian returned to Antioch alive.*

Mediolanum
2 August, 260

"Something must be troubling you." Philip, Greek tutor to Gallienus' children, said, putting down a scroll he had been lecturing from and frowned at Marinianus, youngest of Gallienus' and Salonina's sons. "But obviously it's not your lack of preparation for this lesson."

"I've just turned sixteen, Philip. Why hasn't my father called me to join him?"

"When he feels the time is right," Philip began, remembering that Gallienus had opposed taking Marinianus on his urgent pursuit of the Juthungi.

"My brothers were already riding with my father by now," Marinianus persisted.

"Maybe you'll be riding sooner than you expected." They both turned in surprise at Salonina's voice. "I've just received a message from your father this morning," she continued, addressing Marinianus. "We're to join him in Carnuntum."

Marinianus' face lit up. "How soon can we leave?"

"I've told Fulvianus to be ready in ten days. He'll command our escort, again."

"Oh." Marinianus couldn't hide his disappointment. He turned to Philip. "Can we end the lesson now?" Philip nodded, realizing he had lost Marinianus' attention for the rest of the day.

"He's a quick, energetic student, just as you were," Phillip said after Marinianus rushed from the room. "Who can blame him for wanting to be with his father?" Philip looked expectantly at Salonina.

Salonina sat on one of the benches to face him. "I won't miss Mediolanum, Philip,"

"It's not Rome," Philip conceded, "but the theatre has given us excellent entertainment. And actors provided almost as much drama as some of the gladiators." He smiled conspiratorially.

"Are you referring to their fighting, or her affair?"

"I find the latter much more entertaining than the former," Philip replied. "Greek culture takes a dim view of adultery. Personally, I think it's scandalous that the wife of your husband's cavalry commander sleeps with a gladiator." He frowned at the thought then shrugged. "But apparently you Romans don't find it that unusual."

"He's a Dacian and so is she," Salonina said, as if their common homeland justified the affair. "Pharsala may even have known him personally before he became a gladiator."

"Probably a criminal," Philip said, scornful of the man's history, "or a slave."

"Neither," Salonina said, a little too quickly for Philip's comfort. "I'm told he enjoys fighting."

"Killing people is probably closer to the truth." Philip thought for a moment. "Surely Pharsala doesn't believe those myths about gladiators' virility?"

"She says they aren't myths." Salonina blushed and smiled. "Now," she rose and turned toward her quarters, "I think I'll finish writing to Saloninus."

Later, when Salonina put down her pen, she stared at a fresco covering the room's far wall, three mounted men and a pack of dogs stalking a lion near a woodland meadow. But instead of admiring the scene she was thinking about her sons. *Saloninus turns eighteen this December. Will I get to see him in Rome again this winter?* His infrequent letters were filled with stories of fighting alongside Silvanus and Postumus against the Franks, some of whom had penetrated deep into Gaul's heartland. And his occasional comments about the two generals reinforced Salonina's earlier observations of friction between Silvanus and Postumus. She knew Postumus was difficult to get along with. *Everyone, except Aureolus, complained about him, although he was always courteous to me. Now that Marinianus is sixteen, he's consumed with the desire to ride into battle with his father, just like Saloninus and Valerian before him. Valerian would have been twenty this September*. Salonina tensed as she thought of her eldest son, whose birthday was three days before her own. *Would his presence in Pannonia have prevented Regalianus' uprising? What would he be doing, if he were still alive*? She pictured him riding proudly beside his father at the head of a cavalry column with Imperial banners fluttering behind them.

Salonina had not seen her husband since the first of March, when he left Rome expecting to fight against Regalianus. She found it unnerving how suddenly and dramatically their lives could change. Instead of a civil war Gallienus had repulsed an invasion of Roxolani, then rushed north after retreating Juthungi. She understood from his letter, sent to her on 19 July, that he had managed to catch them before they crossed the Danuvius River, retaking a great deal of their spoils and freeing many of their captives.

I wonder if Maximus found Prisca, Salonina thought. She was pleased that Gallienus had invited General Maximus to join his army to search for his wife. He'd been so desolate in Rome last winter without her. *Was Prisca still alive, had she been one of the captives already taken across the river*? Salonina tried to imagine what being a prisoner might have been like, but found herself unable to understand being totally dependent on the whims of a barbarian. She shook her head to clear those disturbing thoughts and returned her attention to Gallienus' last message. He had said he was planning to cross the Danuvius to fight the barbarians in their homeland. Many times during their interminable winter in Carnuntum, Salonina had stared at the vast wilderness across the frozen expanse of that river. *Could it possibly have been five years ago*? What had unnerved her was the realization that barbarians could walk across the frozen river wherever they chose and whenever they wished. A shiver ran through her as she tried to picture Gallienus somewhere beyond the river.

Pompeia, Salonina's head of the household staff, interrupted her musings with a message that had just arrived from Rome. "It's from your father."

Salonina smiled, relieved for a reason to brush aside her

troubling thoughts of Prisca's unfortunate ordeal, anticipating happier news from her father. "Stay Pompeia," Salonina said, expecting to share some tidbit of gossip from Rome. Eagerly she broke the seal and opened the scroll. Her face turned ashen and she gasped. The scroll fell from her lap onto the floor.

"What is it?" Pompeia asked, alarmed by Salonina's reaction.

"Poor Valerian…"

"Is he ill?"

"Captured!" Salonina whispered. "By the Persians!"

"May the gods protect us," Pompeia cried, unconsciously covering her mouth with one hand.

"Can he survive the rigors of captivity?" Salonina wondered aloud.

"He seemed to have aged so much since his wife died."

"Or stand the shame of slavery?" Salonina looked at Pompeia, voicing the question they'd both thought immediately—the emperor was regarded as the intermediary between the gods and the people. That he could become a slave of their enemy was inconceivable.

Pompeia began to tremble. Over twenty years earlier, Emperor Maximinus and his soldiers had marched through Emona on their way to Rome to crush a rebellion supported by the Senate. On their way, Maximinus had allowed his soldiers to ransack the cities. A small group of soldiers had broken into her parents' home looking for food. Pompeia's mother had seen the soldiers coming and had hidden Pompeia and her sisters in their root cellar. Crouching in the dark, holding her two younger sisters, Pompeia could clearly hear soldiers' voices and her mother pleading with them to take what they wanted, saying that they had nothing. "But you do have something we want," one of the soldiers had said. She had heard everything: chairs scraping, sandals thudding on the wooden floor, soldiers' laughter, her mother's cries. Afterward the soldiers had started to ransack the kitchen. One of the men began pulling on the door to the root cellar which he mistakenly thought was jammed. Finally, he yanked the door free and took a step into the darkness. As he stood motionless, waiting for his eyes to adjust to the dark, a voice from outside had shouted something and the soldiers had run from the house. Pompeia never forgot that moment of helplessness, the terror of the darkness, then silence and finally relief.

Salonina, who had been quiet, now spoke. "Can Gallienus survive this disaster?" she asked, more to herself than to Pompeia. After Governors, Ingenuus and Regalianus betrayed Gallienus, Salonina was suspicious of all of her husband's generals. She was acutely aware of Rome's violent history of uprisings by ambitious men who had both influence and power. *Will other generals betray Gallienus? Will he be able to suppress them*? Salonina had no illusions about what would happen to people close to Gallienus if he were to fail. It angered her that men she most feared and distrusted had been promoted to positions of power and prestige by either Gallienus or his father. If it weren't for them, the generals would still be common soldiers. For some men even that wasn't enough. The more they got, the more they wanted. "Tell Fulvianus I've changed my mind," Salonina snapped. "I want to leave Mediolanum as soon as possible."

2-2
Counterattack, Cross Purposes
Pompeiopolis, Cilicia
10 August, 260

"Do you trust his information?" The younger Macrianus looked anxiously at Callistus.

The early morning sunlight sparkled across the Mare Cilicium. Callistus leaned against the ship's railing and stared north at a coastline that ran roughly east-west. As the ship edged closer to land, he watched the coastline slowly emerge from the blue-grey haze.

"Yes. That's why I've brought him on the expedition—and why his sons are being held by the authorities in Seleucia until we return." *And I brought you with me so your father will* support this effort adequately.

The man being discussed was Severus, the ship's captain, who had first reported a Persian attack at Aigeai. He had brought his trireme, a smaller warship powered principally by rowers, alongside to report on the Persians' current location and activities.

"He knows his sons are being held?" Macrianus arched his eyebrows.

"No point in doing it, if he didn't," Callistus smiled.

Rubius and Severus joined them along the railing. "Zephyrion lies east of us," the fleet commander pointed toward the rising sun. "If the Persians have already sacked that city,"

"Which your captain assures us they have," Callistus interrupted, nodding at Severus.

"And which I have no reason to doubt," Rubius replied, before finishing his sentence, "then Pompeiopolis is their next logical target." They all stared in silence as the ship continued northeast and the coastline grew steadily more pronounced. "That's Pompeiopolis," the commander eventually pointed ahead of them. "You can see where the port lies against hills on this side of the city."

"Where can you put the ships ashore, Severus?" Callistus asked him.

"Let's take a closer look. You can judge for yourself."

Callistus studied Severus intently before answering. He was a short thin man with a long face browned by years of exposure to sun and wind. Probably of Syrian parentage, Callistus guessed. *Is he trying to prove his trustworthiness, or is he trying to deliver the leader of the invasion force into Persian hands?*

Rubius nodded toward Severus' trireme, tied alongside. "You'll attract less attention in a smaller ship. I'll sail east—make the Persians think we're running away from them. Once we're out of their sight, I'll turn out to sea and sail back west. I'll keep the fleet hidden until you've determined where you wish to go ashore."

"You think this is wise?" Callistus asked the commander. *Could Rubius and Severus both be conspiring against me?*

The commander shrugged. "You wanted to see the coast. It's

your decision."

"Very well," Callistus decided. *If I think I've been betrayed, Severus will die with me.* He climbed aboard the smaller ship, leaving Macrianus and the rest of his staff behind then watched the two vessels draw apart. While the larger ship moved east, the trireme glided closer to a hostile shore.

Callistus studied the coastline, hills, fortified port, and the city of Pompeiopolis. The occasional creaking of the ship's timbers and the rhythmic dipping of oars in and out of the water were the only sounds he could hear as the ship slipped toward the city. Callistus looked at the ship's captain with a raised eyebrow.

Severus smiled at Callistus' discomfort. "You have to get in close to see what's really going on."

Callistus nodded, outwardly impassive, inwardly uncertain. *Would Severus beach the ship and give me to the Persians for some sort of reward? Or would he have me killed before reaching shore? Should I remind him his sons are being held hostage?* He realized the impracticality of that. *If he's planning to betray me, then he's already decided to accept their deaths.* He moved a little closer to Severus and fingered the dagger on his belt for comfort.

The rowers propelled their ship smoothly and effortlessly past the city's walled harbor. "It looks like the Persians have started their siege," Severus frowned. "Ordinarily, the eastern side of the city would be the logical point to land, flat sandy beaches there, not like beaches on the west side. But now, with the Persians on the eastern side of the city, we'd be driven into the sea if we tried to land there. I didn't see anyone west of the city—probably because of those hills. They'd shield us from the Persians' view. Shore is a bit more treacherous, all the more reason the Persians wouldn't pay any attention to it. You could probably land there unopposed—if they aren't expecting a landing."

That all seems reasonable, Callistus thought. *But is he trying to lure me into a trap?*

The trireme moved closer to the sandy beach east of the city. Callistus was beginning to believe that Severus actually intended to beach his ship there. Some of the Persians on the shore were calling to them and gesturing for the ship to come closer. He stood tensely beside Severus, alert to any sudden movement by some of the crew to overpower him. Unconsciously, he rested his hand on the hilt of his sword. Callistus realized that if he jumped overboard or was pushed into the water wearing his armor, he would drown. His only hope, if attacked, was to kill Severus before taking his own life. Water splashed in nearly a dozen places near the ship, startling him. A school of fish? Severus barked an order to the helmsman, who swung the ship right, to a course parallel to the beach.

"Arrows," Severus explained, pointing at the splashes close by. He shouted something at the Persians in Farsi. Callistus recognized a few of the words—insults! Severus turned to Callistus and grinned. "Have you seen enough, General?"

Callistus exhaled. "Were you taunting me as well?"

"Most of our families were captured by the Persians at Aigeai." Severus ignored the question and waved a hand at his crew. "Maybe some of them are still alive..." his voice trailed away.

"I lost my family when Shapur took Antioch," Callistus managed to say, surprised at the emotion these men's recent losses awoke in him. "We'll land west of the city, as you suggested, and attack the Persians at dawn tomorrow."

11 August, 260
Pompeiopolis

"You didn't even try to rescue the prisoners?" Callistus asked the young Macrianus late the next afternoon, not bothering to hide his disgust. The general wiped perspiration out of his eyes streaking dirt and blood from his tunic across his forehead.

"But we captured Shapur's harem," the young Macrianus countered, "and an incredible amount of treasure that he's stolen along the way!"

"I'd rather have freed the emperor," Callistus frowned. "Of what use is Shapur's harem to me?"

With effort Macrianus stifled a smile, assuming that Callistus was speaking figuratively.

"My group got separated from the rest of the army. We had to march all the way from the beach," Macrianus reminded Callistus. "When we broke through to clear ground, we found ourselves almost on top of Shapur's harem and baggage train."

Before battle Callistus had ordered him to remain at the shore in charge of camp guards, despite Macrianus' request to participate in the battle. Then, Callistus had called for Macrianus to reinforce his left flank when fighting with the Persians was heaviest.

"There was only a small force guarding the harem. I don't know who was more surprised," Macrianus chucked as he recalled the astonished expressions on the Persians' faces, and their panicked flight. "They must have thought we were a much larger force. I felt there'd be many more men guarding the prisoners, and that they'd have been alerted to my coming," Macrianus concluded.

"You should have left the harem and supplies unguarded," Callistus said, angry that his best chance to rescue the emperor had been lost.

"There was no one to help me."

"We were fighting hand-to-hand. That is why we came here, in case you'd forgotten. We could have slaughtered them all, if Shapur hadn't turned his rout into a somewhat organized retreat." Callistus' disappointment was obvious,

Macrianus shrugged. "It was my first battle. I thought you'd be pleased with what I'd done."

Callistus studied Macrianus dejected face. He questioned Macrianus' logic, but decided that Macrianus' actions could be attributed to inexperience. In any event, an opportunity for rescuing Valerian had passed. Shapur would not be that careless protecting his assets again. "It's done now," Callistus grunted and turned away. He would send the harem and spoils back to Seleucia, then have the ships return with reinforcements. His fight with Shapur was far from over. Callistus thought of sending Macrianus to Seleucia, then decided against it. Macrianus was still of value to him as a hostage, but he was unwilling to give him any further position of authority.

Macrianus watched Callistus walk away, bellowing a string of orders to his tribunes. He remembered his father's concern about Valerian being rescued, then thought about the situation after capturing both spoils and harem. He realized that if he had found Valerian, he would not have been able to kill him outright, but he recalled hearing that Persians often killed their prisoners when they were forced to retreat.

2-3
A Serious Turn of Events
Colonia Agrippina, Germania Inferior
21 August, 260

News of Valerian's defeat in Syria had just reached Postumus in Colonia Agrippina in a letter sent from Rome on July 23. Before Silvanus could decide what to tell the legionnaires, the story swept rapidly through the campsite. Rumors of revolts and renewed barbarian invasions dominated discussions around campfires and in taverns. Men grumbled about the possibility of having to march east and fight Persians, a trip that might mean several years' absence, leaving their families alone and inadequately protected against any invasions. But for Postumus nothing had really changed. He still commanded insufficient forces to prevent Franks from breaching Rome's borders and raiding deep into the countryside. The real significance of that disaster in the east was that Gallienus would not return legionnaires he had taken from the provinces two summers earlier. Indeed, he might even demand more troops to counter further Persian aggression.

That evening Postumus lay on his cot, arms folded behind his head, a single candle flickering on a small table beside him and considered what Valerian's defeat and capture might mean to the rest of the empire. Usual consequences of the empire's weakening came quickly to his mind—more barbarian incursions, more revolts by ambitious generals or governors. *Would Gallienus go east, or send an army with some of his generals? What would the Marcomanni do if Pannonia suddenly lay nearly undefended? What would the Franks do if his legions along the Rhenus had to send more of their men to Syria?*

Postumus thought of his own prospects. *As a general I serve at the pleasure of the emperor, but as emperor the powers would be mine.* He considered Rome's recent history. In the last twenty years Decius overthrew Philip. Aemilianus overthrew Gallus. Valerian overthrew Aemilianus. All of them took legionnaires from their provinces and marched on Rome. But the list of unsuccessful attempts is longer than the list of successes—Ingenuus and Regalianus being the most recent. *What would Gallienus do if I revolted? He'd send an army, or come himself, despite his serious problems in the east and a threat along his northern border. How much cavalry would he bring? Could I defeat him?* He brooded for a while on his chances of winning a pitched battle against Gallienus. Leaving his northern border vulnerable, would alienate the local population, perhaps even a significant part of the army. That reminded Postumus of one more significant obstacle, the army's loyalty. Postumus sighed and shook his head. *Saloninus was popular with the soldiers. No reason for the army to suddenly switch allegiances. Too many things working against me. For now, I'd better address the immediate threats and defeat the Franks.* He leaned over and blew out the candle.

North of the Danuvius River
22 August, 260

General Claudius chuckled as he gave Aurelian, head of Gallienus' cavalry forces, a friendly punch on the shoulder. "They should have recognized it as a bad omen, when that chieftain ran out between our armies and challenged you to a duel."

"A bad omen for him," the usually stern-faced General Aurelian answered, smiling. "Did you see his look of surprise when the first arrow struck him in the neck?"

"And the expressions of his kinsman when they rushed out to rescue him?" Volusianus, head of Praetorian Guards and Gallienus' chief-of-staff. chuckled.

"I couldn't tell if their distress was due to his death, or from all the arrows that greeted them." Claudius was still chuckling.

"Maybe it was because they were the first to see your charge," Volusianus suggested to Aureolus.

Aureolus nodded, relishing the surprise and confusion his attack had produced on the Roxolani's flank. "Same tactics we used against them at Verona."

"And when they fled into the forest—seeking safety." Aurelian's face broke into a broad grin.

"They were really running into the Quadi's homeland," Claudius finished the sentence. Everyone present knew the Quadi would regard the Roxolani as invaders. The generals threw back their heads and roared. It had been a most satisfying day's work.

Their army was camped at the edge of Quadi and Marcomanni homelands. Cooking fires burned brightly. Soon the army would take their evening meal. Gallienus and his generals sat outside his tent reviewing their day's battle against the Roxolani horsemen. Gallienus anticipated sharing stories later with the soldiers in the lingering twilight hours. He gazed contentedly at his generals. Finally, order seems to be restored. The Juthungi, Alamanni, and Roxolani have all paid for their invasions. Regalianus' rebellion ended favorably and without another battle where one Roman legion fought against another. "I think we'll let the Quadi deal with what's left of the Roxolani," Gallienus decided.

"Why not attack the Marcomanni?" Aureolus asked. "We're here."

Volusianus held up a hand, his face now more serious. "The purpose of crossing the Danuvius was to punish tribes that invaded the empire. The Marcomanni have given us no cause to fight them, lately. Why stir up trouble where there isn't any? And speaking of the Marcomanni," Volusianus remembered suddenly, "Attalus is sending us an emissary. I expect him to arrive tomorrow morning."

"I'm rather looking forward to a period of peace," Gallienus said.

"Excuse me, sir. A messenger from Rome to see you." A tribune approached Gallienus and the generals. "Shall I have him come back in the morning?" Gallienus waved for the tribune to bring the messenger forward.

A chill flashed through Gallienus' body as he looked at the messenger's expression. "Are you aware of the contents of this message?" he asked, studying the man's face. It was half question, half accusation.

"I've not read it, sir, but news is all over Rome." The messenger stood rigid while Gallienus held the unopened message. "I was told, under penalty of death, not to reveal what I knew to anyone until you'd seen it."

Gallienus spread the message out in his lap and read silently. He pursed his lips, rubbed his chin, then read it again. Afterward he neither moved nor spoke. "No reply at this time," he said finally, looking up at the messenger and dismissing him with a wave of his hand. He glanced at the expectant generals. "I always knew my father was mortal," he said. Then he tossed the message to Volusianus.

"Emperor Valerian has been defeated and captured," Volusianus announced.

Lost in his own thoughts, Gallienus stared at the ground while Volusianus read the message of Valerian's defeat and capture to his generals. *How do I deal with this disaster?* he wondered. *Abandon the western half of the empire and attempt a rescue? Is he even still alive? What can I actually do*? He quickly ran through an analysis of his governors' and generals' loyalty. Gallienus looked up. His generals stared at him with expressionless faces, expecting some comment. He cleared his throat. "When the Goths killed Emperor Decius, none of us thought the empire would ever be more imperiled. It appears we were wrong." He stood abruptly and began pacing. "This would be an ideal time for any barbarian tribe to invade. The defeat of two Roman armies in nine years, first by the Goths, now by the Persians, is certainly enough to encourage any aggressive barbarian chieftain. But who might attack us now?"

"Maybe the Goths in the east," Volusianus suggested.

"Or the Marcomanni here, along the Danuvius," Aureolus said.

"And there's always the Franks in the west," Aurelian added.

"My assessment, as well," Gallienus nodded. "Then there's the possibility of some rebellious governor or general. I can think of only two serious possibilities," he continued. "Postumus and Macrianus, and both are deeply engaged fighting their respective enemies." He stopped, as if considering both men's predicaments, then looked suddenly at the generals. "It could even be one of you." No one dared cast a surreptitious glance at anyone else. No one spoke. No one moved. Each was uncertain of the others' intentions, and each feared the emperor might accuse him of disloyalty. Gallienus paused for a moment. "But I know of no reason to doubt any of your loyalties."

"What will you do?" Volusianus asked quickly, relieved the danger for them seemed to have passed. He felt it was inappropriate to offer his sympathy that Gallienus' father was the first emperor in Rome's thousand-year history to be defeated and captured by an enemy.

"Nothing, actually." Gallienus smiled.

The answer surprised Volusianus. He'd always known Gallienus to be a man of action, sometimes even a bit impetuous, but inactivity was not one of Gallienus' faults.

"We'll say that my father was treacherously seized by the Persians when he went to negotiate with Shapur," Gallienus said. "That's true, as far as it goes. The fact that he'd been defeated first doesn't need to be mentioned to anyone."

"Then you plan to stay in Pannonia and Moesia?" Claudius asked.

Gallienus sat down again and nodded. "After two revolts and ten years of invasions, I'd be a fool to leave this area right now."

"And it's the most central location, in case of any future revolts or invasions," Aurelian said.

"We don't know whether your father is alive or dead,"

Aureolus returned to the subject of Valerian. "Will you send a rescue force?"

Gallienus frowned. "I have to balance the welfare of the empire against the possible freedom of one man, even if that man is my father." After a lengthy silence he added, "I'm open to suggestions from any of you."

"You'll tell the army yourself?" Volusianus asked. "Everyone will have heard the rumors before the day's out."

"First thing tomorrow."

"What about the Marcomanni emissary?" Volusianus asked.

Gallienus stroked his chin. "After I've spoken with the troops." He rose and started to walk away. "I need some time alone." He wandered about the campsite, unaware of the Praetorian Guards shadowing him at a discreet distance, and looked toward the eastern sky, darkening on the edge of night, then across the vast expanse of forest. He tried to envision the great disaster that had occurred somewhere out there and thought of his father. Anger surged through him that his father had left him to deal with this crisis in the east. Pity followed. Valerian had tried to do something beyond his ability. Prisca's warning of Valerian's plan to replace him as co-emperor came to his mind. *My own father distrusted me, just as he did all of his generals!* He clenched his jaw. *Threats to the empire are external, but the threats to me, and my family, are internal. I could lose support of my governors, my general staff, or the army. despite what I said to them, can I still count on my generals' loyalty? What if one, or all of them, decided to revolt? Sending them away would be more dangerous than keeping them close. Father refused to trust his generals, yet none of them betrayed him—as far as I know.*

Meanwhile, the generals, who had all remained sitting outside Gallienus' tent, discussed the situation among themselves. "He might choose to do nothing," Claudius said, "but others may not be so inclined." He looked around the group for agreement.

"And what would you do?" Aurelian asked. Claudius shrugged. He had no immediate response.

"I think until we know of something happening elsewhere, that staying in the center of the empire is the best action to take," Volusianus said.

They mulled it over in silence. "Who could revolt?" Claudius asked the group. "Postumus?"

"As Gallienus said, he's got his hands full with the Franks," Aureolus said. "Besides, Silvanus and Saloninus are with him."

"That arrangement didn't work so well with young Valerian and Ingenuus," Aurelian said.

"Well, what about Macrianus?" Volusianus asked.

"He may think he's a general," Aurelian scoffed, "but he's never commanded troops in the field that I'm aware of."

"And the Persians have shown no signs of retreating, as far as we know," Aureolus said. "I think they'll keep him busy."

Volusianus shook his head. "When he said it could be any one of us, I've never felt my life hang on another man's whim before—especially around Gallienus."

Claudius shrugged. "He was just being dramatic. "It's his nature to trust his generals and governors. Whereas Valerian was proclaimed emperor by an army he'd gathered from the provinces. That's why he never trusted his generals."

"If it weren't for Valerian and Gallienus, we'd still be senior centurions," Aureolus mused. "We owe our rank and our status to them."

"The only way any man could mount a successful revolt would be with a military force under his command," Aurelian observed.

"And with support of his legions," Claudius added.

History shows another option, Volusianus thought uneasily, then relaxed as he thought it through. *The only way an assassination by a Praetorian Prefect ever succeeded was if he thought the emperor wasn't doing an adequate job.*

"Gallienus is very popular with the troops," Claudius was saying. "As long as he proves himself capable, there's little to gain and much to lose, by trying to overthrow an emperor."

Claudius' comment reminded Aureolus of a conversation he once had with Postumus six years earlier when Postumus had said he doubted Gallienus could hold the empire together if any-thing happened to Valerian. Aureolus wondered what Postumus would be thinking when he learned of Valerian's defeat and cap-ture.

"It took two months for this news to reach us," Aureolus said to the others. "I wonder if something is already happening somewhere in the empire because of this."

2-4
Loyalties Tested
Palmyra, Syria
24 August, 260

The full moon, just risen, bathed the city's marble buildings in golden hues and cast long shadows across the Grand Colon-nade's three hundred-fifty columns. A light breeze stirred the flames from torches surrounding Odenathus, Zenobia, Herodian, and General Zabdas. They sat cross-legged on a blue and white carpet. A message lay on the circular brass table around which they had gathered.

Zenobia inhaled deeply. She smiled as she looked across the city's flickering fires to the date palm trees at the edge of the city, then to the consuming emptiness of the desert beyond. She loved to gaze from this plaza atop Odenathus' palace into the night and imagine caravans working their way to Palmyra from exciting and distant places. But tonight she was impatient. This was a night for important decisions.

The situation seems to have changed," Odenathus said, pointing at the message. "You may read it, Zabdas." He pushed the message toward his senior general, letting his mind wander while Zabdas reached for the message, coughed once discreetly, and read aloud to Queen Zenobia and Prince Herodian.

From: Titus Macrianus, Pro Consul of Asia
To: Septimius Odenathus, King of Palmyra
I am pleased to report the landing of a Roman army near the city of Pompeiopolis in Cilicia, and the subsequent victory over Shapur there on 11 August. Two subsequent landings and attacks against Persian forces were made, one near Sebaste on the 14th, and a second at Corycus on the 18th. Over three thousand Persians were killed. These defeats have caused Shapur to begin a withdrawal from Cilicia. Aside from inflicting significant Persian casualties we have recovered a considerable quantity of spoils, and even Shapur's harem. Further attacks against Shapur's army in Cilicia are either under way or being planned.

I urge you to come with your son, your generals, and your army to take part in a future campaign, under my command, against Shapur at such time as his retreat toward Persia brings him closest to Antioch.

"It seems Macrianus forgot to include you in his battle plans," Odenathus teased Zenobia.

She scowled. "I doubt it was an accident. His attitude toward me at Emesa was dismissive and insulting. None of our allies would have thought to make such statements."

"Perhaps he felt your six-month-old son might keep you from the battlefield," General Zabdas suggested. "Maybe it was merely an oversight on his part."

"It's Macrianus' job to make sure all diplomatic niceties are addressed," Zenobia objected. "Can't he even do that?"

"He doesn't really know you, my dear," Odenathus soothed, patting her arm.

After Valerian's failure to contain Shapur's attack, Palmyra had remained largely uncommitted, waiting to see what, if anything, Callistus and Macrianus could do to stop the Persian advance. Considering his earlier rebuffed offer of alliance with Shapur, Odenathus considered an eventual confrontation with the Persians inevitable.

"Who do you suppose is leading these attacks?" Odenathus wondered. "Callistus?"

"What the Romans did was risky and daring," Zenobia said immediately. "Neither of those words comes to mind when I think of Macrianus."

"You're not the only person he misjudged at that dinner in Emesa," Odenathus said, recalling Macrianus' opinion of Shapur's intentions.

Zabdas shifted his position and wrinkled his brow. "I find his invitation to join in a joint campaign troubling, considering his lack of any battle experience."

"But now is clearly the time for action," Zenobia said. "After my sword practice this afternoon, I offered sacrifices to Alat. The priestesses judged this to be an auspicious time for battle. Besides," she smiled, "you'll show the Romans that you've sided with them, by eliminating your main rival."

Odenathus nodded. "Shapur is retreating, apparently without his whole army intact. His soldiers will be tired after a long campaign. We have fresh troops and the element of surprise. If I'm going to attack, now is the time." He smiled at the others. "Perhaps, we could also relieve Shapur of some of his spoils."

"Do you suppose he's gotten another harem?" Herodian asked. The thought of spoils suddenly intrigued him. He reached for several dates from a nearby platter before looking back at his father.

Zenobia shook her head in disgust. "Instead of dreaming about pleasures of the flesh, you should be pleading with your father to lead this campaign himself, like he did against Nehardea. If we fought with Macrianus commanding, you'd probably end up like Valerian. I doubt you'd be thinking seriously about a harem if you were Shapur's prisoner."

Herodian glared at her. There was something more than hate that she could read in his eyes. Her step-son was a year older than she, and Zenobia shivered at the thought of her fate if anything were to happen to Odenathus. She pointedly turned her back on Herodian and faced Odenathus, looking at him expectantly.

He mulled the matter over in his mind, before looking at his general. "I think we know the queen's opinion on this matter. Your thoughts, Zabdas?"

"I favor the queen's position, sire." Zabdas responded without hesitation.

"Because she's the queen?" Odenathus asked.

"Because her judgment is sound," Zabdas said, diplomatically, bowing to Zenobia.

"Herodian?" Odenathus looked at his son.

"I'll support your decision, Father," Herodian shrugged. "Where would you attack Shapur?"

"That depends on how soon we can be ready to march and how far Shapur has retreated," Odenathus rubbed his chin. "And yes, Zenobia," he smiled, "I never seriously considered fighting under Macrianus' command."

Zenobia's black eyes sparkled at the thought of a great battle with the Persians. "According to the message, Shapur could have started his retreat as early as the 12th or as late as the 18th."

"He'll have prisoners and plunder," Zabdas said, considering their effect on Shapur's march.

"Although without a harem to distract him," Zenobia feigned sympathy, "he might be moving faster."

"He'll have to cross the mountains east of Cilicia," Zabdas continued. "Harem or not, prisoners, plunder, and the mountains will slow him considerably. I'd be surprised if Shapur hasn't already addressed his harem shortages."

They discussed the time required to gather forces from the Syrian villages and warriors from the desert tribes, then estimated the time required to march north toward Edessa and Carrhae where Shapur would pass on his way back to the Persian capitol of Ctesiphon.

"With luck we'll catch him before he turns east," General Zabdas concluded.

"Will you tell Macrianus of your plans?" Zenobia asked her husband. "If not, he might think we're about to attack Antioch."

"I suppose I ought to send him some sort of a message." Odenathus yawned. "Tomorrow should be soon enough."

2-5
Revelation
Aquileia, Gallia Cisalpina
26 August, 260

Maximus and Prisca arrived in the city of Aquileia on the afternoon of August 26. Not finding a private house which took in overnight guests, they chose a deversorium that also offered shelter for their animals. Maximus purchased an entire room to avoid sharing it with other travelers. While he dictated a courtesy message for one of his slaves to take to the city prefect informing him that a Roman general and former consul was staying in Aquileia for the night, Prisca lay back on the bed and closed her eyes. Moments later she sat up abruptly twisting her shoulders back and forth and groaned.

"What is it now?"

"I'd hoped the bed bugs would be fewer here than at last night's lodging, or the night before that."

Maximus scowled and pointed a finger at Prisca. "You've been unhappy ever since Gallienus left us in Vindobona and asked me to take care of matters in Carnuntum. That was… almost four weeks ago."

Prisca stood and rubbed her back against the wall. "I've had nightmares about my time in captivity, and weeks of hard travel with little sleep," she pointed at the bed, "have been difficult for me. You haven't been the easiest person to travel with either."

"I've been searching for you ever since you were captured at Arretium, hoping that you were still alive and still inside the empire. When I learned that you were with Gallienus at Augusta Vindelicum, I was overjoyed. I expected you would feel the same way. But you didn't seem to share that feeling. It was a painful surprise. I've wondered what the reason for that might be and my conclusion is also very disturbing."

She tensed. "What do you mean?"

"Before you knew I was there, you reached out and put

his hand to your cheek. Over the next two weeks, I watched you staring at him when we were at dinners together. And you were particularly irritable for days after we left him."

"He'd rescued me just before I was to be offered to their gods in a sacrificial fire. For the next four weeks I ate at the emperor's table when we dined with local officials. I became very used to it."

"And slept in his bed as well, I assume," Maximus said.

"Yes. I did," Prisca said matter-of-factly. "I thought you'd died defending Arretium, that our villa there had been looted and burned, and that our slaves had been killed or captured. Our daughters and their husbands were in the path of the barbarian invasion. I didn't know if they were alive or dead either." She paused and rested her face in her hands for a moment, then took a deep breath and looked at Maximus. "I'd been a slave for almost a year when Gallienus rescued me." Prisca paused again to see if Maximus was really hearing what she was trying to tell him. "For a brief time with Gallienus I was well treated, I felt safe, and I lived well. You might not be able to understand or appreciate any of that, but I have no regrets."

Maximus was quiet for some time, then took a deep breath. "I think I'll check on the animals."

When he had gone, Prisca sat on the edge of the bed. What she remembered most vividly about the time between being rescued and being reunited with Maximus were the banquets and more intimate dinners. She had dined with the provincial governor and with the city prefects, along with their wives and other notables from each city that they traveled through. She smiled as she recalled looks of appraisal from the men and of envy from the women when she entered the rooms on the arm of one of Gallienus' generals and was seated as an honored guest. Despite Gallienus publicly treating Prisca with the respect due to her, the women deduced their relationship and some had approached her quietly later seeking favors from the emperor. Prisca had found the feeling of power intoxicating and addictive. Having to surrender that power and influence so suddenly and unexpectedly had been extremely difficult. She had come to feel what it must be like to be empress and felt a flash of jealousy. She doubted that

Salonina fully appreciated the power she could wield as empress, or that she would be inclined to use it if she did.

Although theirs had been an arranged marriage, Maximus had shown her affection and treated her well. She had grown to love him. She still loved him. But she was finding it difficult to reestablish their lives together and feared the quiet life at their villa in Arretium would be intolerably dull. She was still uncertain whether Maximus could ever fully accept the fact that she had been the mistress of a Germanic chieftain named Galtis. *And what would he do if he learned I've been having an affair with Gallienus… for years?*

She had been enslaved as a Juthungi chieftain's mistress for almost eleven months, had spent one month with Gallienus after being rescued from a sacrificial fire, and now… she faced an uncertain life with Maximus.

***

She was startled when the door opened and Maximus returned. Prisca looked up. "The animals are adequately quartered, I presume."

Maximus ignored her comment. "What troubles me is that you don't seem to have any regrets for what you've done."

"For what? Surviving? You had to know what had happened to me if I were still alive."

"I should be having trouble accepting you back after you've been a slave for a year… and a mistress for a month. Instead you seem to be unable to accept being back with me."

Prisca shrugged. "Gallienus was considerate and caring, unlike the treatment I'd had in captivity. For a brief time, life was glamorous and exciting, compared to nearly a year of drudgery, hardships, fear, and the growing likelihood that I'd be a slave forever."

"All that's over now."

Prisca shook her head. "I still have nightmares about slavery with Galtis, about the sacrificial ritual, and crossing the Danuvius River into a life of slavery."

Maximus nodded. "But you're going back home to Arretium."

Prisca exhaled, looked down at the floor, and spoke softly, "I don't know if I can endure the quiet routine there."

Maximus took several deep breaths then frowned. "Are you saying you no longer want the life we've shared together, or that I'm not enough for you... or both?"

"My life has changed so dramatically over the last several months that I don't know what I want right now." Prisca paused, took a deep breath, and looked up at Maximus.

"So you'd like to go back to Rome and be Gallienus' mistress...'

"It worked well in the past..." Prisca caught herself when she saw Maximus take a step backward and stare at her. Suddenly her eyes widened as she realized what she had just said.

"How long has that been going on?" Maximus asked finally.

"How do you think you got your position as prefect in Rome?"

"That was years ago!"

"Or your consul posting the following year? How do you think that our son's first military assignment happened to be on Gallienus' personal staff? Or that our daughters' husbands got good postings when they joined the legions?"

"I see," Maximus said. "How did this happen?"

"Gallienus stopped at Arretium to ask your advice on who to appoint to one of the provincial governors' positions, almost six years ago.

"I assume I was away."

"Everyone was away... but me. I invited him in. We had a pleasant conversation over several glasses of wine. I mentioned how you felt being at the end of your career. He offered to appoint you prefect of Rome the next year. I thought you'd appreciate the assignment, and I was excited to go back to Rome. I also asked if he could help Quintianus find a suitable posting when he joined the army. When he said he might be able to help, I realized he expected a favor in return."

"Let me guess."

"You don't have to. I knew what he wanted. If I refused him, he would have withdrawn both offers. He might even have been one of those vengeful emperors who confiscate your 94property and have you executed for the most trivial reasons. If I accepted his offer, it might have just been a one-time encounter."

"Which wasn't the case I gather."

"Later it became clear that he wanted more. That's when I used the relationship to get you the consul position as well as the good assignments for our daughters' husbands."

"And after that?"

"It was a little late to say 'no' at that point."

"So then you did it for pleasure…"

"If my sexual encounters were gaining benefits for you and the children, I felt I deserved to enjoy them—and get something for myself at the same time."

"Which was?"

"Opportunities to be in Rome with all the excitement and to enjoy the prestige that came with your positions."

Maximus shook his head and reached for the door. "I could divorce you…"

"Do that and you'll lose your connection to Gallienus," Prisca countered. *I'm bluffing, but he won't be certain of that. He's benefited from my relationship… more than once.* She took a deep breath and shuddered then looked up when Maximus opened the door. A slave standing just outside their door handed him a message.

"What is it?" Prisca asked when she saw him frowning.

"An invitation to dine with the city prefect."

"Unfortunate timing."

"Along with the empress."

"Salonina, here?" Prisca exclaimed. "Tell him we can't make it."

Maximus turned to the messenger. "We would be delighted to attend."

2-6
Dinner with the Empress
Aquileia, Gallia Cisalpina
26 August, 260

Prisca stared at her reflection in a silver mirror, absentmindedly combing her hair. *But he won't be sure of that.* Shaking her head in disgust, she tossed her comb onto the dresser and used the remaining minutes powdering her face to cover the redness in her cheeks. Prisca took a deep breath before rising, unsatisfied with her appearance. *It will have to do.* She massaged the muscles at the base of her neck, trying to ease the tension. *I wish there were some way to decline tonight's dinner invitation,* she sighed, knowing there was none.

That evening Salonina greeted them warmly at the villa of Aquileia's city Prefect. "What a delightful surprise meeting the two of you here." She sensed something was amiss as soon as Prisca and Maximus had entered the garden. "When our hosts," she nodded at Clodia and her husband Cestius Gallus Antony, "told me you were here, I insisted that we all dine together."

"Our surprise is only exceeded by our pleasure," Maximus said to Salonina. He glanced politely at Antony and Clodia, then waited for Prisca to comment further. *His smile is there, but the warmth is missing,* Salonina noticed.

"Most fortunate we met you here," Prisca agreed, *rather than have you arrive unexpectedly at Gallienus' camp while I was sharing in his quarters.*

The diners reclined on couches around a table in the garden. Mint leaves, strewn along the pathways, released their own fragrance as the scurrying servants crushed them underfoot. Two young men playing flutes accompanied a woman who sang while she gently plucked the strings of a lyre. Servants brought trays loaded with the first course.

Salonina reclined at the left corner of the back table, the place of honor, which put her nearest to her host. He offered her a platter of mushrooms and olives. She shook her head then passed it on to Marinianus. Salonina watched the tray as her son offered it to Maximus, on the couch opposite Antony and Clodia. He declined and instead helped himself to beans and raw carrots. "There's so much to catch up on," Salonina said turning her attention to study Prisca's face. *Is the stress she's showing from her time in captivity? It must have been a terrifying experience. How long has she been free?* Salonina wondered.

Prisca forced a smile. She had entered the garden walking beside Maximus, rather than arm-in-arm as they customarily did, and unconsciously headed toward the table's place of honor. When Maximus put a hand on her shoulder, she had shrugged it aside. Then Maximus caught hold of her elbow firmly and steered her to her assigned seat. She desperately hoped that Maximus' reminder had gone unnoticed and that the Prefect and his wife, overly solicitous to the empress and her son, had missed the whole incident. She recalled several dinners she had hosted with Gallienus in the provinces where she had treated some of the Prefects' wives condescendingly. Prisca felt the beginning tightness of a headache. *Perhaps some more wine would help.* She refilled her glass as the servants cleared dishes, then brought a smoked white fish and snails cooked in pungent garlic.

"I must ask if all of you have heard the dreadful news from the east?" Salonina looked sadly around the table.

An embarrassed hush fell over the room. Musicians even stopped playing. Torches cast flickering shadows across nearby shrubs and bushes in stillness and continued silence. Prisca could hear dishes clattering in the kitchen. Clodia looked angrily at the head servant, who disappeared immediately.

"Yes, a few days ago," Maximus finally broke the quiet. "I know how concerned about Valerian you and your family are," he spoke to Salonina, then nodded gravely at Marinianus. "Do you have any of the details of the battle?"

At the mention of battles, Prisca felt a surge of anger at Gallienus. Prisca was acutely aware of the power and prestige she had been forced to relinquish. Her headache began to throb. Now her eyes ached too. *He cast me off so easily,* she reflected, recalling the awkwardness of an unexpected reunion with her husband nearly six weeks earlier. Gallienus had returned her to

Maximus as if she meant nothing to him. *After all I've done for him, the personal risks I've taken, and all the things we did together.* She scowled and reached for her wine. *How could I have misjudged his feelings for me so completely?* She looked up from her glass and glanced surreptitiously at Salonina, knowing that she would be joining Gallienus in Carnuntum. *Was there something more I could have done? Will I get another chance with him?*

"I can tell you about it, Uncle Maximus," Marinianus said eagerly. "I read some of the reports."

"The details of Valerian's battle really don't interest me," Salonina spoke softly, her face reflecting anxiety. "It's what might follow that concerns me most. What do you think will happen, Maximus?"

He considered her question carefully.

"Did Valerian really try to negotiate with Shapur?" Antony asked Marinianus.

"Yes, and he was seized under a flag of truce," Marinianus nodded importantly.

Clodia waved her hand for the musicians to begin another song, then signaled the head server to remove the dishes. Slaves brought bowls filled with water and rose petals for the guests to wash their hands.

Prisca retreated into her musings. Readjusting to life with Maximus had been difficult. She had found herself ambivalent about Maximus' attentions and confused by her own feelings. *No matter how hard he tries, he can't offer me the life that Gallienus did. But I can't admit that to him. Still, it must be very painful, after all he went through, to find me indifferent toward him. Can I ever accept my life as it is now?* She let the thought go, afraid of what its answer might be.

"It's difficult to know how men will react when they're actually faced with this sort of situation," Maximus said at last. "Some will see this as an opportunity."

"I could get that answer from any of my servants, Maximus. What do you really think?"

He arched an eyebrow. "Probably at least one revolt, maybe more, and no reason to think there won't be barbarian invasions.

This is a very dangerous time."

While Maximus spoke, Prisca stared at her husband and thought of their earlier argument which erupted when Maximus finally confronted her about her involvement with Gallienus. "I thought you were dead and I slept with the emperor because he gave me no choice." She had stood facing him, rigid and unapologetic, returning his gaze without blinking. "Maybe it was out of necessity," he'd eventually conceded, "but did you have to take such pleasure from it?" "What makes you think I took any pleasure from it?" she'd countered. "It's obvious from the way you've acted ever since our reunion." It had ended there, with Maximus stalking out of the room, threatening to divorce her. When he had returned moments later, Prisca thought he had come back to talk things out. Instead he dropped the dinner invitation onto the table beside her. They had not spoken since their argument.

"I'm told Valerian was reluctant to trust his subordinates," Salonina spoke, almost to herself. "Isn't there also a danger of trusting them too much?" she voiced her fears to Maximus as diplomatically as she could, considering Antony's and Clodia's presence.

"We need capable governors to defend our provinces," Maximus replied. "Those who abuse their powers must be dealt with quickly and harshly—as your husband did with Ingenuus. Anything less would be seen as a sign of weakness, in which case there'd be no reason for them not to try again."

Another course began arriving on steaming platters. Cooked beets and onions first, followed by roasted hares served in garum, a widely popular fish sauce. Shortly afterward, the last plate of the main course was served—a spit-roasted swan garnished with chopped shallots, rosemary, pepper, and thyme.

"How lovely." Salonina said as she glanced around the table, while considering Maximus' previous comments. Clodia beamed jubilantly, delighted with Salonina's admiration. Antony and Clodia had been anxious, concerned that their meal with the empress might not be perfect. Clodia then motioned to a poet, hastily obtained for the dinner's entertainment. He began to recite verses from the Aeneid. But after a few minutes, when Salonina's annoyed frown suggested to Clodia that his voice was a distraction, she waved him away.

Still preoccupied by her revolving thoughts, Prisca gazed into her wine glass. *My relationship with Gallienus is apparently over. Now my marriage is on the verge of collapse. Where would I go if he divorced me? Could I ever face the people in Rome again? Could he?*

Antony took advantage of the ensuing silence to sample one of the hares. He looked at Clodia and murmured approvingly as he swallowed his first bite. Salonina studied Prisca's down-turned face and her furrowed brow. *She's still beautiful, even after her time in captivity,* Salonina marveled. *But why is she unhappy? I would have expected her to be joyful being together with her husband again. And why did she almost take my place at the table tonight? Enough talk of Rome's problems; it's time I learned what's going on around me.*

"You've said nothing during this whole discussion, Prisca." Salonina's voice startled Prisca out of her reverie. "I was certain you'd have an opinion on the empire's present situation. And you've hardly eaten anything at all. Are you ill?"

"So much has happened recently." Prisca shook her head, looking up to meet Salonina's gaze. "A year and two weeks ago, I was taken prisoner at Arretium."

Poor girl, Clodia thought, *I don't even want to think what they must have done to her*. "How extremely fortunate that you and Maximus are together again," she effused, "considering that either of you could have been killed, or worse," she directed the last to Prisca. "You both must be delighted to be reunited."

"I was," Maximus answered, before Prisca had a chance to speak. "I am," he corrected himself quickly, then turned to glance at Prisca.

"Since Arretium was sacked I've been trying to deal with lots of changes in my life," Prisca looked at Salonina before glancing back at Maximus, "even now." Maximus studied the food on his plate with sudden interest. Conversation lapsed.

Salonina changed the subject. "Where was my husband when you left him?"

"He'd planned to go to Vindobona, then Carnuntum, before

mounting his campaign across the Danuvius River," Prisca replied reflexively. "But he told me he changed his mind after Aurelian's legionaries joined him."

"Really?" Salonina's eyes widened, surprised that Gallienus had apparently shared his operational plans with Prisca. "Did he tell you that?" she asked Maximus.

Maximus shook his head, but then added quickly, "He crossed the river at Vindobona, instead. I'd guess he's somewhere in the barbarian heartland right now. I was sent to Carnuntum with orders to install legates and a governor loyal to him. There was no need of staying after that, so we were returning to Arretium, and that's how we happened to be here."

Salonina considered Maximus' account, nodded, then looked at Prisca again. *She knew Gallienus' plan and Maximus had not. What else does Prisca know?* "Tell us of your ordeal with the barbarians, if it's not too upsetting."

Prisca hesitated to speak at first, but consented after Salonina's gentle coaxing. Salonina listened intently as Prisca told them how she had been captured when barbarian tribes stormed Arretium last August, and had been enslaved by Juthungi. "Ever since I was captured, I thought Maximus had died defending the city," she said.

As she continued her story Antony interrupted. "Most fortunate that their chieftain, was his name Galtis, took you away from his young warriors." Prisca detected more than a trace of a leer in his smile.

"I thought so too, until the end of the ordeal," she replied.

"You were a slave to a barbarian chieftain!" Marinianus exclaimed in the following silence. "What was that like? What did you do?"

Clodia giggled nervously, then quickly covered her mouth to hide her embarrassed smile. Maximus stared ahead stonily. Prisca looked expectantly at Salonina, hoping she might squelch her son's question. "I did what I had to do, to survive," Prisca said, when Salonina did not respond. But her reply was intended for Maximus rather than Marinianus.

"Why don't you let Prisca continue with her story." Salonina gently chided Marinianus before nodding for Prisca to continue.

Prisca talked about her brief freedom during the battle at Mediolanum, when Romans had routed the Juthungi army, then defeated the Alamanni. "When the mountain passes were blocked by snow, we were forced to spend a winter outside Sabiona." Prisca told of her desperate winter and a lack of food that left her with a constant, gnawing hunger.

Clodia looked sympathetically at Prisca. "How did you ever endure?"

"The only alternative was to give up and die, Clodia. Many did." Prisca shivered involuntarily when she recalled bone-chilling cold and her threadbare clothing.

"I expected a Roman attack in the spring. Instead, the barbarians kept moving closer to the Danuvius River and I'd almost given up hope of being rescued."

"The army was rather busy with other things, Regalianus' revolt and a Roxolani invasion, as I recall," Antony interposed.

Prisca frowned. "I had no way of knowing any of that." Antony shrugged in acknowledgment. She told them of her increasing despair and of her vow to drown herself rather than to cross the Danuvius into slavery. Salonina nodded approval of Prisca's vow. "Just as I'd come to terms with that, I was taken by barbarian priests and told that I was going to be sacrificed to their gods."

"Why didn't your chieftain try to protect you?" Marinianus asked, eyes wide.

"He said the welfare of the tribe was his responsibility," Prisca drew in a deep breath, held it for a minute, and then let it out slowly, "and that the situation called for a great sacrifice on his part. He told me I should be honored to have been chosen."

"Can you tell us about the sacrifice" Antony asked. After noticing disapproving stares from around the table he added, "It might help us understand the barbarians more completely."

Prisca looked to Salonina for guidance.

"Our host," Salonina nodded at Antony, "would like to know the details. I have no objection, if you're comfortable sharing them with us."

Prisca could sense Maximus' tension. Both Antony and

young Marinianus stared at her intently. Clodia squirmed uneasily. Salonina watched dispassionately, as if she were about to listen to the recitation of some Greek tragedy. Prisca licked her lips, then cleared her throat. "Perhaps, some of it." She had the full attention of everyone now. "I was taken to an oak tree and suspended by my wrists from a limb." Prisca hesitated.

"No need to go on if it's too difficult for you," Salonina offered.

"I was told it was to be a ritual burning," Prisca continued, her eyes distant, as if she hadn't heard Salonina's comment.

"Like the Celts used to do," Antony interrupted. "You were governor of one of the Germania provinces, Maximus. You must know about the Celts burning prisoners."

"I was governor of both provinces, Antony," Maximus corrected him stiffly, "and the Celts were subdued long before I got there."

Let Prisca tell her story." Clodia looked disapprovingly at her husband, then smiled encouragement at Prisca. "Please do go on." No one spoke while Prisca took a deep breath, struggling for the courage to continue.

"Then Galtis appeared beside me with a lighted torch, waiting for a signal to light the fire," she said haltingly.

"Did he?" Marinianus' question broke the silence.

"Of course not, dear," Salonina answered, mildly irritated, "otherwise Prisca wouldn't be with us now. What did happen?" she prompted.

"We heard trumpets in the distance, then galloping horses coming closer. When Galtis turned to look, I was able to kick his shoulder. He stumbled before he could draw his sword, but he dropped the torch and the fire started anyway." Prisca stopped for a moment, drained her wine glass, and surveyed her rapt audience. Antony's eyes were fixed on Prisca. He absent-mindedly patted the beads of perspiration from his forehead. Clodia's brow was compressed in a mixture of horror and sympathy. Maximus remained silent. Prisca doubted he had even moved since addressing Antony earlier. Young Marinianus was staring at her, mouth open, and eyes wide. Salonina gave no indication of her frame of mind.

Prisca spoke slowly, phrasing her next words carefully. "In the confusion…one of the Roman horsemen cut me free, but I fell and landed at the edge of the burning wood and rolled clear of the fire just in time to trip the priest. He'd rushed back at us with his knife drawn."

"How lucky someone was able to get you in time. Did your rescuer survive the attack?" Clodia asked, biting her lower lip.

Prisca nodded. "The priest was killed. Galtis escaped. I was picked up, covered with the horseman's cape, then left in the care of several junior officers. I've had nightmares about it ever since."

"Not surprising," Salonina agreed.

"Did anyone ever find Galtis?" Marinianus asked.

"They never found his body. My nightmares stopped suddenly sometime during our trip from Carnuntum. I can only guess what that might mean."

The hostess breathed a sigh of relief and smiled brightly. "What a terrible experience, but that's all behind you now."

"I hope you're right," Prisca murmured.

Clodia looked around, suddenly remembering her responsibilities as hostess. She waved for the head servant to bring the next course, then indicated that the musicians should begin playing again. One by one the dishes were removed. Platters appeared piled with grapes, almonds, and apricots. Servants refilled the diners' glasses with a mixture of wine, honey, and spices.

An odd comment, Salonina thought. She reached for several grapes before turning to Maximus, smiling. "It must have felt wonderful to rescue your wife from such a terrible situation."

"I … wasn't actually there," Maximus frowned, drained his wine glass, and lowered his eyes.

"Oh? Where were you?"

"After the battle near Verona, your husband split his forces. He chased the Juthungi with the cavalry. I went with Aurelian's legionaries following the Roxolani. We met rather by coincidence near Lauriacum."

"I must have misunderstood." Salonina looked expectantly at Prisca. "Then who rescued you? Did you know him?"

Prisca hesitated and swallowed hard. "Yes. It was Gallienus."

"My husband cut you down from the tree himself!" Salonina exclaimed, her eyes widening.

Clodia covered her mouth in an astonished expression. She looked from Prisca to Salonina and back. Antony gaped at Prisca, then glanced surreptitiously at Salonina, who seemed to have forgotten the almond in her fingers. Maximus closed his eyes.

The musicians paused, then continued uncertainly. The head servant grasped the arm of a young slave girl walking toward the table with a platter of honeyed cakes and held her back.

"He was the first one to reach us. If he hadn't rescued me when he did, I would have died in the fire." Prisca could tell that Maximus was lying rigid beside her.

Clodia quickly waved toward the head servant. "More wine, and the honeyed cakes, too." A pointed glance at the musicians sufficed to resume their music. She cleared her throat to comment.

But Salonina broke in before she could speak. "So…" she looked speculatively at Maximus and thought *that changes things at bit*, "when were you finally reunited with Prisca?"

"After we fought the Roxolani," Maximus studied the apricot he held in his hand.

Salonina eyes were still on Maximus, but her thoughts were elsewhere: *Gallienus sent me news of those two battles, but he never mentioned Prisca. And that's just the sort of gossip he likes to share. Why had Prisca been so reluctant to say that Gallienus rescued her? And Maximus' beloved wife is alive and restored to him contrary to all expectations, yet both of them are clearly miserable and ill at ease.*

Clodia's voice interrupted Salonina's thoughts. "Where in the world did they put you?" Clodia asked.

"What do you mean?"

"I remember accompanying Antony on campaigns. Dreadful time." Clodia frowned at the recollection. "But you were picked up by the cavalry. There couldn't have been any other women that could keep up with the army. Where did you sleep?"

Prisca stared blankly at Clodia.

"They have extra tents," Maximus interjected. "Especially after experiencing a few casualties." He looked from Clodia to Salonina and was disturbed to see her watching him closely.

"So you were one of only a few women in the camp," Antony noted. "For how long? Five weeks?"

"Closer to four," Prisca contradicted him. "But no, there were other women there who had been prisoners of the Juthungi." Suddenly her temples were pounding again. *Damn this headache*, Prisca cursed silently, then rubbed her aching eyes. She reached for her wine glass.

"How did you spend your time?" Clodia asked.

"During the days I helped the other women adjust to their freedom. At night there were dinners with minor dignitaries in the various cities," Prisca waved a hand casually. Antony cleared his throat loudly, shifted on his cushion, and scowled at Prisca. Clodia stiffened, stung by the implied affront.

'Minor dignitaries'? Salonina pondered, while she reached for a bunch of grapes. *Those people have the same social status as she and Maximus.*

Prisca suddenly realized she had insulted Antony and Clodia. Her face reddened. "We entertained the governor of Noricum and Gallienus' generals several times," she added, attempting to explain.

Salonina quickly looked up from the grapes. "'We' refers to you and my husband, I assume?"

"Yes," Prisca nodded, hoping to move beyond her insult to Antony and Clodia. "He was interested in…"

Salonina held up a hand. "No need to go into details; I think I understand." She stared at Prisca contemplating the implications of what Prisca had said.

"Can you tell us about fighting the Roxolani, Uncle Maximus?" Marinianus asked eagerly. "What was Quintianus doing? Was he with my father or with you?"

Salonina restrained her initial impulse to close the conversation. *Where was Prisca's son while she was spending so much time with Gallienus?*

"He asked to be with me when I joined Aurelian," Maximus

said, pleased for a chance to talk about his son and distract from the tension. "And Gallienus graciously agreed to let him come. The fight with the Roxolani was very similar to the battle near Verona," he began.

"Unfortunately," Salonina interrupted Maximus, "I'm afraid we'll have to conclude this lovely dinner now," she smiled apologetically at Clodia and Antony. "We have to leave early tomorrow. Perhaps," she said to Marinianus, "you can get the details from Quintianus himself."

The others began scrambling to their feet when Salonina rose. She waved for them to sit as she stepped away from the table.

"Enjoy life at Arretium together," Salonina looked down at Prisca and Maximus. Then she turned to Antony and Clodia and smiled politely. "Thank you both. It's been an unforgettable dinner." Antony and Clodia escorted their guest of honor to the villa's entrance, leaving Prisca and Maximus alone at the table.

Prisca let out a long sigh. "Thank the gods that meal is over," she said, confiding with Maximus as they had done over the years. "At least Salonina doesn't suspect anything." Tears began to flow silently down her cheeks. "We've got to leave somehow."

"Clodia will understand," Maximus said, taking Prisca's hand stiffly and helping her stand. *Unfortunately, I think Salonina now knows everything she needs to know.*

2-7
Marcomanni Treaty
North of the Danuvius River
27 August, 260

Attalus, the Marcomanni chieftain, frowned and shook his head. "So far you've only offered us lands along Rome's borders. I see no advantage to any of them over what we have already. My young men won't be content to sit and defend your borders for you." He shrugged and held his hands out, palms upward to Gallienus. "They're warriors." Attalus glanced briefly at his chieftains before turning back to the Romans. "My priests told me the auguries were favorable for discussions today. Have you nothing else to offer me?"

The wooden structure they were negotiating in belonged to Attalus himself. Red, white, and grey clays had stained geometric patterns onto the large wooden planks that formed the walls. Smoke rose slowly through a hole in the center of a thatched roof and drifted lazily upward, carried away by the early afternoon breeze. Shields hung on the wall behind Attalus and four of his chieftains, just above their narrow, short spears. The Marcomanni leaders sat on benches behind wooden planks laid across triangular supports that formed a simple table. Drinking horns and metal plates were strewn over the table and between the chieftains' helmets, which were laid in front of each man. All were fully armed, despite this being a peaceful negotiation. Across a dirt floor and beyond the fire in a giant pit at the center of the hall, a smaller table had been arranged for Gallienus and his four generals. Volusianus forced himself to ignore barking dogs and shouts of children playing nearby in order to concentrate on the negotiations. The day before, Marcomanni priests had proclaimed that day inauspicious for discussing treaties, and Attalus had turned them away, refusing discussions of any kind.

Gallienus raised his eyebrows and looked to his generals. They huddled together and spoke softly to one another.

"What about a grant of land inside Pannonia?" Volusianus suggested finally, the beginning of an idea taking shape in his mind.

"Where?" Gallienus asked.

"Somewhere around the center of the province, maybe near Volgum, on the southwest corner of Lake Pelso. The Roxolani destroyed most of the city and the surrounding area last spring. A large contingent of Marcomanni cavalry there, loyal to the emperor, might well discourage a third rebellion by the Pannonian legions."

"And provide us another mobile strike force," Aureolus interjected, pleased at the prospect of increasing his cavalry.

"Are you comfortable with such a large non-Roman force permanently settled in the middle of Pannonia?" Aurelian asked.

"I'd rather have an ally in Pannonia than an enemy on my northern border, especially now," Gallienus said then paused to think.

"Will the governor of Pannonia be willing to work with your arrangement?" Claudius asked.

Gallienus thought for a moment. "I'll bring Heraclianus from Dacia to govern Pannonia. He'd be capable of dealing with this sort of arrangement."

The proposal was made. Further negotiations dealt with sovereignty, the number of warriors Attalus would provide for Gallienus' use, and who would lead them. Attalus leaned back until his shoulders rested against the wall, put his feet on the table edge, and clasped the back of his neck with both hands. "Food and drink will help us evaluate this proposal further," he said. A glance to his right brought a slave to his side almost immediately; after a few hushed words the slave vanished.

"That must be the sword you took on the battlefield," Attalus pointed admiringly at the weapon strapped to Gallienus' side. An ivory grip showed above a sword trimmed with silver and sheathed in a red leather scabbard.

"It belonged to an Alamanni chieftain," Gallienus replied, glancing at it casually.

One of Attalus' chieftains spoke to him from the chieftains' table. Atttalus smiled and nodded. "The stories of how you came by it were almost legends by the time they reached us," Attalus said looking back from his chieftain. "One of them said that you fought the chieftain personally, and took the sword from the dead man's hand yourself."

"Partly true," Gallienus said, a slight smile on his lips.

"Which part would be true?"

"I did fight their leader personally," Gallienus stared off as if trying to recall the event. "Mederich, that was his name." He nodded and looked back at Attalus. "The last I remember, he swung an ax at me and I knocked him off his horse just as his blow struck. I don't actually know who killed him."

"A pity," Attalus' eyes twinkled, as if he had known the actual story from the beginning. "But then, legends are always so much more dramatic. I'm told you wear a medallion, taken from an Alamanni chieftain on the battlefield. Would it also belong to this Mederich?"

Gallienus nodded. "Yes, I…" He trailed off and stared at the tall, willowy young woman with golden hair who had just entered Attalus' hall. Her ankle-length indigo dress was sleeveless and held at the waist by a thin leather belt. She walked confidently to Attalus' side and put a hand on his shoulder. When she bent down so her face was close to his, Gallienus noticed that she wore a necklace of small shells, doubtless imported from some distant ocean. At some point in the conversation, she turned her head and looked at the Romans—not a shy glance, but openly and with interest. She smiled, without any hint of self-consciousness, when she saw Gallienus staring at her.

Volusianus shifted uneasily beside him and cleared his throat. "You were speaking of the medallion you took from the Alamanni," he reminded Gallienus, jolting him from his reverie. "The medallion," Volusianus prodded, a note of impatience in his voice. "The question was whether you'd also taken it from Mederich?"

"Same man. Same battle," Gallienus shrugged, causing a lapse in the conversation.

Attalus looked up, smiling affectionately at the woman. He whispered something to her. She nodded then turned away and left the hall. "My daughter," Attalus inclined his head at the departing figure. "She'll supervise the food and drink," he explained, when no one spoke.

Soon two slaves appeared, removed the meat from the fire pit, then cut it into small strips which they piled on two trays. Then two other slaves entered with small loaves of bread, one tray for each table. Other slaves brought beverages. The Romans were served wine, the Marcomanni all took beer in their drinking horns, poured from an amphora large enough to require a strong slave to carry and pour it.

"Her husband died hunting a boar almost a year ago," Attalus tilted his head in the direction that his daughter had departed.

"I'm looking for a marriage that would be worthy of her," Attalus wiped foam from his beard and took another drink from the human skull he used instead of a horn favored by most of his chieftains. "It's no one you knew," Attalus pointed at the skull and laughed when he saw Volusianus' expression. He was distracted by one of his chieftains, and leaned over to listen to him. They exchanged a few words, before Attalus rubbed his chin, then looked over at Gallienus appraisingly.

"Perhaps a marriage between our families would bind us together and strengthen the treaty—assuming we can come to an agreement, of course."

"I would be honored to take her as a consort," Gallienus countered.

Attalus scowled. "She's the daughter of a chief! She'll be no one's consort while I'm alive." He touched the hilt of his sword to emphasize the point.

Gallienus held up both palms in front of him. "I have a wife. Roman law forbids another."

Attalus relaxed. His scowl disappeared. "You could divorce her, if you wished."

"I don't wish to."

"Unfortunate," Attalus looked disappointed. "With marriage come privileges."

"And responsibilities," Gallienus added. "She would be treated with the greatest respect and well cared for as a consort of the Emperor. You have my word on that."

Attalus shook his head angrily. "It would be an affront to her honor—and to mine as well!" He reached for his drinking skull, found it empty, and gestured impatiently for the amphora. "We take only one wife ourselves—but for persons of high rank there are sometimes exceptions."

"Such as?" Gallienus arched an eyebrow.

"Perhaps you could marry her according to Marcomanni laws and customs." Attalus grinned at the brilliance of his suggestion. "In the eyes of Roman society you wouldn't be married to a second woman, while Pipa, my daughter's name by the way, would be married in the eyes of our people. Everyone would be satisfied. Everyone would be happy."

After considering Attalus' proposal for a moment, a smile crept across Gallienus' face.

"Not everyone would be satisfied," Volusianus whispered urgently, alarmed at this sudden turn of events, "and not everyone would be happy." Gallienus glanced to his right side, as if surprised by the intrusion. "Besides the fact that you already have one wife, marriage to any non-Roman citizen is legally impossible," Volusianus reminded him, looking quickly to his right at the sober nods of the other generals. "Not only would it go against our laws it would be deeply offensive… to everyone."

"Attalus' suggestion solves the issues for them as well as for us," Gallienus countered.

How will your wife feel about to this?" Volusianus asked him softly. "She'll be neither satisfied nor happy."

"I'll still be married to her according to Roman law; nothing will have changed," Gallienus persisted. "She'll come to understand that this…formality…was necessary to finalize an important alliance."

"Consider for a moment what you're asking of this Marcomanni maiden."

Gallienus looked puzzled.

"You're taking her away from everything she's ever known: her friends, her family, her entire tribe. Instead," Volusianus said, "she'll be alone in a hostile Roman world. She barely knows our language. And she'll be forever in conflict with Salonina, no matter how gracious your wife may be."

"I realize this is an unconventional step, but it would, indeed, bind our families together and strengthen the treaty. We had nothing to hold Chrocus to his agreement almost six years ago despite giving him land." Gallienus nodded to himself. "Sometimes people have to make sacrifices for the good of their countries," Gallienus said, after considering Volusianus' entreaties.

"It's not altogether clear to me that she has to marry anyone to make this treaty to work," Volusianus objected.

"A treaty with the Marcomanni eliminates a serious threat on my northern border," Gallienus said. "Then I might be able to take an army east and reclaim territories my father lost to the Persians. Your counsel is valued, Volusianus, especially when you challenge my views and positions. But…"

"My fear is that this 'marriage' will bring strife and unhappiness for everyone involved," Volusianus interrupted.

"Clearly, we see the matter differently," Gallienus interposed, abruptly concluding the exchange. He looked across the table to find Attalus watching him intently. "I would be honored to accept your offer."

"Excellent!" Attalus grinned broadly. "Tomorrow morning, I'll take your offer to the assembly for discussion and final approval."

North of the Danuvius River
31 August, 260

Volusianus frowned, unmoved by the nearby celebration and gaiety. Seated at the table of honor to Volusianus' left, Attalus smiled broadly. His fierce blue eyes, accentuated by his sunburned face, twinkled with merriment. Attalus was a heavyset man, taller than Gallienus by half a head. He slammed his drinking skull down emphatically, sloshing beer onto the wooden table. Casually, he wiped the foam from his sandy blond beard with his sleeve, while he leaned toward Gallienus to share an amusing story. Gallienus held a nearly full drinking horn and was smiling at Attalus' anecdote, his head cocked to hear the story better.

A beautiful young Marcomanni woman sat beside him, staring straight ahead. Gold bracelets jangled when she sipped from her drinking horn and gold earrings danced when she turned to her right to speak quietly with the Marcomanni women beside her. Even seated it was clear that she was tall, like her father. A wreath of flowers graced blond hair that fell to the center of her back in a long braid. Hand-stitched purple embroidery, almost matching Gallienus' cape, lined the borders and hem of her short-sleeved, white linen dress. Despite being engaged in a raucous conversation with Attalus, Gallienus reached his right hand out to pat the young woman's hand. Startled, she looked toward him and forced a smile, while fingering a large amber pendant at her throat, a recent gift from Gallienus. Then she turned and resumed her discussion with the women next to her.

A table of honor had been placed at one edge of a large clearing in the forest, with afternoon sun at the guests' backs. Volusianus sat with Aureolus, Claudius, and Aurelian at a table perpendicular and to the right of the head table. Marcomanni chieftains and their wives filled a similar table, directly across from the Roman table. Volusianus had first glanced at their wives as a matter of curiosity, but found himself studying the warriors intently, unconsciously assessing a potential foe, a habit of many years. The men were enormous and, for the occasion all of them had filled their hair with what smelled like rancid butter. Even at festive gatherings they remained armed. Sword belts were buckled across close-fitting short-sleeved linen shirts and short trousers, and their legs were bare above ankle-high boots. Throwing axes were hooked under their right arms, and round shields lay beside each man. Despite their appearance they were in exceedingly good humor, laughing, joking, pounding each other on the back, and drinking great quantities of beer.

Slaves from many nationalities darted among tables serving beer and meats cooked over fires to Volusianus' right. He wondered how many slaves were Roman citizens and, if so, whether Gallienus would try to do anything about freeing them.

His thinking was distracted by naked Marcomanni boys who filed quickly into an open space between tables and began a dangerous dance with swords and lances. Warriors shouted their approval and began chanting rhythmically, while pounding on the tables with their fists and knives. As the dancers spun and weaved between their weapons, Volusianus marveled that no one was seriously injured or killed. He had heard that a youth who had done poorly at the dance might go into voluntary slavery.

Volusianus sampled the beer and grimaced at its bitter taste. He caught a passing slave by the arm, put his beer on the platter and ordered wine. While he waited, he ate roast boar and dark bread to clear the aftertaste from his mouth. He looked at the generals beside him, and was not surprised by their dour expressions.

Could we have said anything else, insisted more strenuously against this? he wondered again. *So much has changed since we heard about Valerian's defeat, hard to believe it was just nine days ago, and now we have a treaty with a barbarian tribe that's been our enemy since Augustus' days.* He thought back to the most recent Marcomanni invasion, six years ago, when Attalus and his army had reached Ravenna, in northern Italia, before turning back. *Now,* he looked around at the rejoicing Marcomanni and stern-faced Romans, *we have this.*

Smoke from cooking fires blew in Volusianus' direction, carrying the smell of roasting meat, and bringing him back to the present. He noticed that the naked dancers were gone, and slowly grew aware of the general din of revelry around him. A crash from the chieftains' table caused him to tense and start to rise, instantly alert for trouble. But he eased himself back into his seat as unobtrusively as possible when he saw one of Attalus' chieftains had passed out and fallen face-forward onto the table. The man lay motionless, oblivious to the shouts of good-natured derision around him. *It's time for the 'married' couple to take their leave,* Volusianus thought, *before the fights break out.* Fortunately, Gallienus had arrived at the same conclusion and rose. After making elaborate departing comments to Attalus, he left with Pipa on his arm. Shouts and cheers of the Marcomanni warriors followed them. Now it would be socially acceptable for the generals to depart. At a nod from Volusianus, they rose in unison and began making their way toward the Roman camp. He looked around one last time at the sight of Rome's newest ally, and shook his head. *They all drink too much, sing too loudly, and reek of their foul beer and rancid butter.*

"Why didn't any of you support my arguments against this marriage?" Volusianus reproached them all as sounds of celebration diminished behind them.

"You were nearest to him," Aureolus offered lamely.

"There wasn't anything else to be said," Aurelian added, "except maybe to ask him what his father would think about it."

"Your opinions would have reinforced mine," Volusianus scowled, refusing to accept their excuses.

"Nothing would have helped," Claudius disagreed. "He'd made up his mind." Each of them was deep in thought about events of the past several days as they neared camp. The sun had just set behind trees in the west and the day's heat faded rapidly.

Volusianus broke their silence, probing the generals' reactions. "All right, none of us thinks what he did was necessary or wise. Now that it's done, what happens and what do we do about it?"

"If the emperor shows no respect for the law, how can we ask others to respect it?" Claudius asked, shaking his head.

"You see this as a salacious act, but I think Gallienus sees it as a tactical necessity," Aureolus said.

"The emperor sets an example for everyone in Roman society," Aurelian spoke in support of Claudius' position. "Some might question his judgment, his soundness of mind, or his respect for Roman values."

"Are you one of them?" Volusianus stopped abruptly, confronting Aurelian.

"I was thinking more of the Senate," Aurelian shrugged. "This is a social issue, not a military one."

"Precisely," Volusianus agreed. "The security of the empire may soon be challenged as never before, and we're arguing about a social issue!"

"What will the Senate think?" Aurelian continued. "Just after hearing of Valerian's defeat in the east, they learn that his son has decided to take a second wife—and a barbarian princess at that! They may be less understanding than we are. They already don't like Gallienus. It was Valerian that they really liked."

"As I see it, it's up to us, the senior generals, to hold the empire together." Volusianus looked at each of them in turn.

"And we won't be able to do that without the support of this emperor." Aureolus' unexpected comment surprised the others. "I agree with both your positions," he nodded at Volusianus and Claudius, "but the last thing we need now is civil war."

"No one is suggesting that," Claudius affirmed. "Gallienus has my support, despite my criticism. My concern is rather with the flagrant disregard of things that make us a civilized country."

"If there's no country to defend, then there's no culture to be concerned about," Volusianus summed up the argument as he saw it. Gravel crunched under their feet while they walked on in silence.

"How do you suppose he'll justify this with Salonina?" Aurelian suddenly wondered aloud.

"And what will happen if he takes Pipa with him when he goes to Rome," Claudius mused.

"I'm wondering what it's like being in bed with Pipa now," Aureolus leered, unaware of his own wife's dalliances with a gladiator.

"You're married, Aureolus," Claudius turned on him sourly. "You should be able to answer that question yourself."

"Have you taken a good look at her?" Aureolus persisted.

"Your wife or Pipa?" Volusianus chuckled.

"She's a decent young woman who's been placed in a difficult situation, not of her own choosing, Aureolus," Claudius said primly. "Speculation on that matter is disrespectful to her and thus inappropriate for general discussion."

They passed through the gates of camp and separated, after saluting the night guard. Each man headed to his own quarters. Before entering his tent for the night, Volusianus reviewed the conversation with the generals in his mind. *They aren't questioning his ability as a leader—at least not aloud. And no one welcomed the prospect of a usurper seizing control. The option of one of us, one of them really, overthrowing Gallienus was never implied. And that*, Volusianus thought with a sense of relief, *was my biggest concern with the generals.*

3-1
Pursuit and Proclamations
Hieropolis, Cilicia
02 September, 260

Cries from the wounded were subdued by morning. The seriously injured had died the day before or during the night. Callistus walked slowly along a colonnaded road of Hieropolis, sacked, burned, then abandoned yesterday by Shapur and his army. Smoke still drifted skyward from smoldering fires. Dogs and vultures fought over corpses lying in streets and alleyways. The baths to Callistus' left had been damaged, but not completely destroyed. The temple of Artemis Perasia, opposite the baths, was untouched, as was the amphitheater carved into the side of a mountain a few hundred yards ahead.

"Set up the hospital tent there," Callistus growled, pointing to the amphitheater. Like other cities in Shapur's path, Hierapolis had been stripped of everything of value, skilled artisans, horses, grains, meat, money and other treasure, anything the Persian King thought would be useful to him.

"Aren't you going to the amphitheater?" young Macrianus asked when Callistus veered off the main street and started up a steep and winding road that led to a rocky crag above the city.

"The men know what to do," Callistus said, trying to mask his heavy breathing from the young man. "You can stay with them, if you want. But stay out of their way."

"Why go to the citadel?"

"I want to know where Shapur has gone and get a sense of the ground ahead of us." Callistus glanced enviously at Macrianus who seemed unaffected by the climb or the late morning heat and humidity. Callistus had come to use Macrianus as his second-in-command, although he continually denied Macrianus' requests to command troops in battle again. And Macrianus asked questions about everything—not to challenge his authority, as Callistus had originally thought, but to learn his thinking. "I know logistics and supply lines as well as anybody," he had explained to Callistus. "But now I want to learn strategy." *He's intelligent and a quick learner*, Callistus reflected, *but his good fortune in one minor skirmish made him think he's competent to command troops in battle.*

Three weeks earlier Callistus had led an amphibious landing near Pompeiopolis, surprising Shapur's forces who were besieging the city, and had defeated them. But Shapur managed an orderly retreat with much of his army, captives, and booty intact. Callistus then initiated two quick amphibious assaults west of Pompeiopolis, surprising other parts of Shapur's army and killing over three thousand Persians. Meanwhile, Shapur had left Cilicia moving toward the safety of Persia, using a more northerly route for his withdrawal. Callistus had pursued him in a series of forced marches. The recent destruction of Hieropolis told Callistus he was finally on the verge of making contact with the Persians.

"Do you think Shapur went this way," the question intruded on sounds of their leather soles crunching on the path's loose stones, "in order to join other parts of his army?"

"I doubt he knows where any of them are," Callistus said. "I'd guess he's looking for other cities to pillage. He has to be short of supplies."

"What if he did, somehow, meet other parts of his army?" Macrianus persisted with his concern.

"Then he might become the hunter, instead of the hunted." Callistus stopped climbing and tried to catch his breath while he thought about Macrianus' question. Below him Hieropolis nestled in a valley carved by the Pyramus River, which snaked off to the south and vanished into the distant mountains. The river was navigable to the sea, and Callistus had expected to receive both supplies and reinforcements from Macrianus' father, who was still comfortably lodged in Antioch. Callistus had dispatched a messenger down the river as soon as he had reached the city to remind the senior Macrianus of his urgent need for support. He felt uneasy about his dependence on Macrianus even though his success against Shapur would be in the elder Macrianus' interest.

What does Macrianus need with thirteen thousand men? It's been a struggle to get him to give me the ten thousand men I have now, even though I'm the one facing the enemy. Is he worried about a Persian attack on Antioch? Is he afraid of Odenathus? As far as Callistus knew, Odenathus had neither offered support to the Roman effort, nor sided with the Persians. Remembering stories of Odenathus' spurned offer of allegiance to Shapur years earlier, Callistus found the prospect of Odenathus siding with Persians highly unlikely. *Does Odenathus know of our successes against Shapur yet?* Callistus wondered. *What will Odenathus do when he learns of Shapur's defeat and retreat?*

"What are you thinking?" Macrianus asked.

Callistus frowned and resumed his climb toward the citadel before replying. "Maybe your father would pay more attention to a request from you for food and reinforcements."

"I'm sure he values your reports and requests every bit as much as he would mine."

"Perhaps it would change his mind if he felt you might get hungry and your safety was at risk."

"I thought we had an advantage." Macrianus' voice showed a concern absent from his previous remark.

"Shapur's a brilliant general. From what I've been able to learn, his army is comprised largely of horsemen. Ours is mostly foot soldiers."

"I'm aware of that," Macrianus shrugged, unable to draw the same conclusion as Callistus had.

"A battle on open plains would work to their advantage, just as it did against Valerian. It all depends on how strong they are." Callistus shook his head at Macrianus' failure to appreciate this issue. "Of course, if your father had sent me more legionnaires…" Callistus let his sentence trail off, hoping Macrianus might be inspired to write to his father.

"If Shapur goes south instead of east, wouldn't Antioch be a possible target for him?"

"Maybe," Callistus conceded. As they neared the summit, Callistus thought about the senior Macrianus. *Certainly he'd fear a Persian attack on the city. That's why he's withholding reinforcements. But will Macrianus venture out of Antioch and attack Shapur if he passes east of him?* Upon reaching the summit, Callistus climbed the citadel's western rampart. He set his elbows on the top of the heavy stones, rested his chin on his hands, and surveyed the surrounding countryside. Beyond the city, cotton fields and meadows lined both banks of the river. To the north, west, and south, mountains filled his view, their blue-grey peaks blurring with haze on the horizon.

Shapur is retreating. Perhaps there'll be another chance to free Valerian, if he's still alive. It seems that Roman order is about to be restored here. He thought of the senior Macrianus' earlier refusal to ransom Valerian. *What will happen if Valerian is either dead or doesn't return?* Callistus frowned while considering those possibilities. *Gallienus would eventually choose a successor of his own to command in the east. Would Macrianus willingly surrender the power and authority he has now? Or would he be rash enough to break with Rome and declare himself emperor? It would mean an eventual confrontation with Gallienus' forces. Certainly Macrianus wouldn't act without Odenathus' support. What would Odenathus do? What would I do? Attack Macrianus as a traitor or support him?*

He shook his head clearing away those thoughts, and walked briskly to the eastern rampart. In the distance Callistus saw a small cloud of dust off to the east. "There it is," he pointed and looked at Macrianus, glad for a distraction from his unsettling thoughts. "The Persian rear guard."

"I see them." Macrianus sounded excited. "How far away are they?"

"No more than five miles. It looks like they're headed toward Germaniceia, and all those captives will slow them down.

They could be there in… maybe four days. I know Germaniceia: there are three important mountain passes open near there, and it's on the edge of an open plain."

"They'll be exposed to attack," Macrianus concluded. He started to speak again, when the clatter of boots distracted them both. They turned to watch a messenger scrambling toward them, gasping for breath as he ran up the remaining steps.

"Supplies from General Macrianus," he panted, after saluting Callistus.

"Where are they?"

"Seized by Shapur, yesterday, sir," the messenger said, still breathing heavily.

"Catch your breath, then give me a complete report." Callistus turned abruptly back to the rampart, unsure that he could mask the disappointment on his face. Wistfully, he watched the dust from retreating Persians dissipate while he waited to learn the magnitude of this disaster.

"It was only three of the supply barges, sir," the messenger resumed after a few minutes of heavy breathing, "the ones that were at the docks unloading. The others stayed in the middle of the river. The Persians tried to board one of them but your arrival scared them away."

"How many are left?" Callistus asked.

"Another four," the messenger answered.

"Any word about others?" Macrianus interrupted.

"No sir."

After dismissing the messenger, Callistus stared eastward again, considering his predicament.

"We're the second army marching through this area," he said, laying out the facts plainly to Macrianus. "Wherever we go, Shapur will have taken everything of value before we arrive. There'll be nothing left for anyone to eat, even if we could have bought and paid for it."

Macrianus nodded. "I understand. We're totally dependent on supplies from my father."

"And there's not enough to sustain everyone I have with me," Callistus said. "I could sit here and wait for another shipment to arrive."

"That doesn't strike me as an option you'd willingly select," Macrianus observed.

"I could leave part of the army here on reduced rations waiting for resupply, and press on with the rest of the army and most of the supplies," Callistus temporized.

"Why not take the whole army and all the supplies?" Macrianus wondered aloud. "Then we could take what we need from Shapur after we defeat him."

"And if Shapur retreats without fighting?" Callistus countered. "Or if we can't defeat him? Either way, we'd starve."

The young man returned his gaze and seemed to be weighing the various options.

"You're the supply general's son," Callistus challenged him. "Got any brilliant suggestions?

Macrianus shook his head, for once glad that he wasn't in charge. "What will you do?"

Antioch, Syria
03 September, 260

"To the new emperors of Rome," the senior Macrianus smiled as he raised his wine goblet in a toast to his younger son, Quietus. "I'm sure your brother will share your enthusiasm when he learns of the army's proclamation."

"Are you sure this was wise?" Quietus asked. "I have no experience leading legions, let alone an army." He bit one of his fingernails and squirmed in the large wooden chair. Valerian had used it when presiding over meetings in this small room.

"You're almost thirty now. Gallienus was about your age when he became emperor," Macrianus patted his son's hand reassuringly. "And he had no experience with legions or armies, either. Opportunities like this never come to most men."

News of Callistus' victories over the Persians and Shapur's steady withdrawal meant that the east might actually survive this Persian onslaught. That's when Macrianus first realized that Valerian's defeat might work to his personal advantage.

"Why didn't you or Callistus take the title, Father?"

"Callistus?" Macrianus scoffed. "He'd never be accepted because of his common birth."

"And your lameness prevented you from being acceptable?" Quietus guessed.

"But you and your brother are perfect choices," Macrianus shifted the subject away from his leg. "You're both high-born—through your mother, of course—and you're young and victorious over the Persians."

"But neither of us played much of a part in the victory," Quietus worried.

"That's not important. The army supports you."

"What about General Callistus? Won't he be angry that we've taken the title of emperor?

"What can he do now?" Macrianus shrugged. "I'll make him your Praetorian Prefect."

Odenathus' message had arrived in Antioch the day before. In it, Odenathus declined Macrianus' offer to join him in a joint attack against Shapur, saying he preferred to attack the Persians with his own army. *So much the better*, Macrianus had smiled to himself as the last unknown fell into place. Macrianus then called for a messenger and told him he wished to address the legions the next morning. A second messenger was instructed to summon three centurions, each with considerable gambling debts. When he spoke to the men separately, he suggested that he could solve their problems, in exchange for a small favor the next morning.

Early the next morning he gathered his troops together. In front of them all, he recounted the success of the amphibious landings in Cilicia and Shapur's continued retreat toward Persia. Peace, he said, was nearly at hand. After the cheers subsided, he told them of Odenathus' message and the Palmyran king's plans to attack Shapur independently. The army cheered again. When the army grew quiet, several men shouted out his name and proclaimed Macrianus the next emperor. The army picked up the cry and in moments was chanting his name in unison.

"I cannot accept your kind offer, brave soldiers," he said when he could finally make his voice heard over the legionnaires. "But I accept your nomination in the name of my two sons." It happened as he had hoped it would. After the briefest of pauses, several men began shouting the names of Macrianus and Quietus and the army joined them.

But that was yesterday. Macrianus reviewed his current situation: *Shapur was in retreat, considerably weakened; the masses would welcome prospects of a return to peace; and Odenathus had committed to the Roman side. Callistus was away and could probably be consoled with the title of Praetorian Prefect, especially when he, Macrianus, had nominated his two sons instead of taking the title himself. He would solidify their position in the east and then see what, if anything, Gallienus might do to challenge him.*

"What should I do next?" Quietus fretted.

"Let me worry about that," Macrianus said. "For now, I'll take care of everything."

3-2
Palmyra's Response
Palmyra, Syria
05 September, 260

The priests of Bel, Yarhibol, and Aglibol had consulted with their gods at daybreak and assured Odenathus of their favorable dispositions toward his confrontation with Shapur. Likewise, Zenobia's sacrifices to the chief goddess, Allath, had predicted a victory. Shortly afterwards, the clatter of horses' hooves and the sound of a war chariot's iron-rimmed wheels rolling over the stone street quieted murmurings of the expectant crowd—anxious women and excited children lining Palmyra's Grand Colonnade. The crowd strained to catch a glimpse of their king as his chariot rode past them. Odenathus, dressed in chain mail armor, stood erect beside his charioteer, who struggled to keep four black stallions from breaking into a gallop. Odenathus' face alternated between light and dark as his chariot rode through morning shadows cast by the Corinthian columns lining the street. Palmyra was going to war. Herodian sat astride a magnificent chestnut stallion to the right and slightly behind his father's chariot. General Zabdas rode to Odenathus' left. Protocol required the queen to follow further back in the procession.

Row after row of Roman cavalry and legionnaires marched a short distance behind Odenathus, some from the local Palmyran detachment, the bulk from III Gallica Legion that Valerian had entrusted to Odenathus just over two years earlier. Warriors from desert tribes, dressed in flowing robes and armed with crescent-shaped swords, followed on swift camels. Behind them the famous Palmyran archers rode Arabian horses, their bows unstrung, hanging at their waists in cases designed to carry both bow and arrows. Support forces came next: men carrying long scaling ladders on their shoulders, donkeys pulling siege engines, the supply train, and the camp followers.

Odenathus had ridden no more than a quarter of the way down the Grand Colonnade, when a lone rider trotted up on his right and edged close to his chariot. The clatter of this horse's hooves was out of place and totally unexpected. *Perhaps an assassin had chosen this opportunity to approach him. The horse was certainly close enough to his chariot.* Although tradition demanded that Odenathus stare straight ahead, the rider beside him represented a serious breach of protocol. Odenathus glanced quickly to his right, suddenly alert to a threat on his life. "You're supposed to be further back in the procession," he hissed at the rider.

Zenobia smiled sweetly at her husband. She nudged her horse between Odenathus and Herodian. "Move over, Herodian. A queen should ride beside her king." Her dark eyes sparkled with challenge. She sat on a magnificent white Nubian mare, the embodiment of a warrior queen. Her burnished chain mail flashed brilliantly in morning sunshine. A helmet, lined with purple and covered with jewels, was secured to her saddle. Her purple robe, draped across her shoulders and partially covering her sword and shield, was clasped with a diamond buckle. Despite his annoyance, Odenathus grinned as he gazed at her.

Zenobia glanced contemptuously at her stepson, Herodian, draped in the robes of the court, not in his battle armor. She shook her head, although she kept her thoughts to herself. Odenathus noticed Zenobia's glance at Herodian. "How he does in battle will be the deciding factor," Odenathus said indulgently.

She almost smiled at the thought of Herodian in a pitched battle with the Persians. *Yes, that will be the deciding factor*, she thought. A few days before their departure, Herodian had suggested that he remain in Palmyra to represent the royal house while the king and the army were gone. Zenobia had learned this from Maeonius, the disgruntled son of Odenathus' brother. She knew Herodian did not care for the hardships of campaigning and was more a lover of luxury than of fighting, yet Odenathus seemed blind to Herodian's shortcomings. However, when Zenobia had challenged Herodian's suggestion to remain in Palmyra, Odenathus rejected it outright and said, "Vorodes will command here in my absence, as he has in the past."

For Zenobia, the issue of succession grew more critical each year. Herodian was now twenty; Zenobia's oldest son merely four. *If Herodian becomes King of Palmyra, my sons will be killed, and I'll be at Herodian's mercy.* She shivered. *I'd be wise to give him no reason for resentment.*

The army had passed through the eastern gate of the city to an area of salt flats. The desert lay beyond. Zenobia loved its vast open space, an affinity that was a legacy from her nomadic relatives. She thought of caravans making their way to and from distant, exotic cities. Instinctively, she looked to the north: somewhere out in that desert, they would find Shapur returning from his conquests in the Roman provinces. There would be a great battle. A flush of excitement rushed through her.

3-3

The Other Woman
Carnuntum, Pannonia
18 September, 260

"How can you drink that?" Gallienus teased Pipa as she wiped foam from her lips with the back of her hand. Since she disliked the Roman practice of reclining when she ate, they were sitting in chairs at a small table for their midday meal in the villa Gallienus had requisitioned for Pipa and her entourage.

"Father says wine is for men who can't afford beer." She bit into a slice of roast boar and drained her glass to emphasize her point. "It tastes better from a drinking horn," she nodded at her empty glass, "but I suppose I can adjust." Pipa cocked her head and looked at Gallienus with a mischievous grin. She'd been very surprised that she was enjoying life with her new husband. When her father had told her about the marriage he had arranged with Gallienus she had been dismayed, not because the marriage was arranged-- that was expected among the leading families of various tribes in order to strengthen alliances—but because it was to a Roman. They seemed so humorless, disdainful, haughty, and untrustworthy. She was greatly relieved when the emperor proved to be an attentive and engaging partner, eager to try new ways, and interested in her, her people, and their customs.

Gallienus gazed into Pipa's piercing blue eyes. In just over two weeks he had come to realize what a remarkable young woman she was, and he was grateful for this time to devote to her alone. He loved her spirit, her sense of humor, and her grasp of strategic situations. Her perspective on tribal reactions to Rome's defeat in the east was especially insightful, and she had proven to be a keen judge of character as well. Her braided hair hung over her brown linen dress, nearly reaching the small of her back. The dress set off the amber pendant, given to her as a wedding gift, matched amber earrings, her father had given her. He leaned back in his chair, content to be with her. "I never asked your father about his drinking skull," he mused. "All he ever said was that it was no one I knew."

"Father used to let me drink from it when I was little." Pipa smiled at the memory. "It was too big for me to handle and I spilled a lot of it. He'd laugh at that and pat me on the head."

"Whose skull was it?"

Pipa's face clouded over. "Tudrus, the Quadi chieftain, an evil man but a fearless warrior. He took great pleasure in burning our homes and torturing his captives, especially women and children."

"How did your father come by his skull?"

"Tudrus was pushing us out of our homeland until father led some of our warriors into battle. There was no clear victor. Father challenged Tudrus to fight him, chieftain against chieftain, in front of both tribes."

"Courageous."

"He wasn't even our chieftain then," Pipa laughed, "but the Quadi didn't know that."

"What happened?"

"Father won. He has an ugly scar from a sword wound on his chest that almost killed him." She paused, then her expression brightened. "But he still had enough strength to sever Tudrus' head with one blow from his ax."

"Why drink from it?"

"He gains the dead man's strength whenever he drinks from it." Pipa took a small bite of cheese, and smiled at him. "It's also a reminder to every one of his victory."

Gallienus sipped his wine, contemplating Pipa's last remark. It reminded him of the staff meeting Pipa had attended with him earlier in the day.

"What are you thinking?"

"I liked your comment to General Claudius at our meeting."

Pipa frowned. "He didn't know what he was talking about. It's the Goths, not the Quadi or Iazyges, as he seems to think, that Rome has to fear in the future. I said it as nicely as I could."

"And you supported your assertions admirably," Gallienus chuckled. "I think he took it well."

"Your general Aurelian wouldn't have been so receptive, I think," Pipa said.

"He is stern. How does Aureolus impress you?"

Pipa considered his question for a moment. "He has a very high opinion of himself," she shrugged. "But father seems to think he's capable."

"They all are." Gallienus stared into his wine glass. "That's why I keep them close to me." When he looked up at Pipa he smiled, content to set his concerns for the empire aside for a while.

Pipa changed the subject to one of more immediate concern to her. "You said Salonina was coming tomorrow."

"In the morning," Gallienus nodded.

"You can persuade her to accept this arrangement?"

"I've made plans for the meeting and how I'll introduce the subject."

"It would probably be wise not to be dressed in Marcomanni clothing when you first see her, and you will wash the gold dust out of your hair, won't you?"

Gallienus nodded. "Once she understands the strategic necessity of the treaty and the 'marriage,' I'm sure…"

"Excuse me sir, but there's someone to see you," the Praetorian Guardsman stepped uncertainly into the room.

"I said I wasn't to be disturbed," Gallienus scowled.

"Your orders were clear enough, sir," the man began, "but under the circumstances…'

"Tell whoever it is to wait," Gallienus waved the man away peremptorily.

A commotion ensued in the atrium. "I've waited long enough!" A woman's voice carried clearly above the noise. A look of horror flashed across Gallienus' face. The only sound that followed was the clatter of sandals across the mosaic floors.

Salonina swept across the threshold. "I was told you were here…" she began, annoyance from the confrontation in the atrium still on her face. She stopped abruptly. Only her eyes, wide in disbelief, betrayed her emotions. She stared at the two of them together, then fixed on her husband, taking in his brown tunic, trousers fastened by a wide leather belt, and the gold dust sprinkled liberally in his hair. Then she studied the woman sitting beside Gallienus, young, trim blond, not wearing anything a Roman lady would have chosen. The woman returned Salonina's gaze with no outward sign of shame or embarrassment. Salonina took a deep breath. "I see you've taken a mistress in my absence." Her conversational tone belied the hurt and anger she felt.

Gallienus leapt to his feet, and rushed toward Salonina. "What a pleasant surprise! I wasn't expecting you until tomorrow," he said reaching his hands out to her.

"I can see that." Salonina made no effort to respond to his gesture.

"So much has happened since you started your trip," Gallienus began. He took Salonina by the shoulders and pulled her close to him. When he felt her shoulders tense, he released his hold and stepped back to face her directly. "I had planned to sit down with you, alone, and explain…discuss… what I've done and the reasons for doing it."

"Who is she?" Salonina demanded, ignoring Gallienus' attempt to placate her. She nodded in Pipa's direction, without actually looking at her.

"This is Pipa," Gallienus turned to face the seated woman directly, "the daughter of the Marcomanni chieftain, Attalus."

"Is she your hostage, then?" Salonina continued looking at Gallienus, speaking as if Pipa were not even in the room.

Gallienus turned back to face Salonina while he searched for the appropriate words. "It's a bit more complicated than that, actually."

"I can't wait to hear your explanation. But this is hardly the place for it."

Gallienus glanced at Pipa.

A difficult but revealing moment, Pipa thought. *He owes Salonina an explanation for what's going on. But he's also made a commitment to me. Will he show me the dignity and respect I deserve?*

Pipa's eyes bore into his. Her expression was expectant, challenging. Gallienus realized how important his handling of this moment was to her, as well as to Salonina. He hesitated. Pipa sighed. *If I hope to have any sort of relationship with Salonina later, I suppose I need to help him exit gracefully now.* "The timing for our introduction has been most unfortunate, Salonina," she addressed the empress, who flinched at Pipa's use of her name but still did not look at her. "I think you should both retire to your villa, Gallienus," Pipa continued. She rose from her chair, moved to stand beside Gallienus, and put a hand on his shoulder. She looked at Salonina, but spoke to Gallienus. "It would be more appropriate if you explained our relationship to her there."

Salonina turned abruptly and left the room without saying a word. Gallienus looked from the departing Salonina to Pipa and back to Salonina again. "Go with her," Pipa urged. "I think you have some convincing ahead of you."

Salonina remained silent during the carriage ride to their villa, trying to keep her face impassive to mask her continued struggle between hurt and anger. Although she occasionally glanced toward Gallienus, she heard nothing of what he was saying. *I've been so looking forward to being with Gallienus again, and I expected he'd feel the same way about me. Instead, I find him with a barbarian girl! What did Gallienus mean when he said their relationship was more complicated than her being a concubine? What is she to him and how will that affect me? Instead of helping Gallienus face problems of the empire, I have a personal issue to face—alone. My marriage, my whole way of life. Is it all over?*

After what seemed an interminable ride, they arrived at Gallienus' villa. Salonina stepped from the carriage and walked past a small group of people without a nod or greeting of any kind. She passed wordlessly through the atrium and into the room Gallienus had chosen.

When they were finally alone, Gallienus reached out to take her in his arms. "I've missed you."

"So I saw." Salonina stepped back and walked purposefully around the square table dominating the room and stopped a quarter of the way around. Salonina took a deep breath, then turned to face Gallienus, her arms folded.

"Wine?" Gallienus asked hopefully. Salonina shook her head. He called for wine anyway, then sat rigidly in a chair on his side of the table and studied her face.

"Barbarian clothes don't suit you," Salonina frowned, struggling to ignore the knot in her stomach. She took a deep breath. "Now tell me what's going on."

Gallienus leaned forward, put his elbows on the table, and rested his head on one hand. "We've both been thrust into positions we never asked for, nor expected to be in." He spoke softly without his usual exuberance. "I've done things recently that I consider vital to the survival of the empire. And I'd made careful plans to explain them to you when you arrived—tomorrow morning." He looked at her questioningly.

"I could tell by the way the messenger acted that something wasn't right. So I ordered Fulvianus to march all night," Salonina said. "You weren't at this villa to greet me, and everyone here gave me strange looks. I was afraid something had happened to you, so I demanded to be taken to where you were."

Gallienus cleared his throat and reached forward, palm up. "That wasn't the way I'd intended it to be."

"I was worried and I came to Carnuntum to support you. This is a dangerous time for both of us. I've thought constantly of the risks, revolts and dangers of invasions. I fear for Saloninus' safety in Germania. Then, at a dinner in Aquileia learned of your recent affair with Prisca," she paused, watching Gallienus' expression for some sort of reaction. He crossed his arms and briefly pursed his lips. She sensed his discomfort, but his face betrayed no further emotion. The fact that he hadn't denied it confirmed her suspicions. "Couldn't you have waited a few more weeks for me? Did you have to put her in your bed and at my place at the dinners?" Gallienus started to speak. Salonina held up a hand. "We'll discuss all that later." She stood rigidly, lips compressed, holding his gaze. The tightness in her chest made breathing difficult. "And when I arrived here, I found you dressed like a barbarian, lounging with a barbarian girl. Have you've lost your sense of reason or your perspective?" She paused and took a deep breath. "Why have you done this, especially with everything else that's going on?"

"It's precisely because of what's going on that I've done this. Let me tell you now what I'd planned to say to you tomorrow." Salonina gave a barely perceptible nod, and sat in a chair on her side of the table. "In the past, the defeat of a Roman army has encouraged revolts or invasions, sometimes both. Occasionally, an emperor's generals have taken matters into their own hands."

She didn't respond.

"The Franks are now running through Gaul. Postumus has more than he can manage with them already," he continued.

"And who knows where Shapur is or what he's doing in the east. I haven't heard anything at all from Macrianus." Gallienus took a breath and shook his head. "The main threats locally are from a Marcomanni invasion and from the restive province itself. Pannonian legions have revolted three times in the last ten years. I think I've reached a solution that will work."

"Does this have anything to do with the girl I just met, by any chance?"

"Yes, everything. My solution to the issues in Pannonia was to conclude a treaty with the Marcomanni. They'll provide a substantial force of auxiliaries for the army. In exchange, I'm letting them settle on land near the western edge of Lake Pelso. Some of my generals thought it unwise to settle a former enemy so far inside the empire. But the large Marcomanni military force in the center of Pannonia that's loyal to me should discourage further provincial unrest."

"And is their loyalty somehow connected to the barbarian girl? Is she your hostage?"

"A hostage—in a manner of speaking," Gallienus temporized. "This is an important treaty for the reasons I've mentioned," he began, "but it's vital that it endures, since we're allowing a large number of outsiders to settle well inside the empire. We have the usual assurances, and I think Attalus and I have developed a mutual trust and respect for one another. But holding a hostage implies a lack of trust on some level. More of a commitment was required on both sides to ensure the terms of the treaty were honored: it needed a gesture of good will, trust, and friendship. To that end, a marriage was suggested."

"A marriage!" Salonina's eyes narrowed. She studied Gallienus' face, her chest tightening again. "Between whom?"

"Pipa, and me," Gallienus admitted reluctantly.

"Oh." Disbelief, hurt, and anger surged through Salonina's body. She closed her eyes, took a deep breath, struggling to master her emotions and reveal nothing in her response to him. "Have I been divorced?"

"Of course not!" Gallienus sounded surprised by the question.

"Are you planning to divorce me?" She could recall no

emperor divorcing his wife since Severus Alexander had thirty-five years earlier. But he was only an adolescent, she remembered, and the divorce was more his mother's doing. *However, Gallienus still has the right to divorce me if he chose to.*

"Of course not!" Gallienus said emphatically. "I told Attalus I'd be honored to have her as a concubine, but he took the suggestion as an insult to his daughter and as an implied insult to himself."

"What about the insult to me?" Salonina blurted.

"It seemed for a time that the whole treaty agreement was in jeopardy," Gallienus continued, ignoring Salonina's question. "Then, someone suggested the marriage be conducted according to Marcomanni customs and traditions."

"What about our customs and traditions?" Salonina countered. "Roman law only recognizes one wife, as you well know." She took another deep breath before continuing. "And only to another Roman citizen. This charade of marriage to a second wife is an affront to me. How do you think others will regard it? No one will recognize it as legitimate with…"

"That's exactly the point," Gallienus broke in before she could finish.

A thought occurred to Salonina. "Won't they all be granted citizenship? You're offering land to these people inside the empire."

"Yes, but she wasn't a citizen when the marriage rites were performed. The marriage was only intended to be recognized and accepted by the Marcomanni people, and they realize the marriage isn't recognized by Roman law. No Roman would take this marriage seriously."

"It's serious to me!"

"Please understand that she's an important part of an alliance that I felt was crucial to the empire. Her relationship with me means I'll be able to trust the Marcomanni while I'm engaged elsewhere." Salonina held his gaze. "None of this was intended to change our marriage in any way," he added when she made no response.

"It can't help but change it. You married her, and she's

young enough to be your daughter!"

"I love you, Salonina. I've always wanted you to share my life, to have you as my companion, confidante, and advisor. If the gods will it, my wish is to grow old with you." He rose from his seat.

"It's hard to reconcile what you've said with what I've seen." She rose and faced him.

"You've always had a keen grasp of power and politics. Please think strategically about this. Securing the center of the empire enables me to go where I'm most needed, east or west." He paused to see if Salonina was hearing what he was saying to her. "The 'marriage' part of the treaty is unconventional but necessary. With it, the Marcomanni under Attalus will guarantee Marcomanni support. They will fulfill their role as allies."

"What role will she fulfill?"

"I expect her to advise me on issues concerning the Marcomanni, and other tribes as well," Gallienus said, moving a few steps closer to her. "You're my wife. You're the empress."

"Where will she stay?"

"In a separate villa, along with her Marcomanni retinue."

"You'll be spending time with her, as well as with me?"

"I'll spend some time with her, of necessity, more with you, of course."

"So, I won't be dining with her?"

"Not unless you wish to."

"I don't think that likely."

"Pipa was forced into the middle of a complex situation, not of her own making," Gallienus said in her defense. "She understands and accepts your preeminence, and her role as a 'secondary' wife."

Salonina shook her head. "Regardless of my feelings, or your assurances, I'll have to endure you having a second relationship that looks like a marriage. Everyone can see it whether they appreciate the nuances of 'strategic necessity' or not."

"If we can't hold the empire together, I won't live to grow old with you," Gallienus said. "I'll issue coins with both of us on it together to show devotion to each other, mine to you especially. They'll emphasize imperial harmony."

Salonina paused a moment. "You won't bring her to Rome, will you?" She stood inches away from him looking steadily into his eyes.

"I'm sure she'll want to visit with her family when we go to Rome."

"I understand—but I still don't like it," Salonina conceded, drawing in a breath. She stood gazing at Gallienus' face, at his features that she knew so well, and exhaled slowly. Reluctantly she let him hold her, and felt his warmth and strength against her, and she sensed his shoulders relaxing slowly. Still, a knot in the pit of her stomach refused to release. *I want to believe what he's telling me. But he has disappointed me twice—that I know of. I can understand what he says, but it's what he does that will show me where his heart is.*

3-4
Battle Recollections
East of Edessa, Mesopotamia
24 September, 260

Odenathus burst into the hospital tent and strode to its center where a stretcher had been placed. "I've come to see my wife," he announced. An elderly Egyptian man bent over the wounded queen, whose blood matted in her long, black hair and covered most of the left half of her face. It had spilled down the front of her silver chain mail, almost as far as her sword belt. Odenathus stared down at his unconscious wife, then glanced anxiously at Zenobia's personal physician. "How is she?"

The doctor was gently removing chain mail covering Zenobia's head and neck. "A blow to the head. You can see the gash in her helmet." He nodded to a corner of the tent where he'd tossed it when she was first brought in. "I'll know shortly whether it's serious."

Odenathus walked over and bent down to retrieve the bloody

headgear. "She'd be furious if she knew how you treated her helmet," he half smiled.

"I'm hoping she has that opportunity." The physician dropped Zenobia's chain mail casually on the floor beside her stretcher and began cleaning the blood from her hair. Odenathus felt hot desert winds stirring through the tent—all four sides had been raised to keep heat down as much as possible. Just outside, a subdued throng of Zenobia's warriors, who had fought with and rescued Zenobia, milled about hoping for encouraging news of her recovery.

While the physician worked, Odenathus studied the damage to his wife's helmet: a small gash on the top left side with jagged edges. He ran a finger lightly along the uneven tear on Zenobia's helmet, noticing the purple lining inside caked with blood. After setting her helmet carefully on a small table, he returned his attention to his wife and to her physician.

The Egyptian took in a deep breath, let it out slowly. "A scalp wound," he announced. "If the blow had hit the helmet a few inches closer to the center, her head would have been split open."

"A few inches in the other direction, and it would have missed her head altogether." Odenathus' smile masked his great relief.

"Perhaps severing her left arm," the Egyptian countered. "She's very lucky, although she might not think so when she wakes up. *If she wakes up*, he thought, keeping that concern to himself. "Her neck will probably be sore, as well as her head. She complained of a pain around her ribs," he added. "That area's badly bruised but it's nothing serious, praise the gods. She doesn't remember how it happened."

"She's spoken to you, then!"

"She's drifted in and out of consciousness several times." The physician shrugged. He returned his attention to Zenobia and soon ceased to notice Odenathus lingering beside him.

* * *

"Do you want to keep it?" Odenathus asked Zenobia the next

morning, nodding at her damaged helmet.

"Of course." She winced at a stab of pain produced by her emphatic answer. "I plan to use it," she murmured, "unless it can't be repaired." She rubbed her neck, trying to ease a pounding in her head. "What about the battle? Where's Shapur? When will we attack him again?"

Odenathus held up his hands, delighted at his wife's enthusiasm and apparent return to her normal self. "One thing at a time. We won a great victory, thanks in no small part to you."

Zenobia sighed and closed her eyes for several minutes. He thought she'd fallen asleep. "Is that all you're going to tell me?" she asked impatiently, suddenly opening her eyes again.

"Shapur is in retreat. After your injury, I decided to let him escape. I don't want the Persians leaderless, otherwise civil war will break out. That would be disastrous for the caravans. I'm satisfied that he's been considerably weakened, and I doubt he'll be a threat to us any time soon."

After leaving Hieropolis three weeks earlier, Shapur had filled a gorge with Roman captives and crossed over the gorge on a human bridge. From there he'd changed directions and moved south, sacking the city of Nicopolis. Antioch lay before him to the south, a four days' march, but Shapur chose to bypass it, recalling his entrance into the city unopposed years earlier. *Better to move east and deny the Romans behind me a chance to unite with defenders of Antioch in front of me.* He'd passed through Zeugma, still in ruins from the earthquake that devastated it earlier that summer, and crossed the Euphrates River, where his line of march had brought him to the gates of Edessa. Last June, he had bypassed the city on his way to Cilicia, so the city remained in Roman hands. Since then, the Romans had reinforced Edessa's garrison. Now, it blocked his retreat.

Shapur knew his army was tired and its morale was low. Hoping to continue his march toward home without having to do battle with the Edessa garrison, he had sent a message to the Roman commander.

Soldiers of Edessa, why choose to oppose my passage when that action will result in loss of life on both sides and, in the end, merely slow my return to Persia? In exchange for granting my army safe and undisturbed passage past your city, I will present you with all the Roman coinage I've gathered on my campaign. I do not offer you these things out of fear, but rather because I plan to attend a religious festival in Ctesiphon, and I don't wish any further delay on my journey home.

The garrison complied, and Shapur had marched past Edessa unopposed.

Four days later, on the 24th of September, Odenathus attacked the Persians east of Edessa. General Zabdas had led the right wing, Herodian the left. Zenobia, who commanded the reserve forces, sat beside Odenathus at the center of the army. Whether the Persian counterattack had chosen Herodian's side by chance or by design, the Palmyran left flank quickly faltered. Odenathus had merely looked at Zenobia, pointed in Herodian's direction, and said "There." And she was off, her shouted order clearly audible above the din of battle. Sun glinted from her burnished chain mail as her white Nubian mare led the attack. Warriors from the desert tribes followed on their swift camels, crescent swords drawn and shouting wildly. Odenathus had watched their robes flowing in the wind, his gaze lingering only long enough to satisfy himself that a contingent of his Palmyran archers had followed the camels. Then, he had returned his attention to the desperate struggle raging in front of him.

"You saved Herodian's life yesterday," Odenathus was saying to Zenobia. *Surprising*, he thought, *knowing how she feels about him.* Zenobia had never cared for her stepson, and since having sons of her own, regarded Herodian as a mortal threat to their chances of succession to the throne.

I didn't do it intentionally, Zenobia thought. Aloud she said, "It would have unnerved the soldiers to see their leader fall in battle, even though it was Herodian." She scowled, trying to recall Herodian's later actions on the battlefield.

"We captured three of Shapur's governors," Odenathus continued, "a lot of his spoils, and a number of Roman citizens."

"Was Valerian among them?"

"No, but did I mention that we took part of Shapur's harem?"

"That doesn't really excite me." Zenobia rubbed her neck again. Her eyes narrowed and she stared accusingly at Odenathus. "What are you planning to do with them?"

"I gave them to Herodian," Odenathus grinned at her suspicions. "I've since been told they're claiming to be captured Roman citizens." He sighed. "I suppose I'll have to check into that later."

"Well, I don't have to ask where Herodian is right now." Zenobia tried to smile. "And who is commanding the army?"

"General Zabdas has taken command in my absence."

Zenobia let out a sigh of relief. "When will we fight again?" she asked, suddenly trying to sit up. "Oh!" She sank back on the cot putting a hand to her head and trying to stabilize the wave of nausea.

"I don't think you'll be ready for battle any time soon." Odenathus patted her leg soothingly. "We'll go as far as Nisibis. After we retake that city, we'll man it, then retire for the winter." He rose abruptly. "I have matters to deal with. I'll come back when I can."

Zenobia cursed her pounding head and dizziness. To distract herself from her discomfort, she closed her eyes and relived the battle scene, trying to recall missing pieces. This time images came to her vividly, as if she were actually fighting the battle again.

She had raced straight for Herodian's battle standards. Her sword slashed the neck of a Persian who'd just knocked Herodian's sword from his hand. She saw blood spurt from the man's wound before her horse's momentum carried her beyond them and into the melee. Zenobia was dimly aware of shouts of her warriors behind her, rising above the general din of battle. Horses' hooves churned sand from the desert floor into great clouds, and winds carried it eastward, toward Persian forces, obscuring her view beyond an immediate area in which she fought. She only glanced back toward Herodian, then immediately turned forward—just before a Persian lance pierced her shield with a loud crunch. She remembered tightening her grip on the shield bracing just before the impact. With a searing pain the lance lodged in her chain mail, slightly below her ribs. She could still hear that crunch of a lance piecing her shield and again experienced searing pain she had felt as it caught in the chain mail. The force of the impact broke the lance with a loud crack—she remembered that sound clearly, too. Her next recollection was lying face up on the ground, gasping for breath. She knew her life depended on how rapidly she could recover.

Even now in the safety of the tent, she began to perspire as she recalled seeing a second Persian horseman rushing toward her, his lance aimed at the center of her torso. Summoning all her strength, she had slashed down with her sword then rolled away, fully expecting to feel the sting of another lance, sure she had moved too late. But her sword stroke had knocked the tip of the lance into the sand beside her. The blur she saw must have been the rider, tumbling from his horse. Adrenalin surged through her. Springing to her feet, she was astride this fallen rider with the alacrity of a tigress seizing an antelope. She planted her knee on his chest and sank her dagger into his throat. She sheathed her knife, grabbed the man's shield, and rose quickly. Steadying herself, she looked desperately for a horse. Then her eyes met Herodian's. He sat on his horse watching her struggle as though she was a participant in the gladiatorial arena. *How long has he been watching me?* flashed through her mind. His fascination with Zenobia's predicament caused him to ignore the battle raging around him. While he watched, his bodyguards fought furiously to protect him. Herodian and Zenobia silently held each other's glance until he broke contact, suddenly distracted by something he saw behind her. Instinctively, she spun around, raising the Persian shield even before she knew what threatened her. Her last recollection was the crash of a sword shattering her second shield, and a flash of light.

Zenobia opened her eyes, took a breath, and felt her ribs

were the lance had nearly penetrated. Now she understood why they throbbed. Eventually, the ache in her head would fade away and eventually hair would grow back to cover her scalp wound. But she would never forget Herodian's dispassionate expression while he idly watched her fight for her life.

3-5

Opportunity of a Lifetime
Southeast of Viennensis, Narbonensis
27 September, 260

Postumus' and Silvanus' combined forces had pursued a large barbarian raiding party to Lugdunum, a city in southern Gaul. There, refugees fleeing north surprised them with news of a second group of barbarians approaching a town south-east of Lugdunum. Anxious to prevent their enemy from combining their forces, Silvanus split the army into two groups again. While he and Saloninus moved slightly west to attack one group, Postumus had conducted a forced march across the Rhodanus River, and through a town called Viennensis, before the enemy reached it. Beyond the town he found open ground amid rolling hills, adequate to field his army and waited for the enemy. There, three days ago, Postumus had intercepted the barbarians, heavily laden with spoils, and defeated them after a bitter, but decisive, battle. In his report to Silvanus announcing his victory, Postumus had casually mentioned dividing the spoils among his legionnaires.

Silvanus' immediate reply demanded that Postumus collect all distributed items from the soldiers and deliver them to him, so that Silvanus could return them to their Roman owners. Initially, Postumus bristled at the command then relaxed, leaned back in his chair, and nodded to himself. "Tell General Silvanus I'll comply with his order," he had replied to the messenger, "but Silvanus and Saloninus must be standing beside me on the parade field when I give the order to confiscate the spoils."

Silvanus' directive had provided Postumus with an opportunity that never came to most men. *The army won't be happy about this,* Postumus thought after the messenger had departed. *Soldiers resent being separated from their booty. But when they learn the order came from Silvanus, they'll understand I had nothing to do with it.* He tried to envision the legionnaires standing on the parade field, their newly gained wealth lying at their feet. *Doesn't Silvanus realize how dangerous this order is?* Postumus shook his head, incredulous, and reviewed his assessment of the army's reaction. *If they accept Silvanus' order, then no one will suspect that I entertained thoughts of revolt. But if they mutiny, then I'll be their logical choice for successor. And if I don't accept, they may very well kill me. But if I accept the soldiers' offer and declare myself emperor, then what do I do next?* He thought again about the perils of marching on Rome, leaving his northern borders lightly defended, and having to fight Gallienus with his own small army. When the idea came to him, it was so simple he was amazed that he had not thought of it before.

What if I only claimed the western part of the empire, I wouldn't need the Senate's confirmation. I wouldn't need to march on Rome. I could leave the problems of the east and center to Gallienus, block the mountain passes on my eastern border with loyal troops, and form an independent empire of Gaul. I wouldn't threaten Gallienus directly, nor expose this countryside to further Frankish invasions. No one has ever tried this before. I think I can do this!

30 September, 260

Postumus looked up from a pile of messages strewn across a small table inside his tent. "Notify me when they've arrived," he said to one of his orderlies, then made a show of returning to his correspondence as the man saluted and stepped outside. Postumus dropped an unread document onto the table. There was nothing further for him to do but wait. He sipped water from his field kit, wiped his lips with the back of his sleeve, and loosened his tunic. He stared through the open flap of his tent at the activities of an encamped army, familiar with the routines, oblivious to the particulars.

"The troops are assembled, sir."

"The emperor's son and General Silvanus are there?"

"Yes sir," the man replied. He cleared his throat uneasily. "General Silvanus was quite irritated that you were keeping them waiting."

Postumus grinned. "We wouldn't want to irritate the general, now would we?"

3-6
Choosing Sides
Nisibis, Mesopotamia
13 October, 260

"General Zabdas wishes me to inform you that Nisibis has fallen," a messenger reported, after reining in his horse and saluting Odenathus and Zenobia.

"Did they surrender, or did we take it?" Odenathus asked, returning the messenger's salute. The king and queen sat astride their horses just beyond the range of arrows from the city wall. Zenobia commanded reserve forces gathered behind her. Odenathus' personal retinue of soldiers was beside her reserves. She had insisted on participating, assuring Odenathus that she was fully recovered from her earlier injuries. How difficult can a siege be? she'd thought to herself.

"We breached the walls, sir, then managed to open a gate," the messenger said enthusiastically. "Prince Herodian led the army into the city himself," he added.

"He'll sack the city," Zenobia whispered to Odenathus. "I thought you didn't want that to happen."

Odenathus nodded. "Remind my son of my instructions to leave the city intact. Then find General Zabdas," he said to the messenger. "Tell him to restore order inside the city any way he can." The messenger saluted, wheeled his horse around, and galloped toward the city.

Wonderful! Zenobia thought. *Herodian avoids the danger of battle, but leads the way into a defeated city. Doubtless, there'll be no adverse consequences for disobeying his father's orders.* She took a deep breath and shuddered at the sharp pain she still felt in her ribs. Her right hand involuntarily reached over and touched the spot where a Persian lance had struck her nearly three weeks earlier. An image flashed through her mind of Herodian's cold gaze on her as she fought for her life during the battle outside Edessa.

Another messenger rushed up to them. "Horsemen approaching from the west, sir! We can't tell who they are yet."

Odenathus strained to see what the messenger was pointing at. He watched while a small cloud of dust grew larger. *Is it part of Shapur's army returning home?* Odenathus wondered. *Who else could it be? And most of my army's inside the city, looting!* "Find General Zabdas," he called to yet another messenger, his calm, authoritative voice masking his concern. "Tell him we may have a Persian raiding force approaching our flank. Have him bring me as much of the army as he can, quickly?"

"In the meantime," he looked at Zenobia and flashed the broad grin he always showed before going into battle. "It's just you and me!" He barked a few quick orders to deploy Zenobia's reserves and his retinue of bodyguards to face this unknown threat, spreading them in a line to face oncoming riders, whoever and how many they were. Zenobia returned Odenathus' smile, her dark eyes flashing with anticipation. She drew her sword, rested its hilt on the saddle in front of her, then glanced around her. There were no other forces to support them, nor was there any sign of General Zabdas. *He can't possibly arrive in time*, she thought, picturing Zabdas inside the city vainly urging troops away from their looting and pillaging. *Perhaps we can retreat inside the city... if it comes to that.* She glanced quickly at the city gates.

"They're riding under a banner of some sort," Odenathus said a few moments later.

"Are they riding in formation?" Zenobia asked.

"Yes, and they're coming at a trot, not a full gallop."

"That's the banner of the emperor," an aide confirmed.

"You're certain of that?" Odenathus frowned. "Last I knew Valerian was Shapur's prisoner, and Gallienus was thousands of miles away."

"Macrianus!" Zenobia exclaimed. "He must have claimed the title for himself."

The Roman formation drew to a halt just beyond arrow range. Each group eyed the other warily. *We seem pretty evenly matched*, Odenathus thought, instinctively gauging the strength of this group opposing him. He glanced expectantly toward the city.

A horseman approached them, emerging from the dust kicked up by Roman horses which drifted toward them on a westerly wind. When the man determined that this force was, indeed, Odenathus' soldiers, he returned to the Roman side. A man wearing a purple cape rode forward, escorted by a small group of horsemen.

"It's Quietus!" Zenobia said when the man's horse brought him near enough to be recognized.

"You can sheath your sword, Queen Zenobia," Quietus said when he drew closer. "That's no way to greet an Emperor of Rome." Zenobia stared at him, amazed and amused at the presumption of this inexperienced young man. "The army proclaimed my brother and me co-emperors over a month ago," Quietus added by way of explanation. Zenobia nodded, amazed at this unexpected turn of events. Slowly she sheathed her sword and again, fixed her gaze on Quietus.

"I'm flattered you rode all this way to deliver the news yourself," Odenathus said. "Reinforcements would have been more useful to me at the moment." He too, stared at Quietus.

"My father wishes to know…." Quietus began, then looked around uncomfortably. "I'd prefer a place where we can discuss matters, alone."

"We're in the middle of a siege." Odenathus frowned and waved his hand toward the city. "Privacy's a bit hard to come by just now. Anything you wish to say to me can be said in my wife's presence," he added.

Quietus scowled at them, but eventually agreed with Odenathus' suggestion to withdraw all supporting personnel.

"You said your father wished to know something?" Odenathus prodded Quietus, who suddenly seemed to be searching for words once the three of them were essentially alone.

"Perhaps I misheard you earlier," Zenobia interrupted. "I thought you and your brother were the emperors?"

"Yes, and I have come in person to receive your oath of loyalty." Quietus looked expectantly at Odenathus. "As one of the new emperors," he added when Odenathus said nothing.

An image flashed through Odenathus' mind of Shapur casting his gifts into the Euphrates River years earlier. Odenathus' subsequent allegiance with the Romans had proven beneficial to both of them—he protected Rome's interests along their eastern frontier, and Rome supported him against Persian encroachment. He had been fortunate that Shapur had chosen to attack the province of Cilicia, instead of Palmyra, after Valerian's disastrous defeat. Odenathus had held his forces close at hand, while the Romans dealt with Shapur themselves. Then he'd received the improbable news that the Romans had actually attacked Shapur and forced him to begin a withdrawal. Odenathus recognized Shapur's retreat as his opportunity to cripple the Persian army, thus safeguarding Palmyra's future.

Now Quietus comes to me with this preposterous claim! If I side with him, then my survival will depend on his forces defeating Gallienus. Odenathus grimaced when he thought of Gallienus' battle-hardened forces and talented generals confronting Macrianus.

"To my knowledge Rome already has two emperors," Odenathus said, "and I've pledged my support to them."

Quietus stiffened. "You refuse to recognize us, then?" He turned, almost reflexively, and glanced at his horsemen as if looking for their support.

A prearranged signal? Odenathus wondered. He reached his right hand across his waist to rest it casually on the hilt of his sword. Odenathus studied the younger man. *To swear allegiance to Quietus places me at odds with Gallienus. Refusing allegiance to Quietus places me at odds with him. What would Quietus do if*

I refused? Try to seize me, and claim I rebelled against Roman authority? Is that why he's come here?

"Are you with us or against us?" Quietus pressed Odenathus.

And if I refused to commit myself either way? Odenathus exhaled slowly, tension slipping out of his body. He flashed a broad smile at Quietus. "I have no intention of interfering in your personal attempt to seize power from Gallienus, if that's your wish. Defending my kingdom, and Rome's eastern frontier, is my primary concern."

Quietus nodded, considering Odenathus' comment.

"Do you think Gallienus will allow your revolt to go unchallenged?" Zenobia scoffed. "Have you forgotten what he did when Ingenuus revolted?"

"Gallienus can't abandon the empire's center." Quietus dismissed her challenge casually. He glanced at the queen appraisingly. "He's got an unruly province to control, and hostile barbarians north of the border."

Zenobia arched an eyebrow. "Are you planning to sit on the throne in Antioch, waiting for Gallienus to send an army when it suits him?"

"That brings me to the other reason for coming," Quietus said, turning his attention to Odenathus again. "My father is planning to take an army west next spring. We'll defeat Gallienus on the battlefield." He looked confidently at each of them in turn. "But we couldn't make that commitment if your loyalty was in doubt. For now, neutrality will do, I suppose."

"Who will command this army?" Zenobia asked. "You and your brother?"

Quietus looked at Odenathus. "Perhaps you would be interested in commanding some portion of the army yourself? Of course we'd expect you to bring a considerable number of your forces with you." He arched an eyebrow, assuming the offer was an honor Odenathus would find irresistible.

"What about General Callistus?" Zenobia asked. "He drove Shapur out of the Roman provinces. Isn't that the sort of man you'd want leading your invasion?"

"Callistus will remain here, commanding the forces in the

east, until we return."

Odenathus shook his head. "My duty lies here, with Palmyra."

"So, your father and the two of you will lead this army yourselves?" Zenobia was incredulous. "With what sort of command experience?"

"My brother has learned a great deal about leading men while with General Callistus," Quietus said. "And I shall acquire the knowledge I need between now and the time we confront Gallienus. It's important for emperors to lead their troops in battle," he added primly.

Zenobia looked across Quietus and caught Odenathus' eye and put a hand to her face to hide her smirk.

"We will still expect you to support our effort with troops," Quietus ignored Zenobia's reaction, "the customary twenty percent."

"I'll need every man I have to defend what we've fought to regain from the Persians," Odenathus countered.

"That won't do."

"My interests coincide with Rome's interests, along Rome's eastern border, Quietus. "

"I'm well aware of that. That's why I'm willing to accept your pledge of neutrality. We're confident of our victory," Quietus continued, "but we can't prevail without an adequate force. We'll be recruiting soldiers from the four legions south of you." He watched Odenathus' face to see if Odenathus grasped the implications of the statement.

Odenathus had. *Soldiers from four legions south of me, marching through Syria to reach Antioch,* Odenathus reflected. *I can't block their passage without a fight, which I don't want. And a force that large could commandeer any part, or all, of my legion if they chose to.*

"You may have the men you request, from my legion," Odenathus agreed reluctantly.

"Rome's legion, Odenathus," Quietus said.

"I'll want them back when you return."

Quietus shrugged. "I'll refer that request to my father."

"Come back to me when you're victorious against

Gallienus," Odenathus snapped. "I'll give you my oath of loyalty then." He reined his horse around and he and Zenobia trotted toward the city of Nisibis.

4-1
Defections
Carnuntum, Pannonia
19 October, 260

Gallienus burst into the room where Claudius and Marcus Aurelius Heraclianus, the recently-appointed Governor of Pannonia, waited. "My apologies for keeping you from your afternoon baths, gentlemen." Gallienus cast his purple cloak toward one of the chairs at the table and knelt by the nearest brazier warming his hands. "I see you haven't been inconvenienced, Heraclianus," Gallienus quipped, noting Heraclianus' neat, clean appearance. "It's good to see you again," he said, grasping Heraclianus' arm. The emperor had just completed a three-day march from the city of Brigetio, east of Carnuntum. Volusianus and Aureolus followed the emperor into the room without fanfare and made their way to the nearest chairs. They were all cold, tired, and dirty.

"There are some perks to being a governor," Heraclianus noted, taking Gallienus' comment as a friendly barb. "Since your message arrived, I've been gathering answers to the questions you sent me."

"Your trip from Vindobona was uneventful?" Gallienus turned from the brazier to look at Claudius.

"Without incident," Claudius nodded wearily at Gallienus. "Isn't Aurelian with you?" he asked.

"He's coming from Aquincum." Gallienus rubbed his hands together, stood, and walked casually to the table. He drew out a chair, eased himself into it and sighed with relief, then took a moment to consider his friend. An image flashed into Gallienus' mind of a late-August sun casting shimmering mirages above a dry, dusty field, the Plains of Hades, where he and Heraclianus had defeated the Carpi in a pitched battle four summers ago. *Heraclianus hasn't aged much,* he thought, *still as thin and muscular as I remember him.* His narrow face, hooked nose, and pointed chin would have given Heraclianus an austere look, if it weren't for his genial personality. Gallienus smiled at the image before focusing on current issues. "You've had the most time to review this development, Heraclianus. Tell us what you've learned."

Heraclianus moved to his place at the table with a slight limp, a wound to his right thigh that he received during another major battle with the Carpi eighteen years earlier. He quickly consulted one of the scrolls lying in front of him, then looked up at the four other men. "This message came from our spies at the port of Seleucia outside Antioch. It said Macrianus' troops had proclaimed his sons joint emperors."

"When?" Claudius interrupted.

"The message left Seleucia in early September," Heraclianus answered, "probably a day or two after the event itself happened."

"An unusual development," Volusianus noted. "I would have expected Macrianus and Callistus as the more likely co-emperors."

"From what I've been able to piece together from these reports," Heraclianus waved at the pile of scrolls on the table, "it seems that Callistus was pursuing Shapur when the proclamation was issued, and that Odenathus was marching north from Palmyra at the head of an army."

"So Callistus and Odenathus weren't directly involved?" Gallienus considered the implications for a moment.

"We have to assume that they're co-conspirators," Volusianus interposed.

Any word of Odenathus' battle with Shapur?" Aureolus

asked. "It should be over by now, one way or the other."

Heraclianus shook his head.

"A victory would make Macrianus' hold on the East more secure." Aureolus' comment voiced everyone's unspoken assessments. "A defeat might mean that it's Persians we'll have to worry about. What do you intend to do?" he asked Gallienus.

The generals waited. Gallienus yawned, stretched back in his chair, and seemed to contemplate Aureolus' question as if it were the first time the subject had come to his attention. "Either way we'll have to liberate the east, I suppose. Which we can do, now that our center is secured by the Marcomanni treaty," he added with a self-satisfied smile. "How many men could we have ready by next spring, Volusianus?"

"About eight thousand legionnaires from the troops we brought from Germania and Britannia…"

"And maybe another eleven thousand from all the Danuvius legions," Heraclianus added.

"Just the overall picture for now," Gallienus held up a hand to prevent the two generals from delving into details.

"Our advantage will be in cavalry," Volusianus noted, and turned toward Aureolus.

Aureolus scratched his head. "About four thousand of our own cavalry, maybe five thousand from the Marcomanni," he said.

"Nearly twenty thousand foot, nearly ten thousand horse." Gallienus considered the numbers. "Can we get more troops from Postumus?"

"He can't really spare them," Volusianus noted. "But we have time to draw support from Africa." He thought for a moment. "There are all sorts of details to consider: a huge logistics effort, money to pay the soldiers, how many legionnaires to guard the frontiers, who will command them…"

"How long will it take to march an army to Antioch?" Claudius directed the conversation away from minutiae.

"Three to four months," Volusianus said. "I remember Valerian taking about that long when he marched east."

"What sort of forces can Macrianus field?" Aureolus asked.

As the generals were calculating Macrianus' strength,

Heraclianus suddenly interrupted. "This planning could be avoided altogether." They looked up at him from their calculations, surprised. "Why not wait for Macrianus to come to us? We could intercept him as he marched toward Rome."

"Assuming that Shapur has been subdued…" Claudius said.

"It's worth waiting a few more weeks for that information," Heraclianus countered. "Let Macrianus take the risks of a long march. Let him deal with logistics issues, along with threats of disease."

"His men will be tired after months of marching," Aureolus agreed, "and we could choose the battle site ourselves. I can think of several."

"Pardon me, sir," one of Gallienus' tribunes entered the room.

"Yes, Quintianus?" Gallienus asked, annoyed at the intrusion.

"A messenger from the west just arrived, sir. He said it was most important."

Gallienus nodded. A lean young legionnaire stepped into the room and looked around the table for the emperor. He walked up to Gallienus and saluted. "General Silvanus sends his respects, sir," he said, then presented Gallienus with a scroll. Despite a cold, gray day outside, the man's face was covered with sweat, mixed with dust from the road.

"Stay a moment," Gallienus ordered. "I may have questions for you." He broke the seal and opened the scroll with a flourish, then read silently. "What?" he exclaimed. "Are we now to do without Postumus' sour disposition?" He grimaced then handed the scroll to Volusianus.

Volusianus quickly scanned the message. "It seems that Postumus has revolted."

Has this ever happened before? Aureolus searched his memory. *Will both Macrianus and Postumus march on Rome? Could we survive simultaneous revolts at both ends of the empire?* He looked up from his musings. Volusianus was explaining the details of the revolt to the others.

"…and in the confusion after the revolt, Silvanus and

Saloninus fled toward Colonia Agrippina intending to rally support of the troops remaining in the north."

"Where did Silvanus send this message from?" Aureolus asked.

Volusianus looked irritated. "Augustodunum, on the first of October, as I just mentioned."

"My mind had wandered," Aureolus mumbled with a shrug.

"It should have taken them about two weeks to reach Colonia," Volusianus continued.

"They may already be there then," Aureolus observed, to show he was now fully engaged in the discussion.

"If they weren't intercepted by Postumus' soldiers," Claudius cautioned. The others stared at him. "An unpleasant possibility," he responded to their disapproving looks, "but one we have to consider."

"And the insurrection may already have been suppressed, or it may already have succeeded," Volusianus said, feeling it best to air the rest of the disturbing possibilities.

"How soon could we march against Postumus?" Gallienus asked.

The generals glanced at each other uneasily.

"I'd caution against that." Heraclianus finally ventured. "We couldn't reach them for weeks."

"It would mean a winter campaign, into hostile territory," Claudius added, reinforcing Heraclianus' misgivings, "without adequate supplies or adequate planning."

Gallienus frowned at his generals' advice, but did not override them. "Your thoughts, Volusianus," he said, to his Praetorian Prefect.

"I agree with the others."

Gallienus looked down at the table, rubbing his chin thoughtfully. The generals watched as he weighed their arguments for caution against his desire for action.

"I suggest we make plans over the winter and be fully prepared to respond to simultaneous insurrections next spring," Volusianus suggested.

"We understand your wish to restore order to the province immediately, and we share your concern for your son's welfare,"

Claudius voiced Gallienus' thoughts. "If Silvanus hasn't rallied support of the northern troops by now, then we can only hope he'll barricade himself inside Colonia and wait for our rescue in the spring."

"There's another reason not to act now," Heraclianus added. "It would be advisable for you to shore up your support in Rome this winter, reassure the Senate and your allies. It's vital they believe you have plans to deal with everything that's happened since June."

The generals all watched Gallienus intently in the short silence that followed.

"It might be best if you gave this news to your wife in person," Volusianus advised cautiously, "before she hears it from someone else."

Gallienus licked his lips and nodded reluctantly. "Before I go," he said to Volusianus, "Send the following message to Postumus…."

* * *

Salonina sat watching Phillip lecture her youngest son, Marinianus, at the opposite side of a large table. They were in the same room in which Salonina had first learned of Gallienus' "marriage" to Pipa, as part of his Marcomanni treaty. It still reminded her of that painful encounter, but Phillip preferred it for his lectures.

"Knowing your own limitations is vital for a great leader," Phillip was saying.

"What if you have none?" Marinianus challenged.

"Only fools think they have none."

"Are you saying that my father has weaknesses?" Marinianus asked slyly. "Or that he's a fool?"

"Even the gods have weaknesses," Phillip reminded him, then continued with his lecture.

She watched while they discussed qualities of leadership. Phillip had described Marinianus as a quick and energetic student on more than one occasion and Salonina smiled as Marinianus listened intently to Phillip's comments, challenging him on certain issues, asking for clarification on others.

A rapid clatter of sandals on mosaic floor intruded, and Gallienus strode into the room. She had not seen him for days while he was inspecting two legions stationed east of Carnuntum. He had sent a message to her earlier saying that he had arrived, and was going straight to meet with his generals. The man who delivered the message had also relayed the news of Macrianus' revolt to her, but she had heard the rumors long before that. Salonina rose to greet him, delighted that he was back from his journey, but before he even took her in his arms, she sensed something was wrong. *What now?* she wondered with dread.

"You look troubled," she said, pushing herself away from his embrace after an appropriate interval. "Have the Marcomanni revolted too?" she asked playfully.

"Worse," Gallienus answered, failing to respond to her jest.

"What could be worse than that?" Marinianus asked, knocking his chair over in his haste when he rose to join the conversation.

Gallienus looked at Marinianus as if seeing him for the first time. He let out a deep breath. "You'd better stay for this as well." He put a hand on his youngest son's shoulder.

"Postumus has revolted," he said to them both.

Salonina sank onto the nearest chair. Especially mindful of Marinianus, she struggled to suppress an upsurge of tears. "What's happened to Saloninus?" she whispered.

Gallienus quickly explained what they knew and didn't know about the revolt and its final outcome. When he had finished, Gallienus glanced to where Phillip had been standing. He had discreetly exited.

"What are we going to do?" Marinianus' face flushed with eagerness and excitement at the prospect of action, adventure and the rescue of his brother.

"We'll talk of it later," Gallienus said, patting his son's shoulder. "For now, the rest of this discussion is between your mother and me." He looked at the painting of Venus behind Salonina and remembered their confrontation here a month earlier. "They'll try to rally support of the troops in the north," he said to

Salonina after Marinianus had gone.

"Will they be successful?"

"They may have already arrived in Colonia," Gallienus tried to sound optimistic. "Perhaps the revolt has already been suppressed."

"What if it hasn't?"

"We won't know anything for several weeks, at least."

"Why aren't you going to help him?" Salonina demanded angrily. "Pannonia is secure now with the Marcomanni in the middle of the province. You've told me that yourself."

"I discussed an attack with the generals, but a winter campaign without adequate supplies would probably be disastrous, as well as unsuccessful."

"Isn't there anything you can do?"

"I sent Postumus a message demanding that he open the mountain passes for me," he said. Salonina stared at him blankly. "They're blocked with forces loyal to him. If Postumus opened the passes, I could take an army into Germania and meet him in battle. That way we'd learn which of us is stronger." Gallienus stopped talking and studied Salonina's face, unsure if she had even heard his comments.

Valerian was eighteen when he died. Salonina's thoughts drifted to her eldest son and his death during Ingenuus' revolt two years earlier, and then back to Saloninus' plight. *Please the gods, it can't happen again.*

"…. we're preparing for a campaign next spring…" Gallienus was saying to her.

"What about Macrianus?" Salonina interrupted him, suddenly remembering the revolt in the east.

"I'll have to face them both."

"I don't think I can stand to spend a winter in Carnuntum," Salonina said. "And you should go to Rome to reassure the Senate."

"That's what the generals recommended. I think we can be ready to leave by the first of November."

"Without taking the Marcomanni woman," Salonina reminded him warily."

"Yes, without the Marcomanni woman," Gallienus agreed. He sat beside Salonina and took her hand. Neither spoke for a time, then he kissed her and reassured Salonina that she was his principal love and concern. Then he rose and apologized for having to leave to deal with business.

Salonina remained sitting at the large table, staring toward the picture of a sea battle on the far wall without actually seeing it. Although the thought of a long dreary winter in Carnuntum was unbearable for her, she didn't relish the thought of visiting Rome either. There was the embarrassment of Valerian's defeat and capture, revolts on both ends of the empire, and the common knowledge that her husband had taken a 'second wife,' a Marcomanni woman—a barbarian. As if that weren't enough, Salonina would have to endure the sympathy of other wives at her second son's predicament. *I understand that nothing can be done to help him until spring,* she thought, *but knowing what he'll have to endure this winter will be difficult.* She tried to picture how he looked the last time she had seen him. Then another thought brought tears to her eyes. *His eighteenth birthday will be this December.*

4-2
Explanations
Antioch, Syria
02 November, 260

"…and after Odenathus' recent victory over Shapur near Edessa," Macrianus summed up his argument to General Callistus and his two sons, "I've decided to take an army west next spring and defeat Gallienus." He surveyed his audience self-confidently. "I asked Callistus to consider the details of such a plan a few weeks ago. It was only a contingency plan at the time, of course." He nodded for Callistus to comment.

"None of these figures matter," Callistus growled, pointing at the scrolls on the table in front of him, "until we know where

Odenathus stands."

Macrianus glanced at his younger son. "I've just returned from a meeting with Odenathus," Quietus said importantly. "He agreed not to interfere with our efforts to overthrow Gallienus. He even agreed to supply his share of legionnaires for the effort."

"Did he, now?" Callistus frowned at Quietus. Then, reluctantly he shuffled through the scrolls in front of him, picking up one that he studied for a moment, before addressing Macrianus and his two sons. "We can gather about thirty thousand men now that I can count on Odenathus' share of legionnaires. That number includes what remains from the army Valerian took into battle, the remnants of the legions at Samosata and Zeugma, men recruited from the four legions south of Syria, auxiliary troops, and men from the legion at Melitene."

Macrianus held up a hand. "Tell my sons about our training plans," he said, interrupting Callistus' calculations.

Callistus paused, frowned briefly, then shifted subjects. "Between now and sometime next spring we'll recruit and train nine cohorts—just over four thousand men," he added when the sons stared at him blankly. He took a breath, shook his head, and then continued. "These nine cohorts will defend the eastern borders—supported by what's left of the four legions I've already mentioned. We'll bring about half of the new recruits with us and leave experienced soldiers as their replacements." Callistus tossed the scroll onto the table.

"So we go west with thirty-thousand men," the young Macrianus said, impressed with the number. "How long will it take us to get there?"

Callistus shuffled through the scrolls again. "About a hundred days, assuming we encounter no opposition on the way, that the Bosphorus crossing goes smoothly, the weather cooperates, and there are no serious outbreaks of plague." He looked up at the three men and smiled grimly. "A lot of assumptions."

"We'll leave around the first of March," Macrianus senior said, unconcerned with the issues Callistus had mentioned. "That way we can fight a battle around the end of June and be in Rome by the end of the summer." He rubbed his hands expectantly.

"What did Odenathus say when you asked for troops?" Callistus asked Quietus, while Macrianus was mentally savoring the image of riding triumphantly into Rome and receiving the Senate's accolades.

"He said he would give us his oath of loyalty after we had beaten Gallienus."

Callistus smiled at Odenathus' reply. "Anything else?"

"He refused our offer to lead the army," Quietus added without thinking.

"What?" Callistus demanded sharply, causing Quietus to blanche. Callistus turned to Macrianus accusingly. "We agreed I was to be in charge of the military side of this!"

"It's vital to have an experienced general commanding our forces here," Macrianus said smoothly, although Quietus' gaffe embarrassed him. "Your success against Shapur will serve as a deterrent to further Persian aggression. I had planned to discuss this with you myself." His outward calm and assurance masked Macrianus' discomfort. He realized Callistus was the better general, but feared Callistus might claim the title of Emperor for himself after defeating Gallienus.

"I'm the Praetorian Prefect," Callistus bellowed. "I should be leading this expedition!"

"My elder son and I will lead it jointly," Macrianus answered, pointing to young Macrianus sitting just to his right.

"Neither of you have any experience leading large forces in battle!" Callistus protested, pounding the table with his fist. Scrolls scattered everywhere. "This is folly!" He glared at Macrianus' smug expression. Callistus thought back to mid-September, when his pursuit of Shapur had brought him back to Zeugma. The city lay abandoned and in ruins from an earthquake two months earlier. Callistus had expected to be met there with reinforcements from Macrianus. Instead, only a messenger had been waiting for him. That's when he learned that he was now the Praetorian Prefect—and that Macrianus' two sons had been proclaimed emperors by Macrianus' troops. When Callistus had asked why he'd received no reinforcements, the messenger had told him it wasn't necessary since Odenathus was marching north to confront Shapur himself. At the time Callistus wondered if the soldiers' proclamations had been orchestrated or were really spontaneous. The timing of the proclamations was certainly suspicious. *Should I have opposed his rebellion?* Callistus wondered. *No*, he rationalized his decision yet again, *Macrianus probably anticipated that possibility. I would have had to lay siege to Antioch with a smaller army than his, and my troops might not have supported me. In any event, I'm committed now.*

"An emperor should lead his forces in battle," young Macrianus broke the silence.

"Only if he knows how to win," Callistus shot back.

"I thought we were both commanding the army," Quietus objected.

"One emperor stays in the east while the other goes west," Macrianus explained. "Since your brother is older, and had battle experience with Callistus, he's the logical choice to go."

Callistus winced at Macrianus' reference to the young Macrianus' battle experience with him. *Does Macrianus think that a few weeks chasing a retreating enemy will give his son the skills he'll need to triumph over Gallienus?* "I should be leading this army, Macrianus." Callistus objected again. "It's been less than six months since we've been confronting Shapur, and you're already breaking your word."

"Actually, our agreement was that you would fight the Persians, which you have done," Macrianus countered. "Your skills and abilities will be best put to use here," he concluded with finality.

"At least choose someone with experience to command then," Callistus implored him. "Young Macrianus is not the man to lead this army, emperor or not."

"You knew about this." Quietus accused his older brother hotly.

"Enough!" Macrianus barked. "I will command the army, assisted by my son," he nodded at the younger Macrianus. "You," he pointed at Quietus and Callistus, "will remain to defend the east. Now that we've settled that," he rose from the table, "there are other matters that urgently require my attention." Quietus and young Macrianus rose to leave with their father.

Callistus remained seated despite protocol calling for him to rise when an emperor rose. Quietus seemed on the verge of commenting about it until his father silently shook his head. The father and two sons left the room to Callistus and the scrolls, which he absentmindedly began to collect. He was thinking about what would happen after the two Macrianii marched west with their army. *Is there any chance that Macrianus can overcome Gallienus? What would happen if Macrianus was defeated? Would Shapur invade again? When would Gallienus come to impose his order in the east? Would Odenathus join me in resisting an attack by Gallienus?* Callistus felt tightness in his stomach. His fate lay in the hands of less capable men who were already making poor choices.

4-3
The Senate and the Philosopher
Rome
20 December, 260

Shafts of late-morning sunlight streamed through high windows of the Curia Julia, meeting place of the Senate, illuminating the interior of the long, rectangular building and reflecting off a patterned marble floor. Gallienus sat on a raised dais at one end of the room opposite the massive doors. Senators sat facing each other on graduated benches along both long walls, senior members occupied lower benches in the front closest to the dais. Gallienus was speaking. "'Your father was defeated and captured by the Persians. Now there are revolts in both eastern and western provinces. Why should the Senate support you under these circumstances?' That's the question I'd be asking if I were sitting in your place. I've come to answer that question, and to assure you the empire is in capable hands—my capable hands." He looked expectantly around the room, anticipating the senators' murmurs and grumbling. "Perhaps I was mistaken in assuming there was any discontent or misgivings at all…"

"We were allowing you time to answer the question you posed yourself, before asking any ourselves," Nummius Bassus responded. "But I would personally like to hear about the, *unfortunate*, situation in the east."

Gallienus nodded at Bassus, one of two men he'd appointed as consul two years earlier and father of Cassius, the young cavalry officer who'd proven so incapable during the campaign against the Marcomanni. Gallienus briefly wondered what had become of the young man after he'd dismissed him for cowardice. "My father was an administrator, not a general," Gallienus said. "The unprecedented disaster there and current revolts are attributable to him. He should have entrusted command of the army and conduct of the war to one of his generals."

"A harsh assessment," Bassus replied, "considering your own inexperience at commanding armies when you were named co-emperor."

"I have competent generals."

"Your father had competent generals as well," Bassus countered.

"Unlike my father, I trust them to do what they're trained to do."

"How will you address the eastern provinces problem then?" Bassus asked, voicing another common concern.

"I expect that problem to come to me." Gallienus walked down the middle of the marble floor that separated the senators, paused, then turned to face one of the groups. "I anticipate Macrianus will march west—here, to Rome." He turned away from them and continued down the aisle before stopping to face another group. "He'll hope to gain your recognition as emperor." Gallienus proceeded further down the aisle, until he was nearly at the far end of the building and turned to face the whole senate. "The only way he'll reach the Senate is if I send you his severed head."

Gallienus considered Bassus' second questions, as he walked slowly back toward the dais. "Before I can seriously consider any action in the east I'll have to deal with Postumus' revolt."

"Isn't he from one of those tribes along the western ocean?"

one of the senators asked derisively.

"Yes," Albinus answered the unidentified senator. "But don't let his heritage mislead you." Albinus had recently finished a three-year assignment as governor of Rhaetia and was due to become Prefect of Rome in a few weeks. "Just because he's not a Roman by birth, doesn't mean he's not a capable and dangerous opponent."

"Certainly he wouldn't expect the Senate to acclaim him emperor," the unidentified man persisted.

Albinus frowned. "If he came with an army of ten thousand men behind him and suggested the Senate proclaim him emperor, you might see that issue differently."

"We heard Postumus sent you a message," another senator interjected, addressing his question to Gallienus. "What did it say?"

Gallienus snorted. "Postumus declined to meet me personally on the field of battle. He said he didn't wish to make war on Romans."

There was a bit of muttering and then Junius Donatus, the junior consul, spoke. "Traditionally after a Roman setback there have been attempts to seize power, and attacks from the barbarians along undefended borders. How will that be different this time?"

"For now, the Franks are Postumus' problem. He'll deal with them, or they'll deal with him for me. The winter weather is harsh there, and I'll assess the situation next spring. The only credible threat along the Danuvius would have been the Marcomanni, and I have concluded a treaty with them." Gallienus looked around the room smugly.

"Surely rumors about marrying a barbarian princess were wild exaggerations?" Bassus' feigned incredulity barely masked his disapproval.

"They're true. I did it to strengthen the bond between myself and the Marcomanni chieftain," Gallienus shrugged. "They understand this marriage isn't recognized according to Roman laws."

"One can only wonder what the empress thinks of this 'technicality,'" Bassus muttered to a senator beside him.

Gallienus heard the comment and walked down the Curia Julia's center to stand directly in front of Bassus. "The empress understands the importance of this treaty more clearly, apparently, than many in this room."

"Is it wise to allow a former enemy to settle such a large group of outsiders so far inside the empire?" Sulpicius Justus asked.

"I've changed them from enemies into allies. They will dampen nearby legions' enthusiasm for revolt. We've had three revolts there in the last seven years, one led by your son-in-law being the most recent." Gallienus let the comment hang in the air before continuing towards his chair between the consuls.

"Will you continue your father's policies?" asked Nummius Aemilianus Dexter. He'd been senior consul the previous year and would soon depart to Asia as proconsul. "Valerian was a friend of the Senate and believed strongly in traditional Roman customs, and its religion."

"I plan to end the Christian persecutions, if that's what you are referring to."

"Surely you're aware of the dangers Christianity poses to the empire!" Dexter exclaimed.

Gallienus gazed across the sea of faces. *How little these men know about various beliefs in the world.* While walking through the camps at night, he had heard about many strange beliefs. *No hope of convincing this self-righteous group that these beliefs and practices form an essential part of the army's morale.* He decided to answer the question on the basis of effectiveness. "The persecutions have gone on for over two centuries. To what effect? Under my father, Christians got stronger and more cohesive. When they're left alone, they persecute each other. As long as they pay their taxes and don't cause civil unrest, we should leave them alone. There are better ways of dealing with them than persecution."

"What ways?" Bassus asked.

"If we leave them alone, perhaps they'll be more receptive to philosophy of some kind—Plotinus' teachings for example," he suggested, naming the most fashionable philosopher in Rome.

"Christianity is, after all, just one of the many varieties of oriental mysticism." Gallienus had not yet heard Plotinus speak, but Salonina was an attendee at both his public and private gatherings. At home, she had enthusiastically and succinctly summarized what she heard. Gallienus had thought of endless rambling official reports he had been subjected to and wished he could send Salonina to those meetings while he went to hear Plotinus.

"I agree that Plotinus' teachings are superior," the voice of Rogatianus interrupted Gallienus' thought. Several other senators sitting near him murmured approval. All were adherents of the philosopher's teachings. Plotinus had convinced Rogatianus to renounce his considerable wealth, as well as an important government position, in order to pursue higher spiritual and intellectual states. *If Plotinus' teachings have that effect on some senators, then I should make time to hear him. That would please Salonina, too.*

Gallienus stopped midway down the senate floor and looked at each side of the room in turn. "I'm willing to answer any other questions you might have now."

"My son was due for an appointment to a position in the army," a man from the back row complained, "but he was denied. Several of my colleagues have had similar experiences. Is this a mistake, or part of some new policy?" Gallienus didn't recognize the voice.

"Now that army service means fighting barbarians, most senators prefer living on their estates, or working in civil careers," Gallienus said, stepping closer to the speaker. "The same could be said for their sons."

"The arduous life isn't for everyone," the man agreed, "but some men wish to pursue a military career."

"Membership in the senatorial class does not guarantee military competency," Gallienus replied. "Some men wish to dabble in it. Their leadership has been amateurish." He thought of his cousin Julianus and the problems Julianus created in Germania Superior, and of Cassius who had abandoned Gallienus' left flank at a crucial time during a battle with the Marcomanni. "Even a conscientious man may not have the ability to lead. I've seen it in the west. Now we've seen it in the east."

"Are provincial governors' posts and proconsul assignments also being withheld?" The man sounded indignant. These prized and lucrative assignments had long been the exclusive privilege of senators. Not surprisingly, losing them to the military class was a bitter disappointment to those still ambitious for political careers and amassing wealth.

"Command of a legion or a province are now arduous assignments that require frequent marches and battles," Gallienus said.

"Are you saying that senators and their sons can't fight or lead?"

"Not necessarily. But I pick leaders based on their proven abilities. Taking the next available senator or senator's son just because he expects a military assignment is a luxury we can no longer afford."

"Is there any truth to rumors that you plan to appoint a consul who isn't a member of the senate?" another voice spoke out from the other side of the room.

"I can't speak to the rumors, but my Praetorian Prefect," Gallienus turned and waved toward Volusianus with his right hand, "will join me as a consul for the coming year."

You've asked us to believe you can deal with simultaneous revolts, at the same time as you invite an enemy to occupy land well inside the empire…" Bassus said.

"A former enemy of Rome," Gallienus corrected him. "And let me remind you of my victories over Alamanni, Marcomanni, Juthungi, Roxolani, and Carpi tribes. Sometimes I was greatly outnumbered. As to suppressing rebellions, I point to my dispatch of Ingenuus."

"In the course of this meeting you've told us you're planning to allow Christians to perform their rites unopposed, against your father's wishes. Then you said you would deprive us from any chance of military careers," Sulpicius Justus added.

"You shouldn't find that surprising, Justus, considering how your son-in-law abused his privileges," Gallienus replied.

"You've flaunted our laws and traditions, taking a second wife," another man complained, "even though you tell us she's not officially recognized as such."

"We're seeing a decrease of our authority, something your father would never have seriously considered. Rome will lose its central importance."

"My father… isn't here. The responsibility to restore peace and prosperity rests on my shoulders now. I will choose my leaders on the basis of merit, not birth or rank. And for those who might think to oppose me, let me remind you, high birth does not protect anyone when it comes to insurrection. I think that about sums it all up." He stalked from the room without entertaining further questions.

Saecularis was first to follow him from the Curia Julia. They walked together into brisk air and dim, gray afternoon light, before descending the steps. Volusianus and his entourage of Praetorian Guards hurried closely behind them. Saecularis was concerned about the Senate's reaction to Gallienus' comments. *At least he was decisive and made his positions clear*, Saecularis thought. "What are you planning to do next?" he asked Gallienus, expecting a tactical or strategic reply.

"It's time I pay Plotinus a visit."

* * *

"…action is always the shadow of contemplation and an inferior substitute for it.…" Plotinus addressed a crowded room in Flavia Gemina's villa. She was one of his adherents. Gallienus and Salonina sat in the front row closest to Plotinus. Four nearby senators listened intently to his discourse. Greek scholars sat alongside them along with several wealthy landowners who were helping support Plotinus. Behind them others, including many women, were crammed into the largest room in Gemina's villa. Even Lysisca was there—Gallienus had seen her standing near the back of the room when he'd first entered. Their eyes had met, but neither acknowledged the other. He thought briefly of their meeting several days earlier when she told him sentiments of certain senators.

But Gallienus was not really focused on Plotinus' words. This morning's discussion in the Senate about Christians was still on his mind. He wondered how many in this room might actually belong to Plotinus' sect. He had seen gatherings at the big temple of Cybele and Attis, and some at the temple of Isis and Osiris. A few of the people here had even traveled to Eleusis to be inducted into the Great Mysteries. Others doubtless belonged to one of the other mystery cults, Dionysus or maybe Orpheus. All these beliefs were now accepted in Rome, but had initially been opposed by the Senate's old guard.

"…God is not external to anyone," Plotinus was saying, "but is present within all things, though they are ignorant that He is so."

Gallienus glanced at his wife, a smile on her face as she listened, occasionally nodding agreement. He smiled in response to her obvious enjoyment and interest. The campaign had exhausted her physically and emotionally and it pleased him to see that their recent time in the city had restored her. *Of course she's interested in Plotinus' comments,* Gallienus mused. *He's teaching Plato's philosophy.*

Plotinus' voice rose with enthusiasm. "It is only through the renunciation of worldly pleasures, that one can achieve a high spiritual or intellectual state."

Gallienus was amazed that some people had already been sufficiently impressed by Plotinus' rhetoric to take action, Rogatianus for example, one of the senators Gallienus had addressed earlier that day. Others had freed slaves, given away personal fortunes, and followed lives of meditation and self-denial.

"…the man in the street must submit himself for the general good, to be ruled with justice by the state…"

Gallienus nodded his approval. *I agree with that.*

"…the soul flees from sensuous beauty as Odysseus fled from the snares of Circe."

Don't agree with that…

Plotinus was widely known for discussions on geometry, arithmetic, mechanics, optics, music, and astronomy. Besides his intellect, he had arbitrated many disputes and accepted the guardianship of children belonging to some of his disciples.

Gallienus found himself shaking his head. *For someone that brilliant, he has some strange ideas. He's a vegetarian, never goes to the baths, thinks poorly of food and drink—even worse of sexual pleasures. He eats little, sleeps little. None of that appeals to me!* Breaking from his musings, Gallienus realized that Plotinus had changed subjects.

"Darkness is merely the absence of light, and evil merely the absence of good. Things are evil only insofar as they are imperfect. Human perfection and happiness are attainable in this world," Plotinus contended, "without waiting for the afterlife."

Gallienus raised his eyebrows, then glanced at Salonina.

"Perfection and happiness, which are seen as synonymous by the way," Plotinus added, "are achievable through philosophical contemplation."

And the renunciation of personal pleasures, of course.

"Finally," Plotinus said in conclusion, "all people return to the Source, that from which all things spring. On returning, their energy, the essence of all, is broken up and recombined into other things."

From sudden sounds of people moving and talking around him, Gallienus realized that Plotinus had ended his talk. Most people started to leave, but a small group hovered around Plotinus engaging him in personal conversations. Gallienus rose, took Salonina's arm, and began to move toward the door. Plotinus noticed him leaving and detached himself abruptly from the group.

"May I have a word with you?" Plotinus asked earnestly. Gallienus nodded. "I've been thinking of founding a commune, a city of philosophers, living under a constitution such as the one set out in Plato's Laws." He looked expectantly at Gallienus.

"Commendable. But you don't need my approval to do that."

"There's an abandoned city in Campania," Plotinus said, rubbing his hands. "I was wondering if you could grant it and the surrounding land to me."

"Whose land is it?"

Plotinus shrugged, tilted his head as if the matter were of little concern to him. "We'd need money to survive, and slaves, of course, to work the land, so we could concern ourselves with philosophical pursuits and not with base distractions."

"'Base distractions?'"

"Menial labor, that sort of thing," Plotinus waved a hand, "anything that interferes with contemplation and enlightened discussions. I was sure you'd understand."

"What about donations from your converts?" Gallienus asked, glancing at Salonina, who was smiling at him. *Has Plotinus already spoken with Salonina about this?* He considered the proposition for a moment. *It might be worth supporting his request if Plotinus took some of the troublesome senators with him, but which ones would join him? I could actually lose some of my supporters.* He frowned. *A rather high price for something that might not work to my advantage.*

Before Plotinus responded Gallienus said, "I'll think about it," careful not to make any commitment, as he worked his way toward the door.

4-4

A Dreary Night
Colonia Agrippina, Germania Inferior
04 January, 261

"Can't this wait until morning?" Laelianus growled.

"Your orders were to wake you, if it was important, sir."

Laelianus held the covers around him, while struggling to awaken from a deep sleep. Sleet, mixed with freezing rain pummeled the villa's roof. The wind howled, and he winced at the occasional gusts, an involuntary reaction from sleeping in tents most of his life. He rubbed his eyes and sat upright. Years of training had taught him to respond quickly to interruptions at all hours. "What is it?"

"A centurion from the defending garrison wishes to speak with you, personally."

"I'll meet him in the atrium," Laelianus replied. Reluctantly he rose from the warmth of his wool blankets and stepped into the cold dark room. *I seem to be growing soft as I age*, he thought while dressing. *Perhaps I'm just coming to appreciate the privileges of the more senior ranks.* Ulpius Cornelius Laelianus, the legate of XXII Primigenia legion, was commanding the siege of Colonia Agrippina, which had been under way for just over two months. Rather than actually trying to storm the walls of the city, his legionaries had merely surrounded it, waiting for the city to exhaust its supplies and surrender, or starve.

Laelianus heard the clack of his boots on the mosaic floors as he walked through the quiet villa. As he entered the atrium, he could hear the wind shrieking even louder. Candles lighting the atrium flickered wildly with the wind, causing shadows to play eerily across the walls and floor. Water gushed through the opening in the roof into the central basin in the atrium's floor. The wind-driven rain and sleet splattered onto the nearby marble floor, making it treacherous to walk on.

He studied the man waiting for him there, a young centurion with sleet still clinging to his cape. "Did we ever serve together?" Laelianus asked.

The centurion shook his head.

"Why have you come to me at this hour?"

"I've brought you something." He turned and called to a man outside. Two burly soldiers entered, dragging two bound men. Saloninus and Silvanus stood dejectedly between their captors, arms tied behind them, their heads bare. A drop of rain from Silvanus' drenched hair had rolled from his forehead and balanced precariously at the end of his nose.

Laelianus gazed at the two prisoners. Until the end of September, they had been the two senior officers in all of Germania. His pulse quickened, but he said nothing.

"A gift for General Postumus," the centurion said, waving a hand at the prisoners behind him.

"It would be Postumus Augustus, now," Laelianus corrected him. "So, are you surrendering the city?" he asked before the centurion could rectify his error.

The centurion nodded. "The gates have been opened."

"Wake the senior centurion," Laelianus said, abruptly turning to an orderly standing nearby. "We'll have to occupy the city tonight." He looked at Silvanus and Saloninus for a moment considering what to do with them. "Put them in one of the servant's quarters," he said to a second orderly, "and post two guards at the door." He returned his attention to the centurion. "I'll take them to Postumus Augustus in the morning." *I don't want their blood on my hands*, he thought.

Laelianus recalled his initial meeting with Gallienus, over six and a half years earlier, when Gallienus had first come to Germania Superior. At that time, he had marched south from Moguntiacum in response to a report of an enemy incursion. But when he arrived at the site of the burned village, he had found the emperor there instead of the enemy. Gallienus' willingness to let him speak candidly at that first meeting had impressed Laelianus. And he could even forgive Gallienus for giving Julianus a group of men to lead. He had watched Gallienus mature into a competent leader in the course of many battles they fought together. The last great engagement he remembered was against an invading army of Franks one spring three and a half years ago. Laelianus admired and respected Gallienus but, when the question of allegiances arose last September, he had acknowledged the reality of the situation in Germania.

"What about us?" the man asked, referring to the fate of the garrison who had defended Colonia Agrippina.

"You've made a wise choice," Laelianus replied, patting the centurion on the shoulder. "Postumus Augustus will be pleased not to have to storm the city walls." He thought for a moment about the man's question. "If you swear allegiance to Postumus Augustus, you'll probably be reunited with your legion."

"He'll kill them, won't he?" the man nodded after Saloninus and Silvanus.

Laelianus shrugged. "Unless he decides to ransom them."

* * *

In Rome a day later, in the hours just before dawn, Salonina awoke with a start, desperately clutching her bedding close to her. Although the room was chilly, she was drenched in perspiration. She felt her heart beating wildly and looked quickly around the dark room, feeling that she wasn't alone. Salonina held her breath and strained to hear any sounds of movement. Finally, she convinced herself that there was no one else in the room besides her sleeping husband. *Where am I?* she wondered for a moment. *What woke me? Oh… that dream again!* She closed her eyes and willed herself to recall any parts of it. A knot tightened in her stomach as a few fragments slowly came to her, followed by progressively more and more details.

A large wolf chased its prey across an open meadow. The pursued animal, desperate and bloody, raced toward a small thicket offering the only chance of refuge from its determined pursuer, and somewhere nearby a den of wolf cubs had been left unprotected.

She stifled a sob and a tear ran down her cheek when she also remembered that someone had died.

4-5

Defensive Considerations
Treveris, Belgica
01 March, 261

"Maybe the Franks and Gallienus won't attack at the same time, yet we have to prepare for exactly that," Postumus said, rubbing his chin. He turned to his lieutenants. "I'll depart for Colonia Agrippina in five days. Marius, you bring half of the legionnaires from the eastern two legions. A blacksmith by trade, Marius, like Postumus, was short and stocky. Unlike Postumus, he was clean-shaven and easygoing.

"Victorinus, the same from the western two, and make sure you both bring German mercenaries. I want all the cavalry I can get to counter whatever Gallienus brings against us—a thousand at least, two thousand would be better." His bearing and mannerisms indicated that Victorinus came from a wealthy family. Instead of becoming a wine merchant like his father, he had chosen a military career. He wore a full beard, was slender, and taller than either of the others. Both Marius and Victorinus nodded, rose, then departed.

Sounds of sandals on tiled floors faded until silence filled the room. The tranquility suited Postumus, giving him an uninterrupted interval to reflect on past events and to ponder the future. He had had very few chances to do that since late September of last year, when he confronted Silvanus on the parade ground and the troops had supported him. His pulse quickened recalling the excitement and exhilaration of the early days: rallying soldiers to his side, seizing mountain passes, and besieging Colonia Agrippina where Silvanus and Saloninus had taken refuge. *I would have enjoyed having them brought to me bound like common criminals, instead of being executed by some overzealous subordinate. Perhaps I could have ransomed them.* But after he learned they had been killed, he had felt relief rather than remorse.

Better now that I control the country, he thought contentedly, *without my authority and privileges dependent on the pleasure of someone else.* He smiled, remembering his pleasure when emissaries from Hispania had come to Treveris to express their desire to join him. *Why not Britannia as well? It's beyond Gallienus' grasp. Maybe next year I'll visit the island myself, convince them of the wisdom and benefit of joining me.* Then Postumus thought about the overtures he had made to the legate commanding the legion in Rhaetia. The man owned land in Germania, and had served in the legions along the Rhenus with Postumus years earlier. A considerable number of his family still lived around Treveris. Postumus had promised the legate a position of influence and had lightly touched on his "concerns" about the legate's holdings and his family's welfare if Rhaetia remained loyal to Gallienus. If the legate could seize Rhaetia, perhaps other provinces might follow his example?

He thought of the coming battle between Gallienus and Macrianus. *If Macrianus wins, I'll attack him before he reaches Rome and asks for the Senate's blessing. His army would be tired from a long march and weakened after a big battle. But if Gallienus is victorious, he'll come here. If I had both Britannia and*

Hispania on my side, then how many more legionnaires could I add to my army? Enough to turn back Gallienus' attack? Postumus took a deep breath. A surge of apprehension ran through him. *He's never lost a battle. Could I defeat him?*

Offensive Considerations
Carnuntum, Pannonia
02 April, 261

Pipa sat in her villa's atrium, anticipating Gallienus' arrival after he had spent the winter in Rome. Rather than pace the floor, she distracted herself by throwing battle axes at a wooden target shaped in the form of a soldier. One of her attendants returned the axes after each series of throws. She had not seen Gallienus since he left for Rome at the end of October, and was keen to rekindle his ardor for her. Pipa intended to fully utilize the several weeks she would have him all to herself—except for the army and the generals, of course. Part of her blue linen dress slipped off her shoulder. "Humph," Pipa snorted as she pulled the sleeve back to cover her shoulder. "Impossible to look good for your husband and still throw axes well."

Concentrating on the target, Pipa grasped the next axe firmly and threw it with extra force. "Yes!" she exclaimed after a resounding 'thunk' and she saw the axe lodged firmly in the middle of the target's torso.

"Remind me never to argue with you," Gallienus quipped from the entryway.

She turned to face him, the next axe already in her hand. "This wasn't exactly the way I'd planned to greet you."

"Everything will be fine, once you put the axe down."

An attendant quickly removed the weapon from Pipa's hand.

"I've missed you," she said after regaining her composure.

"I can see that," he nodded after the retiring attendants.

She rushed to greet him and threw her arms around his neck. "Thanks to Woden that you're safely here."

"Mercury deserves at least some of the credit." He tossed his purple cape onto a nearby chair, kissed her and held her close.

After a long embrace, she offered refreshments—smoked

meat, bread, cheese, wine for him, and beer for herself.

"Tell me about the rumors," she said after a draught of beer.

He sipped his wine. "What have you heard?"

"Did you really challenge Postumus to fight you?"

"Yes."

"Did he accept?" Her eyes sparked briefly at the thought of the individual combat, but her face turned serious when she considered the grave risk that a fight-to-the death would pose to her personally.

Gallienus shrugged. "I haven't heard from him lately."

"People are saying that Postumus and Macrianus formed an alliance, and that Macrianus has already started marching toward us."

"Probably no… and probably yes." He ate a bite of bread, drained his wine glass, and looked at her appraisingly. "It's wonderful to see you."

Pipa reached across the table, took his hand, and smiled. "Let me show you how wonderful it can be. Come." She rose and led him to her bedroom.

Once inside she held him tightly. Despite the warmth of his body, she shivered as he kissed her neck and earlobe. She pushed him back. "Let's get you undressed." Pipa began urgently tearing at his clothes. "Oh damn. Help me with this," she exclaimed while fumbling with the strap on his sword belt. When she finished helping Gallienus out of his clothes, she put one of her hands on the knot holding her dress in place. "Now help me with this one." She wiggled out of the dress and slid it away with her foot.

"Women's clothing seems so much easier to remove," Gallienus noted appreciatively.

"They're designed with different purposes in mind. You wouldn't want your clothes falling off in the middle of a battle, would you?" They caressed each other's naked bodies eagerly, then she threw her arms around his neck. "By the gods you feel good," Pipa said as she reached up and gave him a lingering kiss before pushing him onto the bed and straddling him. She leaned over and gazed into his eyes. "I've been waiting for this moment since you left me last fall."

He ran the fingers of one hand across her shoulders and down her back. The other hand massaged one of her breasts. "I hope I meet your expectations." Before he could finish the thought, Pipa kissed him on the lips.

"Move up a bit. Yes, there," she said, then settled onto him. "Oh yes!" Gallienus' hands grasped her hips tightly. Neither of them moved until Pipa began to rock back and forth. Gradually her pace grew more urgent. Finally she stopped, shuddered, and gave a loud cry of pleasure. After a few seconds she collapsed into his arms. Silence and stillness followed.

Pipa awoke with a start to find herself lying on her back in the darkness with Gallienus' head resting on her chest. He was already asleep. She sighed contentedly and stroked his hair until she, too, fell back into a deep sleep.

When Pipa came to the table for breakfast, she found Gallienus dressed in a Marcomanni tunic and trousers, absorbed in a pile of messages and reports. She put a hand on his shoulder and massaged it affectionately. "You're still here, so it wasn't a dream."

"Where else would I be?" he asked, putting a hand on hers and smiling. "You slept well."

"Best night in a long time. I'm starved." She signaled to one of her assistants. "Bring bread and cheese, and some beer, maybe a bit of wine," she added glancing at Gallienus.

"None for me." He set the scrolls aside and pointed to two items wrapped in soft animal furs. "I've brought you a few things."

After a bite of cheese and a sip of beer, Pipa smiled and accepted the gifts, choosing to unwrap the smaller one first.

"It's a scarab bracelet," Gallienus explained, as Pipa studied it admiringly, then wrapped it around her wrist. "The stones were carved in a distant land called Aegyptus. I don't know where the silver clasp was made."

"I've never seen anything like it," Pipa said, holding her wrist up and turning her arm back and forth.

"That was for your feminine side," Gallienus said. "The other is more suited to your warrior heritage." He signaled to one of Pipa's attendants while Pipa unwrapped the second package.

"A dagger," she exclaimed, pulling the small knife from its decorated leather case.

"The handle is made of carved ivory and the blade is the same metal that Celts made their swords with." He gave Pipa a few moments to examine the craftsmanship and feel of the knife. "It's balanced to be a superb throwing knife. Try it." He pointed to the target that she had used with her throwing axe the night before.

Pipa hefted the blade, felt its balance, then threw it suddenly and forcefully at the target, just as her father entered the room. The blade struck the target beside Attalus with a thud. Attalus' eyes widened. He instinctively dropped into a crouch and drew his sword, before he realized he wasn't the target. He glared at Pipa, who tried to look concerned, but was struggling to refrain from laughter.

"It's all right," Gallienus said to Attalus. "She did the same thing to me last night, but with one of your throwing axes."

Attalus sheathed his sword, broke into a grin, and strode into the room. "Good to have you back," he said and gave Gallienus a bear hug.

"I'm sorry if I frightened you," Pipa said and offered her father food and drink.

"Nice throw," Attalus observed, pulling the knife from the target and feeling its balance. "Maybe the target was a bit too close to the door. Your next visitor might not be so lucky." He ignored the bread and cheese, but accepted a horn of beer and took a long drink. "My daughter must be glad to see you back, too," he smiled. "I was around to see you earlier this morning and they said you were both still asleep." He straddled a chair. "Now that you're here, we can get down to some serious fighting."

"You didn't even ask about his trip," Pipa protested.

Attalus grabbed a loaf of bread, tore off a piece and began to eat. "Must have been a good trip. He's here in one piece." He washed the bread down with a sip of his beer, then wiped his sleeve across his face. "My men are ready to fight now. When can we start?"

"After I learn when Macrianus left Syria I can estimate when and where I can attack him."

"Then there'll be time for a feast to welcome you back," Attalus said.

"I rather like that idea," Gallienus agreed.

Attalus asked about various rumors that Pipa had queried Gallienus on the night before. She contentedly watched the two men talking and recalled the last time she had seen Gallienus, just before his departure for Rome in early November. *Salonina gets Gallienus all winter, and I have to share him with her from April through October, but for now he's all mine,* Pipa thought contentedly.

"What about attacks from both sides at once," Attalus was asking, "or one side attacking while you're involved with the other?'

"Those are problems I'll have to work on when I know Macrianus' departure date. Right now I want to know the condition and morale of the men, generals, and the Marcomanni."

"We're ready to fight."

Gallienus nodded. "I assumed as much. What do you hear about attacks from north of the border?"

"We've heard no word of any threats," Pipa responded when Attalus was caught with a mouthful of bread.

"Good. For the present, we prepare and we wait."

"Excuse me, sir," an orderly interrupted. "General Volusianus wishes to see you."

Carnuntum, Pannonia
11 April, 261

Gallienus spent the following days conducting a thorough review of the legions' training and battle readiness. Today he was observing the cavalry's operations, which Aureolus was eager to show him.

"I've spent much of the spring recruiting," Aureolus told Gallienus, as they watched the men performing various training drills. "I've been anticipating battles against other legions since Macrianus and Postumus will be our next likely adversaries."

"Most likely," Gallienus agreed.

"Larger cavalry forces will be the deciding factor against both of them, just like they were against Ingenuus."

"We'll have our hands full with Macrianus," Gallienus said. "I've heard he may have up to thirty thousand troops."

Aureolus grinned and waved at the men performing in front of them. "You deal with Postumus. Leave Macrianus to me."

A messenger approached them and handed Gallienus a scroll which he studied for a moment. "We now have Macrianus' departure date," he said while rolling up the scroll.

"Shall I terminate the exercises?"

"No. Continue. We'll discuss the matter after we have breakfast, tomorrow."

Gallienus' War Council
Carnuntum, Pannonia
12 April, 261

"Forget about the little man from the east who walks with a limp and never led an army in his life," Attalus urged Gallienus then pounded his fist on the table. "Postumus is your enemy and the murderer of your son. Honor demands he be killed, preferably by your own hand." That last thought pleased Attalus considerably. He smiled and nodded to himself, then said no more.

"Point taken about avenging Saloninus' death," Volusianus responded. "But Macrianus is the one marching against us. Postumus claims he only wants land west of the Alpes mountains."

"Hah!" Attalus snorted. "You'd trust the man after the things he's done to you?" He glanced at Marinianus, Gallienus' third and only surviving son, and shrugged.

Gallienus cleared his throat. "Volusianus and I have had all winter and the duration of the march from Rome to consider alternatives." He looked from Heraclianus to Aureolus, to Aurelian, and finally to Claudius. "I'd be surprised and disappointed if each of you hadn't thought about this over the winter. Every option we considered had risks associated with it." He nodded at Volusianus, who began to discuss alternatives.

"We now know that Macrianus left Antioch on the first of March, so we can expect him to be somewhere near us in a little more than three months, depending on how hard he marches his men, and how he manages to get his army across the Bosphorus straits."

"So we can expect him to be near Mursa about mid-June or a little later," Aureolus noted, rubbing his hands. "What better place to meet him than on the plains of Mursa, where we defeated Ingenuus?"

"And we considered the attack on Postumus, as well," Volusianus said. "It's almost eight hundred miles from here to Colonia Agrippina."

Claudius whistled. "If we marched at twenty miles a day it would take over a month just to get there."

"And if we left Carnuntum right now," Heraclianus said, "we'd have a bit more than two months to march into Germania, defeat Postumus and march back to block Macrianus from getting to Rome."

Aurelian shook his head. "That won't work. We'd need almost three months just getting there and back."

Macrianus has too big an army for a holding force to resist him, let alone survive," Aureolus said.

"What if we all attacked Macrianus, then turned our attention to Postumus?" Claudius asked.

"Postumus will be fighting the Franks, from time to time," Attalus said. "What better time to attack him than that?"

"I don't have the exact figures for a march from Mursa, but let's say it's a thousand miles. Mid-June, twenty miles a day with a few days' rest along the way, about sixty days' travel time," Volusianus concluded.

"Assuming a two-week campaign to defeat Postumus, then we'd be leaving there around the first of September, getting back here around mid-October at the earliest," Aurelian said.

"No need to come home after we've beaten Postumus," Attalus scoffed. "We'll stay there. Enjoy the local hospitality."

"We have to at least consider the possibility that a victory might take longer than planned. We don't want to be in hostile lands in late autumn," Volusianus explained.

"Enough talk. What are you going to do?" Attalus asked Gallienus.

"We have a slightly unusual situation, facing two hostile Roman armies, one on each side of us," Gallienus said. "Now that we know Macrianus' departure, we can figure the best time and place to attack him. And I intend to attack Postumus myself before this year is out."

"I want to be with you when you slit his throat," Attalus said, his face beaming in anticipation. "How will you do it?"

"Slit his throat?"

"No. After all this discussion," Attalus waved a hand around the room, "how will you attack Postumus and Macrianus in the same summer?"

"We'll attack them both, at once," Gallienus said shifting his gaze from Attalus to the rest of the generals.

"You plan to divide our forces, then?" Claudius voiced the obvious, with a hint of concern. He looked from Gallienus to Volusianus questioningly.

"There is an element of risk in that approach," Volusianus conceded, "but we've estimated the strengths of our adversaries and compared it to our own."

"Of course you'll take me with you—won't you?" Attalus asked Gallienus.

"Yes. You, Volusianus, and my son will all be with me," Gallienus said. The others looked expectantly at Gallienus.

"Each of us would like the opportunity to lead an army against Macrianus," Claudius said. Heraclianus, Aurelian, and Aureolus nodded agreement.

"Why don't you send Aureolus," Attalus suggested. "He's good with horses and he can't wait to get back to this Mursa place."

Gallienus ignored Attalus' unsolicited opinion. "Each of you would be an excellent choice for this assignment," he said to all three men. "Heraclianus…"

Heraclianus' face brightened.

"I want to you remain to govern your province. I want a steady hand there for unforeseen contingencies." Heraclianus nodded reluctantly.

"Claudius, I'll need your help. You'll come with me."

"Aureolus will command the army against Macrianus," Gallienus said. "And your reasoning was correct, Attalus. About half of his force will be horsemen."

"Aurelian, you'll go with Aureolus."

"How will we compare to the opposition?" Aurelian asked. Gallienus turned to Volusianus.

"This was one of the options we considered over the winter," Volusianus said, while shuffling through a number of scrolls beside him. "The emperor will have eight thousand five hundred—about five thousand of them will be foot soldiers, two thousand Praetorian Guards, Attalus and a thousand of his horsemen, and five hundred archers. Our spies estimate that Postumus has about nine thousand legionaries, some of whom will probably stay along the frontier, and only a couple hundred cavalry, although he might have recruited some German mercenaries."

"And Aureolus?" Heraclianus asked.

"Twenty-four thousand total—almost fourteen thousand foot soldiers, about five thousand cavalry, and another five thousand Marcomanni horsemen," Volusianus said. "Our last estimate was that Macrianus left Antioch with something over thirty thousand men, but almost no cavalry. That's why Aureolus seemed like the best man to lead the opposition against him."

"Both groups outnumbered," Aurelian noted. "Do we have any contingency plans?"

"We expect Macrianus to have some losses along the way, desertions, sickness, and his men will be tired after their long march," Volusianus replied. "We don't think Macrianus has any experience commanding a large group of men in battle, and doubt he'll expect us to meet him with so much cavalry." A silence followed and Volusianus sensed that no one felt comfortable asking about Gallienus' numerical disadvantage. "As for the group against Postumus," he added, "we think he'll have to leave a number of them along the borders."

"I gather there's no contingency plan, then," Aurelian persisted.

"We expect both groups to be successful," Gallienus said,

effectively closing the meeting.

The generals filed out realizing that they would be facing two Roman armies, both superior in numbers to their own.

Defeat of either force could have disastrous consequences for this regime to survive—for all of us to survive. Aurelian shook his head. *Gallienus and Aureolus will be too far apart to offer each other any timely support.*

4-6

Precarious Predicament
South of Adematunnum
Border of Germania Superior & Lugdenensis
11 June, 261

Attalus galloped up to the meeting place where Gallienus, Volusianus, and Claudius had been reviewing the battle they'd just fought, and planning their next moves. Chairs were spread outside Gallienus' tent in the middle of their improvised fortifications. The Marcomanni chieftain swung off his lathered horse and stalked toward the gathered men. He threw down his helmet and cursed loudly while he ripped off his gloves as if he could no longer bear to wear them. His hair was matted with sweat. Mud had splattered his face and the front of his body. He swore and scowled fiercely. Attalus' command of Latin profanity, Gallienus noted, had become rather proficient.

"There were too many of them, and they fought like my warriors," Attalus said, unmindful of the fact that he was late and interrupting an ongoing discussion. "They couldn't have been Roman!" He fixed his eyes on Volusianus for several seconds before speaking. "You supported my retreat admirably, general. My compliments." Then he looked at Gallienus. "When will we attack them again?"

"One thing at a time," Gallienus held up a hand. "First, we think Postumus' cavalry were mercenaries, probably Franks."

"Second," Volusianus added, "there were far more of them than we expected, so we weren't surprised that you couldn't envelop them."

"I thought five thousand of your horsemen and warriors would be sufficient," Gallienus shrugged apologetically at Attalus.

"And we couldn't hold the center because their foot soldiers outnumbered us," Claudius explained.

"I never thought you planned to hold the center," Attalus countered.

"We'd intended a controlled withdrawal," Claudius agreed, "so that your horsemen could swing around behind them. When that didn't happen…" he let the sentence go unfinished.

"Then we should have brought more foot soldiers," Attalus interjected.

"I gave all but one legion to Aureolus, along with all my Roman cavalry," Gallienus said, holding Attalus' gaze. "Even then, I was afraid he'd be outnumbered by Macrianus' troops."

Attalus scowled. "I hope Macrianus doesn't have German cavalry with him, as well."

"There's no point arguing past decisions," Volusianus intervened. *Gallienus was advised against dividing his forces, but he chose to do it anyway.* "What's important now is to determine our next actions carefully—and quickly—before Postumus deprives us of any options."

"What have you decided?" Attalus asked, grabbing a chair and straddling the seat, with its back facing the others.

"Another attack isn't wise," Claudius said. "We're either outnumbered or too evenly matched."

"You aren't going to remain here?" Attalus waved a hand around the open fields outside the city of Adematunnum, horrified at the prospect.

"We could probably hold the city," Volusianus began, "but Postumus might get other forces and press the issue. We'd risk being surrounded and isolated."

"Maybe he'll have to deal with a Frankish invasion," Attalus suggested.

"We can't depend on that happening," Volusianus cautioned.

"You can't attack. You can't stay here. What can you do?" Attalus asked sourly. "I'd attack them tomorrow!" The thought made him break into a broad smile. "They'd never expect that."

"We're withdrawing," Gallienus said. He was surprised that Postumus had forced him to retreat. He was second-guessing his faulty assessment of Postumus' strength, and his decision to split his forces, against the advice of his generals.

Attalus stared at Gallienus speculatively, his face impassive. "You've considered the implications of a retreat, I assume." The emperor withdrawing after any battle could have serious consequences, could encourage the opposition, and it might demoralize the emperor's army or his support. And to withdraw from a battle against a province in revolt would be taken as a sign of weakness.

Gallienus was acutely aware that Postumus' reputation would be enhanced at the expense of his own, and that those near him would be watching him closely to see how he dealt with this setback. "We've picked a defensible position inside Germania Superior. We'll wait there until Aureolus' forces arrive."

"Where?"

"About three days' march," Gallienus pointed to the road running south-east from the city of Adematunnum. "The road crosses a river—there. The town of Vesontio is on the other side. We'll keep most of the army on the far shore and defend the bridge. Postumus can't cross it, and we won't have to storm it when we return."

Attalus stroked his beard, considering Gallienus' comments. "How long?"

"After Aureolus defeats Macrianus, maybe a month," Gallienus replied. "And he still hasn't fought that battle, according to my most recent communication."

"You think he'll beat Macrianus?" Attalus asked.

"I'm counting on it."

"And you think he'll bring soldiers to you, assuming he wins?"

"I'm counting on that, too." Gallienus said, his serene smile masking his knowledge of the great risk he had taken by placing his trust in Aureolus.

Vesontio
Germania Superior
15 June, 261

Pipa leaned against the far edge of the small pool, her outstretched arms resting on its black marble rim in a conscious attempt to appear relaxed. This was the first chance she'd had to spend more than a few minutes alone with Gallienus since his withdrawal from Adematunnum. Time together in the baths seemed an ideal setting to Pipa: intimate, relaxed, and the least likely place for any interruptions. Even his guards had withdrawn discreetly when she'd slipped out of her clothes and stepped into the pool with him. Sunlight streamed through small windows high in the walls casting shafts of light onto her golden hair and the rippling waters around her. If they had been in the public baths this pool would have been much larger, but it was located in a private villa, loaned to Gallienus by a wealthy city resident.

Gallienus sat erect, his brow furrowed, and his arms folded across his chest. He stared past Pipa through the mists rising from the pool. Despite the calming effects of the warm water, the tension would not leave him.

"What are you thinking?" Pipa asked. Her smile did not hide the concern in her voice. When he didn't answer her, she stretched out a foot and ran it across his thigh, then asked her question again.

He was suddenly aware of Pipa, immersed in the water to her waist, staring at him. At first, her intrusion on his thoughts annoyed him. Then he looked at her foot, took a deep breath, and smiled. "I was thinking about Postumus' last message to me."

"Which message was that?"

"I'd challenged him to settle this matter by fighting me personally." his voice trailed off.

"Father and I both thought that was marvelous!"

"It would have been much simpler if he'd accepted," Gallienus continued to stare into the mists rising from the warm water. "Less Roman bloodshed, and I would have avenged the death of my son."

Gallienus spoke little about Saloninus' death, but Pipa knew it weighed heavily on him. He had told her that he often regretted his decision not to invade Germania last autumn, right after learning of Postumus' revolt. His choice had been the prudent course of action, but the fact that he had done nothing at the time made his son's subsequent death more painful.

"But Postumus refused you," Pipa said. Gallienus remained silent. The surface of the water rippled slightly as Pipa moved her foot slowly up to Gallienus' chest and pushed an elbow, causing him to unfold his arms. "There's more on your mind than a duel with Postumus."

He took a deep breath. "This is the first chance I've had since the battle with Postumus to review my decisions and why I made them."

"Think out loud," Pipa urged. "I need to know as well."

He arched an eyebrow.

"My safety and the safety of the Marcomanni depend on what you do next."

He looked surprised at first, then nodded. "You have every right to be interested, and concerned."

"I'll help you think it through. There's no risk in sharing your thoughts with me," she added with a smile.

For the first time, Gallienus felt some of his tension easing slightly. "I didn't expect Postumus to have so many mercenary horsemen," he conceded grudgingly. "Maybe I was too impetuous."

Pipa nodded without comment.

Gallienus shrugged. "Perhaps I could have delayed my attack against Postumus, but I thought he might march for Rome while I was waiting for Macrianus' army."

"So why are we in this place now?"

"It's a defensible position, and I'm staying here so everyone will know that the issue with Postumus isn't over."

"I like that. What will you do next?"

"I'll attack Postumus again with reinforcements Aureolus will bring. After I've defeated Postumus, I'll restore the provinces to my rule."

"What about Postumus?"

"I'll kill him myself."

Pipa accepted his statement as a matter of course. "When will Aureolus join you?"

"After he fights his battle with Macrianus. There was no word of any battle in his last message."

"What if Aureolus loses?" Pipa felt his body tense. He shifted his position unconsciously, causing her foot to slip off his chest and splash into the water.

"Let's hope it doesn't come to that…" he said forcing his tone to sound casual.

Despite the warm water, a shiver ran through Pipa's body. She paused briefly and deliberately repositioned a foot on his other thigh before continuing. "Can you hold on until Aureolus comes?"

"It would appear that I have no other options right now."

Pipa thought for a moment. "Father told me about rumors that the Franks have invaded. Do you think that's why Postumus hasn't attacked you?"

"It's possible. He may have gone north himself."

"You probably never thought that a Frankish invasion could help your cause." She hesitated; a brief smile played across her lips then vanished. "What will happen in the rest of the empire, while you're here waiting for your general Aureolus to bring you more soldiers?"

Gallienus exhaled audibly. "You're asking a lot of questions."

"Your generals are asking them, if not to you then to each other. Haven't you been asking them yourself?"

"Of course. When Roman legions are fighting each other, it encourages barbarians to invade—present company excluded, of course," he hastened to add.

"The Franks are already invading—although they're Postumus' problem at the moment," Pipa replied, ignoring the slur. "The Persians have been repulsed, and we're your friends now," she said, referring to the Marcomanni and their recent treaty. "Who else are you worried about?"

"Postumus will become emboldened by his victory,"

Gallienus suggested.

"That might work to your advantage. He may underestimate you later."

Gallienus smiled at Pipa's perception. "I've considered that, as well." He frowned for a moment. "My… defeat might encourage my 'friends.'"

"Who?" Pipa asked, missing his sarcasm.

"Ambitious generals, questionable allies, those in the Senate who oppose me," he waved a hand at an imaginary host of adversaries and grimaced. "Some of them—or all of them—might begin to question my abilities, if they haven't already done so."

"Who are you thinking of, besides Postumus and Macrianus?" she asked.

"It could be any number of people, Pipa. It's a big empire."

She considered the possibility of other revolts or betrayals. "Has this defeat affected your confidence?"

He shook his head. "I'm more concerned about the army's confidence in me."

"I don't think they feel that way, nor does Father." Pipa hesitated. "I felt there were two reasons not to split your army." She frowned and let her voice trail off.

"My generals only mentioned tactical considerations."

"But what if Aureolus declared himself emperor? After all, he's got most of the army with him now, and Pannonia doesn't seem to like you. My father's warriors were your deterrent against an uprising there, but most of them are here with you."

Gallienus considered Pipa's analysis, shook his head, then tried to reassure her. "A leader has to take some risks, Pipa. Aureolus would have to convince Heraclianus, and Aurelian to betray me as well."

Macrianus convinced his generals to support his revolt. She paused. "You've worried enough for one day." Her leg slipped off Gallienus' thigh. She leaned across the pool, put her hands on his shoulders, kissed his lips, then drew back slightly searching his face for some reaction to her overture.

"You're right." He leaned over to kiss her more ardently.

"Let me take your mind off battles won and lost, and

generals loyal and treacherous." She pulled herself onto his lap and held him tightly. *For a while, anyway*, she thought.

4-7

Reunited

North of Vesontio, Germania Superior

29 July, 261

Gallienus, Volusianus, Aureolus, Claudius, Attalus, and Pipa, were all gathered outside of Gallienus' tent, in the twilight of a summer's day. They were all leaning toward Aureolus, who was speaking. "… and then," he paused to savor the attention of his spellbound audience, "Macrianus begged his troops to kill him and his son, rather than to fall into our hands."

"A pity you couldn't have killed them yourself." Attalus looked at Gallienus, the disappointment showing in his expression.

"But the interesting thing was who did kill them," Aureolus paused again. "It was the Pannonian deserters!"

"Soldiers who've revolted against me three times now," Gallienus observed sourly.

"They were the last to stop fighting," Aureolus nodded. "So they were nearest to Macrianus."

"Probably killed him hoping to gain my forgiveness," Gallienus said.

"No doubt," Aureolus agreed. "I executed the legates, by the way." He glanced at Gallienus, who frowned at the comment. "But I forgave the soldiers, in your name," he hastened to add.

Gallienus nodded.

"And after they surrendered, the whole army cheered 'Gallienus!'" Aureolus concluded, waving his hands at an imaginary army.

"Have I understood all this correctly?" Attalus inquired. "You met an army much larger than yours, but you had more cavalry he did…"

"A lot more."

"Then you surrounded his army. One of your cavalry groups charged their center, and a signiferi--- you said it was a signiferi-- that fell?

"A standard-bearer," Aureolus nodded, "the man who carries the flag for a battle group."

"Ah," Attalus nodded comprehension.

"Why did he drop it?" Pipa asked.

"Probably a javelin struck him. His standard fell with him."

Pipa smiled at the confusion and the major impact of this simple act. "And then the others thought it a sign of surrender."

Aureolus nodded. "The others dropped their banners, too," he grinned, recalling the event. "The battle was essentially over at that point. I left Aurelian in charge of both armies and came with the cavalry, so as to make the best time."

"Congratulations on your great success," Gallienus slapped Aureolus on the shoulder and grinned, the execution of the rebellious legates now forgotten. His sentiments were echoed by the others in a series of enthusiastic commendations. "And with so little loss of life, on either side," Gallienus marveled.

"Aureolus' victory eliminates the threat from the east," Claudius said.

"Except the loyal troops he left to garrison the eastern provinces," Volusianus cautioned. "What will you do with Macrianus' army?" he asked Gallienus.

"We'll integrate them into other units after we've dealt with Postumus," Gallienus pointed at the distant campfires of Postumus' army flickering in the waning evening light.

"Tell me about your battle with Postumus," Aureolus said.

"We'd planned to have our center fall back while Attalus swept around their flank. But Postumus brought mercenary horsemen that blocked the flanking movement."

"That's new for Postumus. Who were they?" Aureolus asked, his interest piqued at this unexpected development.

"One of the Germanic tribes, we think."

"It's fortunate you arrived when you did," Gallienus said to Aureolus. "I advanced the army west from the bridgehead at

Vesontio when I knew you were nearly here. As you can see, we got halfway to Adematunnum before Postumus' forces resisted us. I knew then that Postumus had returned."

"We think he's brought a larger force than he had before," Volusianus added, "but with the cavalry and Marcomanni horsemen Aureolus brought, we have about ten thousand more men than we did during the first battle."

"If you hadn't come this afternoon," Claudius said, "we might have had to defend against an attack by Postumus without you."

"Perhaps he still thinks he's stronger," Gallienus looked hopeful. "Your arrival so late in the day gave me an idea. That's why I ordered you to leave the cavalry you brought well back from the front lines," he explained to Aureolus. "Perhaps we can lure Postumus into a trap."

* * *

Three days later Postumus attacked.

Early morning sun had filled the sky with a crimson glow, but by the time his soldiers were formed up and ready to advance, dark rain clouds raced low across the sky. The various units' banners and pennants strained against their poles and snapped in the wind blowing from the west. Noises, normally lost over the distance between armies, carried across the open field, making Postumus' army sound much closer than it actually was.

Gallienus watched them come toward the place he had chosen for this battle, where the ground rose from west to east, giving him a clear view of Postumus' strength and disposition. Gallienus and part of his army were in plain view on the slight incline. Postumus saw a force nearly as large as the one he faced during his first encounter. Behind the visible force, the terrain fell away, concealing Aureolus' newly arrived cavalry from Postumus' sight. They were behind a hill to Gallienus' right. Attalus and two thousand Marcomanni warriors were on Gallienus' left.

Gallienus had ordered Attalus to charge around Postumus' right flank when attacking soldiers threw their javelins. As soon as Attalus started this maneuver, the remaining Marcomanni warriors were to charge from their concealed position behind the hill. As soon as they reached the battle line, Aureolus' forces were to begin their assault. Once Postumus was forced to commit his troops to halt the Marcomanni attack on his right, then he'd leave his left flank open for Aureolus. The weakest part of Gallienus' plan was the center of his army, which would be forced to make a controlled retreat very soon after the battle began.

Gallienus felt his pulse quicken as Postumus' legionnaires neared his line. He glanced at the dark sky and gave a quick prayer to Jupiter, the sky god who controlled rain and lightning: *O, noble Jupiter, ruler of the sky, and of the weather, may it be your pleasure to withhold your rains until this battle is done.*

The attack seemed like a dream from Gallienus' vantage point: Postumus' steadily advancing legionnaires suddenly broke into a run. They threw their javelins, drew their swords, and made contact with Gallienus' own line. It was a few seconds before the shouts and the crash of shields striking shields reached him.

"They have two legions to our one," Marinianus looked anxiously at his father. He wiped sweat from his eyes, then looked back to Postumus' advancing legions.

"Claudius will spread his troops out, now that he's seen what Postumus is bringing to bear against him," Gallienus said to his son, without taking his eyes off the advancing army. "It looks like he's holding a legion in reserve," he noted to Volusianus. "Be ready to support Claudius with the Praetorians, if he needs them."

Volusianus pointed to their left flank. "Looks like the same number of cavalry as he had before, and a much smaller force on the right."

"Enough to create havoc behind our lines," Gallienus said. "Watch them."

"General Claudius won't be able to hold out long against two legions," Marinianus fretted.

"Just long enough to get our horsemen around their flank," Gallienus said. "It will require some careful timing." He glanced up at the menacing clouds, then at Volusianus.

"I'd say Postumus is planning to simply overwhelm us,"

Gallienus said. "No diversions, no deceptions. He's a good general, but he lacks originality."

"He did put German horsemen to good use," Volusianus noted.

"Yes. There was that," Gallienus conceded. They watched the advance of eight thousand disciplined men. *What a tragedy, Gallienus thought. All Roman, or our auxiliaries.*

Gusts of wind rippled across the grass-covered fields, blowing dust from the soldiers' feet low and fast toward Gallienus' forces. He felt warm wind on his face, heard it whipping through his Imperial banner behind him. He smelled sweat mixed with leather; his hands were moist on the horse's reins. His horse pranced nervously back and forth. He spoke soothingly to it and stroked its neck.

"Attalus couldn't wait," Volusianus snorted beside him, amused by Attalus' impetuousness. "He began his charge before their soldiers started to run."

Gallienus saw Attalus in the distance, racing ahead of his warriors, spear in hand. The memory of a battle six years earlier, when Attalus had led a nearly successful charge against his own left flank, flashed through his mind

"He's getting some of his men past the Germans," Volusianus noted approvingly.

A roll of thunder to his left made Gallienus turn to see if the rains had come. Instead of rain he saw the rest of Attalus' horsemen race over the crest of the hill behind and to his left. They swept over the hilltop and galloped to join Attalus' forces in an undisciplined mass. Gallienus watched them for a moment, and then turned to his son. "Let's see what Postumus does now," he shouted above the noise of the battle, a continuous din, below him.

"He's sending part of his reserves to block them," Marinianus shouted back.

"But not all of them," Volusianus added, his voice clear despite the noise.

"Keep a group covering that cavalry unit on our right," Gallienus shouted to Volusianus. "And send half of the Praetorians down to support Claudius," he added. He looked anxiously at

Claudius' legionnaires fighting against a force twice their size. They were already yielding ground.

The Praetorians now were trotting toward Claudius' desperate struggle. *Hold on…a little bit longer*, Gallienus willed them. Another rumble like thunder sounded close to Gallienus' right side. It wasn't the Praetorians. They were in front of him by now. "Look there, Marinianus" Gallienus pointed to his right in time to see Aureolus cresting the hill at the head of over 4,000 cavalry troops. Unlike the Marcomanni's headlong gallop to the enemy, they rode at a trot, maintaining their formation until just before beginning their final charge.

"He's seen them," Volusianus called to Gallienus. "Postumus is sending the last of his reserves to face Aureolus." The last of Postumus' reserves were running quickly to their own left flank to prevent Aureolus from sweeping around their left side. It would be some moments before the two forces actually came together. Gallienus looked to his left to see what Attalus had been able to accomplish. The German horsemen and Postumus' reserves had managed to contain Attalus prior to the second wave of Marcomanni reaching the battle line.

Gallienus pointed to the Marcomanni horsemen. "I think they're about to break through,"

"Yes!" Marinianus shouted. "Postumus' flank is collapsing!" His voice sounded unnaturally loud. The wind had stopped blowing. In the complete calm, the air felt oppressive and humid.

"I think it's a retreat," Volusianus contradicted him. "But it might yet collapse."

Gallienus scanned the whole battlefront quickly. "They're giving way in the center, too." The men on Postumus' flanks were beginning to turn and run. He grinned and pounded a fist into his other hand. "I've got him now!"

Limp banners stirred with a cool breeze. Gentle at first, it rapidly grew stronger and more insistent. The first clap of thunder was indistinguishable from noise of the battle. Then a jagged bolt of lightning lit the dark clouds to their left, quickly followed by another clap of thunder. Raindrops, large at first, fell intermittently to the ground. Then sheets of driving rain shrouded everything beyond a few feet in front of them.

"We've got to get off of the hilltop!" Volusianus shouted and pointed at the clouds.

"Move toward Claudius," Gallienus commanded. "Bring the Praetorians." They made their way down the hill toward the place they had last seen Claudius fighting. Lightning struck on the peak of the hill behind them in a series of jagged flashes. Heavy rain obscured their view and flooded the field. Softer ground turned to mud. Rain cascaded down the hill. Horses' hooves tore at the soggy grass. Progress slowed once Gallienus reached flat ground. Rain continued, and the direction to proceed became less obvious. They found the dismounted Praetorians first, those who had been ordered to help Claudius. Eventually, using the Praetorians as a guide, they located Claudius.

"I ordered the men to halt," Claudius shouted to Gallienus. "They were exhausted, and I couldn't see enough to command a charge."

"We'll regroup and pursue them when the rain passes," Gallienus shouted back.

"It can't last much longer," Claudius agreed.

"How are the men?"

"Their ranks held," Claudius said, pride lighting up his weary face. "Reinforcements were helpful!"

"Postumus started a retreat just before the storm," Gallienus said, tight-lipped, pointing into the rain ahead of Claudius' legionnaires. "Then his ranks broke and he fled! We had him, Claudius!" Gallienus had dismounted. He paced back and forth, impatiently waiting the storm's passage. Each time he reversed direction he scowled and looked up at the sky.

"We'll finish it soon," Claudius said to cheer his impatient emperor. "The rain seems to be slackening." Winds abated. Thunder and lightning moved to the east, but rain continued in a steady, heavy downpour. All Gallienus could do was to continue to pace as he considered how he would reorganize his army to pursue Postumus.

"I think I can see Aureolus," Aurelian finally called to him. He pointed behind Gallienus. The rain diminished slightly and Gallienus turned to see Aureolus walking his horse deliberately through the battle lines toward his banner. The cavalry that Aureolus had left behind him were still out of sight. Both Claudius and Gallienus looked in the opposite direction to see if Attalus was joining them from the other side of the battlefield. By the time Aureolus reached them, Attalus was approaching on his mount. When he arrived, Attalus slipped off his horse and tossed the reins to one of Gallienus' surprised tribunes. He paused to hand his helmet to one of his assistants and then wiped the dirt and sweat from his face with his sleeve. His entire tunic was soaked with rain and sweat. Blood covered the right leg of his trousers.

"We almost had them," he shook his fist at the rain clouds. "How soon 'til we pursue them?" he asked Gallienus.

"Are you wounded?" Claudius asked, pointing at Marcomanni chieftain's leg.

Attalus looked casually at the blood on his leg, surprised at the question. "Not mine," he grinned, then looked up at the sky. "It's passing."

The rain slackened. Gradually the previously obscured battlefield came into view. Gallienus remounted and stared at the bodies lying sprawled on the ground where the battle had raged so recently.

"Hard to tell whose they are from here," Claudius commented. "Most are probably Postumus' soldiers who turned and fled." They watched a few wounded limping away from the battlefield. Those that couldn't walk were trying to crawl.

"They're all ours. That's the tragedy," Gallienus said.

"Today, they were the enemy," Attalus growled. "The tragedy would be letting Postumus escape."

"One tragedy is enough for today," Gallienus agreed, setting aside his concern for casualties and remounting his horse. "Send scouts ahead while we regroup, Aureolus. We'll march as soon as your men are ready, Claudius."

He turned to speak to Attalus, but stopped and looked to see what the generals were staring at. A lone rider galloped toward them from the crest of the hill. As he drew nearer, the generals edged closer to Gallienus, anxious to hear what news the messenger was bringing so urgently. A pathway cleared between the rider and Gallienus without orders being given. The rider slowed his exhausted horse to a walk. Volusianus could see tension etching Gallienus' face, although he sat erect and impassive. *No messenger gallops to the emperor with good news*, he thought sadly. He waited tensely as the rider approached.

"What news are you bringing with such speed?" Gallienus asked the messenger. The messenger took a deep breath, then saluted the emperor. "The Governor of Rhaetia sends his respects, sir, and reports that the legion under his command has declared its allegiance to Postumus." The man stopped and looked around the battlefield, as if expecting to see Postumus himself.

"He's not here," Gallienus said, following the messenger's eyes. "Was there more to the message?"

"The Governor is under siege in Augusta Vindelicum, sir."

"Take care of this man," Gallienus said to his tribune, Quintianus, before facing his generals. "An unexpected complication, it would seem."

"Rhaetia can wait," Attalus urged. "We've just defeated Postumus; now we must destroy him. Can't your governor hold out for a few weeks more?"

The question struck a nerve. Gallienus had told his son, Saloninus, to hold out through the winter, only to learn that the city of Colonia had turned him over to Postumus in early January. "I can't let another province fall," Gallienus insisted.

"Why not?" Attalus asked. "We finish here, then go to Rhaetia. Kill enemy there too."

"Tuscus has only been governor there for seven months," Gallienus said. "I'm not sure he's tough enough to sustain a siege."

"Better to let the rebels kill him, then," Attalus scoffed. "Save you the trouble of replacing him yourself."

"If I don't act decisively in Rhaetia, other provinces will decide to follow Rhaetia's example," Gallienus declared.

"The eastern revolt has just been suppressed," Aureolus reminded Gallienus.

"And now we're about to put down the one in the west," Claudius added.

Attalus scowled and spat on the ground. "How much more decisive do you need to be?"

Gallienus considered their comments for a moment. "I agree. We should pursue Postumus and finish what we came here to do…" he began.

"I'm glad that's settled," Attalus said. "My warriors will be ready to march on your orders." He started toward his horse.

Gallienus held up a hand, causing Attalus to turn back and stare at him, a mixture of bewilderment and frustration on his face. "Rhaetia is centrally located. If other provinces in that area joined them, they'd split the empire in the middle. Italia itself would be threatened. If Italia is threatened, Rome will be threatened. I can't allow Rome to be sacked."

"What will you do then?" Attalus asked. "Go to Postumus, or go to your governor who cannot control one stinking legion?"

"Both—at once," Gallienus reluctantly concluded. "Aureolus will command here. I'll take the legionnaires and put down the rebellion in Rhaetia myself."

Claudius glanced at Volusianus, before reminding Gallienus. "Postumus has four legions at his disposal, along with a large number of German horsemen. If he's given a chance to regroup, he could put a larger army in the field than we have."

"I request the honor of destroying the German cavalry myself," Attalus interjected, stepping closer to Gallienus, who put a hand on Attalus' shoulder and nodded agreement.

"Even with the Marcomanni horsemen, we could still be outnumbered," Volusianus cautioned.

"He's capable of another victory," Gallienus waved a hand toward Aureolus.

"You'll have to move quickly, then," Claudius said.

Gallienus turned to Aureolus. "You'll command the cavalry and all of Attalus' warriors. Attack Postumus and destroy him. Then, leave Claudius to restore order in the provinces, and return to me at Augusta Vindelicum." Aureolus nodded. No one else raised further objections. "I'd prefer not to split my forces again," Gallienus concluded, acknowledging their grim faces, "but I feel it's necessary."

The meeting concluded, the generals returned to their respective commands. Attalus lingered behind. "Need any of my horsemen to protect you?" he asked.

Gallienus put a hand on Attalus' shoulder. "I'll have Volusianus and my Praetorians," he said.

Attalus considered the situation for a moment. "You'll take Pipa with you?" he asked in a confidential tone. "She can ride a horse as well as any Roman."

"Of course."

"Do you think Aureolus can manage this job?" Attalus asked.

"He defeated Macrianus," Gallienus replied. "And Macrianus had the larger army."

"He was lucky," Attalus growled. "What about avenging the death of your son?"

Gallienus tensed. His face hardened. "Aureolus will have to take my revenge for me. I must stand between anyone and Rome." *And that includes any victorious general at the head of a large army.* Out loud he added, smiling at Aureolus, "After your victory over Macrianus, I have confidence in your ability to defeat Postumus."

4-8
Revolt and Reaction
Carnuntum, Pannonia
31 July, 261

Salonina reviewed the situation since she had reached Carnuntum on May 15th, two weeks after all the generals and most of the soldiers had left the city. Gallienus had gone west with an army to defeat Postumus. *He took Claudius, Volusianus, Attalus, and, probably Pipa as well,* she thought. Every time she imagined Pipa with Gallienus, sharing his thoughts, feelings, concerns, and his bed it angered her. *She's where I should be right now,* Salonina thought and remembered another time when Prisca had probably filled that role while she, herself, had been languishing at Mediolanum. *That will have to change; I'm not going to be left behind again.* She had cursed the slow-moving wagon train that had brought her from Rome to Carnuntum and determined from now on to move with part of the army close to Gallienus.

Aureolus had left Carnuntum the same day as Gallienus with a large army, heading south to intercept Macrianus who was marching from Antioch toward Rome. For a little over five weeks, she had been nearly alone in Carnuntum, anxiously awaiting any news of the two important battles.

When the first reports arrived, she thought maybe ignorance was preferable: news of Gallienus' defeat reached the city on the 27th of June, delivered to her by the grim-faced Governor Heraclianus himself. She had asked if he would take some refreshments and felt relieved when he declined and departed. As soon as he had gone, she sank into the nearest chair. She felt a tightness in her chest. *This was the first time that Gallienus had ever lost a battle!* Her breathing was labored and left her lightheaded and dizzy. *Was Gallienus' wounded? How serious was his situation? Would Postumus attack him again?* There were too many questions, and no one in Carnuntum could answer them. She had seen no visitors for two days and ate little. At the end of the second day a personal message from Gallienus had arrived assuring her that he was well and that the battle had been more of a draw, which he would set right once Aureolus arrived. Salonina remembered the wave of relief that had washed over her. On rereading the letter, she realized that, had Gallienus' camp been overrun by Postumus' troops, Pipa could have been killed or captured, the fate of the defeated. Salonina remembered Prisca's harrowing story of captivity and degradation. She thought of her recent decision to stay close to Gallienus during his campaign and wondered if she really had the courage to face the risks.

The letter from Gallienus reassured her about his immediate personal safety but she continued to dwell on the implications of the defeat: *What will the Senators be thinking? Valerian lost a battle in the east; now Gallienus has lost one in the west. Will he lose the Senate's support? Will he lose his generals' support?*

Will there be more revolts? She longed to confide in someone, but whom? She had the occasional company of Aureolus' wife, Pharsala, and Aurelian's wife, Severina, but she couldn't ask them the question uppermost in her mind: Will your husbands remain loyal to my husband after this defeat? Nor could she share her fears with Pompeia, the head of her domestic staff. A careless slip of Pompeia's tongue later and the whole household would know how anxious she was.

Five days later, on the second of July, word of Aureolus' great victory over Macrianus reached Carnuntum. The report said he had defeated a much larger army with minimal casualties. Now, worries about the possible results of Gallienus' defeat were replaced by fears of what might happen after his general's victory. *Will Aureolus' success eclipse Gallienus' authority*? Salonina had wondered. *At some point Aureolus would learn of Gallienus' failure; would he still go to Gallienus' aid? Would he help Gallienus defeat Postumus*? She was relieved that Aureolus, despite having the perfect opportunity to revolt with a great victory and a powerful army under his command, had remained loyal. The last report said that Aureolus was riding west with the cavalry to join Gallienus in his campaign against Postumus and that Aurelian had taken over the command of Aureolus' remaining infantry, along with the army formerly led by Macrianus. *Will Gallienus have attacked Postumus by now? He has to win that battle*!

Salonina also had a personal reason to wish Postumus defeated and killed. The blood of her second son was on his hands. She thought again of Saloninus. Images of him as an infant, then as an adolescent flooded her mind. On the 30th of April, they had shared a family dinner: her father, Gallienus, and their two sons. She had objected to Gallienus' plans to make the dinner a larger affair. During dinner Saloninus talked enthusiastically about his adventures leading soldiers and fighting along the empire's northern borders and even offered his father some advice on how to deal with Macrianus and his invading army. Gallienus had been uncharacteristically quiet for a few seconds before complimenting him on his suggestions. Salonina smiled at the thought. *He looked so handsome and mature that night*. She let out a deep sigh and wiped a tear from her eye. *The last time I saw him was the next morning before he left for Colonia Agrippina.* She thought of her eldest son, Valerian, who had been left in the protection and care of Ingenuus, here in Carnuntum! At first, she thought Ingenuus had killed Valerian after he revolted. Much later she learned that Valerian had actually died of wounds received in battle some time before the revolt. *At least he wasn't murdered,* she thought. *I've lost two sons, both alone, on distant frontiers. Now Marinianus is riding with his father. He'll probably spend his 17th birthday on a battlefield in Gaul. Somehow I must keep the same tragedy from happening to him.*

Aurelian had returned to Carnuntum on the 26th of July with an army of over forty thousand soldiers. Four days later the news of Rhaetia's revolt arrived. Rumors spread, growing more ominous with successive repetitions. Some said the neighboring province of Noricum was also on the verge of revolt, and was only waiting to see what reaction Rhaetia's revolt would provoke from Gallienus. Others told of an army preparing to attack Carnuntum, thus increasing the latest provinces in revolt to three. None of the stories were substantiated by any of the officials, nor were they denied. Salonina knew as much as anyone did, but that was only the contents of a message Heraclianus, showed her yesterday. "What will you do?" she had asked him.

"I've instructed Aurelian to proceed west and suppress this insurrection with whatever troops he feels necessary." He saw the anxiety on Salonina's distraught face. "It's most fortunate that he returned from fighting Macrianus with most of the army a few days ago. I take that as a good omen." He smiled encouragingly.

"What of the rumors?"

"Probably just that." Heraclianus shrugged. "We've heard nothing to substantiate any of them."

"You'll keep me informed?"

"Of course." Heraclianus nodded his head slightly at Salonina.

She had left the governor's villa late in the afternoon feeling somewhat reassured. But her night had been nearly sleepless and this morning she sat in the villa alone with her thoughts, unaware of the morning meal laid out in front of her. Salonina took a deep breath and gazed at the roses cascading down trellises along the edge of the garden. She closed her eyes and turned her face to the warmth of the sun. News of Rhaetia's revolt had arrived at the provincial capital the previous day in a private message to the governor. By this morning everyone in the city knew about it. Salonina took a deep breath. A stirring at her side broke her reverie; one of the slaves was trying to remove the breakfast dishes without disturbing her. Suddenly Salonina felt hungry. "Leave them a little longer," she said. "I think I may take something after all." The slave bowed and retired silently.

She picked half-heartedly from the choices laid out in front of her. Suddenly she wondered, *What did Gallienus have for breakfast....and Marinianus? Had they had the meal together?* She felt intensely lonely. She did not even know where her husband and her only remaining son were. *How can I join them?* She thought of Aurelian, soon to be taking his powerful army to Augusta Vindelicum. *Will he remain loyal after he suppresses the revolt in Rhaetia?* "Rhaetia," she repeated to herself as she gazed at the grape she was holding in her fingers. "Aurelian is going to Rhaetia. I can go with him!" She sat up straight on her bench, energized. Salonina dropped the grape, clapped her hands several times, and waited impatiently for an attendant to answer her summons. "Tell Pompeia to come to me at once."

"Is everything all right, my lady?" the servant asked, alarmed at Salonina's sudden urgency.

"Yes, yes! But we have much to do, and little time to do it," Salonina replied, her mind racing with thoughts and plans.

"You wished to see me, my lady?" Pompeia's question interrupted her concentration. She had no idea how long Pompeia had been standing beside her.

"Send a messenger to General Aurelian. Find out when he plans to leave. Inform him that I will accompany him on his campaign to Rhaetia.

Pompeia's eyes widened.

"You'd better send a messenger to the governor, too," Salonina added, ignoring Pompeia's expression. "We have a lot of preparations in the meantime."

Maybe my presence will help assure Aurelian's loyalty, she thought after Pompeia had left her, although she was under no illusions about that. *Whatever happens, this will get me closer to Gallienus*. And Salonina was certain that eventually, Gallienus too, would go to Augusta Vindelicum.

5-1
A Great Gift
Palmyra, Syria
15 August, 261

"What had you expected from Macrianus?" Zenobia asked her husband at the beginning of their war council

Odenathus, Zenobia, Herodian, and General Zabdas sat cross-legged on a blue and beige carpet in a private room at Odenathus' palace. The message of Macrianus' defeat lay on the low, circular brass table around which they were gathered. Warm desert winds wafted through nearby windows, billowing silk curtains and blowing Zenobia's black hair into her face. She brushed it away repeatedly and unconsciously, the annoyance failed to interrupt her excitement.

"More of a fight, I guess. He had a substantial army with him," Odenathus said, stroking his beard while recalling news that the battle had ended quickly and with little loss of life on either side. Two notable exceptions had been Macrianus and his son.

"His army is now loyal to Gallienus," General Zabdas said. "Amazing how quickly allegiances shift, isn't it?"

"I'm not surprised at all," Zenobia replied. "In Gallienus they finally have a competent leader."

"Several of his generals could also be described as

competent," Zabdas added.

Odenathus had called this meeting immediately after returning to Palmyra, where news of Macrianus' defeat at the hands of Aureolus awaited them. He had been campaigning against Persians since the spring rains ended. First he restored the city of Dura Europus to Roman rule, then led his army north along the Euphrates seizing Shapur's outposts of Circesium and Nicephorium.

"The report said a number of cities were abandoning Quietus' cause," Zenobia said, her eyes sparkled, barely able to contain her delight at Quietus' predicament. "I always thought of him as a presumptuously arrogant, inept boy."

"The gods have given us a great gift and a unique opportunity," Odenathus agreed.

"If we act quickly," Zenobia said, her voice full of anticipation.

"What's to fear from Quietus?" Herodian asked derisively. "His cause is finished."

"He could still command a substantial army," General Zabdas replied, "if he marched south and combined his soldiers with legions in Judea, Arabia, and Egypt."

"But that won't happen," Odenathus declared. "Have the army ready to march in five days," he said to the general.

"Then I should begin preparations at once," Zabdas rose from the table, acknowledging the king's command. He bowed and departed the room leaving Odenathus, Zenobia, and Herodian to discuss the situation further.

"There's another compelling reason to crush Quietus," Odenathus mused.

"What's that?" Herodian asked.

Rome!" Zenobia agreed. She looked at Herodian and shook her head. "We do it to gain Gallienus' favor."

"Why do we need Gallienus' favor, Father?" Herodian asked, deliberately ignoring Zenobia. "You've said he was defeated by Postumus."

"We know he was defeated. We know he's still alive. And we know he's still in the territory he was trying to reclaim,"

Odenathus explained patiently to his son. "That tells me a lot about the man and his intentions."

"Gallienus didn't even feel it necessary to confront Macrianus himself," Zenobia added. "He sent one of his generals to do the job, and that general remained loyal to Gallienus, even after his victory and Gallienus' defeat. Can't you see any of the dangers or opportunities we're facing?" she asked, incredulous at Herodian's lack of perspective or urgency.

"Dangers?" Herodian scoffed. "Rome is a long way away, and they still have Postumus' revolt to deal with. Maybe," he added stubbornly, "Postumus will defeat Gallienus again."

"That's possible," Odenathus considered his son's question for a moment, "but unlikely in my mind. No, the sentiment in the east is swinging to Gallienus. That's where our future lies."

"Then what's the risk she mentioned?" Herodian pointed at Zenobia with his thumb, as if she were one of the household slaves.

"Oh really, Herodian!" Zenobia exclaimed. "We have to convince Rome that we're their ally, before they conclude we're one of their enemies."

"Then we must defeat Quietus' forces," Herodian said to his father, as if the idea were his own.

"And tell Rome that we've done it," Odenathus confirmed.

"Otherwise, they'll think we supported Macrianus," Zenobia explained.

"Didn't we?" Herodian challenged.

"Our responsibility was always the defense of Rome's eastern border," Zenobia said. "If the question ever comes up, we can say we only supplied a few legionaries for their effort, from the legion under our command."

"If we defeated Quietus and swore allegiance to Gallienus, would he really believe us?" Herodian asked his father.

Zenobia looked at her step-son and thought *It's like I'm explaining an obvious fact to an adolescent, rather than the crown prince.* "What else can he do, Herodian?" she asked him sweetly.

5-2
Reunion and Accusations
Augusta Vindelicum, Rhaetia
26 August, 261

Gallienus and his only remaining son, Marinianus, stepped out of the governor's villa and into the city street. Their meeting with Marcus Tuscus, Gallienus' recently appointed governor of the province, and General Aurelian had covered details of the revolt and how Aurelian had suppressed it. Gallienus glanced at the bustling street with idle curiosity, watching carts rumble past him amidst the throng of people, all eager to get somewhere in a hurry. Late afternoon shadows crossed the street and people walked through light and dark neither noticing nor caring. The shadows meant cooler temperatures, and for that Gallienus was grateful. He had just arrived in the city with his legionaries after a hot and dusty day-long march.

A sudden scuffling sound nearby interrupted his reveries. Someone rushed toward them from the nearby shadows. Marinianus, closest to the stranger, instinctively pivoted and drew his sword.

"Is that any way to greet your mother?" Salonina chided him, almost as startled as Marinianus. She studied him appraisingly, while he sheepishly returned his sword to its scabbard. "Look at you. What a handsome young man—and seventeen years old now." Salonina instinctively wiped a smudge of dirt from her son's face, then gave him a long hug. "I'll always be your mother," she reminded him when she released her grip. Marinianus pulled away self-consciously as Salonina turned to look at Gallienus. "Thank the gods you're both unharmed!"

Thank the gods I knew that Salonina was here! Gallienus thought to himself. Aurelian had tactfully mentioned her presence in the city when he sent word to Gallienus about his suppression of the revolt, helping Gallienus avoid another unexpected and awkward meeting between Pipa and Salonina. The interlude with Marinianus and Salonina had given Gallienus time to compose himself, and sheath his own half-drawn sword, unnoticed, he hoped.

"I've been so worried about you both," Salonina continued, "especially when I heard of your battle with Postumus."

"An inconvenient setback," Gallienus said with a wave of his now-free hand.

"You are all right, aren't you?" She looked them both over to assure herself they were, indeed, unharmed. "I could tell you were surprised to see me here," she laughed at Marinianus' embarrassment.

"Surprised—and delighted," Gallienus interrupted. "The governor arranged a villa for us. We expected to find you there." He smiled warmly at Salonina, pleased to have her finally back with him.

Salonina threw herself into his arms and buried her face in his shoulder. "I'm so happy we're together again," she said, her voice almost a whisper.

Marinianus cleared his throat nervously and suggested that, perhaps, he should return to his duties. Gallienus glanced at him and nodded imperceptibly.

"Such a handsome young man," Salonina beamed, as Marinianus walked away, accompanied by several tribunes, all his own age.

"I see a lot of you in him," Gallienus replied, "a quick energetic student—both in his studies and in battle." He held her tightly. *It's been almost six months since I've seen Salonina!* "I'm glad you've come," he said, stroking her shoulder. Life was about to get more complicated for him, he realized. Gallienus could already sense tension created by having Salonina here reclaiming her position, along with Pipa and her resentment at being displaced. Besides the domestic issues, affairs of state weighed on him. He was relieved that Rhaetia's revolt had been suppressed, yet disturbed by Postumus' escape. *Despite risks, she took the initiative to come with Aurelian. Now we can share everything openly, just as we've always done.* He realized how much he'd missed her. "I'm glad you've come," he said again, more emphatically.

"I'd rather be with you, regardless of the dangers, than

facing the uncertainties alone," Salonina said. She searched Gallienus' face. *He appears happy to see me*, she thought. *And he doesn't seem to have changed, despite his loss to Postumus. How will I fit back into his life, after he's spent months with Pipa? What does he plan to do now that the revolt here is suppressed?*

"Let's walk," Gallienus suggested. "The villa isn't far." He offered her his arm then put his hand over hers as they strolled toward the villa, unmindful of Praetorian Guards and Salonina's attendants, trailing behind at a discreet distance.

"When I got to Carnuntum, the city was almost deserted," she began, the words tumbling out. "Then, I heard about your loss, and didn't know if you were alive or dead, or if you or Marinianus had been hurt, or how serious it was, or what you were going to do next!" She stopped to catch her breath, then continued. "I worried whether you'd lose support in the Senate, or if your generals would rise up against you, or whether there'd be more revolts, and how much you could withstand." She stopped for several breaths, then said more quietly, "I thought a lot about Saloninus, and that made me think about Valerian, and then I'd worry about Marinianus." She paused again. "When we heard of Aureolus' victory, I had a whole new set of things to worry about! Would his victory eclipse you? Would he revolt against you? Then, when he didn't, I was afraid he wouldn't come to your aid! When he did, I worried about your next battle with Postumus and how that would turn out."

Gallienus smiled. "You certainly have been busy while I've been away."

"I so wanted Postumus dead. I felt I could have killed him myself to avenge Saloninus," she said in an intense whisper. Then, composing herself, she continued in her usual voice. "That's not all. When I heard of the revolt in Rhaetia, everyone wondered if other provinces would join them. Then, when I learned that Aurelian was taking a large army to suppress them, and all the same fears came back, only this time about him. So, I decided to come along," she added proudly. "That way I'd get to be with you and maybe my presence would distract Aurelian from any thoughts of betraying you. It must have worked because we're here together and everyone remained loyal." She gave him a smile of joy and happiness. "It was a bit silly, looking back on it, although the dangers seemed real enough at the time. But everything has turned out all right," she concluded.

Gallienus didn't respond. He was frowning and staring straight ahead. His silence immediately aroused Salonina's suspicions; she looked at his face, suddenly concerned. "What is it?" she asked, now alarmed. "Did I say something wrong?"

"All of those dangers are still real enough, Salonina. Actually, everything has not turned out alright. Perhaps we can talk about it over dinner."

Wonderful! Salonina thought nervously, as they entered the villa and passed through the atrium. She was too preoccupied to admire the gardens of the inner peristyle, or to notice the retinue of servants now trailing behind them into the triclinium, where they would take their evening meal. *Something's not right, and I haven't even mentioned Pipa! Could that be what he's referring to?*

They sat on the edge of one of three couches and waited silently while servants brought water to wash their feet. Salonina bent down and took a cloth from one of the servant girls, who had just dipped it into the warm water. She stared at Salonina aghast, horrified that Salonina might wash her own feet. Instead, Salonina slowly and deliberately began wiping the dirt from Gallienus' face. He closed his eyes, took a deep breath, and relaxed, a smile returning to his lips. Bread had already been served and servants were pouring wine sweetened with honey into crystal goblets by the time Salonina finished. She and Gallienus reclined together on the couch.

"Because of the revolt, there was nothing available besides what we could obtain locally," Gallienus said, apologizing in advance for the simplicity of the meal

Salonina nodded absentmindedly as she sipped her wine and glanced around the dining area. She found the yellow and black mosaic floor unattractive, even though it had been carefully coordinated with the yellow border around red frescoed walls. The picture on the wall to her left, the longest wall of the room, was of some unfamiliar goddess or perhaps the matron of the villa.

Fortunately, Salonina thought, *I won't have to look at that during dinner.* She was resting on her left elbow, and would be looking at the fountain instead. Salonina watched Gallienus reach for the platter of smoked fish. He tasted a morsel, nodded, then reached for another. *He's preoccupied with eating and I want to find out about Pipa,* Salonina thought. *How shall I direct the conversation?* "When I heard of your loss," she began, "I was beside myself with worry. But after your message assuring me you were alright, I began to think about the camp followers and the risks they were exposed to. I could have been there with them. I'd never seriously considered that before. I could have been killed, or captured. Was… anyone harmed?"

Gallienus shook his head, his mouth full of raw carrot. "No one was ever at risk," he was finally able to say.

Salonina exhaled deeply, reached for her honeyed wine. *That means Pipa is alive and well,* she thought, feeling both disappointed and guilty that she could wish death or enslavement on anyone.

"I don't want to expose you to that danger," Gallienus was saying to her.

"If I stayed away from your battles, then I'd never see you," Salonina countered, reaching for a plate of olives and mushrooms. *And Pipa would have you all to herself.* "Besides," she added, "these were Romans. I know Postumus, after all."

"Unfortunately, that doesn't guarantee anything in a battle," Gallienus said. *Postumus made no effort to ransom Saloninus. What would he have done if he'd captured Salonina?* "Still, I had hoped to bring you along," he began.

"But you took Pipa instead."

"Not instead," Gallienus protested. "You hadn't arrived from Rome."

"Perhaps her death or capture wouldn't have the same impact on the empire as mine?" *She's not going to get favored access over me, just because she might be expendable!*

"Disastrous for the alliance, perhaps," Gallienus agreed, "but certainly not for the Empire. I had Attalus and a thousand of his warriors with me. It was politically expedient to take her along.

My…arrangement with Pipa shows our commitment to the treaty. If I dishonor her then I risk alienating Attalus and jeopardizing the alliance." He thought for a moment. "Things were a little *uncertain* after my first battle with Postumus. Thank the gods I didn't send for you or you might have ridden into the middle of the Rhaetia revolt yourself."

Salonina frowned while considering his response. *Does this issue he mentioned have anything to do with his relationship with Pipa and with me? Where do I stand with him after Pipa's had him to herself for months? It's so frustrating having to be guarded in our conversations when I talk about Pipa. We've always been open with each other in the past.* She stifled a small sigh. *At least I'm with him now and not alone in Carnuntum! I'll have to deal with the inconvenience of Pipa somehow.* "Was Pipa helpful to you after your first battle with Postumus?" she asked trying to sound casual.

"How do you mean?" Gallienus asked, surprised by the question.

"Was she supportive? Did she have any advice, or suggestions, as I would have?"

Gallienus paused to think while servants cleared away dishes from the first course and began serving the main course. An image of Pipa in the bath at Vesontio flashed through Gallienus' mind, and he recalled her concern with his future successes. "Generally speaking, she wants the same things as you do."

I'm sure she does! "Is she here?" Salonina asked, serving herself beets and onions.

"Yes, of course."

"In this villa? Now?"

"She has her own quarters," Gallienus held up a hand in protest, "with her own staff."

"She knows I'm here?"

Gallienus nodded, savoring his trout. He recalled Pipa's dark expression when she learned that Salonina would be in Augusta Vindelicum and how she rode silently beside him afterwards.

"And?"

Gallienus sighed. "Let me tell you about Pipa," he said.

Salonina tensed and held her breath.

"When I first arranged the Marcomanni treaty with Attalus, Pipa's 'marriage' to me served two different purposes. For the Romans, who, as you know, don't recognize our relationship as a marriage, she's a hostage. For the Marcomanni, the ceremony lent dignity and honor to her relationship with me. More importantly, it demonstrated a Roman commitment to them as well."

"I think we've been through all this before." Salonina took a breath, and then asked her question. "Is there more to the relationship than that now?"

"She's brought a great deal more to the relationship than I first imagined," he replied.

"Oh?" Salonina braced herself for the worst. She could feel her heart begin to race, but struggled to maintain an outward air of composure.

"She has remarkable insight into the Germanic tribes, their customs, their issues, at least remarkable to me," he said enthusiastically. "I'm much better informed about them than I ever was before!"

"That's it?"

"There's something else about Pipa, that I've come to realize," he added seriously.

Salonina braced herself again, but knew she had to find out. "And that is?"

"Naturally she has my interests, Rome's interests at heart," he continued.

"Naturally!"

"But there's something more." He stopped eating and frowned for a moment. "Pipa has other interests as well."

"Really?"

"She has the welfare of Rome and the welfare of her own people to consider, a double loyalty, if you will. Anything I say to Pipa, even in confidence, could well get back to her father, especially if she felt it had a bearing on Marcomanni security."

Salonina let out a long sigh, trying not to show her relief and her feeling of triumph. "I see what you mean." *Yes! My husband doesn't fully trust Pipa!* "Then things will return to normal now that we're together."

"I'm afraid not," he said, thinking about Postumus' escape.

"What do you mean?" Salonina asked, immediately tense and on her guard again.

"It's very sensitive. Maybe I'd be wise not to even discuss it right now."

"No issue should be too sensitive to share between a husband and wife, especially when our lives could depend on its outcome," Salonina objected. "I haven't seen you since the first of March. Have you lost confidence in my judgment and discretion in that time?"

"No, not at all," he answered quickly, then looked at her thoughtfully. "I've become accustomed to keeping my concerns to myself. I can't trust others to truly share their opinions with me. Even the generals have their own interests to protect, so they temper their advice with their expectations of what they think I want to hear. You're the only one I can speak to openly. Your fate is totally entwined with mine."

He put his right hand on her shoulder and massaged it affectionately.

"Is this what you said we'd talk about over dinner?" Salonina asked, nuzzling her cheek against his hand.

"No. It's Aureolus."

"Aureolus," she said, relieved of one concern, only to be troubled by another. *I've been preoccupied with things more important to me than Aureolus.* "Why is that topic so sensitive?"

"Last night one of my generals accused Aureolus of treachery!"

"How could that be? After his victory over Macrianus, that makes no sense!"

"I didn't think it did either." He reflected for a moment. "After I'd defeated Postumus, I learned of the revolt here. So I left Aureolus with most of the army to finish the job. I've known for several days that Postumus escaped. Last night Attalus insisted that Aureolus deliberately allowed it to happen."

"Can there be any truth to it?"

"It could have been an honest mistake."

"What if it wasn't?"

"I'm constantly weighing risks and alternatives with my generals and governors," Gallienus said. "I can't be everywhere at once, so I have to send competent generals into the field with sufficient armies to defeat our enemies. Maybe that will be my undoing someday."

Salonina's face darkened and she furrowed her brow unconsciously while she thought about his last comment. "Trust is a perilous issue," she said at last. "You've been betrayed four times already: Ingenuus, Regalianus, Macrianus, and Postumus, five if the charges against Aureolus are true."

"It's dangerous, I know that," he said, "but entrusting armies to my generals is no more dangerous than my father's refusal to trust anyone. I'm aware of the history of emperors' violent deaths, just as you are. Despite my plans to the contrary, I realize I may not die in bed." He smiled at her wryly.

Salonina shivered.

"I regret that my becoming emperor has put you in a dangerous situation," Gallienus said, his smile gone. "It was never my intention."

"I'm willing to share the dangers with you, but I expect you to share your concerns and problems with me, just as we've always done."

"That's a great relief to me," he said kissing her shoulder. It had been months since he could really speak freely with someone who understood him and whose concerns were his as well. Then a frown swept over his face. "You've hardly touched your dinner," he said.

"I don't seem to have much of an appetite," she apologized, as her thoughts drifted back to her dinner with Prisca in Aquileia.

Gallienus looked disappointed that the dinner had failed to please her. He signaled the staff to remove all the dishes.

"What you've said about Aureolus confirms my fears about loyalty," Salonina said, relieved to know her position was not in jeopardy. "You have a delicate balance to maintain with very powerful and capable men around you—all those egos, jealousies, and mutual suspicions. Attalus seems especially volatile and the least accustomed to taking orders from anyone. He can't be making your job any easier." She paused, thinking. "Frankly, I haven't trusted any of them since Ingenuus revolted three years ago. Both Aurelian and Aureolus left their wives in Carnuntum. Whenever we were together, the question I most wanted to ask them was whether their husbands would remain loyal to my husband." She laughed at the absurdity of that situation. They were both quiet for a time. "After an accusation of treason, wouldn't either Attalus or Aureolus have to go?" she finally asked. "

Gallienus nodded.

"But Aureolus," she looked at him sadly. "You've known him forever."

"Not forever, exactly, but for a long time." He mused for a moment, "And it's not only our long friendship, I owe a lot of my success to Aureolus. We formed the cavalry together. Rome has always relied on infantry, a big army and big set battles, but that's not the way barbarians fight. As you know, they're everywhere at once, so we had to reorganize the army into smaller, more mobile units. Aureolus and I spent a lot of time figuring that out." he trailed off.

"What will you do?"

"I'll have to hear what everyone has to say first. Then I'll try to untangle the mess of conflicting reports, see if I can learn what really happened and why. It's hard to know without being there. Everything happens so fast in a cavalry engagement. You can miss seeing something and the chance is gone—and timing is everything. Horses won't charge a bristling line. You have to know exactly when the moment of hesitation comes in enemy ranks and exactly where it is so you can break through. Aureolus' timing has never been off. His instincts are unerring, or they always have been." Gallienus was still for a moment thinking that Attalus, too, was an experienced cavalry man. "Of course it's always trickier to fight Roman legions, since they've trained with our cavalry. I'll know more when Volusianus reports back to me; I sent him to talk with Claudius about the battle. Whatever I decide, not everyone will agree."

"Does Pipa know about this?"

"Now that her father's here, she must know everything."

Servants arrived with silver platters of grapes and a small

dish with cakes drenched in honey, and a different type of wine, this one mixed with water. *What sort of advice will Pipa give Gallienus, and will it be different from mine?* "What are your plans, after the meeting?"

Gallienus regarded the apricot he was holding. "From here I'll go back to Carnuntum, personally supervise the restoration of the whole province."

Our time together begins again here, in Augusta Vindelicum, Salonina thought happily. Then, another thought came to her. *This is where Gallienus' relationship with Prisca began, and they were riding toward Carnuntum, too!* "Isn't this where you rescued Prisca?" she asked.

Gallienus nodded, and put down his half-eaten apricot. "The battle took place where the army is camped now," he said, and recalled Aureolus' part in the victory over the Juthungi. "I won that battle with Aureolus' help."

Interesting, Salonina thought, sampling one of the honeyed cakes. *This summer I was in Carnuntum waiting for Gallienus while he was on campaign with Pipa. Last summer I was in Mediolanum waiting for Gallienus, while he rescued Prisca here and she played at being his wife for nearly a month!* Her face flushed, and her jaw tightened. The event was still painful for her to think about, even though Gallienus had eventually returned Prisca to Maximus. Salonina suddenly remembered the dinner she and Prisca shared in Aquileia. *That was exactly one year ago today,* she realized.

A messenger entered the room. "Yes, what is it?" Gallienus asked, setting his wine goblet onto the table a little harder than he intended.

"A message from Pipa," the man said, eyeing Salonina uncomfortably. "She's wondering when she can expect to see you tonight."

Gallienus felt Salonina tense beside him, the honey-cake in her hand frozen halfway between her mouth and the plate. He glanced quickly at Salonina, then back to the messenger, hesitating before he replied. "Extend my regrets to her," he told the messenger. "I won't be available tonight."

Salonina relaxed gradually, after the messenger had gone. She lifted her chin, clearing away thoughts of Pipa, Prisca, and Postumus. Then she took a bite of her cake and a sip of wine. A chill ran through her as she realized her fears and suspicions about the generals' loyalty seemed to be coming true. *Will there be others?* she wondered.

"What are you thinking about?" Gallienus asked, leaning close to her and kissing the back of her neck.

"How closely our fates are intertwined," she murmured, closing her eyes and snuggling against him. "I want to be with you wherever you go, whatever the risks might be."

5-3

A Hearing

Augusta Vindelicum, Rhaetia

03 September, 261

The evening he arrived at Augusta Vindelicum, Aureolus had reported to Gallienus' quarters. He had only begun to speak of his encounter with Postumus when Attalus burst into the room, contesting Aureolus' account of events. Aureolus denied his charges. Attalus persisted. Gallienus had to separate the two men and terminate the meeting, saying they'd discuss the matter in detail tomorrow. All his generals were ordered to meet at the Governor's villa the next morning. It was customary to have a generals' meeting after a defeat, and they were never pleasant, but this was a meeting that promised to be especially difficult.

Aureolus sat at the end of a large rectangular table in the governor's quarters and glanced uneasily to his right at Claudius, Attalus, the two men whose accusations against him had resulted in this meeting, and Marinianus. He looked to his left at Aurelian, Governor Tuscus, and Volusianus, but could read nothing from their expressions. Gallienus, at the far end of the table, was the only man in the room who seemed at least somewhat sympathetic to his situation. He cleared this throat and addressed the group.

"The ground was unsuitable for cavalry." He shrugged. "I couldn't take hold of him," he said, referring to his recent unsuccessful encounter with Postumus.

"Describe the situation for us," Gallienus said.

"Flat land, trees on both sides of us, but much closer than when we first fought Postumus," He paused briefly, recalling the details of the battlefield. "We were on a road that led from Vesontio, behind us, to Adematunnum. well behind Postumus. His forces backed up against a river with a single bridge across."

"So there was no battle?" Gallienus asked, puzzled that Aureolus would come to Augusta Vindelicum without having fought Postumus.

"Actually, we fought briefly," Claudius clarified, "before a truce was declared, and Aureolus sat down to talk with Postumus."

"I could have gotten around his flanks," Attalus interjected.

"I think that highly unlikely," Aureolus snapped back.

"But he," Attalus continued, glowering at Aureolus, anger barely controlled, "refused to release my horsemen."

Aureolus is my best cavalry commander, Gallienus thought. *If he said the ground wasn't suitable for cavalry use, then I should have no reason to disbelieve him. Yet Attalus does most of his fighting on horseback.* "You were there, Claudius. Your assessment?"

Claudius looked briefly at Aureolus, sitting just to his left, then to Gallienus at the far end of the table. He hesitated, accusing Aureolus of deliberately allowing Postumus to escape would be a charge of treason, punishable by death. "I feel the engagement was slow to develop and tentatively prosecuted."

"Claudius wasn't in command," Aureolus objected. "It was my responsibility to determine the best course of action. When you don't have the responsibility," he looked pointedly at Claudius, "you don't see the situation with the same perspective."

"Maybe," Claudius conceded, his eyes on Aureolus, "but that's still my opinion."

"So there was a battle?" Volusianus questioned. The night before, after hearing Attalus' accusations, Gallienus had asked

Volusianus to check with Claudius for his version of events.

"More of a skirmish," Aureolus answered. "We were dismounted and fighting them on foot when Postumus requested a meeting. I thought he might want to negotiate terms of surrender, since we were pretty evenly matched."

"You didn't bother holding a meeting before you fought Macrianus," Attalus scoffed. "Yet you keep boasting that Macrianus' army was much larger than yours."

"Different terrain, then," Aureolus looked past Claudius to the middle of the table where Attalus sat, "and Macrianus' army wasn't well led."

"We weren't well led when we fought Postumus, either," Attalus grumbled.

Aureolus raised his eyebrows and looked sympathetically at the others. "Unfortunate that Attalus doesn't understand the finer points of Roman battle tactics."

"He failed to defeat our enemy," Attalus pointed an accusing finger at Aureolus. "I understand that part well enough!"

Aureolus' face darkened, but Gallienus interceded. "I told you to defeat Postumus," he said. "Why didn't that happen?"

"We were fighting against our own legions," Aureolus explained, turning his attention to Gallienus. "I felt I might achieve another victory with only minor casualties."

"When we fought against Ingenuus at Mursa, you didn't propose a meeting," Volusianus said. "We were fighting Roman legions there, too."

Aureolus shrugged. "Gallienus was in command at Mursa,"

"So you agreed to a meeting, with Postumus," Volusianus stated, returning the discussion to the present. "From what happened, it appears that Postumus wasn't agreeable to surrendering."

"That was not at all clear to me when we first met."

"A demand for surrender should have taken less than a minute," Attalus interrupted again, "yet it dragged on long enough for Postumus' soldiers to flee. What were you talking about all that time?"

The question went unanswered and an oppressive silence followed. "Is this really necessary?" Aureolus finally asked.

"Yes. We all need to know," Gallienus replied, his face weary.

Aureolus looked around the table, took a breath, and nodded. "There were some formalities and pleasantries exchanged, the normal sort of things that precede a negotiation session."

"Why did you think Postumus would surrender at all?" Aurelian suddenly asked. "It would have meant his own execution."

Gallienus glanced at Aurelian. *When I met with him yesterday*, Gallienus recalled, *he commented on the strangeness of Postumus' escape.*

"I've already explained my rationale for agreeing to a meeting," Aureolus dismissed Aurelian's question, with a wave of his hand.

"Did you actually address surrender?" Aurelian persisted, looking to his right, directly into Aureolus' eyes.

"It was discussed." Part of what Postumus said flashed into his mind. "After you've defeated Macrianus and me, Gallienus might regard you as a personal threat and have you assassinated. Join me; I'll make it worth your while." Aureolus had given no indication of his willingness to join Postumus, but the suggestion of his further value to Gallienus had been an unsettling thought.

They all think Aureolus made a pact of some kind with Postumus, Gallienus suddenly realized. *This isn't a meeting about incompetence, it's a meeting about treachery!*

"He took no one with him," Attalus interrupted, "so we don't really know what they said to each other. And we were ordered not to move our warriors during their meeting."

"Standard procedures," Aureolus snapped.

Gallienus held up a hand for silence. "Your comments, Claudius."

"What Attalus said is essentially correct," Claudius replied.

"Yet not moving soldiers during a meeting is standard procedures," Gallienus pointed out.

"Postumus didn't think so," Attalus countered. "We tried to tell him," he jerked his thumb at Aureolus, "but he refused to receive our messengers while Postumus' troops crossed the river."

"My view of the bridge was blocked by a line of German

horsemen. Postumus told me they were his honor guard."

Claudius shook his head. "I still don't understand why the meeting lasted as long as it did."

"It's not hard to figure out," Attalus scoffed. "There was no demand for surrender. They were plotting together!"

"You're questioning my integrity, my judgment, my loyalty!" Aureolus shouted, standing so rapidly that his chair fell over behind him.

Attalus leapt to his feet. He sprang toward Aureolus, instinctively reaching for the war axe he customarily wore on his belt. Claudius, seated between the two, was barely able to keep the men apart. Marinianus rose to help him with Attalus, while Aurelian pulled Aureolus back to his chair. Attalus stopped struggling but glared at Aureolus for a moment. "Lucky for you we left our weapons at the door," he growled, then sat down and nodded an unspoken apology to Gallienus.

"What did you think," Volusianus inquired, addressing Aureolus, "when you realized Postumus had used the time to withdraw his troops?"

"Apparently my trust in his honor was misplaced."

"Perhaps Aureolus has to claim he was betrayed," Claudius asserted, "in order to avoid the accusation of deliberate collaboration."

"Maybe he just doesn't want to admit he was outwitted by Postumus," Gallienus suggested to Claudius. "We all get into bad situations from time to time," he added, now looking at everyone at the table. "Occasionally mistakes are made. We all know luck plays a part in all conflicts."

Claudius and Aurelian exchanged glances silently.

"This wasn't a matter of luck," Claudius said. "He could have pressed the attack."

"Would you have pressed the attack?" Volusianus looked down the table at Claudius.

"There would have been significant casualties, on both sides."

"Would you have done it?" Aurelian repeated the question very deliberately.

"Yes, I would," Claudius said with a single nod of the head.

"Why did you feel you owed Postumus safe passage after he'd betrayed you?" Aurelian persisted.

"I was reluctant to seize him after giving my word of a truce—like Shapur did to your father," Aureolus addressed his reply to Gallienus. "But Postumus' horsemen suddenly surrounded us, gave Postumus a horse, then rode across the bridge before I could react."

Aureolus came to me at Vesontio, Gallienus thought, *after I'd lost a battle and he'd won one. Why would he betray me now*?

"You went after him, of course?" Volusianus suggested, knowing the answer already from his earlier talk with Claudius.

"No," Aureolus said. "His forces had crossed the river by then. The bridge was defended, and the river banks were guarded by German cavalry."

"His troops were in the open then, in flight," Volusianus continued, expanding on what Claudius had told him, "but you didn't try to intercept him before he reached the city. Wouldn't that have been favorable ground for using cavalry?"

"I felt it inadvisable to pursue him that far."

"Why?" Aurelian asked.

"It was nearly dark by that time."

"But Postumus had foot soldiers and we had horsemen," Claudius said.

"Adematunnum is a fortified city."

"You surrounded the city the next day," Claudius countered, "but then abandoned the siege."

"Why?" Volusianus asked.

"We didn't have siege equipment, and I felt the legions along the Rhenus might come to Postumus' aid at any time."

Could their accusations be rooted in jealousy? Gallienus wondered studying Aureolus' face. *Or are they correct*?

"If I was in command," Attalus declared, "I'd have executed both Postumus and Aureolus on the spot."

Gallienus frowned but said nothing.

Aureolus smiled thinly at Attalus. "As you can see, we're more civilized than that."

"Will you keep a general on your staff that deliberately

allowed an enemy to escape?" Attalus glared at Gallienus.

Aureolus looked around at the grim faces staring at him. "You can't seriously believe the word of a barbarian chieftain over the word of a Roman general!"

No one spoke.

Claudius finally broke the silence. "I've heard nothing from Attalus that I could take issue with."

"We're discussing questions of judgment, made on the field of battle." Aureolus countered. "As a result, an adversary escaped—but we'll be able to deal with that next year. You're making much more out of this than is justified."

"I disagree," Claudius said. "There were too many unusual circumstances to dismiss the matter as a lapse of judgment."

Is it possible that events happened the way Aureolus described them? Gallienus wondered. *I've never had any reason to doubt his actions before. On the other hand, Claudius and Attalus were with him. There'd be no reason for them to conspire against Aureolus, would there? Can I afford to disregard them*? He looked around the table at the grave men, then shifted in his seat. "We've heard from the left side of the table," he said, acknowledging Attalus and Claudius. "I'm excluding my son from voicing an opinion on such a grave matter," he added, before turning to Volusianus, sitting immediately to his right, and arched an eyebrow.

Volusianus returned his gaze for a moment, then gave a subtle shake of his head.

"I need more than that," Gallienus insisted.

"General Aureolus no longer enjoys my support," Volusianus said.

"Governor," Gallienus prompted Tuscus, who had thus far not taken part in the discussion.

"It's difficult to know," Tuscus temporized.

"By the gods!" Gallienus exclaimed, scowling at Tuscus. "If it were easy to know, I wouldn't be asking everyone's opinion!"

Tuscus took a deep breath and licked his lips. "Then," he looked uneasily at both men, "I would give my support to General Claudius," he concluded.

Gallienus nodded. "Aurelian?"

"I wouldn't want to find myself in a battle with Postumus uncertain about Aureolus' motives and loyalties." There was neither doubt nor hesitation in Aurelian's reply.

Aureolus eyes were wide with disbelief at the charges being leveled against him, and by Gallienus' lack of support. "Consider my victories in the past," Aureolus appealed to Gallienus. "At Mursa against Ingenuus, at Mediolanum against the Alamanni and the Juthungi, at Verona against the Roxolani. I've just won a brilliant victory over Macrianus, against a much larger army. I came to you at Vesontio. Your victory over Postumus wouldn't have been possible otherwise."

"All true," Gallienus agreed, leaning back in his chair and drumming his fingers on the table. *I've trusted Ingenuus, Regalianus, and Postumus. All of them betrayed me—and two of my sons have died because of that. I never had any reason to distrust them either, but Aureolus! What could Postumus possibly offer him that I haven't given him.*

"I won't serve under Aureolus' command in any future battles," Attalus declared, interrupting Gallienus' thought. Then, turning to Gallienus he continued. "If you support him and disregard everything I've told you, I'll take my people back across the Danuvius—even if we have to fight to regain our lands. There, at least, I'll know my friends from my enemies."

Gallienus hesitated, his fingers falling silent on the table. *This situation is serious*, Gallienus realized, as he glanced at the men watching him intently. *I owe Aureolus my successes and he saved me after my defeat. But if I keep him, I'll lose an ally and I'll probably be assassinated before the end of the day.* He drew in a deep breath and exhaled slowly. "I can no longer allow you to retain your present command, General Aureolus."

"But I'm your cavalry commander! Who can possibly replace me?" Aureolus appealed to Gallienus.

"General Claudius will assume that position—effective immediately. Guard," he summoned over his shoulder, "escort General Aureolus to my tent for final arrangements. Gentlemen," he addressed the generals, "see to your troops." *The men are used to serving under different generals, but they might be restless when they learn of Aureolus' dismissal, especially if they think it unjust.* Gallienus rose abruptly, turned away from the table, and walked out of the villa.

* * *

"I didn't think he'd do it," Aurelian said to the remaining generals, after Marinianus, Attalus, Tuscus, and Aureolus had followed Gallienus out of the room. "He seemed to believe Aureolus' excuses despite his actions."

"Maybe he wanted to believe him," Volusianus suggested. "This was the man who created his cavalry. Gallienus couldn't accept the fact that Aureolus would betray him. Aureolus was victorious over Ingenuus and Macrianus, despite what seems to be his treachery with Postumus. No wonder he wouldn't put him to death or fully disgrace the man."

"He had to replace Aureolus," Claudius agreed. "I think he realized that."

"He did," Volusianus confirmed.

"Still," Aurelian said, "it was hard for him to do it."

"But he did it," Volusianus replied.

"Congratulations on your new assignment, Claudius!" Aurelian said. "Were you surprised?"

Claudius grinned. "Yes. I hadn't expected that. He paused. "We'll have plenty to keep us busy next year. We still have Postumus to deal with."

"And maybe we'll find Aureolus with him next year," Volusianus added, shaking his head.

"A pity it's too late in the year to start another campaign and finish Postumus now," Claudius said glumly. "We can't afford to give anyone an opportunity to betray us a second time. Fortunate that you executed the legate in Rhaetia, Aurelian."

"I knew Gallienus wouldn't like it, but it had to be done," Aurelian said.

"We'd better 'see to our troops.' I don't expect any trouble," Claudius said. "On the march back, they were disgusted with the outcome, they felt they had Postumus cornered, and were frankly puzzled by Aureolus' inaction. It was so out of character." Their chairs scraped on the mosaic floor as they all pushed back from the table. Claudius wondered what Postumus had offered Aureolus and, after Postumus' treachery in the meeting, would Aureolus ever trust Postumus' word in the future.

"Do you suppose Gallienus would lead an expedition east himself?" Aurelian speculated as they moved toward the door. "Quietus is still there, and he hasn't renounced his claim as emperor, as far as I know."

"Can he risk going east when Postumus is still alive?" Claudius asked. "Wouldn't Postumus cross the Alpes and march on Rome in his absence?"

"That would be Gallienus' concern," Volusianus agreed.

"Perhaps he'd send one of us with an army," Aurelian suggested.

"After Aureolus' treachery," Volusianus mused, "I wonder if he'll ever trust anyone to command a large army on his own."

"Wouldn't it be nice if the gods provided us with the solution to a problem once in a while," Claudius remarked wistfully, "instead of just handing us another problem?"

5-4
Final Reflections
Emesa, Syria
30 October, 261

General Callistus gazed over Emesa's eastern rampart and tried to discern where flickering stars filling a black sky met campfires of Odenathus' army. A chilly desert breeze lifted a corner of his cape and occasionally carried a whiff of smoke. Laughter from Odenathus' soldiers drifted across open spaces between city walls and the army's encampment. Camaraderie around Odenathus' campfires accentuated Callistus' loneliness. He pulled his cape tighter around him. Nearly a year-and-a-half ago Callistus had gazed at Shapur's army from another city's walls. He had thought that June night would be his last. Tonight he was sure of it.

Three summers ago I dined on this rampart with Valerian, Macrianus, Odenathus, Zenobia, and others. So much has changed since then, he thought, taking a deep breath. *At that time, Odenathus was uncomfortable being situated between an indecisive ally and a determined enemy.* A smile crept over Callistus' face. *That was the first time I'd met the fiery young queen Zenobia. It was her suggestion that Valerian make her husband governor of Syria, and that's how Odenathus came to command the legion at Raphnae.* Callistus considered the irony and regretted there was no one to share it with: one of the dinner guests was now besieging the city intending to kill another of the dinner guests.

Callistus reflected on choices and consequences—leadership and loyalty, fate and fortune. *A title, emperor, king, even general, means little if you aren't wise enough or strong enough to hold it.* Over the last two years four influential men made miscalculations that significantly changed the situation in the east, while one other had survived the reversals and grown stronger because of them.

He thought first of Valerian. *He should have recognized his limitations and left the fighting to his generals.* Valerian's disastrous defeat enabled Shapur to ravage countless cities in Cilicia without any serious opposition. *What would have happened if Valerian had let his generals fight Shapur?* he wondered. Then Shapur grew overconfident and made a serious error in judgment. Shapur had split his forces into several marauding groups, and Callistus' amphibious landing and subsequent attack at Pompeiopolis had nearly defeated Shapur. After that, he'd been steadily driven back toward Persia ahead of Callistus' relentless advance. *What would have happened if Shapur had kept his army intact?* Callistus realized he was pacing along the rampart, grimfaced. He pounded a fist into his open palm, then pivoted and began walking the opposite direction. *I would have liked to kill Shapur myself!* Callistus' family had died at the hands of Shapur's army nine years earlier when the Persians had marched west, unopposed, to sack Antioch. Callistus bitterly resented losing the opportunity to personally avenge their deaths. But before he could exact his revenge, Odenathus and Macrianus interceded: Odenathus had supported Rome by attacking Shapur during his retreat. Macrianus had directed Callistus to return to Antioch with his troops. Despite his initial victory over Valerian, Shapur returned home, twice defeated, first by me at Pompeiopolis, then by Odenathus east of Edessa. Bringing a captive Roman emperor home as part of the spoils was probably the only thing that saved Shapur from insurrections when he returned.

Then, Macrianus had declared his two sons as emperors, thinking that a local victory could lead him to distant successes against a battle-tested emperor and Gallienus' experienced legions. *What would have happened if Macrianus had remained loyal to the emperor?* Looking back on it now, the revolt seemed less remarkable than it did at the time. Macrianus made no attempt to rescue Valerian after Shapur's victory, and even refused to negotiate a ransom. Callistus thought about Macrianus' two sons, trained as logisticians like their father, impressed with their own self-importance, and with virtually no military experience between them. *They were given titles, but were neither wise enough, nor strong enough to keep them.*

Even Callistus had not been exempt from miscalculations and their consequences. *I, too, abandoned Valerian and Gallienus. The price for my loyalty was command of the eastern army.* But Macrianus reneged on that agreement and led the army against Gallienus himself. *Could I have defeated Aureolus? Perhaps, but I would rather die at the hand of a Roman general than be killed by a desert king.*

Odenathus had kept his forces in Palmyra when Shapur ransacked the province of Cilicia two summers earlier, but had attacked Shapur when he was retreating ahead of Callistus' forces later that fall. *Was Odenathus lucky, or shrewd? He certainly was a genius for waiting until it was clear who would win.* Then, Odenathus had managed to support Rome's interests without explicitly supporting Macrianus' claim to the title of emperor. He'd sent only a token number of legionaries with Macrianus' army and remained behind to defend Rome's eastern borders. When the news of Macrianus' defeat reached Odenathus, he again attacked the losing side. This time the losing side had been Callistus and Quietus.

News of Macrianus' defeat reached his son, Quietus, and Callistus at Antioch on the third of August. The messenger had told them that many cities were openly abandoning their support for Quietus. *It was only a matter of time until Antioch, too, turned against us*, Callistus had realized immediately. *Our only chance of surviving lay in gathering our forces immediately and joining with the legions in Judea, Arabia, and Egypt. If we could have gotten through Syria before Odenathus blocked our path, it might have worked.* Quietus had shown his true character during that time of crisis. Perhaps he was consumed with surprise and grief. Whatever the reasons, he was indecisive and failed to appreciate the implications of his father's defeat, and the grave peril it put him in. But Odenathus had been waiting for them at Emesa as they marched south in early September. Quietus had tried to convince Odenathus to join him and resist any Roman army that Gallienus might bring to reclaim the east. Callistus could still remember hearing Odenathus' deep laugh after he listened to Quietus' proposal. "Draw up your battle lines," he had said to Quietus, the smile now gone from his face. "We'll see who the gods favor now."

Callistus' three thousand foot soldiers were heavily outnumbered by Odenathus' army of light and heavy horsemen. *It must have been much like that when Valerian's foot soldiers faced Shapur's horsemen at Carrhae,* Callistus realized. While Quietus wore the cape of an emperor, it was Callistus who actually commanded the soldiers. *And I'd just managed to form up my legionaries when Zenobia led a charge on my left flank. She was, indeed, a spectacle— sword drawn, dressed in silver mail, galloping toward me on a white horse.* Callistus had managed to block Zenobia's attack by drawing heavily from the center of his force, all the while retreating toward the walls of Emesa. The city had thrown open the gates and allowed them to enter. Emesa had now been under attack by Odenathus' army for two months. Callistus had hoped Odenathus would tire of the undertaking and depart. But Odenathus was clearly unwilling to abandon the siege. Callistus had wondered how long the city would continue to support Quietus. Earlier today he had gotten his answer.

The town's militia had seized Quietus, killed him, and thrown his body over the city wall. Next, they'd come for Callistus, with the same intention. Callistus had confronted the armed residents with a small band of body guards, swords drawn, ready to fight. While the militia had hesitated, Callistus realized the futility of his situation. The town was not willing to tolerate his presence. So he sheathed his sword and announced to the citizens of Emesa that he would personally surrender the garrison to Odenathus, at dawn tomorrow. Odenathus would spare the garrison and the city, Callistus was reasonably certain. But he was under no illusions about what would happen to him. He sighed and gazed out at the stars and campfires.

Fate seems like the blowing desert winds, Callistus thought. *For a time, they blew for Valerian, then Shapur, then they shifted and blew for Macrianus and me. Now they've shifted again. How long will they'll blow in favor of Odenathus…and Gallienus?*

5-5

Natural Disasters

Carnuntum, Pannonia

27 April, 262

Moonlight sparkled off water cascading from courtyard fountains. Salonina entered the courtyard quietly, pausing to stare at the outline of her husband across the garden, silhouetted by the full moon.

"Why are you here?" Salonina asked, her voice just above a whisper. If he heard her, he didn't answer. She walked up behind him and reached out to put a hand on his shoulder. Gallienus turned to look at her. She studied his face in the dim light. What would cause him to leave Pipa's quarters—her bed more likely—at this time of night? A quarrel perhaps? "I was informed that you'd returned," she began, when he didn't answer immediately, "and so I came to find out what was wrong."

"This." He pointed to a message lying on the garden wall beside him.

Salonina bit her lower lip, hesitated for a moment, took a deep breath, picked it up, and walked to the nearest torch, held it close to its flickering light, glanced first at the closing and noticed that it was signed by one of the consuls in Rome. Next she held the message close to the flickering light of a single candle burning on the table.

> Rome has been shaken by earthquakes. Libya, too, was shaken, but reports from Asia tell of terrible earthquakes with sounds of thunder and a roaring as if coming from the earth itself. Buildings were destroyed or disappeared completely with great loss of life. Salt water filled some of the fissures and flooded many coastal cities.
>
> We have consulted the oracles, and made sacrifices to Jupiter. In addition to restoring the damage, we now have famine and pestilence to deal with.

Salonina dropped the message and leaned against the garden wall. "It must have happened just after we left the city," she gasped, one hand partially covering her mouth. "Father was still there! Do you suppose….?" She struggled to breathe, feeling as if a weight were pressing on her chest.

"No. Tremors in Rome weren't as serious as the quakes in Asia. Besides, if anything happened to him, we would have heard about it," Gallienus said to reassure her. *Even though that's probably just an initial report*, he thought grimly.

Is this why he came back from Pipa's? Salonina wondered.

"The earthquakes in Africa and Asia would have happened well before the one in Rome; it would take longer for that news to reach us, of course. I came as soon as I learned because I knew you'd be concerned about your father, as am I, and I wanted you to hear this from me!"

"An earthquake happened once while I was studying in Athens," she recalled. "It wasn't nearly as large as these must have been. Still, it was terrible—we didn't know where to hide or to find shelter. Most of the people lost everything they had. Afterwards," Salonina's face darkened, "there wasn't enough food to keep all the survivors alive. Many that didn't starve were lost to sickness." She wrapped her arms around herself and shivered involuntarily.

"Didn't the governor help, or the emperor?"

"It seems they weren't interested." She shook her head. "We have to help," she said, looking to Gallienus for a solution.

"I'll have to send an emissary to each affected area with money to help them rebuild. They're too widespread for me to go everywhere. Maybe I'll empower the emissaries to suspend local taxes for one or more years."

"Why not just send the money to the Proconsuls of Africa and Asia?" Salonina asked. "You appointed them, after all."

"To make sure the money's spent where it's needed," Gallienus said, "and to remind the people that it's the emperor who is aware of their troubles and cares about their welfare."

"That's good," she nodded. Then she sighed deeply and shook her head. "We've endured a plague for years, then food shortages because there's not enough people to tend the fields, and now these earthquakes. Why are the gods so angry?"

"Actually, earthquakes are supposed to be natural events that have nothing to do with the gods' displeasure," Gallienus said, holding up a hand as if to ward off Salonina's suggestion. "That's what the writings of Seneca, Pliny, and Lucretius say."

"I've read them," Salonina replied, "I think they borrowed their ideas from Aristotle. They speak of underground winds, and lakes, and rivers, cold air forcing out hot air that sometimes breaks the earth's surface. Their logic seems convincing, but what evidence do they offer?" She paused, still skeptical. "How many people do you think believe these writers?"

"Certainly the educated and well informed."

"You're educated and well informed. Do you believe them?"

Gallienus paused, then said, "It's in my interest to believe them."

"But most of the people will believe one or more of the gods are displeased for some reason." Salonina paused. Neptune is the god of earthquakes—and he has a quick temper. Maybe he's angry at us for some reason. *Juno is the goddess of marriage and the protector of the empire as a whole. Maybe she's displeased with Gallienus for marrying Pipa in violation of his marriage vows. could the earthquakes and other issues actually be an omen against Gallienus' fight with Postumus*?

Gallienus was lost in his own thoughts. *I've tried to seek the gods' favor in everything I've done, and I've done fairly well, considering the challenges I've faced. Could the earthquakes signal some god's displeasure that I've failed to rescue my father? Or failed to even try to secure his release? If so, why didn't it happen last year?* He shook his head. "I'll consult with the priests, then offer sacrifices to Jupiter," he said.

"Do you think your generals will take the earthquakes as omens?" Salonina asked. "They're capable soldiers, but not what I'd consider sophisticated thinkers."

"I suppose their reactions will be an indication of how the troops feel," Gallienus said after a moment's thought. "If so, I must convince them that earthquakes in Africa and Asia have nothing to do with fighting Postumus in Germania. If the soldiers begin to think I've lost favor with the gods, then they'll lose their faith and trust in me!"

"What did Pipa say about this news?" Salonina asked suddenly.

"Interesting that you would ask." He looked at Salonina speculatively.

"Her reaction is probably the same one you could expect from Attalus tomorrow. It might be useful to know in advance how at least one of your generals is going to respond."

Gallienus nodded and smiled at Salonina's perception. "She said earthquakes were caused by Loki, their god of strife, who was bound inside a cave for murdering Baldr, their god of light. A poisonous snake above his head drips venom onto his face, but his wife catches the venom in a bowl." he paused.

"Surely there's more?"

"Yes. Every now and then his wife has to empty the bowl, and that's when Loki jerks his head and struggles against his restraints. It's his struggling to keep the venom off his face that causes the earthquakes."

"Maybe Loki's wife should find a larger bowl, or another husband." Salonina frowned at the quaintness of the explanation. "Besides, that's a highly localized explanation for something that's happening all over the empire."

Gallienus smiled and held up his hands. "You asked me what she said."

"From what you've told me, there doesn't seem to be any way to appease their god," Salonina concluded, "or to somehow seek his favor." She paused, then looked up at Gallienus. "So you'll still meet with your generals tomorrow to plan your attack on Postumus?"

"He escaped me once," Gallienus said, rising from the table and pounding a fist into the open palm of his other hand. "I don't intend to let that happen again."

"It won't bring Saloninus back," Salonina said sadly, "but I'll feel better knowing that the man who killed our son has paid for it with his own life." She sat looking at her lap for a few moments, then looked up. "Are you worried about Claudius commanding the cavalry?"

"I won't know if he's able to command horsemen in battle until he proves himself," Gallienus replied. "Fortunately, I also have Attalus."

Salonina rose from the table and moved close to him. "Come to bed now," she whispered, placing a hand lightly on his arm. She looked up at his face and noticed a few flecks of gold dust in his hair, then caught the scent of Pipa's perfume. *And as long as he has Attalus*, Salonina thought, *he'll also have Pipa.*

5-6
A Change of Plans
Carnuntum, Pannonia
28 April, 262

"This came late last night," Gallienus said, handing a message to Volusianus, and glancing at his generals gathered around a large table at the governor's quarters. "Several other earthquakes have been reported in Asia Minor, Libya, even one in Rome, but there's no mention of earthquakes in any region that would affect our campaign against Postumus. So from our point of view tactically, they're of little consequence."

"They must be more significant than 'of little consequence,'" Attalus snorted, "since you left my daughter's bed in the middle of the night."

Claudius and Aurelian exchanged uncomfortable glances. Attalus couldn't see Volusianus' face, since he was engrossed in the message.

"Salonina's father was in Rome," Gallienus said, noting Heraclianus stifle a smile. "I knew the matter would be of great concern to her."

"What has your mother told you about earthquakes?" Claudius asked Aurelian. "We know she's a priestess in the temple of the Sun God."

Aurelian shrugged. "Only that they occur in dangerous and uncertain times."

Attalus smirked. "What a perceptive deity, this sun god of yours!"

"Couldn't she have given her own son something more specific?" Volusianus asked, shaking his head.

"We don't have time to await another opinion from Aurelian's mother," Gallienus interrupted, closing the subject.

"Perhaps these earthquakes have some connection with blood-red sunsets we've been seeing," Volusianus suggested. "Some of the men believe they're an omen of some sort. This news will add to their fears."

Salonina was right, Gallienus thought, looking at the

concerned faces of the men around the table. *These men may be great generals, but they're as convinced as any of their soldiers that earthquakes are caused by the gods' displeasure. A rational approach will get me nowhere with them.* "First, I intend to put things right with the gods," Gallienus announced. "After we conclude this meeting, I'll discuss the matter with the priests. They may want to consult the Sibylline Books in Rome, see if there's a prophecy that refers to this event. They may suggest something we can do to appease the gods and avoid calamity to the state." Sibylline Books were a collection of prophesies by Sibyl, a Greek seer, purchased by the last king of Rome, around 500 BC. The books were consulted during times of crises. Predictions described within the text themselves were never revealed to the public. "I'll make appropriate sacrifices to Jupiter," Gallienus continued, "and have the auspices determine if this is a favorable time to attack Postumus."

"There'll be famine and disease in those areas," Volusianus muttered, still thinking of earthquake victims.

"Prompt help from Rome might discourage uprisings by some of the local leaders," Heraclianus suggested.

Gallienus nodded. "I'll send emissaries to affected locations with money to help local recoveries and authority to provide tax relief, if they feel it necessary. I want people to be thinking of the emperor's generosity, not about whether some god is displeased about one thing or another."

"Help from Rome may distract earthquake victims," Claudius said, "but there's still talk of omens in our soldiers' ranks. How will you deal with them?"

"Why would Neptune be causing these earthquakes?" Aurelian wondered aloud, inadvertently revealing his own beliefs. "And what would he accept for appeasement?"

"You can't appease the gods for causing earthquakes," Attalus scoffed. "They're caused because Loki strains against his chains in a cave—to keep the serpent's venom off his face," he added, as everyone gaped at his explanation.

"Have none of you read Aristotle?" Gallienus exclaimed in frustration at the men around the table. "Or Lucretius, or Pliny, or

Seneca? They all say earthquakes are natural events. There's no reason to infer any divine action in them at all!"

"Whatever we might think," Claudius replied, "most of our soldiers still believe gods cause earthquakes, for reasons of their own."

"We don't want our soldiers to believe you've lost the gods' favor." Heraclianus added. "I suggest some personal reassurances that you have things well in hand."

Gallienus considered Heraclianus' advice.

"Offer sacrifices to Jupiter at the next full moon, in the presence of the men," Heraclianus continued his theme. "Maybe even have auspices do their reading at that time. If the signs are favorable, then everyone would want to know of it."

Gallienus studied the faces of the men around the table nodding agreement. He sensed a feeling of relief among his generals. *Salonina was right*, he thought, *and Heraclianus has given me a sound suggestion.* "Then we'll do that," he said. "Now, we still have time to consider our plans to defeat Postumus before the midday meal." He signaled to an aide, who brought in a large map which he spread out on the table. "I intend to send two armies against Postumus, one here," he pointed at the center of the map, "through the middle of the country, the second there," he pointed at the upper right part of the map, "along the Rhenus River. Either of the forces should be sufficient to—now what is it, Quintianus?" The tribune had entered the room and stood waiting for the emperor to acknowledge his presence.

"There's a messenger outside who says he has urgent news, sir," Quintianus said. "You told me to interrupt you, if I felt the situation was important."

Gallienus nodded for the messenger to enter. He read the message, then tossed it onto the table and frowned, lost in thought for a moment, before looking up at the generals. "It seems that Byzantium's prefect has been forced to flee the city," he said. "But he only calls the matter a 'disturbance'" Gallienus drummed his fingers on the table and rested his chin in one hand. "This will interfere with my plans to defeat Postumus. How utterly inconsiderate of him!" he exclaimed.

"A disturbance could mean anything from city riots to full-scale revolt." Volusianus said.

Gallienus sighed. "We'll have to assume the worst."

"You're going to split your forces again?" Attalus' question broke the silence.

"Yes. We're much stronger now than we were at this time last year."

"I understand the urgency in resolving the Postumus revolt," Heraclianus said, "but a convincing argument could be made for deferring that matter until Byzantium is pacified."

"Proceed."

"Postumus has already revolted and is fully in control of his area, despite your vigorous, and nearly successful, attempts to dislodge him last year," Heraclianus chose his words carefully.

"But the longer he's in control of Gaul, the harder he'll be to dislodge," Aurelian objected. "Not to mention the example he's setting for the rest of the empire."

"That's why it's important to respond immediately to this outbreak in Byzantium," Heraclianus countered, "to show that other revolts won't be countenanced. For now, Postumus can easily be contained beyond the Alpes Mountains."

"And the Franks will probably attack him again this year," Volusianus added. "That would force him to commit his forces along his northern frontier."

"Probably," Claudius agreed, "but we can't count on that."

"After our victory over Macrianus, we have over sixty thousand men at our disposal, if I have my figures correct," Gallienus said, looking up from the detailed report of his current troop strengths that Volusianus provided for this meeting.

"The number includes legionaries, cavalry, Praetorian Guards, and Attalus' warriors," Volusianus clarified.

"Surely that's sufficient strength to overwhelm Postumus and suppress a 'disturbance' in Byzantium," Gallienus challenged his generals. The silence in the room was broken by Quintianus' second intrusion. "What? Again?" Gallienus stared at Quintianus with a mixture of disbelief and irritation.

"There's another message for you as well, sir," Quintianus replied uneasily.

"Maybe a second messenger bringing the same news," Volusianus speculated. Sending multiple messengers with the same message was a common practice intended to ensure that the news actually reached its destination. "Did you happen to determine what news the man is bringing?" he asked Quintianus.

"I did, sir." Quintianus handed the message to Gallienus, who broke the seal and read in silence.

"Now *this* is disturbing," Gallienus said, looking up quickly from the latest message. "The Prefect of Aegyptus has forbidden the grain fleet to sail for Rome."

"He can't do that!" Volusianus exclaimed. "That exceeds his authority!" He looked at the others. "Why, that would be an act of treason."

"So it would seem," Gallienus said, pausing to read further. "It says here that the city of Alexandria is strongly divided in their loyalties, but it's clear that Aemilianus has decided to revolt."

"This grain fleet—it's important?" Attalus inquired. He'd grown accustomed to the generals guarding their reactions and emotions, but he'd noted immediate concern on all their faces at this news.

"Rome depends heavily on grain from Aegyptus," Volusianus explained. "It would be a disaster if Aegyptus were to fall into hostile hands!"

Attalus shrugged and looked around the table. "So now we forget about Byzantium—and Postumus.?"

"We'll have to rethink the whole situation," Gallienus said, careful to maintain his composure. "We now have two provinces in revolt: Postumus' and Aemilianus,' three if we consider the 'disturbance' at Byzantium to be serious," Gallienus said finally. "And the eastern part of the empire isn't exactly stabilized, although we've got Odenathus in Palmyra, who's sworn his allegiance to me."

"Do you plan to replace him with a Roman commander?" Aurelian asked immediately. The other generals nodded agreement. "It could become troublesome over time if Odenathus is allowed to remain the dominant force there."

"Right now I'm more interested in replacing people who

have declared against me rather than the ones who have declared for me."

"Clearly, regaining Aegyptus and restoring grain deliveries must be our first priority," Volusianus stated, looking to Gallienus for confirmation.

"I was willing to divide my forces into two armies," Gallienus mused, sensing the opportunity to attack Postumus slipping away. "But the situation is a bit more complex now." Whatever else I do, I'd be wise to leave a large central reserve force, in case further revolts break out.

"What will you do about the grain fleet revolt?" Volusianus prodded Gallienus.

"A quick response is vital. I just haven't figured out how." Gallienus said at last.

"What about Odenathus?" Aurelian asked. "He's much nearer to Alexandria than we are."

Volusianus shook his head. "We've urged him to attack the Persians, and Odenathus plans to campaign against Shapur's army this spring. He'll be engaged with Persians before we could communicate our wishes to him."

"There's also the danger that he'd keep control over Aegyptus after suppressing the rebellion there," Claudius added.

"Then a quick response is going to be problematic," Heraclianus said. "It took Macrianus over 100 days to reach Sirmium, and he wasn't coming all the way from Aegyptus."

"I'm thinking more of an amphibious operation," Gallienus announced. "But I haven't determined whether it's best to launch it from Aquileia, or have the troops march to Rome and depart from the port of Ostia. Your thoughts, gentlemen?"

"How many men?" Claudius asked.

"Around a legion of well-trained, experienced men should be adequate," Gallienus said.

"If they came from the army Macrianus brought with him, they'd be more accustomed to fighting in summer heat," Aurelian suggested. There were murmurs of agreement around the table, and Gallienus nodded his assent.

"Around five thousand men," Volusianus mused. "We'll

need… maybe sixty ships, unless we can commandeer some of the larger merchant ships. That's a lot of ships and they'll need a lot of supplies. Aquileia is certainly closer, but can Aquileia supply the ships or the support—especially on relatively short notice?"

"I rather doubt it," Gallienus agreed.

"Why don't we send a messenger to the Consul in Rome," Volusianus suggested. "Faustianus is a capable man. Tell him to round up enough ships at Ostia to transport a legion, and to gather supplies to support it."

"And he'll have time to make necessary arrangements while the army marches from here to Rome," Heraclianus smiled at Volusianus' solution. "Who will command them?" he asked. Everyone looked at Gallienus, each hoping to hear his name mentioned.

"I think the man for this task is Theodotus."

"An unexpected choice," Volusianus finally managed to reply, his comment reflecting everyone's surprise.

"Who is this man?" Attalus asked Gallienus. "And why do you choose someone I don't even know for something everyone says is so important?"

"He's commanded a legion, and he fought with me at Mediolanum against Alamanni and Juthungi," Gallienus replied, "and at Verona against Roxolani, again at Mursa when we defeated Ingenuus. I could go on."

"Have I ever fought with this man?" Attalus demanded.

"More likely against him," Gallienus chuckled, "before we were friends, of course."

"If you think he's the right man, I have no problem with the choice," Attalus conceded. "I have no interest in this far-away place anyhow."

"Theodotus is an Aegyptian," Volusianus pointed out. "That could prove useful to the campaign."

"Does Theodotus have any experience with a naval operation?" Claudius asked.

"Who among us has had *any* experience with a naval operation?" Gallienus frowned and looked around the table.

"It's the only way to respond quickly to something that far

away," Heraclianus said, after mulling the situation over.

"Any other thoughts concerning the Aemilianus matter?" Gallienus asked. "Then I'll need to speak with Theodotus immediately," he said to Volusianus, "and I'd like you to start on that message to Rome, right after we conclude our discussion."

Volusianus nodded. He signaled to Quintianus, standing by the door, to summon Theodotus.

"Since you've chosen Theodotus for something this important, I presume you have other plans for the rest of us," Heraclianus said to Gallienus.

"We have two other issues to contend with," Gallienus replied, his attention focused on Volusianus' troop strength report on the table. They all watched him expectantly. Silence in the room was broken only by the sound of Gallienus shuffling through the papers. "First, we'll consider Byzantium," he said, finally looking up at his generals. "I think four wings of cavalry should be sufficient. Claudius, you'll command them." *So I can see how well he manages horsemen in battle.*

"What about the rest of my cavalry?" Claudius asked, surprised and dismayed that his new command had been divided before he'd even had occasion to lead it in battle.

"I'm giving them to Aurelian," Gallienus replied, his mind still on the Byzantium operation. "I'll take the Praetorians, of course, and two thousand of your warriors, Attalus. Now as to Postumus," Gallienus consulted the papers on the table before looking up again. "Aurelian, Attalus, your assignment is to prevent Postumus from marching on Rome. That's it. You're to take the two remaining cavalry wings and two thousand Marcomanni warriors to Mediolanum. I'll give you five legions as well—two from the eastern legions that Macrianus brought, three from the western legions." *Attalus can watch Aurelian, in case the thought of marching on Rome crosses Aurelian's mind. And dividing the legions between east and west should prevent any conflicts of loyalty from arising.*

"Shouldn't I be commanding all of the cavalry?" Claudius asked, "since you assigned them to me."

"I don't expect that Aurelian's actually going to need them,"

Gallienus replied. "But if Postumus tries to force his way to Rome, then Aurelian will need all of them. I do expect that you'll need four wings at Byzantium. You can sit with two cavalry wings in Mediolanum and do nothing, or you can fight with four cavalry wings in Byzantium. I assume you'd prefer the latter." Claudius took a deep breath, nodded, and said nothing.

"You're taking no foot soldiers," Heraclianus commented to Gallienus.

"I want to travel quickly," Gallienus replied. "And I want to be in Rome by this fall—to celebrate ten years as emperor."

Fifteen hundred cavalry, and twenty-four thousand legionnaires, Aurelian thought. *Clearly the largest force of any assigned so far.* "What do you wish me—us, to do, specifically," Aurelian corrected himself, after a glare from Attalus.

"I've already told you," Gallienus said. "Prevent Postumus from marching on Rome. What you do and how you do it, I leave to your judgment and discretion."

"Why don't you give the smaller command to someone else?" Attalus asked, "And attack Postumus yourself?"

"I'm sorely tempted," Gallienus replied. "But too many things are happening already. And if Theodotus isn't successful, then I'll have to send another force against Aemilianus. That will have to come from Aurelian's troops, since he's the closest to Rome."

Attalus gave a barely perceptible nod, then looked at Aurelian appraisingly.

"According to my calculations," Volusianus said to Gallienus, "there are quite a few men available that you haven't yet accounted for."

"Just over four legions," Gallienus agreed, "and another two thousand Marcomanni horsemen. They're to remain in Pannonia, under your command, Heraclianus, to defend your borders, and in case another unforeseen event arises." He closed the meeting, dismissed the men, and reviewed the empire from west to east.

The legionnaires should discourage Postumus from marching on Rhaetia or Pannonia. The Marcomanni horsemen will discourage the Pannonian legions, or Heraclianus, himself, from any ideas of a third revolt in Pannonia. I've tried to address the issues and provide contingencies where I can. There'll be a lot of generals with a lot of armies marching all over the empire this summer. I hope I haven't misplaced my trust in any of them..

6-1
Decennalia
Rome
10 September, 262

"What are you doing here?" Attalus exclaimed, glancing around his campsite, alarmed that others might have noticed this unexpected arrival. He blinked, staring at the figure outlined by the morning sun, then unceremoniously grabbed her arm and pulled her into his tent and out of sight.

"I wanted to see this city, and the parade, Daddy." Pipa smiled wearily. Dust from the long ride covered her face and clothes. "An emperor doesn't celebrate his tenth anniversary every day!"

"The agreement we made with Gallienus was that you would never to come to Rome!" Attalus struggled to keep his voice lowered. "If you're discovered, it could jeopardize our treaty as well as your marriage."

"I won't be obvious," Pipa assured her father, "and you can deny that I was ever here. Besides, Gallienus won't divorce me."

Attalus snorted. "You're that confident of your power over him?"

"Yes. He won't dissolve the treaty he has with you. It's too important to him. And I don't want to see Gallienus embarrassed any more than you do. Coming here now was an opportunity I couldn't pass up."

"How did you get here?" Attalus asked, dropping the question of 'why,' doubting he could get a straight answer from her.

"Gallienus wanted to send me back to our settlement when we reached Poetovio," she said. "After he left, I dismissed the Roman escort. Then, my warriors and I disguised ourselves as a band of merchants and followed Gallienus to Rome."

"How did you find me?"

Pipa grinned. "I asked people where the barbarians were camped." She paused and looked around. "I could use something to eat, and a bath."

"A bath!" Attalus laughed. "Aren't you the Roman lady now?" He watched, as she ripped a piece of bread off a half-eaten loaf from last night's dinner, and washed it down with some of his beer. *She never dared drink from my horn before*, he thought, amused at her brazenness. "What about the disturbance in Byzantium?" he asked.

Pipa glanced up from a second piece of bread and frowned. "A trifling event. Nothing that should have required a general's presence, let alone the emperor's." She drank more beer. "What about the revolt in Egypt?"

"Nothing, yet."

Pipa wondered if that was significant or not, then returned to her father's drinking horn. "And Postumus?" she asked, wiping her lips with the back of her hand.

"Busy fighting the Franks." Attalus grabbed a piece of meat from his disappearing meal, then reached across the table for his drinking horn and drank from it himself.

"Any further earthquakes in the west?" Pipa asked, pulling his drinking horn back to her and smiling at her father.

"Loki has been quiet." Attalus frowned, thinking. "I'll have to disguise you somehow," he said finally. "The triumphal parade is five days from now. I don't want you recognized when you march with me!"

"Humph!" Pipa snorted, shaking her head. "I've been marching for two months. I want to watch the spectacle. And I don't want to be stuck on some street fighting for a view with the rest of the crowd. Get Gallienus to give you seats for a delegation to watch the event. There must be some place important where people go to watch this sort of thing."

"You will be discreet," Attalus pleaded with his daughter, suspecting it was a futile request. "That's where Salonina will be sitting—and there'll be others with her who know you too."

Rome
15 September, 262

"Soldiers of the Empire," Gallienus addressed his legionnaires on the Campus Martius just outside the city, "for the last ten years you've managed to put down your wine and stop chasing prostitutes long enough to defend Rome's borders." He paused and smiled at the soldiers' cheers. "You defended Rome's borders against foreign invaders and have overcome traitors who've attempted to overthrow the order. Every man has done his part valiantly. My gift to you this morning is to give a short speech and send you off to your breakfast. After our triumphant march through the city today, you'll be given a victory feast. Tonight, I expect most of you will disappear into the city to spend your newfound wealth on more cheap wine and loose women. Soldiers of the Empire: I salute you!"

The soldiers dismissed, Gallienus and Marinianus ate a quick meal of pork, grapes, and cheese, then dressed in triumphal white linen togas, and made sacrifices of incense to Jupiter, before starting their day of triumphal celebration.

* * *

"When will they come?" Salonina asked, turning away from the feats of street entertainers in front of her to look at her father, Saecularis. They were waiting for Gallienus' triumphal procession to enter the Circus Maximus, along with two hundred thousand other eager spectators. All Triumphal parades began, Salonina knew, with the emperor entering the city through the Triumphal Gate. It would then wind along city streets, passing through various theatres along the way, to provide a better view of the spectacle to the crowds. After entering the Forum, the procession would stop on the Capitoline Hill, at the Temple of Jupiter Optimus Maximus. Leaders of the defeated armies would then be executed, before the emperor entered the temple to present his laurels to the god and offer sacrificial animals in Jupiter's honor.

Shadows from upper levels of the Circus had nearly all receded, and morning chills had long since vanished. Nummius Faustianus, the junior consul of the year and Nummius Ceionius Albinus, prefect of Rome, sat beside Salonina and Saecularis.

"The people will tell us," Saecularis answered Salonina's question, although there was already quite a commotion throughout the stands. The pantomimes' lewd and suggestive gestures drew cheers and howls of laughter from the multitudes, while actors and jugglers received shouts of approval and applause for their feats and skills. Salonina glanced around, studying the crowd. Magistrates sat with their wives to her left, while a number of Senators and their wives sat on her right. She recognized most of them. A few looked back at her and smiled or waved acknowledgment. A flash of anger surged through Salonina's body when she recognized Prisca. *Why did she have to be here?* Salonina wondered as she studied Prisca's appearance. *She still looks beautiful*, Salonina noted, much to her disappointment. Their eyes met and Salonina forced a smile to her face before twisting in her seat to look at the crowd behind her.

Spaces had been reserved for provincial dignitaries, even for some foreigners who wished to attend this event. Up and to one side, she noticed a group of about twenty Marcomanni men and women. By now she was quite familiar with their manner of dress. *Why aren't they marching with Attalus*, she wondered, studying the group suspiciously. *Of course! The women wouldn't march along with the soldiers. But why are any Marcomanni women here at all?* Although the group was too far away to identify anyone clearly, one of the young women looked vaguely familiar. With a hood covering her hair and shading her face, it was impossible to be sure, but the way she tilted her head and stood with her hands on her hips were traits she remembered from the few times she had actually seen Pipa. *Gallienus promised me she'd never come to Rome*! Salonina fumed, assuming that the woman actually was Pipa. To distract herself from thoughts of Prisca and Pipa, she turned to Faustianus. "Congratulations on your efforts to outfit Theodotus' amphibious operation," she said, forcing herself to speak in a conversational tone. News had just reached Rome of Theodotus' victory in Aegyptus, somewhere near Thebes.

"You're most kind," Faustianus replied, smiling at Salonina's recognition. "I expect your husband will make Theodotus the next governor of the province." The rest of his remarks were drowned by blaring trumpets as soldiers marched through the gates where chariots customarily burst into the Circus. A collective roar from the crowd then overwhelmed even the trumpets. Behind them, women, carrying torches and dressed in white flowing robes, walked beside ox-drawn wagons filled with more acrobats, jugglers, and boxers. Many of these performers spilled out to entertain some part of the crowd before dashing back to rejoin their wagons.

"I'm so glad you weren't hurt in the earthquakes!" Salonina patted her father's arm and leaned her head against his shoulder. "And Rome seems to have escaped without great damage."

"The gods smiled on both the city and on me," he replied, squeezing her hand affectionately. "Gallienus was wise to send help to the less fortunate regions."

"My idea," Salonina said, smiling. "By the way, what do you think of my new pendant?" she asked, proudly showing the large blue stone hanging at the end of a long gold chain. "I bought it in the market yesterday from a Syrian merchant who gave me a very good price on it!"

Saecularis frowned. "I can see why," he said, taking the stone in his fingers and examining it carefully. "I think it's glass, not a real gem." Saecularis allowed the bauble to fall back onto Salonina's chest. "Perhaps Gallienus can bring the man to justice for you," he suggested when he saw Salonina's pained expression. "Could you recognize him, if you saw him again?"

A deep roar resonated through the Circus, quieting the entire arena. Ten lions padded into the Circus, each led by enormous black men. Bears followed. The crowd gasped when one of the trainers stopped in front of Salonina's seat and coaxed his bear onto its hind legs. The bear's head appeared directly in front of Salonina, who shrank back involuntarily. She recovered quickly, however, and, leaning forward, patted the bear on the head before the trainer tugged at the bear's collar, pulling him down and away. The crowd had laughed at her initial reaction, then cheered her courage.

Cheetahs, wolves, zebras, wildebeests, and antelopes entered after the carnivores. Another shout of approval came from the crowd as giraffes emerged through the gates, their long necks lowered to allow them entry. The giraffes, too, stopped when they reached Salonina's seat. Their heads towered over Salonina and her entourage, as they eyed the crowd curiously. One of them leaned down and snatched a mouthful of food from the hand of a Senator's wife. The crowd laughed and cheered while the embarrassed trainer pulled his giraffe away quickly. Camels followed led by men in long flowing desert robes who did not stop anywhere, avoiding any opportunity for a camel to spit on one of the dignitaries. Ten African women dressed in gaily colored native dress trailed behind the camels, each wearing a large boa constrictor draped around her neck. Huge tigers, led by tall men in Indian garments including turbans, ended the animal procession. The gladiatorial procession followed.

Fifty women in golden cloaks marched into the Circus carrying weapons representative of the types to be used by the gladiators during succeeding days' games—spears, daggers, tridents, nets, and swords—both straight, and shaped like scimitars. More women entered carrying shields—some small and round, others large and rectangular, requiring two women to support them. They held the weapons high above their heads, or waved them at the crowd.

"Wise not to arm the gladiators," Albinus muttered, over the cheering crowd.

"There are twelve hundred of them," Faustianus said, waving a hand at the expanse of gladiators streaming into the arena, elaborately dressed in gold-embroidered women's clothes.

"Not the sort of group you'd want running around the city waving swords at the populace," Saecularis murmured, "Especially dressed like that!"

"One of Gallienus' pranks I suppose," Albinus speculated, to no one in particular.

Although gladiators were considered one of the lowest social orders, they were widely admired for their bravery by both men and women. Many wives of high social standing had had affairs with gladiators, as graffiti on their barracks' walls proudly proclaimed. The gladiators walked with a confident swagger, smiling broadly, waving enthusiastically in acknowledgment of the crowd's adoration.

"Here come the elephants," Salonina exclaimed, as the last gladiators passed her and these large beasts lumbered methodically across the arena in single file. Each elephant sounded a trumpet call as it passed near Salonina's seat, startling white sacrificial lambs that trotted nervously beside the elephants.

After white oxen plodded through both side gates, captured warriors trudged sullenly through the large central gate. "A pity Gallienus didn't capture any kings," Albinus said impulsively. He immediately regretted the comment as the thought of Valerian being paraded through some Persian city hung in the air.

"Tell me who the captured warriors are," Salonina said to her father, changing the subject of their discussion.

"The tall ones with light skin, blond hair, and long beards, are Goths," Saecularis answered, pointing. "You can't tell from here, but most of them have blue eyes, although some are actually closer to green."

Salonina watched the huge men pass by her seat. They were bound, and escorted by armed legionnaires. Most wore short tunics and ankle-length trousers tied at the waist with a belt that would normally carry swords, daggers, and axes. The ones with more colorful clothing must have been wealthier men, Salonina thought. "Weren't they the ones who killed Decius and destroyed his army?"

"Probably not these Goths. But yes. That was almost twelve years ago, and in Pannonia. And these must be Alamanni," he nodded at the men behind the Goths. "They look more like the

Celts than either the Goths or the Franks."

Salonina studied the men being pushed forward: they were shorter than the Goths, with darker hair, beards, and darker complexions. Their long hair was gathered into knots on the top or side of their heads. Their arms and legs bore tattoos of wild animals, and they wore earrings and necklaces. She could see arm bracelets on many of the men because of their short-sleeved tunics. "Did you capture any of these men when they tried to take Rome?"

Saecularis shook his head. "I think most of these men were captured in the battle at Mediolanum. There are only about two hundred here, but we captured many more than that, as I recall."

"The rest must have been sold as slaves," Salonina speculated.

"Or killed," Saecularis shrugged, "or sent to fight in gladiatorial games."

"What does the knotted hair signify?" Salonina asked.

"Only free men in their society can wear the knotted hair. Now these men," he pointed to the group of captives following the Alamanni, "are Sarmatians, nomadic tribes that migrated from somewhere northeast of Rome's frontier."

They were about the same height as their Roman guards, Salonina noted, but thinner, and with long dark hair and full beards. Their trousers and kaftans were of loose-fitting cloth. Some wore pointed felt hats that drooped forward on their heads. Others wore a sort of scale armor that draped over their shoulders and down to their knees.

"The scales of their armor," Saecularis remarked, "are made by splitting their horses' hooves, then sewing the pieces onto an undergarment with sinews from their horses or oxen. It's light and very effective against swords and spears. They're horsemen, of course, and they even cover their horses in the same sort of protective armor."

"What does the red color signify?"

"It's worn by their military aristocracy, just as our generals wear a red cape." They watched the men shuffle past. "Gallienus defeated them once around Verona and then again near the

Danuvius River."

"Aren't those women with them?"

"Yes," Saecularis agreed. "Both their men and women are warriors."

While the remaining Sarmatians marched past, Salonina tried to imagine what life as a nomad might be like, especially when women were expected to fight alongside men. It was so contrary to everything she'd known and experienced that she soon abandoned the exercise. Besides, the Persian captives were now coming into the Circus. They were tall and thin with dark complexions, dark curly hair, and full beards. Some wore helmets and full suits of armor with leather belts. Even their boots had protection.

"Their armor is made of metal, not animal hooves, you can be sure," Saecularis commented on the Persians' head-to-toe chain mail. "The ones with only leather kaftans and trousers are archers. They're usually lesser nobles or commoners. They don't have enough money to equip themselves or their horses well enough to be part of the heavy cavalry."

Salonina found herself thinking of Valerian fighting against warriors such as these. *Is he still alive*, she wondered sadly. "How did we get them?" she asked her father about the captives.

"From Odenathus." Saecularis answered. "He even sent several of the nobles that he captured when he fought with Shapur, actually not too far from where Valerian fought with Shapur himself."

"What are *they* up to?" Salonina asked. About six people had emerged from between the white oxen as the Persians prisoners approached, and were making a show of examining each of the Persians carefully. "Mimes?" Salonina suggested. After each elaborate examination, they'd look to the crowd, point to the person and shrug, feigning amazement and wonder with open mouths. Then they'd move on to another man and repeat the process.

"Find out what they're doing," the Consul, Faustianus, growled to a nearby legionary. The man saluted and hurried off, returning a short time later, short of breath, but with an answer.

"They say they are looking for the emperor's father," the

soldier reported.

Faustianus' expression darkened; he leaned over and spoke to the soldier, but his voice was drowned out by a roar from the crowd around him. Gallienus had entered the arena!

Four white horses pulled a chariot decorated with gold and ivory. Gallienus, wearing a toga embroidered with stars and his head wreathed with a laurel crown, stood on the right side of the chariot waving an ivory scepter at the crowd. The charioteer on his left had been personally selected by the emperor for this honor because of his bravery in battle. Gallienus' son, Marinianus, rode beside him on a white horse, in ceremonial armor with a crimson cape draped over his shoulders. Five hundred soldiers behind his chariot carried gilded spears and a hundred others carried banners that fluttered in a light breeze.

"Aren't they magnificent!" Salonina enthused.

"They are indeed," Saecularis answered proudly. After a moment he added, "I'm surprised that Marinianus is wearing a general's cape. Isn't Gallienus going to make him a Caesar as he did for Valerian and Saloninus?"

Salonina shook her head. "The idea for that was more Valerian's."

It would be a logical thing to do, Saecularis thought. *Perhaps Salonina is resisting the appointment after what happened to Valerian and Saloninus.* He shrugged and decided not to pursue that topic further.

Senators marched behind Gallienus' soldiers dressed in white togas with purple borders. There were priests, too, carrying statues from their temples.

"If you want to be at the Capitol to watch the sacrifices and the execution of prisoners, you should go now," Salonina suggested to her father.

Saecularis shook his head. "Gallienus will do fine without me."

Legionnaires, dressed in white and separated into distinct detachments, marched behind the priests and Senators. Each group was led by a man carrying an eagle pendant that indicated which legion his legionnaires represented. They were loudly singing ribald songs about Gallienus. This was customary during triumphs, but Salonina, despite her attempts to remain impassive, winced as the soldiers approached her and the lyrics became audible:

> He leads his men to victory, by using foot and cavalry. Then when he's not opposing foes, to prostitutes and bars he goes. To drink and joke with every kind of person there that he might find. So Senators your wives take care, or else their favors he'll ensnare. With kings he walks, with maids he lies, his treaties even gain him wives. He dyes his hair to make it gold; his younger wife will make him old.

Salonina turned and looked sadly at her father as the legions marched past them. At first he thought she was trying to ignore the soldiers' songs, but when she spoke to him, in a tone so low that only he could hear, he realized that she had something else on her mind. "Did you know that in the last hundred years only four other emperors celebrated a tenth anniversary?"

He thought for a moment. "That sounds about right."

"It is right," Salonina asserted. "I had Philip research the matter."

"Four plus Gallienus, that accounts for half of the century."

"And of those four," Salonina interrupted him, "three of them were later murdered, not one of them lived long enough to celebrate twenty years! What can we do to prevent that from happening to us?"

Saecularis wanted to put an arm around Salonina's shoulder. He knew of Rome's history of violent successions, and was acutely aware that the victor frequently killed all his predecessor's close associates. He'd considered the matter himself more than once. "I don't see what more Gallienus could be doing," he said finally. He looked at her with great fondness. "Believe me, I wish I had a better answer for you."

So do I, Salonina thought, holding his hand more tightly. *So do I.*

The crowd's excitement diminished markedly after the emperor and his entourage passed through the Circus Maximus, yet there was still enthusiasm for the legionnaires. Many of the spectators had served in one or more of the represented legions. Some had sons or husbands still under arms, but few had any direct connection with the auxiliary soldiers, who followed the legionnaires. These men came from Rome's client states and allies. Some were even mercenaries recruited from Rome's enemies. All but the mercenaries were promised Roman citizenship after twenty-five years of service, and their sons frequently joined regular legions. As excitement passed, many spectators suddenly realized they were hungry and began leaving the Circus, in search of one of the concession stands below the seating or just outside the arena, despite the fact that there was to be a public feast that night provided by the emperor. Even nearby prostitutes began recruiting a brisk business.

During this lull, Attalus majestically entered the arena astride a black stallion. He rode alone for perhaps twenty paces, far enough to attract the crowd's attention by his singular appearance. He was too far from the stands for the people to notice his fierce blue eyes and sunburned face, but they were struck by his size, his blond beard, and the long blond hair, which protruded below his helmet. Sun glinted off his polished breastplate, the reflection running randomly across the crowd as he slowly rode forward again. Unlike many of the participants today, he was fully armed. A sword belt buckled across his short-sleeved tunic. He carried a round wooden shield with a shiny metal boss in his left hand, along with his horse's reins. Spears protruded from their sheath on his right side. In his right hand he held a mighty war axe that he waved at the crowd.

Then, Attalus stopped. He returned his axe to its place on the right side of his belt, drew his sword, and pointed it high in the air. A roar erupted behind him. Marcomanni warriors burst through all three gates uttering fierce war cries. They galloped toward Attalus, who had urged his mount forward into a canter. When Attalus reached the area where Salonina sat, he drew his column to a stop, and waved a hand to silence his warriors. He turned his horse to his left and saluted the dignitary stand. Suddenly there was a cry from high in the stands. The voice rang clear and loud yelling to the Marcomanni warriors in a language unfamiliar to the Romans.

Attalus recognized her voice. *She promised to be discreet*, he thought ruefully. At first he looked uncomfortable, but then he broke into a broad grin. *That's my daughter. Her greeting deserves an answer!* He waved his sword enthusiastically in her direction. Without warning, he wheeled his mount to the right and spurred it forward. The Marcomanni warriors galloped after him, exiting the Circus in a cloud of dust.

Salonina sat with her lips compressed into a thin line and her brow furrowed. She turned again, to where the Marcomanni maiden had shouted her greeting to Attalus, as if for confirmation of her suspicions. But the whole group was standing and they were beginning to leave the Circus. *He promised me she'd never come to Rome!* Salonina thought furiously.

When the triumphal procession reached the foot of the Capitoline, important captives would normally be led away for execution. The lesser prisoners could be sold as slaves or later put into the arena to fight as gladiators. Sometimes they were even granted Roman citizenship. Today, Gallienus had chosen to spare the Persian royalty. The enemy captured at Mediolanum and most of the Persians were destined to fight in the gladiatorial ring.

Gallienus then entered the Temple of Jupiter, where he placed his triumphal wreath on the statue of Jupiter Optimus Maximus and offered thanks for his victories and ten years as emperor. Animals were then sacrificed to the god, and other offerings were also made to Jupiter. Later in the day, feasts were held, one for the Senators on the Capitoline Hill, another in the city for the people and the soldiers. When his feasting was done, Gallienus was given a musical escort back to his home, where Salonina waited—with questions she wished to ask him.

6-2

The Last Fight

Rome, Coliseum
17 September, 262

"Why did you include them at this event?" Salonina asked, over blaring trumpets announcing their arrival, as she and Gallienus entered the Coliseum and began to descend the steps toward the emperor's box. The crowd erupted into a collective roar of approval. Gallienus was the sponsor of the games and his arrival was the signal that the afternoon's entertainment would soon begin.

"I know we've been entertaining dignitaries for days," Gallienus replied. "Maximus and Prisca are still powerful allies and I felt it was important to share an afternoon with friends of the family to keep them on our side."

Prisca was much more than a 'friend of the family!' Salonina fumed inwardly. She held Gallienus in a proprietary way as the two of them moved toward their places, where Maximus and Prisca were already seated.

"I don't think we've seen them since…" Gallienus paused and wrinkled his brow. *The last time I saw them was when I returned Prisca to Maximus, but when did Salonina last see them?.*

"Since when?" Salonina asked, watching Gallienus' expression closely. I remember the last time I saw them, she frowned. *Dinner together in Aquileia where I learned that Gallienus had allowed Prisca to occupy my place.*

"I don't think we've all been together since… well… sometime before Prisca was captured by the Juthungi invaders," Gallienus mused, regaining his composure.

Gallienus and Salonina moved toward their elaborate seats at the front of the imperial box. Once they were seated, ceremonies that opened the afternoon events could begin. Salonina took her seat to Gallienus' right, her father was behind her right shoulder, Maximus sat next to Saecularis, and Prisca was to Maximus' left, behind Gallienus' left shoulder. Salonina settled herself and greeted her father. She felt the warmth of the early afternoon sun beating down on her, despite a protective awning that shielded the imperial seats. She prayed to the wind gods for a gentle breeze and wondered how long it would be until the sun dipped below the opposite side of the Colosseum. "It's going to be a hot afternoon," she said to her father.

Saecularis nodded agreement then asked, "Where's Marinianus? I thought he'd be with you."

"He and Quintianus are doing something together," Maximus interjected.

Hearing the name, Salonina remembered that Quintianus was a tribune on Gallienus' staff. *And he's Prisca's son! She probably knows everything that's going on with Gallienus.*

While Maximus engaged himself in discussion with Salonina, Gallienus looked behind at Prisca. Her dark eyes sparkled mischievously, seemingly acknowledging some shared secret and, as she moved her head, her golden earrings danced.

"We haven't seen each other in two-and-a-half years." A fleeting sadness showed in her eyes. He gazed at her appreciatively and remembered the feel of her red hair in his hand. She flashed him a dazzling smile and leaned forward. "You know we haven't seen you in over two years."

Her eyes and smile reminded him of pleasant times they'd spent together before he had encountered Pipa. "It's nice to see you again," she continued her voice quietly enthusiastic. Her eyes held his gaze expectantly. When he just smiled and looked at her she added, "I'm thrilled to be in Rome again with all the excitement and activity!"

"We've seen precious little of Rome ourselves," Salonina interjected, frowning at Gallienus' back, then turning to face Prisca directly, "with all the turmoil on the borders." *Prisca never seems to age*! Salonina thought irritably when Prisca smiled politely at her. *And she's as trim as she was the last time I saw her. Here she is again, and I thought she wasn't an issue anymore. Clearly I was mistaken about that*!

"I think there's always excitement wherever the emperor goes," Prisca said, turning her eyes back to Gallienus. Prisca fingered her right earring casually, then ran her hand slowly across her neck and down the center of her dress, pausing to toy with the emerald pendant, a gift from Gallienus, that hung between her breasts. When his eyes followed her hand, Prisca knew she still was able to attract him. She gazed about the stadium, drinking in the feelings of that power. *I've missed this! she realized*, intoxicated again by being at the center of the empire and so close to the man who ruled it.

Salonina studied Prisca's flushed face. She recognized that Prisca was trying to entice Gallienus, and with disquieting success. She realized suddenly, *she's in love with the power and the influence. She had a taste of that when she was alone with Gallienus along the northern border, and may have convinced herself that she loves Gallienus. But he's really the means to her ends.* An official, looking up expectantly at them from the arena, drew Salonina's attention away from her thoughts. "The game," she said urgently to Gallienus, whose back was to the arena. He turned to face the waiting authorities and casually waved a hand in their direction. Then he turned back to address Maximus and Prisca.

"You weren't here this morning for the animal hunts," Gallienus chuckled. "A huntsman tried to show us his skills as an archer by killing a bull."

"Not a particularly difficult feat for a competent marksman," Maximus commented.

"Exactly!" Gallienus agreed. "But he missed the bull ten times in a row!"

"Then what did he do?" Prisca asked, leaning forward slightly, so that Gallienus shifted his gaze to her. She imagined what it would be like to be close to him again.

"He gave up."

"He must have run out of arrows," Prisca speculated, before Maximus could comment.

"An excellent observation!" Gallienus paused. "As you suggested, he only had ten arrows with him. I sent him a wreath and had a herald announce to the crowd, 'It takes great skill to miss a bull so many times.'"

Maximus smiled. "Perhaps the award will inspire him to improve his marksmanship."

"Or maybe he'll bring more arrows next time," Prisca

suggested with a melodious laugh.

"I never attend the noontime execution of prisoners," Gallienus continued, "so I had the next event delayed until the start of the afternoon activities. That fellow there," he turned back to the arena and pointed to a man being bound to a stake, "cheated Salonina in the market."

"He cheated you?" Prisca exclaimed, looking at Salonina in amazement. "Didn't he know who you were?"

"Apparently not," Maximus observed.

"He'd just come to Rome from somewhere in the east," Salonina explained.

"So you're going to expose him to a wild beast," Prisca mused, looking at the large cage being wheeled into the arena and placed in front of the bound man. "That should put an end to his cheating in the marketplace."

"A lion," Maximus guessed, "from the size of that cage."

Gallienus nodded. "That's what the merchant was told to expect." He leaned forward and waved a hand signaling an official to proceed. A hush hung over the expectant crowd. Slowly the cage door swung open. At first there was no sign of activity from within. Finally, a rooster strutted out of the cage. The bird stopped at the entrance, blinked at the crowd, then casually began scratching the sand in front of him for signs of food. Salonina stared, open-mouthed, at Gallienus, who seemed quite pleased with the outcome.

A herald entered the arena and loudly proclaimed, "He practiced deceit and has now suffered it!" The crowd roared with laughter.

"You're letting him go free?" Salonina exclaimed. "What about him cheating me?"

"Do you want me to have him killed?"

"No, but now everyone will think they can cheat the empress without consequence."

"He won't last long in the market, now that everyone knows he's dishonest," Prisca suggested to console Salonina, imagining how she'd feel in the same situation. Salonina turned from Prisca and looked into her lap, fighting the tears that threatened to come. It was Gallienus' understanding she wanted, not Prisca's.

Blaring trumpets announced the gladiators' arrival. Wild cheering erupted from the crowd, especially when one of their favorites entered the arena. *I'll find some way of dealing with that cheating merchant myself,* Salonina decided. The thought enabled her to put aside her disappointment, for the time being.

The gladiator procession marched two-abreast around the Coliseum's inner perimeter before forming two lines that faced Gallienus' side of the arena. The crowd grew quiet as the inspection of weapons began. The gladiators laid their weapons on the ground in front of them while the host of the games inspected them all for authenticity. Today Gallienus had bestowed this honor on Volusianus, his Praetorian Prefect, who now paced slowly through their ranks, stopping occasionally to tug on a man's armor strap, pick up a sword and inspect its blade, or to share a joke or comment with a man here and there. When he was satisfied that all was in order, Volusianus turned to a referee and nodded. The man brought forth a large brass bowl and the gladiators took turns drawing lots from it to determine their opponents. Meanwhile, the waiting gladiators performed warm-up exercises, practiced their attack maneuvers, or performed tricks with their weapons and shields to amuse the crowds and distract themselves. To add to the excitement and deliberately build tension, musicians played trumpets, curved horns, and a water organ.

Prisca admired Gallienus' profile while he surveyed the activities in the arena. *Even though Maximus is content to be at Arretium, maybe I could convince Gallienus to give Maximus another assignment, perhaps a second Consulship.* Prisca smiled at the thought. *That would bring us back to Rome, closer to Gallienus.*

Once the pairing of the combatants and their order had been determined, Volusianus turned and strode purposefully off the arena floor toward his seat. The crowd cheered: the games were about to begin. When all but the first two combatants had left the ring, trumpets blared. "Advance," shouted the referee to the two armed men.

"This match is between Lucanius, the Thracian, and a fellow named Rubrius," Saecularis said, intruding on the long silence that had followed the merchant's release. He'd already made a note to speak with the city prefect and suggest that Albinus revoke the merchant's license. He consulted his copy of the program that had been circulated before the game. It listed featured gladiators and included their records in the arena. "Ah yes, here it is," he continued. "We've all seen Lucanius fight over the years, but this Rubrius fellow is new to Rome. He fights as a Hoplomachus. The program says he's from Numidia, so he'll be accustomed to the heat of the arena. And he's got an impressive record of victories," Saecularis concluded. Before turning his attention to the arena, he summoned a runner to place a bet on the Thracian gladiator, despite the fact that the men with the small shields generally lost their contests.

The terms "Thracian" and "Hoplomachus" referred to two different classes of gladiators. They wore different types of armor and used different types of weapons. Key parts of each fighter's body were protected against minor wounds that would hinder his use of the weapons particular to his class. The crowd's interest was equally divided between the two men facing each other and how each fought against an opponent with different strengths and weaknesses. Both men wore loin cloths and broad-brimmed metal helmets with visors that completely covered their heads and faces. The helmets provided protection but were hot and restricted the wearer's field of view. The Thracian swaggered to the center of the ring. He was the larger of the two men. He had a small round shield, and metal scales that covered the sleeve of his left hand. Both his legs were protected by metal greaves. A belt attached around his waist supported his loin cloth, and the Thracian's short, curved sword was already drawn and held loosely at his side. He had the advantage of years of fighting in this arena, and expected the Hoplomachus to start cautiously. His slow advance seemed to confirm the Thracian's assessment. The Hoplomachus held his large rectangular shield close to his body, leaving only his head and sandaled feet visible while he moved forward. His gladius, the short straight sword used by the legionaries, was still in the belt at his waist, and he grasped a spear in his right hand. Beside his shield he had a metal greave on his left leg and leather bands wrapped around his right hand, right wrist, and right ankle. As the Hoplomachus moved forward, he studied the Thracian closely, looking for an opportunity to attack.

Slow music from the water organ mimicked the Hoplomachus' deliberate movements. Occasional shouts from the crowd urged one or the other to action. The Thracian raised both hands urging the crowd to respond more vociferously. The spear was arcing toward the Thracian before most of the spectators realized it had been thrown. In a sweeping movement the Hoplomachus drew his sword and rushed at his opponent hoping to capitalize on a moment of confusion. Belatedly, the water organ changed from its methodical pace to a more urgent beat, punctuated by the blare of the horns. The arena erupted with a collective roar.

Surprised and off balance, the Thracian took a step back, turned to his right side, and leaned away, desperately trying to avoid the spear. A strike to his body would be fatal, but if the spear lodged in his small round shield, even that would be worthless to him: he would be defenseless. He held his shield up at an angle hoping to deflect the spear with it. But the Hoplomachus had thrown his spear very slightly to the right of the Thracian, forcing him to cross its path in order to deflect it with his shield. The spear grazed his left upper arm as it passed between the shield and his head. He glanced at the wound for an instant before returning his attention to the charging Hoplomachus. He darted across the path of the Hoplomachus, dodging the man's gladius thrust, then pivoted counterclockwise trying to slash behind the Hoplomachus' large shield. The quick, unexpected move was partially successful and the Thracian drew blood from the other man's left side. Both men then stood their ground facing the other warily, as they each composed themselves for their next moves.

Volusianus returned to his seat. "What have I missed?" he asked eagerly.

"The Hoplomachus tried to end the contest with his opening attack," Prisca replied. The others were watching the early sparring with sudden interest. "He's making the Thracian take him more seriously. But he might have done better to keep the Thracian guessing."

She thinks like a legionary, Gallienus thought on overhearing Prisca's assessment.

The contest in the arena returned to cautious sparring. The Hoplomachus seemed content to wait for the Thracian to make the next move. Bored by the inactivity, Gallienus turned to face Maximus.

"What are the Senators saying these days?" he asked. "I doubt that I can get an objective answer from any of them, even the ones who support me."

"After the revolt in Aegyptus was suppressed, most of their discussions have been about Postumus' breaking away—how and when you'll subdue him. Some even mention Postumus' ability as a general and quietly wonder if he's planning to march on Rome himself," Maximus replied carefully, choosing not to mention comments he'd heard about Valerian and his continuing captivity.

"He won't do that for several reasons," Prisca interposed, shaking her head. "He has the Franks threatening his borders, so he can't take his army away from the frontier—he'd lose the people's support when barbarians destroyed their cities and towns. Besides, he has no blood relative to succeed him, so he's not going to risk a march on Rome without support at home that he can trust. His attention will be on the northern borders until you're ready to confront him again." She could tell by Gallienus' approving look that he agreed with her appraisal. A smile crept onto her face. "You looked superb on your triumphal chariot," she said to him.

"Thank you, I know."

"I was surprised not to see any Juthungi prisoners," Prisca continued. "Wouldn't it have been wonderful to parade their chieftain as your captive?"

Gallienus nodded, but didn't reply. Although his face registered no emotion, he regretted not having any prisoners of high rank, despite all the battles he'd won.

I hope he doesn't think I'm diminishing his achievements in any way, Prisca thought anxiously. She leaned forward and spoke to him in a lower tone. "I have fond memories of the time we spent together after your victory at Augusta Vindelicum." Her dark eyes regarded him suggestively. "Life in Arretium is a bit dull by comparison."

What are they talking about? Salonina wondered, looking uncomfortably at Prisca, whose face was far too close to Gallienus. A sudden shout from the crowd caused them all to turn their attention back to the arena.

The Thracian had rushed directly at the Hoplomachus, who'd braced himself and held his ground. At the last moment, the Thracian had shifted to his right, again trying to get around the large shield. But the Hoplomachus had anticipated the move and shifted to his left, directly into the path of the Thracian. The unexpected impact caused the Thracian to fall to the ground. But he rolled away from the Hoplomachus who had been knocked in the opposite direction by the larger man's weight. The Thracian was upright and on one knee before the Hoplomachus could charge. Dirt mixed with the sweat and blood on his left arm, but the Thracian's sword and shield were ready to meet the Hoplomachus' advance. And seeing that the Thracian had recovered from his fall, the Hoplomachus chose to pace himself and wait for another opportunity. Gladiators learned from experience to avoid unnecessary exertions. Sweat inside their helmets affected their vision and, over time, fatigue slowed their reactions.

Gallienus watched the contest for a few more thrusts and parries.

"There were some men poking around in the ranks of the Persian captives during the triumph," Maximus said to Gallienus, when the gladiators had returned to their sparring. "I didn't understand what that was about."

"They said they were looking for the emperor's father," Gallienus said tersely. His expression darkened. "I had them arrested."

"I see," Maximus said. The offenders would be tried before the urban prefect and undoubtedly convicted, he realized. For the lower classes, death for a capital offense could be burning, crucifixion, or exposure to the wild beasts. If they counted on Gallienus' reputation for tolerance, they were seriously mistaken, Maximus mused. *I doubt Gallienus will use a rooster on them*!

Salonina heard Gallienus' response and turned to look at him. All that was visible was his back, as he was still facing Maximus. Gallienus' reaction to the capture of his father greatly puzzled her. *As far as I know, he's done little or nothing to rescue Valerian, yet he acts violently against anyone who implies that he should. He seems indifferent to Valerian's fate, yet he must feel guilty about not trying to rescue him.*

Prisca understood Gallienus' sensitivity to this issue and felt more sympathetic than the others. She remembered overhearing Valerian speak of replacing Gallienus as a co-emperor six years earlier, and the warning she had sent Gallienus at great personal risk. *It's not surprising to me that he hasn't tried to rescue a father who planned to replace him*, she thought, and nodded sympathetically at Gallienus. Prisca had never mentioned the event to Maximus. She assumed Gallienus had kept the information to himself, as well. "I understand," Prisca said softly.

Gallienus' expression softened. The distasteful situation already put out of his mind. He turned to watch the fight for a few minutes.

By now the gladiators had moved to opposite sides of the arena, and the Thracian stood near the spot from which he'd originally begun the fight. Fatigue and the wound on his left arm were beginning to take their toll. He realized that his movements were becoming more and more defensive. Some of the crowd began to chant, "He's had it." Others still cheered the Thracian on. Suddenly he dropped to one knee and lowered his shield arm. The Hoplomachus rushed him immediately, sensing this was his opportunity. But as they made contact the Thracian thrust upward and lifted the Hoplomachus' shield high enough to make a slashing attack underneath it. His blade cut across both of the Hoplomachus' thighs, drawing blood immediately. Fans of the Thracian roared their approval. Action slowed as both men drew away from each other.

"Has Claudius proved himself a capable successor to Aureolus?" Prisca said quietly to Gallienus.

Salonina noticed Prisca's conversation with Gallienus out of the corner of her eye. *What is it now?* she wondered. A glance at Maximus confirmed her suspicion that he was displeased about it as well.

"Claudius has my confidence," Gallienus replied guardedly, "but he's hardly been tested, so far."

"By the way," Maximus spoke up quickly, trying to limit Prisca's exclusive dialogue with Gallienus, "I saw an attractive young woman in the Circus Maximus the other day."

"You have to be careful about all the pretty women you see in the Circus," Gallienus replied with a smile at Maximus' interruption.

"This one was watching your triumph with a group of foreigners," Maximus persisted. "They all rose and she shouted to one of the barbarian leaders in a foreign tongue. The leader looked back at them and waved. It seemed they knew each other."

Gallienus shifted in his seat as he recalled his earlier discussion on the same subject with Salonina.

"He was leading the first group of auxiliaries on horseback—an impressive looking man, for a barbarian," Maximus continued.

That was Attalus, Salonina thought, her lips compressed and her brow furrowed. *It's bad enough that I think Pipa is in Rome; I don't want anyone else to be thinking that*!

"That was Attalus," Gallienus confirmed, "the chieftain of the Marcomanni tribe, the one we formed an alliance with two summers ago."

"It must have been his wife," Maximus speculated.

"His wife died years ago."

"Obviously a daughter, then."

"He has a daughter," Gallienus agreed, "but she's not in Rome." He turned away from Maximus abruptly and gave his attention to the progress of the two gladiators.

I asked Attalus if Pipa was here, Gallienus thought as he attempted to lose himself in the gladiatorial contest. He remembered Attalus' shrug and enigmatic reply. "I came straight from Mediolanum with Aurelian. Pipa was last with you." Gallienus watched the contest for a few thrusts, feints, and parries. He sensed their fatigue and saw the gleam of sweat from their bodies and places where blood had mixed with dust from the arena. *Both men have done quite well, he thought. Very nearly matched.*

Prisca leaned close to Maximus while Gallienus' attention was elsewhere. "Of course it was Attalus' daughter," Prisca whispered, "but he doesn't want to talk about her in front of Salonina. Her name is Pipa and Gallienus 'married' her as part of the Marcomanni treaty."

Maximus' eyes widened in amazement. "How do you know about Attalus' daughter?" he whispered back.

"I know all about Pipa," Prisca whispered.

She must know who Pipa is, Salonina realized when she saw Prisca whispering to Maximus, and his look of surprise. *Quintianus obviously tells her everything. And she knows things before I do. I'll urge Gallienus to move Quintianus. He must be due for a promotion of some sort. Somehow he has to go.*

Maximus shrugged and returned his attention to the gladiators. Prisca felt she was being watched, looked up and met Salonina's cold stare. She averted her eyes and looked into her lap, suddenly jealous of Salonina's relationship with Gallienus.

What can I do to arrange a meeting with Gallienus, alone? Prisca wondered. *A chance visit when Salonina isn't around? Or is there some way to make him think inviting me is his idea? What will I say when we're alone? What do I want?*

The Hoplomachus felt his thigh muscles tightening from the wounds he'd received. Both heat and loss of blood were wearing him down, he realized. He determined to make a final rush at the Thracian, concentrating on the man's wounded shield arm. He judged the Thracian to be nearly as tired as he was. Summoning as much strength as he could, he leapt suddenly forward, thrusting his shield ahead of him aggressively. His gladius crashed repeatedly down on the Thracian's small shield, forcing him backwards. As the Thracian dodged quickly to his right, he stepped onto the spear cast by the Hoplomachus at the beginning of the fight. He slipped and fell hard onto his back. Before he could regain his feet, the Hoplomachus stood over him, his sword pointed at the Thracian's throat.

"What a bad bit of luck," Maximus exclaimed to Prisca, who had long been a fan of the Thracian. When she stared at him vacantly, Maximus realized she had no idea what was going on in the arena. Anger welled up inside him. He turned away from her and looked back at the prostrate gladiator in the arena, wondering idly if Gallienus would spare the man or not.

The Thracian cast his shield aside and raised a finger of his left hand toward the emperor, a sign of his surrender. The crowd erupted with mixed cries of "Set him free," and "Execute him." The Hoplomachus looked to the emperor for a life or death decision. Generally, the emperor sided with the will of the crowd, and they sometimes favored setting a defeated man free if he'd fought well, or if his defeat were due more to chance than to his opponent's skill. The crowd seemed equally divided.

"I can't make an objective judgment on this one," Gallienus said, shaking his head. "I've been too distracted with all our discussions. Why don't you decide, Salonina." She masked the feeling of horror that ran through her body. She'd paid scant attention to the contest either. As she stared dumbly at Gallienus, she caught a glimpse of Prisca intently watching Gallienus and the emotions of the day suddenly overwhelmed her. She'd been embarrassed in front of 50,000 people when her husband released the merchant who'd cheated her. She felt relatively certain that Pipa, the 'second wife,' was in Rome and that others knew it too. Finally, she'd been forced to watch Prisca flirt with her husband in front of everyone.

Abruptly she turned to the waiting Hoplomachus and thrust out her arm giving him a thumbs down. "Cut his throat," she cried out.

A lull in the shouting followed as the knowledge of her decision spread through the crowd. The spectators quieted, anticipating the ritual procedure about to follow. "I'm rather surprised at your decision," her father said quietly from behind her. "He did the best he could with what he had." Saecularis paused and shook his head sadly. "He was planning to retire, you know. This was to be his last fight."

"I... didn't know."

"The bulletin mentioned it at the end of his personal summary," Saecularis explained gently.

Salonina felt a sinking feeling in her stomach. *A man is about to die because I made a decision based on my emotions, and not because of anything he did or didn't do himself.*

The defeated gladiator looked toward her briefly, then he tilted his head back exposing his neck to the victor's knife. "Do it quickly," Salonina found herself whispering urgently to the executioner.

The winner received a palm branch from the emperor along with a payment of gold coins. Then, he hobbled around the perimeter waving the palm high over his head. Although there were twelve more contests to be played that afternoon, Salonina rose abruptly and left the arena.

6-3
In Hostile Lands
Colonia Agrippina, Germania Inferior
01 March, 263

On the same day Gallienus began his march from Rome to retake the rebellious provinces in the west, Postumus was considering his spring and summer strategy. If Gallienus were to attack, he would be moving through lands under Postumus' control. Thus Postumus would soon know the direction Gallienus was coming, the size of his army, and an approximately when Gallienus' army would pose a threat. But an attack by the Franks could come at any time and at almost any location along his border. So Postumus planned to neutralize the Frankish threat first, if possible.

He thought of his minor victory over Gallienus, then of his two subsequent defeats, one in which he had escaped during a thunderstorm, the second when he had escaped from Aureolus' battlefield. *The fact that I've resisted both the Franks and Gallienus this long suggests that the gods favor me,"* he said aloud before lapsing into thought again. *If I defeat Gallienus, then I could march on Rome. Spain and Britannia have already joined me. Perhaps if I left a small holding force to defend my borders, that would discourage a revolt while I was away.*

Outside Ctesiphon, Persia
17 June, 263

"You can't be serious!" Odenathus exclaimed, looking at his young wife in amazement. "He's only seven years old!"

"He's almost eight," Zenobia countered, "and he wouldn't actually do any fighting. He'd be there to see how a great king leads his army in battle."

Odenathus held up a hand. "I can't watch a child and oversee a battle at the same time! This is Shapur we're fighting. I'm not willing to accept any distraction."

"It's really quite unusual," General Zabdas added gently, siding with Odenathus. "Even you might become distracted, worrying about your son's safety."

Zenobia glared at Zabdas. "I never get distracted in battle."

"We're here to reopen the caravan routes," Odenathus interrupted brusquely. "I have to fight the Persians to do that. If the caravans stop, our kingdom will perish! I want Vaballathus to have battle experience, but he's too young now. I won't permit it!"

Zenobia recognized that Odenathus' usual good humor was exhausted and did not pursue the matter further, but she refused to acknowledge Herodian's triumphant expression as he and Zabdas rose to leave Odenathus' tent. *Then I'll place Vaballathus beside me, she decided. I do command the reserve forces, after all.* She looked at Odenathus, bent over a small table in the center of the tent as if studying his battle plan. *He probably expects an argument,* she realized. "I think I'll take a walk," she said calmly. Odenathus glanced up from his papers and nodded, a hint of relief on his face.

She stepped from the dim light of the tent into cool fresh air and lingering twilight. Stars flickered faintly in the eastern sky. *Somewhere over that horizon is Ctesiphon,* the Persians' winter capital, she thought. *And in the morning we'll face Shapur in battle*!

Last winter Shapur's son, Bahram, had provoked this confrontation by closing trade routes, and Shapur had declined to reopen them when he returned from suppressing an eastern revolt.

She wandered through the campsite, ignoring her guards trailing discreetly behind her, and nodding distractedly at the greetings soldiers offered when she passed between their campfires. She was thinking about the meeting she just left and their son's future. It wasn't the battle that caused her anxiety—she relished that opportunity. *Shapur is the adversary, but Herodian is my enemy! Despite his ineptitude, he's old enough to be king—and Vaballathus is too young. If Herodian succeeds his father, he'll kill my sons. What Herodian would do to me, I shudder to think. But I must get Vaballathus, not Herodian, to the throne. I keep hoping Herodian will do something to convince Odenathus he's unsuitable to be king... or that he dies in battle, unlikely as that is: Herodian never takes any risks.* That thought caused memories of a battle nearly three years earlier to flood over her. After she had rescued Herodian's forces from Persian counterattack, an enemy lance had knocked her to the ground, and she found herself assaulted by at least two Persians. As she lay on her back fending off sword blows, she chanced to glimpse Herodian sitting on his horse, watching her fight for her life as though she were a gladiator in the arena. *I have to stay alive, to protect my children*, she resolved, *but I can't be passive myself. That's a sure way to get killed in battle. I must convince Odenathus to appoint my son as his successor. Otherwise...terrible things will happen.*

Encampment Outside Colonia
Agrippina, Germania Inferior
15 July, 263

"What is it?" Salonina asked. She looked across the table at Gallienus, who showed no interest in his breakfast. They were alone in the emperor's campaign tent. "You seem discouraged."

"I've been laying siege to Colonia for a month now!"

Gallienus pushed the plate of cheese and bread away and looked up at Salonina. "Postumus eludes me despite my victories over him," he said, his usual exuberance notably absent.

Salonina thought about what had transpired during the last five months. Late in March, Gallienus had joined a portion of his army near Mediolanum. After crossing the mountains, he'd marched north intending to engage Postumus wherever he could force the rebellious general to battle. While Gallienus went north, the remainder of his army had marched westward from Pannonia, under the command of Heraclianus, the provincial governor. The two forces met near Treveris and together they had advanced on Postumus, who had consolidated his forces outside Colonia Agrippina. Gallienus had defeated Postumus decisively in the subsequent battle. Postumus fled, along with most of his army, into the walled city. "What else can you do?" she asked finally.

"Usually there are two choices." Gallienus shrugged. "Overwhelm the city's defenses, or starve them out. In this case I must overwhelm them. Sieges are bad for soldiers' morale, and tying the army down here leaves the rest of the empire vulnerable to attacks, or revolts. Today we'll try to breach the walls." He studied her face for a moment, as if expressing this plan of action had freed him from his concerns. "You look like you had a restless night, too," he said.

"I didn't sleep well," Salonina agreed. *Should I burden him with my dream, again?*

"The army awaits you," Volusianus announced as he entered the tent.

Salonina glanced up briefly, then looked anxiously at her husband. She wondered whether to say, "Good fortune," or "Be careful," but merely smiled and nodded as he left her. As she sat alone in the tent, silence settled around her. Routine noises of the encampment were suddenly audible: shouts from the centurions, footsteps of men marching, then, an occasional voice from the few men left to guard the campsite. The anxiety she always felt when Gallienus went off to battle swept over her. Salonina thought of her dream: wolves, again, but she could recall nothing more than that when she awoke in a sweat. She rose from the table and stepped outside to distract herself. *Maybe I'll share my dream with Gallienus when he comes back this afternoon.*

* * *

Marcianus, a promising young officer in Gallienus' body guards, burst into Gallienus' tent just after the midday meal, ignoring the usual protocol. "What is it?" Salonina gasped, alarmed by his grim expression.

"The emperor's been wounded!"

Panic surged through her body, jolting her to her feet. Her face paled, and she grasped the edge of the table for support. She refused Marcianus' offer of help and sank back into the chair she had been sitting in. She struggled to keep her emotions in check, for now, and to present an image of dignity and composure. *If his wound was fatal*, she managed to think, *someone more senior would have been sent to me… probably.* She willed her voice to sound calm. "How serious is it, Marcianus?"

"Not fatal, nor is it insignificant, I'm afraid."

"What happened?"

"He was struck by an arrow during the assault."

"That's all you can tell me?"

Marcianus shrugged. "I'm afraid so."

Infuriatingly vague! Salonina suppressed her irritation with the greatest of efforts. *But details aren't important at the moment.* "Where is he now?" she asked instead.

"He's being carried to the medicus' tent for treatment. I'll take you there."

* * *

Marcianus walked ahead of her quickly, shouting to clear a pathway through the milling confusion of legionaries. When they noticed Salonina, they immediately moved out of her way and silently watched as she passed by. It felt like a dream to her. When they reached the medicus' tent, Volusianus was standing just outside the entrance. She glanced at him without speaking, then tried to step around him to enter the tent. He held out an arm, blocking her path.

"It's best to wait here, for the moment," he said gently but firmly. "The medicus is trying to remove the arrow."

She took a deep breath and restrained her impulse to push by him. "How is he?" she finally asked, watching Volusianus' face closely to discern his true feelings.

"We won't know until the medicus has treated him."

"The emperor isn't supposed to be in the thick of battle himself! How could this have happened?"

"Normally he wouldn't have been so close," Volusianus agreed. "But he led the men during their assault. When he turned away from the city walls to rally the men behind him, his back was momentarily exposed, and unprotected. That's when the arrow struck him."

"That sounds serious!"

"The fact that he's still alive is very encouraging."

A commotion behind them interrupted their discussion. Pipa pushed her way to the front of the crowd that had formed a few feet away. She hesitated, then walked slowly but deliberately across the last few feet of open space and stopped when she stood face to face with Salonina. Pipa said nothing, but looked at Salonina's face questioningly, and Salonina saw the look of concern, mixed with fear, on Pipa's face. Although they were rivals, she felt a fleeting impulse to reach out and embrace Pipa, the only one who knew exactly how she felt herself. Instead, she chose not to acknowledge Pipa's status publicly and gave Pipa an imperceptible shrug. "We don't know yet," Salonina said. "I'll see that you're kept informed of his situation. Right now all we can do is wait."

* * *

Early the next morning Volusianus called the generals to his tent.

"You're proposing to take matters into your own hands?" Heraclianus asked, stroking his beard. The casual phrasing of his question belied the seriousness of the matter.

"Our hands," the Praetorian Prefect corrected him, looking at Claudius, Aurelian, Heraclianus, and Attalus. "We should decide the best course of action to take—until the emperor recovers."

"What does your healer say about Gallienus' condition?" Attalus asked. He sat furthest from Volusianus, his arms folded across his chest.

"An arrow wound to the lower side of the back." Volusianus rattled off details given to him earlier that morning. "We don't think it pierced a lung from the way he's breathing. There's no blood in his urine, which means the arrow missed the kidneys. A wound there or to the liver would be fatal, so we're cautiously optimistic right now."

"What about Marinianus?" Aurelian asked, returning to Heraclianus' original question. His expression and tone revealed neither his thoughts nor his opinions. "He's almost nineteen."

"The emperor's son is accustomed to taking directions from others," Volusianus replied. "That was obvious to me when he took no action yesterday, or failed to call for a meeting this morning. That's why I haven't included him in this discussion."

"So you'll just tell him?" Claudius asked.

"That as a temporary measure we're managing the affairs of state." Volusianus looked each man in the eyes, deliberately attempting to gauge their acceptance or resistance to his proposal. Whatever their opinions might have been, no one objected. He felt a sense of relief.

"What about Salonina?" Heraclianus asked.

"Her first concern will be Gallienus' health," Volusianus predicted. "Her second will be Marinianus' safety."

"In the middle of an attack on a rebellious province, I think she'll understand our reasoning." Claudius said, indicating his support for Volusianus' position.

"So, who is actually in charge now?" Attalus asked.

"We should all agree to any actions we take," Volusianus replied.

"Who will decide when there's no time for these meetings?" Attalus persisted.

"As Praetorian Prefect, that responsibility would normally fall to me," Volusianus said. "But I propose to act in concert with all of you." He paused, awaiting an objection. "If anyone has another suggestion, now would be a good time to voice it."

"That works for me," Attalus growled. "What about the siege?" he asked. "We aren't going to run away like scared rabbits just because one of us got hit by an arrow, are we?"

"That's what Gallienus would want," Claudius said, "to continue the siege, I mean—not to run like rabbits."

Aurelian nodded agreement.

"For now, it makes sense," Volusianus concurred.

"We should consider the possibility of invasions or revolts elsewhere, once news of his wound circulates," Heraclianus said. The question was intended to suggest foreign invaders or a revolt by some distant provincial governor. But each of the generals realized that any one of them, with the exception of Attalus, might try to assume power himself, should Gallienus succumb to his wounds.

"Worth considering, but later, in my opinion," Volusianus replied. "Too many uncertainties."

"What shall we tell the army?" Claudius asked.

"That Gallienus is recovering and the siege will continue."

"How do you expect the empress and her son will react to this news?" Attalus asked.

"I'll stress that it's only a temporary action—but they'll have to acquiesce," Volusianus replied.

Attalus considered Volusianus' comment, then asked, "And what about the emperor?"

"When he's able, command will be restored to him." Volusianus waited for other questions. "If we're all agreed," Volusianus concluded, "then I should inform Salonina immediately." The men all rose and silently filed out of Volusianus' tent.

Attalus walked back to the Marcomanni campsite, lost in his own thoughts. Arrow wounds to the back were serious, he knew from years of fighting experience. What would happen to our treaty, if Gallienus died? he wondered. *What would happen to Pipa? Who would try to succeed Gallienus? Marinianus? He* snorted, shaking his head dismissively. *Too young and inexperienced! One of the generals? Probably more than one would try.*

He thought of the brief civil war that brought Valerian and Gallienus to power, just over ten years earlier. *Whose side would I take*?

* * *

A few days later Salonina nearly collided with Volusianus as she stepped out of the tent where Gallienus was recovering. "Any progress with the siege, General?" she asked the Praetorian Prefect.

"Some." He returned her smile pleasantly. "The siege engines are beginning to take effect and we're digging tunnels in several places."

"No further plans to storm the wall?"

"Not until part of it is destroyed, either by the siege engines or the tunneling collapsing somewhere.

"So it's just a matter of time, then?" Salonina asked, recalling Gallienus' concern about invasions or revolts elsewhere while the army was preoccupied here.

"Yes," Volusianus nodded, "a matter of time." *As long as we can bring down a wall somewhere before the campaign season ends*, he thought, *or before dysentery breaks out in the camp*. He took a deep breath, then exhaled slowly. *Everything else depends on the emperor recovering from his wounds.* "How is your husband this morning?" he asked.

"Still very weak. The medicus said recovery would be slow, but steady."

"That's encouraging news!" *As long as he doesn't develop a fever, he should recover completely.* Images of a struggle for succession flashed through his mind, and a frown furrowed his brow. He was suddenly conscious of Salonina watching his face closely. He cleared his throat. "I'm told that you've been visiting the wounded soldiers."

Salonina's face brightened. "They seem to appreciate it."

"More than you know," Volusianus murmured.

She looked at him uncertainly.

"They've told me your visits have cheered them considerably." He paused. "If you'll excuse me, I need to speak with your husband for a few minutes."

6-4
An Unexpected Visit
Colonia Agrippina, Germania Inferior
20 July, 263

The afternoon sun still felt warm on her back when Salonina finally left the hospital tents. She felt renewed after spending time with the wounded men. They helped her forget her own worries, even if only temporarily. In turn they clearly welcomed her visits and made no requests of her when she spoke with them. Now she wandered through camp, not relishing the prospect of another afternoon alone with her thoughts and concerns. Near the emperor's tent, a large raven perched atop the flagpole that flew Gallienus' banner. Her pulse quickened. A raven accompanied Andrasta whenever they met. Salonina looked around expectantly, but saw no one familiar, aside from the soldiers standing guard outside the tent.

"We tried to scare it away," one of the guards apologized for the raven's presence. "We feared it brought a bad omen of some sort."

"But the bird keeps coming back," a second guard added. "It first came right after a slave girl asked for an audience with you. We said you'd return later, and she left."

"What did she look like?" Salonina asked, trying to keep the urgency from her voice.

"Blond hair and blue eyes," one of the guards said. "A very attractive girl, although her clothes were rather shabby."

"And a bit taller than you," the second added.

"Did she say anything?"

"Nothing." The guard shook his head. "We thought it strange to see an unfamiliar slave-girl in the camp."

"When she returns," Salonina said feeling hopeful, "bring

her to me at once." She glanced up at the flagpole and gasped. The raven was gone. Salonina entered the tent, and began pacing back and forth expectantly. The raven must belong to Andrasta. But she was shorter than me, with red hair and green eyes. It's unlikely the guards would confuse those details, Salonina thought dejectedly. Clearly it's not Andrasta. Who else could it be?

The wait seemed interminable to her, but Salonina's visitor arrived within the hour. When the guards ushered the girl into her presence, disappointment clouded her face—clearly this was not Andrasta. "Who are you?" Salonina asked.

"I'm Domitia," the girl answered. When Salonina showed no recognition of her, she continued to explain. "I was a slave at the villa you lived in when you were in the city years ago." She paused to point in the direction of Colonia Agrippina. "You bought me from the owner, then gave me my freedom. Now I'm Andrasta's apprentice."

"You were the one who first brought Andrasta to me!" Salonina exclaimed. Domitia smiled and bowed slightly at Salonina's recognition. "But why are you dressed as a slave now?"

"A slave can go anywhere," Domitia answered. "Dressed as a Druid, I would not have gotten through your campground gate."

Salonina understood. "When I saw the raven, I thought you might be Andrasta," she confessed her disappointment.

"That's why I'm here," Domitia replied enthusiastically. "When I learned of your husband's wound, I felt you might wish to speak with Andrasta, yourself. And since you gave me my freedom, I took the risk of coming to see you." Domitia paused. "Andrasta agreed to meet with you—if you wish it." She arched an eyebrow and waited for Salonina's response.

"I would, Domitia! When can she come?" Salonina asked eagerly.

"This time you must go to her."

"But why? She's always come to me before."

"In the past there was no civil war," Domitia pointed out. "You were in a villa, inside the city—not in a military campground surrounded by thousands of soldiers. And the Romans have outlawed Druids for centuries. Andrasta is willing to meet with you, but she's unwilling to risk her life to do it." Domitia took a breath and looked expectantly at Salonina. "What shall I tell her?"

"What if I guaranteed her safety?" Salonina offered.

Domitia shook her head. "That was her condition for a meeting,"

I can't just walk through the gates by myself, Salonina frowned while she considered how to comply with Andrasta's precondition. *Even if I disguised myself, I'd probably be recognized, and that would raise questions, even suspicions. Better to do it openly.* She took a deep breath, then nodded at Domitia. "Where does she wish to meet?"

"On the other side of the river…" Domitia shifted uncomfortably.

Salonina gasped. "That's hostile territory!"

"The whole of Gallia is hostile territory for you right now," Domitia reminded her.

"Perhaps a grove of trees, maybe at the edge of the clearing around the campsite?" Salonina suggested.

"If Andrasta agrees to that, then I'll lead you to her tomorrow morning."

"I'll have to leave the campsite with an armed guard," Salonina cautioned.

Domitia frowned. "They would have to be kept at a safe distance."

"That would suit both our purposes," Salonina agreed. *No one must know who I'm seeing or what I'm being told.* Domitia bowed slightly, then left. Salonina rose to make arrangements for an escort, and considered how she'd explain her intentions to Volusianus.

The next day, shortly after her morning meal, Salonina, with a small contingent of soldiers and several women of her personal retinue, walked through the main gate where Domitia was waiting. She led them to a grove of oak trees at the edge of a clearing nearest to the river. The morning was sunny and warm. A few clouds drifted across a blue sky, and a single raven circled overhead. When the group was about a hundred yards from the clearing, the raven swooped down past Domitia and cawed loudly. It alighted on a tree branch and watched the group of women and soldiers in the open field. Domitia stopped and turned to Salonina. "Your guards must stop here," she said. "If you wish, you may bring your women with you."

"That won't be necessary." Salonina turned and instructed the legionaries and her retinue to wait where they were. "I won't require your assistance," she said over the legionaries' protestations, "I'm meeting a friend. If I need you for any reason, I'll raise my arm—like this." Then she and Domitia continued walking toward the oak grove and a figure wearing a brown hooded cloak who sat on a fallen log watching them. As they drew closer, the raven flew down to Andrasta's shoulder, and Salonina could see Andrasta nod occasionally as the raven looked from Salonina to Andrasta. The priestess rose as Salonina and Domitia approached, and the raven spread its wings and flew back to a branch above her. The priestess removed her cloak, letting it fall to the ground behind her. "Empress," she said, with a faint bow when Salonina drew near.

They faced each other silently for a moment. Salonina remembered the penetrating stare of Andrasta's green eyes. Her long red hair fell down her simple white tunic. As far as Salonina could remember, Andrasta was dressed exactly as she'd been during their previous meetings. The gold chain at her neck held a strange golden disc that Salonina had admired in the past. Mistletoe was pinned to her tunic on her right breast and the triskele was pinned on the left. For some reason Salonina recalled that its three radiating arms represented land, sea, and sky. A crescent shaped knife hung from the brown leather belt at her waist, along with a cloth bag of herbs, and the leather pouch that held Andrasta's runes.

"Surely you didn't request this meeting just so you could stare at me."

Andrasta's comment brought Salonina back to the present and she smiled. "No, of course not." Salonina collected her thoughts. "You're aware of my husband's situation?"

The raven cawed and flapped its wings. Andrasta glanced at the branch over her head, then turned back to Salonina and nodded. "Yes."

"She foresaw the emperor being wounded," Domitia interrupted enthusiastically, when Andrasta didn't elaborate. "I had a dream about your husband and asked Andrasta to read a rune about what it meant. She drew teiwaz—it warns of injury on the physical level!"

"Why didn't you tell me?" Salonina demanded sharply.

"I came to warn you," Domitia replied quickly, "but when I got to your campsite, it had already happened."

"Could you have convinced your husband to avoid the battlefield that day?" Andrasta shrugged. "Or not to turn toward his soldiers? It's doubtful that your knowledge would have prevented the event from happening."

"At least I could have tried," Salonina protested.

"It cannot be changed now," Andrasta frowned dismissively. "In the past you've brought a dream to me. Have you had it again?"

"Only parts of it," Salonina admitted, "and the details leave me as soon as I wake up."

"Then your dream is not ready to reveal itself to you," Andrasta noted. "You wish to speak with me about the present… and the future, I presume?"

"Yes!" Salonina forced herself to put Andrasta's advance knowledge of Gallienus' injury aside. "Are you suggesting that his wound was preordained by the Fates?"

"No," Andrasta said impatiently. "I've told you before that our lives unfold on an ever-changing path—yesterday's actions brought you to today, and today's actions determine where your path will lead in the days ahead."

Salonina considered Andrasta's comments. A light breeze rustled oak leaves above them. "Will my husband die?" Salonina asked directly.

"Yes."

Salonina's face drained of color.

"That's not the question you really wish to ask me."

Salonina thought for a moment. "Will he…survive this wound?" she asked. Then she licked her lips and asked, "And what would happen if he didn't?"

The raven flew down, alighting on Andrasta's shoulder. It eyed Salonina intently. Before Andrasta could answer, it shifted its position and cawed several times.

"I can deal with your first question, but the second involves the paths of others," Andrasta said. "Since you don't have a dream for me, you can draw one rune for your first question, and then, based on what it indicates, we can decide what to do next." Salonina took a deep breath and gave a barely perceptible nod. The Druid closed her eyes and began what sounded to Salonina like a prayer in a foreign tongue. All the while, Andrasta held the leather pouch of runes that she had removed from her belt. When she was finished, Andrasta opened the leather pouch and held it out for Salonina. "Think carefully about your question, then search through the runes until one feels right to you. Draw that one out and hand it to me."

Salonina sifted the oak tiles through her hand while she concentrated on the question she'd already asked Andrasta. Finally, she selected one, gingerly pulled it from the pouch, and handed it to Andrasta. The raven leaned over and peered intently at the rune. "Isa," Andrasta said tonelessly, studying the rune for a moment before looking at Salonina. "It stands for ice. The world we live in was created when fire and ice came together. While ice can be a destructive force, it's also necessary for our survival."

"I associate ice with winter," Salonina said, shivering involuntarily. "That suggests..."

"Death is a possible interpretation," Andrasta agreed, anticipating her thought, "but I think other runes would be more appropriate for that conclusion." She paused. "I see it more as winter preceding spring. Under your husband's present condition, the winter represents his convalescence before spring, his recovery." She smiled kindly at Salonina. "It's hopeful. Now, we can continue with your second question which, I assume, would be 'What happens next?' Is that about right?"

"Yes," Salonina agreed, as relief washed over her.

The raven suddenly spread its wings and flew out to the field, where it circled over the soldiers that had escorted Salonina. It returned to Andrasta's shoulder and cackled several times.

Salonina followed Andrasta's gaze, now fixed on her escort. The legionaries were watching her intently, but remained where she'd instructed them to wait for her.

"Despite what you've told them, they'll become restive soon," Andrasta commented. "Therefore, draw three more runes: one for the past, one for the present, and the last for the future."

"Why draw runes for the past and the present?"

"Each rune affects the one that follows it."

Salonina considered Andrasta's answer, and then nodded. "This reading will be on my husband's behalf," she specified.

"I assumed as much," Andrasta replied. Again she held out the pouch for Salonina and wordlessly took the rune that Salonina selected. "This rune is called wunjo: it stands for glory. Your husband's past endeavors have brought him success, and therefore the glory this rune represents."

A smile crept across Salonina's lips. *Almost anyone in the Roman world could have told me that,* she thought.

"You did pick the rune yourself," Andrasta reminded her, sensing Salonina's skepticism. "The more important point of wunjo, to my mind, is that it cautions against overconfidence. What has been done does not guarantee what will be done."

"That's good advice," Salonina agreed, "but still not prophetic."

"It's not intended to be. Its significance will be tied to the next rune you select. As you choose it, consider your husband's present situation." Again she offered the pouch to Salonina, and waited silently while Salonina selected her next rune.

Andrasta studied the rune that Salonina handed to her. "An interesting selection. It's called perp. Generally it's referred to as the 'dice cup' because of its shape. So it involves mystery—the unknown outcome of tossing the dice—as well as things hidden that would reveal themselves after the dice are cast. Since the rune for 'the present' involves decision and action, it fits well with the idea of casting the dice." The raven cawed. Andrasta paused. "Yes…. Before we go into the possible meanings, there's another view of perp I wish to mention."

Salonina nodded.

"Some people refer to this rune as the 'womb of the goddess.' If this drawing were for you, I might dwell on that aspect more deeply. But we can consider the analogy of birth or rebirth for either gender. As with tossing the dice, rebirth represents an opportunity."

"But tossing the dice involves risk," Salonina interjected.

"You can't win if you don't toss the dice."

"Is the chance of gain worth the risk of loss?"

"Life forces us to cast the dice, whether we wish to or not," Andrasta pointed out. "So let me continue with my thoughts on what this rune might indicate on physical, mental, and spiritual levels." She paused to make sure she had Salonina's attention. When Salonina said nothing, Andrasta continued. "Physically, this rune is concerned with fertility and may also deal with pregnancy."

"I think we can dispense with those possibilities in this case," Salonina smiled. *Unless it dealt with Pipa!* Her face darkened at that possible complication to her life. *But, no, this is Gallienus' reading, not Pipa's.* She relaxed and exhaled a breath of relief.

"My thoughts as well," Andrasta was saying. "Several things come to mind when I look at the mental aspects of perp. While the birth analogy suggests a new beginning, it's more a matter of going in a new direction. A difficult life experience may convince someone to approach some matter differently in the future. The dice cup suggests chance and opportunities, which accompany all choices we make. Often a new direction involves giving something up in order to get something else."

"Do you get any sense of what he'd decide to give up or let go?"

The raven cackled several times while it swayed back and forth on Andrasta's shoulder. She raised her eyebrows and pursed her lips. "How many times has your husband tried to defeat Postumus?" she asked.

"The most recent battle was his third victory."

"Along with one defeat, as I recall."

"A minor setback," Salonina interjected stiffly.

"Each time Postumus has eluded capture or death," Andrasta continued, disregarding Salonina's tone. "And the current effort has nearly killed your husband instead."

"But Postumus murdered my child! Gallienus would never leave the death of our son unavenged!" Her voice carried into the clearing startling the legionaries. Their leader rose and looked anxiously in her direction. When nothing further happened, he relaxed and the group resumed their uneasy vigil.

"The decision, whatever it might be, belongs to your husband,"

"And that would mean leaving the empire divided," Salonina continued.

"I merely offered one possible situation that he might choose to put behind him. Perhaps you can think of another?"

Could it mean getting rid of Pipa? Salonina wondered with a sudden surge of hope. *Or could it be me? That would certainly involve a new direction*! Hope changed to uncertainty; she frowned.

"He took a second wife." Salonina's voice trailed off. She bit her lip and her eyes moistened. "Could it refer to her, or to me?"

As Andrasta considered Salonina's question, her translucent green eyes stared, unfocused past Salonina, as if looking into some different realm of reality. "Has there been any recent discord?" she asked finally. "Some recent turmoil involving that arrangement?"

Salonina paused, recalling Pipa's unexpected and unwelcome visit to Rome. "Neither of us likes the situation, but we've both had to adapt to its reality."

"Then I think this rune addresses a different issue," Andrasta concluded.

Salonina took a deep breath, then exhaled slowly. Relief, mixed with disappointment, washed over her.

"There's a spiritual aspect of perp as well," Andrasta continued. "It suggests an interest in exploring the unknown, perhaps learning the secrets of life—or of the afterlife."

"We don't think a great deal about the afterlife," Salonina said.

"So much of life's meaning escapes you," Andrasta shrugged. "What a pity."

"Perhaps this refers to our interest in Plotinus and his teachings," Salonina suggested. "We've both attended a number of his lectures."

"I see this as more of a new interest." Andrasta sounded doubtful, her gaze was again unfocused and distant.

"I'd like to return to your comments about making a decision and choosing to give something up," Salonina said. "Could we explore that further?"

"Fortunately, we don't have to know what your husband's decision will be, what he chooses to give up, or what spiritual path he follows, in order to draw the third rune," Andrasta prompted Salonina to move on, "only that he has to make a decision, and that, according to perp, it involves a beginning of some sort." Andrasta glanced at the men in the open field. "We must move on," she pointed out, offering the bag again. "What I say of the future is what the runes say to me, and to my teacher." She patted the raven affectionately.

Salonina hesitated before reaching into the pouch to draw the final rune. "What will the rune for the future tell us?"

Andrasta exhaled impatiently. "I won't know until you draw it."

"It was more of a general question," Salonina clarified herself. "Will it suggest what will happen, or what might happen?"

"That's actually very perceptive." Andrasta smiled approvingly at Salonina. "More the latter, based on the choices and actions taken in the present." The raven cawed and flapped its wings. "Yes, yes; I'm aware of that," Andrasta said, looking thoughtfully at the bird for a moment. "I must add," she said to Salonina, "that it's not the only outcome possible."

"Then what use is it?" Salonina asked, disappointment in her voice.

"It could be advisory, or it could be a warning. Let's see what you draw before you ask anything further." Andrasta presented the pouch to Salonina, who touched many runes before she selected one that felt right to her. Salonina realized her heart was beating rapidly when she handed the rune to Andrasta, who glanced at it for only an instant. Andrasta's head turned quickly to the raven, who had been leaning over to see the rune for itself. "Hagalaz!" Andrasta said, raising an eyebrow. "The rune of elemental destruction." She seemed to forget about Salonina and instead listened to the raven's repeated cackling, nodding her head from time to time. "This rune stands for hail," she finally said to Salonina.

"Hail and elemental destruction don't sound very promising," Salonina said, concerned with both the rune and with Andrasta's reaction to it.

"It depends." Andrasta's reply lacked the reassurance Salonina had hoped for. "You could also see 'destruction' as a necessary step—one that makes room for the new to grow."

"Are you referring to death?" Salonina shifted uncomfortably on the log where she was sitting.

"As I said earlier, we all die at some point," Andrasta shrugged. "There'd be little value in the rune pointing out what's obvious to all of us. The 'destruction' and 'making way for the new' aspects of hagalaz reinforce the warning against complacency that I spoke of with wunjo, and past glories." Andrasta pursed her lips, then continued. "To understand hagalaz more fully, think of it this way," she began. "We come to this life with lessons to be learned. The adversities, hardships, and losses we experience are sometimes misinterpreted as punishments by the gods, rather than as divine reminders of what we have chosen, spiritually, to work on." She paused to see if Salonina understood her.

"We would call this 'fate,'" Salonina said. "And that suggests predetermination."

"Then why have you sought me out to find meaning in your dream, or to draw runes and ask me what they stand for?" Andrasta asked, arching her brow. "Life is a journey and we choose our paths. If you truly believe that your path is fixed at birth, then I urge you most strongly: don't seek to learn what you cannot change!" Andrasta paused for Salonina to consider what she'd said, and to decide if she wanted to proceed.

"I don't understand what you mean by lessons," Salonina

said finally. "But I agree that we make choices and that they influence the rest of our lives."

"Then we can continue," Andrasta said. The raven suddenly left her shoulder and flew back to the tree branch over Andrasta's head. "The gods give us opportunities to learn these life lessons. If we fail to learn from one situation or event in our lives, then other, more serious situations will be put before us. You've already experienced some hardships and losses in your life, but probably never thought of them as a lesson."

Salonina thought of the deaths of her first two sons, and then of hardships caused by Ingenuus' and Regalianus' revolts, Macrianus, Postumus, and Aureolus' betrayals. "Could this lesson be about trust and betrayal?" she wondered aloud.

"Your husband will have to determine that," Andrasta said. "Think of hail's destructive nature as clearing a path—making way for better things. The life challenge is to learn from the hardships and losses without being overwhelmed by them."

"What do you foresee, based on what the runes have told you today?" Salonina asked.

"The gods rarely provide second chances in life, but when they do, failing to learn from a second chance will have a worse outcome than the first. Hagalaz predicts this. Your husband became emperor through a series of unusual circumstances. I believe the gods have bestowed upon him a perilous privilege. And while I rarely quote your emperors, one of them once said something that seems appropriate to your husband's situation 'controlling the legions,' he said, 'is like holding a wolf by the ears.' In a way, your husband is like the leader of a pack of wolves. He will fare well, only so long as he retains the confidence of the rest of the pack."

Several caws from the raven overhead intruded on the silence following Andrasta's analogy. "Your escort is growing restless," Andrasta said. She rose abruptly and pulled on her hooded cape before turning to face Salonina. "How he will do that, I cannot say."

6-5
A Different Approach
Outside Ctesiphon, Persia
01 July, 263

"Why don't you let Herodian conduct negotiations with Shapur?" Zenobia asked her husband. She and Odenathus sat outside their tent with General Zabdas and Herodian, discussing a message Shapur had sent to them earlier that evening. Odenathus' army was encamped near Ctesiphon, which they had besieged for the last two weeks.

Odenathus stared at Zenobia, speechless for several seconds. "I… wasn't expecting that from you," he finally managed to say. Shapur's message suggested a meeting to discuss terms that Palmyra wanted in order to lift the siege. Zenobia looked at the astonished expressions on all of their faces and bit her lip in order not to smile. Her reason for this suggestion was far from innocent, but she wanted to make them think otherwise.

She recalled their victory over Shapur two weeks earlier and his retreat to Ctesiphon's safety. Vaballathus, her young son, had been with her during the battle. He'd been frightened, even though there'd been no direct threat to him. Zenobia doubted that he'd learned anything about leading men in battle, which was her reason for wanting him there. *Fortunate he hadn't been with Odenathus and Herodian after all*, she admitted to herself.

"I realize now that Vaballathus is far too young to assume any leadership positions." Zenobia paused to look briefly at Herodian, "Therefore we need to groom the logical successor in the arts of war and negotiation." She waited for their reactions.

Odenathus looked relieved at the prospect of his wife and eldest son finally existing in harmony. Yet, considering how long they'd been at odds, he wasn't completely convinced that her change of position was genuine. Zabdas said nothing, but the twinkle in his eye and his barely-concealed smile suggested he recognized Zenobia's intentions. Herodian looked surprised but guarded. "Naturally I want Vaballathus to become king," she admitted to Herodian, "but you're old enough to succeed your father now, if anything should ever happen to him. So our job, your father's and mine, is to see that you get every possible exposure to a king's responsibilities while your father is able to instruct and guide you through them."

"What do you think?" Odenathus asked Zabdas. Zenobia held her breath and maintained her outwardly congenial expression while they all waited for Zabdas' reply.

"The experience could be beneficial for him," Zabdas rubbed his chin as he answered, "but Shapur is a wily and capable adversary. I'd suggest you be beside him, in case some unexpected issue arises," he added, so as not to offend Herodian.

Odenathus considered Zenobia's suggestion and Zabdas' advice. "Are you up to that?" he asked Herodian.

His son shrugged and nodded. "Sure," he said unenthusiastically.

"Then we'll discuss our position after lunch," Odenathus said.

"But…" Herodian began to object.

Zenobia could not help herself. "You'll have time to play with your concubines later." She patted Herodian's hand and smiled sympathetically.

"We'll meet with Shapur tomorrow morning," Odenathus announced, concluding the meeting.

* * *

Zenobia made a pretext of needing to inspect her soldiers, but actually she sought time alone to consider her new approach to Herodian. Part of what she'd said was true: it was obvious that her son was too young, by at least ten years, while Herodian was old enough for succession today. More importantly, she realized that her past criticisms of Herodian had only strengthened Odenathus' attachment to his eldest son. It was time to appear to be an ally rather than an antagonist, to profess support for Herodian and encourage his development in diplomatic and military affairs. Her intention was to let Herodian reveal his incompetence. There was a risk in this approach, of course. If Herodian were successful, he'd garner Odenathus' support for him, rather than diminish it. However, knowing Herodian as she did, Zenobia had no doubt that in due course he'd fall short in some capacity. Opportunities for failure would present themselves and she'd do her best to see that Herodian missed none of them. If all of that was insufficient to convince Odenathus that Herodian was unfit to rule, then she would have to find another other way to ensure Herodian never become king.

She dismissed poison, although she rather enjoyed the image of Herodian writhing in agony on the palace floor. Poison would be too obviously her doing. Death in battle was a promising outcome, but Herodian was notoriously cautious. She considered discreetly contacting the Persians to identify Herodian's armor and where he would be on the battlefield. But that was a risky and unreliable approach. Word of the contact might somehow work its way back to Odenathus, and there was still no guarantee that the Persians would, or could, act decisively on that information. She could try to encourage Herodian into taking a more aggressive role in battle, appealing to his ego and convincing him to demonstrate that he'd inherited his father's skills and daring. That failing, she might persuade Odenathus that Herodian should learn and demonstrate those abilities so that he'd have the confidence of his soldiers. There were several problems with this approach. It was doubtful Herodian would ever accept such a challenge on his own. Odenathus might not agree with her reasoning, and after their recent victory over Shapur, it seemed unlikely there'd even be another opportunity to fight the Persians. If another battle ever presented itself, she'd have to hire an assassin, someone within the ranks of his soldiers, who could make his death seem accidental somehow. She could promise the person money or a position of power as enticement. Later, of course, she'd deny any association with the assassin, in the unlikely event that he himself actually survived. The only other activity Herodian engaged in that was even mildly dangerous was hunting, and that he did only because his father was such an avid hunter. Maybe there was someone with a grudge against Herodian? Suddenly she thought of Maeonius, a nephew of

Odenathus, who had once argued with Odenathus and Herodian over some issue she could not now recall. A disgruntled member of the royal family. He might be perfect for her purposes. Zenobia smiled. She turned and started walking briskly back to the meeting that Odenathus had said would take place after lunch. *It's time I got to know Maeonius better. He and I have may some things to talk about.*

6-6
Complications
Encampment outside Colonia Agrippina
Germania Inferior
01 August, 263

The medicus met Salonina and Volusianus outside Gallienus' tent. "He developed a fever late last night." The medicus frowned wearily as he reported Gallienus' condition.

Salonina flinched noticeably. She glanced briefly at Volusianus' impassive face, then back to the medicus. "What are you doing about it?"

"We're giving him tea made from barley, as much as he can drink. We keep the wound clean with wine, and rub it with olive oil. Several times a day, I put a hot compress on it, a mix of malva and honey. When the compress cools, we clean the wound with wine and olive oil again. In the afternoon, I serve him artemisia infused in wine. The wine seems to extract the beneficial ingredients of the plant," he explained.

"Is there anything else you can do?" she implored.

The medicus paused. "I could cauterize the wound…"

Salonina winced and held up her hand. "I hope that won't be necessary. I'd like to see him now."

"Of course." The medicus bowed slightly, pulled back the tent flap, and gestured for her to enter.

Salonina stepped into the dim light followed by Volusianus and the medicus. Several candles flickered on small tables beside

Gallienus' cot. While her eyes adjusted, Salonina was more acutely aware of scents and sounds: garlic and myrrh, oregano, salvia, peppermint, and violet—all herbs or flowers used by the medicus to treat a variety of ailments. Two of the medicus' assistants talked together in hushed tones in one corner of the tent.

"Have any prayers been offered?" Volusianus asked the medicus. "And I don't see any amulets near him," he added looking anxiously around the tent.

"I pray to Aesculapius daily," the medicus replied staring directly at Volusianus. "But what I do makes more of a difference than what I ask of him." The medicus paused and shrugged. "If the god of healing answered all my prayers, everyone would recover." He refrained from saying more, lest he affront Volusianus' beliefs.

"What will happen?" Salonina asked.

"He may lose consciousness, or become delirious. If the fever doesn't break," the medicus sighed and looked sadly at Salonina. "You may want to get him back to Rome. We're doing what we can for him here, but this," he swept a hand around the tent, "isn't the best place for recovery. And there would, of course, be more help available in the city." He nodded toward Gallienus. "Why don't you suggest it to him?"

Salonina walked over to the cot and knelt by Gallienus. She put her hand on his arm and looked anxiously into his face. He opened his eyes and smiled weakly at her.

"How are you feeling?" she asked, trying to mask her anxiety. For a while he said nothing.

He studied her face, then finally spoke. "Not one of my best days."

"We'll get you back to Rome," Salonina patted his hand. "You can recover there."

"I want to stay here," he said, then closed his eyes.

Salonina turned to glance at Volusianus. He stood just behind her and stared down at Gallienus. She couldn't read his expression. The medicus also remained in the tent, but at a discreet distance. "You must go," she whispered to Gallienus, her tears welling up. "I want to get you home where you'll get better treatment." She gazed down at her husband's pale face. She had no idea what would happen to Marinianus if Gallienus died outside the walls of Colonia Agrippina while his army besieged a rebel general in one of his cities. *We don't want to be here if something were to happen to you,* she thought, wiping the tears from her eyes. She looked down at her husband's face. *I want to get you home, where we'll all be safe.* "Volusianus," she spoke to the Praetorian Prefect, "convince my husband that he should return home now."

Volusianus shifted uncomfortably behind her. "If he commands me to remain here, then I'm bound to obey his order."

"You told me you and the generals were taking matters into your own hands, at least for a while," she reminded him. "Isn't there anything you can do?"

"If he becomes delirious or slips into unconsciousness, as the medicus said he might, then we'd be forced to make a decision for him," Volusianus answered.

Color drained from Salonina's face but her voice was calm. "Won't that be too late?"

Volusianus looked inquiringly at the medicus' face. The medicus shrugged his shoulders, turned and left the tent. Salonina looked down at Gallienus, who had fallen into a restless sleep. After a few moments' silence, she allowed Volusianus to escort her to the tent's entrance. She ducked through the opening ahead of Volusianus and collided with Pipa, who stood just outside the tent talking with the medicus. The jolt startled her back to the present. She glanced at Pipa with surprise, then annoyance. At first Pipa was also too surprised to react. They stood face to face for a moment. Salonina saw Pipa's questioning look. "Ask him," Salonina nodded at the medicus. Until then she hadn't noticed the unknown man standing beside Pipa. Salonina paused to stare suspiciously at the unfamiliar person. He was tall and thin, dressed in a leather tunic and leather boots. A narrow animal skin draped around his neck hung nearly to his knees. Beneath his long blond hair and beard Salonina could just make out a talisman on his chest suspended from a leather cord. His belt held a small dagger and a leather pouch. Salonina wondered if it contained runes or held something else entirely. She noticed that he held an object wrapped in a dark cloth in his hands. After inspecting this strange man, she looked from him to the medicus and frowned. The medicus understood her concern and nodded to her. Salonina then brushed past Pipa and her companion.

"You may offer your amulets and prayers. But leave your dagger outside, and I must see what you have in your bundle," the medicus growled before letting Pipa and her priest enter the tent, "Do nothing more unless I agree to it first." He followed them into the tent saying "He needs his sleep. You can only stay a short time."

* * *

"I would have told you earlier," Volusianus said to the other generals, gathered outside his tent that evening, "but I thought the siege should continue as usual, so Postumus wouldn't suspect anything." He paused and took a breath. "Gallienus wants to continue the siege. He was quite clear about that when I spoke with him this morning."

"Better to take the city and kill Postumus now," Aurelian agreed, "so we don't have to come back and try all this again."

They considered the implications of Gallienus' fever. In the course of their military careers, Aurelian, Claudius, Attalus, and Heraclianus had all seen comrades wounded and occasionally develop fevers. The possibility of death was known to them all.

"What did the medicus say?" Heraclianus inquired, breaking the silence.

"He suggested moving Gallienus to Rome for further treatment and recuperation."

"Then we should consider departing for Rome before cold weather arrives," Claudius said. "We'll have to cross mountains with an injured man."

"Why don't some of us stay and continue the siege without him?" Attalus proposed.

"He wants to be here himself when Postumus surrenders," Volusianus shrugged.

"It seems the Fates are against Gallienus taking Postumus,"

Claudius mused. "Three times Postumus has been defeated. Three times he's escaped."

"He won't this time—unless we let him!" Attalus disagreed emphatically. "But, since we're all thinking about it, what happens if Gallienus dies?" He looked at each of the generals. No one seemed inclined to answer him. "How does it work?" he asked them again.

"How does what work?" Heraclianus asked.

"Will his son succeed him?" The following silence answered that question for Attalus. "Then it's fair to say that one of you will try to claim the title," he concluded.

"If Gallienus died here," Heraclianus temporized, "there could be revolts or invasions anywhere in the empire. Probably both," he added.

Attalus considered this answer for a moment. "So there's no peaceful way to change leaders." Attalus rubbed his chin then looked at the men around him. "You'd be fighting among yourselves for the position."

"If Gallienus dies, then this is not the place any of us wish to be," Volusianus said. Not in the middle of a hostile province, when each of these generals would suddenly be suspicious of all the others.

But Attalus had his own concerns. "Will my treaty be honored by the successor? Or will I have to take my people north of the Danuvius? If that happened, I'd no longer be your ally—or your friend." He glared at the generals accusingly.

"Only the successor could answer your question," Volusianus said honestly, "but he'd be foolhardy not to honor the alliance."

"All this talk assumes that Gallienus will die," Claudius interrupted. "Aside from suggesting that Gallienus goes to Rome, I still don't know what the medicus said about his condition." They all looked at Volusianus.

"The medicus has done as much as he can. We'll have to wait to see if the fever breaks."

"While we wait," Attalus persisted, "what are we going to do? Someone's got to make a decision." The generals turned from Attalus back to Volusianus.

He was silent for a moment to consider the siege's possibility of success, transporting a sick man all the way to Rome, and the ambitions and mutual suspicions of these generals if Gallienus were to die. "We'll have to depart on the 15th of August if we want to cross the mountains before snowfall," he said. "Even then, we won't reach Rome until the end of November. That leaves us less than two weeks to breach the city walls."

6-7
Allies' Assessment
Outside Colonia Agrippina, Germania
2 August, 263

Attalus barged into Pipa's tent. The look on his face told her this unexpected visit wasn't social.

She stood up. "He has a fever, doesn't he?"

Attalus nodded.

"I wanted to put my hand on his forehead this morning, but the Roman medicine man said it might awaken him. He only let us stay a few minutes," she said, biting her lower lip. "The priest thought it might be a fever."

"They plan to leave for Rome in two weeks."

"Then I should go with him," Pipa declared, starting to rise.

"I said *he* was going to Rome," Attalus reminded her, grabbing her arm before she could move away. "Gallienus told you not to go there, and Salonina certainly doesn't want to have you there."

"I'm married to him," Pipa protested.

"So is she," Attalus countered. "And in Rome, no one will acknowledge your claim to him. You know that." He straddled one of the chairs beside the small table. "Have you any beer?" he asked. She nodded. "Good," he said. "Bring me some, and two glasses. We need to think about this whole situation."

They sat at her small table while a slave girl brought beer, two glasses, and a loaf of bread. The girl had not even finished serving when Attalus drank deeply from his glass. He wiped the foam from his beard with his sleeve and waited until the slave left before speaking. "They say it's for his recovery."

"But that's not this real issue, is it?" Pipa sipped from her glass and broke a small piece of bread from the loaf.

"He could die in Rome," Attalus frowned. "He could die before he even reaches Rome!" He considered the situation and drank more beer. "That's what everyone is thinking, although no one admits it."

How serious do you think it is?"

He shrugged. "Not even their medicine man could say."

Pipa considered his answer. "My welfare depends on his survival," she said finally.

"As long as I'm around, I'll protect you. But let's consider alternatives." He stopped, frowned, and looked around. "Have you no cheese?"

"You didn't ask for any." Pipa clapped her hands. "Bring us cheese," she said as the girl reappeared at her summons. She looked at her father's glass. "And more beer," she called after the girl.

"If he survives, everything will be as before," Attalus said, staring at his empty glass. "You weren't supposed to be in Rome anyway, so no one will ask why you weren't there."

"And if he doesn't," Pipa continued, accustomed to her father's reasoning process, "then I'd be safer in Pannonia with the rest of our people." She nibbled at her crust of bread and sipped her beer while she thought. "As would you," she looked from the half-empty glass to her father.

"Until a new leader is chosen," he agreed, "and we learn if he honors our treaty."

"I can't see his son succeeding him." Pipa paused while the girl returned with beer and cheese, then sipped from her refilled glass. "Is there no designated successor?"

Attalus shook his head.

"So there'd be a civil war."

"Yes, I think so." Attalus tore off a corner of the cheese wedge and took a bite.

"Who then?" she asked.

"That," Attalus said while he chewed his cheese, "is exactly what the generals are wondering themselves."

"Who will we support?"

Before responding Attalus drank half of his glass, then set it onto the table harder than he'd intended. He drew his sleeve across his face again and smiled at his daughter. "The winner, of course!"

7-1
Succession Schemes
Rome
11 August, 263

"I got a message from Quintianus this morning," Maximus announced casually over their midday meal taken in the villa's garden enjoying the warm summer day.

"Really?" Prisca raised an eyebrow. She put down the fig she'd just bitten into and gave Maximus her full attention. A message from their son was a rarity. "What did he say?"

"It seems that Gallienus was felled by an arrow during their siege."

Prisca caught her breath. Her heart raced. "What does that mean, exactly?"

"Apparently he was leading an assault on the city himself. He must have turned around to face his troops, because the arrow hit him in the back somewhere. It seems…"

"Is he alive or dead!" she interrupted. "Quintianus must have mentioned that detail somewhere in his message?" *What would Gallienus be doing so close to the battle himself?* A shiver ran through her. She bit her lip. A deep sadness swept over her as she realized how much she had missed him. *If he dies, I'll lose the influence I've had—and so will Maximus and Quintianus.*

When she looked up, Maximus was watching her. "The

arrow was successfully removed." He paused, then glanced back at the message. "He's recuperating now." He looked up again to study Prisca's face.

"Let me see that," Prisca said. She leaned across the table and seized the message from is hand. She read it twice, then put it down abruptly and looked at her husband in frustration. "He doesn't say how bad the wound was anywhere in here!"

"He probably didn't know."

Prisca took a deep breath and asked, "How serious do you think this is?"

"The fact that he didn't die immediately is encouraging." Maximus reached for a pork sausage, ate it slowly, then sipped his date wine. He looked at the bread and cheeses on the table, but took several almonds instead. While he ate them, Maximus thought back to his military experiences. "As long as he doesn't develop a fever, he'll probably recover," he said finally.

"What would a fever mean?"

"It often leads to death."

"'Often,' as opposed to 'always'?"

"Yes."

Prisca unconsciously swirled her wine glass and tried to envision Gallienus lying in some medical tent with Salonina and Pipa alternately hovering over him. Another thought suddenly came to her. *Gallienus' successor might kill Gallienus' supporters! It's happened before.* "Who would succeed him, do you suppose?"

"One of his closest generals, I imagine."

"Which one?"

"Anyone but Attalus."

"Not Marinianus?"

Maximus shook his head. "I doubt the generals would accept him."

Prisca pursed her lips. "Another civil war… in just ten years!"

Maximus didn't answer her immediately. He, too, was thinking how new emperors sometimes eliminated past emperor's allies and friends. "The last time it ended relatively quickly," he said, "but the empire wasn't fragmented then. As I recall, Valerian took no reprisals against Aemilianus' family or supporters."

In the last civil war Maximus had been a private citizen and did not have to make any decisions. He lapsed into silence, thinking that his appointment to the consulship last month to finish the second half of Dexter's year might have been a particularly ill-timed honor. If Gallienus died and the generals fought for the title, he could see no way to avoid taking sides. Even if the conflict erupted in the provinces, repercussions would be felt in Rome.

Meanwhile Prisca was having her own thoughts. *It's bad enough to lose a mentor and a patron, but to think of another civil war and the chance of losing everything!* Prisca shuddered as she considered their precarious position. It forced her to recall being captured by the Juthungi in the summer of 259, another time in her life when she thought she had lost everything. She had been a slave of the chieftain for over a year and had nearly died during the winter when the Juthungi camped outside Sabiona. When the snows melted and they had marched north toward their homeland, she had vowed to drown herself in the Danuvius River rather than cross it and spend the rest of her life in captivity. Then, when they were less than a week's march from the river, her captor had offered her as a sacrifice to one of the barbarians' gods. And she had nearly died before Gallienus had personally rescued her from death by fire. Prisca could clearly remember the bone-chilling cold of the winter as well as the heat from the first flames of the sacrificial fires. There were many things in Prisca's life now that she could do nothing about, but if her life and security were again threatened, she was not about to accept the situation passively. *What can I do?* When an idea finally came to her, she took a deep breath and relaxed a little. *What if Maximus succeeded Gallienus? He'd be a logical choice for succession! He's a consul now and a friend of the Senate with a distinguished military career. If the Senate united behind him, then Rome might avoid civil war. This could be a once-in-a-lifetime opportunity for Maximus. And Quintianus might become his logical successor!* The fact that Prisca would also become empress did not escape her, but she convinced herself that this was a secondary consideration. Prisca sat straighter in her chair, relaxed the tension she experienced in her shoulders, and pushed her food aside. She looked at Maximus. "Do you see any way to a smooth transfer of power then?"

"Unlikely, I'm afraid. What are you thinking now?" he asked, familiar with Prisca's leading questions.

"Remember when Nerva succeeded Domitian as emperor?"

"That was over a hundred years ago," he replied after a moment's thought.

"Wasn't he was a consul at the time?"

"Yes," Maximus agreed, "but…"

"But it was a peaceful transfer of power."

Maximus searched his memory for specifics of the event. "As I recall, the only way Nerva survived a revolt from the army was to adopt Trajan as his heir."

"That's because Domitian was murdered," Prisca replied, "and the army liked Domitian. Besides, Nerva was never much of a military man."

"Where are you going with this idea?"

"So, aside from the generals, if anything happened to Gallienus, then you'd be in a logical position to succeed him, wouldn't you," she proposed. "If Gallienus died from a fever, then the army couldn't blame you for it. Besides, you have a distinguished military record yourself."

"Don't forget there are two consuls," Maximus pointed out. "And Albinus has more current military experience than I do."

"He's too old to want the title."

Maximus shook his head. "I've already done my part for the empire."

"You could help avoid a civil war. Isn't that a worthy service to the empire? Think of the lives you could save and the destruction you could prevent!"

"I might prevent a civil war," Maximus said. "A number of ambitious men would like to succeed Gallienus. And the penalties for coming in second are rather severe," he reminded her.

She looked at him doubtfully.

"Look at Aemilianus—he tried to seize power from Gallus, a man clearly unfit to be emperor." Maximus took a breath then continued. "What happened to him?"

"He was successful," Prisca replied, recalling the revolt just ten years earlier. "Gallus' soldiers murdered him when Aemilianus' army approached the capital."

"But what happened next?" Maximus pressed her.

"Well… Valerian was marching south with an army to support Gallus. But obviously he was too late."

"And when Valerian neared the capital, Aemilianus' troops murdered him." Maximus leaned back in his chair and studied Prisca's expression.

"Nothing like that is going to happen this time," she replied confidently.

"What would I do if any of Gallienus' generals marched on Rome with even a part of the army that's in Pannonia? What if Attalus came along with six thousand warriors?"

"There are several generals on Gallienus' staff. If the Senate declared you the emperor, they'd have someone to unite behind, rather than fighting among themselves."

"But would they? It's hard to enforce a good idea without troops to convince doubters of its merit."

"So you agree that it's a good idea then?"

"It has its appeal," Maximus conceded, "but it's unlikely to succeed. You'd probably survive a failed attempt, but Quintianus and I certainly would not. Do you want me to be emperor that badly?"

"What I want," Prisca said, "is for Gallienus to survive. If he doesn't, then I'd like to avoid another civil war which might prove fatal to us, whoever wins." She looked at Maximus grimly. "Whoever wins, we risk losing everything." Neither of them spoke for a while. Prisca reached up to massage the tension in her neck. Her expression softened and she seemed to stare at some unseen object as another wave of sadness swept over her. "I'd hoped Gallienus would rule for a much longer time."

It was clear to Maximus that Prisca still had deep feelings for Gallienus. He recognized—and appreciated—the benefits her relationship with Gallienus provided for Quintianus, and for himself. He disliked the situation intensely, but felt powerless to stop it. "I realize that," he said.

7-2
A Palace Visit
Rome
1 December, 263

What is she doing here? Salonina thought as she stared with surprise and amazement at Prisca among a small group of dignitaries that had come to welcome them back to Rome. They stood in the large antechamber that had been Valerian's waiting room. Carpets covered mosaic floors, busts of previous emperors stood in corners of the room, and above a great ebony table at the far wall, the fresco of a Roman battle was clearly visible. Braziers burning along the walls provided some relief from winter's cold. Albinus and Maximus, the two Consuls for this year, were there and Prisca had insisted on accompanying her husband. They'd been greeted by Salonina, her father, Saecularis, and Volusianus. After the greetings, the men had congregated together and talked of last summer's battle and the subsequent siege. That had left Salonina alone with Prisca.

"We've come to welcome you back—and to wish the emperor a speedy and complete recovery," Prisca said to Salonina, who stood stiffly in front of her.

"But what are you doing in Rome?"

"Maximus was appointed to replace Dexter as consul for the second half of the year. Gallienus made the appointment himself," she added when Salonina still looked at her in amazement.

Why didn't I know of this? Salonina wondered and immediately suspected Prisca of engineering the appointment when she and Gallienus were last together in Rome. *I'll have to ask Gallienus why I wasn't made aware of this situation.*

"Maybe he made the appointment before getting wounded," Prisca offered, sensing continued confusion and surprise. "He would have had other things on his mind after that." Prisca had

had other things on her mind after that as well. In mid-August, when Maximus told her of Gallienus being wounded, she had conceived her plan for a peaceful succession of power. She had begun gathering support for her plan among the senators, through their wives, after the message announcing Gallienus' fever and his intention to return to Rome arrived in early September. She took a breath. Today, she would learn if the whole undertaking should be abandoned, or if she needed to redouble her efforts to gather support. "Would it be possible," she asked tentatively, "for me or perhaps my husband, to see him?"

"He's probably asleep," Salonina replied. "The medicus wants him to get as much rest as possible. And, as I assume you know, we've just completed a long, arduous journey.

"I'd really like to wish him well."

I'm sure you would, Salonina thought, *especially when he's in bed*! "The medicus has insisted that he really needs his rest," she said instead.

"Of course," Prisca said. "Maximus and I were extremely concerned when we heard of Gallienus' wound, and then of his fever—especially when we learned he was returning to Rome. Pardon my saying this, but it seemed to imply that he was coming home to die! After word of his fever became widely known, rumors that he was already dead broke out almost immediately."

Salonina stared at Prisca, wondering how many people had concluded what she herself had feared. Prisca nodded sympathetically, but continued on. "The city was quite restive for some time," she said. "I was surprised there were no invasions, insurrections, or riots."

"His fever broke just before we began the march home, and his condition has improved steadily after that," Salonina assured her.

"Then why isn't he here now?" Prisca asked, clearly skeptical of Salonina's explanation.

"He caught cold when we crossed the mountains."

"Of course," Prisca nodded. She continued to look at Salonina expectantly.

Prisca's disbelief was so obvious that Salonina felt like slapping her mocking face. She took a deep breath and clasped her hands behind her back. As she very carefully steadied herself, she realized that she could actually use this troublesome but well-connected, gossipy, and socially active woman for her own ends. Salonina smiled sweetly at Prisca. "Perhaps you'd like to see him yourself." *After Prisca's comments about coming home to die, it might be important for people to see for themselves that Gallienus is not only alive, but recovered from both his wound and fever. His cold*, she realized, *would be misconstrued by some, but he'll be fully recovered from that in a week or two.* She looked at the men who were still involved in some sort of discussion. "Come with me."

Prisca followed Salonina down a tiled hallway, past a dormant inner peristyle garden, then to the entrance of Gallienus' room, where braziers provided heat for the guards standing outside the door. Salonina opened the door and moved quietly inside. Gallienus was propped up against the headboard looking at a scroll. Many others lay at the foot of his bed. "There's someone to see you," Salonina said softly stepping aside to reveal Prisca standing behind her. Gallienus looked up from his bed expectantly. A faint smile played across his face briefly, before he looked at Salonina, who was watching his reaction closely.

"I hadn't expected to see you so soon," he said. "We only arrived late yesterday." He put the scroll aside and looked at Prisca's expression. "Is something wrong?" he asked.

"I expected you to be half-dead," she almost whispered as she took a few steps toward his bed. "The messages," she began, "It was difficult not to succumb to all the rumors that were flying around the city." Seeing him in bed instantly flooded her memory with more intimate and exhilarating times spent together. "I'm so happy to see you're better," she said kneeling next to Gallienus' bed. She was aware that Salonina was standing next to her, doubtless watching everything she did. Prisca felt guilt, that she had pursued her plan for Maximus to succeed Gallienus so actively for nearly three months. "When Maximus was governor of the Germanias," Prisca said pursuing a more neutral subject, "he used to say that the ride to and from Rome was almost as hard as a summer campaign," she smiled at Gallienus' reaction.

"I would agree with that," Gallienus nodded pleasantly.

"Salonina said you'd caught a cold. How are you feeling now?"

"I still tire quickly, otherwise I'm almost as good as new."

Prisca nodded her understanding. There were many questions she wanted to ask him, but not with Salonina there. She put a hand on Gallienus' arm. "I hope—we all hope—that you recover quickly and that things will be as they were before."

"It's time he got some rest," Salonina said abruptly. She ushered Prisca to the doorway and back to the palace atrium.

While they walked, Prisca considered the ironies of the situation. *His fever broke the day after we got word of his wound, and he recovered about two weeks after we got word of his fever! All my succession efforts were undertaken when he'd already recovered!*

Meanwhile, Salonina was having thoughts of her own. *First I have to put up with Pipa while we're on campaign, now I'm faced with Prisca here in Rome! I'm not sure which is worse: a barbarian with a fictitious marriage, or a Roman woman with connections and ambitions!*

When they reached the atrium, Salonina stopped and turned to face Prisca.

"I appreciate you letting me see him," Prisca said before Salonina could speak. "It meant a lot. As I told him, he looks far better than I expected. I was very concerned."

I'm sure you were, Salonina thought. "He recovered steadily ever since his fever broke. I trust that the news of his recovery will help to quiet the city."

"I do hope you'll let Maximus and me visit him again from time to time," she said. "We both are concerned with your health and his."

"Thank you, but he'll recover just fine if he's left to himself."

"But having people visit raises a person's spirits. Surely, you're not going to exclude him from seeing anyone now that he's among so many friends."

Salonina sighed, realizing that she might not be able to even if she wished it. "As long as that's the only reason for seeing him," she added.

Prisca eyed Salonina suspiciously. *Is she alluding to my succession plan? Or to my relationship with Gallienus after he rescued me from the Juthungi? Or to my long-running involvement with Gallienus? Does she know anything, or everything?* Prisca wondered as she and Maximus left the palace and stepped into Rome's busy streets. Salonina's comment could refer to so many different things.

Salonina watched Prisca and Maximus leave the villa and disappear into the crowded streets. She thought for a moment of the dinner she'd had with Maximus and Prisca in Aquileia three summers earlier. She had become convinced that Prisca had been intimate with Gallienus for several weeks after he'd rescued her from a barbarian sacrificial ritual. *I thought I'd be returning to the safety of Rome and a time of quiet convalescence. Instead, I find Prisca, who wasn't supposed to be in Rome at all! And there's every bit as much competition and intrigue here as I had on the frontier!*

7-3

A Great Deal Explained
Rome
28 December, 263

"Welcome to Messalina's" the Superintendent of Women said perfunctorily when Gallienus entered. He told her who he had come to see, and she consulted a master schedule on her desk for a few moments. Then she glanced up briefly. "Lysisca wasn't expecting you quite this early," she said and nodded at a stone bench nearby. And she immediately returned to the work that had preoccupied her before he had entered. *Apparently Lysisca didn't tell her who I was*, Gallienus thought. While he waited for a slave girl to return with wine he had been offered, he decided that anonymity was generally a good thing.

Small torches along the walls lit a dim entry causing shadows to play across colorful frescoes. Braziers struggled to overcome December's cold air. Nearby garden lay barren, although a fountain at the far end still splashed continuously. A comment by Saecularis, Salonina's father, had prompted this visit tonight. Saecularis had overheard parts of a conversation in the baths about a plan for succession. He mentioned it to Gallienus and suggested that he inquire around about it. Gallienus also needed to get away from the constant care and attention he was receiving at the palace. Salonina had rolled her eyes when he said he was "going out" for part of the evening, but then thought it indicated he was returning to his old self. Usually he went to Messalina's alone, but tonight he wanted a trusted member of Volusianus' guards to accompany him. The man had been instructed to act as a companion, not as a guard on duty.

A slave girl approached him bringing wine. Gallienus offered a glass to his legionary escort, who declined. She poured it for Gallienus then turned to leave. "Here," he said and placed a gold coin into her hand.

"Oh, thank you!" The girl's face broke into an astonished smile. She studied the coin for a moment, turning it over twice before looking at Gallienus again. "Has anyone ever told you that you look like the emperor?"

Gallienus grinned, "I get that a lot."

As the girl departed, she nearly brushed against a man who stepped clumsily out of a room and into her path. At first Gallienus thought the man was drunk, then he noticed that the man walked with a distinct limp. Obviously he had been a legionary at some point in his life. "What're you lookin' at?" the man growled as he stopped in front of Gallienus. The burly man sitting beside Gallienus rose abruptly and faced the man, a hand on the knife hilt at his belt. A flash of understanding came to the injured man and he muttered something under his breath as he turned away and headed toward the door.

"Anyone you know?" Gallienus asked his companion.

"Never seen him before, sir," the man replied. He sat down beside Gallienus and lapsed back into silence.

Gallienus sipped his wine, then stared at the glass as he

thought of the battles that Rome was constantly forced to fight. *There must be thousands like him*, Gallienus thought. *Men who are neither killed, nor able to continue fighting any longer*. He pondered the difficulties such a man would have just staying alive, and promised himself that he would look into the matter later.

"And what have you been up to since I saw you last?" Lysisca stood in front of him and interrupted his thinking. She looked him over critically, saw no obvious injuries. His posture was erect but she thought his face seemed weary. His eyes looked hollow to her and she noticed traces of grey in his hair.

Gallienus glanced at his escort and nodded. "I think I can take it from here, Marcus. Thank you." The man stood and saluted before retiring wordlessly.

"Haven't you heard?" he asked Lysisca as he rose slowly to his feet. When he stood, they were so close they almost touched. He gazed into her eyes, smelled her perfume, felt, and heard her breathing. She smiled at him but deliberately delayed answering, allowing her proximity to be experienced and his anticipation to build.

Finally, she nodded. "The fact that you're here is encouraging. You can tell me how much you've recovered," she put a hand on his cheek, "or you can show me."

"The latter would be more convincing."

"Come," she said, stepping back and taking hold of his hand. She led him to her room. "You remember the way don't you?"

"It hasn't been that long," he quipped, although he hoped that he hadn't come too soon after getting over his wound and his cold, or too late to learn about the plot Saecularis mentioned to him.

"No, it hasn't," Lysisca agreed, masking her own anxieties: *He's recovering from a serious wound. In the past he's wanted information as much as he's wanted sex. If I deny that I've heard anything, he'd doubt my credibility, how much shall I tell him? What if he asks for names? This is the most powerful man in the world. I need to be extra attentive, as well as on my guard.*

The door clicked shut audibly behind them as they entered

Lysisca's room. A light fragrance of perfume greeted Gallienus, along with a feeling of warmth and seclusion. Candle light flickered across two wall tapestries. He could see the reflection of Lysisca's body in the large mirror between them. Gallienus followed her across a carpet that covered much of her tiled floor, then stopped beside her bed and a few feet away from the mirror. He smiled, anticipating her seduction ritual.

Lysisca stood facing the mirror in a way that gave Gallienus a view of both her front and her back. Slowly she pulled the pin out of her hair letting it fall across her shoulders then shaking it loose.

"After word of your fever reached the city," Lysisca began softly, "there was a lot of speculation as to whether you'd live or die. It was very worrying. I'm so glad to see you." She unfastened the pin at her shoulder and held it a moment before letting her dress fall to the floor. She watched Gallienus' face as he admired her reflection in the mirror.

"There was some of that among my generals as well," he said. He reached out and put a hand on one of her bare shoulders, then stepped forward and kissed her neck. Lysisca shivered slightly from his touch.

"No plots or intrigues?" he asked.

"Were there any among your generals?" she asked, deflecting his question for the present.

"Probably." He caressed the back of her neck and lightly massaged her shoulders. "You must have heard something," he prompted her.

Lysisca turned and faced him, pausing long enough to allow him to take in her naked figure. Then, she threw her arms around his neck and pressed herself close to him. "Let's talk about that later," she suggested before putting her head against his shoulder and kissing his neck. He felt her hair against his cheek. A shiver ran down the side of his body, and he was aware of being guided to Lysisca's bed.

"Just lie still and enjoy yourself," she whispered, after noticing the wound on his back. "I'll take care of everything."

Much later, Lysisca felt a great sense of relief as she lay beside Gallienus, feeling his rapid heartbeat, then listening to his rhythmic heavy breathing.

"For a while, I thought I might have expected too much of myself." The sound of his voice surprised her.

"You did just fine," she purred, running her hand gently through his hair. She took a deep breath, exhaled slowly, and lay next to him without speaking for a long time. Gallienus reached out a hand and idly caressed her body. She waited anxiously, wondering when he would return to the discussion they had interrupted not long ago.

"We were talking earlier about plots and intrigues," he said casually. He felt her body tense. "You suggested that we talk about it later."

Her pulse quickened. "What would you like to know?"

"If there's any of either in this city, then surely you would have heard something about them."

Anything I tell him might result in some of my clients being hauled off to prison...or worse, she thought, *even if my information is sketchy—or maybe even inaccurate*. She tried to keep her voice conversational and not to reveal her concerns. "Most of what I've heard is from people making an occasional comment about what they've heard someone else say. There have been a lot of rumors as well," she took a breath and smiled at him. "The fact that you're here disproves at least one of them."

"All that's to be expected." Gallienus ran his fingers lightly up her arm while he waited for her to say more. It appeared to him that she was reluctant to offer information voluntarily. "What have you heard that I should know about?"

Lysisca was quiet for a moment. "There was only one bit of information I heard that deserves more than passing attention."

"A plot?" He rolled onto his side and faced Lysisca.

"I'd call it more of a scheme," she replied. "A succession plan, actually."

"It must be very interesting." His fingers gently massaged her shoulder, then ran to the back of her neck.

"Someone had proposed a plan of succession—not a plot to overthrow you—but rather a way to transfer power to someone else in case you died, or were already dead."

"Why would someone do that?"

"You weren't expected to live," she reminded him. "It was an attempt to avoid another civil war, so I was told."

"Did it have a lot of support?"

"I don't know, really."

"Who does it involve?"

"When you first asked me for this sort of information, I told you I'd lose my business if I gave you names." She held her breath, wondering if he would still honor that agreement. "At the time you said names weren't what you were interested in," she added.

"Plots can get very nasty, Lysisca."

"This wasn't a plot," she protested.

"Someone who helped to prevent it could be rewarded, handsomely." The cold expression she saw when he looked into her eyes sent a chill through her body. "On the other hand, someone who withheld information from me…" His meaning was clear to her.

"If word ever got out that I was supplying information, including names, to you, then you wouldn't have to shut my business down," she said. "Clients would stop coming. Then I'd have no further business and you'd have no further information."

"Perhaps a hint?" he suggested softly.

Lysisca realized that this was a grossly unequal contest of wills. *He could close my business or throw me in prison if he chose to.* She gave a sigh of resignation. "It was one of your Consuls."

Gallienus rolled onto his back, winced involuntarily, and stared at the ceiling. "That was very good," he congratulated Lysisca. "An excellent hint, and yet you gave me no names!" Gallienus lay quietly, considering her revelation. He thought first of Albinus, his senior Consul for the year. "Too old," he muttered to himself. "And Albinus has been loyal to me for years. What about Dexter? No, he asked to be replaced last summer. That leaves Maximus!" He frowned and scratched his head. "That doesn't sound like something Maximus would even think of," he continued his rational aloud, "let alone try to get support for." He looked over at Lysisca. "You're sure about this?"

"I wouldn't have said it otherwise."

Could my involvement with Prisca have any bearing on Maximus' loyalty? he wondered. *Could this be a way for him to take his revenge on me? If it were a plot, then Quintianus would be in a position to help him immeasurably. On the other hand, would Maximus risk his son's life like that?* "You're certain this wasn't actually a plot against my life?" he asked.

"I explained it to you as I understood it," Lysisca said. "Maximus frequents this establishment, too, but he prefers a different woman," she added. "And my girl told me that he never mentioned anything like this to her."

"No one considering that sort of thing would, unless he was stupid—or drunk."

"I've seen my share of men who were both," Lysisca snorted.

"Did you ever suggest that the girl ask Maximus about it some time?"

Lysisca nodded. "He was visibly surprised and upset when she did."

"It could have been an act."

"Possibly, but my girl didn't think so. It was curious," Lysisca added as she studied his reactions, "but it sounded like most of the promotion was being done by his wife."

Gallienus exhaled deeply, then nodded, and frowned. "That would explain a great deal!"

7-4

Questioning Motives
Mediolanum, Gallia Cisalpina
30 April, 264

"Do you think he's lost his nerve? I've seen it happen before." Aurelian's question hung in the air. He had just completed transferring slightly over fourteen thousand legionaries, three full legions, from their winter campsites in Pannonia to Mediolanum and joined Claudius, who had set up his own camp several weeks earlier. He had five wings of Roman cavalry and two thousand Marcomanni warriors, nearly six thousand horsemen in all. This was the first time the generals had had an opportunity to discuss the situation privately since arriving.

Claudius studied the wine in his glass before replying, as if he expected to find the answer to Aurelian's question there. "I understand what he's done and why," he said finally, "but I don't like it."

"Nor do I," Aurelian said after considering Claudius' comment for a moment. "He's been in the provinces fighting someone ever since he became emperor—until this year."

"He's still recovering from his wound," Claudius continued. "I haven't seen him draw a sword since he's been back on his feet. He nearly died after all."

Conversation lapsed while both men considered Gallienus' recent past.

"A serious wound, nearly dying, and lingering physical issues might be enough to make someone more cautious."

"He's gone to Athens to indulge in some ritual." Claudius said. "Do you know anything about the Eleusinian Mysteries, other than the name?"

"It's a secret cult," Aurelian nodded. "People who participate in the mystery seem to feel that death is not the finality we take it to be."

"I can see why it appeals to Gallienus."

"He's always been fascinated by all things Greek."

Claudius wondered if there was any validity to the idea of immortality. Then he looked curiously at Aurelian. "How do you happen to know so much about this secret cult?"

"My mother explained it to me once," Aurelian shrugged. "She's a priestess to the Sun god at the temple at home, as you know."

"Ah, yes," Claudius nodded his comprehension. "Then she would know about that."

The sun descended below the horizon and evening air grew chilly as they sat in silence. Finally Aurelian pulled his cape closer around him. *I'll have to make the rounds of my legionaries soon*, he thought. He cleared his throat. "Since Gallienus will be in Athens through September, there'll be no campaign this season against Postumus, and we're camped in Mediolanum just to block Postumus from marching on Rome. Why do you suppose he didn't send one of us with an army to finish the job?"

"Fear of being upstaged by a victorious general?" Claudius speculated. "Maybe he wants to be there himself when Postumus is defeated."

"Or maybe he's thinking that the last time he gave a general an army he was betrayed," Aurelian said, and he frowned as he thought of Aureolus and how he had let Postumus escape.

"Remember how hard it was for Gallienus to relieve Aureolus of his command?" Claudius asked. "The fact that Aureolus had deliberately let Postumus escape was obvious to everyone but Gallienus. He could barely bring himself to acknowledge the treachery."

"Do you think he ever realized that Aureolus betrayed him?" Aurelian asked.

"I don't know," Claudius paused, "but Gallienus wouldn't have been out of line if he'd executed him on the spot."

"That's what I would have done." Aurelian stretched. "I better check on my men," he said rising stiffly from his chair. "I suppose the empire will survive, fragmented as it is, for another year while Gallienus recovers from his wound." Aurelian shrugged. "Let's hope Gallienus is up to confronting Postumus next year."

7-5

Archon of Athens

Athens

02 July, 264

Gallienus sat in the receiving room of the Prytaneum,

residence of the Eponymous Archon in Athens. He gazed at the Acropolis through the building's entrance, and marveled at how he came to be here.

Salonina had suggested Athens as a suitable place for Gallienus to recover from his wound and fever. Once the Athenians learned of his plans, they elected him Eponymous Archon, the chief magistrate of the city, who shared power with two other principal archons, the Basileus (concerned with religious rites), the Polemarchos (military commander), and six other lesser archons with judicial functions. Shortly after their arrival in Athens, he and Salonina had experienced the Lesser of the Eleusinian Mysteries, and in the fall would be initiated in the Greater Eleusinian Mysteries, a secret cult of Demeter and Persephone that had existed for nearly two millennia.

The Prytaneum was regarded as the religious and political center of the community, the nucleus of all government, the official "home" of the people, and for centuries the location of the city's sacred fires. Columns and statues lined the receiving room's marble floor, a large rectangular hall with a chair, almost like a throne, at the center of one end and an entrance door at the center of the opposite wall.

Gallienus adjusted his crown of myrtle, then frowned as he considered his clothing, a short-sleeved, ankle-length white linen tunic, fastened by a gold belt at his waist, and trimmed with gold along the hem and ends of the sleeves. "What's next, Demetrius?" He looked expectantly at a short, stocky, balding man in his late forties who coordinated the Archon's meetings. Demetrius consulted his scroll and cleared his throat.

"We've finished the proclamations, appointments, and all current challenges—much more rapidly than is usually the case, I might add. There's a man named Herennius Dexippus to see you, Archon Basileus for this year. Your Praetorian Prefect is here as well."

"Bring them to me." He watched a tall, lanky man with ruddy complexion entering the room beside Volusianus. "Good of you to come, Dexippus," he said when the two men were standing in front of him. Although Gallienus had exchanged correspondence with Dexippus, this was the first time they had formally met. Dexippus showed an easy smile and exuded an air of self-confidence that reminded Gallienus of Aureolus.

"Welcome to Athens," Dexippus said with a slight nod of his head.

"This is the man with the disturbing news about eastern developments I've been telling you about, Volusianus."

"We talked briefly while we waited to see you," Dexippus said. He glanced around the room. "It's much as I remembered it. I was Eponymous Archon myself a few years ago. It's good for the ego to have a year named after your term in office."

"A little like the Romans naming their years after the two consuls who served," Volusianus said.

"You fought bravely against Goths in the past, Dexippus," Gallienus said.

Dexippus shrugged. "I was fighting to protect my family and to preserve my homeland."

"Two worthy causes," Gallienus agreed.

"And we've heard stories about a number of your impressive exploits. My sympathies on your wound but surviving your fever was commendable," Dexippus said. "In Athens, you have chosen a wonderful place for your recovery."

"It was actually my wife's suggestion. Perhaps we should compare war stories over dinner."

"It would be my pleasure," Dexippus agreed, "although I'm sure that's not the reason you asked to see me today."

"Regrettably not. The Amber Route runs through the Goth's homeland. A decrease in amber in Rome led me to believe there was some unrest in that area, which several amber traders confirmed. Some of my spies have told me about unrest in the east as well, but their details were sketchy. What do you know about this, Dexippus?"

"It seems that a sudden population growth put pressure on tribes near our eastern borders to move west. They're largely Goths, but also a tribe known as Heruli. The two seem to be in competition with each other, and the latter group has some experience with ships, as well as moving over land."

"If that's accurate, there could be trouble around the Pontus

Euxinus," Volusianus said.

"It is accurate," Dexippus assured him, "so we may even expect trouble in the waters around the Mare Aegaeum."

"I heard they might act together," Gallienus said.

Dexippus frowned. "That would be far worse."

"When is this supposed to happen?" Volusianus asked.

"Within the next few years."

"Preparing for that possibility takes time," Volusianus replied.

"Fortify some of the cities near the water," Dexippus suggested.

"And begin getting the navy ready for war," Gallienus added. "I'll have Volusianus contact you in the next couple days to set up a detailed planning meeting."

"Excellent," Dexippus said and tuned to go, then turned around. "Oh, I almost forgot. I understand that you and your wife are taking part in the Eleusinian Mysteries. In fact, I officiated at the Lesser Mysteries myself this year." He nodded as if to acknowledge to himself that he had covered the points he intended to talk about during the meeting.

After Dexippus left the room Gallienus turned to Volusianus. "You didn't have much to say during that discussion."

"I was wondering…" Volusianus cleared his throat, then hesitated. He glanced away briefly before he began again.

"What's on your mind?"

"We all know you need to recover from your wounds. I suppose it doesn't matter whether you do that in Rome or in Athens. And we realized at the start of the summer that your decision to attend the Eleusinian Mysteries would mean no campaign against Postumus this year."

"Then what is troubling you, Volusianus?"

"I wasn't aware you'd be assuming the responsibilities of Eponymous Archon, as well."

Gallienus smiled. "An unexpected honor. I couldn't refuse the opportunity."

"And the next archon won't assume his responsibilities until sometime next July, I believe?"

"That's correct," Gallienus agreed.

"Going a second year without attacking Postumus could encourage other revolts or invasions, when people see that you've done nothing to retake Gallia." Gallienus stared at him without responding. "I've made a quick calculation of the logistics required to mount a campaign against Postumus if we began from here next July," Volusianus continued. "It would be fall, at the earliest, before we could complete the march to Germania and challenge him in the field. Four years ago," he paused, recalling the time when Gallienus learned that Postumus had revolted and was besieging his son in Colonia Agrippina, "we concluded that starting a campaign in the fall was unwise."

Gallienus frowned and mulled Volusianus' comments over in his mind. "As I recall, we got word of Postumus' revolt in October of that year. At that point it was nearly winter."

"In any event," Volusianus persisted, "a mid or late fall operation would not, in my opinion, be advisable."

"A reasonable assessment," Gallienus agreed, then fell silent for a moment. "So we both agree that a late fall campaign is unwise."

"Then, Postumus' control of Gallia will go unchallenged both this year and next?" Volusianus voiced the obvious as a question. "Do you think that's wise?" He waited for an answer but got none. "Have you given any further thought to my suggestion of putting an army in the field commanded by one of your generals?" Volusianus' question interrupted the silence.

Gallienus dismissed the suggestion with a wave of his hand. "We've talked about this before. Why bring it up again?"

"Our plan was for a single season," Volusianus reminded him. "I'm concerned about the loyalty of the legions—and the trust of your generals."

"What legions? Which generals?"

"There's no disloyalty or trust issues now, that I'm aware of," Volusianus held up both hands. "But I know the generals are uncomfortable leaving Postumus in place, as am I. And I fear that prolonged inactivity could have a number of undesired results."

"What would you suggest?" Gallienus asked.

Volusianus looked Gallienus directly in the eye. "Give me an army. Let me defeat Postumus for you." Gallienus stared at him for what seemed an eternity, then shook his head.

"No. Postumus has all he can do to keep the Franks from overrunning the province. And he seems inclined to restrict his interests to Gallia," Gallienus said.

"Britannia and Hispania have joined him, not an insignificant part of the empire," Volusianus countered. "Do you think Postumus will always be content with just part of it?"

Gallienus held up a hand. "I'm content to leave the situation with Postumus as it is for the time being. He has the Franks to deal with. Claudius and Aurelian will discourage him from trying to reach Rome, and the central part of the empire is quiet now. I'm not in Athens exclusively for my recovery. Neither are the honors of being an Archon nor the privilege of attending the Eleusinian Mysteries the reasons for my visit. Rumors of trouble coming to this area appear to be true and we have a chance to prepare for it now. That's my principle reason for an extended visit to the east."

Volusianus realized further discussion was pointless. Then he drew himself up fully erect, saluted formally, and withdrew wordlessly. The sound of his sandals on the marble floor echoed off the room's walls. At the doorway Volusianus stopped. He hesitated a moment. Then he wheeled about to face Gallienus and spoke so he could be heard clearly across the room. "I'd be derelict in my duties if I didn't speak my mind. There is strong disagreement with your decision not to engage Postumus this year, either by yourself or by one of your generals. I think it's going to be worse when a second campaign season passes without acting." He stopped to catch his breath.

When Gallienus started to respond he held up a hand. "I beg leave to finish." Volusianus was Gallienus' most trusted general and closest advisor. Although he was frowning, Gallienus nodded for him to continue. "Inaction is both a tactical error, and a morale error. One year will raise eyebrows but, due to your wound, people can understand why you're not acting. Ignoring Postumus for a second year will suggest to the world that you've accepted his revolt. Further," he stopped for a breath, "the people of Gallia will come to think of Postumus, not of you, as their ruler.

Postumus himself might be tempted to advance his control over the whole empire, not just over Gallia, Hispania, and Britannia. Odenathus might decide Rome is too weak and indecisive for him to bother with. And why should the barbarians fear Rome, when Rome doesn't seem willing or strong enough to retake a province? Their conclusion would be the same regardless of whether it's an issue of will or weakness. Then there are your soldiers. The legionaries are young and trained to fight. Remember how Maximinus murdered Emperor Severus Alexander and his mother when Alexander tried to bribe the barbarians instead of fighting them." Volusianus continued, not expecting Gallienus to reply. "As for your generals, they're tough, capable men who've risen from the ranks themselves. You and your father made them what they are, but there's a limit to their loyalty. At some point they might decide they could do your job better than you." He stopped for a moment knowing that what he'd just said might result in the generals being relieved or arrested. "At present there are only dissatisfaction and restlessness. I'm telling you what I fear might happen."

He felt suddenly spent, just as he did after a fiercely fought battle, when he had the time to think about how close to death he had just been. Now he realized that he had severely criticized his commander and suggested revolt among Gallienus' generals and unrest among his legions. He took another breath and looked at Gallienus, who stared at him, uncharacteristically speechless. Volusianus didn't know if his career was over or not. *Either way, I've done my duty as I see it,* he thought. "With your permission, sir," he said, saluting Gallienus again, and without waiting for an acknowledgement, pivoted on his heel and retired.

As soon as the door closed behind Volusianus, Demetrius entered the room. "I trust everything went well with your general," Demetrius said solicitously, although he had overheard everything. Demetrius stopped when he noticed Gallienus staring vacantly into space, apparently unaware of his presence. He waited a few moments, then cleared his throat and shuffled the papers in his hands. The noise broke Gallienus' reverie. He sat upright abruptly.

"Your wife is waiting to see you."

Gallienus sighed. He suddenly remembered that he had invited Pipa to come to the Prytaneum this afternoon, since he was planning to spend the evening with her. "Yes, I'll see her now."

Demetrius bowed slightly and retired.

While he waited for Pipa's entry, he reflected on Volusianus' concerns of trust, loyalty, and Postumus. His thoughts turned to Aurelian and Claudius, well over a thousand miles away, and together commanding slightly over twenty thousand men. *What's the likelihood that either or both of them would revolt?* he wondered. *My plans to block Postumus included a balance of forces and generals both in Mediolanum and in Pannonia.* He scratched his head unconsciously. *Aurelian and Claudius could revolt and march straight to Rome and would probably be there before I even learned about it.*

Gallienus shifted in his chair and reached back to rub the spot where the arrow had struck him last summer. *I could replace Aurelian and Claudius in Mediolanum next year before they devise a succession plan of their own, but who could I trust in those positions?* The phrase brought an ironic smile to his face. That was the term Prisca used last fall when she conceived her own succession plan! Only hers was different. *That's what she told me.* He thought about the meeting with Prisca after he had learned of what she had done when she thought he might die. He had accused her of organizing a plot to make Maximus emperor. Her smile suggested she thought he was joking, but when she realized he was serious, a look of astonishment swept the smile from her face and fear briefly showed in her eyes. But Prisca had seen nothing wrong with her idea, and defended it vigorously. "We wanted you to live," she had insisted, "but we didn't want another civil war and we didn't want to be killed by your successor if you died!" He remembered studying Prisca's face and searching for any betrayal of emotion. She had returned his gaze, confident and unapologetic, and he believed her. *I can still see her dark penetrating eyes and the flash of the smile she sometimes showed me.* He had reached out and touched her cheek, and she had put her hand over his and held it. The thought of her efforts and resourcefulness made him smile. *Of course her plan would never have succeeded. But she tried to make the best of an uncertain situation.* He thought about risks that people close to him were exposed to, willingly or otherwise. People loyal to one emperor were sometimes considered a threat by his successor, especially if the successor came to power by violent means—the usual course of events.

"That crown of myrtle looks a bit uncomfortable."

Gallienus looked up, startled by Salonina's voice. He reached up and unconsciously adjusted the wreath. "The emblem of inviolability, you mean?" he asked, concerned that she had entered the room unnoticed and now stood directly in front of him. "It itches."

"You seemed surprised to see me."

"I was."

She looked at his white and gold tunic, his sandals, and the myrtle crown appraisingly. "You look rather handsome dressed as an Archon. I'm sorry I didn't come to see you yesterday, but I thought your first day would be very confusing."

He willed a smile onto his face. "You're aware, I assume, that Greeks don't take kindly to their women interrupting business."

"I'm a Roman woman. And while I appreciate Greek culture, I have no use for their primitive notions restricting women to the hearth and home." Salonina paused. "I thought you'd be done by now."

He looked uneasily at the door where Demetrius had disappeared, before looking at Salonina.

"When I was growing up, I never dreamed I'd get the chance to experience the Eleusinian Mysteries," Salonina said. "Everyone who's ever been a part of them told me the experience changed their lives forever. And it's so exciting to be sharing the experience with you."

He smiled, pleased at Salonina's enthusiasm.

"I thought we could discuss some of our preparations for the Greater Mysteries over dinner tonight," she said. "There's so much to learn, and I have questions about several rituals."

"I'm afraid… that won't be possible." He took a breath and

exhaled it slowly. "I've made arrangements to see Pipa tonight," he said, anticipating Salonina's disappointment. "I thought I'd mentioned that to you this morning."

Salonina's smile left her face as she tried to conceal her disappointment. "It seems like such a waste," she said, letting her voice trail away.

"Seeing Pipa?"

"Well, that too, but I meant bringing her to Greece. How could she possibly appreciate Greek art, culture, or philosophy? Thank the gods she doesn't speak a word of Greek, otherwise she'd probably want to participate in the mysteries herself."

Gallienus hoped his surprise at Salonina's speculation didn't show. Pipa had, in fact, wanted to take part in the Mysteries—especially when she learned Salonina was involved herself. Even though he had told Pipa that participants were required to speak Greek, she refused to accept his explanation and wanted him to waive this one requirement by Imperial decree. Gallienus realized that he, too, was grateful that Pipa did not speak Greek. There were four months of preparations and rituals between the April initiation at the Lesser Mysteries and the revelation of the Greater Mysteries in September. The idea of five months of potential close-contact encounters between the two women, and later the certainty of contact during two nights together in the same hall made him shudder. Pipa had shown some interest in the city, its architecture, and its history, but none in Greek culture which she regarded as a weakness rather than a refinement—reason enough for the Greeks to have been conquered by the Romans.

"I'm afraid it will have to wait," Gallienus said to Salonina.

"What will have to wait?"

"Our discussion. Exploring the Mysteries with you will be my priority and my pleasure—tomorrow, after I've finished here."

Salonina searched his face. "Fine!" she responded, resigned to the fact that his mind was made up, although in her mind it wasn't fine at all. *Once more I have to wait to be his priority and his pleasure.* She started to leave, but stopped and turned back to face him. "Oh, if your conversation with Pipa should happen to lag tonight, why not ask her opinion about redemption in

Aeschylus' play *Oresteia*. That should be interesting." She turned away from him but stopped when she saw Demetrius standing at the door, ashen-faced.

"What's troubling you, Demetrius?" Gallienus asked.

"There's a woman in the waiting room to see you,"

"I thought you said you were done for the day," Salonina said to Gallienus. "Who is it?" she asked Demetrius.

"She claims to be your wife," Demetrius stammered, directing his reply to Gallienus. "I tried to send her away, but she was insistent. And there's a dreadful man with her who threatened me physically if I didn't listen to his daughter."

The door to the waiting room flew open and banged against the wall. "Where have you run off to, Demetrius, you insolent son of a ……" Attalus bellowed, as he burst into the room. Demetrius cowered behind Gallienus' chair. Attalus paused uncertainly when he noticed Salonina staring at him with a mixture of surprise and horror on her face. "Perhaps," he suggested, suddenly uncomfortable, "I've come at a bad time."

"Your timing is perfect, Attalus," Salonina replied, recovering her composure. She looked past Attalus to where Pipa stood in the doorway. "I was just leaving." She looked at Gallienus once more, sadness and disappointment in her eyes; then she walked from the room without further comment. An awkward silence filled the room.

"Sorry if I interrupted anything important," Attalus said to Gallienus. "Since you'd invited Pipa to come, I didn't think—and he," Attalus pointed at Demetrius, "never said anything about Salonina being here." He glared at Demetrius who stood beside Gallienus looking as if he expected an apology. "None of this changes my impression of you," Attalus growled at Demetrius.

"We'll work this out later," Gallienus nodded at Demetrius.

Demetrius arched an eyebrow, and hesitated for a moment before bowing slightly. He kept his eyes on Attalus as he walked from the room with as much dignity as he could muster. But he hurried when he was closest to Attalus, who glared at him menacingly. Demetrius kept his eyes on Attalus as he passed and nearly collided with Pipa who had entered the room shortly after

Salonina departed.

Pipa dodged Demetrius, then walked around Gallienus' chair looking at him critically. "So this is how the Greeks dispense justice?" she mused.

"For over nine hundred years. I thought you'd enjoy seeing the building's magnificent architecture, detailed mosaics, elegant statues," he pointed needlessly around the room, "and the way I'm dressed."

She looked at the art and architecture indifferently, then studied Gallienus' appearance. "You're far more impressive in armor," she said finally.

"That would be more 'imposing,'" Gallienus suggested, disappointed at Pipa's lack of enthusiasm.

"We don't need all this to decide who's right and who's wrong," Attalus frowned, looking around the room. "We sit on logs, around a campfire. I think our truth is at least as real as the Greeks'."

Gallienus sighed at their lack of appreciation for craftsmanship and nuanced expressions of Greek statues.

"Greeks are just one more of your conquered people." Attalus replied. "They're fortunate you haven't enslaved them or destroyed their cities. If Demetrius is any example of what their men are like, I'm surprised they lasted as long as they did."

"There was a time when the Greeks ruled almost the entire known world."

"Those men I'd like to have known," Attalus conceded.

"I hope you won't get too comfortable with this way of living," Pipa said, putting a hand on Gallienus' shoulder. "It weakens the will." She studied his clothes for a moment. "You… won't come with us dressed like that, will you?"

"Wait for me in the receiving room." *I came to Athens for rest and recuperation*, he thought, after Attalus and Pipa left. He rubbed his chin and looked around the empty room for several moments. Then he stood, took a deep breath, removed the crown of myrtle and tossed it onto a chair before walking out of the room alone.

7-6
Oracle at Delphi
Epirus, Greece
10 July, 265

"The god Apollo himself speaks through me," the Pythia, priestess of the Delphi Oracle, intoned before slipping into her trance. "Therefore, heed his message." She adjusted herself on a tripod perched over a chasm in the earth and inhaled vapors rising from a fissure below her while she studied the man standing a few feet away.

Priests had earlier determined that Gallienus' sacrificial goat offering was acceptable to the god, and that this was an auspicious time for prophesy. They had then escorted the priestess to the temple, accompanied by Gallienus and she had stopped at the hearth of the eternal flame where, centuries earlier, Orestes had slain the son of Achilles. After burning an offering of laurel leaves and barley meal on the hearth, she had descended into the Adyton, a holy chamber below the temple, where Apollo's prophesy would be delivered through her. She was thin, about thirty years old, with short dark hair. In one hand she held a sprig of laurel, sacred to Apollo, in the other a dish of holy water from the nearby Kassotis spring. Her white, short-sleeved, ankle-length dress was partially covered by a pale blue wrap draped over her head and ending mid-calf, leaving her bare feet exposed.

"Welcome to my temple, Emperor of Rome, guardian of the civilized world, protector of this sacred oracle. You are favored by Zeus, my father, although you know him as Jupiter."

Gallienus had long sought an opportunity to visit Delphi. *I'm at the most famous oracle in the world, speaking directly with the god Apollo*! A shiver ran up Gallienus' spine. He cleared his throat and shifted self-consciously before answering. "I'm here to…"

"There's no need to explain, Gallienus," the Pythia interrupted. "I know why you're here."

* * *

"If you ask me, it's a long way to come, just to listen to some woman in a cave answer a few questions," Attalus said to the two generals with him. He sat on the steps of the temple and tossed a pebble at a nearby pigeon. Volusianus watched the pigeon flutter a few feet further away. Heraclianus, recently transferred to Gallienus' staff, smiled at Attalus' comment, as he watched people entering and leaving the temple. Meanwhile, Attalus studied the city around him, not with a Greek's awe nor with a Roman's respect, but rather as a potential conqueror. City walls were not overly high, he had noticed, and the city was not defended by any troops. Morning sunlight glinting off Apollo's nearby statue caught his attention. *Must be made of gold! Enough to pay my entire army, after I melted it down*, he thought with a smile. *And Delphi's Treasury buildings must have a fortune in them from all the donations*. Attalus shook his head and took a deep breath of the clear, cool air. In Athens by this time temperature would be uncomfortably hot.

"For their important decisions Greeks, and many others, come to Delphi." Volusianus' explanation intruded on Attalus' musings.

Heraclianus chuckled. "It's been said that the Oracle, 'the Pythia' they call her, neither reveals nor conceals. Rather she indicates."

"Sometimes prophesies have been given directly," Volusianus added, "and sometimes in verse. Ambiguity protects the Oracle. Unpleasant truths can anger powerful, ambitious men who come seeking the god's advice. A king once came to ask if he should make war against one of his neighbors. The Pythia told him that if he did 'a great empire would be destroyed.' Turned out to be his own."

"I could get as much from my own seers," Attalus shrugged, no longer impressed, "probably much cheaper—and they would come to me." He considered Heraclianus' comment for a moment, then asked "Why is this Oracle called the Pythia?"

"Greeks regard Delphi as the center of the earth. Many centuries ago, this place was guarded by a giant python, which

Apollo had to kill before he could claim Delphi for himself. For a while the site was actually known as Pytho, after the dead serpent. The 'Pythia' is a title that pays respect to the dead serpent, also female," Heraclianus explained.

Volusianus glanced impatiently into the temple. Somewhere inside, below the temple's main floor, Gallienus was still alone with the oracle. No Roman soldiers had accompanied him, and, while Volusianus expected no violence in this sacred place, he was always uneasy when Gallienus went anyplace without guards. "We aren't leaving Greece any too soon for me," Volusianus said with a sigh.

"I agree," Attalus said. "Greeks are too consumed with festivals and games to have any time left for fighting."

"And since he's been here, Gallienus hasn't missed any of them," Heraclianus noted, "the Nemean games last July, the Eleusinian mysteries in September, the Dionysia this spring." He paused. "Now we're at Delphi, and next month we'll be at the Olympian Games. And Salonina has encouraged all of it." He shook his head glumly.

"There were reasons for him coming to Greece other than recovery, but we've ignored more pressing issues elsewhere," Volusianus said, casting another glance toward the Oracle's chamber. "His concerns about a Gothic invasion haven't materialized, although we've fortified a number of cities and left their fleet in a better state of readiness."

"You'd think we were at peace everywhere, from the coins he's minted," Heraclianus said to Volusianus. "Last fall's issue said, 'Peace Secured', and the ones minted in Mediolanum this spring with 'Salonina, Empress of Peace' on them."

"How do you suppose the generals at Mediolanum reacted to that?" Volusianus speculated.

"What difference does it make what you put on a coin?" Attalus asked.

"Propaganda," Volusianus said. Attalus stared at him blankly.

"The soldiers are paid in coins," Heraclianus explained. "What coins say on them is intended to influence their thinking and later, when the coins get into circulation, the population's thinking."

"Well we are at peace right now," Attalus frowned, "although we shouldn't be."

"Maybe Gallienus wants everyone to think the problems are solved."

Volusianus cleared his throat, interrupting Heraclianus. "What do you think the Oracle has said to him? He's been with her for quite a while."

* * *

"You are wondering whether to go West or East from here," the Pythia said to Gallienus.

"Yes. To defeat Postumus or confront a Gothic threat."

"If you cross the waters to Asia Minor like Alexander, then another general will cross the mountains like Hannibal." The priestess paused and breathed fumes emanating from the chasm below her.

That's why I've left a good bit of my army at Mediolanum. He nodded, reassured at the Pythia's validation of his assessment.

"But neither of those threats is your most dangerous foe." She fixed her gaze on him.

Gallienus stared at her. *What haven't I considered?* "Then who is?"

"You've picked good generals, Gallienus, but not always loyal ones."

He frowned and thought of the generals who had already betrayed him. Ingenuus and Regalianus each revolted when they were governors of Pannonia. Macrianus revolted after Valerian's defeat in the east. Then Postumus revolted in Gallia, and later Aemilianus in Egypt. Only Postumus still remained undefeated. The others were all dead, except Aureolus who had been forced to relinquish his command after Gallienus' generals accused him of treason. Gallienus shook his head, and looked up to see the Pythia watching him.

"Trust bestowed does not assure trust repaid."

"Then who can I trust?" he asked, throwing up his hands.

"Those closest, least."

"It's impossible to rule this empire without relying on others!"

The Pythia gazed into the dish in her lap that held water from the sacred Kassotis spring without commenting. She remained motionless until Gallienus thought she had lapsed into a trance. Finally she looked up and into his eyes. "Beware of being twice betrayed," she said.

"By whom?"

The priestess sighed and shook her head. Her shoulders drooped forward. "He's left me," she said. She closed her eyes, her head bent forward, and she spoke softly. "I see—nothing more."

* * *

Gallienus emerged from the temple's dim light into brilliant morning sunlight. He paused on the steps and blinked while his eyes adjusted. Attalus stood, casually tossing his handful of pebbles onto the ground. Heraclianus was now fully alert and watching the emperor.

"What did she tell you?" Volusianus asked, when Gallienus seemed acclimated to the daylight.

"She said to trust no one," Gallienus answered lightly. "After the session, a priest who witnessed the Oracle's pronouncements had dictated it to a scribe." Gallienus held up a scroll the priest had given to him, but didn't offer to show it to anyone.

Attalus snorted.

"You got that advice from your father in Rome years ago," Volusianus noted, glancing at Heraclianus. He wondered what the Oracle had actually said, and why Gallienus was reluctant to share it.

"I did," Gallienus replied. He stood silently, gazing into space, puzzling over the Oracle's prophesy of a second betrayal. *Perhaps Salonina will be able to make sense of what the Oracle told me, or maybe Pipa.*

"That was the only thing she told you in all that time?"

Attalus marveled. "These Greeks do have a way with words."
The comment caused Volusianus and Heraclianus to chuckle.

Their laughter brought Gallienus back from his reverie. He realized this was not the time to mull over Pythia's comments. He would decide later what, if anything further, he would share with them. For now, he smiled at their jokes, took a deep breath, stretched, and looked admiringly at the gleaming Temple of Apollo, at the huge amphitheater rising majestically above them, over to Apollo's great golden statue, and then down the valley covered with grey-green olive trees. *I've got what I came here for. Now I can return to Rome and focus my attention on Postumus.* "No need to stay here any further," he said. "We'll go to Mycenae before the games begin at Olympia in August. I'd like to see King Agamemnon's ancient home." He paused. "Do you think Achilles ever set foot there?" he asked the gathered generals. Before any of them could think of a suitable reply, he turned and began descending the steps.

North of Colonia Agrippina, Germania Inferior
31 July, 265

I've had two years of successful campaigns against the Franks, Postumus thought with pride and satisfaction. He sat alone in his tent and drank red wine from a simple cup, still wearing the clothes he had worn during his just-completed battle. The thought of a bath was appealing, but it would have to wait until he returned to the Roman side of the river. For now, he felt content to relax with nothing more important to do than to drink wine. *And Gallienus has made no move to attack me for two years!* Postumus finished his wine and poured more from the pitcher on the table in front of him. *Why has he spent two years in Athens instead of coming here? Has he given up all thoughts of reclaiming Gallia?* Marius and Victorinus, his closest generals, thought so.

Postumus frowned. *Maybe they're right, but I can't ignore the possibility of his returning.* Postumus had originally claimed that he sought no lands east of the Alpes Mountains. The fact that he continued to honor this pledge was really due to barbarian attacks and to Gallienus' placement of soldiers at Mediolanum. But since his recent victories over the barbarians, Postumus began thinking more about challenging Gallienus. *If there were only some sort of distraction elsewhere in the empire. Then he'd have to take soldiers from Mediolanum.. That would be the time to make my move!* Postumus stretched to ease the tension of his aching muscles. Unconsciously, he wiped sweat and grime from his forehead with a sleeve of his tunic. *I'll issue some coins, he decided, see how the soldiers react to them. What should they say?. 'Ruler of the East' and 'Peacemaker of the World' should do for starters.* His spies had told him of Gallienus' coins issued in Mediolanum proclaiming Salonina 'Empress of Peace.' He smiled at that indication of wishful thinking. Gallienus' vision of peace conflicted with his vision of an empire united under his rule! *The Fates have allowed me to survive each of Gallienus' attempts to retake Gallia. Now he no longer tries.* He drained his glass. *Perhaps the Fates will also allow my vision to prevail over his.*

7-7

Goths

Outside Ctesiphon, Persia

13 June, 266

He's reading a message—in the middle of a siege, Zenobia mused, watching her husband from a distance. The sounds and confusion of battle had forced Odenathus to lean close in order to hear what the horseman who had just galloped up to him was saying. He'd nodded at the man, then accepted a message that the man offered before dismissing him with a nod. Messages frequently came to the King during a battle, but they were always verbal—short, concise communications. Now Odenathus had shifted his attention away from the siege of Ctesiphon, broken the seal on this message, and was actually reading it. She realized it must be of considerable importance and rode quickly to him from her place at the head of the reserve forces. Her son, Vaballathus, trailed along behind her, following his mother's instructions to stay close to her at all times.

Zenobia reined her horse to a stop on Odenathus' left side, and studied his sweaty, dust-covered face while he read. Herodian sat astride his horse on Odenathus' right side, uninterested in the siege, but suddenly curious about the message and its contents. Odenathus continued to read, frowned, and shook his head. He unconsciously lowered the hand holding the scroll, allowing it to rest on the saddle in front of him. He looked up, surveying the battle around him, then raised his hand and read the message again. He took a deep breath.

"What does it say?" Zenobia demanded loudly in order to be heard above the din of battle.

"It's from Rome."

"Has Gallienus defeated Postumus?"

Odenathus didn't answer immediately. Instead, he lifted his helmet and wiped sweat from his forehead.

"Did Postumus defeat him? Is Gallienus dead? What is it?" Her voice grew increasingly urgent.

Odenathus looked from the message to Zenobia. "There's been an invasion."

"Oh. That's it?"

Odenathus wanted time to think about Gallienus' request and how he would respond to it. He turned to Herodian. "Supervise the siege while I consider this matter."

"Me?" Herodian asked. "But what about the message?"

"Do it now!" Odenathus snapped.

Reluctantly, Herodian reined his horse around and left the discussion.

"Who invaded? Where?" Zenobia's questions intruded on Odenathus' thoughts. He sighed. As long as Zenobia was beside him, there was no chance he would be able to read it uninterrupted.

"The Goths attacked a city on the south shore of Pontus Euxinus," Odenathus replied, "about the same time we left Palmyra."

"And?"

"Gallienus wants us to engage them."

"Doesn't he know where we are, and what we've been doing?"

"I've tried to keep him informed," Odenathus looked at the message again, "but it took over a month for this to reach us. Who knows what information he had when he wrote it."

Zenobia considered their situation and Gallienus' request. "After all the battles we've fought to get this far! The victories over Shapur and armies his supporters brought to help him. Then to abandon the siege and just leave!"

Odenathus considered her objections for a moment. "I can't ignore his request, Zenobia."

"Does he realize it will take us at least a month to reach them?"

"Probably longer," Odenathus agreed.

"The Goths might well be gone before we even get there."

"Clearly this is important to him. I doubt he'd make the request lightly."

We're only a couple of weeks away from victory here; why leave now?" Zenobia thought. But she knew Odenathus' relationship with Gallienus gave him freedom to act largely as he wished.

"All right," Zenobia sighed. "Which city? How many of them are there? Are they coming south toward us, or going in some other direction? Or does anybody know?"

Odenathus looked at the message again. "A town called Polemonium, west of Trapezus, it says. They headed south, after sacking the city. The message doesn't say how many there are, but apparently Gallienus doesn't consider his two legions on the Armenian border sufficient to confront them, or maybe he doesn't want to commit the legions and leave the area vulnerable to further attacks. He doesn't say."

"He's asking us to march our army through provinces controlled by other governors," Zenobia said. "How will they respond to that?"

"Gallienus has given me the title of Corrector Totius Orientis, that grants me authority to supervise civil administration of the whole eastern part of the empire."

"The governors won't like that."

"But it gives us the authority to pass through their provinces."

"We've never been through any of the country beyond Antioch." Zenobia smiled. "Maybe we should ask Shapur for directions. He's been further north and west into the provinces than we have."

"I'll have to get someone who's traveled with the caravans and knows the country. We'll take mounted troops, leave the foot soldiers in Palmyra."

"Why should we abandon our siege to help Gallienus with his problems?" Herodian interrupted. He'd returned to them unnoticed with all the confusion around them. "Why can't he go there himself?"

"His problems are our problems," Odenathus replied. "What are you doing here? I put you in charge of the siege."

"I left General Zabdas in charge," Herodian said casually. "Your message seemed important, and if he's listening," Herodian jerked a thumb at Vaballathus, who had followed his mother from the reserve forces, "then I should know what's in it too."

Odenathus frowned at Herodian for a moment, but let his action pass without comment. "The emperor asked for our help," he explained to Herodian. "And bringing our army through Asia Minor will increase our prestige throughout the area, at the same time as we're helping the emperor."

"Perhaps someone should return to Palmyra—make sure all stays quiet at home while you go that far north," Herodian suggested, thinking of the long march from Ctesiphon to wherever the barbarians might be,

"Your place is with your father at the head of the army," Zenobia objected. "The soldiers will expect that." *I'm not going to let Herodian miss another opportunity to get killed in battle, whether it's by the Goths or by the Persians, and nothing fatal will happen to him while he's lounging with his harem at Palmyra.*

Odenathus nodded agreement with Zenobia, but he was preoccupied with another matter. "There's no indication that this siege will end any time soon. However, it's an embarrassment to Shapur and a drain on his nearby resources. I'll negotiate an agreement with him, not give up what we've fought so hard to win without concessions in return." He was lost in thought a while longer. *If Shapur learned we were quitting the siege to help Gallienus with a distant problem, we'd get nothing from him.* "Herodian," he said firmly, "resume command of the siege, and send General Zabdas to me. We have some planning to do."

Heraclea, Bithynia
18 September, 266

"They're escaping!" Zenobia exclaimed. The city of Bithynia, rising on the edge of a headland to their left, had obscured their view of the harbor. But the road, where Zenobia, Odenathus, Herodian, and General Zabdas had paused, now curved to reveal a natural harbor filled with boats, full of departing Goths. Some of the warriors were still on the beach, loading the last of their captives and booty into small boats. Five large boats, still tied to piers along the edge of the harbor, were in the final process of getting underway. Many other ships filled the outer harbor, awaiting the last of their comrades to join them.

A warrior glanced up, saw the column of Odenathus' warriors, and pointed excitedly in their direction. Word of Odenathus' presence swept through their ranks. They began rushing to complete their loading and escape before Odenathus' forces could intercede.

"This is your chance to attack another enemy of Rome!" Zenobia shouted to Herodian. "They're already in retreat," she added, aware of his natural reluctance to engage any enemy.

"If they're already retreating," Herodian equivocated, "why risk taking any casualties?"

Zenobia looked to Odenathus, who waited for Herodian to take the initiative.

"We can't just watch them leave, not after coming all this way," Zenobia exclaimed. She turned to her soldiers and shouted, "Follow me," then urged her horse into a gallop, with no further word to Herodian, or to Odenathus.

Her son, Vaballathus, raced after her, his sword slashing the air over his head. He had recently started displaying his mother's aggressiveness and was eager to show his courage after his previous encounter with the Persians three years earlier.

What does he think he'll accomplish? Herodian mused, watching Vaballathus trail after his mother. *He's only ten years old! Maybe he'll get himself killed. That would do me a favor.*

Zenobia raced down the road, then onto the sandy beach. Some of the nearby Goths drew their weapons and readied themselves, but she galloped past them and into the surf, pursuing the boats that had just been launched. When she'd ridden alongside the last of the boats, she slashed her sword at warriors on the side nearest to her. A Goth faced her as the boat continued to glide into deeper water. He had drawn his dagger and waited for the moment to make his attack, but Zenobia thrust her sword into his belly first. In a boat just ahead of Zenobia, a tall and muscular Goth with long blond hair stood precariously in the stern of his heavily laden boat. While Zenobia struggled to free her sword from her victim, he took aim at her with his battle ax.

Vaballathus shouted a warning from behind his mother. Zenobia held up her shield, anticipating the blow, and leaned forward, her head resting on the Goth's shoulder to brace herself against the impact of the ax. If the blow knocked her into the water with the armor she was wearing, she would drown. Even though her helmet was firmly in place, she saw greasy blond strands of hair in front of her face and nearly gagged at the stench of his unwashed body. The crash of the axe on her shield pushed her even closer to the Goth. She looked at her shield, split with the ax still lodged in it, and useless against another ax blow. She threw it into the water on the left side of her horse. The distant Goth grabbed an ax from the man beside him. Zenobia let go of her sword and pushed the impaled Goth into the water. She reached for a javelin from behind her saddle, aimed at the distant Goth, and threw it with all her strength. The javelin arced through the air and struck the man in the shoulder while his arm was pulled back to throw the second ax. He screamed with pain, dropped the ax, and fell into the water behind the boat.

The occupants of the farther boat did not stop to rescue their comrade while he thrashed in the water, and tried to pull the javelin from his shoulder. Zenobia glanced away from him and looked to find the man with her sword lodged in his stomach. He was treading water beside her horse, blood flowing from his wound and swirling in the water. Zenobia bent over and grasped the hilt of her sword. She put a foot on the man's chest and pulled. When the sword came free, she almost fell over backwards, but caught her horse's mane with her left hand. She became aware of whizzing sounds overhead and splashes in the water in front of her. Palmyran archers! No wonder I haven't had to deal with another ax attack. The Goth she hit with the javelin had managed to pull it free. She decided to take him prisoner, sheathed her sword, and urged her horse deeper into the water. The Goth had slipped below the surface, his wet clothes dragging him down, but he struggled and finally managed to get his head above water. Zenobia grabbed him by his long yellow hair and began dragging him back to shore. He pulled a dagger and twisted around to stab her. She pushed him away and he immediately began flailing in the water.

"Drop it," she shouted in Aramaic, and then in Greek, when he didn't respond to her first command. He looked at her in amazement, realizing for the first time that he had been fighting a woman. He saw her watching him, just far enough away so that he could not reach her, and showing not the slightest interest in helping him while he was armed. He dropped his dagger; she moved forward and reached out to him again. When he took hold of her wrist, he yanked hard, trying to drag her off her horse. Although she resisted his pull, she was leaning precariously toward the Goth who still held her tightly. He grinned at her as he lifted his legs to push against the horse's stomach. She was almost overpowered when a second horse moved behind the Goth and the rider stuck his sword at the man's throat.

"Let her go or you die!" Vaballathus shouted to the Goth in Greek. He had been close enough to hear Zenobia's earlier exchange. The Goth dropped Zenobia's arm and spun around to face Vaballathus. His surprise turned to disbelief: he was fighting a woman and a child! In an instant, Zenobia regained her balance and again grabbed the man by his hair.

"If he struggles, kill him!" she shouted to Vaballathus in Greek so the man would understand.

* * *

Zenobia's warriors met her when she and Vaballathus dragged the Goth into shallower water. The small skirmish on the beach had ended while Zenobia confronted the departing boats. The last of the ships, now beyond arrow range, sailed into the open sea. The Goths trapped on the beach had fought Odenathus' troops, rather than surrender. The wounded screamed or moaned as they writhed on the sand before death ended their agonies. Some of the Goths had fallen into the water, where they drowned or died from their wounds. Treasure that had been seized during their summer of sacking cities lay scattered near the remaining boats. The women and children whom the Goths were planning to take home for ransom, or to sell as slaves, huddled together comforting each other.

Odenathus met Zenobia as she and Vaballathus brought their prisoner to shore. Although exhausted, she was still exuberant. Odenathus' face broke into an approving smile.

"Good of you to save one of them for questioning," he grinned. "But for a while I wasn't sure who was going to prevail."

"Thanks to Vaballathus, I'm still here." Zenobia nodded at her son. "You were exceptional out there," she said to him, putting her hand on his shoulder. Vaballathus broke into a grin at her praise.

"Today you fought like a warrior!" Odenathus added gravely, nodding his approval. Then he turned to the Goth. "Where are the boats going?" he demanded. The man stared at him, uncomprehending.

"He speaks Greek," Zenobia informed Odenathus, repeating the question to him in that language. The Goth looked at her and smiled. "To our homeland, with your women and your treasure."

"But not you."

"I'll go to the warrior's hall," he boasted.

"Not unless you die with a weapon in your hand," Zenobia

contradicted him. "Answer our questions and maybe we'll let you die like a warrior."

He scowled at her, but nodded reluctantly.

"Where did you come from?" Odenathus asked.

"The north shore of this water," he said, pointing behind at the departing ships, "along the Nearer River—you call it the Tyras."

"Why did you come now?"

"We heard Odenathus planned to march against the Persians, and we knew the emperor had left Athens for Rome, and taken his army with him."

"This is Odenathus," Herodian said, proudly pointing at his father.

The man studied Odenathus for a moment. "Maybe," the Goth conceded, "but you certainly aren't the emperor," he snorted, pointing a finger at Herodian.

"Can I kill him now?" Herodian asked, starting to draw for his sword. He was stung by the man's insult, and emboldened by the fact that the Goth was unarmed.

"No!" His father held out an arm.

"Then what are we going to do with him?" Herodian asked, trying to hide his disappointment. "You don't want to take him all the way back to Palmyra, do you?"

"We'll send him to Rome, along with some of the treasure," Odenathus replied, "a gift to the emperor."

"And the women?" Herodian asked, hoping to augment his harem.

"They're Roman citizens," Zenobia interjected quickly and emphatically, although there was nothing to prevent Herodian from enslaving any of the women if Odenathus allowed him to do so.

Herodian looked at his father.

Odenathus looked at Zenobia, then Herodian, and shook his head. Herodian pouted. "What do we do now?" Herodian asked, looking reluctantly away from the freed women and the spoils not loaded onto the ships.

"We've done what we were asked to do." Odenathus replied.

"Now we can go home."

7-8
Part of a Larger Plan
Rome
26 November, 266

"Do you think that's wise?" Salonina asked Gallienus, surprise mixed with concern on her face. She held an apricot in her hand that she had been about to eat but, instead, waited for his answer. Alone in the Imperial Palace dining hall during their midday meal, they could speak freely about whatever was on their minds. Braziers near their couch struggled to overcome the cool November air. Salonina shivered briefly and longed for the warmth of spring. Gallienus' voice brought her attention back to the present.

"It's part of a larger plan," he said, as he bit into a piece of bread covered with goat's cheese. "Let me explain the situation as a whole before you make any judgments." He washed down the bread and cheese with wine from a golden goblet, then resumed his explanation. "None of my spies suggest that Postumus will do anything next year other than stay in Gallia and fight the Franks."

"I pray to the gods daily that he dies violently!" Salonina burst out, surprised by her own vehemence. "You will avenge Saloninus' death, won't you?" she continued more evenly.

"I've tried three times. Last time I nearly died!"

Salonina thought of Gallienus' arrow wound and subsequent fever that caused him to abandon their siege of Colonia Agrippina. She bit her lower lip and furrowed her brow. "But that was four years ago. What kind of message do you send to the world when you've allowed Postumus to take Gallia, Britannia, and Hispania for himself?"

"I want Postumus defeated as much as you do," he nodded. "Early next year I'll send several expeditions to secure the mountain passes into Gallia."

"Only that far?" Salonina didn't try to hide her disappointment.

"I expect the main threat to come from the Goths next year," he said. "Dexippus warned me of that when we were in Athens and has sent frequent updates. I'll deal with Postumus after I've restrained the Goths."

"Dexippus was such a charming man, and so helpful when we were experiencing the Mysteries in Eleusis." She sipped wine from a crystal goblet and thought fondly of her time in Athens.

Gallienus waited to see if she intended to make further objections or comments.

"Oh," she said, recognizing his impatient expression, and setting her glass on the table. "I'm distracting you from explaining your plan."

He smiled, then resumed. "I'll go to Pannonia in the spring, probably to Poetovio."

"Like a spider in the center of her web?"

"Exactly. From there I can get to the most serious threat quickly. I'll leave troops in Mediolanum, of course, to keep Postumus in Gallia. By appointing Volusianus as Prefect of Rome, he'll be my backup, the way your father was when the barbarians got to Rome eight years ago.

"Is Volusianus happy about the assignment?" Salonina asked.

"I think so. It's quite an honor for him although he'll miss army life, and I'll miss his advice and counsel."

"Do you think Heraclianus will make as good a Praetorian Prefect as Volusianus?"

"I'll have Aurelian and Claudius with me, in case he doesn't," Gallienus replied, scratching his head. "But he did well as governor of Pannonia and as a general in Dacia before that."

"Which brings us back to my original question. Do you think it's wise making Aureolus governor of Rhaetia?"

He shrugged. "The position will be open in January. I can't leave it unfilled."

"Isn't there someone more suitable, or at least less

controversial? The generals won't like your choice. Don't they still regard him as a traitor?"

"Yes. But I could never bring myself to believe that."

And I never could understand why you couldn't, thought Salonina, remembering when Aureolus was in command of an army with orders to kill or capture Postumus. When Aureolus returned empty-handed, all of Gallienus' generals accused him of treason.

"Yet you dismissed him."

"I felt I had to."

"What's different now?"

"If Aureolus were in collusion with Postumus, then why didn't he go to Postumus after I relieved him of his command?"

Salonina thought for a moment. "Maybe Postumus didn't really want Aureolus at all."

"Why wouldn't he want him?"

"Maybe he felt that Aureolus couldn't be trusted in a difficult situation. And if Postumus could discredit Aureolus in your eyes, then he'd have eliminated a dangerous adversary. You wouldn't use him any further. Postumus could ignore him."

"Think how Postumus will feel having one of the two people he's most wronged in charge of a province beside him."

"Wouldn't that provoke Postumus to take some sort of action?"

"Aureolus will only have one legion under his command, not enough men for Aureolus to threaten Postumus by himself." A moment of silence followed.

"How will you convince your generals that this is a good idea?" Salonina asked finally.

"After the Goths are repulsed, I plan to use Aureolus as part of a two-pronged assault into Gallia: he'll attack from the north through Rhaetia and I'll attack from Mediolanum through the mountain passes," Gallienus explained. "Then, we'll both get our revenge on Postumus. That should satisfy the generals."

"Once Aureolus has gotten a little power back, will that be enough for him, or merely whet his appetite for more? You must be absolutely certain of his loyalty to you."

Gallienus did not reply immediately. Then his voice was so low that she would not have heard it had they not been sharing a couch. "Since I've become emperor, Salonina, I've never been absolutely certain of anything, or anyone. I doubt I ever will be again." He was quiet for a moment. Salonina watched him silently, holding her breath so as not to disturb him. "But I have to give powerful people more power. I pray to the gods daily that they remain loyal and don't destroy us from within. I'm certain the people outside our borders are ready to take advantage of any person or any point of weakness that we allow."

She leaned across the table and patted his hand. "You know I have as much interest in your success as you do. But I feel that making Aureolus governor of Rhaetia isn't wise! I don't see that it gains you a great deal, but I feel that the risk is significant." She hoped her reservations would cause him to have second thoughts. "However you feel about Aureolus, remember, he betrayed you once. The generals won't look favorably on you giving him a chance to betray you a second time."

8-1
Improvident Decision
Beside the Orontes River Near Antioch, Syria
27 November, 266

Smoke from many campfires drifted on a light breeze, carrying smells of roasting meat and fresh bread. Overcast skies had threatened rain before sunset, although none had yet fallen. Tonight was darker than usual with neither moon nor stars. Those furthest from the fires felt the chill. Everyone was dressed for the cold, except the dancing girls, swaying sensuously in front of Herodian in their diaphanous costumes. On his twenty-sixth birthday, a banquet was being held in his honor. Even dignitaries from Antioch had come to participate in the celebrations, bringing great quantities of wine and several of Antioch's best belly dancers.

Men clapped in time to rhythmic drumbeats of hour-glass shaped dharboukas. Mandolin-like ouds accompanied them, along with cane flutes. The men laughed much and drank deeply of wine captured from the Goths at Heraclea.

Odenathus sat cross-legged in the middle of a center carpet, Herodian to his right, General Zabdas to his left. A Roman delegation from Antioch sprawled uncomfortably on a nearby carpet, unaccustomed to sitting on the ground. Other carpets were occupied by important sheiks and leaders of Odenathus' army units.

Zenobia was not expected to attend the gathering. Her son had been cut during sword practice when he failed to parry a sword thrust by his opponent. It wasn't life-threatening, but Zenobia had decided to stay with him to ensure he received every appropriate medical attention, as well as the right prayers from the priests. At the time, neither she nor Herodian regretted her decision. Later in the evening, when Vaballathus was sleeping comfortably, Zenobia felt she had done all she could for him. An appearance at her step-son's birthday celebration would show her support for him, she thought. It would be appreciated, at least by Odenathus and the soldiers.

She paused when she reached the celebration's edge, not far from Odenathus, to take in the scene from the shadows. Drumbeats carried over other sounds and she heard dinner guests' laughing and clapping. Zenobia caught a whiff of smoke, the cooking meat, and fresh bread. She suddenly remembered she hadn't eaten since the morning meal. *Perhaps a glass of wine or two and a few skewers of lamb. Then I can take my leave of them.* She watched Herodian leering at the dancing girls, stuffing food into his mouth, and washing it down with copious amounts of wine, clearly enjoying himself. *He takes his pleasures well enough. A pity he doesn't act like a warrior on the battle field.* Zenobia frowned. *He's only half a prince and would only make half a king.* She shivered at the thought.

Other guests were enjoying themselves, too. She could tell by their animated expressions, loud laughing, and the way they waved their glasses around, spilling much of the contents. *Too much wine already*, she thought. She was considering whether to turn around and leave when Odenathus struggled to his feet, intent on making a speech. He swayed slightly as he looked out at the crowd gathered in front and to the sides of his carpet. General Zabdas reached up to steady him.

"Warriors of Palmyra, men of the desert, tonight, we celebrate my eldest son's twenty-sixth birthday." Odenathus' voice carried to all the men attending the celebration. He paused and looked down at Herodian approvingly. Cheers arose from some of the guests, followed by polite clapping from the Roman delegation. "We've nearly finished our long march that drove the Goths into the sea," Odenathus continued to more cheers and shouts. "And before that," Odenathus paused and drank from his goblet, "before that," he paused. "there were great victories over Shapur. Even his supporters, who sent their own armies to help him, couldn't deter us." The cheers and shouts from the men were more enthusiastic now. "I've just learned that, instead of leading another army out to confront us and regain his honor, Shapur has begun building another city." Odenathus drained his goblet. "Shapur, is no longer fit, to claim the title 'King of Kings.'"

The men present began to chant "Odenathus, King of Kings," repetitively, the chorus growing louder and louder. Odenathus gazed at his army with approval and let their chorus of support and loyalty wash over him.

"Yes," Odenathus shouted back to them, a broad grin on his face. "I claim the title of 'King of Kings' for myself!"

Herodian rose to stand beside his father. Raising his glass he shouted, "To the King of Kings!"

Cheers and chanting resumed.

"I've been beside you through all these battles," Herodian said to his father, his words intentionally lost to the others amidst their cheering. "Valerian shared power with Gallienus. Make me "King of Kings" with you."

Odenathus met Herodian's gaze for several moments.

Zenobia felt herself grow tense and alert.

"And as a birthday gift to my son Herodian," Odenathus continued putting a hand on Herodian's shoulder, "I declare Herodian to be King of Kings, as well!" he shouted. Herodian looked at his father and broke into a broad smile. Odenathus' declaration was met at first with stunned silence. Men stared at each other, amazed. Then sporadic cheering began.

Zenobia realized her multi-year effort to undermine Herodian had been nullified in a single evening of drunken revelry. Now there was no hope for her son's succession or for her own future safety. *You've betrayed me*, she thought, staring at Odenathus with a mixture of sadness and anger. *When you die, my sons die, and I'll die along with them, after Herodian has raped me*! Zenobia sighed. She had tried criticism, then encouraging Herodian to reveal his inadequacies. Neither had worked. Now she would be forced to try something else. She turned and left Herodian's celebration. *It's time I spoke with Maeonius*, she thought.

8-2
A Tragic Accident
Palmyra, Syria
18 April, 267

"General Zabdas requests an audience with you, madam," the messenger bowed at the entrance to Queen Zenobia's private quarters. The musicians who'd been playing for her stopped at the interruption.

"You may bring him to me," Zenobia replied, waving the musicians away with her hand. The midday desert breeze stirred nearby silk curtains and wafted incense throughout the room, but she was aware of neither at the moment. *General Zabdas has been on the hunting trip near Emesa with Odenathus, Herodian, Maeonius, and others*, she thought as she readied herself for Zabdas' arrival. *It's odd that Zabdas returned from the hunt with news of Herodian's death. I expected Odenathus would tell me himself when he came back.* She took a breath and prepared to give Zabdas a convincing show of surprise and sorrow at the news. When he entered the room, she was struck by the look on Zabdas' face. *I didn't realize he was that fond of Herodian.* She frowned. *I'll have to watch him in the future.*

"The hunting trip—there's been—a tragic accident, my Queen!" General Zabdas said, grim faced.

"What could have happened to… him?" she asked, feigning concern. She had started to say "Herodian," then caught herself at the last second.

"He was killed by his nephew, Maeonius," Zabdas said,

"during the banquet."

"Nephew? Don't you mean 'cousin?'?"

"I'm quite sure Maeonius was your husband's nephew."

"What are you telling me, Zabdas?" she demanded, eyes wide with genuine surprise.

"That Odenathus was killed by Maeonius," he said. "I know it's hard to believe, but I'm afraid it's true!"

"No!" Zenobia exclaimed. "Not Odenathus!"

Zabdas nodded. Zenobia paled, sagged, and reached for the nearest piece of furniture for support.

His words of sympathy went unheard.

It was supposed to be Herodian! Zenobia thought. Finding the end of a nearby writing table, she edged toward a chair and eased herself into it. Her heart raced. Breathing was shallow and rapid. "Not Odenathus!" she said again, almost in a whisper. Her mind refused to grasp what she had just heard and confirmed. "You're sure? Couldn't there be some mistake? Were you there?" She looked desperately at Zabdas.

Zabdas was still in shock himself, having just lost his king so unexpectedly. "We were on a hunting trip, as you know," he began. "For some reason Maeonius shot at game before Odenathus several times! Naturally, your husband was insulted, and took away Maeonius' horse after the third time."

What was Maeonius thinking? Zenobia wondered.

"That angered Maeonius," Zabdas continued, "and when he threatened Odenathus, he was removed from the hunt and restrained."

"He actually threatened Odenathus? What did he say?"

"Who can remember now?"

"So he insulted his uncle, then threatened him," Zenobia shook her head, more mystified than Zabdas by Maeonius' actions. "But you said he'd been restrained."

"Later Herodian requested that Maeonius be allowed to join them during the evening banquet. That," Zabdas concluded, "was when Maeonius attacked and killed your husband with a dagger." He stopped talking and fidgeted as if reliving the events himself.

"Could no one stop him?"

"It happened so quickly," Zabdas shook his head sadly, "and

everyone thought that the insults of the hunt were forgotten. It was completely unexpected."

Thoughts swirled through Zenobia's head. *Maeonius failed. What if he'd been taken alive? What if someone interrogated him?* "What became of Maeonius?" she asked.

"He was killed immediately," Zabdas assured her. "Thank the gods you weren't with them!" he added. "You might have been killed as well." *Unusual that Zenobia didn't accompany Odenathus on this hunting trip. I wonder,* Zabdas thought suddenly. *Was that just a coincidence?*

Then our agreement dies with him! Zenobia held her breath and watched Zabdas, waiting for further details. When he offered none, she exhaled slowly then spoke. "I suppose Herodian will have to begin making funeral preparations."

"That won't be possible," Zabdas looked at her surprised. "Herodian was killed by Maeonius as well.

"Herodian, too?"

Zabdas nodded. "I'm sorry. This whole affair has been quite unexpected and upsetting. I thought I'd already mentioned his death."

"I'm quite sure I would have remembered that," Zenobia said. *Both Herodian and Maeonius dead!* Relief swept over her. *Yet Odenathus is dead too!* She struggled, barely able to keep her conflicting emotions of relief and bereavement under control.

"The whole affair was rather unusual," Zabdas mused. He looked at Zenobia with interest. "What do you suppose prompted Maeonius to do what he did?"

"I'm as surprised as you are at his actions. I understand he had feelings of jealousy," Zenobia ventured warily, bringing herself back to the present, "but I didn't know why or who was involved."

"What do you think he hoped to gain from it?"

She shrugged. "Since he's dead, we'll never know."

"Yes," Zabdas agreed, watching her face closely. "The dead tell no tales."

Zenobia tried not to show any reaction and hoped her face didn't flush, although it felt hot. "Now Vaballathus will succeed as king," she said, changing the subject to deflect Zabdas' thoughts.

Zabdas decided to drop the issue of Maeonius' motives. There were more immediate issues to deal with. "He'll need a regent to act for him until he's of age, of course," Zabdas nodded. They looked at each other while the thought hung in the air. "It will be both difficult and dangerous for you," he said finally.

"Do I have your confidence?"

Zabdas thought for a moment before nodding. "Yes. But a great deal depends on your husband's allies. Will they be willing to transfer loyalties to you—a twenty-six-year-old queen with an eleven-year-old crown prince? If they perceive weakness or hesitation...." He paused. "Shapur might try to take advantage of the situation himself. Perhaps he'd attempt to convince Odenathus' allies to support him. And there's also the question of Rome."

"What about Rome?"

"Will the emperor be willing to transfer your husband's titles and responsibilities to you or your son? Or will he send someone of his own choosing as a replacement?"

"Will I have the army's support?"

"And of the nobility," Zabdas assured her.

"Then I'll have to make the rest of it work," Zenobia said. She sighed deeply. "Would you begin preparations for the funerals, Zabdas? I need some time to myself."

When Zabdas had gone, she rose and stood at the window gazing past the city, beyond the Grand Colonnade, date palms marking the city's edge, to the Valley of the Tombs, the city's burial site. She'd never considered that she would see Odenathus placed in one of those graves. Now it was about to happen.

She recalled how excited she had been when she first learned she was betrothed to him, and the first time she had actually met him. He seemed so young and vigorous, handsome and charming then. She thought of their wedding, the birth of their sons, of the animals they had hunted and of the battles they had fought together, and of Odenathus' rise to power and influence over the entire eastern part of the Roman world. Then, she truly felt the emptiness that his death created, the loss—now and forever—of her friend, lover, and confidant. From this day onward she would have to face the world without him. She buried her head in her arms and wept.

When her tears were gone, Zenobia thought of Herodian and Maeonius. *Thanks to the gods that Herodian can threaten me no more and that Maeonius takes his secrets to the grave!* Zenobia wondered for a moment if Maeonius might have revealed anything about the plot to his father, Vorodes. *No. If Vorodes suspected anything he would have alerted his brother, and Zabdas would have known about it. Still, I'll have to deal with Vorodes.*

Despite her intense and conflicting emotions, there were other pressing matters that required Zenobia's attention. *Everything could yet be lost*, she realized. Odenathus had grown into his position, establishing and cultivating his alliances over time. She would have to step in, having little personal experience in state-craft and no personal rapport with his supporters. Could she convince them to accept her leadership now and to eventually support her son? Her lip quivered when she thought of Odenathus again. *I'll have to teach Vaballathus to hunt myself, and now he'll need a tutor.*

Zenobia knew she'd have to act quickly and decisively. *First Rome,* she thought. Although she had a secretary, this message was too important for anyone else to know about. She sat at her writing table, sniffed, and wiped tears away. Then she adjusted the parchment, picked up her pen, and dipped the quill into a nearby inkwell, while she considered the words of her first message to the emperor of Rome.

> To: Publius Licinius Gallienus, Augustus
> From: Septimia Zenobia, Queen of Palmyra
> I regret to inform you…

8-3

The Spider's Web

Poetovio, Pannonia Superior
29 May, 267

" When springtime comes, men go to war. It's what we do. So why are we sitting idly in Poetovio," Attalus spoke the city's name with distaste, as if he'd bitten into an over-ripe fig, "when we could be fighting someone somewhere else?" He looked for an answer to Gallienus, Claudius, Aurelian, and Heraclianus, who had recently been transferred from governor of Pannonia to Gallienus' Praetorian Prefect.

Gallienus had chosen Poetovio for its central location, a cross-roads town on the Dravus River, along the border between Pannonia and Noricum. "From here I can go southwest and be in Mediolanum in just short of a month, or go northwest to the border between Postumus and the barbarians in just over a month. If I go northeast, I could be in Carnuntum in a week and a half, and going southeast I could get to the Pontus Euxinus in about a month-and-a-half." The five men were sitting around a table studying a large map. Gallienus pointed to the various places as he spoke.

"Where would you go?" Heraclianus asked Attalus, amused by his impetuousness.

"Gallia comes to mind. I've yet to see Postumus' head on the tip of anyone's spear."

"We've sent forces to clear the passes," Heraclianus replied. "After we've seized the passes, we can enter Gallia in force."

"Then why aren't we right behind them?" Attalus demanded.

"Because I think the main threat will come from the east," Gallienus interrupted. He tilted his chair back and took a deep breath, savoring the scent of roses blooming in nearby gardens. *It's good to be with the army again,* he thought. Gallienus was in cheerful humor, having arrived at the army camp outside the city yesterday, and was enjoying the routine, purposeful activities of the camp after months of posturing Senators and formalities of Rome. Being here brought back memories of earlier campaigns, of hardships shared, and of battles won. He respected his generals, and realized that he had missed Attalus' opinions and his way of speaking his mind—something he rarely saw in Rome. And he was eagerly anticipating time with Pipa, although she would probably complain that he wasn't spending enough time with her, while Salonina had already suggested that he spent too much time with Pipa when on campaign.

"Ah, the Goths! Giant men, fierce fighters." Attalus rubbed his hands together. "If that's what you think we'll be doing, we should be going east to meet them."

"We have to know their intentions first."

"You should have asked me that. I know their intentions! They want to attack your cities and towns, to make slaves of your women and take your country's treasures. That's their intentions!"

"I rather suspected something like that," Gallienus chuckled. "It's not a question of 'what,' rather a question of 'where' and 'when' they intend to do these things. That's what I'm waiting to learn. They could come by land, or by sea, and their points of attack could be very different. What if they did both?"

"Where would you go if you were leading them? You've got some experience in these matters," Claudius ribbed Attalus. Thirteen years earlier Attalus had crossed the Danuvius River with an army of Marcomanni warriors and ravaged much of Pannonia. He had reached Aquileia and was poised to invade Italia itself, only turning back because of the onset of winter.

"Those were the days," Attalus grinned, scratching his long blond hair as he considered Claudius' question. He stood suddenly, absent-mindedly knocking his chair backwards onto the mosaic floor, and began pacing around the rectangular oak table that dominated the room. "No point in returning to the southern shore of the Pontus Euxinus so soon. They probably took everything worth having last year. Not much on the eastern part of that sea either. They could come by land, down the western side of the Pontus like Cniva did years ago, or put to sea as they've done in the past." He stopped pacing to look at the generals. "I've never had any reason to use ships myself, so I don't appreciate them much. But, I'd say this: they may not have much of a plan when they set out. They'd go where they thought there was treasure and take it if they could. If not," he began pacing again, "then they'd just move on and try some place else."

"Consider the differences between what we want and what the Goths want," Gallienus mused.

"For what purpose?" Attalus asked.

"To see if there's a way to use their desires against them."

"I don't know that I've seen much difference," Attalus replied. "We raided and burned your cities and towns. You attacked and burned our villages."

"We do make occasional forays into enemy land. They're intended to discourage our enemies from raiding our land," Gallienus said.

Attalus nodded. "Most of our warriors saw no reason to grow crops or raise cattle when they could take them from someone else. When we went to war we were looking for glory, prestige, wealth. You fight to maintain your lands. We fought for what we could take from that land. It never entered our minds to stay anyplace we'd conquered." He rubbed his chin thinking of the differences from his perspective. "How will you use their desires against them?" Attalus asked finally.

"We know what they want, and we know from past experience that they don't have the ability to lay siege to a walled city. That's why I've been so interested in fortifying those cities most likely to be at risk," Gallienus said. "Once we know where the Goths are going, then we'll take the army there to protect the unfortified cities—and to drive the Goths into the sea."

Attalus considered that for a moment. "Whether they come by land or by sea, we could still move closer to them."

"Before we decide to do anything, let's hear what Marcianus has to say about the Goths," Gallienus said, and nodded to Heraclianus, who picked up the message that came the previous evening from the eastern city of Tomis. He cleared his throat and gazed at the others before beginning.

"Just give us the essence of it," Gallienus interrupted.

"Very well," Heraclianus nodded, then glanced back at the message. "It's from Marcianus, governor of Moesia Inferior..."

"He's become a competent general," Gallienus interjected. The others nodded. All but Attalus were familiar with Marcianus' abilities. "This isn't the same person who tried to overthrow the empire six years ago," he noted for Attalus' benefit. "That was Macrianus; this is Marcianus. You'll hear no more of Macrianus."

Attalus gave Gallienus a sideward glance. "As I recall, Macrianus was killed during the battle."

Gallienus nodded. "Killed by Aureolus," he added to emphasize his support for his former cavalry general. Heraclianus looked at Gallienus, trying to mask his frustration with the frequent interruptions. "Please continue," Gallienus said as if nothing was amiss.

"This message was sent on the 10th of April," Heraclianus began, scanning the message for the date and other pertinent information. "Marcianus' forces repulsed an invasion of Goths near Tomis, and drove them back to their ships."

"Where is this place?" Attalus asked.

"On the shore of Pontus Euxinus," Aurelian said pointing to a map. "At the far end of Moesia Inferior."

"How many?" Claudius asked.

"Marcianus estimated several hundred ships, but says that counting ships was secondary to what he was actually doing."

"Didn't he say that not everyone had gotten off the ships to fight, in his opinion?" Gallienus prodded Heraclianus.

"I was just coming to that part."

"Let's see if we can get some idea of the troop strength," Claudius rephrased his question. "Several hundred ships… maybe three hundred. The ships on the Pontus are generally fishing boats and cargo ships, aren't they?"

"Dexippus once told me that they might get between thirty-five and fifty men on each ship," Gallienus said.

"That's useful," Claudius noted, then continued. "Three hundred ships with fifty men on each ship. That gives us about fifteen thousand warriors, tops."

"Less those that Marcianus killed at Tomis," Attalus added.

"Where did they go after Tomis?" Aurelian asked.

"To the South."

"Only a couple cities along the coast south of Tomis,"

Claudius nodded. "Presumably Marcianus alerted them."

"And they've been fortified, much like Tomis," Gallienus said, reminding them that he hadn't been totally idle during his stay in Athens. He nodded to Claudius and Aurelian. "You were doing much of the work to make those places secure."

"So presumably Goths will land here and there, testing defenses of local cities," Claudius continued. "If Attalus is correct in his assumptions, then the only course of action for them, aside from going home,"

"They wouldn't do that without something to show for their efforts," Attalus interrupted.

"then my guess is they'll try going through the Bosporus and into the Propontis," Claudius said. "That should be interesting!"

"Why 'interesting?'" Attalus asked.

"The Bosporus is tricky to navigate," Heraclianus explained. "Endless winds from the Pontus Euxinus blow strongly there and currents run from shore to shore a number of times before reaching calmer waters. If the Goths are piloting those ships themselves, they may not realize that."

"So they all might end up on the rocks?" Attalus asked with a trace of disappointment. "And I was hoping to destroy them in battle." He pounded a fist into his open palm.

"Some, probably," Claudius agreed, "but not all of them. They'll learn. You'll have your fight Attalus."

"Let Marcianus deal with the Goths," Aurelian interjected. All eyes turned to him, images of Gothic ships on the rocks of the Bosporus temporarily forgotten. "He has four legions under his command."

"He'd have to leave some men protecting his northern borders," Heraclianus noted. "There might yet be a land attack for him to deal with."

"Do we expect one?" Aurelian asked.

Well, no, not that I'm aware of." Heraclianus paused and looked to Gallienus for confirmation. Gallienus shrugged.

"We don't expect a land attack and we don't know where the Goths are going," Aurelian continued. "We've only made the roughest of guesses about their strength."

"What if it's more than we thought?" Heraclianus asked.

"What if it's less?" Aurelian countered. "Think about it, Heraclianus. If the Goths land on the Asian side of the Propontis, we're not likely to cross and try to engage them. They'd probably be gone long before we got there. And the north side only has a couple cities—Byzantium, Selymbria, Perinthus, and Bisanthe— all fortified and well defended."

"You're suggesting a campaign against Postumus now?" Claudius asked, as he considered Aurelian's suggestion.

"We're planning to campaign against the Goths, although we don't know where they are, or where they're going to be," Aurelian said. "We know where Postumus is."

"The Goths are invading. Postumus shows no interest, at present, of crossing the mountains," Heraclianus pointed out.

"We could use Rhaetia as a base of operations," Aurelian continued. *Aureolus should be eager to help us*, he thought, deciding to keep that sarcastic comment to himself.

"Before we leave the Gothic matter there are several things I need to consider," Gallienus continued. "The Goths may threaten the Mare Aegaeum, if they enter the Propontis."

"If they manage to get through the Bosporus, then getting through the Dardanelles will be another dangerous passage," Heraclianus said.

Gallienus listened to Heraclianus' comment without replying. "I want you to draft a message to Theodotus in Aegyptus," he said to him. "Tell him to have his fleet ready to face enemy vessels later this year."

Heraclianus nodded, making several notes to remind himself of Gallienus' orders.

"Whatever else happens, I want trade routes to stay open," Gallienus said. "And tell Theodotus to increase escorts on the grain fleet. That has to get through to Rome." He lapsed into thought, considering what else might be required. He was about to reply to Aurelian's suggestion when a tribune entered the room. "Yes, what is it?" he asked irritated by this interruption.

"A message from Palmyra, sir," the man said, saluting and handing him the scroll.

"What could Odenathus want?" Gallienus wondered aloud

while he fingered the seal on the message. He broke it open and set the scroll on the table in front of him. "My, my," he said, looking up at the generals. "It's from the queen!" He frowned as he glanced down at the rest of the message. Then he rubbed his chin and stared into space.

"The queen's news displeases you?" Attalus asked, finally breaking the tense silence.

"Yes," Gallienus said, returning from his reverie. He took a breath, and looked at the expectant faces of his generals. "It seems that Odenathus is dead."

Each of the men thought of what the loss of a powerful ally might mean for the empire. "A great deal depends on how he died," Heraclianus said. "Was it peaceful or violent? And if violent, by whom?"

"Yes. How did it happen?" Claudius asked.

"Killed by a drunken nephew during a banquet," Gallienus said.

"Why?" Aurelian asked.

"Arguing over the wine, maybe," Gallienus speculated. He ran a finger down the scroll. "No, she doesn't say."

"Then his eldest son has succeeded him. What's his name?" Heraclianus asked.

"Herodian, I think," Claudius said. "Something like that, anyway."

Aurelian shook his head. "He wasn't much of a fighter from what I recall."

"Apparently not," Gallienus said, examining the scroll again. "He was killed by the same man."

"So who's next in line?" Attalus asked. "This Odenathus must have had more than one son."

"The next son is eleven," Gallienus said, pointing at the message. "Zenobia says she'll function as regent until he's old enough to become king. She's taken the liberty of passing the titles I gave to Odenathus on to her son." He frowned. "'I assume that you'll want an orderly transition of power,' she says."

"Can she do that?" Attalus asked.

"She thinks so," Gallienus said, "although I'll have to decide if I agree to it."

"What else did she say?" Heraclianus asked.

"She assures me she has the support of her army and nobility, and pledges her loyalty to me." There was a moment of silence while they all considered the possibility of this statement being true.

"What do we know of this Zenobia?" Attalus asked.

"She used to hunt and fight alongside her husband," Aurelian said.

Attalus grinned. "I like her already!"

"I understand she's young, I think about the age of her stepson, and quite attractive," Claudius said, winking at Attalus.

"I have several friends who served in Syria," Aurelian continued. "They told me she drinks with the officers and sometimes marches with the soldiers, and that she lives like a Persian, but banquets like a Roman."

"My kind of woman," Attalus said, admiration in his voice. "But, can she rule?"

"That remains to be seen," Gallienus said. "We've lost a capable ally in Odenathus. I doubt I can count on any meaningful support from Palmyra for a while. But at least, while she's busy getting control of her own people, I think I can count on no immediate threat from that quarter, either."

"Wait and see if she survives the palace 'infighting' for succession," Heraclianus agreed.

"Let me see if I understand your situation," Attalus said. "You have a usurper in Gallia, a man of questionable loyalty in charge of Rhaetia, and Goths—who knows how many—running around, who knows where." Gallienus nodded. Attalus continued. "And now you've got an inexperienced young woman trying to lead the eastern provinces." He looked at the generals, then back to Gallienus.

"That about sums it up," Gallienus said. "But it has been my good fortune to have all of you with me, as well as other capable men all across the empire—Volusianus in Rome, Theodotus in Aegyptus, Dexippus in Athens, and Marcianus in Moesia. At this moment, the Goths are the only ones who threaten us."

"What will you do now?" Attalus asked.

"Wait," Gallienus smiled. "Before the spider moves, something has to disturb her web."

8-4
A Meeting with Zenobia
Poetovio, Pannonia
30 May, 267

"Goths threatening us from the east and an uncertain ally in Syria, are a dangerous combination," Heraclianus noted as he and Gallienus inspected city defenses.

Gallienus reigned in his horse and feigned interest in part of Poetovio's wall. He wiped sweat from his forehead, then directed his attention to Heraclianus. "I agree. What are your thoughts about Zenobia?"

Heraclianus pursed his lips while he considered an answer, then scratched his chin. "I suppose someone should visit Zenobia, determine if she intends to continue her support for you, then offer our help if her response is favorable. That's assuming she can hold onto the position herself."

"Excellent assessment." Gallienus nudged his horse forward and continued his tour of the city walls. "I want you to lead the mission."

"What about my duties as Praetorian Prefect?"

"Claudius or Aurelian will fill in while you're gone. "

"I really don't think I'm the right person…"

Gallienus held up a hand. "You're the most appropriate person because you're my Praetorian Prefect." He paused until Heraclianus understood and nodded. Then he continued. "Your stated mission will be to discuss her responsibilities for leading the eastern provinces and to offer support, but your real mission is, as you mentioned, to judge if she's capable of holding onto the position. If you have any doubt, take command of the east yourself. You must not reveal this until you get face-to-face with her alone, otherwise you'll never get to see her—or you might suffer an 'unfortunate accident.' Sail from Aquileia with a century of legionnaires. More would arouse suspicion. I'll write a letter authorizing you to take command of the legion at Raphnae if you decide Zenobia is unable to assert control or if her allegiance is doubtful."

"Negotiations aren't my strongest skills," Heraclianus protested.

"It's most important that you not be refused," Gallienus interrupted, annoyed by Heraclianus' reluctance. "List your qualifications for the leadership position and indicate my trust in you. But whatever you do, don't alienate her, unless you feel the need to replace her."

Imperial Palace, Antioch, Syria
11 July, 267

"Queen Zenobia welcomes you to Antioch, general."

Heraclianus nodded while he studied the dark-skinned young man who greeted him, and decided he must be of Bedouin descent. Heraclianus recalled that Zenobia came from Bedouin parents and wondered if that was significant in her attempt to maintain power.

"We received your message. The queen looks forward to meeting with you." The young man smiled broadly.

"Today?"

"Oh no sir. The queen has not yet reached the city."

"Tomorrow then?"

"I'm afraid that is not possible either, sir," the messenger said, a look of concern on his face.

Heraclianus frowned. "When then?"

"Four days from now, sir."

"Here, at the palace."

"Yes, yes, here." The messenger's head bobbed up and down.

Heraclianus relaxed slightly. "When?"

"The afternoon, sometime after lunch. I will see you then, sir." The young man slipped out of the palace and disappeared into the crowd on the street.

Three days later the young man returned to the palace. "I'm very sorry, sir. The queen is unable to come today. She asks that you come to Emesa and meet her there. Is this possible?"

Heraclianus struggled to conceal his irritation. "She will meet me there?"

"Yes, yes, at Emesa. Contact Nishru, the head priest at Emesa. Queen Zenobia will meet with you afterwards." The man watched Heraclianus' reactions closely.

"Very well," Heraclianus reluctantly agreed. "I'll leave Antioch tomorrow."

"That would be good, sir. And may I inquire for Queen Zenobia, what is the purpose of your visit?"

Heraclianus had been expecting this question. "To extend Emperor Gallienus' good wishes and offer any assistance she might require."

The young man looked perplexed. "But all that could have been expressed in a letter, sir, not by a senior official with a hundred soldiers."

"Eighty," Heraclianus said. While he appeared to be a mere messenger, this young man seemed to know Zenobia's thoughts and concerns. "There will undoubtedly be matters of mutual interest that require a face-to-face meeting."

"Of course, sir. Might I ask the nature of these matters so the queen will be better able to speak to those issues that caused you to come all the way to Syria in person?"

"I'd rather not disclose the specifics to anyone other than Queen Zenobia herself."

"I understand, sir. I will convey this to the queen," the man said. He inclined his head in a slight bow, then left the room.

Heraclianus frowned, then motioned to one of his aides. "Send a tribune to the legion at Raphnae. Get the legate's assessment of Zenobia's chance of maintaining power. Imply that I am empowered to act if the situation should require it."

Emesa, Syria
24 July, 27

Heraclianus shaded his eyes as he gazed over the southern city walls across an open expanses of desert. He watched a cloud of dust that signaled the arrival of some group of animals and people, probably another caravan, but maybe Zenobia herself.

When he arrived two days earlier, he had contacted Nishru who said he had no knowledge of a firm meeting date. He was told to expect Zenobia, maybe on the 27th.

As the dark cloud grew closer, Heraclianus could make out a train of camels—another caravan. He shook his head and left the wall.

***

Three days later, as Heraclianus left Nishru's palace and descended the steps leading to the city's main street, Zenobia's young messenger appeared beside him. Relief overcame Heraclianus' frustration. "I was beginning to think you wouldn't come. When can I meet with Queen Zenobia?"

"The meeting is not possible now." The young man shook his head, his expression grave. "She's had to resolve some minor tribal misunderstanding."

Heraclianus' face darkened. "When?"

"Hard to say," the man broke in before Heraclianus finished his question.

"Then I'll go to Palmyra and meet her when her campaign is finished."

"No!" Zenobia's messenger shook his head emphatically. "A Roman general and strange soldiers would upset the situation there right now."

"She must need help."

"If she needs help, she will call the legion at Raphnae herself!" she said. "Do not come to Palmyra."

Heraclianus grabbed the man's arm as he started to leave, but the young man wrenched it free, slipped into the mass of people on the street, and disappeared. Heraclianus suppressed his emotional response with difficulty and made a professional assessment of the situation. Clearly Zenobia did not wish to meet with him, perhaps because she did not wish to hear what he had to say, maybe she was not planning to continue Odenathus' support, or possibly she was just struggling to maintain her power. *How would my appearance at Palmyra upset the balance of power?* he wondered. *With only a century of men, I could easily be overwhelmed by hostile forces, whoever they might be. And what was the significance of the man's comment about Zenobia seeking support from the legion at Raphnae herself?* He took a deep breath and shook his head, wondering what Gallienus would do in this situation. *I suppose I should talk with Nishru, get his advice about what to do next.* He turned around and ascended the palace steps once more.

Aquileia, Gallia Cisalpina
10 September, 267

"… and that concludes my assessment." Heraclianus glanced around for a sense of how his report had been received. Claudius seemed indifferent. Aurelian did not even make eye contact with him. He read disappointment on Gallienus' face and felt disappointment himself, both at failing to achieve one of Gallienus' first important assignments, and at being out-maneuvered by a woman.

Gallienus shrugged. "That's essentially what we heard from our sources, but without the details you've provided. She's held onto her power, by the way, but hasn't been as helpful as her husband was." He let the silence prevail then rubbed his chin. "There have been some changes in the command structure that I'll have to explain. Tomorrow will be soon enough, I suppose. You must be tired from your long trip."

Heraclianus took the hint and left Gallienus' tent. Once outside he lingered long enough to hear Gallienus comment to the other generals. "Well, he warned me that negotiations weren't one of his strengths."

"Apparently not," Claudius replied. "He couldn't even convince her to meet with him."

Gallienus shook his head. "I sent him there to keep an ally, not to make an enemy. If I wanted that result, I could have written her an insulting letter myself."

Heraclianus burned with shame as he walked to his own tent.

8-5
Enticement
Augusta Vindelicum, Rhaetia
18 February, 268

Aureolus stared at the most recent correspondence from Postumus, and ran his finger down the scroll until he found the words he was looking for.

> Have you given any consideration to what you will
> do when your current term as governor expires? I think
> you're right that you will never again rise to your ear-
> lier position of prominence as long as Claudius and
> Aurelian enjoy Gallienus' trust and confidence.

He sat alone at a rectangular oak table in the governor's villa and watched candles flicker wildly as wind drove sleet against glass of the closest windows. Nearby, braziers barely overcame the chill and gloom of the night. Aureolus hunched his shoulders and pulled his cape more tightly around him. Just over a year ago Gallienus appointed him governor of Rhaetia, the province adjacent to the eastern border of Postumus' self-proclaimed empire. Aureolus' fingers idly traced the edge of the scroll and thought about Postumus, a friend and comrade in arms since Gallienus first arrived in Germania. Perhaps their close relationship had been because both came from humble origins, not from Roman aristocracy. Postumus had even saved his life once during a minor skirmish with a band of Alamanni horsemen. Some of

Gallienus' generals found Postumus irascible. So when Silvanus drove Postumus to revolt, Aureolus understood the reasons, although he disagreed with the action. The fact that Postumus still controlled Gallia was the reason he was no longer Gallienus' cavalry commander.

Nearly seven years earlier, Gallienus defeated Postumus with the help of cavalry that Aureolus brought after his own spectacular victory over Macrianus' rebel army. Before leaving the battlefield to suppress another revolt, Gallienus transferred command of the army to Aureolus, ordering him to pursue and dispose of Postumus. But Postumus escaped, along with much of his army, and Aureolus returned to Gallienus in Rhaetia empty-handed. During a gathering at the table where Aureolus now sat, Gallienus' generals accused him of treachery and of deliberately letting Postumus escape. Although sympathetic to Aureolus' explanations, Gallienus had reluctantly relieved him of his command.

Treachery! Aureolus thought bitterly. *One error in judgement, after all those years of loyal service.* He scowled, shook his head, then took several deep breaths, forcing himself to relax before rereading another portion of Postumus' message.

> If you hold any ill feelings toward me because you lost command of your cavalry, I'd like to rectify that situation. I offer you a future with me.
>
> There will be many opportunities for battle for you here in the Gallic Empire.

Postumus had sent his first letter last spring congratulating Aureolus on his assignment as governor, and mentioned that seizing the Gallic Empire had happened when soldiers acclaimed him emperor following Silvanus' unreasonable demands. He assured Aureolus, that Saloninus' death was an unfortunate decision by one of his lesser officers. The rest of Postumus' first message had included only pleasant banalities. It surprised Aureolus that he continued the correspondence, and he assumed Postumus was trying to rekindle their earlier friendship. But the tone of Postumus' successive messages had changed during the course of the year. Aureolus again glanced at the message delivered to him earlier this morning.

> Gallienus has ceded the province of Gallia to me. He hasn't challenged my authority for over two years and is unlikely to do so this year either.
>
> My sources suggest Gallienus may be forced to confront a large Gothic invasion from the east. His power and authority decline as mine continue to grow. While he allowed Odenathus to rule the east as he pleases, I have drawn Britannia and Hispania to me.

Aureolus pushed the scroll away and leaned back in his chair, recalling life just after his command had been taken from him—the shame he'd felt returning in disgrace to the land of his ancestors, how his friends had pointedly avoided him, how his wife offered him only tepid support, and the petty assignments Gallienus had given him there. *It was because of the cavalry, and my leadership, that we won victories over barbarians in Germania, and defeated rebel armies under Ingenuus and Macrianus! Now I govern a small province with one legion, and no cavalry at all.* He pounded the table reflexively.

A slave immediately entered the room thinking he wished something, jolting Aureolus back to the present. Instinctively, he pulled the scroll closer to him as if shielding its contents from the slave's eyes. "Yes, have someone tend to these braziers," he said. No doubt Gallienus had given him the governorship over the objection of his generals, and he should be grateful for that, at least. But he could expect no significant assignment when his term as governor expired. Postumus was right about that. With Gallienus, he had been the leader of the cavalry from its inception. He wondered what Posthumous was prepared to offer him. *Was it a position of similar authority? What were the possibilities for advancement?* Two older slaves entered the room, further interrupting his thoughts, and refilled the braziers, bringing Aureolus some relief from the chill. Their task complete, the slaves departed as silently as they had come. Aureolus reread Postumus' closing comments.

> The Fates have given us this singular opportunity to rise up together and seize power from one who can no longer wield it effectively. All we need is the resolve and the courage to act together.

He considered Postumus' suggestion, and the situation across the empire. Gallienus was probably going east to fight an army of Goths. *Would Gallienus fall to the Goths*? If Gallienus survived, then a successful revolt against Gallienus would mean the death of his friend and benefactor. Aureolus had known Salonina well, and had watched Marinianus, their one remaining son, grow into a young adult. Of course Marinianus, too, would have to be killed.

With Postumus, there were possibilities for greater glory. Thoughts of fighting Goths, or Persians, at the head of his own great army filled his mind. All his privileges and opportunities were due to Gallienus—not that he hadn't earned the recognition and advancements. And Postumus had not directly offered, or even hinted, at what his position would actually be. Instead he had made vague promises and implied possibilities. Still…

Aureolus idly ran his fingers along the table's polished surface. He frowned and held his breath for a long moment, then sighed, drained his glass of spiced wine, now only lukewarm, and poured himself another. He dipped a pen into the nearby inkwell, hesitated, and began to compose his response to Postumus.

Treveris, Belgica, Gallic Empire
02 March, 268

"Aureolus has agreed to join us," Postumus exclaimed, stabbing his finger at a scroll in front of him, with an elfish grin filling his bearded face. He looked at the men gathered around the table—Victorinus, Marius, Laelianus, legate of the Moguntiacum legion, and commanders of three other legions under Postumus' control. The men looked back at him expectantly.

Incredible! Laelianus thought. *I'd have bet a month's wages against that ever happening.* "Congratulations," he said when no one else could think of an appropriate reply. He waved his hand around the room. "We had no idea he was even considering that."

Postumus chuckled. "It's taken me months to convince him."

"What do you expect to happen next?" Laelianus asked the question on all their minds with a sense of foreboding.

"The Fates have placed a great opportunity before us," Postumus replied. "I've learned that Goths have been gathering ships all winter for an invasion of considerable magnitude. When they strike, it will draw Gallienus to the east and the garrison in Mediolanum will probably be reduced to support his effort. With Aureolus threatening my flank, I'd be reluctant to move against Mediolanum myself. But now," he paused dramatically and glanced smugly at his army commanders, "there's a much better way."

"Have Aureolus win the forces over there for us," Laelianus nodded, impressed with Postumus' scheme. *We're about to become part of an empire-wide revolt!*

"Exactly," Postumus said. He reached for a map. While he spread it on the table, chairs scraped the mosaic floor as men stood and leaned forward for a better view. "Gallienus was due to leave Rome yesterday, and march to Poetovio like he did last year. Our key to act will be when he moves east from there, maybe sometime before the end of this month. Aureolus' task is to move south and win the loyalty of forces around Mediolanum. Then he'll open the mountain passes west of Mediolanum for us to cross," he pointed to the map again.

"There's a bridge east of Novaria that could be a problem," Victorinus noted, pointing to a river just west of Mediolanum.

"I've already mentioned that to Aureolus."

"What will we be doing in the meantime?" Marius asked.

"We'll march south along the western side of the mountains." He drew a line with his finger from Treveris down the map to the mountain passes in the southern part of his Gallic Empire. The men looked at him expectantly. "I'll go over how many men we'll take in a minute," he said. "After Aureolus opens the passes and clears the bridge," he nodded at Victorinus, "then we'll combine forces with Aureolus in Mediolanum and be in a position to either defeat Gallienus, or to march on Rome."

"Which do you expect to happen?" Marius asked.

"Both," Postumus replied. "I just don't know which will happen first."

That will be a fight to the death, Laelianus thought. *Both Postumus and Aureolus will have betrayed Gallienus—no quarter asked or given, and high casualties on both sides.* "What if Aureolus fails?" he asked.

Postumus beamed. "That's the beauty of this plan! If he's unsuccessful, then we turn around and return home." He ran a finger back up the west side of the mountains toward the Rhenus River. "No invasion, no casualties, no provocations to Gallienus."

"What's to keep Aureolus from marching on Rome without us?" Victorinus asked.

"That is a risk," Postumus conceded, "but Aureolus has no allies in Rome, and Volusianus is there, along with Gallienus' son, so Praetorian Guards will be there, as well as some other local defenses. I doubt Aureolus would feel comfortable confronting them with the forces he has now, or will get if Mediolanum supports him. Besides, I told him not to move until I've dealt with my connections in Rome."

"Do you have contacts in Rome?" Marius asked.

"Maybe," Postumus said and stared stonily at Marius. "Sit down everyone," he said to the others.

"You said you'd come back to the details of our march," Laelianus prompted him.

Postumus nodded at Laelianus. "We'll need an army to carry out our part of the agreement. I want you to gather men we'll need from each legion," he glanced at the other legates. They nodded their understanding.

"How many men? Where do you want them? And when?" Laelianus asked.

"It would be better if my army were considerably larger than Aureolus' army," Postumus temporized. "Have them in Treveris ready to march by…mid-April."

The legates exchanged uneasy glances. *Gallia, Britannia, and Hispania weren't enough for Postumus*, Laelianus thought sadly. *This could involve years of fighting and massive casualties*. "How many men?" he pressed for a definitive number.

Postumus stroked his beard. "Bring everyone but the auxiliaries," he said.

Laelianus leaned forward putting his elbows on the table and looked at Postumus. "That will leave our frontiers exposed and vulnerable," he objected. *Not only the frontiers, but also the cities, and our families*! The legates all realized the implications of such an action.

"A standard practice," Postumus waved a hand dismissively at Laelianus. "If you want to succeed, you take enough men to ensure success. Others have done it before—Valerian, most recently."

With disastrous results for those left behind, undefended. "How long can the legions expect to be away?"

"Impossible to say."

All summer at the very least, and that's if everything goes according to plan. "Is it, prudent, to leave only auxiliaries behind?" Laelianus asked.

"We've had significant victories over the Franks in the last few years." "But they keep coming." *Some of the auxiliaries are Frankish mercenaries. How long will they remain loyal when the rest of the army is gone*?

"Until I can return the legionnaires, the auxiliaries will have to deal with the situation," Postumus growled. "If you're not up to this task, I'll pick someone else." He starred at Laelianus.

"I didn't say I wouldn't do it," Laelianus said, holding eye contact with Postumus and forcing an outward calm. "It was rather my intention to point out certain… issues that a withdrawal might create locally." *Postumus is consumed with ambition, and his family isn't along the border so they won't be in any immediate danger. Better to have control of this withdrawal than to watch my men be stripped away from me.* Laelianus nodded. "All but the auxiliaries, Treveris, mid-April."

Poetovio, Pannonia
23 March, 268

"The Goths have sailed," Gallienus announced to his generals, then resumed reading the scroll, just presented to him by a fatigued, sweaty messenger. Claudius, Aurelian, Heraclianus, and Attalus had originally met that morning at Gallienus' quarters to discuss a planned training exercise. All present realized that this discussion would be entirely different. Gallienus cleared his throat, "It came from Olbia." he said pointing to the scroll on the table in front of him, "so we all know what that means."

The city of Olbia lay on the northwest shore of the Pontus Euxinus beyond the empire's borders and under Gothic control. The previous year Goths successfully passed through the Bosphorus and attacked Byzantium, then sacked several cities along the southern coast of the Propontis. Their attacks were finally repulsed at Cyzicus, then they were defeated in a naval engagement as they retreated.

Survivors returned home to spend the following winter along the northern coast of Pontus Euxinus. *A report from one of his spies*, Heraclianus thought, shifting in his chair as he waited to hear details.

"Goths, Heruli, and warriors from several other tribes reportedly set sail. Estimates run between five hundred to six thousand ships."

"Well that narrows it down considerably," Attalus observed. "One of my men could have given you better details than that."

"Your men aren't there," Gallienus replied. "Not all the ships were leaving from Olbia. Your estimates?" he asked the group.

"The first number is probably too low, the second is probably too high," Claudius ventured.

"I doubt the entire Pontus holds six thousand ships,"

Aurelian said.

"Troop strength?" Gallienus asked.

Heraclianus scratched his head. "Between thirty-five to fifty men per boat, as I recall," he explained. "These will be fishing boats and small cargo vessels, not troop transports."

"So, somewhere between seventeen thousand and three hundred thousand," Gallienus calculated.

"Even a mid-range estimate is a very large force," Heraclianus said.

"All the more enemy to kill," Attalus smiled thinking about spoils to be taken from the dead warriors: gold arm bands, fine swords and armor, maybe even some of the treasure they had pillaged from hapless Roman citizens. The fact that he needed none of those things was completely beside the point. He slapped his hands onto his thighs to clear the pleasant thought away for now. Claudius was speaking.

"What do you figure our strength to be?" Claudius asked Heraclianus. As the Praetorian Prefect, it was his responsibility to keep track of these figures.

Heraclianus glanced at several scrolls on the table in front of him before speaking. "We have seventeen thousand legionnaires with us now, along with six thousand horsemen, that's half our cavalry and half Marcomanni horsemen," he glanced appreciatively at Attalus, who merely nodded his acknowledgement. "In addition, there are two thousand Praetorian Guards, who can fight mounted or on foot.

"About twenty-five thousand," Aurelian commented. "Favorable odds against the low estimate." He looked at the other generals who, like him, were all thinking about the higher estimates. "What did we leave at Mediolanum?"

Heraclianus shifted through the scrolls on the table, then took one, scanned it quickly. "Eleven-thousand legionaries and fifteen hundred cavalry," he looked at Gallienus.

"Adequate to deter Postumus," he replied with a shrug.

"What forces can Marcianus bring from Moesia?" Claudius asked.

"He commands four legions, about nineteen thousand men,

but he'd probably leave half of them to protect his border."

"Alright, let's say about eight or nine thousand men," Claudius said. "That's twenty-six thousand foot and eight thousand horse, altogether."

"Last year Goths were apparently testing our defenses," Gallienus observed. "And whether we're facing the low estimate or the high estimate, we don't have the luxury of deciding whether to fight or not—unless we're willing to see the empire fall." He paused for emphasis. "Our best opportunity, maybe our only one, is to meet them on ground favorable to us, before they get well established."

"When do you want to march?" Heraclianus asked.

"In two days," Gallienus said. "They haven't stopped along the western shores of the Pontus Euxinus this time, so that's not their objective. Two years ago they ravaged Cappadocia and Galatia. I doubt they'd return there so soon with such a large force. It suggests to me that they intend to force their way through the Propontis and into the Mare Aegaeum."

"Then Macedonia may be their destination," Aurelian concluded.

"It could just as easily involve the cities in Lydia, on the other side of the Mare Aegaeum," Claudius pointed out.

"Probably both with a force of any size," Gallienus said.

"Will you ask Zenobia for help if they attack Lydia?" Aurelian asked.

"If we're involved with the Goths in Macedonia, I'll have to. This would be a good opportunity to prove her loyalty to us."

"What if she doesn't respond?"

Gallienus drummed his fingers on the table. "Then I'll have to replace her."

* * *

"We've only been here a week," Salonina protested. She struggled to overcome the anxiety she felt when Gallienus went off to war—each farewell possibly their last, leaving her alone with her fears and uncertainties. Salonina thought about her first two sons, Valerian and Saloninus, both dead because her husband was emperor, although neither had died on the battlefield. *At least Marinianus is safe in Rome as a consul, not a figurehead leader in some far-away province.*

"That's about what my generals said," Gallienus said. "Last year they wanted to move. This year they're surprised when I want to leave quickly." He held his arms out to her. While they held each other close, he felt her rapid heartbeat and listened to her deep breathing. Her head rested on his shoulder and her hair smelled clean and fresh. Gallienus took a deep breath then spoke to her again. "We've been expecting this invasion, and I've got to stop the Goths before they destroy the empire."

"You'll take Attalus and his horsemen?"

"Of course."

That means Pipa will be riding with him while I lag behind! "Can't the legions in the area deal with it?"

He shook his head. "Too many enemies. I've ordered Marcianus to take his soldiers south and engage the Goths. I'll either join him, or cover his borders if the Goths decide to attack while he's away."

"I'll lag further and further behind until you stop moving." *That will mean he's fighting one or more battles. What will I find when I get there?*

"I'll be fine," he assured her, although they both knew it was an empty promise.

To distract herself she asked, "Will the west be safe while you're so far away?" She felt him tense momentarily, and immediately regretted the question.

"That will be up to the people I've left there."

Maybe for an emperor the battlefield is one of the least dangerous places to be, Salonina thought while she hugged him tightly. "I'll follow you wherever you go. Your fate is my fate."

8-6

Complications

Moguntiacum, Germania Inferior

30 March, 268

and therefore, consider this a declaration of war between us.

Laelianus exhaled, crumpled the message he had just drafted to Postumus, and threw it on the floor along with his two previous drafts. He sat alone in his quarters within the legion's barracks. Before starting to write, he left specific instructions with his orderly that no one was to disturb him under any circumstances.

Once Postumus got the message, there would be no turning back. Throughout his career, Laelianus had faced difficult decisions, although none had ever involved the lives of so many people. He took a deep breath and considered the situation he now faced. Whichever course he chose, blood would be shed. To refuse Postumus' order would result in a civil war against Postumus, a life or death conflict against other Romans, many of whom were his friends. And it would not be resolved until either he or Postumus had been killed. That was the risk he faced personally. But to strip the borders of their defenses and join Postumus in Treveris meant a civil war against Gallienus. Laelianus knew what would happen to his and others' families if he left them defenseless along the borders for an extended period of time. Either the Franks or Alamanni would attack. They would loot, burn cities and towns, rape the women, and enslave or slaughter everyone else. He frowned and shook his head to clear the thought.

Legates commanding the two other legions stationed along the Rhenus River shared Laelianus' misgivings. They had discussed the impact of withdrawing all their forces while the three of them rode north from Treveris after their meeting with Postumus on the second of March. Each legate had subsequently sent half of his legionnaires to Moguntiacum, in support of Laelianus' planned revolt. Laelianus rubbed his hands together and held them close to the lamp illuminating his small table. Although it was nearly April, the air was still chilly.

What will Postumus do after he gets this message? What should I be doing? Will the other legates continue to support me? Maybe I should make overtures to Gallienus about rejoining the empire. That might prevent a war of succession among the other legates if Postumus was killed. Laelianus smiled at his series of thoughts. So many things to consider! *But none of these issues will matter if I don't first defeat Postumus.* After drumming his fingers on the table for several moments, he dipped his pen into the ink bottle and began again.

> I believe that a leader's primary responsibility should be the safety and welfare of the land and people which he governs. Further, the acquisition of additional power should not come at their expense. Your order to remove all legionnaires from their positions along our borders poses an unwarranted danger to the citizens, therefore, I refuse to comply with your directive.

Laelianus reread his latest draft and shrugged as he waited for the ink to dry. *It will have to do*, he thought. *If Postumus had only asked for a fraction of my legion, I would have grudgingly accepted the order.* He smiled grimly as he envisioned Postumus' reaction to this message: he could see Postumus' lower lip begin to quiver and his face redden just before he broke into a fit of profanity.

"You have a visitor, sir…" his orderly's announcement intruded on Laelianus' thoughts.

"I told you, no interruptions!" Laelianus snapped, angry that a simple order couldn't be obeyed.

"I don't have time to wait until it's convenient for my legates to see me," said an angry voice. A momentary shock ran through Laelianus' body when he recognized Postumus' voice. Brushing past the orderly, he strode into Laelianus' quarters and stopped in the middle of the room. Laelianus leapt to his feet and tried to cover the message lying on his desk with his pen and inkwell. Postumus glanced with a frown at the crumpled pages Laelianus had tossed onto the floor.

"I wasn't expecting visitors at the moment, sir," Laelianus stammered. *What is he doing here now? Does he know of my intention somehow? Maybe he's guessed at it?* "How… can I be of service to you?" he finally managed to ask.

"I heard you might be having problems getting my legionnaires to Treveris," Postumus said, looking at Laelianus closely. Postumus' aides had urged him to be more suspicious of his reliability after Laelianus' comments during their conference earlier in the month. "So I decided to come and see for myself."

"They're not due to arrive until mid-month," Laelianus countered. *He doesn't know! He's just suspicious.* Laelianus relaxed a bit inwardly and regained some of his composure.

"How many legionnaires are here so far?" Postumus demanded. "I didn't see what looked like four legions in camp just now."

"Half of the Vetera and Bonna legions have already been transferred here."

"Where are the rest?"

"I've left half of each legion at their posts until the last possible minute. The legion at Argentoratum hasn't moved north to join me yet, but I expect them within the week."

Postumus thought about Laelianus' actions for a moment. Finally he nodded a grudging agreement. As he did so, he noticed the paper on Laelianus' desk and nodded towards it. "The paperwork never seems to end. I thought it would when I became emperor, but there's more now than ever. That one seems to be giving you trouble," he grinned, glancing at the papers on the floor again.

"It's to a, colleague," Laelianus temporized. "An issue regarding his performance." He shrugged as if the message were merely a routine annoyance to be dealt with.

"They're always hard to write," Postumus sympathized. "Just tell him exactly what you feel and what you expect from him. That's what I do."

Laelianus nodded. "I've tried to do that."

"Back to the reason I came," Postumus dismissed the matter of correspondence. Laelianus held his breath and waited for Postumus to continue. "The men didn't seem to me like they were ready to march any time soon."

"It's only a six-day march from here to Treveris," Laelianus objected. "I wasn't planning to leave until the 9th or 10th."

Postumus wrinkled his brow and looked as if he were about to comment, when an orderly appeared at the door. "A message for the emperor," he announced, handing Postumus a scroll. Postumus scanned it quickly. His lower lip began to tremble, his face reddened, and he burst into a string of expletives. This may disrupt all my plans! He tossed the scroll onto Laelianus' table, then pounded a fist into his open palm.

"Trouble, sir?"

"The Franks have crossed the river, west of Colonia," Postumus growled.

"Do you want to take men from here to deal with it?"

Postumus considered Laelianus' offer, then shook his head. "No. They'd slow me down. Your decision to leave men along the border turns out to have been a fortunate one for me. I'll go north and lead the effort with the troops that are still there. I'll call for reinforcements if I need them. Otherwise get the troops ready to be in Treveris by mid-April."

Lealianus nodded. "Is there anything else I can do to help you?"

"Paper." Postumus said.

Laelianus looked at him uncomprehending.

"For a message to Victorinus and Marius in Treveris," Postumus said irritably. "If I don't tell them, they'll never think to go to Colonia on their own initiative. I'll use what you have on the table," he said, shooing Laelianus away from his message on the desk lying in plain view. Postumus walked around the table and reached for the chair that Laelianus had been sitting in.

"Let me get you a clean sheet," Laelianus said, snatching the paper away as Postumus eased himself into the chair and reached for Laelianus' message. If Postumus had not had other things on his mind, he might have found that behavior peculiar. Laelianus dropped the message he'd been composing onto his cot behind the table, then quickly found several clean pages which he almost threw onto the desk in front of Postumus.

"I've found that if you want to avoid confusion or misunderstanding," Postumus growled, taking the paper without looking up at Laelianus, "then you have to write this sort of thing yourself." He picked up Laelianus' pen. The only sound in the room after that was scratching of a pen across page.

A Day's Ride South of Augusta Vindelicum, Rhaetia
20 April, 268

Wild flowers covered roadside meadows and blossoms adorned fruit trees in nearby orchards. Mild, sunny weather matched Aureolus' mood of optimism and anticipation. He turned in his saddle and gazed at three quarters of his legion marching behind him, as if looking for confirmation that this was not some fantastic dream. His pulse quickened at the thrill of again leading a group of armed men. True, it was only part of a legion, and there were scarcely any cavalry with him, but at Mediolanum all that would change. He was pleasantly surprised at how easily he had been able to convince these men to adopt his own, personal cause, even though the legion was assigned to the province of Rhaetia, and thus already under his command. He knew that convincing foot soldiers at Mediolanum would be more difficult. He would have to rely on his personality and reputation to sway them over. The force at Mediolanum, he had learned through discreet inquiry, outnumbered the men he was bringing by nearly three to one. But there were cavalry men there, and they had been his men for years. Anxiety mixed with a feeling of opportunity. This was a great gamble—but so were the rewards. *Men who dare to do great things will be greatly rewarded*, he reassured himself. *After winning the Mediolanum forces to my side, the rest will be easy, just clear one bridge, open the mountain passes, and wait for Postumus to join me with an army of his own. Then the two of us will march to Rome and have the Senate declare Postumus emperor before Gallienus even knows that it happened.*

While Aureolus rode south, a lone rider galloped east taking news of Aureolus' treachery to Gallienus, and another man rode north, to alert his Alamanni tribesmen that borders were now open and lightly guarded.

Colonia Agrippina, Germania Inferior
20 April, 268

Postumus frowned as he began reading the message an aide had just handed him. By the time he finished, he could barely contain his rage. He threw the scroll to the ground beside his startled horse and pounded a fist into his other hand. *First the Franks, now Laelianus may disrupt my plans*!

"Bad news, I take it," Victorinus offered blandly. At the end of their intense, two-week campaign, Frankish warriors had finally fled across the Rhenus River. Now, Postumus forces were just outside Colonia Agrippina, tired and dirty from fighting and forced marches. Victorinus sighed. *And I was looking forward to a bottle of wine, a bath, and an evening of female companionship.* He knew better than to say anything further to Postumus just now, or to have someone retrieve the message so he could read it himself. When Postumus was ready, he would tell them what he wished them to know and what they were to do next.

"It's Laelianus," Postumus growled, pounding a fist into his open palm.

"Is he ill?" Marius inquired.

"Worse," Postumus replied, seeing the perfect opportunity to seize the whole empire slipping away, through no fault of his own.

"Dead?" Victorinus asked.

"No. But he will be after I get my hands on him," Postumus said fiercely. *Maybe there'll still be time to take advantage of Gallienus' absence, if I can crush Laelianus' revolt quickly.*

"What exactly is the issue then?" Victorinus inquired.

"He's refused to withdraw legions from the border. If we hadn't come up here to fight the Franks, he'd have control of all three legions along the Rhenus now."

"Has the legion at Argentoratum joined him too?" Marius asked.

"That's unclear," Postumus said. He thought a moment. "I want you to ride down to Argentoratum, Marius. Take some horsemen with you. Tell the legate to march south—to Vesontio. If I can defeat Laelianus quickly, then I'll join him there later."

"And if we can't?" Victorinus asked.

"Then we won't have crossed the mountains and committed ourselves against Gallienus."

Victorinus nodded. "But Aureolus has committed himself by now. I imagine he's already left Augusta Vindelicum."

"An unfortunate situation, for Aureolus," Postumus agreed, without a trace of remorse or guilt in his voice. "There's no way to get word to him before he goes south." He thought about Aureolus marching toward Mediolanum with, at most, one legion of men. *I always thought convincing the men at Mediolanum was the riskiest part of this venture.*

"What if he's successful?" Victorinus asked, thinking of Aureolus at Mediolanum. "Then he'd have a force large enough to march on Rome whether we joined him or not."

A shiver of anxiety swept over Postumus. He was reminded of the issues of trust and treachery that Gallienus had been facing for years. He imagined what Gallienus must think about him and smiled grimly. "Then I'll have to convince Aureolus to wait for us."

Forty Miles North of Naissus, Moesia Superior
20 April, 268

This afternoon was much like most others Gallienus had experienced during nearly a month of marching. He idly watched countryside pass by and studied travelers sharing the road. Some looked up with expressions of surprise and awe. A few waved. Little children ran alongside the horses for short periods, until they tired or their mothers called them back. The rest passed by without showing any surprise or interest that the emperor of Rome and an army were marching through their villages.

Gray clouds raced low overhead, driven by warm winds threatening showers. Gallienus disliked rain even more than heat and dust of summer. It soaked through their clothing during marches. Campgrounds became muddy almost immediately, and provided little relief to tired, cold soldiers. Wet fields hindered cavalry movements, and limited visibility made ambushes more difficult to detect— although Gallienus didn't expect an ambush here, three days' ride from Naissus, an ancient city long considered one of the gateways between the east and west. At Naissus the Via Militaris, which they had been marching on for four days, continued east to Byzantium, while a second road out of the city led south to Thessalonica. Gallienus would have to choose one of those roads, depending on what he learned of the Goths' location and movement.

Day after day, the same thoughts and questions ran through his head, although he knew he could not answer most of them until much later. *Have I made the right assumptions? What have I overlooked? Will I choose the right direction leaving Naissus? What will I find when I meet the Goths? Will I have sufficient strength to defeat them?* His mind returned to his soldiers. *What can I do to keep their morale high on this long, tedious march? Perhaps I should organize some competitions during our next rest day. Maybe the Amphitheatre at Naissus will be large enough to accommodate my army. I could offer some gladiatorial games for them.*

His thoughts drifted to Salonina, traveling somewhere behind him with a small support force and retinue of her own. *How is she? Will she stop at all the cities I've passed through and allow local dignitaries to entertain her?* He hoped she would— otherwise it would be a long, lonely journey for her indeed.

"What are you thinking?" Pipa's voice startled him.

"I didn't hear you ride up."

"I've been with you for some time!"

He looked over and smiled affectionately at her. Pipa's off-white, short-sleeved linen tunic fit snugly across her breast down to her waist, then over knee-length trousers. The thin leather belt at her waist held a sheathed dagger he had given her. Gold earrings danced constantly due to her horse's movements, and golden bracelets jangled during her frequent hand gestures. Pipa's blond hair fell freely over her shoulders. She was always able to distract him from nagging concerns of leadership. She had made it a habit to ride with him during the afternoons. After their midday meals, Gallienus' generals customarily rode at a discreet distance behind them.

"So what were you thinking?" she asked again.

"I was wondering what dinner might be."

She looked at him out of the corner of her eye. "Probably the same as yesterday, and the day before that: pork, bread, beans, and cheese."

"How's morale holding out?"

"Your soldiers don't talk to me as a rule, but the Marcomanni are doing well enough."

They rode in comfortable silence for a while. "Any regrets about how your life has gone so far?" he asked her philosophically.

"I never thought I'd be married to a Roman, let alone an emperor!" She thought for a moment, then added, "I don't feel that I completely fit with either the Romans or the Marcomanni anymore." Her voice trailed off as she brushed a tear from her eye. After a pause she asked, "What will you do after you defeat the Goths?"

"Next year I'll take back Gallia and execute Postumus."

"Then what?"

"Then I've got to deal with Zenobia in the east. Why all the questions?"

"I had a strange dream last night."

"Tell me about it."

"I was in an unfamiliar campground. A raven circled high in the air and below it men were running everywhere without any clear purpose—like no one was in charge of them. When I looked around, I couldn't find you anywhere." She shivered. "I felt very alone—and afraid."

Gallienus was struck by her comment. He had never heard her admit to fearing anything before. "Dreams can be very unsettling," he said, trying to reassure her. "Was there more?"

"That's all I can remember. It made me wonder what my future might be."

"It's with me."

"As long as you're not in Rome, where I'm not welcome. After you've restored the east and the west, you'll probably stay in Rome all year! What will I do then?"

"I haven't been able to stay in Rome any year since I've been emperor." They rode in silence, each considering the other's comments.

"Rider approaching!" one of the tribunes shouted, alerting the men around the emperor. They studied the rider advancing toward them. A feather on the tip of his spear showed that he was a messenger. As he approached them, Pipa stole a glance at Gallienus. His face seemed tense and anxious.

"What news, messenger?" Gallienus demanded, as soon as the man had approached and saluted him. The messenger tried to hand him several scrolls. "Tell me what they say," Gallienus insisted.

It's a bit complicated, sir. First, Thessalonica has been sacked and the enemy is heading east."

"Towards Thracia?" Gallienus interrupted. "There isn't much for them to loot there, unless they're trying to fight their way back home. You're sure it wasn't west?"

"Well, a small part of that group broke away after Thessalonica and did head west."

"That group?" Gallienus interrupted again. "There's more than one?"

"Three that I know of—now four, since the group at Thessalonica split." The messenger waited for Gallienus to consider this information. Eventually, Gallienus nodded for him to continue.

"Athens has been sacked. That group has headed west toward Megara. Where they intend to go after that is unclear. General Dexippus was attempting to organize a defensive force."

"Megara?" Pipa asked Gallienus.

"It's west of Athens. We passed through it on our way to Delphi."

"Remind me, who is this Dexippus?"

"An Athenian general. You may have met him in Athens." Gallienus nodded at the messenger. "And the third group?"

"The coastal cities of Asia—Ilium and Pergamum were mentioned. They were continuing south. Probably they've reached Ephesus by now, or maybe even Miletus."

"Do you know the whereabouts of General Marcianus?"

"South of you, sir, heading toward Amphipolis."

"Where is Amphipolis?" Pipa asked, trying to understand the significance of what the messenger was saying.

"It's on the seacoast, over three hundred miles from here," the messenger said, looking at Pipa with considerable interest. Pipa nodded blankly.

"I assume the same details will be in the messages?" The messenger nodded. "Get something to eat and take some rest," Gallienus said. "I may need your services shortly."

"It's good they split into groups," Pipa commented as the messenger saluted and rode past them.

"I wish he had some estimates as to their numbers."

"Why? Whatever the number is, you'll still attack them."

"It would help to know how to divide my forces, if I have to."

"As you get closer, those estimates will come to you, and they'll be more accurate then," Pipa speculated. "So many cities that mean nothing to me. Tell me what the messenger said so that I can understand it."

"Fortunately, I've been studying maps of the area," Gallienus said. "Everything is well to the south of us, so there probably won't be any fighting for a couple more weeks. In the meantime, we'll continue south toward Amphipolis, which is on the north coast of the Mare Aegaeum, then decide where the most serious threat is. From Amphipolis, Thessalonica will be about seventy miles southwest, also on the coast. Athens will be south of us a little more than four hundred miles. It's near the western part of the same coast. The towns he mentioned in Asia are on the far side of the ocean and of no immediate threat to us."

Pipa heard horses approaching and knew the generals were coming forward to learn the news. *Then they'll want to discuss it among themselves.* "And then the fun will begin!" she said.

Gallienus looked at her, surprised by her remark.

Pipa wheeled her horse to the right and began to ride away. She looked over her shoulder and grinned at Gallienus. "That's what Daddy will say."

9-1
Important Decisions
Amphipolis, Macedonia
12 May, 268

"We're too late," Pipa exclaimed, looking at the city ruins around her.

"Our scouts said the same thing," Gallienus said grimly.

"I'd hoped they would somehow be mistaken." Amphipolis had been built in a bend of the River Strymon which surrounded it on the north, west, and south. Gallienus and Pipa rode at the head of a small group of men, since the scouts had determined no hostile threat remained in the area. A small group of Praetorian Guards accompanied them, along with Generals Heraclianus, Claudius, Aurelian, and Attalus. From high ground inside this part of the city, Pipa could see the river to the west as it flowed into Mare Thracium, nearly three miles south of them. She noticed a single ship approaching the small, empty harbor. *This must be what cities looked like when Daddy was ravaging Roman countryside years ago*! It gave her a different perspective.

"Where would that take you?" Pipa asked, pointing to the road running along the coast and off to their right.

"That's Via Egnatia," Gallienus said, referring to a map of the region he'd studied the previous night. "It goes west to Thessalonica, about sixty miles from here. To the left," he swung an arm toward the east, "the same road runs all the way to Byzantium. Several coastal towns lie along the road and the province of Thracia lies just across the Nestos River."

"How far is that?" Pipa asked.

"About seventy-five miles, maybe four days marching from here." Gallienus paused and looked around. "It seems that the attack happened some time ago."

"How can you tell?"

"No fires burning, or even smoldering, no wounded lying in the streets." Gallienus wrinkled his nose distastefully at the stale smell of charred timbers mixed with the stench of dead citizens. "They've been dead for some time."

"There seem to be some survivors," Pipa noted, pointing to a two-story home destroyed by invaders. Fire had burned through timbers supporting the roof causing it to collapse into the living spaces below. Terra cotta tiles from the roof lay scattered in the street. One of the larger timbers had knocked a huge hole in the front wall, exposing what was left of interior furnishings. Two small children peered out at them curiously, until their frightened mother pulled them out of sight.

"They probably fled before the attack. Now they're coming back to see what's left of their homes and shops."

The clopping of their horses' hooves echoed loudly in the unnatural silence, while they threaded their way through streets littered with remains of buildings. Some had been made of stone, but most had been wooden.

"Where would the Goths have gone?" Pipa asked.

"Either east or west," Gallienus said. "The ocean is south and we'd have seen them if they came north."

"Wasn't your general… Marcianus supposed to be here?" Pipa asked.

"Yes. Maybe the Goths defeated him…"

"We've seen no dead soldiers," Pipa said, glancing around the city. "yours or theirs."

The main road curved to the left then opened into a spacious agora. Closest to them were remnants of what had been merchant stalls before raiding Goths torched them. Buildings lined edges of the market place, the first they came to was a sanctuary dedicated to Clio, a local deity and mother of Rhesos of Iliad fame. Beyond that was a temple to Artemis Brauronia. And at the far end of the agora, was a crowd of people—and soldiers!

Gallienus nudged his horse forward and slowly advanced toward the milling crowd. As they drew closer, he saw one of the soldiers glance up from the child he was attending to. Startled, the soldier leapt to his feet and shouted to a short stocky man nearby, obviously their leader. The man stood, looked toward Gallienus, straightened his uniform, and deliberately approached. A few feet in front of the emperor's horse he stopped, saluted, and gave his name and the legion he was assigned to. He stared at Pipa for a full second wondering why a barbarian woman was riding beside the emperor of Rome.

Gallienus noticed scars on his muscular arms, his uniform streaked with dirt and blood. Heraclianus, Claudius, Aurelian, and Attalus moved forward to hear the man speak. "What are you doing here, centurion?" Gallienus asked.

"General Marcianus left us here to meet you, sir. We've been waiting nearly two weeks. These people," he nodded at the crowd behind him, "are most of the survivors, the ones who fled before the Goths attacked or somehow escaped during the pillaging. They're just returning to the city. We've been treating sick and wounded as best we can. There's no one else to help them."

"Perhaps I could help them," Pipa suggested, knowing that the men wished to learn what had happened and to decide how to proceed. She slipped off her horse and started walking toward the crowd and the assisting legionnaires.

"Stay here!" Gallienus said sharply. Pipa turned back to him, unaccustomed to being spoken to that way. He saw the surprise and hurt on her face and softened his tone. "It's too dangerous for you. They wouldn't understand help coming from someone who's obviously a foreigner to them." Pipa nodded reluctantly as she realized why he'd spoke sharply. She looked around and finally sat on the steps of Artimis' temple to listen and wait.

"Give me a quick summary, from the time you first got here," Gallienus ordered.

"We arrived with General Marcianus on the 25th of last

month with half a legion of men and nearly marched into the middle of an enemy army while they were sacking the city."

"Did you attack them?"

"No. General Marcianus rode forward to see the situation for himself. He told us we were outnumbered by somewhere between five and ten to one and he said it would be pointless to attack with those odds."

"So you held back," Gallienus nodded. "Then what?"

The centurion again glanced curiously at Pipa, then Attalus before continuing. "A few days later we captured a raiding party—well, most of them. The general has a few men on his staff who speak their language, so he brought the survivors back to camp and interrogated them. That's when we learned the bar...," he paused to look at Pipa, who returned his stare with a stony expression, but Attalus' fierce scowl told the man that he understood what was being said and did not care for it. The centurion cleared his throat and then resumed, "… the Goths had split into two groups at Thessalonica."

"Why wasn't I informed of this?" Gallienus demanded.

"I presume the general sent you a messenger, sir; perhaps he was intercepted."

"Did they split evenly?"

"The centurion shrugged. "The … Goths probably didn't even know that themselves,"

"Any estimates of their strength?"

"Only that they laughed when they saw how few men we had in camp."

Gallienus smiled. "That tells us something of their strength. I hope you didn't let them return to their camp after they knew of your strength."

The centurion shook his head. "General Marcianus followed the Goths when they left Amphipolis heading east towards Thracia. He planned to shadow them until help arrived, but I know he hoped to catch them before they reached the bridge over the Nestos River."

"When did the Goths leave?"

The man thought for a moment. "Around the 28th."

Gallienus nodded for him to continue.

"He also sent a small cavalry force to locate the Goths who went west from Thessalonica." He paused to think. "Six days after everyone departed, another half-legion of General Marcianus' men arrived here. They went east on the general's orders."

"Then he has a full legion's strength," Gallienus commented. "Where's the rest of his forces?"

"Another legion is still on the march."

Gallienus paused to consider this information, staring past the centurion without further comment. The man stood rigidly mistaking his thinking for disapproval.

"Heraclianus," Gallienus turned suddenly and addressed his Praetorian Prefect, "find someone familiar with this area to tell us where the Goths could be going—both east and west. And have some of our men help this centurion tend to the sick and injured." He turned his gaze back to the centurion. "You've done well." Relieved, the man saluted and returned to his legionnaires.

The midday sun heated the market place stones. Claudius removed his cape and laid it over his horses' saddle. Aurelian followed Claudius' example.

"Why would anyone want to live in this place?" Attalus complained. "The hot humid summers are unbearable!"

Gallienus dismounted and climbed up to sit on the highest steps of the temple to seek shade and to give him a better view down the street. The others, except for Attalus, followed his example after leading their horses to shade. Attalus remained standing at the base of the steps. He held his horse's reins in one hand and glanced about restlessly.

"We've marched for weeks to fight," Attalus fumed, as he paced back and forth, "but now you're all sitting on the steps of a destroyed temple in the middle of a destroyed city. The enemy has come and gone. What are we waiting for?"

"If we turn east to attack one band of Goths, my friend," Gallienus replied to Attalus, "then we'll have two other groups somewhere behind us. I'd like to know where they are, and where they're going before I turn my back on them."

Attalus looked unconvinced.

"A short wait now won't make that much difference,"

Gallienus continued. "I can't afford to get this wrong." He stopped speaking and watched with sudden interest as Heraclianus approached with two men behind him. He rose and descended all but the last temple step as they drew closer.

"This is Marcus," Heraclianus announced, pointing at one of the men. "He lives in Amphipolis and knows this region well. And this fellow," Heraclianus nodded at the other man, "is a messenger who just arrived by ship with news from the south."

"Good work, Heraclianus!" Gallienus exclaimed before turning his attention to the two men. "What news do you bring me from the south?" he asked the messenger.

"The, enemy," the messenger began, choosing his words carefully. He had noticed Attalus and Pipa standing near the emperor as soon as he approached Gallienus and his entourage. "have landed in great numbers on our shores."

Gallienus held up a hand. "I already know Athens has been sacked. What happened after that."

The messenger nodded. "They moved west, taking Megara. Then, they crossed the isthmus, sacked Corinth, and are currently ravaging all of Achaea."

"They're still in Achaea?" Gallienus asked.

"They were when I left with this news," the messenger replied.

"Hmmm, less than a week ago," Claudius speculated. "They'll eventually have to come north."

"General Dexippus is gathering an army of sorts from the men who tried to save Athens," the messenger said. "He's preparing to confront them when they do. He urgently requests any assistance that you might be able to provide him." The messenger looked expectantly at Gallienus.

"That won't be possible," Gallienus said, after considering the request. "There are two enemy groups somewhere near me that I have to deal with first. Tell Dexippus he'll have to manage himself, for now." He paused. "Anything else you want to tell me?"

"My ship first landed at Thessalonica," the messenger said. "I learned the Goths had tried to sack the city, but failed, so they moved on. The people there said some of the Goths had gone this way, so I decided to sail east, hoping to find some Roman military forces pursuing the… invaders."

Gallienus nodded his approval. "That's good news about Thessalonica. We'd heard it was sacked." Then turned his attention to the man from Amphipolis.

"Marcus was a legionary and retired at Amphipolis," Heraclianus explained, "so he's familiar with the land all around here."

"I noticed your limp when you approached us, Marcus," Gallienus said. "Where did you serve?"

"Mostly along the Moesian borders, sir," Marcus replied. "I fought with Emperor Gallus, he was actually General Gallus then, against Goths when Cniva was their chieftain. That's when I got this," he said, tapping his left leg. "So I retired here and became a wine merchant."

"Fortunate you weren't with Emperor Decius' army," Gallienus replied.

"Why?" Attalus asked.

"Gallus was governor of Moesia Superior when Cniva and his army swept through much of that province, seventeen years ago," Gallienus explained. "Decius and most of his army were killed when he attacked retreating Goths near a town called Abritus in Moesia Inferior."

Attalus grunted.

Marcus nodded. "That was so long ago I thought we might have seen the last of the Goths. But they've killed my family and destroyed most of the city." His lower lip quivered as he looked around the agora. When he had gained control of himself, he continued. "I was away on business when this happened, but I wish that I'd been here to die with them."

"I know what it means to lose family. I've lost two of my sons."

"Nothing will bring them back, nor restore my livelihood," Marcus began.

"Right now," Gallienus interrupted, "I need to know where the Goths have gone, so I can destroy them, and so you can return to your life without further threats."

Marcus drew himself up straight and took a deep breath.

"We were told the Goths divided their forces at Thessalonica," Gallienus said.

"The group who sacked this city went east when they left here."

"And the group that went west out of Thessalonica?" Gallienus arched an eyebrow. "Where would they have gone?"

"West of Thessalonica the roads go west, north-west, and south. They could have taken any one of them."

"So they could be almost anywhere by now," Heraclianus exclaimed.

Gallienus looked at his generals. "Either we pursue the group going east, or we hunt for the group that went west from Thessalonica. Your thoughts?"

Claudius shrugged. "As long as the Goths west of Thessalonica aren't heading towards us, they're not our immediate concern."

"So you'd suggest going east?" Gallienus probed. Claudius nodded. "I believe the map showed favorable terrain for a battle where the River Nestos divides Macedonia from Thracia." He paused. "Do you agree with that, Marcus?"

"A good place for a battle," Marcus nodded. "The River Nestos meanders through rugged mountains, steep slopes end almost at the river's edge, no crossing the river there—for an army anyway. South of the mountains land opens onto a marshy isthmus before reaching the Mare Thracium. There's a bridge across the Nestos, part of the Via Egnatia. At this time of year, the river is full, and the isthmus is swampy. An army with captives and spoils could only get across using the bridge."

"The eastern group is already leaving the country," Aurelian interrupted. "Why not let them go."

"So you're suggesting going west?" Gallienus asked Aurelian.

"Attack the Goths west of Thessalonica before they can join the Goths in Achaea," Aurelian reasoned.

"But we don't know where Goths west of Thessalonica are," Heraclianus objected, "or where they're going."

"Marcianus sent scouts after them," Aurelian reminded him. "They should be back with that information any day now. What if the Goths head for Rome itself?"

"We can march faster than the Goths," Claudius countered. "They'll stop and loot every city and town along the way."

"The garrison at Mediolanum could deal with them if it came to that," Heraclianus said.

"If the garrison left Mediolanum, they wouldn't be a deterrent to Postumus," Aurelian said

"It would take Postumus weeks to march an army south from his northern borders," Claudius said. "The garrison at Mediolanum could confront any Goths that might roam that far, and be back in Mediolanum before Postumus could act."

"What if he'd already marched south?" Aurelian persisted.

"Do you have any information that he's planning to do that?" Claudius asked.

"No," Aurelian conceded, "but it's something that should at least be considered. And the standing orders for the army in Mediolanum are to defend against an attack from Postumus. We could only hope that their commander would act on his own initiative if a hostile army suddenly appeared from the east."

"Valid issues and concerns," Gallienus agreed, after thinking about Aurelian's reasoning for a few moments. "But the more immediate problem is here and now. If we let Goths escape unchallenged, what message does that send to others?"

"They'd see you as weak or indecisive—probably both," Attalus interjected. "Then they'd come in force, before someone else could plunder the land. Think of the turmoil you'd have on the borders next year."

"There's another option," Heraclianus suggested. "Divide our forces and pursue both groups at once."

"Marcianus doesn't have sufficient strength to challenge the Goths himself," Claudius objected.

"He has almost five thousand men with him now and another five thousand on the march," Heraclianus countered. He looked at the skeptical expressions on the men's faces. "In addition to Marcianus' forces we have about seventeen thousand legionnaires, three thousand cavalry, two thousand Praetorian guards, and another three thousand horsemen that Attalus brought."

"The Goths reportedly came in great numbers," Gallienus said to Heraclianus. "I remember you saying that even a mid-range estimate of their strength would be a very large number."

"True," Heraclianus agreed, "but they've split into four groups that we know of: one's in Asia somewhere, another in Achaea, the other two near us right now."

Gallienus considered Heraclianus' argument. "So you're suggesting that we go both east and west."

"Temporarily."

"Whatever else you do," Attalus said, "you can't let the eastern group escape without a fight."

"So let me see," Gallienus summed up his generals' advice, "I have a suggestion that we go west and let the Goths in the east escape, another view that we must do just the opposite, and still another that we do both at the same time, each with convincing arguments as to why that solution is to be preferred. Did I, perhaps, miss anything?"

"As you said," Claudius finally spoke, "a case can be made for each of them."

Gallienus considered the generals' recommendations and reasoning. *The fate of the empire, and my reign, might depend on the outcome of my decision.* Sounds of the legionnaires and the crowd of citizens drifted towards them. Attalus batted a fly from his face, and cleared his throat. "We'll go east," Gallienus finally announced, "with everyone."

9-2
Around the River Nestos
Macedonian-Thracian Border
18 May, 268

The morning star hung low in the dim gray sky. Gallienus watched it fade as night yielded to the dawn. He pulled his cloak around his shoulders and patted his horse's mane, only partially aware of the hushed sounds around him. Steep mountains to his left rose abruptly. Ahead and to his right the Nestos River flowed into marshy ground before emptying into Mare Thracium. The Goth's camp lay directly ahead of him, on his side of the river. Scouts had reported a vast number of people in the Goths' camp—they had acquired a considerable number of horses and wagons—but from a distance they couldn't distinguish between warriors and captives.

Gallienus planned to defeat the retreating Goths on open plains before they could cross the bridge. Only yesterday he had joined General Marcianus and learned that many of the Goths remained on the western shore, although others had been crossing the river for the last two days. During his tour as one of Gallienus' Praetorian guards, Marcianus had distinguished himself and had risen rapidly in the ranks thereafter.

Sacrifices to the gods earlier that morning were favorable for a battle. Gallienus had issued instructions to his generals, and spoken words of encouragement to the soldiers. For the moment, nothing further was required of him. Legionaries marched past his right side on the Via Egnatia. Their shoes on the pavement and an occasional clank of shields against armor were the only sounds he was aware of. A light rain the night before left traces of mist ahead of him. It would burn off shortly after sunrise, he knew, and then they would have the rising sun in their eyes for the early part of the battle. A slight easterly breeze blew the smell of nearly extinguished fires from the Goth's camp, maybe a mile ahead of them. An image came to Gallienus' mind of a few of the Goths rising to stir fires for their morning meal and looking west in amazement as the Roman army swooped down on them.

"General Claudius and his cavalry are in position on our left flank," Heraclianus reported.

"And the right?" Gallienus asked.

"General Marcianus and his legions are moving that way now. Attalus and his men will be right behind them," Heraclianus assured him.

"The center is taking too long to get into position," Gallienus grumbled to Aurelian, who sat astride his horse beside Gallienus and Heraclianus. "I know it's the fastest way to move them, but they're still bunched up along the road."

"There's still enough time for them to be in position before you give the order to attack," Aurelian reassured him.

"Once the legionaries are deployed in the center," Heraclianus said, "then we can form the reserves behind us."

Gallienus nodded. "Let me know when they're ready." Anxiety mixed with his anticipation as he realized he was finally in contact with an enemy who had given him so much trouble over the last few years. *The gods have smiled on me: a large invasion force has split into smaller groups so I can attack and defeat each separately. This group is trapped in front of a river with only a small bridge for them to escape across. After I defeat this group, I'll go back past Thessalonica and find the next group before it can rejoin other forces.*

A tremendous roar of men shouting startled Gallienus from his reverie. Puzzlement gave way to irritation. "I haven't given the order to attack yet!"

"That's not our men," Heraclianus shouted. "We're being attacked!"

Trumpets blared orders and centurions shouted commands to their soldiers. Men rushed to form up their legions with armor clanking as they ran past Gallienus. His horse pranced and whinnied uncomfortably, disturbed by the confusion around him. A whizzing sound similar to angry bees now added its noise as the first enemy arrows started falling around Gallienus and his staff.

"Get the men to spread out—right here," Gallienus shouted to Aurelian. "Then tell the center to fall back. We've got to hold the center together."

Aurelian saluted and galloped off, bellowing orders to his nearby centurions.

"Tell the reserve forces to be ready to support the center," Gallienus shouted to his Praetorian Prefect, while keeping his eyes fixed on the evolving battle situation. Heraclianus reined his horse away from the emperor and gave several brisk orders to his tribunes. Committing the reserve forces so early in battle was a serious decision. No help would be available later on, should any part of the battle line falter.

Gallienus, wanted to be close to this critical part of the action to rally the troops. He spurred his horse toward legionaries bearing the brunt of this surprise attack.

Heraclianus, noticing Gallienus' movement, urged his horse forward to support the emperor. He had nearly caught up when Gallienus' horse staggered, then pitched forward and tumbled, lifeless, to the ground. Gallienus was thrown forward and landed on his back, where he lay motionless.

Heraclianus was beside Gallienus in seconds. The Praetorian Guards closed around both men. Heraclianus lifted Gallienus' head and leaned close to him. "He's only lost his wind," he shouted to the anxious Praetorians. "Bring me another horse!" Gallienus was rising unsteadily to his feet. Heraclianus pointed to his own mount. "Take mine, sir. It's an excellent horse," he said to Gallienus as he helped him into the saddle. "Just stay away from the water. For some reason this horse fears it."

"I'll remember," Gallienus grinned, still somewhat shaken.

A tribune returned with another mount for Heraclianus. He leapt into the saddle and reined the animal around toward the nearby legionaries, who had fallen back and were fighting tenaciously just in front of where Gallienus had fallen. "The reserves are coming forward, and our line is holding!" he shouted. Heraclianus rapidly surveyed the battlefield near them. "I strongly suggest you withdraw from immediate danger," he urged Gallienus. "You'll be better able to direct the battle from a little further behind the front line!"

Gallienus reluctantly allowed himself to be taken back to a safer place. From there he observed the overall situation while catching his breath. The Goths' advance on his center was halted. Roman legionaries had regrouped and recovered from their initial surprise and confusion. Far to his right he could see Marcianus' forces had prevented any Goths from getting around that flank. In fact, Marcianus was moving forward and seemed to threaten the Goth's own flank. And Attalus and his Marcomanni were supporting Marcianus, no they were moving to the right of Marcianus and going ahead of him against a wing of enemy horsemen who were no doubt trying to counter Marcianus' advance. *Splendid! Maybe Attalus can capture the bridge*!

Gallienus glanced to his left flank. Claudius' cavalry was still there, outside and behind the left flank of his legionaries, ready to move on Gallienus' command. He rapidly scanned the situation in the center. "Heraclianus, we should be able to start withdrawing reserve forces," he ordered. "Aurelian seems to have everything under control at the moment."

He strained to see what was happening on his right. Despite earlier rain, dust was beginning to obscure his view. Attalus was engaged with enemy horsemen and Marcianus' men weren't moving, which meant stiff Goth resistance. In the center there was no change, aside from a gradual withdrawal of some forces to reconstitute his reserves. To the left, enemy forces were falling back and to their left. *Probably to support their comrades fighting Marcianus. This is my chance*! "Tell General Claudius to attack," he called to one of his tribunes. As the sound of the bugle call drifted across the plain, Claudius' cavalry sprang into action. Over two thousand horsemen advanced at a trot toward retreating Goths. The enemy's retreat quickly dissolved into panicked flight. Some men threw down their weapons to hasten their escape. Lead elements of Claudius' cavalry broke into a gallop just before catching the retreating Goths. Gallienus watched a volley of Roman javelins caught the fleeing men in their unprotected backs. As they closed on the enemy, horsemen used swords to slash at men who had not even turned to defend themselves. Back to his right enemy horsemen fighting Attalus were slipping back through their own warriors. *They're disengaging from Attalus to reinforce their faltering right side*, Gallienus marveled.

"They must have noticed the right side of their army's collapsing," Heraclianus noted, following Gallienus' gaze.

"Rather remarkable soldiering," Gallienus commented on the enemy horsemen's maneuvering. "Do you think it will do any good?"

"Probably not at this point," Heraclianus speculated. He watched the battle continue to unfold. "Their center seems to be giving ground too." A cheer from nearby legionaries signaled their sense of impending victory as they began to advance. "So far the enemy retreat is orderly," Heraclianus observed. "That probably won't last long though. Do you want me to commit the reserves now?"

"Not yet, but have them ready. I want to be sure," Gallienus said. He shaded his eyes against the sun to see what was happening on the far right edge of his battle line. Attalus and his horsemen were racing toward the bridge. "If he can get there and hold it, there'll be no escape for the rest of their army! Commit the reserves," he shouted to Heraclianus.

While Heraclianus carried out this order, Gallienus scanned the center of his army, then squinted into the sun trying to see Claudius' progress. "Is that Claudius directly behind their army?" he asked his tribune with the sharpest eyes.

"It is, sir," the tribune confirmed, peering into the sun. "He's about to engage the Goth's horsemen!" Gallienus could see enemy horsemen struggling through their own panicked warriors. Most men fled past their mounted brethren, but a few were taking heart and turned to fight alongside their comrades.

"Time we moved forward," Gallienus said, nudging his new horse ahead. "At first we were a bit too close. Now we're too far away."

Heraclianus caught up with Gallienus after committing the reserves to the battle. He strained to see distant parts of the battlefield. "I think Attalus has reached the bridge," he shouted, pointing unnecessarily ahead of them.

"Let's hope Marcianus can get close enough to support him," Gallienus said, tempering his rising optimism. "Desperate men fight desperately." They moved forward slowly, picking their way around bodies of fallen enemy soldiers. "What do you see now?" Gallienus asked his tribune.

"He definitely has the bridge now," the tribune replied.

Gallienus turned his attention to the center. *What will the enemy horsemen do when they realize their retreat's blocked? Will they fight to the last man?* Gallienus urged his horse ahead more rapidly. *I want to be ready for any desperate counter-attack*, he thought. *We've come too far to have this suddenly go against us.* He turned his attention briefly away from the immediate carnage he was passing through and tried to see what the enemy horsemen were doing. "Have they stopped?" he asked, not fully trusting his eyes. "The Goth horsemen—are they standing still?"

"Yes!" the tribune exclaimed. "They've stopped. I think their leader's trying to surrender!"

* * *

What always impressed Gallienus most was the complete quiet and stillness that hung over a battlefield following desperate struggles, confusion, and cacophony of battle. He looked down at men lying lifeless on the field and wondered at what point in the battle that time had suddenly ceased to matter to them. *For a moment I just want to savor being alive and this victory, to visit the wounded, and offer a word of encouragement here and there with my men.*

"Where were you during the battle?" he asked a nearby legionary, who had just killed one of the dying enemy warriors. "The center," the man grinned as he wiped the blood from his blade on the dead man's tunic.

"A commendable job! I feared the line might yield for a time," Gallienus confessed.

"General Aurelian took care of us, sir," the man said, before turning to look for the man who had just groaned nearby. Gallienus moved on.

It's been five years since I last fought a battle! And that was against Postumus outside Colonia Agrippina. How different that battle field was—every casualty was one of my own soldiers! He paused and watched several men helping a wounded legionary. "What's his injury?" he asked.

"A slashing wound," one of the attendants replied without looking up.

"Serious?"

"He'll survive," the man replied, still preoccupied with his task, "if I can stop his bleeding."

Gallienus moved on, careful to avoid blood that pooled around all of the casualties.

I beat Postumus on the battlefield yet couldn't capture the city where he took refuge—the same city my son sought refuge in after he revolted. Anger swelled inside him. *Will I ever be able to retake Gallia and avenge the death of my son?* A nearby scream brought Gallienus back to the present. He looked up to see who the voice belonged to, but a legionary had already slit an enemy's throat with a swift, practiced motion. Bodies of the dead were strewn randomly across the plain in grotesquely unnatural positions. *How many battles have been fought on these grounds before?* Gallienus wondered. *And how long until there's another one here?*

Men greeted Gallienus as he wandered among them and laughed at his stories and comments before he moved on to yet another group of soldiers. A feeling of relief and respect ran among them all. They had served the emperor well. He had led them to victory, and they had survived the battle. *The gods smiled on me twice today*, Gallienus reflected. *They gave me a victory and my life!*

As post-battle adrenalin wore off, fatigue washed over him. *Their initial attack nearly succeeded!* He rubbed his back and stretched tentatively, muscles stiffening from the fall from his dying horse. *That fall could have killed me.* He thought of the many miles his horse had carried him during his march from Rome to Poetovio, and from there to this location. *But the mount that Heraclianus gave to me seems to be an excellent anima—responsive and spirited, yet Heraclianus said it feared the water. I wonder why?*

"Do you have time for a report, sir?"

Gallienus looked up at Aurelian and sighed. *Time to resume my responsibilities.* "Proceed."

"Our casualties were light, most during the initial enemy attack. Enemy losses were much heavier, after their retreat turned into a rout. We've captured a significant number of their survivors—I don't have an accurate count just yet."

"Any leaders among their survivors?"

"None that I'm aware of. What would you like me to do with them?"

"Have them clean up the battlefield. That will keep them occupied for a while, and remind them who was victorious today.

Later, we'll sell them on the slave market."

"And we have captured the bridge across the river!" Attalus boasted from behind him. Gallienus turned to see Attalus standing beside Marcianus. Gallienus studied Marcianus' face—dirty, lined with fatigue, but with a faint smile of confidence. *So Marcianus can handle himself and his legions in battle! What he did today showed courage and initiative*, Gallienus thought. *I should keep him in mind for more responsibility*. He nodded approval to Marcianus, before turning to respond to Attalus.

"Capturing that bridge helped turn the tide of battle elsewhere on the field! Well done, to you both," he exclaimed, slapping Attalus on the shoulder.

"You should have seen their men after they saw we'd taken the bridge," Attalus chuckled. "Many of them threw down their weapons—swords, shields, axes, everything—then plunged into the river and tried to swim across! Of course some of them forgot they couldn't swim, or wore armor. Others were swept away by swift current." He shook his head. "And they call themselves warriors!"

"How many crossed?" Gallienus asked.

"A great many," Marcianus took the question. "But with carts, captives, and loot, it's hard to get an accurate count. Maybe about the same number as were on this side of the river."

"We'll have the same issues they did if we pursue them," Aurelian observed. "Only one way across the river, and they'll be able to put all their forces against any men we try to force over the bridge."

"Wait a while and they'll just go away," Attalus remarked. Everyone looked to him for elaboration. "They don't want to stay here any longer than they have to, especially when half their army's been defeated. Draw back a few miles, wait a day or two, then you can walk across the bridge without an enemy in sight."

The generals looked to Gallienus. He smiled. "That could work. We've had a great victory today, but we're still not done with this group."

"It must have been very dull in the center of the line," Attalus chided Gallienus. "We heard that you tried to take a nap in the middle of the battlefield!"

"I did," Gallienus grinned, "and when I awoke, Heraclianus gave me a splendid horse!" He paused. "It takes years to train a horse for cavalry service. Are you sure you wouldn't like it back, now that the battle's over?"

"I'd be honored, sir, if you would accept him," Heraclianus replied.

"And I have news from your left flank," Claudius spoke up, after Gallienus had acknowledged Heraclianus' gift.

"What have you to tell us?"

"Over three thousand enemies dead, as far as we can tell," Claudius began.

"That's the same as a whole enemy clan!" Attalus interjected.

"When they faltered, and on your orders," Claudius continued, "Cecropius and his Dalmatian horsemen led the charge and attacked with great effect. The enemy took significant losses. In fact, it was Cecropius who received the surrender from the enemy cavalry commander."

"Where is he now?" Gallienus asked, looking around him.

"I brought him with me," Claudius replied, signaling for one of his assistants to bring the man forward.

"I meant Cecropius," Gallienus interrupted.

"Attending to his wounded."

Gallienus nodded approval. "Give him my commendations. It may be a while before I can get to him myself." He turned his attention to the man now standing just behind Claudius. His arms were bound behind him and he was being led by a rope around his neck. He nodded at the enemy chieftain. "What can you tell me about him, Claudius?"

"His name is Naulobatus. He says he's not a Goth but comes from a tribe called the Heruli. Attalus understood some of what he said and he speaks some Greek," Claudius cautioned Gallienus.

Gallienus looked appraisingly at Naulobatus without acknowledging the man's presence. He was thin, half-a-head shorter than Gallienus, with a long mustache and straight black hair that trailed over his shoulders. His ice-blue eyes quietly took in everything around him. His leather belt, studded with silver, ran from his left shoulder down to the belt at his waist. His plain brown tunic ended at mid-thigh partially covering simple linen trousers. A plain gray cape covered his shoulders, held in place by a silver clasp. He stood erect and proud; from his expression one would not have guessed he had just been defeated in battle.

"His sword," Claudius said, handing the weapon to Gallienus. "He gave it to Cecropius when he surrendered."

Gallienus nodded, glanced at the sword, then looked Naulobatus in the eye. "You're rather short for a Goth. Where's your armor?"

"I am Heruli, not Goth," Naulobatus said. "We have no need for armor. For us, a cloak and shield are sufficient."

"Apparently not sufficient for victory."

"We have been undefeated until today," Naulobatus sniffed.

"You hadn't encountered the Roman army until today." The Heruli looked sullenly at him but had no response. "Your attack this morning very nearly succeeded," Gallienus continued evenly. "How did you know we were about to attack you."

"Some of my men discovered you while searching for food," Naulobatus replied, savoring thoughts of their initial attack and near victory. "Some of our warriors wished to take what they'd already gained in plunder and return home. They crossed the river this morning." He spat on the ground in disgust at his comrades' cowardice. "Otherwise we would have defeated you."

"Perhaps," Gallienus said. "Had you been victorious, you would have shown us no mercy, and yet you surrendered. Why?"

Naulobatus shrugged.

"Was this army mostly Heruli warriors?"

Naulobatus nodded. "Some Goths, and a few from other tribes."

"I was told that Heruli had moved into areas previously claimed by the Goths," Gallienus said. "Was that what caused this grand invasion?"

"We couldn't live peacefully in the same area," Naulobatus said. "Nor could we even fight a common enemy together. That's why our army split into groups—Goths wanted to go here," he nodded his head in one direction, "Heruli wanted to go there," he nodded the other way. "Other tribes had their own ideas as well. Nobody was willing to be led by anyone else. If we'd remained together, we'd have been invincible." His voice trailed off wistfully.

Gallienus considered this information and whether it might be useful for him in the future. "Your horsemen fought valiantly against my own cavalry and that of my Marcomanni allies," he said finally.

"They're good horsemen," Attalus interjected. "Not as fierce as we are, of course, but better to have them as allies than as adversaries, if they could be persuaded to join you."

Gallienus looked from Attalus to Naulobatus and was about to speak.

"Messenger approaching!" a tribune shouted. Everyone turned to where the tribune was pointing. A single rider approached them slowly, picking his way through bodies strewn across the battlefield. A feather on the tip of his spear was clearly visible as he drew nearer. Just beyond this inner circle stood a group of legionaries that Gallienus had been conversing with earlier. An anxious hush fell over all of them.

"Maybe he's bringing further word of the Goths' movements," Heraclianus suggested.

"Greetings Gallienus, Augustus," the messenger said, as he saluted the emperor. His words were clearly audible to all who listened.

"What news do you bring me, messenger?"

"General Aureolus has marched south from Augusta Vindelicum in revolt, sir!"

Gallienus took in a deep breath, then exhaled. "He knows how to spoil a perfectly good victory celebration!"

9-3
A New Crisis
River Nestos, Thracian Border
18 May, 268

An angry murmur swept through nearby legionnaires and swelled into loud shouts and curses as news spread to others. Gallienus stood, outwardly impassive and held up a hand for silence, which was grudgingly obeyed. *Betrayed! By a man I trusted, and gave a second chance—against everyone's advice.* Anger surged through him.

Claudius and Aurelian exchanged tight-lipped glances. Heraclianus moved Naulobatus toward one of his guards. "Get him far enough away so he doesn't hear anything further."

Gallienus struggled to maintain his composure. "What a distinctly unpleasant development. When did this happen?"

"The 19th of April, sir."

"And when did he reach Mediolanum?"

"He'd only just left Augusta Vindelicum when this message was sent."

"There's no chance that Aureolus could have just decided to visit Mediolanum, is there?"

"It was clearly a revolt, sir. He took nearly a whole legion of soldiers with him."

"Anything further?"

"That's all that I was given."

Gallienus nodded. "Thank you for your services, messenger." He spoke to one of his tribunes. "See that this man and his horse are taken care of." The messenger saluted and turned away to follow the tribune.

"How quickly could he get to Mediolanum?" Gallienus asked Heraclianus as the messenger and tribune departed.

"Two weeks, if he pushed."

"So possibly by the first week of this month," Gallienus figured.

"We don't know what happened when he got to Mediolanum," Claudius said, offering a thread of hope.

"With only a legion, he couldn't take the garrison by force," Aurelian noted. "He'd have to persuade them to join him."

"He was always very good at that." Claudius said. His comment reflected the other generals' thinking.

If Aureolus won the garrison over and marched on Rome with a force that large, Volusianus would be overwhelmed. The Senate would declare Aureolus emperor, whether they wished to or not, and Volusianus and Marinianus would be killed! It might already have happened. His face flushed as he realized that misjudging Aureolus might result in the death of his one remaining son, perhaps the end of his reign. *What will Salonina say when she learns of this? What are my generals thinking? They tried to convince me that Aureolus betrayed me once before.*

"I knew he had treachery in his heart," Attalus exclaimed. "We should march there now, show him how we deal with traitors! My men can be ready to leave in …"

"We have three enemy armies ravaging Macedonia," Claudius reminded him. "Would you let them continue unchallenged?"

"Treachery is a matter of honor," Attalus replied. "Besides, even I know you'll have a civil war on your hands if Aureolus wins Mediolanum over to him."

"Come to my tent," Gallienus said. Once inside all eyes turned to Gallienus. "Your thoughts?" he asked them, before making any final decision.

"Attalus is right about the risks of a civil war." Heraclianus spoke first. "But we're a long way from Mediolanum, and the whole matter has probably been decided already."

"And if Aureolus was successful?" Gallienus asked.

"Then nothing could stop him from marching to Rome. He may have done it already."

"Attalus is right. If I let his revolt go unchallenged, the whole empire will fall into civil war and chaos," Gallienus said, looking at Heraclianus.

"Up until a few moments ago the agreed upon plan was to defeat the Goth army, group by group," Heraclianus said. "We've met and defeated a portion of them. The rest are who knows where. We chose that approach because a united Goth army might overwhelm what we could put against them."

"The situation has changed," Claudius pointed out.

"I say it's best to remain here and finish what we've already begun so successfully," Heraclianus said stubbornly. "Then we can go west and deal with whatever issue we find there."

"If Aureolus was successful, then we have to crush his revolt as quickly as possible—preferably before the Senate declares him emperor," Claudius said, "but if he's already gone there, then we need to defeat him before he has a chance to attract others to his side."

"Make an example to any other ambitious men with a few legionnaires under their command," Attalus agreed, nodding his head vigorously.

"It's a long march from here to Mediolanum, Claudius. My guess is nearly three months' time if you took the legionnaires," Heraclianus said.

"Mid-August," Claudius nodded. "Still plenty of time for fighting. Suppose Aureolus suggests an alliance with Postumus? Their combined forces would be nearly equal to ours, and they wouldn't have to deal with the Goths right away."

"An alliance? Not likely," Heraclianus dismissed Claudius' assertion.

"Until today a revolt by Aureolus was considered unlikely too," Aurelian noted.

"Postumus would have a long march to Mediolanum, and he'd be leaving his own borders unprotected," Claudius added.

"What about the Goths?" Heraclianus asked. "They'll have had a free hand to ravage Macedonia—or wherever they decide to go next—all that time."

"We know your brother is governor of Thracia," Claudius said. "Perhaps your interest in fighting an enemy here and now is really to keep them from plundering his province. Don't you hold land there yourself?"

Heraclianus' face reddened. He tensed and balled his hands into fists for a few seconds before taking a deep breath. "The Goths to the west will soon be pillaging your homeland, Claudius—yours, too, Aurelian. And Marcianus, you can expect them to pass through your provinces as they return to their homeland. No one will be able to resist them, aside from this army. Of course I'm concerned about my brother and his province."

"Enough!" Gallienus interrupted. He looked angrily around

the men gathered to him. "I need suggestions, not arguments." There was a moment of silence.

"We could leave foot soldiers behind," Claudius improvised, "take only horsemen and move quickly."

"Two months' travel time instead of three." Heraclianus shrugged. "Does that make enough difference?"

"The men left behind could continue to fight the invaders," Aurelian suggested.

"How many men were at Mediolanum?" Claudius asked.

"About two legions and two wings of cavalry, somewhere around twelve thousand men." Heraclianus recited the numbers from memory. "Plus another four thousand if Postumus left his borders unmanned and brought most of his legionnaires," he added.

"How large would your mobile force be?" Marcianus asked Claudius.

"We'd have the cavalry, the Praetorian Guards, and the Marcomanni horsemen," Claudius listed them by groups, and then stopped to calculate numbers. "Just over eight thousand."

No one spoke while they considered that disparity.

"Why don't we take some of those Heruli horsemen with us?" Attalus asked. "You were wondering what to do with them."

"How many could they bring?" Gallienus asked.

Attalus scratched his head. "A couple thousand."

The generals studied Gallienus' face as he considered his options. *What's best for the empire now? I may face long marches and long odds, but whatever I choose, I'll have to act quickly.* He smiled and felt the tension slip away as an idea came to him.

"I'll leave foot soldiers here to pursue what's left of the Goths," he said. "And I'll take a mobile force west. If I get news that Aureolus was defeated at Mediolanum, then I'll attack the nearest group of enemy I can find." He paused. "Then I'll return to deal with the remainder of the Goths."

"When do you wish to depart?" Heraclianus asked.

"We'll have our reckoning tomorrow," Gallienus said. "We'll disperse spoils and commend men who performed exceptionally well during battle. Mobile forces will depart at sunrise the following day."

"Who will command the legionnaires?" Heraclianus asked.

Gallienus looked at the expectant generals around him. "Marcianus, you're the logical choice to command this army. You have troops already under your command, and you're familiar with the local terrain and people."

"I accept this appointment with pleasure," Marcianus said solemnly.

"Claudius will be your second in command."

"With all due respect sir, I wish to decline," Claudius said. "You appointed me commander of your cavalry and I wish to remain in that capacity. And I very much want to participate in the suppression of Aureolus' revolt."

Gallienus weighed Claudius' request for a moment. "Granted," he said finally.

Aurelian spoke before Gallienus could turn and make the same offer to him. "I too, request the honor and privilege of helping you overthrow this traitor."

Gallienus took a deep breath and exhaled slowly while he considered Aurelian's refusal of a command even before he'd made the offer. *Might not be a good time to put someone inexperienced as cavalry commander. And these are my two most experienced and capable generals.* He nodded his assent to Aurelian.

"What are my orders?" Marcianus asked.

"Defeat the rest of this enemy group."

"And then?"

"Find other invaders, engage them, and drive them towards me. After I defeat Aureolus, I'll return to finish what we've started today." Gallienus turned to Heraclianus. "Bring me that Heruli chieftain. Perhaps I can use him and his horsemen to my advantage. I'll meet him in front of the tent."

* * *

"How would I benefit from your offer?" Naulobatus asked after listening to Gallienus' proposal.

"I can make you an ally, or sell you into slavery."

"Only if you survive the coming battles."

"Others will be fighting your tribesmen in my place. Right now I have a revolt to suppress."

"Your traitor is a long way from here. Many days riding and no spoils or women all that time."

"Your days of raiding and pillaging are over, Naulobatus." Gallienus rubbed his chin thoughtfully. "I'll spare you slavery and death. But because of the extraordinary circumstances and the fact that your alliance would be advantageous to me, I'll give you the dignities of a consul of the empire. It would, of course, be an honorary position."

The nearby generals sucked in their breath collectively.

"He's offering this stranger and enemy the status of a consul!" Aurelian whispered.

"Naulobatus wears trousers, keeps his hair long, and speaks abominable Latin," Claudius whispered back, disgusted and indignant.

"This has never been done before," Heraclianus agreed.

"It's just for show," Marcianus whispered. "I think it's rather creative."

"This 'consular' thing is important?" Naulobatus asked Gallienus.

Gallienus nodded. "Only two men are given this high honor. You would be attended by something of an honor guard, to let everyone know of your importance."

Naulobatus nodded, pleased. "Anything else? Perhaps money, or women, or cattle?"

"This is an offer, not a negotiation." Gallienus frowned. "I'll give you this choice—agree to lead your men in battle as my ally, or I'll have you fight to the death in the gladiatorial ring." Gallienus turned to walk away.

"What happens after the battle?" Naulobatus called after him. "Will you sell us into slavery after we've helped you defeat this traitor?"

"Ask Attalus how I treat my allies. He's the Marcomanni chieftain you fought against today."

"Is it true that you married his daughter?" Naulobatus asked. "We heard rumors, but no one believed them."

"Yes, but I don't need another wife as part of our agreement."

Naulobatus' frown slowly turned to a smile. "I think my soldiers would prefer fighting in the open rather than in an arena," he said, "and for pay, I assume we'll be paid!"

"A wise choice!" Gallienus said gravely. He took the sword that Claudius had given him and returned it to Naulobatus. "Since you already know General Claudius," Gallienus said to Naulobatus, "I'll have him work out details of surrender and the swearing of your allegiance to me." That issue settled, he dismissed the men.

Alone for a few moments, Gallienus thought of his previous concerns about dividing his forces and of the bad experience he had against Postumus as a result. *Last time I gave command of a large group of men to one of my generals, it was Aureolus.* He shook his head and sighed. *I can't be everywhere at once. I hope this turns out better!*

9-4
A Brief Reunion
Thessalonica, Macedonia
25 May, 268

"And what brings Empress Salonina to Thessalonica in these troubled times?" the city prefect asked after exchanging greetings. They sat inside the Fountain House, a prominent landmark on the main east-west road near city center. Even though this road was forty-five feet wide, it was jammed with people and carts making their way to and from market.

"Troubled times, themselves, I'm afraid," Salonina replied, shaking her head sadly. She trailed a hand through deliciously cool water of the fountain. "My husband's fighting Goths. I was hoping to meet him around Amphipolis. But then I learned that there's been a revolt in Mediolanum."

"I hadn't heard." The prefect was silent for a time, wondering if that meant Goths might return to besiege his city. "I thought he might try to intercept the part of the Goths who went west from here."

A look of concern swept over her face. "Two groups?"

"Three, actually. One sacked Athens and was still in Achaea, last I heard."

"Not Athens!" Salonina exclaimed, covering her mouth with one hand. "And the other two groups?" she asked after a moment.

"The barbarians that attacked us split after they failed to take Thessalonica. We withstood their attack, even though they used siege equipment against us," he said proudly,

"Well done," she congratulated the prefect. "Where did they go?"

"Some went east from here. Probably the ones your husband is dealing with now. Others went to our west."

"I expect my husband will go back toward Mediolanum. Will the western Goths be a problem for us?" she asked.

"Probably not. About twenty miles west of here the road forks. I've been told the Goths took the north-west road. I expect you'll continue west on Via Egnatia. The road the Goths took goes to Ulpiana--about two hundred miles northwest of here. They'll probably go north toward home from there but—they could also go southwest," he paused, not wanting to alarm her further. "If they went southwest, they'd eventually come to the same coast road you and your husband would be taking."

Salonina considered the Prefect's description of this situation for some time before deciding she would probably miss both the Goths in Achaea and those on the road to Ulpiana. She relaxed visibly. A smile swept over her face as she looked around the city. "I remember visiting Thessalonica as a young girl—I think I must have been about eighteen." She looked to her right where the city rose to the Acropolis, some three hundred feet above them. Olive trees grew where the incline was too steep for houses, and the ground was covered with a sky-blue carpet of nigella in full bloom. "My father was governing Pannonia then, and Themistocles, my tutor, showed me Thessalonica on one of my visits to Athens." In front of Salonina the road continued west, passing through the Sacred Area, where temples to Greek gods were clustered, before reaching the Egnatia Gate. "Themistocles said he could walk from the gate I entered through."

"The Kissos Gate?"

"Yes, that's it. From there all the way to the Egnatia Gate," she pointed behind the prefect and to the west, "in a quarter of an hour, but I never tried. The city is just as I remember it."

"You'd honor me by being my guest. It's nearly time for the mid-day meal and you must be tired and hungry", the prefect inclined his head graciously. My quarters used to be the governor's residence, and King Cassander once lived there. He named the city after his wife, Thessalonike."

"Wasn't she was one of King Philip's daughters?"

"Yes, and Alexander's half-sister," the prefect nodded, impressed by her local knowledge. "The building is just above the Sacred Area. It overlooks Dionysus' temple and has a wonderful view of the harbor."

"It would be my pleasure," Salonina happily accepted his invitation. "And then perhaps I could walk around the market place and reacquaint myself with the city."

* * *

Salonina had just settled into a warm bath at the Prefect's quarters that afternoon, when a slave girl burst into the room. "What is it?" Salonina asked, masking her annoyance at the disturbance.

"There are soldiers in the courtyard, my lady," the girl said, bowing deeply. "They told the prefect that they had come for you."

"Who are they?" Salonina asked, suddenly concerned. She stepped out of bath and began drying herself hurriedly with a towel the slave girl offered her.

"They said they're from your husband's army," the girl replied.

"How did they know where to find me?" Salonina asked while allowing the slave girl to help her dress as quickly as she could.

"The emperor sent soldiers to the city prefect, my lady, to tell him that a Roman army would be camping outside their walls. And the prefect told them you were staying with us." *Surely the prefect would have invited the emperor to dine with him!* Salonina thought. *I wonder why Gallienus declined.*

She was thrilled at the thought of seeing Gallienus, yet felt guilty to be backing out of her social obligation to her host. "Please give my regrets to the prefect," Salonina instructed the slave girl. "Tell him I'll dine with him later, after the emperor has gone."

"He told me to say that he understood," the girl bowed deeply again, then left.

* * *

Twilight lingered. Heat of the day subsided grudgingly. While Salonina waited for Gallienus in front of his tent, she gazed at the Macedonian countryside beyond the campsite Gallienus' troops had constructed. Poppies bloomed, covering large areas with blood-red blossoms where Goths had left the ground untrammeled. Near a stream at the edge of the camp she saw laurel, myrtle, and oleander growing. In the distant north, Salonina could clearly see the Kissos Mountain range. In the early evening tranquility, she found it difficult to picture a hostile army nearby, bent on destroying this city and ravaging its population. She shivered at the thought but was distracted by the sound of footsteps. She turned and caught sight of Gallienus approaching. "It's been such a long time." She threw herself into his arms and held him tightly.

"And I've missed you!" he said. Neither of them spoke while they savored the feeling of each other's embrace.

"I've felt so alone traveling without you," she said finally.

"I told the prefects of each city I passed through to expect a visit from you," Gallienus said. "Weren't you entertained everywhere?"

"They did their best," Salonina agreed. "But it was always a dinner with strangers." Being reunited, even temporarily, reassured her. She drew away from him and looked at him appraisingly, noting with relief that there were no obvious new scars or wounds on his body. "Congratulations on your victory at Nestos! I was so worried about you."

"A partial victory," he shrugged. "I left Marcianus in command of foot soldiers with orders to finish the job." He paused. "I didn't expect to find you in Thessalonica!"

"When I reached Amphipolis they told me about your victory and about Aureolus' revolt. I was certain you'd respond to that personally, so I went west from there, knowing you'd catch up with me eventually." An awkward silence followed her mention of Aureolus. She watched his expression while she waited for his response.

His face darkened and his shoulders sagged. "I should have taken your advice about Aureolus. I considered myself a better judge of his character."

"Loyalty is such a hard thing to determine," Salonina said, "as opposed to good generalship." She thought of Ingenuus and Regalianus, each of whom had tried to seize power when governing Pannonia, of Postumus who revolted while governing Germania, and of Aemilianus who had governed Aegyptus. *But Aureolus was different*, she thought. *Gallienus gave him a second chance, against my advice and the advice of his generals. Aureolus showed his gratitude by betraying Gallienus a second time. Gallienus' decision to trust Aureolus has brought on civil war in the midst of an enemy invasion! What must his generals be thinking?*

"And I'm acutely aware that Aureolus' revolt puts Marinianus in grave danger," Gallienus continued, his thoughts still on Aureolus' betrayal.

"I've thought about that too!" Salonina said quickly. "If Aureolus had gone to Rome then Marinianus would have been killed!" Ever since she'd learned of Aureolus' revolt, she had been trying to hold herself together, but the thought that all three of her children might be dead overwhelmed her. "If he's been killed, then what's the use of going on?" Tears streamed down her face in helpless frustration.

"That's only part of my worry," Gallienus said.

She looked at him, surprised.

"If I were dead that would give Aureolus' claim credibility. My generals would doubtless oppose him, and Postumus might be tempted to become emperor himself. Marcianus now has a large army under his own command. Maybe he'd want to be emperor, too. There could be three or four separate factions competing. And while they fought one against the other, Goths would continue ravaging Macedonia!"

"None of that erases the pain of my loss," she countered.

"It's our loss," he reminded her. "And we don't know whether it's even happened."

Salonina saw the pain on his face and realized his decision to trust Aureolus was reasoned, although deeply flawed in her mind. *He expected loyalty, and was rewarded with treachery, and the results of his decision weigh heavily on him. Besides, it's pointless to argue with him or blame him now. It wouldn't change anything, and would only drive him into Pipa's arms—where he's already spending too much time!* "Maybe the uprising wasn't successful," she said hopefully.

"I've heard nothing from Mediolanum," Gallienus replied. "I'm afraid that suggests that it was."

"Then nothing would have stopped him from going to Rome."

"Unless he's worried about the troops I put there with Volusianus," Gallienus speculated. "Remember how your father held off that barbarian raid outside Rome when he was city prefect?"

She nodded. The thought of her father's success nine years earlier and the hope it gave her forced Salonina to smile through her tears. "How did the generals take the news?"

"No outward reactions."

"You know what they must be thinking."

He nodded.

She put a hand on his arm. "Be careful." He smiled at her and put a hand on hers. "What are you going to do?" she asked after a period of silence.

"I've taken every horseman I can lay my hands on. I can

move much faster that way. I'll find Aureolus at Mediolanum, or wherever he is. After I've defeated him, then I'll return to Macedonia, or wherever the Goths are, and fight them."

"How many men are you taking?"

"Eight thousand horsemen, including Attalus' warriors—plus a group of Heruli horsemen that surrendered after the battle—maybe two thousand of them."

"Not Goths?"

"There were a number of different tribes involved in this invasion. That's how it got to be so large. And because they were from different tribes, that may be why they split into different groups when they got onto our shores."

"How many men will Aureolus have?"

"Up to seventeen thousand, if he took his whole legion out of Rhaetia."

"Oh." Salonina considered the disparity.

"I left some of Attalus' warriors in Pannonia," Gallienus said. "Maybe I can get some of them to join me."

"That would help!" She thought about his earlier comment. "Do you think Aureolus would actually leave his entire province unprotected?"

"He wouldn't be the first to strip a province bare, just to support personal ambitions."

"Won't that invite an attack by the Alamanni?" she asked.

"It might," Gallienus agreed, rubbing his chin thoughtfully, "but I'm dealing with two other crises already. Let's not worry about a third, unless it actually happens."

"Should I stay in Macedonia and wait for your return?"

"Too dangerous, and uncertain," he said. "Cities that have been sacked are hard-pressed to feed themselves, and the rest may be future targets for the Goths. There's a large group of Goths in Achaea now."

"The prefect told me about them."

"It would be logical for them to come north through Thermopylae," Gallienus continued. "They'd pass through Thessalonica if they did. And then there's another group that went west from here."

"The prefect told me they were on the road to Ulpiana," Salonina interjected.

"You're as well informed as I am," he smiled at her. "I could send you to Rome on a ship. You'd be there in time to celebrate Marinianus' twenty-fourth birthday."

"Aren't the seas too dangerous now?"

"The seaborne raiders seem to be staying along the coast of Asia."

"What if some of them change their minds?" Salonina frowned. "And Aureolus may already be in Rome."

"A ship to Aquileia then?" he suggested.

"What if Aquileia's gone over to Aureolus? No," she shook her head in frustration. It was the only decision she could make. "I'll follow the road you take. Maybe I'll meet you returning to Macedonia before I even catch up with you. *" He's just won a battle against an invading army larger than his,* she thought. *And now he plans to fight against a Roman army, also larger than his, with his best cavalry commander leading the rebels.* She felt even more anxious than she usually did when he left her to fight an enemy. *We'll probably have only tonight together, and all the time he's been traveling, Pipa's been with him instead of me!*

"Why are you looking so pained?" he asked.

At first she shook her head, not wanting to admit her fears and jealousy. "We have so little time together," was all she said.

9-5
Before and After
Mediolanum, Gallia Cisalpina
26 June, 268

Aureolus sat alone at a field table in his training camp outside the city. During the morning he had drilled his experienced cavalry. This afternoon he planned to resume training with new cavalry soldiers selected from the existing legionnaires. But plans to eat with his subordinates and discuss training exercises had suddenly changed.

The day was already warm and humid. Sweat on his forehead had mixed with dust from the training field. Aureolus sipped from his glass of watered wine. He picked up a piece of cheese while he gazed indifferently at a basket of fresh bread and a plate of sausages. Instead of food, his thoughts were about a message given to him when he returned to camp. An early afternoon breeze drifted through his campsite, across his sweat-soaked face cooling him slightly. He lunged for the message from Postumus that lay on the table in front of him, catching it just before it blew to the ground. It had been sent on the 16th of June and was only the second Aureolus had received since telling Postumus of his arrival in Mediolanum on the 11th of May. The previous message had been both terse and vague. In it, Postumus had said there had been a slight delay in his departure plans, which he promised to elaborate on when he could. He had also asked Aureolus to keep him informed of the progress he was making.

Aureolus rested his chin on his hand, his elbow on the table, tapping the table with a finger of his other hand. He reread this letter, trying to discern what Postumus was not telling him and why he chose not to.

To: Manius Acilius Aureolus, Commanding General
From: Marcus Cassianius Latinius Postumus, Emperor
      Greetings! Congratulations on bringing the garrison at Mediolanum to our cause! And I note with pleasure that the bridge at Novaria and the mountain passes have been secured. As we discussed earlier, I originally expected to arrive at Mediolanum sometime around mid-May myself.

      But just prior to my departure I encountered some local issues, minor in significance but nevertheless requiring my attention before I take my army south. I will keep you informed of the situation and of my progress. In the meantime, I've been in contact with several senators in Rome (best not to put their names in print) and they are prepared to throw their support behind me. Success is within our grasp! Continue to train your men and wait in Mediolanum for my arrival!

Aureolus frowned. *Did he ever intend to come to Mediolanum? Could he have orchestrated all this with the sole idea of eliminating the threat on his eastern border?* Aureolus sighed. He regretted not having a trusted assistant to discuss such matters with, but Postumus had been the only person he had confided in. *Should I march on Rome myself, without waiting for Postumus? I know Gallienus put Volusianus in Rome with troops. Postumus promised to bring an army. Together we would overwhelm Volusianus. And Postumus said he had influential support in the Senate, although he conveniently omitted naming them. Maybe that was a ruse as well. How long should I wait for him? Would I have any support in the Senate myself?* The question made Aureolus think about Gallienus. *Would he abandon his campaign against the Goths to deal with me? If he learned that I'm still in Mediolanum, that would be an incentive for him to return. Did Postumus intend to leave me here in order to lure Gallienus back? Or maybe Postumus really does have a good reason for not being here.* Aureolus sighed, then stood and stretched. *I'll give Postumus the benefit of the doubt a little longer.*

Outside Mediolanum, Gallia Cisalpina
17 July, 268

The scent of citron blossoms filled the early evening air and flickering torches illuminated the ground in front of Pipa's tent. Its walls were still rolled up and tied, allowing the inside to cool from the day's heat. Pipa sat next to a small table savoring the tranquility and pleasant temperature. Great mountains to the north were silhouetted against a pale evening sky and she could see a faint glow from the lights of Mediolanum to the west. She idly listened to crickets chirping and occasional sounds of laughter from soldiers gathered around campfires while she waited for

Gallienus' arrival. She was accustomed to living this way before meeting Gallienus, although she had grown fond of Roman baths. Earlier that day she had gone to the River Addua, not far from the site of yesterday's battle, to swim in its chilly waters.

One of her father's warriors had killed a boar for her today that she would be serving for dinner tonight, along with plum sauce she had been saving for a special occasion. Pipa had even secured several bottles of wine from a merchant when they passed through Verona. After reviewing her meal plans, Pipa's thoughts went to yesterday's battle.

Gallienus had soundly defeated Aureolus near the River Addua, east of Mediolanum. Aureolus had been seriously wounded and retreated inside city walls, along with much of his army. Just before the battle and during the last few days of the march, Gallienus had been tense, preoccupied, and tired. Last night, before the battle, she did not see him at all. Tonight, he would have reason to relax and celebrate. Although Pipa's previous life involved frequent moving, she was pleased not to have been on horseback all day and relieved to think they might spend a few days here before the long march back to Macedonia. On the positive side, she had enjoyed Gallienus' company for nearly two months!

She frowned, as she thought of similarities between the present situation and one with Postumus five years earlier. Then, Gallienus had defeated Postumus in battle, but Postumus had taken refuge in Colonia Agrippina. Yesterday, Aureolus had also withdrawn into a walled city. Postumus had survived his siege and still ruled Gallia. *How will the present situation end, and when?*

"Why the troubled expression?" Gallienus' question interrupted her thoughts and startled her, but she managed to conceal it. "I was beginning to think you'd forgotten me," she said then gave him a warm smile.

"I could never do that," he said, pausing to admire her appearance: the blue eyes, blond hair falling well past her shoulders, and her smile. Her indigo linen dress, sleeveless and cut low at the neck, accentuated an amber pendant hanging on a golden chain. "I haven't seen you this well dressed in a long time."

"To welcome my conquering hero." She gestured for him to sit by her. "After a long march from Macedonia you've defeated Aureolus in battle!" Pipa looked admiringly at him, then offered him a glass of wine. "You were outnumbered and faced a very talented adversary. Weren't you at all anxious before the battle?"

He took the wine and grinned, realizing that she already knew the answer. "A little," he admitted, "so I had to out-think him."

Pipa signaled to her attendants, who brought cooked mushrooms, bread with honey, and cheese.

"Where did you find mushrooms?" Gallienus asked, filling a small plate eagerly.

"They're wild. You have to know where to look for them," she said, pleased at his enthusiasm. She watched while he tasted them, nodded his approval, then dipped his bread in the juices and ate with gusto.

"And the wine?" he asked. "Surely you didn't find that with the mushrooms."

"From a merchant in Verona." She ate a piece of bread, then took a bite of cheese. "So how did you 'out-think' him?" Pipa prompted, while reaching for her glass of beer.

"I expected him to try getting around my flanks with his cavalry, so I put most of my strength there. And I used some deception that I knew would appeal to his ego."

"Tell me."

"I had my center forces advance on his army but told them to retreat after an initial engagement. When Aureolus saw them falling back, he attacked our flanks, and we met him there with our cavalry. Your father was very aggressive. I think he was trying to kill Aureolus himself. And you should have seen those Heruli warriors charging!" He paused to sip his wine and thought for a moment. "Aureolus must have had some inexperienced cavalry in the fight. After he was wounded, his army retreated. Unfortunately, we couldn't catch him before he got inside Mediolanum. What's this?"

Pipa had signaled her attendants to bring the main course: roasted boar with plum sauce. The bread, mushrooms and cheese remained on the table to be consumed with the meat, since this wasn't a sumptuous dinner.

"One of Daddy's warriors killed it for me," she explained. "When he came to me this afternoon, I wasn't sure whether he'd be bringing meat, fish, or fowl."

"I'm glad it was this," Gallienus voiced approval between bites. "And plum sauce!"

"I'd been saving it for a special occasion." They ate in contented silence.

"Where was I?" Gallienus asked finally.

"Chasing Aureolus into Mediolanum."

"Ah yes." He sipped his wine and stared into the darkness toward Mediolanum, reliving his victory and his pursuit of Aureolus.

Pipa smiled at Gallienus, sharing his feelings of relief and exhilaration. She, too, had been concerned about Aureolus' reputation and the size of his army. "So now Aureolus cowers behind the walls of Mediolanum and your son is safe in Rome!" She studied her glass of beer speculatively before deciding to continue. "I chose not to share my concerns before, but I was surprised that Aureolus hadn't gone to Rome long ago!"

"So was I. Maybe Volusianus and his forces deterred him, or maybe he lost his nerve?"

"But why take the risk of revolting, only to sit here for much of the summer? He had to know about Volusianus' forces in Rome before he revolted."

"What's your opinion?" He watched her, while he ate boar, then used the last of the bread to gather plum sauce.

"He must have been expecting help from Postumus. It's the only thing I've been able to think of, unless he was waiting to see if the Goths killed you."

"That thought had occurred to me," Gallienus nodded, "the Postumus one, I mean. But why wouldn't Postumus have come by now? I've gotten no information at all from my spies and informants in Gallia."

She shrugged. "But Aureolus staying in Mediolanum seems very odd to me." They both fell silent for a moment trying to think of other reasons, but none seemed plausible. "Anyway, it must be a great relief to you that the battle is over," Pipa finally said.

"Yes. But the problem isn't over, Pipa," Gallienus' smile left his face. "This situation here is much like the one with the Goths—both beaten, neither subdued."

"More like Postumus," Pipa said, before she could stop herself. He looked at her quizzically. His look said he expected more.

She signaled for the main course to be removed. Her attendants brought another bottle of wine and filled Gallienus' glass. Then they brought plates filled with almonds and cherries. She smiled at his questioning glance. "Verona," she said.

"You were speaking about Postumus," he said to her.

"Both betrayed you, revolted, and then you defeated both of them."

Gallienus nodded.

Postumus survived that siege and strengthened his position in Gallia, she thought. *And we still have enemy armies ravaging Macedonia. Can Gallienus get either or both situations under control?* "What will you do now?" she asked.

"I sent a messenger to Mediolanum today demanding Aureolus' surrender. While he's thinking about it, I've had the city surrounded, so he won't be tempted to try an escape. Tomorrow I'll move our camp closer to Mediolanum. If he doesn't agree to surrender, I'll begin a siege of the city. It will take a few days to build all the siege equipment."

"Then what?"

Gallienus shrugged. "We'll just have to wait."

"Time will become an issue," she said, then decided not to pursue the matter further.

"Time always is."

She picked up a cherry by the stem while holding Gallienus' eyes with hers. She licked her lips, then dangled the cherry between her teeth and held it there briefly before pulling the stem free and taking the fruit into her mouth. She smiled at Gallienus while she chewed it slowly, then tossed the stem onto the ground. She rose from the table and led him into her tent.

An attendant had lowered her tent's walls when the evening air cooled. A single candle flickered on a small table beside her bed. Once inside, she unfastened the belt at her waist and smiled at him. He helped her slip the dress off her shoulders, then pulled her close to him. Pipa tried to be responsive to his caresses, but she felt conflicted. The dinner had gone as she had hoped and this was her intended outcome. But she was distracted by unsettled questions of time. *How much time does he have*, she wondered, *before his generals grow restless?*

9-6
Siege Preparations and Other Issues
Gallienus' camp outside Mediolanum
17 July, 268

"It seems that Aureolus isn't as good a general as he thought," Claudius chuckled. Aurelian accepted Claudius' offer of wine then sipped thoughtfully. "Well, he hasn't led an army in seven years. Gallienus was right to expect him to attack on our flanks."

"And you were there to meet him," Claudius grinned. "How did it feel commanding cavalry for the first time?"

"Better than fighting on foot. But things happen much faster than leading legionnaires in battle. You have to think a lot further ahead."

Claudius nodded. "Who do you think wounded Aureolus?"

Aurelian shrugged. "A pity he didn't die."

"We wouldn't be here now if Aureolus had defeated Postumus the first time," Claudius frowned.

"He did defeat him," Aurelian reminded Claudius.

"Well, you're right. But he should have killed Postumus when he had the chance."

"Why do you suppose Aureolus agreed to meet with Postumus before Postumus had surrendered?"

"Who knows?" Claudius scratched his head. "Letting him escape was either gross incompetence or treachery—and he hadn't shown himself incompetent before."

"Then it took two years before Gallienus got back to Postumus."

"A bit of bad luck for Gallienus—getting hit with that arrow outside Colonia Agrippina." Claudius shook his head. "I was afraid he was going to die before we got him back to Rome!"

"Yes. I wonder how many factions in the Senate were plotting to succeed him."

"We almost had a civil war on our hands," Claudius recalled. He lowered his voice. "But I think we did the right thing, agreeing to support each other if succession ever became an issue again."

"I agree.' He held his glass out for a refill and waited while Claudius poured. "I would have gone back to finish Postumus off the next year myself. Why do you suppose Gallienus went to Athens instead?"

Claudius arched an eyebrow. "Apparently he was more concerned about a possible attack from the east than he was about Postumus' continued existence."

"Still," Aurelian said, "he should have finished Postumus off before that threat proved real, then there'd be no one trying to spear us in the back now."

"I remember him once saying he was content to let Postumus fight the Franks for him—for the time being."

"Aureolus is really responsible for all our current problems," Aurelian concluded. "Because of him we've lost the west to Postumus. And because of him we're laying siege to Mediolanum when we should be fighting Goths—who are about to invade our homelands!"

"Aureolus couldn't have revolted if Gallienus hadn't reinstated him," Claudius said. He drained his glass and refilled them both.

"Gallienus never agreed with us about Aureolus betraying him. He only relieved Aureolus because the entire staff opposed him." They sat silently for some time nursing their drinks and their resentments.

"I think it was Volusianus who finally convinced Gallienus to relieve him, but even then he didn't want to," Claudius nodded.

"I miss Volusianus." Aurelian said, studying the remains of the wine in his glass.

"He knew what he was doing, and did it well," Claudius agreed. "Maybe that's because he'd come up through the ranks like us—not from the Senatorial class like Heraclianus." They sat in silence for a while.

"Heraclianus must have been a capable general and a competent governor. Otherwise Gallienus wouldn't have chosen him to succeed Volusianus."

"His main distinction as governor was that he didn't revolt, like his two predecessors," Claudius said. "Frankly, I think the job of Praetorian Prefect is a bit more than he's capable of handling. It certainly started badly."

"The mission to see Zenobia?" Aurelian arched an eyebrow and held up his glass to Claudius who shrugged. "Don't you have another bottle?"

Claudius got up and started rummaging through a chest at the rear of his tent. "What a disaster that was," Claudius raised his voice a bit to carry over the clatter he was making. "Aha!" he suddenly exclaimed and triumphantly produced an unopened bottle.

"Gallienus needed someone who was both a high-ranking officer and a skilled diplomat."

"Instead he sent Heraclianus," Claudius snorted. "What are you smiling at?"

"'You can't negotiate with someone unless you first convince them to actually meet with you,'" Aurelian chuckled.

"Wasn't that what Gallienus said when Heraclianus reported back to him?"

"Word for word." Aurelian nodded and held out his glass for another refill.

"Remember the comment he made after Heraclianus left the meeting?" Claudius grinned as he refilled Aurelian's glass.

Aurelian shook his head and sipped his wine.

"He said, 'I sent him there to keep an ally, not to make an enemy. If I wanted that result, I could have written her an insulting letter myself.'"

They were both laughing at the memory when the legionnaire in charge of the night watch entered the tent and saluted Claudius. "I've just completed a routine check of the area, sir. All's well, but when I returned, General Heraclianus was standing in front of your tent. He said he wanted to talk with you, but decided it could wait until the staff meeting the day after tomorrow. Then he just walked away."

19 July, 268

"We hope we can starve Aureolus out of Mediolanum." Claudius began, opening the morning meeting. "But I don't expect that's likely to happen." Heraclianus, Aurelian, Attalus, and Naulobatus, the Herulian chieftain recruited at Nestos, sat on stools crowded around a table covered with a map. Lower ranking commanders stood behind them.

"There are three roads out of Mediolanum," Claudius said, pointing at the map. "This one goes north to Rhaetia, this one west to Gallia, and this one south to Rome. We'll block each of them with one wing of cavalry. Have each wing set up camp a couple miles outside of town beside the road. Make sure they keep a close watch on the city: nothing goes in or out."

"The fourth wing?" Aurelian asked.

"We'll keep that with us here at the main camp, along with the Praetorian Guards," Claudius nodded at Heraclianus, "and also the Marcomanni, and the Heruli. We're closer to the northeast wall of the city here. That's where our siege efforts will be focused."

"Wouldn't it be better to try and breach one of the gates?" Heraclianus asked.

"This is the plan we're working with," Claudius dismissed his question.

"How about the five thousand legionnaires that surrendered to us after the battle?" Heraclianus reminded Claudius. "Don't you want some of them to augment the cavalry?"

"No." Claudius shook his head. "I want them here at the main camp. They'll build most of the siege equipment." He smiled at the irony. "Meanwhile, the emperor wants to see if he can negotiate a surrender with Aureolus. Personally, I doubt it will work, but it's worth a try. Maybe he can convince soldiers inside to turn Aureolus over to us without a fight."

"Will the usual surrender option apply here?" Heraclianus asked.

"Since when do surrendering people have an option?" Attalus interrupted.

"The option is that they can surrender and be granted mercy any time before the first battering ram strikes the city wall," Heraclianus replied.

"And after that?" Attalus arched an eyebrow.

"No mercy is given to anyone when the city falls. The men are killed, the women and children sold into slavery, and the city is destroyed." Aurelian said, then shrugged.

"Even the animals are killed—to make a point," Heraclianus added.

"You'd do that to a Roman city?" Attalus asked.

"Possibly," Aurelian shrugged. "If you make an example of one city, others might think twice before rebelling."

"Gallienus hasn't made that decision, yet," Claudius said. "In the meantime we'll build and dig." The Roman officers nodded.

Attalus tilted his head close to Naulobatus and murmured and gestured a bit. Claudius stopped speaking and frowned at the two of them. Attalus jerked a thumb at Naulobatus. "He ought to know what you're doing,"

"Dig?" Naulobatus asked in his heavily accented Latin.

"Tunnels," Attalus said. "Under the city walls… to make them collapse…fall down…so we can get into the city."

"Ah!" Naulobatus nodded, smiling at the thought.

"We'll want scorpions, ballistae, and catapults," Claudius paused to look at Naulobatus. "They throw stones at the enemy— from the size of your hand," he thrust a clenched fist toward Naulobatus, "to the size of your head," he put both hands to his head for emphasis. "The smaller stones are used against the men on the wall; the larger stones are to destroy their defenses." He looked back at his generals. "We also need a battering ram, and two siege towers to begin with…"

Naulobatus cleared his throat loudly.

Claudius glanced over at Naulobatus puzzled expression. "The ram is to break down a gate or a part of the wall, and the siege towers will be rolled up to the wall for our soldiers to climb out of and onto the top of the city walls. They're all built within sight of the city so the people inside can see what to expect if they don't surrender. Any other questions?" He paused; no one spoke.

"Very well," Claudius continued. "Position your men this morning. We'll start gathering lumber for siege engine construction tomorrow morning." The men rose and began leaving. Aurelian had planned to remain behind to talk with Claudius, but noticed Heraclianus lingering. He decided not to stay, and nodded toward Heraclianus when he passed Claudius on his way out.

"A moment of your time?" Heraclianus said to Claudius, after Aurelian and the legates had filed out of the tent. "There's something more I'd like to discuss with you."

Claudius settled back onto his stool. "Sit," he indicated to Heraclianus, then began rolling up his map to give the Praetorian Prefect time to speak.

Heraclianus stood until he was certain they were alone. Then he took a seat opposite Claudius. "It seems we're once again outside a Roman city besieging a traitor," he smiled sadly. He continued, when Claudius said nothing. "I hope we don't leave the job unfinished this time."

"No one wants to."

"Of course," Heraclianus agreed and was quiet for a while. Claudius busied himself with the map and some papers on the table, waiting for him to continue. "I still think he should attack one of the city gates."

"Tell that to the emperor. It was his decision not to attack there." Claudius regretted the comment as soon as he made it. *That's no way to learn what's on Heraclianus' mind.* "Gallienus knows the city, and he's spoken with the engineers who expanded the wall last year," he said in a more congenial tone.

"If Aureolus survives this siege somehow, then I think Gallienus will lose the support of the legionnaires."

Claudius was suddenly alert and on guard. Heraclianus' comment could almost be considered treasonous. *Is he just speaking his mind, or is he trying to entrap me?* "Then it's up to us to see that he doesn't," he replied.

Heraclianus hesitated a moment. "You're no doubt aware that I came to your tent the other night."

"The orderly mentioned you'd been there." Claudius looked up from his paperwork and met Heraclianus' gaze.

"Perhaps I should have come inside, but at the time I decided it was best not to intrude on two soldiers drinking and complaining."

"I know you didn't come up through the ranks like Aurelian and I did," Claudius said, "but that's what soldiers do."

"Legionnaires aren't the only ones who complain. It seems to be a human condition." Heraclianus hesitated, then went on. "I share some of the same doubts and frustrations you were discussing." Now he looked closely at Claudius. "But it's my job to protect the emperor, and when I hear two senior officers discussing those feelings, it concerns me more than overhearing two legionnaires—or even two centurions."

"Aurelian and I come from the same province. We've been close friends for years. So we can, and do, talk freely with each other about anything that comes to our minds."

"What would you do differently?" Heraclianus asked.

"Now? Nothing."

"What would you have done, then?"

Claudius thought for only a moment. "Since you heard our conversation the other night, you must recall my saying we should have redoubled our efforts against Postumus as soon as possible—the year after the siege failed. Instead, we all went to Athens."

"Fortifying the coastal cities there has doubtless saved a number of lives."

"The emperor didn't have to be there himself to do that," Claudius said.

"Was there anything else you would have done?"

"I would never have entrusted Aureolus with another command. We wouldn't be here now." Claudius shook his head sadly. "But that's the nature of this emperor. He's too forgiving. On the other hand, he is competent. He looks after his soldiers, he's made us all generals, and he's kept us alive."

"That he has, that he has." Heraclianus shrugged, as if the whole issue had been an inconsequential, professional conversation. Claudius turned his attention to the papers on his table. But Heraclianus held up his hand. "By the way," he said casually, "the other night you mentioned my trip to meet with Zenobia."

Now we've come to the real point of this meeting.

"Was the assessment I heard yours, or the emperor's?"

"Gallienus was, disappointed, with the outcome of your trip. You must have known that yourself."

"It was my first assignment after becoming Praetorian Prefect, you know. I was never good at diplomacy, that's why I became a soldier."

Gallienus had hoped you were both, Claudius thought.

"He laughed at me behind my back, and in front of you and Aurelian!" Heraclianus slapped his hand on the table.

Claudius shrugged. "We've all been cut by Gallienus' tongue at one time or another. When he's frustrated he often resorts to sarcastic remarks."

"He treated my failure as if it were a joke to him!"

"What do you want, an apology from Gallienus?"

With effort, Heraclianus restrained his impulse to respond sarcastically himself. He didn't answer the question directly. "First I was sent on that impossible assignment to Zenobia, then I return to find you fulfilling my duties and that Aurelian is commanding the cavalry. I'd been effectively demoted in absentia."

"He needed someone to do those jobs while you were away. It seems that he's satisfied with the current arrangement."

"Then why did he pick me for Praetorian Prefect?" Heraclianus asked.

"Apparently he was impressed with your performance as a general, and as governor of Pannonia."

"It seems that he's changed his mind since then."

"And he felt your background as one of the senatorial class might help pacify the Senate."

"Really! I didn't think he cared about that."

"Generally he doesn't," Claudius agreed. "But here's the conflict he faces with the Senate: they expect their sons to start out as officers, no matter how competent or experienced they are. Gallienus refuses to put his soldiers under the command of incompetent or inexperienced officers, and the army is better for it. Some senators understand his excluding untried men from army commissions, but many others don't. Those senators would gladly see him gone. Gallienus doesn't seem to care what they think, but it's unfortunate that he antagonizes the senators that way."

"His comment about my not being able to negotiate with Zenobia was a stinging rebuke," Heraclianus abruptly returned to the Zenobia matter. "It suggests his lack of confidence in my abilities."

"Only as a diplomat," Claudius tied to soothe him.

"What about his saying he didn't send me there to make an enemy?" Heraclianus snorted.

Claudius shrugged and raised his eyebrows. "Listen, you're still Praetorian Prefect, and you performed competently during the battle against the Heruli. Just manage your assignments during this siege and keep the emperor and his family safe, and you'll be fine."

"Perhaps." Heraclianus rose from his stool, signaling that the discussion was over as far as he was concerned. "But I still feel under increased pressure to perform."

"We're all under increased pressure to perform," Claudius assured Heraclianus as he paused at the opening of the tent, "even the emperor. We all know it, and so does he."

Claudius sat mulling over the situation as he watched Heraclianus walk back to his quarters. He noticed the guard outside Heraclianus' tent talking to another soldier. But he did not see that soldier later mounted a horse and began riding south, toward Rome.

* * *

"Do you think you convinced him?" Aurelian asked after Claudius had shared his private conversation with Heraclianus.

"Not totally," Claudius admitted. "The part about Postumus and Aureolus wasn't really what it was about. It's his pride and Gallienus' sarcastic comments that upset him."

"Should we say anything to Gallienus about it?"

"I already have. Gallienus happened to mention that Heraclianus suddenly seemed moody and irritable so I told him that Heraclianus overheard 'some soldiers' making jokes about his mission to Zenobia."

"And," Aurelian prompted.

"He was quiet for a moment, then said 'Sieges always make tempers flare. There's too much time for wounds to fester.' He told me I was right to tell him about Heraclianus and he expected that we'd be busy soon enough." Claudius paused. "I don't think he felt he could switch Praetorian Prefects right now, even if he wanted to."

Aurelian shrugged. "You know Gallienus; he flares up and then it's gone. I don't think he understands people like Heraclianus. They brood, and the bitterness eats at their insides. Bitterness like that can be dangerous."

9-7
A Visitor and A Siege
Outside Mediolanum
07 August, 268

"A messenger to see you, sir," an orderly announced to Heraclianus from the entrance of his tent. Heraclianus glanced up from a small table covered with papers. Light from a candle flickered across his face highlighting both his fatigue and irritation at being disturbed.

"What does he want?"

A brief exchange followed between the orderly and the messenger. "He says he brings a message from Rome, but refuses to explain it, sir."

"Rome? Doesn't he want the emperor?"

"He insists this message is for you, sir."

Heraclianus frowned, wondering who in Rome wanted to communicate with him. *Somebody probably wants a favor of some kind*, he thought while he tidied up the papers in front of him. "Send him in, then," he sighed.

A tall, slim man stepped into Heraclianus' tent and saluted smartly. "Greetings Marcus Aurelius Heraclianus," he said in a clear, confident voice. "I bring you salutations from the Senate." Heraclianus studied the man with interest. His clothes were of good quality and bore a broad purple stripe denoting his senatorial rank. He returned Heraclianus' gaze with a casual smile. This was no ordinary messenger.

"Don't you wish to speak with the emperor?"

"This communication is for you alone," the man replied. "Do you mind if I sit?" he asked, easing himself into one of the chairs by Heraclianus' table before Heraclianus could reply. "It's been a long ride," he said, as if that explained everything. He looked about the tent.

Heraclianus had the distinct impression he expected to be offered refreshments. "You didn't come all the way from Rome just to bring me greetings," Heraclianus prompted the man.

"I'm instructed to tell you that you have friends in the Senate."

"Of course I do," Heraclianus answered, surprise showing in his voice. "My father's a senator himself, in case you didn't know."

"Your father knows nothing about this visit, although I suspect he'd approve of it. These are 'special' friends—some you undoubtedly know—others I suspect you do not."

"Indeed! Who are they?"

"It's far too *impractical* to mention names at this point—in case my message was to be somehow misconstrued. For now, you'll have to trust that what I tell you is the truth."

"I'll judge that for myself! Proceed."

The man leaned closer to Heraclianus and lowered his voice. "For a number of years the emperor has excluded senators or their sons from serving in the army and thus gaining positions of rank and honor,"

"and wealth," Heraclianus added sourly. "If they later became Provincial Governors, they would return to Rome far wealthier than when they'd left."

"A small compensation for their services to the empire." The man inclined his head and raised an eyebrow as if the matter were entirely inconsequential. "The exclusion from these positions has been taken as a grave insult by many in the Senate."

But Provincial Governors sometimes have several legions under their command, Heraclianus thought, *and that's what concerns Gallienus!* "You'll have to take this matter up with the emperor."

"This has been tried, I assure you,"

"If the emperor is unwilling to modify his policy, then surely I can do nothing to help you."

"But perhaps you can," the man replied, returning Heraclianus' gaze evenly.

"Where are you going with this conversation?" Heraclianus finally asked.

"We're hoping that the next emperor would view the Senate's desires favorably."

"The current emperor shows no signs of dying any time soon. Are you suggesting something?"

"No, no, no," the man protested holding up his hands, "no one's suggesting anything!"

"Then what are you saying?"

"Only that unexpected events sometimes happen. Remember when Gallienus was struck by an arrow and nearly died during that nasty siege against Postumus?"

Heraclianus nodded.

"Right now the emperor has no designated successor. His death—for whatever reason—would probably lead to civil war. We think a man such as you might be worthy of our support— should such an unexpected event occur."

"Why not Claudius or Aurelian?"

"It's doubtful that either of them would reverse the policy we've been discussing."

"But you think I might?"

"We'd expect, in exchange for senatorial support, that you, a member of the senatorial class, would understand and be sympathetic to our situation, just as we would be to yours."

"Why have you come to me with this proposal now?"

"The time to plan for this type of contingency is long before it happens." The man spread his hands as if to emphasize the remoteness of the possibility. "Besides, we have friends in the camp," he said with a disconcerting smile. "And we know how some highly-placed people feel about the emperor's policies." He paused, studying Heraclianus' weary face, then rose abruptly. "I'll take no more of your time tonight, Marcus Aurelius Heraclianus. We'll discuss this matter again, sometime in the future. A good night to you."

In the silence following the man's departure Heraclianus thought about what he had just heard. The topic itself was disturbing enough, but what troubled Heraclianus even more was his suspicion that someone in the camp had relayed information about him to the Senate.

19 August, 268

"Sieges grate on my nerves," Gallienus declared, wiping the sweat from his forehead. "We've been at this one for over a month now."

"Before we get into anything else," Attalus interjected before Gallienus could say anything further, "what can be done about the foul smell in camp?"

"That's the latrines," Gallienus said. It's time to re-dig them—and cover the garbage dump while we're at it." He nodded at Claudius to take that for action. "That's what happens when a large number of men stay in one place for more than a short time."

"One more reason to end this siege quickly," Attalus noted.

"We're almost ready to launch a combined assault against the north-east wall and overwhelm Aureolus' defenders," Gallienus continued with his original topic. "This will be our overall battle plan: we'll create a diversionary attack to the south, and try to collapse the tunnels under the city walls at the same time…"

"How is this collapse done?" Naulobatus asked.

"We burn the timbers supporting the tunnels while they were being dug. When they collapse, so will the ground above them, we hope." Gallienus waited while Attalus explained the procedure to Naulobatus. Attalus eventually looked up and nodded.

"While that's going on, we'll move a battering ram against the wall and try to break through part of it. Then the siege towers will come forward—one on either side of the ram, just before assault ladders are brought to the walls."

Then comes the moment of truth, Claudius noted. *If we fail it may be days, or even weeks before we can mount another attack.*

"How many scaling ladders have you built, Aurelian?" Gallienus asked.

"Fifty, so far."

"Adequate," Gallienus nodded. "They're not too short or too tall?"

"Neither," Aurelian replied, "according to our best estimates of the wall height."

"You've allowed for the depth of the moat?"

"Yes. You know they'll probably drop stones and pour molten pitch on the climbers," Aurelian added.

"The catapults should keep the defenders off the top of the wall," Gallienus replied. "Will they be able to do that, Claudius?"

"As long as we concentrate our attack on two or three main places," Claudius replied.

"Make sure your people know not to shoot at the slingers on the walls," Heraclianus reminded Claudius. "Several of them are our spies. They're sending us messages on the stones they're slinging at us."

"They'll be safe until the main assault begins," Claudius replied, "then anyone on the walls will be shot at." He paused a moment, and resumed when Heraclianus raised no objections. "We've done some minor damage to the walls with the catapults and have thrown some burning rags into the city itself. They started a few fires, but the defenders caught others with wet cloths."

"We'll try that again during the assault," Gallienus said. "They won't be able to defend against all of them."

"Nothing like a burning city to distract defenders," Attalus murmured approvingly.

"Your progress with the tunneling?" Gallienus turned to Aurelian. "Weren't two of them discovered by the enemy?"

Aurelian nodded. "One was flooded. Smoke was forced into the other one."

"How many do you think are still usable?"

"I think there are three, undisturbed, that are underneath parts of their wall. But we hear them digging other tunnels. I expect they're trying to undermine our siege engines, or maybe the larger catapults."

"Should we move any of them?"

"Not yet," Heraclianus shook his head. "If we move them too soon, that would alert the defenders to our planned point of attack. And it keeps them digging in the same places, so we know where they are."

"What about our battering ram?" Gallienus asked Claudius.

"We've tried it against the east wall. It caused some damage, but defenders dropped a padded mat against the wall—we think it was filled with straw. They also lowered a noose and tried to snare the ram with it. We covered the roof of the battering ram with wet animal hides to protect it from their attempts to set it on fire. Of course that only works for so long," Claudius added.

"Any reports of sickness or starvation inside the city?" Attalus interrupted, sounding hopeful.

"Not yet," Gallienus said, glancing at Heraclianus, whom he had made responsible for spies and intelligence.

"As a matter of fact there may be," Heraclianus said. "A deserter was brought to me this morning, just before the meeting began. I can bring him here for questioning."

"Do it now," Gallienus said immediately. "And while we're waiting for your man to arrive, tell us about the siege towers."

Heraclianus gestured an aide to fetch the deserter then turned back to Gallienus. "Nearly complete. We can move them whenever you like. We'll protect them with wet hides once we move them closer to the wall, but they're beyond arrow range now, so that hasn't been necessary."

"They may try to flood the ground when the towers are moved against the wall," Gallienus cautioned. "You've planned to fill in the moat at the attack sites, of course?"

"Yes. The low water has made that job easier. There's no assurance flooding will work for them, unless they've got tunnels right under the towers. We'll have to work quickly, in any event."

"Here comes your man now," Gallienus interrupted. They collectively turned to watch while the defector was led to the meeting site. "State your name, and title" Gallienus commanded when the man stepped forward and saluted the emperor.

"I am Lucius Septimus Julius, sir, deputy commander of a quingeniary ala…"

"Of a what?" Attalus interrupted.

"A cavalry wing with five hundred horsemen," Gallienus explained patiently. "Proceed, Julianus."

"I fought with General Aureolus against Ingenuus, Macrianus, and Postumus."

"And now with Aureolus against the emperor," Attalus interrupted again, scowling at the man. "Don't forget that part!"

Julius glanced condescendingly at Attalus. "Who is this man, sir?" he asked Gallienus.

"An ally," Gallienus replied. "Tell us about the revolt, Julius," he said quickly.

"No one knew that Aureolus was in revolt when he first arrived in Mediolanum. We thought he'd come as an official representative of you, sir. Once here, he convinced some of the cavalry to join him and then bribed or coerced the rest of the army to do the same. I don't think everyone in the army is all that convinced of Aureolus' cause. No one has a grudge against you." He paused to look around at the once familiar faces all staring stonily at him. "In fact, some convincing excuse to change sides might prove effective for many of them. There are quite a few uneasy heads resting on their pillows in the city."

"And what about their bellies?" Attalus asked. "We're six weeks into this siege. Aren't they starving yet?"

Julius paused slightly before deciding to answer Attalus' question. "General Aureolus' food supplies are dangerously low," he conceded. "He's already put the citizens on rations and there's lots of women and children to feed, as well as all of the army. But rationing has only delayed the day when his storehouses will run empty. So, he's been sending groups of horsemen out at night to raid the countryside for food. They've managed to evade the men you've posted to watch the city gates."

"Aureolus can't possibly expect that the emperor will just give up the siege and leave, can he?" Aurelian asked.

"No sir, he doesn't expect that."

"Then sending out foraging patrols isn't a very effective plan for long-term survival," Aurelian noted. "His alternatives are starvation, an outbreak of disease, or his soldiers betraying him to Gallienus. Which is he waiting for?"

"His plan has been to hold out until General Postumus arrives with his army."

"Somehow I have trouble believing that Postumus would accept a position as Aureolus' deputy. I'm beginning to doubt your sincerity, Julius," Gallienus said frowning menacingly.

"It's the other way around, sir," Julius said hastily. "Here, let me show you." He reached into a leather pouch at his belt and took out several coins which he put on the table in front of Gallienus. "You can see General Postumus' face on the obverse side of the coin," he explained to the others, while Gallienus examined the coins, "with the title 'Imperius Augustus.'"

"Aureolus minted these?" Claudius asked, as he turned one of the coins over in his hand. On the reverse side were the words "Loyalty of the Cavalry" above a man sitting on a horse.

Julius nodded. "We thought you knew."

Attalus could tell by the stunned looks on the generals' faces that this was somehow significant. "So?" he asked.

Gallienus finally answered him. "It means that Aureolus and Postumus were planning to combine forces and revolt together."

"Well then, where is Postumus?" Attalus asked.

"He kept delaying his arrival date," Julius said, "but Aureolus believed his promises to come soon.'"

"We're hearing rumors that Postumus is dealing with a revolt of his own," Heraclianus said.

"A pity," Attalus said. "I was so hoping for another chance to get his head on the end of my spear."

"Probably fortunate he's detained," Heraclianus said. "If he'd combined forces with Aureolus' men, we'd be facing a very large army." The generals focused on Gallienus, careful not to look at each other.

"It could still happen," Gallienus cautioned. "If Postumus suppresses his revolt quickly, we might still have to deal with him. That's one more reason I want this siege brought to a successful conclusion—soon."

"So, Julius, why defect now?" Claudius asked Julius.

"I heard that Aureolus planned to kidnap the empress, and use her to negotiate his safe passage from the city."

9-8
A Setback
Outside Mediolanum
19 August, 268

"Salonina isn't due to arrive for days," Aurelian objected.

"He knows that," Julius said. "I was at some of the meetings when all this was discussed. That plan went against my principles as a Roman. I came to warn you about it."

Gallienus leaned close to Heraclianus. "I want you to personally ensure the empress' safety," he said. "Do whatever you think necessary to protect her." Then he looked up and nodded for the man to proceed.

"What about tunnels and raids?" Claudius asked.

"There were tunnels," Julius replied, "but I don't know where they were being dug. And General Aureolus realizes that your siege towers are nearly done. He was planning to attack them."

"When?"

"Very soon."

Gallienus dismissed the man. When Julius had departed, he spoke to Heraclianus. "The siege towers are adequately protected, aren't they?"

"I assigned eighty men to each siege engine," Heraclianus answered.

Gallienus mulled that over for a moment. "Double, no triple that right away."

Sounds of a galloping horse signaled the arrival of a messenger. After a quick dismount, he approached and saluted Gallienus.

"What news is so important at this time of morning?" Gallienus asked. "Has Aureolus offered to surrender?"

"It's the siege towers, sir," the messenger replied. "Aureolus attacked them at dawn this morning!"

"And?" Gallienus asked, careful not to look at Heraclianus.

"Both destroyed."

"And Aureolus?"

"Back inside the city, sir."

"Give us a complete report," Heraclianus demanded, scowling, "not bits and pieces!"

The messenger glanced uneasily from Heraclianus to Gallienus, who nodded for him to proceed. "Some of General Aureolus' men attacked one of the catapults early this morning. The soldiers guarding the siege tower closest to the catapult went to help defend it, thinking they could overwhelm this small force quickly. Once committed, they found themselves facing a much larger enemy force than they'd first seen."

"Lured into a trap," Heraclianus fumed. "I want to see the centurion responsible for defending that siege tower!" he said to the messenger.

"He was killed during the engagement, sir."

Gallienus nodded for the messenger to continue.

"It was a short skirmish. They attacked from behind on horses—we'd dismounted to help the defenders—then they galloped to the siege tower and set fire to it.”

“And the second tower?” Gallienus asked.

“As the first tower started to burn, they rode towards the second one. By then our defenders had formed up and were prepared to meet Aureolus’ force, but suddenly the tower just collapsed!” He looked at them inquiringly.

“Maybe they tunneled underneath it,” Aurelian speculated. “Unless there was a problem with construction.” He looked at Heraclianus. “When did you check it last?”

Heraclianus glared at Aurelian. “I inspected both of them myself, yesterday. They were fine then. And we had no indications of enemy tunneling around them, even though we expected them to try.”

“What happened to the enemy?” Attalus asked.

“They fled, mostly on horseback. We gave chase ourselves but when we neared the walls, we were attacked by arrows and javelins. Most of the horsemen escaped.”

“That’s just wonderful!” Gallienus said. He rose, intending to pace about, but only made a quick turn inside the small tent, before sitting down again. “Anything more?” he asked the messenger. The man shook his head. “Have you any more questions?” he asked the generals. They shook their heads slowly. Gallienus dismissed the messenger with a nod. “It will take weeks to repair them or build new ones, I suppose. That delay helps no one but Postumus and the Goths.” He sat, silently, brooding.

“They were your men, Aurelian,” Heraclianus said, feeling he was being blamed for the failure.

“Under your command, Heraclianus.”

“I can’t be held accountable for troops assigned to me, who fail to follow my explicit orders,” Heraclianus growled, knowing that he could and most likely would be held accountable for any failures occurring under his command, regardless of whose men they were.

“While their intentions and initiative may have been commendable,” Gallienus emerged from his reverie, “in the end they failed to protect what they’d been ordered to protect. I’m, disappointed, in the outcome.” He rubbed his forehead. I wonder why he's reacting this way. "Do you have a plan for the towers?" he asked Heraclianus.

"I won't know until I've seen them myself. Perhaps they can be repaired; perhaps we'll have to build others."

"How long to rebuild?"

"Two to three weeks if we have to start over completely."

"Early September!" Gallienus frowned. "Then there'll be no time to engage the Goths before next spring."

"We gave Aureolus an attractive target and he came out," Attalus said. "Why don't we give him another one? But this time we'll trap him. If we killed Aureolus, then we wouldn't have to storm the city—the men would give up without their leader, and you'd get your revenge." Attalus looked at Gallienus.

"An excellent idea." Gallienus' expression brightened for the first time that morning. "Give me some choices," he said to his generals. "I want this siege ended before winter, so we'll be ready to march against the Goths next spring."

Gallienus is right, Heraclianus thought. *If he fails to capture Aureolus there'll be further revolts, and we still have a serious one that's unresolved. His reign would be finished. I don't see how he or any of us under his command could possibly survive.*

29 August, 268

"This isn't how I'd hoped to welcome you to Mediolanum," Gallienus said to Salonina, as he held her close and listened to the sheets of rain whipping the sides of his tent. The single candle flickered precariously with every gust of wind.

"We're together; that's all that matters to me." She pulled close to him and he wrapped a blanket securely around her shoulders. "I got chilled during the storm," she admitted, sniffling.

"We didn't expect it to last this long."

"I'm so happy to be here with you and finally to be in your arms and no longer traveling. We left Rome on the first of March and I've only had a week's stay in Poetovio, that was late March." Lightning flashed. She started at the crash of thunder that immediately followed. They paused, waiting for another crash of thunder while rain beat steadily against the tent. "I've been on one road or another ever since. Five months of traveling!"

"It might be a short stay here too," Gallienus said. "I hope to conclude this siege soon and return to Macedonia to finish the campaign against the Goths."

She glanced up at the shadowed features of his face. *He looks tired. He needs to end this siege quickly.* "Right now we have each other." Salonina closed her eyes and sighed, holding him tightly.

She'd arrived that afternoon, thoroughly wet from traveling through a cold, heavy rain, which started the night before and turned their campground into a smelly morass. Gallienus' plans for a welcoming celebration and dinner with the generals had been cancelled. Instead, the generals had come individually to Gallienus' tent to offer her their greetings. She had made a point of talking with each of them for a few minutes, trying to learn their minds.

"Have you noticed anything different about Heraclianus?" she asked. "Aurelian seemed as dour as ever, but I felt that Heraclianus was uncomfortable. He avoided looking me in the eye."

"He's under a lot of pressure—we all are." Gallienus paused. "I regret not having Volusianus with me, but I felt I had to promote him to the Rome posting."

"I'm glad he's there to help Marinianus," Salonina said, and let her unease about Heraclianus drop for the present. "As I passed Verona I was thinking about how I was almost captured near there by Juthungi nine years ago. You had just won a tremendous victory over them and the Alamanni."

"So much has happened since then," he said, nodding at her recollection.

"What of the Goths?" she asked suddenly. "I got so little news visiting with all those city prefects. Mostly they just gossiped at dinner."

"Did you hear about Dexippus' victory over the Goths near Megara in early June?" Gallienus asked. A strong gust of wind nearly extinguished their candle. She pulled even closer to him.

"Yes," Salonina smiled. "What a remarkable man: a priest

for the Eleusinian Mysteries, and also a great general."

"His victory blocked their advance to the north. They would have gone through Thessalonica, where I met you for a night. Instead he turned them west toward Delphi, which they sacked some time ago."

"Beautiful Delphi," she murmured sadly. "I hoped to return there someday."

"The Goths moved northwest along the coast road," Gallienus continued. "My last report said they sacked Nicopolis in Epirus."

"I heard that at Aquileia," Salonina confirmed.

"They'll have to follow the west coast road for quite a while before they have a chance to turn north."

"Do you think they'll do that?"

He shrugged. "If they go north, they'll eventually run into Marcianus. Otherwise they'll run into me when I go back east. Then we wouldn't have to go so far to destroy them."

"What do you hear from Marinianus? I thought of him on his birthday. Twenty-four years old this July! Is he enjoying his consulship? Or would he rather be here with you?"

"I think the job suits him, at least that's what his letters suggest," Gallienus replied.

"That's all? Wasn't there more?"

"Not from him, but I have heard rumors that Volusianus relayed to me. There's something going on in the Senate. Nothing specific—some sort of dissatisfaction."

"But they're always dissatisfied with you."

"They seem to like making trouble for me, or maybe they just like complaining."

"Do you think it's anything serious?" Salonina asked.

"It won't be serious unless I can't take Aureolus."

Salonina thought about that, then shivered and curled up against Gallienus. She tried to stifle her yawn. "How did you learn of these rumors?"

Gallienus frowned. "From an informant," he said. "A particularly reliable source." *I can't tell her that Lysisca brought news to Volusianus from her brothel!* He breathed a sigh of relief that

Salonina didn't pursue that line of thought.

"I had a dream…" Salonina's voice trailed off.

"Tell me about it," Gallienus said, not realizing that she was almost asleep.

"What…? Oh, the dream. A pack of wolves chased a wounded boar into a thicket…" Salonina's eyes closed. Soon her breathing became slow and rhythmic.

Gallienus kissed her forehead and laid her gently on the bed. "You can tell me about it later," he whispered and covered her carefully with a blanket.

10-1
Northern Camp, A Plan
Gallienus' Northern Guard Camp
01 September, 268

This is not a good idea—no matter what Gallienus or Aurelian said, Heraclianus thought darkly while riding across gently rolling plains between Gallienus' main encampment, northeast of Mediolanum, and an auxiliary campsite. From there some of his soldiers guarded the northern road out of the city. Olive groves lined this dusty trail created by frequent transits between the two bases. Occasionally they passed open fields of grain waving in waning summer breezes. Heraclianus thought back to the conversation earlier that morning when Gallienus first announced that Salonina would accompany them.

"I thought this was a resupply and reconnaissance trip."

Gallienus laughed at Heraclianus' stunned expression. "It is. We'll leave her in the northern camp while we're on patrol. She'll be safer there."

"She's not as mobile as Pipa is when she's with you." Heraclianus objected. Pipa always rode on horseback, accompanied by a band of Marcomanni warriors. Salonina would be traveling in a wagon. "She'd attract less attention if she dressed as an aide, and rode a horse like everyone else," he suggested.

"More trouble than it's worth." Gallienus dismissed the

suggestion with a frown. "She's not been on a horse since child-hood. Besides, I'll have to bring along a few of her attendants."

They rode in silence, except for the rhythmic plodding of horses' hooves on this dry dirt trail. *At least the wind is blowing dust to the side*, Heraclianus noted. *I can understand Salonina not wanting to be nearby when the latrines are being re-dug, espe-cially when the wind blows the stench toward her tent. But bringing her to a forward camp seems extremely unwise—espe-cially if Aureolus has plans to abduct her.* He looked around at the horsemen Gallienus had selected for this sortie, trying to reas-sure himself. Aurelian, flanked by some of his staff, rode to the left side of Gallienus. Behind them were thirty Praetorian Guards, followed by Salonina and her attendants, then another thirty Prae-torian guards. Naulobatus and twenty-five of his Heruli horsemen came next, ahead of twenty pack animals and their attendants. At-talus' force of twenty-five Marcomanni warriors brought up the rear. Heraclianus wondered briefly if he'd caught a glimpse of Pipa with Attalus' forces, but suppressed the thought.

Gallienus had been adamant about limiting the size of each group. *I suppose the chance of meeting any of Aureolus' men is remote*, Heraclianus thought, *and we'll be joining nearly seven hundred of our cavalry at the northern camp.*

The lead elements of Gallienus' force approached the bank of the Olona River that flowed south from mountains around the city of Comum and into Mediolanum. As the horses picked their way down the river bank, their hooves dislodged small stones that clattered ahead of them down the embankment. The group moved across dry mud along the river's edge then splashed through gently flowing water of the rocky river bed itself. Gal-lienus' horse balked when first coming to the water, but was coaxed through when he was able to follow Heraclianus' horse.

We'll be there soon, Heraclianus thought, *and we're only re-supplying the camp, not expecting a skirmish or battle.*

The group emerged from the river bed and onto a road con-necting Mediolanum with Comum. It was deserted, except for a group of horsemen between them and the main entrance to the Roman camp, a hundred feet beyond the road.

All Roman camps were constructed following a common layout, so everyone knew where they were supposed to go at the end of each day's march. This one was similar to other Roman camps, except much smaller—intended for seven hundred men and horses, not the customary five to ten thousand men. A six-foot trench had been dug around the entire perimeter and dirt from the trench was piled beyond the trench forming a small wall with stakes pounded into the ground on the top of the mound. The camp formed a nearly square palisade about two hundred and fifty feet on each side. The main gate opened to a road inside that led directly to the headquarters building. Another road, just in front of the headquarters ran perpendicular to the main road and led to secondary gates on either side of the camp. Behind the headquarters a lesser road ran to the smallest gate at the rear of the camp.

"Ah, a welcoming committee," Gallienus said appreciatively to the horsemen gathered on the road. "What's gotten all of you up at this hour of the morning?"

"You have, sir," the camp commander smiled as he saluted Gallienus.

"General Aurelian has brought you something to eat," Gallienus waved at the supply train, still making its way through the river behind him. "And as long as we're here, I thought we'd take a look around and see what Aureolus' people are up to."

The commander's eyes widened as Salonina's cart emerge from the river bed.

"I've brought the empress along for security reasons," Gallienus said, anticipating the commander's protest but elaborated no further. "She's still recovering from a cold she caught on her travels from Macedonia, and will need a place to rest."

"Of course, sir," the commander quickly replied, masking his amazement that the empress had been brought to his outpost and wondering what the security reasons were. "She can use my tent, or perhaps she'd be more comfortable using the headquarters tent. If there's anything we can do for her, my men and I will be at her service."

Gallienus, Aurelian, Heraclianus, Attalus, and Naulobatus all entered the camp, leaving most of others outside. Salonina and her attendants proceeded to the headquarters tent. Pack horses followed, and were led to stables, where their supplies would be unloaded and stored in granaries at the rear of the camp. The Praetorians remained just outside the front gate. The Heruli spilled off the road south of camp, the Marcomanni fanned out to the north. They all rested and took their mid-day meal while waiting for Gallienus to issue orders for the afternoon operations.

While Salonina slept, Gallienus ate with Aurelian, Heraclianus, Attalus, Naulobatus, and the camp commander. "Did you notice how low the river was?" he asked them during lunch.

Heraclianus nodded, his mouth too full to respond.

"Do you suppose the culvert is exposed?" Gallienus asked. Besides filling the surrounding moat, the Olona River supplied water directly into the city through an opening in the fortifications that was normally well below the river's surface. "Have you checked that?" he asked the commander.

"No, sir. We were planning to act on a complaint of raids further north. It seems Aureolus' men have been seizing food supplies up near Comum."

"A good chance to exercise the cavalry, Aurelian," Gallienus noted. "They'll have to come south at some point."

"With your permission, we'll go north and intercept them." Aurelian looked eager for the chance. "Do you wish to lead them?" he asked Gallienus.

"That's your job," Gallienus replied. "But I would like to take a closer look at that culvert. The raiders may be using it to get in and out of the city. That would explain why we're not catching them at the gates."

"Couldn't we send someone else?" Heraclianus asked.

"As long as we're here, I'll go myself. During the assault we might be able to get through it and into the city."

"I only have sixty Praetorians to protect you and the empress," Heraclianus objected.

"The only danger I see is being detected when I get close to the city."

"Then I could detail thirty men to protect you, and leave the other thirty to protect the empress." Heraclianus wrinkled his brow. "I'd feel more comfortable if some of the cavalry were left to guard her as well."

"Agreed," Gallienus said.

"How about three troops of cavalry?" Aurelian suggested.

"Will another seventy-two men be enough for you Heraclianus?"

Heraclianus nodded. "Who will command them?"

"May I suggest Cecropius?" the camp commander asked.

"He's a good fighter, but he's a bit aggressive and impulsive," Heraclianus noted.

"There's a problem with that?" Aurelian asked.

"Only that he's commanding a cavalry troop, not Praetorian Guards. And cavalry are trained to attack, not to defend," Heraclianus replied.

"They're Roman soldiers, Heraclianus; I'm sure they'll obey their commander," Gallienus interposed.

"With your permission I'll command the defenses here myself," Heraclianus suggested. "We could send some of the cavalry with you."

"Forty Praetorians should be adequate," Gallienus said. "We'll go down the road on horses until we get closer to the city, then I'll take a few of the men into the riverbed with me and continue on foot."

"Why not use the Heruli and Marcomanni to create a diversion?"

"I was thinking the same thing," Gallienus grinned. "Attalus, take your men to the west of the road. Get them some distance away from the river. Let the city sentries see you. Make a scene if you want. Naulobatus, do the same with your Heruli on the other side of the river. Any questions?" He looked at the men around him. "Good. Give Cecropius his orders. The rest of us know what to do."

* * *

After the mid-day meal Gallienus moved south along the road with forty Praetorians. Marcomanni and Heruli fanned out on either side of the road and all headed roughly south, while

Aurelian departed to the north with most of the cavalry. Quiet settled over the camp and a warm afternoon breeze blew dust from departing men and horses east, away from the fortifications.

Cecropius' face showed disappointment as he watched the cavalry depart, but he made no protest at his orders. "Where would you like me to place my troops?" he asked Heraclianus.

"Tell me your plan."

Cecropius screwed his face up in thought. "I'd put one of my groups on the eastern side of camp facing the road, and two groups to the south—where the threat is likeliest to come from. They'll all have scouts patrolling beyond them looking for anything unusual."

"What about the northern and western sides?"

"I could put men there, if you wish," Cecropius conceded. "But we're concentrating our forces where we think an attack might happen, and the north and west gates themselves will be guarded. If anyone sounds an alarm, one of my three troops can be there quickly."

"All right, we'll use your plan. I'll put two guards at the empress' tent and the rest of my Praetorians along the road, just south of your men."

While the men were moving into their positions, Heraclianus inspected the north gate, then the west gate for security. He judged it to be adequate, then turned and took in the camp as a whole. He walked back to its center, where Gallienus' banner fluttered from a pole just in front of the headquarters tent. Two burly Praetorians stood guard outside Salonina's tent, one in front, one in back.

"Any activity?" Heraclianus asked the guard at the front, nodding at the tent.

"All quiet, sir."

"Good. Take down that banner," Heraclianus pointed at the flag pole at the front of the tent. "We don't want to draw attention to the empress' presence. And make sure there are two men at the tent at all times. I'll send your reliefs shortly." Heraclianus looked around camp one more time. Satisfied, he walked toward the main gate to check on Cecropius' forces and the rest of his

Praetorians. When he reached the road in front of the main gate, Cecropius' men were playing dice.

"You don't mind if the soldiers gamble, do you?" Cecropius asked, glancing up when Heraclianus returned. "It helps keep the men alert. Our guards are properly posted," he added quickly waving a hand from the east through the south. "If anything happens, they'll give us plenty of time to respond."

A number of spirited contests were already under way. *Probably too late to stop it now*, Heraclianus thought, irritated at Cecropius' permissiveness. *Then I'd have bored and sullen troops standing guard.* "Tell them to do it quietly," Heraclianus grudgingly agreed after a moment's thought. "I don't want to alert any enemy to our presence."

10-2
Northern Camp, Another Plan
Gallienus' Northern Guard camp
01 September, 268

While Gallienus moved south along the road to Mediolanum, twenty horsemen concealed themselves in the river bed just north of the camp. They were returning from a raid on Comum, a city about twenty-five miles north of Mediolanum. It had been a successful enterprise and they were laden with supplies. They had interrupted their return to partake of an early mid-day meal.

Statius, their leader, was a short, stocky man, thirty-one years old, who had spent most of his early career with the cavalry under Aureolus' command. When they first dismounted, he had sent a scout to reconnoiter the enemy campsite. Statius planned to rest his group during the afternoon, then attempt to elude sentries and pass the camp that night using the river bed for cover. After their meal, Statius leaned back comfortably against the edge of the river bed and closed his eyes, enjoying the sun's afternoon warmth. He opened an eye to check that the sentries were in position, then closed it with a contented sigh. He had just drifted to sleep when his scout shook him urgently.

"Gallienus was there," the scout said excitedly, "and he brought supplies for the camp—I saw them unloading horses myself."

Statius sat up abruptly, rubbing the sleep from his eyes. "Where is he now?" *If they search the river, we'll never escape!*

"It's all right," the scout put a reassuring hand on Statius' shoulder. "The camp's almost deserted now, and there's only a couple sentries on the north gate."

"Where did they all go?"

"Most of the cavalry headed north on the road. You must have heard them."

"No," Statius admitted. "And the emperor? He must have had Praetorians with him."

"And barbarians, too," the scout added. "Lots of them. But they all went somewhere else, maybe toward Mediolanum. I couldn't tell from where I was. Oh, I almost forgot, when Gallienus arrived he had a cart with him, and there was a banner planted outside the central tent after he left. I think he brought the empress, I mean Salonina, with him!"

"You're certain?" Statius asked.

"I saw female attendants around the headquarters tent, but I couldn't tell who they were attending."

Statius considered the scout's report. "There must be someone guarding her."

"A group of horsemen was outside the main gate, along the road. But only sentries at the north and west gates."

Statius held up a hand to quiet the scout while he considered his options. *Should I ignore this situation and return with the supplies? Or forget the supplies and try to kidnap Salonina—if that's even her?*

"The risks are great," the scout's comment intruded on Statius' thoughts.

"But so are the rewards!" Statius exclaimed. All reservations left him. His pulse quickened and he took a deep breath. "Gather the men," he ordered. When all nineteen men had gathered around him, Statius explained his plan. "We'll leave five men with the supply horses in the river bed. He indicated who was to remain.. "Start moving supplies down the river bed. We'll join you when we can. You seven," he pointed to the men, "will over-power the guards at the north gate and wait there with our horses. I'll take the other seven of you to the back gate—on the west side—and we'll take that gate ourselves. We'll enter camp, seize Salonina—she's resting in the headquarters tent—then escape through the north gate, meet the rest of you there and get our horses. Any questions?"

"Why not take your horses to the back gate and ride in from there?" one of the men asked.

"It would attract attention."

" It's not a big camp, but it's still a long way to drag a strug-gling woman, especially before someone notices," the man persisted.

"All right," Statius agreed. "We'll take horses with us, but we'll walk in."

* * *

Money changed hands as gamblers' fortunes rose and fell. All interest and attention quickly turned to the outcome of the games. One of the luckier gamblers, suddenly tossed the dice onto the ground and swept all his coins into his purse. "I'll be late to relieve the watch if I'm not careful," he exclaimed. He surren-dered his place to another eager gambler, then pushed his way through the crowd and hurried into the camp. Before he reached the center of camp, a disagreement broke out among the gam-blers.

The loser accused the winner of cheating. "You're a liar and a poor loser," the winner replied, dismissively. "You're the liar, and a cheat," the accuser cried, lunging at the other man. The rest of the gamblers quickly took sides, while the two men rolled in the dirt together. Cecropius and Heraclianus both heard shouts and hurried toward the commotion.

The man who had just left the games was running by Sa-lonina's tent when a strap on his sandal snapped. Cursing this turn of his luck, he stopped and leaned his spear and shield against the edge of the tent.

"Hey!" the guard shouted. "What're you doing?"

"Sandal broke," the man answered, pointing at his foot. "And I have to relieve the watch at the back gate."

"While you're doing that," the Praetorian growled, nodding at the man's broken sandal, "keep an eye on the empress for us. No one's come to relieve us, and I've got to take a leak."

"Do it behind her tent," the man replied, unsympathetically. "I'm late."

"With the empress and her attendants around? I don't think so. Look, the two of us will just run out the back gate and do it there. It won't take long, and I'll tell the sentry you're coming." Without waiting for acknowledgment, both Praetorian Guards hurried away.

The man shrugged and laid the strap of his water bladder on a paving stone. He carefully cut a long thin strip off the edge, planning to make a temporary fix by slinging the strip around the bottom of the sandal and tying it on the top of his foot. He had nearly finished when movement caught his attention. He looked up, expecting to see the returning Praetorians. Instead, there was an unfamiliar man coming around the corner of the tent, with a drawn sword!

"Intruders!" he bellowed instinctively, forgetting about his sandal and reaching for his shield. He charged Statius with only his dagger, slashing his knife across the intruder's face. A second man rounded the tent. He crashed into that man with his shield, forcing that man to stagger backwards. He looked to the back gate, expecting help from the two guards. Instead, other unfamiliar men approached him, each holding a sword in his hand. "Intruders!" the man bellowed again and charged at Statius' men, unnerving them.

The man could see the invaders' eyes shift momentarily from him to the Praetorian Guards sprinting towards him from the main gate. Before the Praetorians reached the attackers, the invaders leapt onto their horses. They galloped up the camp road to the north gate, slipped through it unchallenged, and disappeared.

* * *

Statius' horse leapt over the bodies of sentries at the north gate. He picked his way through the underbrush following the rest of his soldiers who all fled toward the river bed. He cursed his misfortune and tried to staunch the flow of blood from the gash in his cheek. *We'll have to ride down the river bed now, he thought. Maybe we can get to the city before they catch up with us.*

* * *

Cecropius and Heraclianus were struggling to break up the fight and calm both factions of angry men when they heard a call for help inside the camp. The accuser, who'd been choking his adversary, suddenly dropped the struggling man, all thoughts of their issue temporarily forgotten.

Cecropius' attention, like most of the others near him, had been on the dice contests, and then on the fight. But alarm quickly spread among the soldiers when they heard a cry for help. Years of training and experience took over. "Mount up!" he shouted as he dashed for his horse. He leapt onto his mount, reined the horse around, and galloped through the main gate, forcing the Praetorians, who were running toward the headquarters tent, to scatter. His troop straggled after him.

Heraclianus dashed after his Praetorian Guards who were sprinting into camp, swords drawn. He was quickly outdistanced by his younger men and paused, gasping for breath partway to the northern gate. He glanced quickly around the camp, his thoughts racing. *Supply horses weren't taken, nothing burning. Their raid was a failure*! Relief washed over him and his breathing became more normal. Then a shock of horror ran through him. *By the gods! Were they trying to capture Salonina? Is she still here? And I forgot to relieve the sentries!* He turned and dashed back toward the empress' tent. Neither of his Praetorians was anywhere in sight. An unfamiliar man wearing one sandal stood there holding a shield and his spear. The front of his tunic was covered with blood.

"What are you doing here?" Heraclianus demanded of the man with one sandal.

"Guarding the empress, sir."

"She's still here?"

"I haven't actually seen her," the man admitted. "But I hope I haven't been defending an empty tent!"

"Where are the guards—the two Praetorians I left here?"

"They went to the west gate, to relieve themselves, sir. Said they'd be right back, but those other guys showed up instead. I chased them away myself," he added proudly.

"Good, good," Heraclianus said distractedly. "Where did they go?"

The man pointed to the north gate. "Your men won't catch them. They were on horses."

"Cecropius!" Heraclianus shouted at the cavalry who were milling around the camp, unsure which way to go. "That way!"

* * *

When Gallienus returned to camp considerably later, he found one troop of cavalry standing guard just outside the main gate. Inside the camp, Praetorian Guards surrounded Salonina's tent. As he approached, he saw Heraclianus standing at the front of the tent, talking with Salonina, seated on a stool beside him. They stopped their conversation as he drew near and Salonina rose to greet him.

"It seems that we've all had a little more excitement today than we expected! The best news is that you're here and un-harmed," Gallienus said to Salonina.

"Where else would I be?" She embraced him smiling, then held onto his arm.

"Cecropius told me briefly what happened here when I met him in the river bed," Gallienus said to Heraclianus. "But I'd like to hear your version of what happened at camp." He tried to dis-engage his arm from Salonina's grasp. "Maybe you could excuse us," he said to Salonina, "while I get a complete report."

"No." Salonina held more tightly to Gallienus' arm. "I've

had enough separation for one day."

She's still shaken from the raid! "I understand completely," he said, putting a hand on her arm. "You can tell us what you saw, as well. But first, Heraclianus."

"I thought the best defense would be placing horsemen outside the camp at the south and east gates. The west and north gates were manned by the normal sentries, and I put two guards outside the empress' tent. I inspected the whole campsite myself." He stopped, hoping for approval from Gallienus. He continued, after Gallienus merely nodded. "We were breaking up a fight among Cecropius' men when the call for help came."

"Why were they fighting?"

"Some disagreement or other." Heraclianus shrugged.

"So, the enemy got into camp, despite all your preparations.."

"Their leader was a very daring and resourceful man," Heraclianus said.

"He was. I had a brief encounter with him in the river bed myself."

"What happened?" Heraclianus asked.

"He came up behind us and attacked the small group I had with me. When the Praetorians on the road answered our call for help, he escaped and fled east, along with most of his men. We chose not to pursue them." Gallienus' composure had returned during the ride back to camp, but he was still felt tense from his brief but desperate fight in the river.

"Where's Cecropius now?"

"Bringing back the wounded."

"We weren't expecting any attack, you said so yourself," Heraclianus emphasized. "But we were prepared for one!"

Gallienus studied his face. "Did they steal anything?"

"Nothing."

"Did they set any fires?"

"No."

Then they were after Salonina! Gallienus realized. "At least you were adequately guarded," he said to Salonina.

Heraclianus realized that Salonina would tell Gallienus about the guards, either now or later. "At the time of the attack," he said, "there was only one man guarding her—a fellow who was repairing his broken sandal in front of her tent."

"That's right," Salonina interjected. "I remember hearing a strange scratching sound and wondered what it was. I peeked out to see what was causing the noise and saw this unfamiliar man cutting something on a rock. Then those other men came and fighting and shouting started. I closed the tent flap as tight as I could, and didn't see anything else."

"He wasn't one of your guards, then?"

"Oh no." Salonina shook her head. "I didn't recognize him at all."

"What happened to the regular guards, Heraclianus?"

"I was told they went to the back gate to relieve themselves. I found their bodies there myself."

Salonina gasped. "They'd been so nice to me and my attendants!"

"Fortunate that such a brave and quick-acting man just happened to be there," Gallienus said. "I'd like to talk with him now, Heraclianus. A resourceful man like that needs to be recognized."

"I don't know who he was," Heraclianus looked down at the ground, embarrassed. "I spoke with him briefly and, when I got back from inspecting the camp, he was gone."

"Make an announcement, then. Say that I want to reward the man who guarded the empress during the skirmish. That shouldn't be too hard."

Heraclianus nodded. "But the guards would have been there if this man hadn't come by," he said. "They'd never have left the empress alone."

The color drained from Salonina's face. "They were after me?"

"Nothing to be concerned about," Gallienus said soothingly, not wanting to emphasize the fact that abducting her was the reason for the attack. "Anyway, I think we've got it sorted out now." He patted her reassuringly on the shoulder, then fell silent. *There's more to this attack than I've been told. Maybe this job is too much for Heraclianus. I don't know what I'm going to do with him until I've learned more.* "Heraclianus, it seems we were lucky here today."

Heraclianus' face flushed. He recalled Claudius saying how Gallienus was quick to reward merit, but that he didn't hesitate to demote or relieve for poor performance. "If I've lost your confidence,"

Gallienus held up a hand interrupting him. "We have other things to think about at the moment." He turned to see Attalus and Naulobatus clattering up the road with most of their horsemen.

"While all of you spent a quiet afternoon doing nothing," Attalus hailed them as he approached, "we've had all the fun," he threw back his head and laughed heartily.

"What makes you think it was quiet here?" Gallienus asked, amused by Attalus' exuberance.

"Did those traitors come here first?" Attalus asked looking more closely at Gallienus, then at Heraclianus. He turned to Naulobatus and grinned. "That would explain the wound you found on their leader's face."

"He's with you now?" Gallienus asked eagerly.

"Well—in a manner of speaking," Attalus hedged.

"I'd like to talk with him," Gallienus said. "Bring him to me."

Attalus shrugged, and moved his horse closer to Naulobatus' mount. He leaned over and spoke to him briefly. Naulobatus nodded and waved one of his warriors forward.

"We killed them all," Attalus explained as the Heruli horseman rode slowly forward. "But that man was clearly their leader," he said pointing to Statius' head, proudly displayed on the Heruli warrior's spear.

03 September, 268

Heraclianus hesitated briefly outside Pipa's tent, fully expecting Gallienus to be annoyed by any disturbance while entertaining Pipa. He hoped he had come before the two of them finished dining. *I could let the matter go until morning, he rationalized, but Gallienus would probably be upset I didn't tell him as soon as I knew.* Heraclianus took a breath and stepped up to the

Marcomanni guard standing just outside Pipa's tent.

"I wish to speak with the emperor," he said to the man.

Anxiety swept across the man's face at the thought of incurring Pipa's ire, and thereby Attalus' wrath. "He very busy now," the Marcomanni guard shook his head. "You come back morning?"

"Now!" Heraclianus insisted, staring into the man's eyes and holding his ground.

The guard scowled then nodded curtly. "You wait," he said before turning and entering the tent. Heraclianus paced impatiently.

Finally, the tent flap opened and Gallienus stepped outside. "What can't wait until tomorrow, Heraclianus?" he asked impatiently.

Heraclianus stared. Gallienus wore Marcomanni clothing, including trousers, and he had gold dust sprinkled in his hair. Heraclianus cleared his throat. "I've just been told about an enemy army somewhere north of Verona!"

"There must be a mistake. The Goths couldn't have gotten that close so quickly."

Heraclianus shook his head. "Not Goths from the east, sir, Alamanni from the north."

10-3
Last Chances
Gallienus' camp outside Mediolanum
04 September, 268

"All of you must have heard about the Alamanni invasion by now," Gallienus said, as he approached the waiting men seated on chairs outside his tent. He had ordered this meeting after hearing Heraclianus' news late the night before. The warmth of the early afternoon sun was tempered by a gentle, steady breeze. Attalus stifled a belch, ineffectively.

"Good lunch?" Gallienus asked.

"Yes. And I was considering a nap, if you hadn't summoned us when you did," Attalus replied, grinning. He stretched to emphasize his point.

"We should have expected as much from the Alamanni," Gallienus continued, "since Aureolus apparently left his borders undefended."

"What's with his hair?" Aurelian whispered, nudging Claudius with his elbow and looking toward Gallienus.

"Gold dust would be my guess."

"He looks tired," Aurelian said.

"Probably didn't get much rest last night," Claudius whispered back.

"…so now we have both an invading army and a siege to deal with," Gallienus was saying. "It's a bit like holding two wolves by the tails, is it not?" he asked, glancing around the assembled men.

"Which tail will you let go?" Attalus asked, clearly excited by the possibility of a battle.

"That's what we're here to discuss." Gallienus looked at Heraclianus. "Perhaps you can elaborate on that news, for us."

"The Alamanni reached Sabiona on the 29th of August," Heraclianus replied.

"How many?" Aurelian asked.

"A 'large army' was all the report said."

"From Sabiona the road leads south, through mountains, to Tridentum, then Verona, as most of you know," Gallienus said, nodding toward Naulobatus, who clearly did not. "From Verona they could go west towards us, south to Rome, or east to Aquileia."

"If they went east, they might run into the Goths—and fight against them, instead of us," Claudius suggested.

An image ran through Gallienus' mind of both armies annihilating each other.

"Not very likely," Heraclianus snorted. "They'd probably join together, like they did with the Juthungi nine years ago."

Claudius started to respond, but Gallienus intervened. "Never mind, Heraclianus; that's not something you'll have to worry about."

Heraclianus tensed and looked from Gallienus to Claudius and then back. *Was that remark significant or merely a casual dismissal?*

"What I'd like you to do, Heraclianus, is calculate the rate of the Alamanni advance," Gallienus continued, and motioned to a tribune to bring him writing material. "Tell me when we'd have to leave here to be in Verona ahead of them. While he's doing that, tell me the status of the siege preparations, Claudius."

"The siege towers will be ready on the ninth of this month."

"You're certain?" Gallienus asked.

Claudius glanced at Aurelian, then nodded. "The earliest we can storm the city is the tenth."

Gallienus scratched his head. "Let's look at our options. Three come to mind. First, storm the city walls, then meet the Alamanni wherever they happen to be. Second, abandon the siege and attack the Alamanni immediately. Third, divide our forces and do both at once." He paused. "If any of you have something to add, now would be a good time to speak up. We must stop the Alamanni, but if we abandon the siege, we'd allow Aureolus and his army to escape. He might even attack our rear. On the other hand, he could take his army west to join with Postumus—that was his original plan."

"Or maybe he'd just march straight to Rome," Claudius interjected. "The Senate would be forced to declare him emperor."

"That too! In sum, then, abandoning the siege might get Aureolus out of Mediolanum, but the consequences are," Gallienus rubbed his chin, "disagreeable." There was a pause. "Have you come up with anything yet, Heraclianus?"

"The 13th of September," Heraclianus looked up from his calculations. "We'd have to leave that day in order to reach Verona a day ahead of the Alamanni."

Gallienus frowned. "A rather tight schedule."

"The Alamanni could advance more slowly," Heraclianus added with a shrug. "Or, they might move more quickly than I've assumed."

"It was you who suggested splitting our forces before the

battle at the Nestos River, Heraclianus. Do you recommend that approach now?"

"No, I don't."

"Why not?"

"Because I estimate Aureolus has about twelve thousand men—nearly as many as we do. He has roughly twice as many legionaries and half as many cavalry."

"You can't afford to lose either engagement," Attalus growled. "Splitting your forces may cause you to lose both." He nodded his head, leaned back, and folded his arms across his chest.

"He's right," Claudius agreed. "A siege defeat would destroy the army's morale, and embolden Aureolus. If we lost many men, it would cripple our offensive capability against the Alamanni."

"Are there any other suggestions?" Gallienus surveyed his staff. Each one shook his head. "Last night, as I was thinking about this problem," He noticed the amused expressions on his generals' faces. "Yes, I know that may come as a surprise to some of you, but I came to the same impasse. We must turn back the Alamanni, we can't leave Aureolus in Mediolanum, and we don't have enough men to deal with both simultaneously. However, perhaps we can use the Alamanni invasion to get the troops we need. About half of Aureolus' men are from Rhaetia. It's their families who have suffered for Aureolus' decision to strip the province of its defenders when he put his personal ambition above their welfare. That news alone may result in a mutiny among those troops, or at least a mass desertion. But since we can't leave any of the enemy at our rear, we must get all of the troops out, and quickly. I think the Alamanni invasion may convince the rest of the troops to abandon Aureolus, too. After all, it's an attack on Rome. But they all need assurance of their safety. I can do that with a decree: a general amnesty for joining us to repel the invaders."

Claudius and Aurelian stiffened and briefly exchanging glances. There was a moment of silence before Gallienus added, "I could use an extra twelve thousand men to fight the Alamanni, and would prefer not to destroy Mediolanum in order to get them. That's why I'm suggesting an amnesty. I'm sure if their safety were guaranteed, the troops and Aureolus would come out."

"Forgive Aureolus?" Claudius erupted.

The outburst surprised Heraclianus. He had never seen Claudius react so strongly. In fact, he had hardly ever seen him react at all before. Heraclianus wondered how Gallienus would respond, but Gallienus seemed to have expected this.

"Yes, Claudius. If we had more time, I could wait for the soldiers to hand Aureolus over, but we don't have more time. The quickest solution is to proclaim a general amnesty… including Aureolus."

"It might be the quickest solution," Claudius protested, "but it's not the right one!"

"Yes," Aurelian agreed. "You've got to get Aureolus out of the city, then kill him!"

"Or kill him inside the city," Claudius said. "It doesn't matter, so long as he's dead. But no amnesty for Aureolus!" Claudius pounded a fist onto the table.

"If you let him out of your sight after pardoning him, he might flee to Postumus and take as many of the soldiers with him as he could," Aurelian pointed out.

"You've beaten each of them in battles before," Attalus observed, "but imagine fighting against both of them on the same battlefield, especially if Aureolus took some of your soldiers with him!"

"Or, he might sabotage our efforts against the Alamanni," Aurelian continued. "I'd personally be very uncomfortable having a traitor in our midst."

"Look how Aureolus repaid you for trusting him a second time." Claudius said.

"Why don't you proclaim your amnesty and then put a knife in Aureolus' belly when he comes out?" Attalus asked. "That would take care of everything."

"A practical solution, yes," Gallienus agreed. "But I can't kill Aureolus after I've offered amnesty to everyone. I'd lose my credibility forever." He smiled at Claudius and Aurelian. "I'm not saying I'd guarantee Aureolus a long and comfortable life." He hoped this remark would mollify them a bit. But Claudius' and Aurelian's faces remained stonily hostile. *Their feelings about Aureolus and how I've treated him haven't changed. I must proceed very carefully now.* He turned to his Praetorian Prefect. "You've said nothing about this amnesty idea, Heraclianus. Have you an opinion on the matter?"

"Storming the city will produce casualties on both sides—losses could be severe. Amnesty would be a good thing if it brought the soldiers out and saved the city from destruction."

"We're essentially agreed on that point," Gallienus said. "I'm interested in your thoughts about how to do that."

"It would be harder to convince the soldiers if Aureolus was excluded from the amnesty, they'd have to revolt against him, and it would probably take longer for a revolt to happen."

"I want a straight opinion, Heraclianus. Do you think amnesty should include Aureolus, or not?"

"Including him might get the troops out fast enough to save Verona," Heraclianus hedged, "and then again, it might not. Either way, the issues that Claudius and Aurelian mentioned are valid and should also be considered."

"Am I to take that as a 'yes' or as a 'no?'" Gallienus snapped.

Heraclianus hesitated. "Well… I think…"

"Why don't you make your offer vague enough so there's room for doubt, or uncertainty about Aureolus?" Attalus suggested to Gallienus. They all stared at him, surprised.

"His response," Attalus pointed at Heraclianus, "made me think of it."

"Yes!" Heraclianus was annoyed by Attalus' interruption, but grateful for his idea. "Offer them amnesty, and say the offer expires the night before we storm the walls."

"Give them an expiration date," Claudius added. "But don't tell them we plan to storm the city the next day! They know what we intend to do. We don't want to tell them when we plan to do it."

"All right," Gallienus took a deep breath and exhaled. "We'll do it that way: an amnesty offer to all the troops. Aureolus can read what he wants into that. It will expire the night of the ninth. If the offer isn't accepted by then, we'll attack Mediolanum on the morning of the tenth. That's settled then?" He looked at his generals; they all nodded. "Any other thoughts?"

"How will you get word about the invasion into the city?" Aurelian asked. "They probably won't believe it at first. In any event, it will take some time for the news and its significance to circulate among the men."

"And Aureolus will do everything he can to discredit the story," Heraclianus added.

"The only person they'll believe is the messenger who brought the news to me, unless we have somebody who actually fled before the invaders?" he looked hopefully at the generals. No one responded. "If anyone shows up in any of your camps, send him to me immediately. Meanwhile I'll have the messenger deliver the news himself," Gallienus rose from his chair and stretched. "Now… if you'll excuse me…"

"Oh, I almost forgot," Attalus said, fishing through a pouch on his belt. "When we brought you Statius' head on a spear the other day, one of Naulobatus' men found this coin in his purse." He produced a silver denarius and handed it to Gallienus, who sat back in his chair. "I've only just come by it," he said while Gallienus inspected the coin. Gallienus turned the coin over and frowned. "Is it important?" Attalus asked.

"Yes," Gallienus replied, handing the coin to Claudius. "Aureolus has given up on Postumus' help."

"He's minting coins with his own image on them," Claudius explained to the others after quickly glancing at the coin, then handing it to Aurelian.

"That means he's desperate and more likely to flee now," Heraclianus said, finally looking at the coin himself. "This is significant, Attalus!"

"Why didn't I think of this earlier?" Gallienus exclaimed. "I've changed my mind."

"About the amnesty?" Claudius asked hopefully.

Gallienus shook his head. "No. What did the Greeks do at Troy when they couldn't take the city?"

"They built the horse," Aurelian said.

"And sailed their ships out of sight," Heraclianus said, a

smile of understanding crossed his lips.

"They left the horse to get into the city by trickery, because the Trojans weren't planning to leave their city," Gallienus explained to Attalus and Naulobatus. "But Aureolus wants an opportunity to do just that."

"So if we appear to withdraw our soldiers, Aureolus may think we've withdrawn to fight the Alamanni." Claudius nodded.

"Then there's a good chance he'll seize that opportunity to try an escape," Aurelian added.

"Especially now that he's given up hoping for help from Postumus," Gallienus finished the thought.

"That could work," Heraclianus agreed. "In fact, I think it probably would."

"Your wish and mine may very well be granted," Gallienus nodded at Claudius and Aurelian, "if we can get Aureolus out of the city. Send word to the cavalry wings guarding the north and west routes out of Mediolanum, Claudius. Tell them to withdraw to the main camp tomorrow." Gallienus thought for a moment. "On second thought, have the western wing join the southern wing, then move them both further south. Their withdrawal will give more credence to our claim that the Alamanni have invaded. But leave just enough men for lookouts, to let us know where and when Aureolus moves."

"What's your plan for the two wings to the south?" Claudius asked.

"They'll prevent Aureolus from reaching Rome," Gallienus said. "Claudius, I want you to command that very important force. Withdraw to Ticinum. You'll have to be on your guard, ready to move at a moment's notice to intercept Aureolus. That should please you." He smiled at Claudius. "We'll begin moving the main camp east in two days."

"Are we still planning to storm Mediolanum on the 10th, assuming there's been no movement from the city by then?" Claudius asked.

"Yes, and if that happens, you'll need to return quickly." Claudius nodded.

Gallienus rose from his chair again. "Now, I think it's time to prepare my message for the soldiers inside Mediolanum."

After the men had left, he entered his tent and sat by the small table that served as a desk. He exhaled deeply and his shoulders sagged. *Postumus in revolt, Aureolus in revolt, Zenobia's allegiance questionable, and now two barbarian armies invading the empire.* He rested his chin on his fist, and closed his eyes, trying to get his thoughts in order.

He considered his most recent danger, the Alamanni invasion—one more crisis caused by Aureolus' revolt and, indirectly, by his own misplaced trust in Aureolus. Gallienus took the silver coin, recently minted by Aureolus, from his pouch. His fingers rubbed over its surface while he stared at Aureolus' face on the obverse side. *My gifted general and former friend, you've overreached this time, and you're causing me no end of trouble!* He turned the coin over and looked at the image of a man on horseback. Above the image he read the words "Loyalty of the Cavalry." Gallienus' jaw tightened. *Loyalty? They betrayed me too!* He stuffed the coin into his pouch. *How could one flawed decision cause so many problems?*

He took another deep breath, exhaled slowly, and reached back to massage the tension in his neck. Finding no relief, he rolled his head in a circle, moved his shoulders forward and back, massaged his temples and tried rolling his head again, and then shook his head. *One thing at a time*, he thought. *The Alamanni won't threaten Verona for a few days. Part of the army is moving in their direction. The rest is packed and ready to move at a moment's notice. My immediate problem is to end this siege and add twelve thousand men to my forces. If this amnesty offer succeeds, I could accomplish that.* He took his stylus and tablet of wax and began composing his message to the army inside Mediolanum.

10-4

Issues and Offers

Gallienus' Camp Outside Mediolanum

04 September, 268

Claudius sat outside his tent reading recent dispatches, pausing occasionally to refer to a map spread across his small table. Movement nearby caught his attention. He glanced up to see Heraclianus approaching, then sat back and waited.

"I just received an update on the Goth's progress," Claudius pointed at the scroll on the table when Heraclianus arrived. Heraclianus looked down at the scroll and map that lay between them but made no comment. "It came by ship—much faster than over land. The Goths reached Appolonia on the 21st. By now they must be heading northwest, along the coast road toward Dyrrhachium. They'll have to go on to Scodra," he pointed at the map, two cities beyond Dyrrhachium, "before they have a chance to turn north. If they don't do that, they'll have to continue along the Dalmatian coast road." He looked up from the map. "Maybe we'll get to fight them sooner than we expected. Unless they fight the Alamanni instead."

"Actually, that's why I'm here," Heraclianus said, glad for the opening provided to him.

Claudius studied Heraclianus' expression while he rolled up the scroll. "What's on your mind?"

"Yesterday during our meeting, Gallienus said something that I thought you might help me understand."

"Remind me of the conversation."

"We were talking about the possibility of the Alamanni joining with the Goths and having to fight a combined army. But Gallienus interrupted me saying it wasn't something I'd have to worry about."

"I remember now," Claudius nodded. "What of it?"

"Did he mean I shouldn't worry about it now, or was he implying that I wouldn't be in a position to worry about it later on?"

"I see how his comment could have concerned you." Claudius put the scroll aside and began to roll his map.

"You're closer to him now than I am," Heraclianus said, a trace of bitterness mixed with anxiety in his voice. "If he intended to replace me, then I expect you'd be aware of it."

Claudius carefully placed the map beside the scroll and sat for a moment before again glancing at Heraclianus' worried face.

"Look, there's been animosity between us ever since you returned from your trip to see Zenobia."

"You displaced me while I was away!"

"It's not a position that I sought, Heraclianus! Nor is it one that I seek to relinquish. But perhaps I can help you to keep from losing your position."

"He's thinking of that?"

"I doubt he'd do anything now, with the siege as well as another invasion to deal with. But you must know Gallienus was unhappy about Salonina's defense at the northern camp. She was almost abducted after all!"

"I considered the camp to be well-protected. I inspected it myself."

"We've already been through all that." Claudius nodded at him with a thin smile.

Heraclianus felt it was a look of disdain, not sympathy.

"Think about it, Heraclianus. Gallienus would have had to negotiate with Aureolus for her release, and that would probably have involved safe passage for him into Gallia." He watched Heraclianus' face while he considered the implications.

"How can I convince him not to relieve me?"

"Show him you're competent." *How many times do I have to tell him that?* "Gallienus moves people up and down according to merit. That's why we're all where we are."

Heraclianus licked his lips. "Would you speak to him, on my behalf?"

Claudius paused for a moment, considering this request. "I'll do something more useful than that. What's going on now is important. I'll give you a list of things you should do before we leave on the Alamanni campaign."

A messenger appeared suddenly at his side. "General Claudius, sir. If you'll excuse me, the emperor wishes to speak to his Praetorian Prefect."

Claudius glanced from the messenger to Heraclianus. Color had drained from his face, but he recovered quickly. He mumbled a farewell and turned to the messenger. "I'll come with you now."

As they walked away Claudius shook his head. *That man needs much more than a list to get him through the next few days*, he thought, before returning to his dispatches.

05 September, 268

Three horsemen rode slowly down the road that approached Mediolanum's northern gate. Earlier in the day heralds had circled the city telling men on the walls to expect an address to them before midday. When the horsemen were just beyond arrow range, they paused long enough to be certain that the sentries would allow them to come closer without firing on them. Then, one of men nudged his horse and rode deliberately forward. The others followed. Even though the morning was gray and humid, the leader wore a purple cape that covered his shoulders and draped over the back of his stallion. The man to his left was a messenger who carried a white flag tied to the end of an upright spear. The man to his right was a herald who held a scroll. They stopped a stone's throw from the gate.

Gallienus regarded the faces of the men gathered at the top of the city wall for a long moment before nodding to the herald. "The Emperor wishes to deliver a message to the soldiers inside the city," the herald said loudly to his audience on the wall. "This message," he briefly held the scroll high over his head "will be left for you to post inside the city for everyone to see." Slowly he lowered the scroll then unrolled it with a flourish. He looked up at the men on the wall before beginning to read in a loud, clear voice.

From: Publius Egnatius Gallienus, Augustus
To: Soldiers of Rome
The Alamanni have invaded Rhaetia. This news came to us two days ago, when the Alamanni had reached Sabiona and were heading south toward Verona. Those of you who came to Mediolanum from Rhaetia have only Aureolus to blame for leaving your families unprotected. You are all asked to abandon this

futile attempt at revolt. Furthermore, if you all join now in the defense of the empire, to defeat the Alamanni who are threatening Rome, we offer you amnesty from participating in this revolt. Join us to confront the real enemy.

Those of you who came from Rhaetia will be allowed to return there—after you have helped defeat the Alamanni. We must respond to this invasion soon.

That gives me little time to await your response. Therefore, this offer of amnesty will expire at the end of four days' time. If you refuse to defend your empire, you will be considered traitors and will be treated as such.

Again, this offer of amnesty will expire at the end of four days."

Gallienus studied the men staring back at him from the top of the wall as the herald slowly wrapped up the scroll. He could not tell if their silence was due to the shock of the news or if they did not believe what they had just been told. "Is there anyone among you brave enough to leave the city walls and receive this message from my hand?" he called to them. When no one came, he held a hand out to the herald and accepted the scroll from him. He spoke quietly to the man on his other side, who tossed his spear onto the ground and took the scroll. "This man," Gallienus pointed to the messenger, "brought me the news of the Alamanni invasion. He saw it himself and can vouch for the truth of this announcement. You can talk with him yourselves." Gallienus and the herald then turned, and rode slowly back to their waiting companions.

06 September, 268

Claudius maneuvered his horse through the organized confusion of military camp while men prepared for a march just after daybreak. As he rode, orderlies approached him seeking answers or decisions to a never-ending stream of issues and problems. He found Heraclianus sitting on a chair where his tent had been pitched, writing. A crowd of tribunes hovered around him. Beyond that group, legionnaires were dismantling and packing everything.

"Good morning, Heraclianus. What a scene out there, like market day in the provinces! It's time we were on the road again. From the problems I've been dealing with, you'd think we'd never moved camp before."

The Praetorian Prefect looked up, surprised. "I thought you'd be gone by now."

Clearly he wishes I were! Aloud Claudius said, "I've drawn up the list I promised you. Make sure the following things are taken care of." He held out a paper.

Heraclianus nodded, took the paper, glanced at it briefly then set it on a disorganized pile of papers at the edge of his table.

This sudden indifference concerned Claudius. "I have one suggestion," he said. "Gallienus is desperate to end this siege so he can march full strength against the Alamanni. If you can get Aureolus out, the soldiers will come out. It's their families who have been killed, and the soldiers are being offered amnesty. I can assure you that whatever has happened between you and Gallienus will be forgiven, if you get Aureolus out of the city and kill him."

"I know what my objectives are."

Claudius stared intently at Heraclianus. *He's a different person today.* "I hope so. In any event, I'll be rejoining you on the 10th when we storm the city, assuming Aureolus hasn't fled by then."

"He may not have to flee. I overheard Gallienus talking to his secretary. If the soldiers don't come out in four days, then Gallienus plans to send Aureolus a secret, but official, letter assuring him of his inclusion in the amnesty."

"You heard him say that?" Claudius exploded. "You can't let that happen!" He poked a finger in Heraclianus' shoulder to emphasize his point. "You must lure him out first."

Heraclianus smoothed over the spot that Claudius had been poking, then looked up. "Is there anything else?" Heraclianus turned away before seeing Claudius' expression. He had a hard time concealing his satisfaction at being able to annoy his nemesis.

* * *

Later that morning, after the sun illuminated distant walls of Mediolanum, Claudius intercepted Aurelian as he rode out of camp to inspect siege equipment. "I'm off to Ticinum before noon," he said, to explain his sudden appearance.

Aurelian looked quickly at Claudius then signaled to one of his tribunes. "Ride ahead," he ordered, "and tell the men to begin pulling the siege engines back. Tell them we intend to post guards on the equipment before we withdraw." The man saluted and rode away. He and Claudius moved ahead of the others. "Aureolus would expect us to do that," he said.

"Do you think those men," Claudius gestured with his chin to the city in front of him, "will come out without a fight?"

"I'm not sure they're convinced the amnesty offer is genuine," Aurelian said when they were comfortably alone.

"I've just spoken with Heraclianus."

"And?"

"He put my list of suggestions on top of a pile of papers that I'm sure he isn't planning to read."

Aurelian nodded.

"He told me he'd overheard Gallienus talking with one of his secretaries," Claudius continued, "and said Gallienus was planning to offer a letter of amnesty to Aureolus, the day after the deadline passed!"

"That's what Heraclianus says," Aurelian cautioned. "That would mean Gallienus had deliberately chosen to act against our expressed concerns. He said he wouldn't do that."

"Actually, he just implied that he wouldn't."

"Any chance Heraclianus is mistaken? Or could he be misleading you?" Aurelian asked.

"What would he gain?"

"Maybe he's trying to create doubt or insecurity in your mind. Or," he added voicing his real guess, "maybe he just wants to distract you."

Claudius considered Aurelian's comment, then shrugged. "If that's what he was trying to do, it succeeded." He paused. "That reminds me, I've been putting a lot of pressure on Heraclianus. I want him to get Aureolus out of that city and kill him. If Heraclianus thinks Gallienus intends to replace him, he might feel compelled to act himself, before being disgraced even more. So if he thought Gallienus might bring charges against him for failing to defend Salonina at the northern camp…"

"Is Gallienus actually planning to do either of those things?" Aurelian looked startled.

"Who knows?" Claudius shrugged. "We do know he's disappointed with some of Heraclianus' performance. So does Heraclianus. The point is to get him motivated to act decisively against Aureolus. Heraclianus has to kill Aureolus before he gets an amnesty letter from Gallienus, assuming there actually is one. But I'm concerned about Heraclianus. All this may be too much for him. I don't trust his judgment."

Aurelian looked away for a moment. They were approaching the siege engines. Soon they would be within hailing distance of the sentries.

"A lot can happen in all the confusion that's going on right now," Claudius concluded.

"I'll keep a close eye on him," Aurelian assured him. "If anything happens, I'll send word to you right away."

"I'm glad you'll be here." Claudius reached out to Aurelian and they grasped arms in friendship. "In any case, I'll see you in four days." Then he reined his horse around and began riding south toward Ticinum.

* * *

"I just overheard some legionnaires talking about an Alamanni invasion!" the tall, slim, messenger from the Senate said to Heraclianus. "Is it true?"

"So we've been told." Heraclianus sat inside his tent, baggage neatly piled along one of the sides, and regarded the man's confident face, illuminated only by the candle that flickered on

the table between them. *Why has he come back now?* he wondered.

"It was quite a surprise to find your camp deserted," the messenger smiled. "Fortunately, the men guarding the siege engines
told me where to find you."

"We're moving east to get closer to the Alamanni." Heraclianus said. *No need to tell him the rest of the plan.*

"The Senate doesn't know about this latest disaster yet. Is
Gallienus trying to suppress the news?"

"We only just heard it ourselves. The information must have
been sent to Rome already."

"You don't know?"

"That wasn't my job," Heraclianus said tersely.

"Shouldn't it be?" the messenger asked, arching an eyebrow.
"I mean, isn't that part of the Praetorian Prefect's duties?"

"Gallienus doesn't see it that way."

The messenger sensed Heraclianus' bitterness. "We in the
Senate have a higher regard for your abilities, Marcus Aurelius
Heraclianus. I understand you've been under a lot of pressure
during this siege."

"We've all been under a lot of pressure."

"But you especially. And it seems you were unfairly singled
out, from what I understand," he sympathized.

What's he referring to? Heraclianus thought back over the
last couple weeks. *It must be the meeting when we learned the
siege towers had been destroyed!* The messenger was regarding
him expectantly, waiting, it seemed, for him to understand the
reference and its implications.

"We think you were blamed for failures that could have happened to anyone."

"How do you know about that?"

"We have our sources."

*Who at that meeting, or close enough to eavesdrop, was
sending information to these senators?* Heraclianus wondered.
The thought of being spied on was unnerving.

"Have you had a chance to consider my proposal from our
previous meeting?" the messenger asked.

"I've had a lot of other things on my mind—the siege, the Alamanni invasion—we just learned that Aureolus is issuing coins claiming himself to be emperor now." Heraclianus frowned, suddenly suspicious. "Did the Senate have anything to do with this current revolt by Postumus and Aureolus?"

"I really couldn't say." The messenger shrugged and held his palms up toward Heraclianus.

Wouldn't say is probably more correct. They stared at each other, each waiting for the other to continue. Finally, Heraclianus asked, "What, exactly, was your proposal again?"

"That we'd be willing to support you as the next emperor—provided that you allowed senators and their sons to enter the army as officers again. Indeed, any action you might choose to take would be a good thing for the empire." The messenger let the thought hang in the air. "It would have our backing." He watched Heraclianus' face closely.

He's expecting a commitment from me! Heraclianus realized in the silence that followed. *Am I willing to take that risk? Do I want a group of senators, whom I don't even know, to realize I'm discussing treason with one of their representatives?* "You're asking a lot from me," Heraclianus said. "I'll have to give it some thought."

"But you won't rule it out?"

"I'll think about it."

"By the way," the messenger smiled, rising from his chair, "how many Praetorian Guards do you have here, under your direct command?"

"Enough," Heraclianus replied. "Why do you ask?"

"Just wondering. Good night, Marcus Aurelius Heraclianus."

10-5
A Decision and a Visit
07 September, 268

"You'll be in charge while I'm gone," Gallienus told

Heraclianus earlier that morning. "Claudius is at Ticinum. Aurelian is inspecting siege equipment for me."

Heraclianus was surprised at this news, but it was Gallienus' appearance that made him gape. "I knew nothing about this," he stammered. "Let me arrange an escort for you."

Gallienus laughed at Heraclianus' amazed expression. "That won't be necessary. I'm going with them." Gallienus waved at Attalus, Pipa, and twenty Marcomanni warriors. "That's why I dressed as a Marcomanni warrior myself. We didn't get a chance to inspect the culvert in the north wall last time we were there. I still want to know if I can use it as an entryway if we have to attack the city. I think a small band of Marcomanni will attract less attention than a Roman detachment. I'll be back this evening."

As soon as Gallienus had left, a dispute arose between Naulobatus and his Roman liaison officer. Heraclianus was called to the nearby Heruli campsite to settle the matter. *Better to work out these misunderstandings quickly*, Heraclianus thought, during his ride back to the Roman camp. *We don't need a disgruntled barbarian ally during our next battle. They can be so temperamental! A pity we have to work with them at all.*

His thoughts returned to Gallienus and his own prospects. *Gallienus obviously trusts me with this position, as he has with others in the past. But can I be sure he won't dismiss me after these emergencies are over, just because of a few unfortunate issues, as Claudius implied? If I killed Aureolus and delivered his army to Gallienus, would that assure my position? If Claudius is telling the truth about being dismissed, the stakes are enormous. But how do I capture or kill Aureolus? Maybe Claudius is wrong about me losing my post, but can I afford to take that chance?* His thoughts were interrupted by the challenge of the guards at the main gate. Heraclianus had demanded that everyone approaching the gate be stopped and challenged, despite the fact that the guards all recognized him. He gave the password and casually acknowledged their salutes as he entered camp. He thought of his options ranging from doing all in his power to please Gallienus to doing all in his power to eliminate him. *If I try to remove Gallienus and fail, death and dishonor are certain. If I do nothing, both outcomes are still possible. At least if I act now, I'd have the Senate's backing. Fleeting though their support might be, it could be enough. Maybe that messenger from the Senate was right: what's good for me is also good for the empire!*

* * *

I should do it now, while Claudius is away, Heraclianus thought while he walked down the first row of Praetorian Guards, lined up for late-morning inspection. Long ago he had discovered that daily inspections were a good time to think. Although surrounded by people, no one ever interrupted him. Partway down the second row something caught his attention. He stopped to examine the man in front of him. "There's rust on your helmet," he growled before continuing down the ranks. *Maybe I could even offer Aureolus an alliance. Of course it would have to be a temporary thing.* He paused in front of a man in the second row, could find nothing wrong with his armor or appearance, then moved on. *Aureolus could be useful against the Alamanni, since I'll have to eliminate Claudius and Aurelian.* He smiled briefly at the thought, then decided to compliment the man in front of him. Near the end of the last row of Praetorians another thought came to him. He stopped and frowned at the unfortunate Praetorian who happened to be there. A flicker of anxiety showed in the man's eyes, but he remained rigid and outwardly calm. *But what if Aureolus comes out of the city before amnesty expires? I suppose I'd have to kill him before he got to Gallienus.* Heraclianus adjusted a strap on the man's uniform and nodded grudging approval of the rest of his appearance.

The inspection completed, he spoke to the man in charge of this unit. "On the whole, they look fairly good. Drill them this afternoon. I want everyone ready for anything that might happen in the next few days." He returned the man's salute, turned on his heel, and walked toward his tent. Until then he had not noticed the change in the weather. High, wispy clouds were moving across previously clear sky. One more uncertainty. *Will it rain before we assault the city? Rain could fill the moat and soften the ground. I hate fighting in the mud!* Heraclianus walked briskly back to his tent to complete his routine administrative duties. He sat in front of his tent and reviewed several dispatches, absent-mindedly waving away the flies that buzzed around his face, then issued a string of orders to his tribunes, and finally sat back to consider more important matters.

The amnesty offer expires tomorrow night, the 8th, and we plan to storm the city on the morning of the 10th, three days from now. Claudius won't return from Ticinum before the assault. His group will move directly up to Mediolanum. Then, we need to de-part on the 13th, to reach Verona before Alamanni can attack the city. I think the night of the 9th should give me time to put a plan in motion. If I blamed Aureolus or some of his soldiers for the death during a night skirmish, that would deflect suspicion from me. And if no one found the body for a while, then so much the better. I might have to charge someone with negligence, but, then again, I might not. He stretched and rubbed an ache in his shoulders. *I could do it myself—no, better to find someone else to take the blame if necessary. Using the Praetorians would immediately place me under suspicion, just like that senators' representative hinted. Maybe the Senate would even accuse me of complicity later, so they could nominate someone else.* He scratched his beard and stared vacantly ahead. Who else could I use?

A tribune came up behind him. "Excuse me, general."

"What is it?" Heraclianus jerked, startled by the interruption.

"A man wishes to speak with you."

"Did he give you his name?"

"It's Cecropius, sir."

"What's he want?"

"He didn't say, but he seemed most agitated."

"All right, I'll see him."

Cecropius approached Heraclianus, saluted smartly and stood stiffly at attention. Heraclianus shuffled through some dispatches on his table while he thought about Cecropius— *something of a bar room brawler, and he drinks and gambles more than the average legionary.* The anxiety on Cecropius' face and his fidgeting told Heraclianus that something serious both-ered him. "You don't look well, Cecropius. Are you ill?"

"I wish it were only that, sir."

Heraclianus waited for a direct answer, but quickly grew impatient when none was forthcoming. "Well then, why are you here?"

Cecropius took a deep breath. "I've gotten into a bit of trouble."

"Can't your legate help you?"

"It's trouble with the legate, sir. That's part of the problem."

"Gambling involved?"

Cecropius nodded.

"Drinking?"

"That too."

"I'm busy, Cecropius. Just tell me what happened!"

"The legate asked if he could join us in a game of dice last night. Naturally we agreed. After a few throws, I was convinced the legate was cheating. By then we'd all been drinking for some time. I may have said a few things I regret now. When the legate called me a liar, I jumped up and lunged at him, didn't even think about it. The others told me they grabbed me before I got close to him."

"Did you actually threaten him?"

"I don't remember exactly."

"But your legate says you did." Heraclianus realized that Cecropius faced serious disciplinary actions. "I assume he's planning to bring charges against you. For what, exactly?"

"I don't know, sir."

"What do you want me to do about it?"

"You're my only hope, sir. I've got no recourse with the legate! I thought, hoped, you might be able to help me somehow, considering my record of fighting and all that?"

"Battlefield fighting as opposed to bar room fighting, I assume?" Heraclianus remarked dryly. But Cecropius was in no frame of mind to appreciate a play on words. Heraclianus studied him with sudden interest as an idea came to him. *Maybe the goddess Fortuna brought this man to me at just this moment. He needs a favor—a big favor—and he commands a detachment of Dalmatian Horse, known for their loyalty to Gallienus.* He looked sternly at Cecropius. "Normally I don't interfere with disciplinary issues at lower levels." Cecropius shrunk perceptibly in front of him. "But perhaps I could get the charges against you reduced or dropped altogether—if you were to volunteer for a particularly dangerous assignment."

Relief and hope washed over Cecropius' face. "Name it, sir,"

Heraclianus leaned closer and spoke in a conspiratorial tone. "You've probably heard that the emperor hopes to lure Aureolus out of the city?" Cecropius nodded. "Well, I could use a group of horsemen, such as yours, who would be ready to intercept Aureolus if he tries to flee. It's my belief he'd be most likely to make his attempt at night. It could be a very dangerous assignment. Are you interested?"

"Count me in," Cecropius replied immediately, suddenly hopeful.

"Then I'll talk with your legate. I think I can convince him to drop or at least reduce the charges against you, since you've volunteered for a risky mission which is so important to the emperor. In the meantime, have your horsemen ready to respond to my summons on short notice." Cecropius smiled broadly, saluted, and departed. *I'll need to work a little more on Cecropius, but for now, let him think his problem is solved*, Heraclianus thought after the man had gone. He pondered details of how to manage Cecropius. Then, he went to speak with Cecropius' commanding officer.

08 September, 268

A pack of snarling wolves pursued an injured boar across a large meadow. Blood streamed from a gaping wound on the boar's flank. It mixed with dirt and branches as the boar desperately sought to evade its determined pursuers. The distance between wolves and boar narrowed as the boar grew weak from loss of blood. The lead wolf snapped at the boar's hind leg, but was still a step behind it. Before the wolf could try again, the boar veered right and dived into a dense thicket, quickly working itself into the heavy cover. The wolves circled the thicket searching for a way to get inside without encountering the boar's slashing tusks. Soon they grew restive and, ignoring their wounded prey, began snarling then fighting with each other. Several drew blood from their new adversaries.

Salonina opened her eyes to a gray light of dawn, drenched in sweat despite cool morning air. Instinctively, she reached for Gallienus before remembering he wasn't there. Her mood swung from loneliness and bitter disappointment to anger and back. She recalled him saying that today he would be reviewing plans for attacking city, then inspecting siege engines. She would not see him until their evening meal. As she washed and dressed, she wondered how to fill the day until she could share her dream with him. She picked unenthusiastically at breakfast. *Maybe a walk will take my mind off that dreadful nightmare.*

Soon Salonina started out with her guards walking ahead and her attendants trailing behind. Outside the camp she found a stream that disappeared into nearby woods and decided to follow it, over the objections of both her escorts and attendants. The solitude of the woods did not calm her. Thoughts still tumbled through her mind, each replaced rapidly by others: the dream's meaning, Gallienus with Pipa, the upcoming assault on Mediolanum, the future battle with Alamanni, then another confrontation with Goths. She felt anxious about her future and very much alone. "Please, Juno," Salonina whispered to the goddess who protected the women of Rome, "help me through this uncertain time."

She leaned over the bank and noticed several small fish nibbling at the plants along the edges. Then she glimpsed a raven's reflection in the water. Surprised, she looked up at the nearby treetops. A large bird gazed down on her. Unconcerned by her sudden movement, it cawed and flew lazily off into the woods ahead of her. Salonina watched it go. *Such odd behavior for a bird, so completely unafraid of me. Only Andrasta's raven acted like that! Could this bird possibly belong to her? Where should I go to find her? What should I do?* Then she relaxed and laughed at her own anxiety. *The raven found me. Andrasta will too*! Salonina fumbled in her pocket for a fig, left over from her morning meal. She took a small bite, and ate it slowly while she waited.

Before she had eaten half of her fig the raven reappeared,

swooping down suddenly to alight on a low branch a few feet in front of her. It cawed, flew to a more distant branch, and waited for Salonina to follow. The bird led Salonina, followed by her attendants, to a clearing in the woods where it perched on a bush in the clearing's center. This time it did not move when Salonina approached. She looked around expectantly. Giant oak trees rimmed the open space. The stream she had been following ran into the clearing's center, its water splashed among the rocks on a shallow sandy bottom. "We'll stop here," she said to her guards and attendants. "I'd like all of you to stay near the edge of the clearing, there." She pointed to the place from which they had just entered, then she sat on a large, flat rock beside the stream, close to the raven's bush. She searched the far side of the clearing for any signs of life. Only leaves rustling in the trees and gurgling water in the brook broke the stillness. A shiver ran through her. She wasn't sure if from the cool air or her anticipation.

Suddenly the raven flew off. The beating of its wings startled Salonina. The bird flew to the far edge of the clearing and vanished in the thicket beyond. Salonina stared at the place where the bird had disappeared, and began to wonder if she should have followed it, but finally a shape separated itself from the darkness of the surrounding forest. Salonina stood as a slender figure dressed in a brown, hooded cloak entered the clearing and walked slowly toward her, a raven perched on the person's shoulder. Salonina's guards sounded an alert but she held up her hand. "It's all right! I've been expecting someone." She glanced at the approaching figure and hoped that what she said was correct. "I want all of you to stay at the edge of the clearing and wait for me there," she repeated. The guards who had started forward hesitated. "Do it now!" she commanded. When satisfied that they were obeying her command, Salonina turned her full attention to the person approaching her. As the figure drew closer and slid back the hood, Salonina could see it was a woman, but not Andrasta. This woman was tall where Andrasta was short, her blond hair and blue eyes differed distinctly from Andrasta's red hair and piercing green eyes. "Who are you?" Salonina asked as the stranger cautiously approached her.

10-6
A Warning and a Curse
08 September, 268

"We saw each other outside Colonia Agrippina, five years ago," the woman said shyly, seemingly disappointed that she had not been recognized. "I am Domitia." She stretched out her hand. Salonina took her hand and peered at the ring. Her own profile was carved in chalcedony. She remembered it, and recalled giving a slave girl her freedom, and this ring, while in Colonia Agrippina years earlier. She studied this young woman's appearance. "I see a resemblance, but you look so different now!"

"Then I was dressed as a slave girl. Now I'm a Druid apprentice," she replied proudly.

"Then Andrasta is with you?"

Domitia nodded.

"What brought you here, now?"

"Early this year General Postumus planned to withdraw legions from his frontier and march south with them. We heard gossip about it in the market place before we fled Colonia Agrippina."

"You were driven away?" Salonina asked.

"Apparently the general learned of Andrasta's reputation as a seer and didn't want her speculating on his movements and intentions. Druids are outlawed by Roman law, so Andrasta feared for her safety."

"Where did you go?"

"Across the river from Moguntiacum. You call the area the Agri Decumates, but it's controlled by Alamanni now."

"But why are you here?" Salonina pressed Domitia.

"I had a disturbing and confusing dream about you and your husband, right after we learned of his victory over General Aureolus at Mediolanum. When I mentioned it, Andrasta asked if I had anything that once belonged to you. I showed her this ring.

Andrasta held it and sat with her eyes closed for a long time. When she returned the ring, she told me she'd had a premonition."

"About what?"

"That your husband was more in danger now, even after his victorious battle. I had to come and warn you," Domitia said. "You gave me my freedom; I wanted to help you if I could."

Salonina's eyes widened. "What sort of danger?"

Domitia wrung her hands. "I don't know, but I convinced Andrasta to come with me. I hope she can explain it to you."

"Thank you, Domitia!" Salonina paused to compose herself. "You've traveled a very long way on my behalf."

"It took nearly a month to get here and I used all the money I had saved to pay for food and lodging," Domitia said proudly.

"I'll see that you have enough to return home comfortably, and then some," Salonina assured her.

"You're most gracious, my lady!" Domitia's smile showed relief and gratitude, then concern. "Please don't reveal our identities or our location to anyone. Druids are outlawed…"

"Yes, you've already told me. I'll be discreet." Salonina looked around the clearing expectantly. "When will Andrasta come to me?"

"When I tell her it's safe to do so." Domitia turned and spoke softly to the raven. It hopped from Domitia's shoulder to her outstretched wrist, then flew to the spot where Domitia had first appeared.

Salonina sat back down on the flat rock beside the stream and waited. *What a coincidence that she came to me now! What will she say this time?*

"That depends on what you tell me."

Salonina's head snapped up to find Andrasta standing in front of her. *She still looks the same: barefoot, that spiraling triskele broach pinned on her white dress, her leather belt with the dagger, the pouch of herbs, and the other pouch with runes that I cast years ago.* "I'm so relieved you've come!"

Andrasta wordlessly let her brown cloak fall from her shoulders, and then tossed her hazelwood staff onto it. "Are you really? I never come when I don't see trouble in your future."

"Bad things did follow your last two visits," Salonina agreed after considering Andrasta's comment. "There was a revolt and my eldest son died. Then my husband was seriously wounded—during a different siege." Salonina sighed. "Both occasions involved Romans who betrayed my husband. Are you bringing me warnings of treachery or death?"

"Maybe neither, possibly both. I value loyalty in those around me," Andrasta said.

"So does my husband."

"For him the stakes are higher."

"Shouldn't loyalty be valued no matter what the stakes?"

"All the more so," Andrasta agreed, "but to work, loyalty has to flow both ways."

"Why doesn't it seem to work for my husband?"

"Actions must have consequences. Wrongs must be righted."

"Such as?"

"I see, for example, that the death of your second son remains unavenged and that the empire is still divided because of a trusted general's treachery. In a way," Andrasta paused to sit beside Salonina, "his present situation is curiously similar: another trusted general has revolted and now takes refuge behind the walls of a Roman city. Last time, the siege was called off..."

"But he was seriously wounded!"

"He recovered yet took no further action." Andrasta peered intently at Salonina. "How do you expect the current situation to unfold?"

"With my husband's victory, I hope!"

"Hope, unfortunately, won't make it happen."

"Preparations have been made to storm the city—if the amnesty offer isn't accepted." Salonina stopped, suddenly realizing what she had divulged.

"Amnesty?" Andrasta raised an eyebrow at Salonina before glancing at the raven. "Forgiveness, for whom?"

"For the men inside the city."

"Including Aureolus?"

"The idea was proposed, then rejected."

"Good. Otherwise there'd be two unavenged betrayals."

Andrasta gave Salonina a long, searching look.

"You had a premonition," Salonina suggested.

"Yes." Andrasta nodded almost imperceptibly. "But no more detail than Domitia has already told you."

"Did you cast any runes?"

"The answers made no sense to me." The raven cawed and flapped its wings. "But you've had a dream about it yourself, haven't you?" Andrasta knew the answer immediately from Salonina's expression. "Perhaps you should tell me about it."

"A pack of wolves was chasing a wounded boar…"

"How many?"

Salonina closed her eyes and searched her memory. "There was the leader and three or four others, maybe a few more. I don't remember exactly."

"An exact count would have been helpful." Andrasta wrinkled her forehead. "Do you remember anything about how the boar was wounded?"

"No."

Andrasta thought for a time. "Continue," she said finally.

"The boar hid in a thicket and when the wolves couldn't get at the boar, they began fighting among themselves. It was loud and violent—and I remember lots of blood!" Salonina shivered at the recollection and opened her eyes.

"Were they fighting among themselves, or did they all attack the leader?"

"Among themselves, but I woke up just after the fighting began."

"Then you didn't see how it ended?"

"No."

"A pity." Andrasta shook her head. "No other details, specifics you can recall?"

"Nothing more."

"Longer dreams give us more to work with," Andrasta mused, "but sometimes they present conflicting information. Short dreams, on the other hand, have fewer details, so conclusions are harder to draw." She looked at the raven, who clacked its bill at her, then looked back to Salonina. "What do you make of the dream?"

"I suppose the wolves are my husband's generals and the boar is Aureolus. But the fighting surprised and frightened me."

"That's what wolves do."

"Between themselves?"

"Has there been any disagreement between your husband and his generals recently?"

"Yes, over the amnesty issue," Salonina said, "but it was resolved."

"Perhaps not."

"Oh! Why do you say that?"

"Wolves turn on their leader if he doesn't show strength."

"Shouldn't they be grateful for their positions and the trust he's bestowed on them?"

"Your dream chose to represent them as a pack of wolves. It was not an accident that it came to you that way."

Salonina considered Andrasta's comments. "But the issues of trust and loyalty have plagued my husband for his whole reign. His father trusted no one. He trusts nearly everyone." She sighed and held up her hands. "What's different about this situation?"

The raven cawed repeatedly and shifted from one foot to the other on Andrasta's shoulder. She nodded at the raven before speaking to Salonina. "Perhaps suggesting amnesty for a traitor strikes one or more of his generals as an intolerable weakness." Andrasta cocked her head awaiting Salonina's answer.

"Is there nothing I can do to protect him?"

Andrasta heard the distress in Salonina's voice. She glanced at the raven, then at Salonina. "Have someone you trust with him at all times." Andrasta phrased the answer to suggest confidence, although her eyes showed something more troubling.

Who do I trust besides Gallienus? Some or all of the generals could be involved in a plot on his life. Attalus—and that Naulobatus--have no thoughts about becoming emperor, but either of them might choose to side with someone else if it were in their interests. Only Pipa has as much interest in Gallienus' welfare as I do, and for the same reasons. She frowned at the thought, but there seemed to be no one else. *Maybe I should suggest that he take Pipa with him during his battles. That will surprise him.* "Which one is the traitor—or is it all of them?"

"Your dream, as you relayed it to me, didn't answer that question."

"When would an attempt be made?"

Andrasta thought for a moment. "The boar was still in the thicket."

"Will it succeed?" Salonina asked, knowing that the dream provided no answer.

"It depends on your husband, and on those who might wish him harm."

"So my warning could prevent a plot from succeeding?"

"You may warn him," Andrasta nodded. "But that guarantees nothing. It is, after all, his fate, not yours."

"His fate is my fate," Salonina protested.

"If you like, I could cast a curse on anyone who tried to replace him by force."

"I'd like to prevent any attempt from succeeding!"

Andrasta was quiet for a time. The raven cawed. "Give him this amulet,." Andrasta said. She removed a wooden disc that hung from her neck on a thin cord. "It's oak, therefore it will give him strength and protection."

Salonina took the disc and turned it over in her hand. Carved characters and symbols on both sides were unfamiliar to her.

"I can't promise that nothing will happen, you understand."

"If someone does overthrow my husband," Salonina's face hardened, "let his reign be short, and let all involved pay dearly for their betrayal."

"That I can do." Andrasta smiled grimly. The raven cackled several times. "Yes. I'll summon Loki's help for this." She turned to Salonina. "He's one of the gods of the underworld. We call him the 'trickster.' This would be the sort of thing he'd enjoy." She walked to the far edge of the clearing, drew the knife from her belt and cut an oak sapling. Domitia joined her and built a small fire while Andrasta seemed to offer prayers of some kind. When she was finished, Andrasta knelt in front of the fire, cut the sapling into three pieces, and tossed them into the fire, one at a time. After watching them consumed by the flame, Andrasta rose and returned to where Salonina remained seated.

"If another dream comes to me, can I speak with you again?" she asked Andrasta.

"No."

Salonina looked hurt, then angry.

"We've accomplished what Domitia wished us to do, and our trip home will take nearly a month." She consulted a bronze disc that she'd just removed from a pouch on her belt.

"What's that?"

"A Celtic calendar." Andrasta held it out for Salonina to inspect. "We're at this point," she indicated a spot on the outermost circle. Salonina studied the markings but they were meaningless to her. "And with luck, we'll arrive home here," Andrasta pointed to the word "Samhain" also written along the outer rim, "just before the celebrations begin."

"I remember Domitia's description of Samhain," Salonina said. "A closing of the old year and the opening of a new one. She said it was a dangerous time when doors between the worlds of the living and of the dead are open and the dead sometimes walk among you!"

"There is a brief bringing together of the past, present, and future times," Andrasta agreed, then paused. "What Domitia told you was part of it. But it's also a celebration when we gather the fruits of the past year and give thanks for the harvest."

"She said it was also a time that one might know the future."

"People often say they wish to know their future, but they're not always pleased to hear it."

Salonina understood Andrasta's meaning and asked no further questions. "I'll get the money I promised for your trip home from the Praetorian Prefect at once."

Andrasta nodded. "Domitia will accompany you to your camp dressed as a slave girl. Please see that no one follows her when she departs."

* * *

Salonina went directly to Heraclianus, interrupting his routine business without apology. "Leave us," she ordered his tribunes. "I wish to speak to the Praetorian Prefect in confidence." She held up a hand when Heraclianus was about to object. "This will only take a short time, and I want it done immediately."

Heraclianus, unaccustomed to seeing the empress so assertive, decided not to protest. "My time is yours my lady." He tried to look amiable.

"Excellent." Salonina ignored his niceties. "I've just completed a session with a," She paused; she had to be careful here. "with a prophet, and I want to give him money for his trip home."

"How much does he want?"

"One-hundred and fifty denarii."

"That's two months' salary for a legionary!" Heraclianus exclaimed.

"Soldiers aren't paid for their prophesies, Heraclianus. Must I bring this matter to my husband's attention?"

"He's not in camp right now." Heraclianus was unnerved by Salonina's determined expression and sighed. "Very well. Where did he come from?"

"Across the river from Moguntiacum."

"Land controlled by the Alamanni now!"

"So I've been told."

This isn't a normal seer, Heraclianus realized, *nor is he likely even Roman. Would he have any information about the Alamanni invasion—or what's happening with Postumus?* "Where is he now?" Heraclianus asked casually. *Maybe I could take him into custody for questioning.* "I might like to speak with him myself."

"I doubt he'd agree to see you," Salonina replied, immediately suspicious. "It was a special favor to me."

"How did he know where to find you?" Heraclianus' expression hid his disappointment.

"He came to where the emperor was, knowing I'd be there too."

"It's interesting that he came to you at this particular time. Did you summon him?"

"He had a premonition."

"A premonition?" Heraclianus arched his eyebrows. "What did he tell you?"

"That my husband was in great danger." Salonina held Heraclianus' gaze, searching for some reaction.

"Indeed!" Heraclianus stared back. *How much does she actually know?* "And what will you do with this information?"

"I'll speak with my husband about it tonight at dinner."

"Of course." Heraclianus stroked his beard and swallowed hard. "I'll have the money sent to you after the midday meal"

Salonina scowled. "Not later, Heraclianus, now! He intends to leave for home immediately. Give me the money so I can pay him and let him be on his way."

After Salonina departed with the money, Heraclianus sat lost in thought, unmindful of tribunes again hovering around him. *Salonina's behavior was abrupt and unfriendly—most uncharacteristic of her. Perhaps I could intercept this seer at the gate as he's trying to leave.* He shook his head. *I don't even know what this person looks like. What could he have told her? It might not affect my plans at all, but I can't afford to take that chance!*

10-7
A Dinner Conversation
08 September, 268

Heraclianus sat at a small table in front of the headquarters tent while organized chaos of camp life swirled around him. Messengers had been bringing a continuous stream of information and requests. A centurion led his legionaries up the main road back into the campsite, calling out a marching cadence. He cursed one of his soldiers as they marched by Heraclianus, causing him to glance up out of curiosity. A merchant squeezed past the soldiers with a cart full of noisy chickens. Two legates, deep in conversation, frowned at several slaves struggling to get by them with a large amphora of wine.

Heraclianus took a break from reading dispatches and

issuing orders. "I spoke with your legate yesterday." He frowned at Cecropius, who stood at attention on the other side of the table from him. "You didn't tell me you'd pulled a knife out of your boot before you lunged at him!"

A flicker of horror flashed across Cecropius' face. "I did what?"

"You may be unclear about what happened during that card game, but your legate hasn't forgotten anything. And your friends witnessed the whole event. Any one of them could support the legate's view of what happened."

"Could, could you order him to dismiss the charges?"

Heraclianus shook his head. "General Aurelian commands the cavalry. It's a matter for him to decide. You know how he is about discipline."

"He'd show me no mercy."

"And I'm certain the emperor wouldn't overrule his legate, or Aurelian, on matters of discipline—especially for someone who tried to kill his superior."

"I didn't try to kill him!"

"You mean you don't remember trying to kill him." Heraclianus paused. "You know the penalties for that as well as I do."

"Yes, sir." Cecropius hung his head, miserable and deflated.

"As the situation stands now there's nothing I can do for you."

Despair swept over Cecropius. He groaned. "Then I'm a dead man! Is there nothing that would change your mind, sir? I'd do anything."

Heraclianus stared at Cecropius impassively. He already had a plan but acted as though he was considering Cecropius' request. He waved the tribunes over and dealt with their business, glancing occasionally at Cecropius. Presently, the group that had gathered around Heraclianus dispersed, and he turned back to the dejected Cecropius. "Perhaps there is one possible way out of this for you."

Cecropius straightened up and looked attentive.

"It's very dangerous and requires a significant commitment on your part. On the other hand, you've already put yourself in a very bad situation with your legate."

"A slim chance is better than none at all, sir."

"Exactly." Heraclianus indicated the chair across the table from him. "Sit there." He lowered his voice after Cecropius was seated. "The emperor's judgment and ability to act decisively have seriously deteriorated over the course of this siege. You probably haven't noticed it yourself, but it's more and more apparent to us in his staff meetings." He studied Cecropius' face.

"I had no idea." Cecropius was suddenly curious.

"The other generals and I have become increasingly alarmed. We could choose to ignore it, but doing nothing with a siege in progress and the Alamanni invasion that seems to be the wrong choice to all of us." Heraclianus paused. "There's only one other alternative for us, and we're all in agreement that we must take it."

Cecropius gaped at Heraclianus. "Replace the emperor?" he blurted out.

"Quiet!" Heraclianus hissed then scowled at Cecropius. He glanced quickly around him. Satisfied that no one had heard Cecropius' outburst, he leaned closer. "Our preference, of course, would be to convince the emperor to step aside voluntarily and choose a successor. But it's doubtful he'd agree to that in his present state of mind. Therefore, we have to take matters into our own hands. The other generals and I would welcome you if you joined us in this unpleasant necessity. And you'd be providing a great service to the empire."

"What service?"

"You command a detachment of Dalmatian Horsemen. You'd be above suspicion."

Cecropius suddenly realized what he was being asked to do, and the high probability it wouldn't end well for him. "So, in exchange for you dealing with my assault charge, you're asking me to murder the emperor for you! That's a pretty uneven exchange of favors." He stood abruptly.

"Sit down, you fool!" Heraclianus glared at him. Cecropius obeyed. "You assaulted your legate with a knife. For that you'll be executed, unless someone steps up on your behalf. I'm the only one willing to help you. I've made you an offer. Take it or leave it!

Cecropius glared back, then blinked. "What happens if I'm successful?"

"I'll have you transferred out of the legate's command. There might even be a reward or promotion in it for you. He watched Cecropius think it through, then turned away to acknowledge another group of anxious tribunes. He held up a hand for them to continue waiting, then returned his attention to Cecropius. "What's your decision, Cecropius?"

If I say 'no' then he'll execute me because of what he's just told me. No one would believe me if I said there was a plot on the emperor's life by all his generals? And who would I tell?

"I want your answer, now."

Cecropius exhaled. "All right, sir. I'll do it."

"Absolute secrecy is essential, Cecropius. If you breathe a word of this to anyone, I'll deny it ever happened. And if you claimed we were plotting against the emperor, it would come down to my word against yours, the claim of a desperate man already in serious trouble. Yes, right now we're having a long discussion in front of a lot of people, but we've been talking about the predicament you're in and possible alternatives for you. There would, of course, be serious consequences for falsely accusing me of treason, in addition to your charges of attempting to kill your legate."

"I came to that conclusion myself, sir." Cecropius exhaled another deep breath and barely nodded a reluctant agreement. "There's no other way!"

"Swear your allegiance to this cause, Cecropius, in the name of Mithras, god of contracts!"

"By Mithras, I swear it." Cecropius looked at Heraclianus warily. "But what do I tell my men?"

"That you've been chosen for an important, independent mission, and they're to be ready to act on extremely short notice. Here's what I want you to do…."

* * *

Candles on the dinner table flickered from cool air that followed Gallienus into his tent. "Something smells good!"

"Probably the mushrooms with garlic." Salonina hastily finished directing the slaves where to place the dishes. Satisfied, she looked at Gallienus, smiled, and studied his face, drawn with fatigue and covered with dirt. But he seemed happy.

Gallienus tossed his cape onto the bed and laboriously removed his chain-mail body armor, which was whisked away by two young boys to be cleaned and polished. He turned to face Salonina. "I thought I'd never get done with those inspections." She rose as he came to her and let him take her in his arms and hug her tightly. He gave her a lingering kiss. She felt the tension of her day slip away and thought he relaxed too. When he released her, he stepped back and brushed the dust off the sleeves of his tunic. "By Jupiter, I miss not being able to bathe," he complained.

"I can tell." Salonina leaned over the table and dipped a cloth into a bowl of warm water. She wrung the water out and washed his hands with it. "Sit and eat. You can tell me about your day." She repeated the process and gently cleaned his cheeks and forehead before sitting across from him. By then he'd eaten three mushrooms and was reaching for a carrot. Salonina picked up a radish and took a small bite, looking at him expectantly.

"Excellent mushrooms! There wasn't much to eat while I was away. I could eat a horse."

"I'm afraid 'horse' isn't on the menu tonight."

He rested his chin on his hand, elbow on the table, and smiled at her.

"Your amnesty offer to Aureolus' troops expires tonight, doesn't it?"

"Yes. I thought it might work." He sighed and ate the last mushroom. "I just hope the rain holds off until after our attack. What a mess that would be."

"Tell me about your plans to assault the city."

"Well, as you know we've withdrawn the legionnaires around the city to make Aureolus think we've departed. Claudius is south of the city to prevent Aureolus from trying to reach

Rome. We'll storm the city on the 10th, then leave on the 13th if we want to reach Verona before the Alamanni get there. It's a tight schedule."

"I hope you can take care of one problem before having to face another," Salonina said, before signaling an attendant to clear the dishes and bring them honeyed wine. "I had an eventful day myself! Remember that Druid priestess?"

Gallienus drained his wine glass. "The one you spoke to at Colonia Agrippina?"

"Yes. I was with her today." Salonina sipped her wine and watched for his reaction.

"She's here?" He set his glass down. "Why?"

"She had a premonition about you and came to warn me." Gallienus arched an eyebrow. Salonina paused while a plate of bread was brought to the table, followed by the main course.

Gallienus inhaled deeply. "Mmmmm. What have we here?"

"It's pheasant, with mustard and pepper, stuffed with sausage." Gallienus restrained his impulse to snatch some from the platter until Salonina had taken a serving herself.

She was pleased by his obvious enjoyment. "Aren't you curious about the premonition?"

"I'm sorry, I was distracted." Gallienus nodded at the table. He swallowed his mouthful of pheasant and washed it down with wine. "Yes. What did she say?"

Salonina kept her voice low so the attendants wouldn't overhear her. "She said you were in more danger after your victory over Aureolus than you were before it."

He tore a piece of bread off the loaf and considered this comment while he ate. "Interesting. Did she say anything about storming the city?"

"No."

"About the Alamanni invasion, then?"

"No! Our discussion was about you and your generals. That's what my dream was about."

"You had a dream? I don't think you mentioned that before."

Salonina related the details of the dream to him, the wounded boar hiding in a thicket, the pack of wolves fighting among themselves just outside, much as she'd told it to Andrasta.

"So my generals are a pack of wolves?"

"Andrasta said wolves attack their leader if they've lost confidence in him."

"Do you think they have?"

"There was the question of amnesty for Aureolus."

Gallienus waved a hand. "That's been resolved. It's not going to happen."

Silence followed his curt dismissal. Salonina finally signaled attendants to remove the remnants of the pheasant and the bread. They brought one final platter and a pitcher of wine mixed with water, then wordlessly disappeared.

Gallienus stared appreciatively at the platter. "Dates, apricots, and pistachios! Where did you get those?"

"Volusianus sent them from Rome. They came yesterday afternoon," *while you were spending time with Pipa*! Gallienus finished an apricot and reached for his wine glass. She returned to their discussion. "If the generals are able to betray you, it's because they know you trust them."

Gallienus set the glass on the table and frowned. "Which generals should I trust and which should I suspect? Did she tell you that?"

"No. She didn't." Salonina said nothing further for a few moments. "I understand how you feel. I've told you to expect danger, but not what the danger is, or from whom it might come."

"Either would have been useful. Both would have been wonderful."

Salonina held up the carved oak disc. "Andrasta gave me this, her own amulet, for you to wear. It will give you strength and protection."

"Her amulet? I'm impressed!" Gallienus took the disc and examined it carefully. "What do all the symbols mean?"

"Andrasta didn't tell me."

"I'll wear it. That will please you, and protect me." He laid it on the table beside his platter. He smiled at Salonina. "Thank you. Did she say anything else?"

"She said to have someone with you that I trust."

"And who is that?"

"Pipa!"

Gallienus nearly choked on his wine.

Salonina waited for his coughing to stop. "All the others could be turned against you somehow—even Attalus. Will you take her into battle with you?"

Gallienus cocked his head, a twinkle in his eye. "She'll be surprised to hear you've selected her! Is this the start of a new relationship between the two of you?"

"I hardly think so!"

10-8
A Dinner Interrupted
08 September, 268

An orderly stepped inside the tent. Candles on a small table guttered, reflecting their light off the man's breastplate. "Excuse me, sir." Before he could finish speaking, Heraclianus brushed roughly past him, and looked briefly at Salonina. A knot turned in Salonina's stomach. She stared stonily back at him.

"Aureolus has left the city," Heraclianus announced before Gallienus could comment on his uncharacteristic brusqueness.

Gallienus leapt to his feet, spilling his wine and scattering dinner dishes. "Where is he now?"

"A messenger told me he's less than two miles away."

"I knew he'd come out!" Gallienus stepped away from the table.

"He has soldiers with him," Heraclianus added.

The boar never left the thicket! Salonina dropped her glass, rose quickly, and slid between the two men. "You're lying, Heraclianus!"

Both men gaped at her. Salonina glared at Heraclianus. He stepped back and cleared his throat, but held her stare.

Is she going to distrust everybody after her dream? Gallienus wondered. "What do you mean, Salonina?"

She turned around to face Gallienus. "The dream. The boar never came out of the thicket! He's lying!'

"The dreams of a woman," Heraclianus sneered.

"If he's telling the truth, have him bring the messenger to you. I doubt there even is one."

Gallienus looked at Heraclianus. "Well?"

He shrugged. "I sent him on to inform Aurelian. If you wish to do nothing, I can confront Aureolus myself. Either way, there's not much time to act."

"Where did you say Aureolus was?"

"Northwest of us, probably less than two miles away by now."

Gallienus glanced from Heraclianus to Salonina, struggling to decide whom to believe. *Do I ignore everything Salonina just told me? Can I afford to ignore Heraclianus' report*? "You said you woke before your dream ended, Salonina? Could this be something more than your dream revealed?"

"I did, and it's possible," *Did I miss anything by waking when I did?* "but my heart tells me I'm right!"

"What if Aureolus really is out there? If I do nothing he might escape, or attack my camp!" He made his decision and reached for his sword belt.

"Let Heraclianus take care of this for you."

"No. After all the trouble Aureolus has caused me, I want to finish this myself." *And Aureolus is a much better fighter than Heraclianus.*

Salonina stepped back from between the two men and looked at them both. She sighed. *Gallienus can't ignore this report!*

"It's a clever ploy, Heraclianus!" She turned to Gallienus. "Take Pipa with you."

Gallienus looked up from strapping on his sword belt. "She couldn't be ready in time."

"Then take Attalus."

"Good idea! No, wait." He adjusted his sword and grabbed his cape from the bed. "I don't want a band of Marcomanni running around in the dark. They might mistake friends for enemies."

"Aurelian then!"

Gallienus threw his cape over his shoulders and pointed at his orderly. "Send for General Aurelian." He adjusted his cape briefly and turned to the front of the tent.

"Your cuirass!"

"There isn't time for my armor!" He grabbed her shoulders and kissed her quickly. "We'll talk when I get back." He rushed past Heraclianus and disappeared into the night.

Heraclianus' eyes met hers briefly. She saw a triumphant look on his face before he turned to go.

"You've been cursed, Heraclianus!" she hissed after him. Salonina stood alone, scarcely aware of shouting and other noises outside the tent. *It all happened so quickly*! Anger welled up. She sank onto her chair and glanced at the remnants of dinner. Andrasta's amulet lay in the midst of the scattered dishes! A great sadness washed over her. *All my efforts to warn and protect him have failed*! She put her head in her hands and wept.

10-9
Except for a Stream
08 September, 268

Outside the tent, Gallienus grabbed the nearest guard by his tunic. "My horse!" His eyes adapted to the dark while he waited. The air was cooler now. Wind had increased and the sky had cleared. Only an occasional cloud raced past a nearly full moon. Heraclianus almost bumped into Gallienus as he emerged from the tent.

"Why haven't you alerted the men?" Gallienus demanded.

"I came to you first."

"How will I find Aureolus?"

"Follow this man." Heraclianus pointed to a nearby mounted horseman.

Gallienus' horse arrived. He grabbed the reins, leapt onto its back, and started toward the main gate. "Have the men catch up with me, wearing their armor."

Heraclianus watched a few of Gallienus' guards trailing after him. "We'll follow you," he shouted after them.

Gallienus galloped through the main gate and onto the west road. Night air rippled his hair and penetrated his open tunic. He shivered briefly and clutched his cape. Yet sweat made Gallienus' hands stick to the reins. His breathing was shallow and rapid. The beating of his heart matched his horse's hooves pounding across dry ground. *At last! A final confrontation with Aureolus. Where is he? Northwest makes sense if he wants to avoid the siege engines and attack my camp. Would he actually attack, or just retreat with his army?*

A fork in the road appeared ahead. Gallienus' guide reined his horse up at the intersection. "That way, sir." He pointed to the right fork. A large bird suddenly flew across Gallienus' path, so close to him that he ducked instinctively. The bird perched on a bush at the entrance to the left fork and cawed urgently at him.

The guide looked at the bird and shrugged. "I'll stay here and tell your escort which way to go." Gallienus nodded and spurred his horse ahead, down the right fork. It led away from the open road into a thickly wooded area.

I hope Heraclianus brings troops before I find Aureolus by myself. The road turned west. As Gallienus rounded the bend, clouds passed away from the moon, bathing the area in a pale light. He saw mounted horsemen blocking the road in front of him.

What are they doing here? Are they Aureolus' men? Since he was nearly among them, and they had made no move towards him, he slowed his horse and continued forward. There were seven or eight horsemen, Gallienus guessed, with one man in front of the rest. Gallienus watched them warily as he neared. Their leader seemed familiar to him. "Cecropius!" he hailed the man and came closer. *He led a group of horsemen at the northern camp when Salonina was nearly captured*! Gallienus relaxed. *I'm among my own men.*

Cecropius remained where he was and said nothing. Gallienus noticed a drawn sword resting across Cecropius' saddle. Hairs bristled on the back of Gallienus' neck.

"Aureolus has left Mediolanum, Cecropius! Haven't you heard?"

"We've heard."

"Then what are you doing here?"

"We've been waiting," Cecropius nudged his horse toward Gallienus. "for you." He rode closer.

"Excellent!" *I misread that situation completely!* "Then follow me."

No one moved, nor yielded ground to him. Gallienus felt the sudden stillness surrounding them. His horse whinnied and shifted nervously. He suddenly realized how alone he was. "What do you want?" he asked Cecropius, who was then almost beside him.

"The end of your reign," Cecropius said just above a whisper.

Gallienus noticed that Cecropius wore armor. Salonina's warning flashed through his mind. He reached for the amulet he'd promised to wear, and felt nothing.

Where are my bodyguards? Where's Heraclianus?

"Horses coming!" one of Cecropius' men shouted. Cecropius cursed and glanced at the road behind Gallienus.

Gallienus spurred his horse ahead, through the surprised horsemen, and fled west.

He gave his horse full rein and glanced over his shoulder. No one was in sight. The angry shouts he had first heard had stopped. *Maybe I've escaped! But where do I go now?* He leaned forward and patted his horse on the neck, coaxing it on. *I'll try to find my way to the siege engines. The garrison there will help me.* He looked ahead for signs of familiar terrain, but this woodland was unfamiliar to him.

What just happened? Heraclianus told me to take the north fork. Cecropius was waiting for me there. Salonina was right. Heraclianus was lying about Aureolus! He said he'd follow with my bodyguards. Was he lying about that too? But Cecropius' men said they heard horses—and they clearly didn't expect that.

Woods ended and the road led into a broad meadow. A stream flowed across the center of the meadow nearly perpendicular to the road. Gallienus could see moonlight reflecting from the water. *At last: open terrain. Now I'll get my bearings.* His horse responded to his urgings and galloped across the meadow. At the edge of the stream, his horse balked so suddenly that Gallienus had to grasp its mane to avoid falling. He spurred his horse. It whinnied, tossed its head, reared on its hind legs, and wheeled away from the water. He reined his horse back to the stream and tried forcing it ahead again. It refused to move. Cecropius' horses broke into the clearing. Gallienus heard thundering hooves, then a shout as they spotted him. They were nearly upon him now.

Calmly, Gallienus turned his horse away from the water to face his assailants. He didn't even feel Cecropius' spear strike his right side just below the ribs. The impact knocked him from his horse. He landed heavily on his back.

The horsemen halted about twenty feet from Gallienus' motionless form. Cecropius rode forward slowly to where Gallienus lay and stopped a few feet away. He looked down for signs of life.

"Is he dead?" one of the men called.

Cecropius circled around Gallienus and stopped, facing his own men. He glanced to his right where Gallienus lay motionless in a pool of blood. "He's not moving."

"We can see that from here."

Weariness suddenly swept over Cecropius. Tension of the wait, apprehension of confrontation, surprise and desperation at Gallienus' near escape, pursuit, catching him, and the successful throw of his spear, were all over. *What do I do now?* Heraclianus had told him where to be and what to do when Gallienus came, but had been vague about what would happen afterwards. Cecropius sighed and prepared to dismount. *"Maybe I'll just slit his throat and be done with it.* "What's that?" he called to his men.

"Horses coming!"

They all looked back to the edge of the woods. A group of horsemen burst into sight. Cecropius rested a hand on his sword while he watched them approach. When he could identify the Praetorian Guards' banner, he took his hand off his sword. Heraclianus had come! Cecropius relaxed and smiled as the Praetorian

Guards galloped toward him. *I've taken care of Heraclianus' problem; now he'll take care of mine.*

"Stay here," Heraclianus ordered his Praetorians when they reached Cecropius' men. He moved ahead alone.

Cecropius' face showed triumphant satisfaction. He expected praise for his accomplishment, until he noted Heraclianus' stony countenance. Heraclianus rode between him and the fallen emperor, deliberately keeping his back to the Praetorians and forcing Cecropius to edge his horse aside. Heraclianus looked down his left side at Gallienus' body. "He's still alive!" he growled.

Cecropius jaw dropped. He looked across Heraclianus' horse trying to see what Heraclianus had seen. He heard the unmistakable 'zing' of a sword being drawn from its scabbard. Instinctively he edged away as Heraclianus' sword thrust at him.

"He killed the emperor!" Heraclianus shouted.

Heraclianus' sword pierced Cecropius' tunic just below his armor. A burning pain shot through his right side. He cursed and drew his own sword, parrying Heraclianus' next blow. "Heraclianus promised to help me if I killed the emperor!" he shouted, dodging another sword thrust. "I'll kill you myself to repay your treachery!" he shouted at Heraclianus, then he lunged, but Heraclianus deflected his blow. Cecropius drew back, knowing a counter thrust would follow.

"Horsemen coming!" a Praetorian Guard called to Heraclianus.

The shout surprised Heraclianus. His back was to the woods but he resisted the temptation to turn and look, but Cecropius faced the oncoming horsemen. Reflexively, he took his eyes off of Heraclianus for a crucial instant. Heraclianus thrust again. This time the blade went deep and Heraclianus put all his strength into ramming it in and upward as far as he could. Blood spurted from Cecropius' wound. He gasped, dropped his sword, and stared dumbly at Heraclianus' face.

Heraclianus watched Cecropius slump in his saddle and slide to the ground a few feet from Gallienus. Only then did he turn to confront the other horsemen.

Aurelian was nearly upon him, with a group of his own

horsemen. He reined his horse to a halt in front of Gallienus and jumped to the ground. He kicked Cecropius' body aside and knelt next to the emperor, bending over Gallienus to assess his wound and search for signs of life. Aurelian's men crowded around him. He waved them back. Gallienus groaned and stirred. Aurelian looked for Heraclianus. *Why is he leaning over Cecropius and not here with the emperor?* He watched Heraclianus withdraw his dagger from Cecropius' ribs.

"The emperor's alive," someone shouted. Aurelian's troops cheered. "He needs medical attention, now!" Aurelian shouted at a tribune. "And bring torches." Aurelian looked back down at Gallienus' wound—it bled profusely. Gallienus looked vacantly into Aurelian's eyes. "Must be serious. I don't feel anything."

Aurelian held Gallienus in his arms. He patted his shoulder. "We're getting help."

So Heraclianus joins a long list of those who've betrayed me! Gallienus thought. He shifted and grimaced when his movement jarred the javelin's shaft. *Heraclianus was clever—counting on my impetuousness and using the Dalmatian cavalry that I thought were loyal.* "Even my horse betrayed me tonight," he said weakly.

Men brought two torches, pounded them into the ground behind Gallienus, then lit them. The flickering light accentuated Gallienus' blood-soaked tunic. Aurelian frowned when he saw the extent of Gallienus' bleeding. Heraclianus pushed his way through Aurelian's men and knelt beside Gallienus.

"This was his doing." Gallienus stared at Heraclianus.

"What are you saying?" Heraclianus exclaimed. "I've just killed the man who did this to you."

"No!" Gallienus barely managed to shake his head. "You put him up to it, told me Aureolus was nearby. You had Cecropius ambush me."

Aurelian looked at Heraclianus. "So that's why you wanted to make sure Cecropius was dead just now."

Heraclianus shook his head vigorously. "He must be delirious."

Gallienus stared at Heraclianus again. "Heraclianus… betrayed me."

"Seize him," Aurelian snapped. Heraclianus leapt to his feet but was quickly restrained by four of Aurelian's men. "Second in command of the Praetorian Guards," Aurelian shouted. "Report to me on the double!" For a moment, he feared a confrontation between his men and the Praetorian Guards.

A man pressed forward. "Here, sir."

Aurelian glanced at the man, recognized him, but couldn't think of his name at the moment. "The emperor has implicated General Heraclianus in plotting treason against him. You're in command of the Praetorian Guard until the emperor decides otherwise. Stay with us now."

The man saluted Aurelian, then looked down at Gallienus. "We all heard what Cecropius said." He deliberately avoided eye contact with Heraclianus. "I'd hoped it wasn't true."

Aurelian nodded before glancing at Heraclianus. "I'll deal with you later."

Another man pushed forward shouting that he was the medical orderly. Men grudgingly let him through. He looked at Gallienus' wound and paused. He pursed his lips as he looked into Aurelian's upturned face. "It might be best if you let him lie flat."

"No," Gallienus whispered. "Leave me this way."

The orderly shrugged. He knelt beside Gallienus and opened his bag.

If they don't stop the bleeding soon, I'll die here, tonight. Gallienus raised a hand.

The orderly frowned. "Be still if you can."

"Take my ring." Gallienus struggled to twist his ring off his finger and dropped it into Aurelian's hand. "Send it to Claudius. He's to succeed me as emperor." He dropped his hand after Aurelian accepted his ring, and closed his eyes for a moment. Then he took a breath and reached for Aurelian's hand. "Tell Salonina…"

"Tell her what?" Aurelian leaned close to Gallienus' ear. He felt Gallienus go limp in his arms.

The medical orderly stood and cleared his throat. "The emperor is dead," he said to no one in particular.

***

When he returned to camp, Aurelian hurried directly to Gallienus' tent. He waved the guard aside and stopped just inside, gazing around him. Salonina sat at the table. Her head lay in her arms which rested on the table. Around her the dishes from their last course lay as they'd been when Gallienus left. One of the candles had burned out, a second flickered weakly.

She raised her head and turned her tear-stained face to the tent's entrance. "General Aurelian!" She tried to wipe away her tears. "I wasn't expecting you tonight."

He took two steps forward, then hesitated before approaching the table. Salonina watched him closely. Suddenly a scene from her past came to her: *It was Aurelian who brought me the news of my eldest son's death! If Gallienus were unharmed, he'd be here himself.* She shuddered.

"It's my sad duty to inform you…"

Salonina closed her eyes momentarily; her lower lip quivered.

"He died in my arms."

She stifled a sob. "Heraclianus?"

"Cecropius threw the spear, but at Heraclianus' direction."

She sat quietly for a time. Aurelian shifted uncomfortably, then added, "Heraclianus killed Cecropius, before committing suicide himself."

She dimly heard Aurelian's words and alarm suddenly showed on Salonina's face. "What about my son in Rome?"

"We'll do what we can to protect him," Aurelian assured her, realizing as he said it that they could do very little, if anything, for Marinianus.

"Who will rule now?"

"Your husband picked Claudius."

"Did he say anything else?"

"He started to give me a message for you. Your name was on his lips when he died."

Tears welled in her eyes. She looked away.

Aurelian lingered for a moment, then left her.

Salonina looked around the table, put Andrasta's charm

around her own neck, then filled a wine glass and drank deeply.

Historical sources are incomplete and sometimes contradictory concerning events for several years following Gallienus' death. My principal sources for the postscript have been Michael Grant's *The Roman Emperors*, Barnes and Nobel, NY, 1985, and Alaric Watson's *Aurelian and the Third Century*, Routledge, NY, 1999.

* * *

Salonina was no threat to Gallienus' successors, and so was not harmed. However, when word of Gallienus' death reached Rome, the Senate ordered Marinianus death and the death a number of Gallienus' supporters, probably including Volusianus. At some point, Claudius ordered killing in Rome to cease, but his directive came too late to save Gallienus' son and many of his unmentioned supporters.

Pipa and Attalus no doubt survived. Since the Marcomanni were allied with Rome, harming either of them would have been both unwise and unnecessary. They, along with Naulobatus and his Heruli warriors, continued to serve as Roman auxiliaries, at least in the immediate aftermath.

Gallienus' soldiers at Mediolanum mutinied when they learned of his assassination and relented only when Claudius offered each of them twenty gold coins, close to two years' salary.

Claudius entered negotiations with Aureolus, who surrendered, hoping to receive clemency from Gallienus' successors—perhaps it was even offered. But shortly after surrendering, Aureolus was killed. Claudius, when hearing about Aureolus' request for a pardon, reportedly said, "He should have asked Gallienus."

Conclusion of the revolt at Mediolanum and Aureolus death freed Claudius to confront the Alamanni. He defeated them at

Lake Benacus, killing up to half of the invaders. The rest escaped to their homeland. Claudius traveled to Rome to inform the Senate of his succession. He ordered the Senate to deify Gallienus, which must have irked them considerably.

Valerian died in captivity, perhaps in 269. Roman sources suggested that Shapur had him flayed, stuffed, then displayed in one of his temples. Instead of further conquests, Shapur seemed content to build several new cities using captured Roman engineers and men.

Early in 269, Postumus suppressed Laelianus' revolt, forcing him into Moguntiacum which he then besieged. Laelianus was killed when the siege succeeded. Postumus' soldiers wanted to sack the city. He denied their demand. Angered, the soldiers killed him then pillaged the city anyway.

Marcus Aurelius Marius succeeded Postumus as emperor of the Gallic Empire. His reign lasted, at most, several months before he was killed in a private quarrel. Victorinus succeeded Marius in the spring of 269.

Claudius' first priority was to rid the empire of Goths, who continued to ravage Thracia, Moesia, and Macedonia. To curtail Gallic ambitions, he sent General Julius Placidianus into southern Gallia, where he opened discussions with Hispania and Britannia attempting to bring them back into the empire. Eventually, both provinces shifted their allegiance back to Rome.

In the spring of 269, Claudius left his brother, Quintillus, in command of the army near Mediolanum, while he marched east to confront the Goths. Marcianus had harassed them ever since Gallienus' victory at Nestos, and had driven them north and west. Claudius joined forces with Marcianus, then attacked the Goths near Naissus, Moesia Superior. Claudius gained a significant victory at Naissus in Moesia Superior. Despite claims of 50,000 enemy casualties, Rome suffered heavy casualties as well, Many Goths were able to escape. Aurelian harried them, attacking when he perceived their weakness. Goths retreated to Haemus Mountains where they were surrounded and forced to spend the winter. The following spring, they attempted to break out, nearly overwhelming Roman foot soldiers. Aurelian' timely deployment of cavalry narrowly averted a disaster.

Meanwhile, the Juthungi invaded Rhaetia and a Vandal invasion near Aquincum seemed imminent. Claudius returned to Sirmium to deal with these challenges, leaving Aurelian behind to eliminate the remaining Goths. He eventually dispatched them as their small groups retreated.

Plague swept the region that spring through summer. One of its victims was Claudius, who succumbed at Sirmium very early in 270. His brother, Quintillus was proclaimed emperor by his troops, and shortly thereafter by the Senate. Aurelian continued to pursue fleeing Goths, forcing them to abandon their sieges of Anchialus and Nicopolis in eastern Thracia before going west to challenge Quintillus' title as emperor. When Aurelian approached Quintillus' army at Aquileia, Quintillus either committed suicide, or was murdered by his soldiers. That November a group of senators met Aurelian in Ravenna to assure him of the Senate's loyalty. Not surprisingly, another change of emperors led to another spate of invasions and revolts.

Zenobia had been solidifying her own power since the death of her husband, Odenathus. Sometime during 270, she decided that Claudius was too busy defending his northern borders to challenge her eastern expansion. She sent her army into Arabia routing Roman defenders. By the end of the year her forces controlled all of Aegyptus. She also pushed into Asia Minor.

In the west, Victorinus earned the reputation of a "compulsive lecher." In the spring of 271 he was murdered at Colonia Agrippina by the husband of one of the wives he had seduced. Tetricus succeeded him.

In the east, Zenobia's forces pushed into Asia Minor, extending her control as far north as Ancyra in western Phrygia.

And in the center of the empire, Vandals crossed the Danuvius River around Aquincum, Pannonia. Aurelian won a decisive victory and Vandals asked for peace terms. Aurelian put the matter to his soldiers, who agreed to peace and to allow the Vandals to leave the empire, but they had to leave two thousand horsemen as Roman auxiliaries, and all their sons as hostages. When five hundred Vandals broke the terms, everyone was killed.

While Aurelian fought Vandals, Alamanni and Juthungi invaded Rhaetia. Leaving a small force to oversee the Vandal withdrawal, Aurelian marched west to confront the new invaders near Placentia (about 40 miles south of Mediolanum), blocking their path back across the mountains. He suggested surrender. They refused, then ambushed Aurelian at night and severely defeated him. The victorious Alamanni and Juthungi then went south along the eastern coast of Italia. When news of Aurelian's defeat and enemy advance reached Rome, riots broke out in the city.

Aurelian pursued the invaders and won a victory north of Ancona in the province of Umbria. He pursued the retreating enemy and defeated them near Ticinum (just north of Placentia). After his final victories against Alamanni and Juthungi, Aurelian went to Rome and forcefully suppressed the riots. Several senators who had supported the rioters were executed and their property confiscated. Once the city was calm, Aurelian turned his attention to the eastern part of the empire. As part of his preparations, he withdrew all the forces from the northern province of Dacia and the province was subsequently abandoned by Rome.

In 272, Aurelian marched across Rome's central provinces, clearing hostile forces out of Thracia along the way. He crossed and retook all of Asia Minor without challenge, except for the city of Tyana. He announced that all cities that surrendered to him would be spared. When Tyana surrendered, he refused to sack the city and showed clemency to all except the leaders of the resistance. Aurelian dispatched a fleet to retake Aegyptus, led by Marcus Aurelius Probus (later to become emperor). Probus returned Aegyptus to Roman rule by early June.

Aurelian first confronted and defeated Zenobia's army east of Antioch, near the Orontes River (sometimes referred to as the battle at Immae). His forces fell back to a marshy area luring Zenobia's heavy cavalry after them. There the infantry fell on the disorganized Palmyrene cavalry. After this victory Aurelian entered Antioch and spent time dealing with administrative and military matters before again confronting Zenobia's army. He granted a general pardon throughout the region, much as he had done at Tyana. He clashed with Zenobia's army again on the plains in front of Emesa, about 120 miles south of Antioch. There, his cavalry was routed and nearly defeated by Zenobia's heavily armored horsemen. When the Roman line yielded, the Palmyrene horsemen gave chase, breaking their own formation. Roman infantry was able to turn and attack the Palmyrenes' flank, decisively defeating them. General Zabdas, along with only a few soldiers returned to Emesa. Zenobia abandoned everything, including the treasury she had brought with her, and fled to Palmyra. At Palmyra, Aurelian offered Zenobia a chance of peace. When she rejected it, he laid siege to the city. Eventually, Zenobia decided her only hope for help lay in a personal appeal to the Persians, reasoning that "the enemy of my enemy is my friend." She fled the city at night on a camel, but was intercepted at the Euphrates River by a detachment of Aurelian's cavalry. Palmyra surrendered without further bloodshed.

Aurelian spared Zenobia, but executed the instigators of the revolt and exacted reparations from the city. Persian envoys also came to him with assurances of Persia's "good intentions" and "seeking assurances of his." Shapur was dying, and Persians wished no outside distractions. Aurelian garrisoned Palmyra with six hundred men and left command of the east to a trusted general named Marcellinus.

When he reached Byzantium, Aurelian learned of a Carpi invasion in Moesia. He immediately campaigned against them, defeating and driving the Carpi across the Danuvius by winter's end.

As he concluded his Carpi operations, news of a revolt in Palmyra reached him. He hastily departed for the east, arriving at Antioch through a series of forced marches in early spring of 273. His speed caught Palmyra's new leaders by surprise, and the city was ill-prepared to defend against him. This time he allowed his troops to loot and burn the city, which never recovered. Aurelian then suppressed a revolt in Aegyptus, and killed their leaders.

By the summer of 274, Aurelian was ready to reclaim Gallia. He joined General Placidianus and marched north in Gallia. Tetricus withdrew most of his forces from his northern frontier and met Aurelian in central Gallia. During fierce fighting,

Tetricus was captured. His battle lines collapsed in the resulting confusion, and his forces suffered serious losses.

Aurelian returned to Rome that autumn and marched both Zenobia and Tetricus as captives in his Triumphal Procession. The empire was finally restored: from Iberia and Britannia, to the Rhenus, the Danuvius Rivers, (having abandoned Dacia), Aegyptus, Syria, and North Africa.

The following year a secretary on the emperor's staff, fearing some serious punishment from Aurelian, forged and circulated a document among the Praetorian officers indicating that they were to be executed. At least one of the men believed the document to be authentic and murdered Aurelian.

None of the emperors who followed Gallienus survived as long as Gallienus until the joint rule of Diocletian and Maximian (284-305), and after that until Constantine from 306-337. Constantine departed Rome sometime after 313, leaving all the senators there, and moved to Constantinople, a city he had built on the foundations of the Greek city Byzantium and which became capital of the eastern Roman empire. Vandals sacked Rome in 455. Constantinople fell in 1453 to an army of Ottoman Turks, commanded by 21-year-old Sultan Mehmed II.

Timeline

248

Goths invade Moesia and into Pannonia
Millennium celebration – Rome
Pacatanius revolts in Pannonia/ Moesia
Jotapianus revolts in Syria
Emperor Philip loses nerve, addresses Senate. Decius sent to
  suppress Moesia revolt
Pacatanius is killed before Decius arrives
Decius repels Goths, restores discipline

249

Decius is proclaimed emperor by his troops
Decius defeats and kills Philip near Verona, becomes emperor
Goths begin invasions due to lightly defended borders;
  initially defeated

250

Gepidae and Carpi raid deep into Moesia; Goths, led by
  Cniva, begin large, coordinated, invasion of Pannonia and
  Dacia
Gallus forces Cniva to withdraw
Decius clears Carpi out of Dacia, then pursues Goths, initially
  inflicting heavy casualties
Goths surprise Decius and defeat him at Beroea, Thracia; he
  withdraws to Novae; army unfit to fight until next year
Valens revolts in Rome; suppressed by Valerian
Goths ravage Thracia; sack Philippopolis
Shapur takes advantage of Roman preoccupations; lays siege
  to Nisibis

Revolt in Khorasan requires his attention, interrupting the
siege. May have occupied his attention for much of next year

251

Decius and a large part of his army are slain at a battle with
the Goths near Abritus
Gallus, the governor of Lower Moesia, is proclaimed emperor
by his troops after Decius' death
Gallus concludes unfavorable treaty with Goths, allowing
them to keep booty and Roman prisoners, agrees to pay
Goths an annual tribute
Plague breaks out in Rome, ravages empire for next 15 years
or more

252

Marcomanni, Carpi, Iazyge tribes attack fortifications and
cities along northern frontiers
Borani and Goths invade provinces of Asia Minor
Aemilianus is governor of Upper Moesia, and perhaps
Pannonia
Valerian is governor of Rhaetia and Noricum
Nisibis captured by Persians
Khosrov II, king of Armenia, is murdered (probably by agents
of Shapur). Son, Tiridates, flees to west. Granted asylum
Shapur invades Armenia
Shapur defeats Romans at Barbalissos, Syria. Roman
incursion into Armenian affairs cited as reason
Odenathus' offer of alliance with Shapur is rebuffed
Subsequent Persian devastation throughout Mesopotamia and
Syria. Antioch sacked

253

Aemilianus, governor of Lower Moesia, refuses to pay tribute
to the Goths promised by Gallus. He then defeats Goths in

battle and is proclaimed emperor by his troops
Coinage in Antioch temporarily ceases this year; resumes in

254

Aemilianus marches to Italia to challenge Gallus, leaving
  borders lightly defended
Gallus sends word to Valerian, governor of Rhaetia and
  Noricum, ordering him to gather troops from the region to
  assist in defeating Aemilianus
Gallus is murdered by his troops as Aemilianus and his army
  approach Gallus in Italia
Valerian proceeds south to confront Aemilianus
Aemilianus is murdered by his troops as Valerian and his
  army approach him
Valerian is proclaimed emperor; designates his son, Gallienus,
  as co-ruler
Plague may have swept through the Goth tribes, since there
  are no further invasions until the late 260's

254

Valerian goes to eastern provinces to confront Shapur in Asia
  Minor
Gallienus leaves Rome for the Germanias, defends against
  invaders
Goths threaten Greece, reach but can't take Thessalonica.
Quadi & Iazyges invade Pannonia
Carpi harass Dacia
Valerian arrives in Syria in Autumn; coinage resumes in
  Antioch

255

Valerian in Antioch
Barbarians attack city of Pityus on eastern Euxine Seacoast.
  repelled by Successianus and his defenders
Gallienus leaves Germanias, campaigns along the Danuvius

Valerian returns from eastern provinces stopping in Danuvian
  provinces. at Sirmium mid-summer
Valerian installs his grandson, Valerian, as Caesar along the
  Danuvius

256

Valerian interrogates Christian martyrs in Rome
 23 Aug: Valerian, Gallienus, may be at Colonia Agrippina
Gallienus campaigns along the Danuvius
10 Oct: Valerian in Rome
Fall: Valerian in Germania
Fall/Winter: Valerian in Rome
Franks invade Germanias
Incursions by Gothic tribes along Euxine Sea and coastline of
  Cappadocia
Shapur's troops besiege Dura Europus
Valerian returns to eastern provinces

257

Gallienus campaigns along Danuvius defeating Carpi, departs
  for Germanias
Gallienus entrusts the young Valerian to the care of Ingenuus,
  the governor of Pannonia
Gallienus arrives on Rhenus to oppose deep barbarian army
  penetration
Gallienus gains significant victories, restores defenses on both
  banks of river
Barbarians attack east coast of Moesia, march south toward
  Byzantium, cross Bosphorus, sacking cities in Bithynia
Siege of Dura Europus ends in Persian victory. City
  abandoned; citizens deported
Valerian mints coins "Victoria Parthica"
August: Valerian suffers series of defeats
Valerian launches new Christian persecutions

258

Gallienus decides to downgrade Ingenuus
Gallienus' eldest son, Valerian, dies early in the year;
  Ingenuus revolts
Gallienus installs second son, Saloninus, as Caesar along the
  Rhenus. Postumus is retained by Gallienus, but western
  theatre placed under nominal authority of son, Saloninus,
  under protection and care of Silvanus.
Gallienus takes a contingent of Rhine troops to the Danuvius,
  defeats Ingenuus at Sirmium, in southeastern Pannonia
  Inferior. Regalianus is installed as governor
Frontier collapses immediately upon his departure
Valerian makes Odenathus 'Vir Consularius'

259

Gallienus remains in Danuvian provinces, reordering region,
  appointing posts vacated by Ingenuus
Gothic raids in either 256 or 259
Franks overrun Rhenus provinces proceeding into Spain in
  some cases
Moguntiacum becomes a frontier city
Alamanni invasion to outskirts of Rome; they are intercepted
  and defeated by Gallienus near Mediolanum
Regalianus revolts
Gothic raiders land in Asia Minor, sweeping east a far as
  Cappadocia
Valerian turns away from Persian frontier, unsuccessfully
  trying to catch the Goths.
Valerian issues coins 'Victoria Parthica'
Nisibis falls to Persians
Army becomes infected with plague
Persians capture Nisibis

260

Regalianus is defeated and killed by Roxolani near Sirmium,
  Inferior

Gallienus defeats Roxolani near Verona
Gallienus campaigns against Juthungi in Rhaetia and Roxolani
near Verona
Shapur launches major invasion of eastern provinces
Valerian is defeated and captured by Shapur near Carrhae
Shapur is virtually unchallenged throughout region
Local Roman generals, Macrianus and Callistus, organize
sporadic resistance
Macrianus revolts in the name of his two sons
Odenathus attacks Shapur's overextended army
Gallienus receives news of father's defeat and capture
treaty with Marcomanni and Marcomannic "marriage"
Postumus revolts along Rhine; Silvanus and Saloninus are
slain

261

Gallienus gathers forces to attack Postumus; is forced to send
a contingent to defend against Macrianus' army that is
marching towards him from the eastern provinces
Gallienus' first campaign against Postumus is unsuccessful.
Aureolus defeats Macrianus. Both he and his son are slain by
his own forces
Gallienus re-engages Postumus with augmented forces; after
initial success, he returns to restore Danuvian provinces
leaving the "mop-up" to Aureolus
Aureolus allows Postumus to escape
Odenathus returns from driving Persians out of Roman
provinces; learns of Macrianus' defeat; destroys local
elements loyal to Macrianus

262

Gallienus directs Pannonian restoration
Lull in Gothic invasions until ~ 267
Aemilianus, prefect of Egypt, revolts
Gallienus dispatches general Theodotus, who defeats and kills
Aemilianus

Gallienus celebrates decennalia with triumph in Rome
Gothic raid on coast of Asia Minor
Gothic attacks 262, 267/268
Odenathus recovers Nisibis

263

Gallienus crosses into Germanias, marching against Postumus.
  He is seriously wounded during a siege and retires.
  Campaign is discontinued
Odenathus campaigns against Persians reaching their capital,
  but is unable to capture it

264

Gallienus visits Greece, participates in Eleusinian Mysteries,
  acts as Eponymous Archon of Athens through mid-265
Gallienus orders defenses to be built for coastal cities

265

Gallienus completes Archon responsibilities, visits Delphi,
  returns to Rome

266

Gothic incursions resume along south shore of Pontus
  Euxinus, then into Cappadocia and Galatia
Odenathus attacks Shapur, forcing him into Ctesiphon, then
  abandons siege to pursue Gothic invaders, surprises them at
  Bithynia.
Odenathus declares himself "King of Kings," grants the same
  title to Herodian

267

Gothic land assault on western coast of Asia Minor

Marcianus, governor of Pannonia, encounters attackers around
  Boeotia
Odenathus and oldest son, Herodian, are assassinated by rela-
tives

268

Massive Gothic and Heruli invasion via Euxine Sea.
  Attacking Bithynia, Macedonia, and coastal regions of Asia
  Minor. A seaborne force attacks Rhodes, Side, Cyprus and
  Crete, while land forces attack Athens and Thessalonica.
Land invasion follows successful sea attack. Philippopolis is
  besieged.
Gallienus takes the main body of cavalry, leaving a contingent
  at Mediolanum
Aureolus revolts in Rhaetia gaining support of the troops left
  at Mediolanum. He is not supported by Postumus
Gallienus wins an inconclusive victory over a force of
  invaders near Nestos River (border between Macedonia and
  Thrace)
Gallienus learns of Aureolus' revolt, leaves Marcianus to drive
  other invaders north
Gallienus grants the Heruli chieftain consular honors, takes
  contingent of his warriors with him to Mediolanum
Shapur moves north along Tigris River with large army,
  Threatening Roman cities in Syria.
Valerian belatedly moves to oppose Persian invasion
Gallienus defeats Aureolus in battle. Aureolus is wounded and
  takes refuge in Mediolanum
Prolonged siege of Mediolanum follows

Cast of Characters

Main Characters in Bold

Aeilianus: Marcus Nummius Aeilianus - fictitious husband of
  Valeria Flavia
Aemilia: Messia Quinta Aemilia - fictitious wife of Egnatius
  Victor Lollianus
Aemilianus: L. Mussius Aemilianus - prefect of Egypt.
  Revolted in 262
Aemilianus: Marcus Aemilius Aemilianus - governor of
  Moesia Superior, 251-3. In 253 he refused to pay the
  annual tribute to the Goths, and subsequently defeated the
  attacking Gothic forces. He was proclaimed Emperor by
  his troops but was eventually murdered by them when
  Valerian approached Rome from the northern provinces
  with an army of superior strength
Albinus: Nummius Ceionius Albinus - Prefect of Rome in
  256, Consul in 263. His assignment as governor of the
  provinces of Rhaetia and Noricum is fictitious
Alexander - fictitious physician assigned to Praetorian Guards
Andrasta - fictitious Druid priestess
Antoninus: L. Junius Aurelius Sulpicius Uranius Antonius
  Priest King of Emesa, rallied forces to repulse Shapur's
  southern offensive in the summer of 253, his troops
  proclaimed him emperor
Antony: Cestius Gallus Antony - fictitious prefect of the city
  of Aquileia, 260
Ardashir - founder of the Sassanid Persian dynasty. In 224 he
  defeated and killed Artabanus V, king of the Parthian
  Empire, to which his father had been a minor vassal. Father
  of Shapur
Attalus - a chieftain of the Marcomanni tribe, and father of
  Pipa, or Pipara
Aurelian: Lucius, Domitius Aurelianus - general who rose

from the ranks during Gallienus' reign

Aureolus: Manius Acilius Aureolus - initially keeper of the Imperial horses, later a cavalry general under Gallienus

Bassus: Tiberius Pomponius Bassus - Senator, Proconsul of Africa under Gallienus, Consul 259, later achieved high office under Claudius

Bassus: Nummius Bassus. Consul 258. Fictitious father of Tiberius Nummius Cassius

Callistus - general serving under Valerian in the east. Chosen as commander by the soldiers who escaped the battle of Edessa, he conducted raids and attacks against Shapur's Army after Valerian's defeat at Carrhae. Nicknamed " Ballista," a reference to an artillery engine of that name

Carvilia Antonia - fictitious wife of Saecularis and mother of Salonina

Cassius: Tiberius Nummius Cassius - fictitious son of Nummius Bassus

Catulus, Quintus Tarquinius Catulus - credited by one source as being a governor of Germania Inferior sometime between 250-259

Cecropius - Illyrian cavalry officer who rose to become commander of a troop of Dalmatian Horse (approximately 64 men), a trusted portion of Gallienus' mobile cavalry force

Celsus - fictitious city prefect of Augusta Vindelicum, Rhaetia, in 253

Chrocus - fictitious Alamanni King extant during the reign of Gallienus and Valerian, according to an account by Gregory of Tours (who died ca 594)

Claudius: Marcus Aurelius Claudius – capable general under Gallienus who rose from the ranks to become Gallienus' chief of staff and head of the cavalry

Clodia - fictitious wife of Cestius Gallus Antony, himself the fictitious prefect of the city of Aquileia, 260

Cniva: Chieftain of the Goths during the invasions of Moesia and Thracia in 250-251

Crinitus: Ulpius Crinitus - a general during Valerian's reign, who claimed to be a descendant of Emperor Trajan. He adopted Aurelian and offered his daughter, Severina, to him in marriage. References to career and family are fictitious

Decius: Gaius Messius Quintus Decius - emperor who was defeated and killed at the battle of Abritus, 251

Domitia - fictitious household servant at a villa in Colonia. Agrippina where Gallienus and Salonina stayed

Eupator: Tiberius Julius Eupator - fictitious king of the Kingdom of the Cimmerian Bosporus, located at the northeastern end of the Euxine Sea

Felix: Nummius Ceionius Felix - a general with Valerian's army in the East reportedly sent to Byzantium to confer about defenses against Gothic invaders. Nothing further is known about him personally. First and middle name, and his relationship to Nummius Ceionius Albinus, as well as his career, are fictitious

Flavia: Valeria Flavia - fictitious daughter of Maximus and Prisca

Fulvianus: Varus Junius Fulvianus - fictitious husband of Valeria Lollia

Gaius - fictitious character in a fight scene with Cecropius at a Vetera tavern

Gallienus: Publius Licinius Egnatius Gallienus - son of Valerian and Mariniana, husband of Salonina; father of Valerian, Saloninus, Marinianus. Emperor

Gallus: Gaius Vibius Terbonianus Gallus - governor of Moesia Superior and/or Moesia Inferior during Decius' reign. Proclaimed emperor by his troops following Decius' death

Galtis: fictitious senior leaders of the Juthungi tribe

Gordian: Marcus Antonius Gordianus - Roman Emperor from 238 to 244. He married Furia Sabina Tranquilina, the daughter of his Praetorian Prefect, Timesitheus. Died age 19

Gratus, Vettius - Consul in 250, fictitious governor of upper and lower Moesia during Valerian's reign

Heraclianus: Marcus Aurelius Heraclianus. A Roman military commander under Gallienus, later became his Praetorian Prefect: 267-268

Herodian: eldest son of Odenathus

Ingenuus: Bassius Naevius Ingenuus - appointed governor of the Pannonias by Gallienus. The first two names are fictitious, although the person is historical

Julianus: Egnatius Victor Julianus - fictitious son of Egnatius Victor Lollianus and Messia Quinta Aemiliana

Laelianus: Ulpius Cornelius Laelianus - historically, either legate of legion XXII Primigenia, or the governor of Germania Superior. He rebelled against Postumus around March, 268, and was killed by Postumus or his troops several months later in or around Moguntiacum. His position as senior centurion of XXII Primigenia in AD 254 is fictitious

Licinius: Egnatius Victor Licinius - fictitious son of Egnatius Victor Lollianus and Messia Quinta Aemilia

Lollia: Valeria Lollia - fictitious daughter of Maximus and Prisca

Lollianus, see Victor

Lucania - fictitious bar maid in tavern in Treveris

Lucius - fictitious Praefect of Mediolanum

Lysisca - fictitious prostitute managing "Messalina's" a brothel in Rome

Macrianus: Titus Fulvius Macrianus - wealthy equestrian and trusted counselor to Emperor Valerian. He served on Valerian's staff as a quartermaster general, principally in a civil capacity due to a deformity or injury in one leg. Father of two sons (Titus Fulvius Junius Macrianus, and Titus Fulvius Quietus) by an unnamed "high-born" wife

Marcianus: Lucius Aurelius Marcianus - historical general and possibly governor of one or more of the provinces of Moesia

Marcus - fictitious centurion of legion XXII Primigenia

Maricq – fictitious senior aide to Shapur

Mariniana: Egnatia Mariniana - wife of Valerian, mother of Gallienus and Valerianus

Marius: Marcus Aurelius Marius - fictitious legate of legion VIII Augusta at Argentoratum

Maximus: Lucius Valerius Maximus - Urban prefect 255, consul 256. The remainder of his career is fictitious

Maximinus: Caius Julius Verus Maximinus - Emperor from 235-238, following the assassination of Severus Alexander in Moguntiacum. A highly successful as a general on the Rhenus and Danuvius frontiers. Considered a barbarian by the elite. The only emperor not to visit Rome. Rebellion in February, 238 due to severe taxation and sentences of death against patricians in Rome. When declared an outlaw by the Senate, Maximinus marched against Rome but was killed by his troops outside Aquileia

Mederich - fictitious Alamanni chieftain, brother of Chrocus

Micipsa - commander of a Moorish cavalry wing, part of Aureolus' cavalry force

Nishru - fictitious high priest from Emesa, Syria

Odenathus: Septimius Odenathus - King of Palmyra, a caravan city-state on the Silk Road from China, in the Province of Syria, located between the Euphrates River and the Mare Phoenicium. A loyal and energetic supporter of the Romans despite Persian military successes in the area. Husband of Zenobia

Pharsala - fictitious wife of Aureolus

Philip - fictitious Greek tutor of Salonina's and Gallienus' children

Pipa - also called Pipara, daughter of Attalus, Marcomanni chieftain. Married to Gallienus in a tribal ceremony to guarantee an alliance between Rome and the Marcomanni

Plotinus - a philosopher and brilliant intellect espousing the teachings of Plato. other interests included geometry, arithmetic, mechanics, optics, music, and astronomy

Pompeia - fictitious head of Salonina's domestic entourage

Postumus: Marcus Cassianius Latinius Postumus - a general in the Germanias during the reign of Valerian and Gallienus. Presumed to be the governor, although the fact Is historically unclear

Prisca: Julia Sabina Prisca - fictitious wife of Valerius Maximus

Quintianus: Lucius Valerius Quintianus - fictitious son of

Maximus and Prisca

Regalianus: Publius Caius Regalianus - governor of Pannonia during Gallienus' reign. The first two names are fictitious

Saecularis: Publius Cornelius Saecularis - urban prefect 258, 259; consul II 259. Considered to be the father of Salonina in this story, although the relationship is unclear

Salonina: Cornelia Salonina - wife of Gallienus, mother of sons Valerianus, Saloninus, and Marinianus

Severina: Ulpia Severina - wife of Aurelian

Shapur I - Shah of Sassanid Persia; son of Ardashir, founder of the Sassanid empire

Silvanus: Tiberius Albanus Silvanus - Praetorian Prefect for Gallienus. The first two names are fictitious

Sophia - fictitious bar maid in tavern in Rome

Statius - fictitious cavalry officer in Aureolus' rebellious army

Stella - fictitious prostitute, owner of a bordello in Treveris

Successianus: Gnaeus Pompeius Successianus - historical figure. His first two names and personal background are fictitious

Sulpicius Justus - Regalianus' father-in-law

Themistocles - fictitious Greek tutor of Salonina and father of Phillip, fictitious tutor of her sons

Theodotus: Aurelius Theodotus - one of Gallienus' generals, dispatched in 262 to suppress a revolt in Egypt. His career is otherwise unknown

Tiberius - fictitious retired centurion employed by Prisca and Maximus

Timesitheus: Gaius Furius Sabinius Aquila Timesitheus – an extremely capable officer of humble origins who rose through the ranks to become Emperor Gordian's Praetorian Prefect, as well as his father-in-law

Tuscus - Marcus Nummius Tuscus. Historical figure, Consul in 258. His role as governor of Rhaetia is fictitious

Valentine - a conversation between Valentine and Salonina regarding her distrust of Ingenuus is attributable to the Continuator of Dio Cassius. His assignment as Prefect of Carnuntum is fictitious

Valerian: Publius Licinius Valerianus - emperor, former head of the Senate, husband of Mariniana, father of Gallienus and another son, also named Valerian. For reasons unknown, Gallienus' brother played no significant role in the regime

Vestralp - fictitious Alamanni chieftain, brother of Chrocus

Vectria - fictitious mother of Chrocus

Victor - Egnatius Victor Lollianus - held high office under Gordian, various offices in Asia Minor between 218-247 . His home was Prusa in Bithynia, urban prefect 254. His relationship as brother of Mariniana is speculative

Victorinus: Marcus Piavonius Victorinus - one of Postumus' generals who briefly became emperor of the Gallic empire

Volusianus: Lucius Petronius Taurus Volusianus - soldier who rose through the ranks to become one of Gallienus' trusted generals. Consul 261, urban prefect 267

Vorodes: Julius Aurelius Septimus - governor of Palmyra

Zabbai - native of Palmyra of Arabian descent. A general and father of Zenobia

Zabdas - Palmyran general

Zenobia: Septimia Zenobia - Queen of Palmyra and husband of Odenathus

Bibliography

Adkins, L. a. (1994). *Handbook to Life in Ancient Rome.* New York: Oxford University Press.

Ando, C. (2012). *Imperial Rome A 198-284 TTThe Critical Century.* Edinburgh: Edinburgh University Press, 2012.

Angela, A. (2009). *A Day in the Life of Ancient Rome.* New York: Europa Editions.

Auguet, R. (1972). *Cruelty and Civilization, The Roman Games.* New York: Barnes and Noble Books.

Ballard, R. (1983). *Exploring Our living Planet.* Washington, DC: National Geoographic Society.

Bray, J. (1997). *A Study in Reformist & Sexual Politics.* Kent Town, S. Astralia: Wakefield Press.

Brzezinski, R. a. (2002). *The Sarmatians.* Wellingborough, Northants, UK: Osprey Direct, UK.

Bunson, M. (1991). *A Dictionary of the Roman Empire.* New York: Oxford University Press.

Burns, T. (2003). *Rome and the Barbarians, 1000 BC-300 AD.* Baltimore: John Hopkins University Press.

Bury, J. B. (1963). *The Invasion of Europe by the Barbarians.* New York: Russell & Russell.

Casson, L. (1994). *Travel in the Ancient World.* Baltimore: Johns Hopkins University Press.

Colledge, M. A. (1967). *The Parthians.* New York: Frederick A. Praeger Puublishers.

De Blois, L. (1976). *The Policy of the Emperor Gallienus*. Leiden: E.J.Brill.

Dodgeon, M. H. (1991). *The Roman Eastern Frontier and the Persian Wars AD226-363*. London and New York: Rouledge.

Donovan, T. (2006). *The Catastrophic Era, Rome Versus Persia in the Third Century*. Baltimore: Publish America.

DuPicq, A. (1946). *Ballle Studies*. Harrisburg: Stackpole Books.

Ed. S.A. Cook, F. A. (1965). *The Imperial Crisis and Recovery AD 193-324, Cambridge Ancient History, Vol. XII*. Cambridge: Cambridge at the University.

Flaceliere, R. t. (1965). *Greek Oracles*. New York: Norton & Co., Inc.

Gerov, B. (1965). La Carriere miliare di Marciano, general di Gallieno. *Athenaeum, vol. 43*.

Gibbon, E. B. (1932). *Decline and Fall of the Roman Empire, Vol. 1 (AD 180-476)*. New York: The Modern Library.

Goldsworthy, A. (2003). *The Complete Roman Army*. London: Thames & Hudson Ltd.

Grant, M. (1985). *The Roman Emperors, A Biographicl Guide to the Imperial Rules of Rome 31 B.C.- A.D. 476*. New York: Barnes and Noble.

Grant, M. (1999). *The Collapse and Recovery of the Roman Empire*. New York: Routledge.

Heather, P. (1996). *The Goths*. Cambridge, MA: Blackwell Publishers.

Herwig, W. (1988). *History of the Goths*. Berkeley: Univrsity of California Press.

Hildinger, E. (1997). *Warriors of the Steppe*. Cambridge, MA: Da Capo Press.

Kennedy, D. L. (1996). The Roman Army in the East. *Journal of Roman Archaeology, Supplementary Series, number 18*.

MacDowall, S. (1995). *Late Roman Cavalryman AD 236-565.* Oxford, UK: Osprey Puublishing.

MacDowall, S. (1996). *Germanic Warrior, AD236-568.* Oxford, UK: Osprey Publishing.

McNeill, W. H. (1976). *Plagues and People.* New York: Anchor Books Doubleday.

Millar, F. (1967). *Roman Empire and Its Neighbors.* New York: Delacorte Press.

Millar, F. (1981). *Roman Empire and Its Neighbors, 2nd Edition.* New York: Holmes & Meier Publishing Inc.

Mommsen, T. (1996). *A History of Rome Under the Emperors.* London: Routledge.

Nicolle, D. (1991). *Rome"Enemies (5), The Desert Frontier.* Oxford, UK: Osprey Publishing.

Norwich, J. J. (1999). *A Short History of Byzantium.* New York: Vintage Books, a division of Random House.

Paretti, L. (965). *History of Mankind, Volume II, The Ancient World.* New York: Harper and Row.

Rawlinson, G. (1885). *Seven Great Monarchies of the Ancient World, Volume III.* New York: John Alden.

Salway, P. (1997). *A History of Roman Britain.* Oxford University Press.

Smitth, J. (2002). *RAIDO The Runic Journey.* Milton, Ontario, Canada: Tara Hill Designs.

Southern, P. (2001). *The Roman Empire from Severus to Constantine.* New York: Routledge.

Stark, F. (1966). *Rome on the Euphrates, the Story of a Frontier.* New York: Tauris Parke Paperbacks.

Syme, S. R. (1971). *Emperors and Biography, Studies in the Historia Augusta.* Oxford: Clarendon Press.

Todd, M. (1972). *The Barbarians: Goths, Franks, Vandals.* New York: Putnam's Sons.

Victor, A. t. (1994). *De Caesaribus.* Liverpool: Liverpool University Press.

Watson, A. (1999). *Aurelian in the 3rd Century.* New York: Routledge.

Webster, G. (1998). *The Roman Imperial Army, 3rd Edition.* University of Oklahoma Press.

Weigel, R. D. (n.d.). *Online Encyclopedia of Roman Emperors.* Retrieved from www.roman-emperors.org/claudgot.

Wilcox, P. (1982). *Rome's Enemies 1, Romans and Dacians.* Oxford, UK: Osprey Publishing.

Wilson, C. (1869). *Sailing Directions for the Black Sea.* London.

Xenophon, t. A. (1956). *About Horsemanship.* translated and published by Denison B. Hull, USA.

Yarshater, E. (. (1983). *The Cambridge History of Iran, Volume 3, part 1.* Cambridge: Cambridge University Press.

ABOUT THE AUTHOR

In 1968, I graduated from the Naval Academy and joined the Navy flight program which included temporary assignments in Pensacola, FL, Meridian, MS, and Kingsville, TX. After earning my wings, I instructed in Kingsville's advanced jet training command, then transferred to San Diego, CA, for training in the F-8 Crusader, a single engine, single-pilot aircraft, the Navy's first supersonic fighter. I joined VF-211, then deployed on USS Hancock in the South China Sea. I flew 68 combat missions in the air war against Viet Nam from June until October 1972. In 1974, I moved to the Naval Postgraduate School in Monterey, CA, for a master's degree in Aeronautical Engineering. In 1976, I went to Virginia Beach, VA, and after training to fly the F-4 Phantom, I joined VF-102, then deployed aboard USS Independence in the Mediterranean. During my tour with VF-102, I had the opportunity to attend the Naval Fighter Weapons School, currently referred to as "Top Gun." I left VF-102 when the ship was in port in Genoa, IT, in the fall of 1979 and went to Newport, RI, for a year-long school at the Naval War College Command and Staff program. The following year I moved to Washington, DC to work at the Naval Air Systems Command as a Deputy Program Manager for several air-to-ground weapons the Navy was developing. My last flying assignment with the Navy was VR-24 in Sigonella, Sicily, a composite squadron composed of heavy-lift helicopters, supporting US efforts in Beirut, Lebanon, C-2 cargo planes that flew people, materials and mail on and off our aircraft carriers operating in the Mediterranean, and T-39 Sabreliners, which flew VIPs and high-ranking military officers throughout the Mediterranean, occasionally into Egypt and the United Kingdom. I flew Sabreliners, thus got to see a considerable amount of the Mediterranean littoral. My family and I visited as much of Sicily and Europe as time permitted. My children learned to ski in Garmisch, Germany, and we visited numerous Greek and Roman ruins in many places. I finished my military career teaching Aerodynamics at the Naval Postgraduate School in Monterey, California.

After retiring from the Navy and a brief exposure to commercial enterprises, I returned to aviation and flew world-wide as first officer then as captain of Boeing 747 aircraft for Atlas Air, a cargo company based in New York city. Only after retiring from commercial flying did I actually begin to write in earnest.

So why is someone who spent his first career at sea or around it, then his second career flying over it, writing about an era that depended principally on land forces? History always interested me and when living in Sicily I had the opportunity to see remnants of ancient Greece and Rome first hand. I was particularly impressed during a tour of Istanbul, called Byzantium then Constantinople during the Roman era. The city withstood twenty-one sieges and I was inspired to write a book I planned to call "The Twenty-second Siege." In the course of research to provide credible background information, I found myself delving further and further into Rome's history. When I reached the third century I became intrigued with a period referred to by many historians as 'The Crisis of the Third Century.' The reign of a father and son who became emperors almost by accident in the middle of this time intrigued me. The father, Valerian, gave his thirty-five-year old son, Gallienus, command of the western half of the empire and told to maintain order, keep barbarians outside Rome's boundaries and protect against revolts by ambitious generals and governors, the latter an all-to familiar occurrence since the time of Augustus. This period and these people were where I chose to write my story. The 22nd Siege will have to wait.

I have three daughters, one son, two grandsons, and one granddaughter. I live in New Hampshire with my wife, Pam.

www.ingramcontent.com/pod-product-compliance
Lightning Source LLC
Chambersburg PA
CBHW070150310726

48976CB00001B/52